*THE DRAGON OF DESPAIR*

TOR BOOKS BY JANE LINDSKOLD

THROUGH WOLF'S EYES

WOLF'S HEAD, WOLF'S HEART

THE DRAGON OF DESPAIR

THE DRAGON OF DESPAIR

JANE LINDSKOLD

A TOM DOHERTY ASSOCIATES BOOK

NEW YORK

THE DRAGON OF DESPAIR

Copyright © 2003 by Jane Lindskold

Edited by Teresa Nielsen Hayden

Map by Mark Stein based on an original drawing by James Moore

A Tor Book
Published by Tom Doherty Associates, LLC
175 Fifth Avenue
New York, NY 10010

www.tor.com

Tor® is a registered trademark of Tom Doherty Associates, LLC.

Library of Congress Cataloging-in-Publication Data

Lindskold, Jane M.
    The dragon of despair / Jane Lindskold.—1st ed.
        p. cm.
    "A Tom Doherty Associates book."
    ISBN 0-765-30259-4 (acid-free paper)
    I. Title.

PS3562.I51248D73 2003
813'.54—dc21

2003040284

First Edition: August 2003

Printed in the United States of America

0 9 8 7 6 5 4 3 2 1

For Jim,
with love, appreciation,
and a whole lot more

A C K N O W L E D G M E N T S

As always, there are many people to whom I owe my thanks for their contributions to the development of this novel. Informally, Jim Moore, Yvonne Coats, Phyllis White, and Linnea Dodson took the time to read the manuscript and provide feedback. Kennard "the mad scientist" Wilson applied his sense of precision to various discrepancies in the glossary. I also appreciated the flood of comments from those readers who let me know what they thought about the story that came before this book.

More formally, my agent, Kay McCauley, remained the bedrock on which I stood. Various folks at Tor Books, including Tom Doherty, Fred Herman, Patrick Nielsen Hayden, and Teresa Nielsen Hayden, provided cogent thought, valuable assistance, and genuine enthusiasm for the unwinding of Firekeeper's story.

Special thanks go to Leyton Cougar and Candy Kitchen Wolf Rescue. They took time out of a very busy weekend to give Yvonne Coats (the world's most patient photographer) and me the opportunity to meet with Raven, their wolf ambassador. You can see some of the pictures from our meeting on my Web site, janelindskold.com, and also learn about the valuable work Candy Kitchen is doing to help save former "pet" wolves from being destroyed.

Extra special thanks go to Raven. Thanks to him, I know firsthand what it's like to be greeted wolf-fashion. It's a pretty extraordinary experience.

IRON MOUNTAINS

Lake Rime

Hope

BARREN
LANDS

Good
Crossing

BRIGHT BAY

Mason's
Bridge

Silver Whale Cove

Forged

Revelation
Point Castle

Fox River

STONEHOLD

Thunder
Island

Half-Moon
Island

Dog
Island

Shell
Island

Shipwreck
Shoals

THE ISLES

Bardenville

Norwood
Estate

West
Keep

Stilled ■ ■ Gateway to Enchantment

HAWK HAVEN

NEW
KELVIN

Eagle's
Nest
Castle

White Water River

Dragon's
Breath

Eagle's ●
Nest

Plum   Zodara
Orchard ■   ■

Flin River

Barren River

● Broadview

S W O R D   O F   K E L V I N   M O U N T A I N S

W A T E R L A N D

Rock
Fort

First
Harbor

Port
Haven

Shoals

Shoals

*Talion
Island*

O C E A N

Map by Mark Stein Studios based on original drawing by James Moore

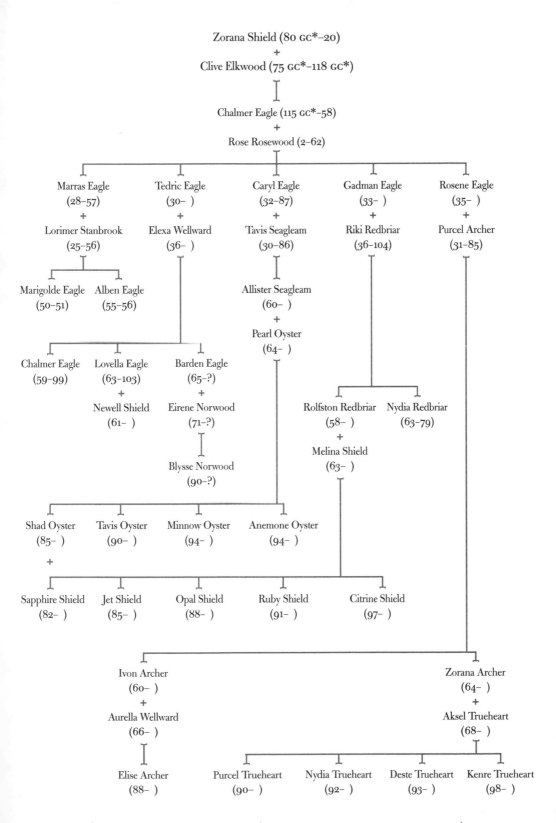

Zorana Shield (80 GC*–20)
+
Clive Elkwood (75 GC*–118 GC*)

Chalmer Eagle (115 GC*–58)
+
Rose Rosewood (2–62)

Marras Eagle (28–57)
+
Lorimer Stanbrook (25–56)

Tedric Eagle (30–)
+
Elexa Wellward (36–)

Caryl Eagle (32–87)
+
Tavis Seagleam (30–86)

Gadman Eagle (33–)
+
Riki Redbriar (36–104)

Rosene Eagle (35–)
+
Purcel Archer (31–85)

Marigolde Eagle (50–51)   Alben Eagle (55–56)

Allister Seagleam (60–)
+
Pearl Oyster (64–)

Chalmer Eagle (59–99)   Lovella Eagle (63–103)   Barden Eagle (65–?)
+   +
Newell Shield (61–)   Eirene Norwood (71–?)

Rolfston Redbriar (58–)   Nydia Redbriar (63–79)
+
Melina Shield (63–)

Blysse Norwood (90–?)

Shad Oyster (85–)   Tavis Oyster (90–)   Minnow Oyster (94–)   Anemone Oyster (94–)
+

Sapphire Shield (82–)   Jet Shield (85–)   Opal Shield (88–)   Ruby Shield (91–)   Citrine Shield (97–)

Ivon Archer (60–)
+
Aurella Wellward (66–)

Zorana Archer (64–)
+
Aksel Trueheart (68–)

Elise Archer (88–)

Purcel Trueheart (90–)   Nydia Trueheart (92–)   Deste Trueheart (93–)   Kenre Trueheart (98–)

* GILDCREST COLONIAL CALENDAR (ALL OTHER DATES HAWK HAVEN CALENDAR)

BOOK

ONE

I

BURNING A TRAIL THROUGH THE SKY, the comet was brighter than any single star, almost brighter than the moon. Certainly, it appeared more purposeful.

There was no doubt about the purposefulness of the young woman who sat watching the comet from atop one of the smooth stone outcroppings that erupted here and there through the forest floor like whales frozen in the act of breaching. Her arms were wrapped around her bent knees so that she made a single form, almost like a rock herself, but unlike the rocks her gaze was fixed on the light in the sky.

To Firekeeper, who knew the stars through all their shifting annual panorama as a city-born woman would know the streets around her own house, the comet was a source of unending fascination and not a little uneasiness. She didn't like either feeling one bit.

Night after night, she found herself drawn to some dark, quiet place where she could watch the comet, as if by watching it she could keep the heavens from doing something else unpredictable. Although the spring nights were yet chilly and damp here in the Norwood Grant at the northwestern edge of the Kingdom of Hawk Haven, Firekeeper didn't find them uncomfortable. She'd lived unprotected through much harsher weather.

Blind Seer, her closest friend, often sat with Firekeeper on these vigils, though the wolf didn't really understand the woman's fascination.

"*A light in the sky,*" Blind Seer grumbled on this night as on so many others. "*That's all it is. Come and run with me. We could terrify the deer.*"

Firekeeper uncoiled herself sufficiently to swat the wolf lightly across the bridge of his long nose.

"*Let them raise their fawns in peace,*" she said, "*so there will be food for the year to come. Surely you haven't fallen so low that you must hunt sucklings and their mothers.*"

"*I was more thinking of the young bucks, spring mad in the pride of their new antlers. They need humbling.*"

Her eyes never leaving the fat white comet with its glowing tail, Firekeeper answered, "*And you a Royal Wolf, greatest of the great, are setting yourself the task of improving Cousin-kind? Our parents would be ashamed.*"

Their argument was interrupted by the sound of feet steadily advancing along the forest trail. Neither wolf nor woman moved, for the tread was as familiar to them as the tall red-haired youth who appeared around a bend in the trail a moment later.

"I thought I'd find you out here," Derian Carter said, greeting them with a casual wave of the hand that was not occupied balancing a tin-screened candle lantern. "Watching the comet again? I promise you, it won't go anywhere."

"Elation tell you where I am," Firekeeper replied, knowing this must be so. She had many places from which she watched the comet. Animal wariness kept her from frequenting any one place too often. Elation, however, could have easily found her.

The peregrine falcon had taken a liking to Derian. Although Elation could not talk to Derian as she could to Firekeeper, she had found ways of making him understand simple things. Derian, in turn, simplified matters greatly by accepting, as most of Firekeeper's human acquaintances still did not, that the bird was as intelligent as most humans.

"Elation might have," Derian admitted before changing the subject. "There's news from across the White Water River. A single courier made the crossing late this afternoon. He came to Duchess Kestrel, figuring she'd pay well to know the last several months' gossip from New Kelvin."

Firekeeper was interested in spite of her initial pique at having her vigil interrupted.

"From New Kelvin?"

The neighboring country was separated from Hawk Haven by a river broad and rocky enough to be difficult to cross even in the best weather. Once snowmelt had swelled the river, the two nations had been effectively cut off for better than a moonspan. Only lately had the river begun to ebb, though many days would pass before normal commerce resumed.

Derian nodded.

"And from how both the duchess and the earl remained closeted with the courier through dinner, the courier had news worth the tokens the duchess has ordered drawn from the Norwood Grant treasury."

"And what did the courier say?" Firekeeper prompted, almost, but not quite, forgetting the comet.

"I don't know," Derian replied, "but we have been requested to meet with Duchess Kestrel and her son as soon as possible. Can you leave your comet unwatched?"

Firekeeper gave him a slight smile, though she knew Derian could not see it in the darkness.

"I can."

A GROUP OF SEVEN was to meet in Duchess Kestrel's study—eight, if you counted Blind Seer, which Firekeeper most certainly did. As she waited for the rest to assemble and stop their idle chatter, the wolf-woman studied her surroundings, automatically noting exits and defensible corners.

This was a room Firekeeper had visited only once before. Unlike the nearby chamber claimed by her son for a similar purpose, the duchess's study was light and uncluttered, its furniture crafted from pale woods rubbed to a high polish and scented with beeswax. The stone-flagged floors were covered in jewel-toned New Kelvinese carpets that seemed to glow in the lamplight. The broad, south-facing windows were curtained in heavy brocade woven in shades of soft golden brown and beige.

In her younger days, Saedee Norwood, Duchess Kestrel, had been a warrior who had won her spurs in a particularly nasty border skirmish with Bright Bay. There was a statue in the garden commemorating those deeds. It depicted a slim-hipped young woman brandishing a sword, an arrogant tilt to her proud head.

But those battles had been long ago. The only trace remaining of that woman was the selfsame sword hanging on the wall behind the desk where the duchess daily dealt with the business of running the large land grant that she had inherited from her father. Bearing children—two of whom had survived to adulthood—had spread Saedee Norwood's once slim form. Bearing the responsibilities of her position had graven lines in her face.

Yet, Firekeeper thought as she watched the duchess greet those she had summoned, perhaps not all traces of that young warrior had vanished. The arrogant lift of the duchess's head was much the same, though tempered with a restraint that might have been alien to her younger self.

There was a similar arrogance in the bearing of the duchess's son and heir, Norvin. Earl Kestrel was a small man—indeed, his mother was taller—and maybe some of his apparent arrogance came from refusing to be seen as weak in a world where strength and size were usually equated.

Firekeeper knew the earl fairly well. It had been he who had led the expedition she had accompanied out of the western wilderness. Initially, she had thought Norvin Norwood taken up with nothing but his own advancement. Later, she had come to realize that—interested as Norvin was in promoting his own good and that of his family—he was also a commander whose troops respected him, a master whose vassals found him fair, and a parent who, though dictatorial at times, strove not to smother his children.

In the eyes of the human world, Firekeeper was one of those children—adopted by the earl soon after his return from the west. Firekeeper did not think of the earl as her father—that place in her heart belonged to the wolves who had raised her—nor did she particularly think of the earl's four children as her siblings. One of these, however, Norvin Norwood's eldest son and heir, had earned the wolf-woman's mingled affection and exasperation.

Edlin Norwood entered the room even as Firekeeper thought of him, his breezy friendliness a decided contrast to his father's and grandmother's studied restraint. Nor did he particularly resemble them, lacking their prominent hawk-like nose. Edlin did share his father's dark hair—though the earl's mixed silver with the jetty black—and the earl's pale grey eyes. Still, no one watching Edlin as he bobbed a quick bow to his grandmother and then collapsed bonelessly into a comfortable chair would have taken him for his father's son.

But Firekeeper respected Edlin. He had been with her and Derian in New Kelvin early in the winter just past and had proven that there was more to him than met casual inspection. However, if Edlin's deeds in New Kelvin had earned Firekeeper's respect, they did nothing to reduce her frustration with him. Soon after Firekeeper had arrived at the Norwood Grant the previous autumn, Edlin had taken a very unbrotherly fancy to her. He'd even—so Firekeeper had heard rumored—told his father he wished to marry her.

The earl had refused without even consulting Firekeeper—though his decision proved much to Firekeeper's relief—but his father's refusal hadn't ended the matter for Edlin. Often he would watch Firekeeper, sometimes covertly, more often forgetting himself and gaping with slightly open-mouthed admiration.

Why Edlin fancied her Firekeeper hadn't the least idea. In a society where women were admired for social grace and elegance—even those who, like Saedee Norwood or Crown Princess Sapphire, had won honor on the battlefield—Firekeeper possessed neither. She donned long gowns, jewels, and other such finery only under duress. Rather than displaying herself to her best advantage on some couch or embroidered chair, she preferred sitting as she was now, on the floor, her arm flung around Blind Seer, her short hair tousled from wind and weather.

Fortunately for Firekeeper, Saedee Norwood had forbidden anyone—even her son—to force Firekeeper to change her ways too drastically. As long as Firekeeper would gown when necessary, used proper utensils when dining at table, and remembered not to bolt her food, the duchess claimed herself content. Firekeeper, in turn, sought to please the duchess, preferring to offer evidence of her willingness to learn human ways on her own, rather than having those ways forced upon her.

Such attempts to please were not alien to Firekeeper's nature. Wolves always submit before those who have power over them. To them this is an expression of respect, not a humiliation. Saedee Norwood did not ask for belly-pissing cringing, only the human equivalent of a jaw-licking tail wag.

Moreover, like her son, Saedee Norwood had proven herself worthy of Firekeeper's respect. The wolf-woman had observed how the duchess enforced the right of individual decision not only for Firekeeper, but for other members of her household as well. At a time when a hundred years of fairly stable government was bequeathing social ritual and restraint as its gift to the younger generation, Saedee was old enough to remember when this had not been so—and wise enough to sacrifice the benefits she could have garnered from a calcifying social order for the greater benefits gained from a vital and active family.

Thus Saedee had made her son, Norvin, her partner in running the Norwood Grant at a time when several of her contemporaries were struggling to maintain a firm hold over their growing households. Equally, she used her authority over her son to keep him from rebuking Edlin too severely for the young man's own idiosyncratic style.

But then, as Firekeeper had learned from Wendee Jay, the Kestrel retainer who served as the wolf-woman's personal attendant, Saedee Norwood herself was an unconventional woman. No one knew who had been the father of her children—Norvin, Eirene, and several others who had not survived beyond infancy. Saedee had not only kept this information to herself—she had also refused to marry, even when offered advantageous alliances for her house.

Firekeeper stretched, wondering just a little about the pedigree of this human family with whom she found herself allied.

Edlin's arrival brought the gathering's number to six. Derian had arrived with Firekeeper and Blind Seer, and both duchess and earl had already been present. Now a slight rap on the door announced the last arrival.

Grateful Peace was a slender and elegant man, almost effete to Firekeeper's way of seeing things. His hairline had receded so far back that he was nearly bald. What hair he retained was bone white. His facial features were startling—adorned as they were with the bluish green lines of several tattoos. Spectacles perched on the bridge of his thin nose and gave him a round-eyed appearance at odds with his air of quiet watchfulness.

He had come from New Kelvin the previous year, self-exiled for choosing to act against the policies of the government he had served for the previous decade and a half.

A solid hit from a crossbow bolt had forced the amputation of Grateful Peace's right arm. While he recuperated, he had wintered at the Surcliffe family vineyards east of Duchess Kestrel's holding. However, when the snowmelt had begun, Duchess Kestrel had invited Peace to join herself and her family at their residence—deliberately waiting to offer her invitation until the White Water River was so swollen that there would be no easy commerce between the Norwood Grant and New Kelvin for at least a moonspan. Grateful Peace was an outcast from his homeland, and no one doubted that there was a price on his life.

Nor, Firekeeper thought, *would Peace be easy to hide. Even though he has stopped painting his face, nothing can hide the tattoos. Though he styles his hair more as men wear it here, still his very bearing and manner of standing is different. He walks awkwardly in trousers, as if his legs still need to feel the touch of robes to know when to break his stride.*

Duchess Kestrel did not keep them waiting long after Grateful Peace had taken his seat.

"I assume that all of you have already heard about the courier who arrived today. 'Courier' may be too polite a term," she added with wry smile. "However, it will do."

"One item of his news was rather shocking," the duchess continued. "Before I reveal it, I must ask that you not speak of it to anyone other than those gathered here. I have chosen to reveal it to you because I would like your advice regarding what course of action I should take."

Nods around the semicircle facing the duchess's desk confirmed the willingness of the gathered to keep her confidence. When Firekeeper realized that this was no general gossip session—as she had first imagined when Derian had spoken to her out on the grounds—she wondered why Duchess Kestrel had wanted her here.

Duchess Kestrel did not offer to answer this unspoken question, only accepted their unspoken promises of silence with a nod of her own.

"Very well," she said with a slight, involuntary sigh. "Melina, once of House Gyrfalcon, has married. Her new spouse is the Healed One, the hereditary monarch of New Kelvin."

Saedee Norwood declaimed these words as if she expected them to cause a sensation, nor was she disappointed. After a moment of shocked silence, there was a tumult of questions and expressions of dismay. Firekeeper believed that she herself had kept silent, but after a moment she realized that the rumbling growl she heard was coming from her own throat.

No wonder. If there was a human Firekeeper hated and despised, it was Lady Melina Shield. She had trouble thinking of the woman by another name, although Lady Melina had been disowned and exiled and so lost both title and right to her House name. Melina had tricked and used Firekeeper— a thing for which the wolf-woman blamed herself as much as she blamed Melina, though this realization made her feel no less bitter.

Earl Kestrel had raised a hand to still the babble and, with a glance at his mother, took it upon himself to answer some of the questions.

"First," he said, his tones clipped, "we are certain that this information is correct. The courier came originally from Dragon's Breath, the capital city of New Kelvin, where the information is, apparently, not common knowledge. However, he has a sister working within one of the Earth Spires and she gave him the news."

Grateful Peace interjected a comment of his own before the earl could continue.

"Keeping such a marriage secret would be less difficult than you of Hawk Haven might imagine," he said, his Pellish excellent but flavored with a melodious accent, rather as if he expected the words to have more syllables than they did. "The Healed One is a semi-sacred person. He appears in public rarely and his affairs are not for common gossip."

"Thank you," Duchess Kestrel said. "You have anticipated one of my own questions. I had wondered how such information could be kept from the people. Certainly servants, at least, would gossip."

"The secret could not be kept perpetually," Peace replied, "but for a few months, perhaps while the Healed One assured himself of support from the Dragon Speaker and some key thaumaturges, for that time it could be kept quiet—a thing rumored, but not confirmed. Many of the servants in Thendulla Lypella"—he used the New Kelvinese name for the Earth Spires, the towering buildings that held the New Kelvinese government—"are slaves and never leave the property. However, as this courier of yours has shown, even slaves have contacts outside of the walls."

After making certain that Grateful Peace had finished, Earl Kestrel continued his discourse.

"Not only are we certain that the news is genuine," he said, "we are fairly certain that we are the first Great House to receive the information. The White Water River remains quite swollen. The courier who came to us risked his life in his hope of reward for being the first."

"As you all must realize," the duchess added, smoothly taking up her son's account, "this information could have serious ramifications for our government."

"Our government?" asked Derian. "You mean for the king?"

Duchess Kestrel nodded. "A woman born of Hawk Haven's nobility has married a foreign monarch. Moreover, Melina is from House Gyrfalcon, first among the Great Houses. Even more significantly, Melina is the mother of one of King Tedric's heirs."

Firekeeper felt herself growling again. Crown Princess Sapphire was indeed Lady Melina's birth daughter, though she had been cruelly used by her mother. Now it seemed that, despite the adoption that should have taken Sapphire far out of her mother's reach, Melina was exercising power over her once more.

Derian frowned, but Firekeeper thought that his concern was less for Sapphire than for King Tedric. Since the autumn before, when King Tedric had honored him by making him one of his counselors, Derian had developed a deep personal loyalty to the monarch of Hawk Haven.

"We will tell the king this news, won't we?" Derian asked.

"Certainly," Duchess Kestrel answered. "Only yesterday I had a packet of letters from Eagle's Nest. Not one mentioned Melina's marriage, nor have the post-riders brought in any news. Therefore, we must act on the assumption that the news has not yet reached the king."

"I say," Edlin said, straightening slightly. "Why would New Kelvin's king need to keep his wedding secret?"

All eyes turned to Grateful Peace.

"A wedding to a foreigner," the former thaumaturge replied, "would most certainly need to be kept secret, at least until the government decided how to present the matter to the public. As you may recall from your visit to our land, we of New Kelvin entertain a somewhat inflated view of our worth in comparison to that of other people."

"Right-o!" Edlin said, grinning. "Sorry. Overlooked that, don't you know."

Earl Kestrel shook his head, disapproving as always of his son's casual attitude. He himself, as Firekeeper knew, would never admit forgetting something—at least as long as he could pretend otherwise.

"May I continue with the business at hand, Edlin?"

"I say!" Edlin said. "Of course you can, Father! I'd be the last to stop you."

Blind Seer was the only one to snigger aloud and only Firekeeper knew the wolf was laughing.

"This news has the potential," Norvin Norwood continued, "to have severe ramifications for our entire kingdom. Princess Sapphire is new to her position. Her mother is feared. This strengthening of Melina's position could greatly weaken the crown princess's support. Therefore, it is important that the news reach the king and his heirs as quickly as possible. The more time they have to prepare, the more wisely will they react."

His pale grey gaze came to rest on Firekeeper and for the first time she understood why she had been included in this gathering.

"Firekeeper," the earl said, "do you think you could get Elation—that peregrine of yours—to carry a packet to the king?"

Firekeeper stiffened. She had dreaded a request like this since the winter before when Elation had deigned to carry a report to King Allister of Bright Bay. For hundreds of years, since before the Plague that had sent the Old World rulers back across the sea and left their colonists to fend for themselves, the Royal Beasts had sought to hide themselves from a humanity that had initially treated with them as friends only to later attack them as enemies.

Her own emerging from across the Iron Mountains with Blind Seer and Elation had been the beginning of the end to that secrecy. True, few knew that the tales that were now widely told were true, not merely a minstrel's fancy, but among those who suspected the truth were some of the most powerful men and women in Hawk Haven. They would not hesitate to use whatever tools they might if those tools would stay a crisis.

"No," the wolf-woman replied bluntly. "I will not. Elation will not. The Royal Beasts are not your servants, any more than King Tedric is their servant. Why not send a pigeon?"

Duchess Kestrel answered for Earl Kestrel, who was frozen with displeasure.

"There are three reasons that sending a pigeon would not be wise. First, it's a bad season for the birds as the weather is very changeable. Second, we have only one bird left who will return to Eagle's Nest and, by our contract with the king, we must keep one in case we need give warning of invasion. Third, this information is too serious to trust to a potentially insecure courier."

Saedee Norwood smiled in a fashion that Firekeeper thought was more akin to a baring of teeth.

"Indeed, the courier who brought this information to us is being detained for a few days. We have him quite comfortable, but have taken care that those who wait on him are the least likely to share gossip."

The duchess turned a kinder smile upon the wolf-woman.

"But Firekeeper, I don't understand your reluctance. Princess Sapphire is your friend. You stood for her at her wedding. Surely you should help her now."

Firekeeper growled, but an idea was taking shape in the back of her mind. She let it grow and answered the first point.

"Sapphire is her own friend first, then Shad's, and the king's, then her family's. Maybe then she remember a few others. No matter, that." Firekeeper bit her lip, for making speeches in human talk was still hard for her. "Everyone know Sapphire's mother—even King Tedric—when she is made crown princess. Why . . . Melina matter now that Sapphire belongs to king?"

What followed was a long discourse on politics, alliances, and the rest, begun by the duchess and her son, but with Grateful Peace adding a few words here and there before it was ended.

Most of what they said went over Firekeeper's head, but she gathered that what Melina had done was so terrible because she had placed herself at the head of another government. At least this would be how many in Hawk Haven and Bright Bay would interpret Melina's actions, though Grateful Peace was quick to say that Melina would not be nearly as powerful in New Kelvin as a monarch's spouse would be in Hawk Haven.

"If she was any but Melina," Firekeeper said to Blind Seer, *"I would be comforted by what Peace says, but Melina will rule where others think themselves the One."*

"So you will have Elation carry their message?" The tilt of the wolf's ears expressed wariness, as if he had scented a puma lurking in the trees.

"Not quite," Firekeeper replied.

She waited until the humans had finished their lecture, then offered the compromise she had come up with a few minutes before.

"Elation not carry message," she said, "nor will I ask her, but I will carry."

She held up a hand to forestall the protests that began almost before she finished speaking.

"I am fast as usual post-horse," she said, "not the gallop relays, no, but as horse jogging on roads, and I not need stay on roads. No great rivers is between here and Eagle's Nest. I can go if not as fast as peregrine flies, as straight."

She stopped, pleased with the image.

Earl Kestrel frowned.

"Blysse, it is time you realized the less than suitable impression such behavior makes. My suggestion keeps your dignity and position in mind—as your own does not."

Firekeeper smiled at him, knowing well that it was his own dignity, as her adopted father, that Norvin Norwood was worried about. What parent doesn't wish to control his children?

"Either I go," she said with polite firmness, "or message no go fast."

Earl Kestrel didn't immediately cease trying to convince Firekeeper to do things his way, but eventually the duchess put a hand on his shoulder.

"Norvin, as easily make water run up hill as try to change her mind. You can't do it. Let us accept this compromise. Firekeeper, when will you go?"

Firekeeper shrugged. "This now, if you wish."

The duchess gave a gracious nod. "Within an hour or two will do. I wish to write out a report and to request that Grateful Peace dictate one regarding his perception of the New Kelvinese reaction when this news becomes widely known."

Derian Carter, who had listened attentively, clarifying terms for Fire-keeper during the more theoretical political discussions, now cleared his throat.

"I can't travel as quickly as Firekeeper," he said, "but I could follow on horseback. I'd been intending to go south soon anyhow, to place an order with my father for mounts for the Norwood stables before he heads to the spring market in Good Crossing. I could carry another copy of the message and speak for you, clarifying points as Firekeeper might not be able."

Earl Kestrel nodded, some of his sourness vanishing.

"We had intended to ask you to do much the same," he said approvingly. "As a ring-wearing counselor to the king, you will be able to gain a private audience."

Derian inclined his head in a bow of respectful acknowledgment.

"He's not as intimidated by our Norvin as once he was," Blind Seer chuck-led. Like Firekeeper he was fond of Derian, and like any wolf he enjoyed see-ing a cub grow into his fur and tail.

Blind Seer's comment made Firekeeper think of something new. Al-though it didn't pertain precisely to the matter at hand, it was related and she thought she might as well raise it now.

"Blind Seer and I go to Eagle's Nest, then," she said aloud, "and from there when telling king is done and questions answered, then Blind Seer and I, and maybe Fox Hair if he wish, we go west across the mountains and see my pack."

She didn't phrase this as request, but Earl Kestrel chose to reply as if she had.

"That would be fine," he said. Clearly, if the wolf-woman wouldn't serve him, she might as well be out of sight. His annoyance at her was apparent in how he quickly changed the subject. "Mother, I was thinking, Derian could carry with him a coop of our carrier pigeons. Therefore, if the king needs to reply he can do so that way as well as by courier."

"I say," Edlin interjected, speaking in Firekeeper's ear so as not to inter-rupt the duchess's reply to the earl. "I say, Firekeeper, can I go with you to see the wolves?"

He looked so eager Firekeeper almost hated refusing him.

"No," she said. "Even Fox Hair will be a problem, but I know he has oath to fill and I would guide his steps. Two humans may be too much."

She stopped then, realizing she had almost said more than she had intended. Edlin, happily, had fixed on the first part of her statement.

"Oath to fill? What?"

Derian nodded. "I vowed at the end of King Allister's War to return to the place where Prince Barden's expedition died and set up a marker for all the dead. Lord Aksel Trueheart has agreed to research the names for me and even to help with preparation of gravestones."

Earl Kestrel, finished with his private discussion with the duchess, had heard Derian's explanation.

"You never mentioned this to me," he said sternly.

"It was a private vow," Derian replied almost apologetically. "When I lettered temporary markers for the battlefield I kept thinking of those graves we left. As you know, we listed the names of those we knew among the dead— Prince Barden and his wife, a few others—but we didn't have a full list of the expedition with us."

Norvin Norwood nodded. Although he had led the expedition to find a prince, he had not been concerned enough about the commoners in the group to carry along their names.

"My sister, Eirene," the earl said, his voice breaking slightly, "was Barden's wife. I would like to send some small trinkets for her grave."

"I would also," the duchess said so quickly that Firekeeper was certain she was swallowing tears. "Sweet Eirene . . ."

Firekeeper sensed the duchess's gaze resting on her and shifted uncomfortably, knowing what the old woman was wondering. Part of the reason Earl Kestrel had convinced his mother to adopt the wolf-woman into the Kestrel line was that there was a good chance that Firekeeper was Barden and Eirene's daughter, Blysse.

The wolf-woman had no idea whether this was true or not but the idea, as always, made her vaguely uncomfortable. She leapt to her feet, suddenly eager to be away.

"I get my things," she said, "and come back for these letters."

No one stopped her as she darted out the door.

II

AS HE RODE SOUTH in the company of a small group from various small holdings in the Norwood Grant, Derian Carter couldn't help but enjoy watching spring unfold. A moonspan before any blossom, even the little white ones that bloomed out of the snow, was a rarity to be treasured. These days it seemed as if every plant that could flower was doing so, from tiny grass flowers in blues and pinks, to the trumpet-headed glories in their mixed costumes of yellow, white, and orange. Fruit trees, too, were bursting into flower: apple, peach, and cherry all rejoicing in the coming of summer.

Spring's spreading wash of color seemed to accelerate the more days he was on the road, for Derian's journey took him not only south, but somewhat east, away from the looming presence of the Iron Mountains, which cradled winter a bit longer in their folds and clefts.

He wondered if Firekeeper, making this journey in advance of him, saw things the same way. She was an odd person—human in shape but sometimes hardly human in her perceptions of the world around her. Would she see the flowers nestled in the grass as he did, bits of bright color that made him smile almost involuntarily after winter's grey, or as useless foliage, poisonous to eat—or as something else he couldn't even imagine?

Certainly she wouldn't have stopped in the towns and villages along the road, luxuriating in the gossipy company of folk glad to see fresh faces and hear the news after winter's cold had kept casual travelers close to home. One thing Derian knew that many city dwellers did not was that winter didn't seal country folk onto their farms—not unless the snow was very deep. They simply traded wheels for sled runners and went about their business.

Indeed, as Derian had learned working with his family business from an early age, for some types of commerce the dead of winter was a very active time. Large loads, whether stone or grain or tuns of wine and ale, were more easily slid across snow and ice-packed roads than hauled over dirt or bogged down in mud.

So Derian listened carefully at every inn and tavern where his group paused, dropped a hint or two, guided a conversation, but nowhere did he catch as much as the slightest hint that anyone had heard of Melina's new and potentially disastrous marriage.

Events from six months before were still being hashed over—the assault on the pirate headquarters in the swamps to the far east, the heroic deeds of Princess Sapphire and Prince Shad, the tragic madness of little Citrine Shield. When Derian's companions boasted that Derian himself had been among those who assaulted the Smuggler's Light, he found himself the center of every circle and used his novelty to probe for other gossip.

But he heard nothing of Melina or New Kelvin. Indeed, none in these relatively isolated towns and farming hamlets knew that little Citrine had been left with the pirates as hostage against her mother's good behavior to allies Melina had later betrayed. Most simply thought Citrine had been kidnapped and held for ransom. After all, wasn't her eldest sister to be the next queen?

Derian didn't enlighten them. If what the courier from New Kelvin had told House Kestrel was true, then there was no need to blacken Melina's name further. Such gossip would only make more difficult the king's attempts to manage the situation to his advantage.

The news would get out in time. Too many of the soldiers who had fought at the Smuggler's Light had grasped some inkling of the truth. Derian simply would not help it spread. Still, his joy in the frolicking of newborn lambs and foals was diminished when he thought of the little girl he'd first met—a girl who had been as lively and enthusiastic as any young creature and who now, by all reports, was driven to extremes of sullen brooding and frenetic activity.

Derian's traveling group reached the vicinity of Eagle's Nest, the capital city of Hawk Haven, midmorning on the ninth day of their journey. They could have pressed on the night before, but heavy rains and the knowledge that the gates would be locked when they arrived made them hold back.

Once they were in sight of the city, Derian broke from the rest, wheeling Roanne, his chestnut mare, toward the city's east side. Prancing Steed Stables, his family's business, was located outside of the east wall and when Derian reined Roanne in under the sign that bore her painted image, he felt as if he was home again.

To Derian's slight disappointment, Colby Carter, his father, was not present at the stables when Derian arrived, nor was Brock, Derian's younger brother. Old Toad, retired from heavy work but still working for the Carter family both at home and at the stables, greeted Derian as warmly as his own grandfather might have done. He took charge of Roanne for Derian, promising to have the mare stabled.

"Actually, Toad," Derian said, burrowing through his saddlebags for the clean though wrinkled clothes he'd put in last night just for this purpose, "if you'll give Roanne over to someone trustworthy, I'll ask you to go up to my parents' house and tell them I'm home. My bags will be coming with one of Kestrel's men, but I've an errand to run for Earl Kestrel before I go to the house."

Old Toad looked at Derian slyly, obviously hoping the youth would say more. It was a matter of great pride for all those associated with the Carters that the heir to the house was so intimate with nobles and even with royalty. Derian, however, said nothing more, and Toad decided to prime his pump with a bit of gossip.

"It's said that the wolf-girl, Lady Blysse, has been seen about the castle these two days since," Toad offered. "Her and her wolf both."

Derian grinned.

"Lady Blysse made her own way here," he said, giving nothing much away. "Not many horses can tolerate Blind Seer close by and she wouldn't leave him behind in the North Woods."

Toad had to be content with this scrap and with the cheerful importance of bringing the news of Derian's homecoming to his family. They set off together, parting when Derian's path took him toward the quarter where House Kestrel maintained its manse.

Derian changed his route as soon as Toad was out of sight, heading straight through the city and up to the heights where Eagle's Nest Castle brooded over her chicks. He'd pulled a knit cap over his red hair and kept from those streets where chance-met acquaintances might recognize him. Happily, it wasn't a market day, so this was easily enough done.

Derian knew he might be being overcautious, but if Firekeeper's arrival was already common gossip—or at least stable gossip, for the stables seemed to get news before anyone else—then he didn't want to add grist to those active mills. The news that Derian Carter, newly made counselor to the king, had rushed to the castle even before going to his parents' house might indeed prove interesting.

And then maybe I'm just getting an inflated ego, Derian thought wryly, but he knew in his heart he was not. He might associate with nobility, but he was common-born and common-bred, and he knew how the least scrap of information was patched into a quilt that covered all the facts—though not always correctly.

The porter on duty proved to be one of those Derian had come to know the year before when Derian had stayed at the castle as part of Earl Kestrel's retinue. He swung open the wrought-iron gate with a grin.

"I was told to keep an eye out for you," the porter said, "though I'd hardly need to be told that once Lady Blysse showed here. She makes the guards edgy she does, slipping both herself and that huge wolf in without any the wiser. The watch captain gave his men the sharp edge of his tongue, he did."

Derian shook his head ruefully.

"And Firekeeper knows well enough that the gate would be opened to her. She just likes causing trouble."

"Show me a chit of a lass," the porter said, closing and locking the gate once more, "or a lad either, who doesn't get joy out of making her elders look foolish."

Derian agreed, thanking the porter for his news before crossing the interior courtyard. He'd met people in the countryside who thought that a castle was just a big fortified building inside a wall. Realistically, a castle was more like a small town. This one had its own bakeries, stables, gardens, smithies, carpenter shops, and all the rest. The stone buildings held quarters not only for the king and his immediate family, but for the legion of aides, servants, advisors, and the like needed to keep the castle in efficient order.

True, much of the staff lived in the city and came up the hill to work, but in a pinch gates like those the porter manned could be sealed and the life of the castle could go on—for a while at least—independent of the city below.

Further, Eagle's Nest Castle was legendary for its security. Songs were still sung and stories told about how Zorana Shield, later to become Queen Zorana the First, had infiltrated the castle, cementing her faction's power during the Civil War. It was no wonder that the watch captain had been furious to have his walls and guards so easily circumvented.

But then no normal army, nor even any normal spy could do what Fire-keeper does, Derian thought. *She climbs like a squirrel, silences guard dogs with a threat, and this all in a silence that makes the blowing of leaves in the wind seem loud.*

Once inside the castle, Derian made his way to the king's audience hall. The herald to whom Derian gave his name was a stranger, but she didn't ask to be shown the counselor's ring or any other form of identification.

"You are expected," she said. "I'll send a message in to His Majesty's secretary, Lady Farand, and I am certain that the king will see you as soon as he finishes with his current meeting."

"That quickly?" Derian replied, surprised.

"The king said he was to be interrupted in the course of his usual appointments," the herald explained, "the moment you arrived. You were to be offered refreshments while you waited."

Derian nodded.

"Will there be a long wait?" he asked. "Because I can just run down to the kitchens myself. No need to bother anyone."

The herald looked a touch startled at his lack of formality.

"If that is your wish," she said. "A runner can be sent for you there as easily as to the kitchen to bring you a tray."

Derian nodded and went. The truth was he didn't want to stand fidgeting in a foyer. Fetching his own bread and beer would be a distraction.

He was finishing up the good-sized meal of cold meats, cheese, and sundry other dainties that a friendly cook had brought him, when a runner came from the herald.

"The king will see you," the boy announced, sliding across the polished stone flags of the kitchen floor and deftly snatching a chunk of cheese from under Derian's fingers.

Derian rose and headed out, nodding his thanks to the cook. She waved her free hand—the other was pinched tightly around the lobe of the runner's ear—and the rest of her attention was given to scolding the boy.

Running up the stone stairs two at a time, mortified that he might have kept the *king* waiting, Derian was relieved to find the herald standing watch before the still closed doors of the king's chamber, but she stepped aside as he came up.

"His Majesty sent a message out to me," the herald said. "His current meeting will be over momentarily. Did you happen to see Lady Blysse in the kitchen?"

Derian shook his head.

"His Majesty requested her presence as well," the herald said with a sigh. "I just hope the runners I sent can find her."

"Did you send one to Holly Gardener's cottage?" Derian suggested.

"And to the gardens," the herald confirmed, her slight, wry smile showing that this wasn't the first time she'd been asked to locate the wolf-woman, "even though for most people today's weather would be excuse enough to stay in by the fire."

"So Firekeeper might have done," Derian said. "She's seen enough bad weather to appreciate comfort."

But Firekeeper hadn't been located when the doors swung outward and those who had been meeting with the king streamed out, arms loaded with books and papers, most still chattering about whatever matter had been under discussion. A few noticed the tall red-haired youth standing to one side, but Derian had practiced effacing himself, and most overlooked him.

"Go on in," the herald said. "The king said I need not bother to announce you."

She looked neither scandalized nor puzzled by this informality and Derian decided that whatever training the castle's heralds received must include a high amount of tolerance for their aging monarch's eccentricities.

To his slight surprise, when Derian entered the conference room, he found it empty but for a single uniformed guard. He recognized him at once as Sir Dirkin Eastbranch, captain of the king's personal guard. Sir Dirkin was a tall man whose square chin and high cheekbones seemed chiseled from his weathered brown skin.

"King Tedric," Sir Dirkin said without preamble, "has requested that you wait upon him in his sitting room."

His studiously calm expression broke into a smile so slight Derian might have overlooked it if he hadn't come to know the man somewhat the summer before.

"The last meeting ran overlong," Dirkin continued, "and the king is wearied of hard chairs and tables."

Derian offered Sir Dirkin a bow.

"It's good to see you, Sir Dirkin. Have you wintered well?"

"Well enough. The cold months have flown by, to be honest, with Princess Sapphire and Prince Shad in residence. There has been much going on."

Derian didn't doubt it. The sporadic letters that residents of the Norwood estate had received from friends and family in the capital city had been filled with accounts of balls, receptions, and less formal social occasions—enough so that Lady Luella, Earl Kestrel's wife, had been quite put out that she and her children were isolated in the North Woods. Accounts of how she had scolded her husband had quite livened the servants' hall.

Earl Kestrel had not given in before Lady Luella's fury, even though House Kestrel maintained a residence in the capital that could easily have been made ready for them. Doubtless he felt that he had earned enough reputation for his house over the previous summer—and all his children but for Edlin, and perhaps Firekeeper, were too young for him to seriously be playing matchmaker. Even if they had been, it would not have mattered. Norvin Norwood was not one of those who believed that marrying off children was the best way to build social status.

If he had been, Derian thought, *we never would have gone west a year ago, nor would Earl Kestrel have risked his life leading cavalry in King Allister's War.*

These thoughts flew through Derian's mind as he followed Sir Dirkin through the conference room and along a minor maze of passages until they came to the king's winter sitting room.

Derian had never been here before—in the summer the south-facing windows would have made the room stifling. In winter, however, they added a pleasant glow of sunlight to the warmth from the fire blazing on the hearth.

When Derian entered, the king was sitting in one of the high-backed chairs nearest to the blaze. King Tedric was a bent man, well into his eighth decade. His brown eyes might have paled with the years, but their gaze remained sharp and he studied Derian as the youth made his bow.

Without rising, he motioned Derian to a chair facing his own, acknowledging the youth's deep bow with a friendly nod.

"Pull the chair back from the fire, if you wish," the king said. "Your blood is still thick and hot, not thinned to whey like mine."

Derian took King Tedric's advice. The room seemed overly hot, even when he pulled his chair away from the blaze. In any case, he had learned that King Tedric, unlike some of the other nobles Derian had met, saved his subtle games for serious matters, not wasting his energy on little matters of etiquette and precedence.

Unless, that is, Derian thought wryly, *he can use those games to set some adversary off balance.*

"I've asked," King Tedric went on, "Firekeeper, and my heirs to join us. Queen Elexa would do so as well, but she's resting. Caught a bad chill this winter. It settled in her chest and she's having trouble shaking it."

Derian murmured his concern. It was sincerely felt, though he hardly knew Queen Elexa. All his life and long before that Elexa Wellward had been Tedric's reliable other self, ruling in his stead when—as last summer—the king had been forced to be away from the capital. Her health had never been sturdy, however, and Derian worried that this illness might be the beginning of a serious downturn. Elexa was younger than her husband, but both were well past the age when the body recovers easily.

King Tedric doubtless read more into Derian's expression than into his polite words.

"Elexa is doing well enough," he said, "though we did have a scare a few weeks ago when we were both down ill. There's no keeping rumors from spreading, not with as many servants as we have, but we've managed to keep the locals from thinking that it might be a good idea to lay in a few extra yards of fabric for mourning garb."

Derian nodded. "I won't say anything that would cause alarm, Sire."

"I know you won't," King Tedric said, a touch testily. "If you were a jabbermouth, I wouldn't have given you my ring. You've become even closer with your confidences since, if I'm any judge—and I am. Doubtless your activities last winter didn't hurt your training in discretion. Tell me about them while we wait for the others. I've had formal reports from all sides, but another personal report doesn't ever hurt."

Derian did as requested, summarizing the events that had led himself, Firekeeper, and several others to suspect Lady Melina Shield of plotting treachery, so that they had followed her across the border into New Kelvin.

He'd told the tale repeatedly by now, editing where appropriate for each audience, so that he had become quite glib. For the king, Derian minimized the details of the journey itself, emphasizing the political aspects. King Tedric nodded, asked an occasional question, but mostly listened.

At first Derian expected the others that the king had mentioned to arrive at any moment, but after a while he realized that the king must have allowed for a private interview in advance. Doubtless this tale—requested so casually, as if to fill an idle moment—was the reason. Derian found part of his mind wondering why, but after he stumbled in his account several times, he forced this distraction from him.

King Tedric waved Derian to a halt as Derian segued from their adventures in New Kelvin to what had happened after they had returned to Hawk Haven.

"I've heard those stories," he said with a sigh, "over and over, set to song, even acted out in a play—if you can believe it. Everyone in Eagle's Nest seems determined to flatter my heirs by praising their heroism."

"I wonder if it's gone to their heads?" Derian thought, then clapped his hand over his lips as he realized he'd spoken aloud.

King Tedric chortled at Derian's expression.

"Sapphire might be tempted that way," the king said, "but two things keep her steady. Three, actually, for her young husband is no fool."

The king looked suddenly sad.

"No. Shad is not a fool," he said, "but it looks as if Sapphire's sister, young Citrine, might have become one. Citrine's mind was weakened by what she endured when she was taken to the Smuggler's Light. Her mother's abandonment threw the scales of reason completely off balance and Citrine has grown worse, not better, since her release.

"Initially, Jet Shield had Citrine's custody—he's the oldest of the family. He has inherited since I declared Melina outlawed—but Citrine worsened under his care. Sapphire requested that she be permitted to bring Citrine here to the castle, saying that she could not easily forget her youngest sister, though by law they are now no longer anything but cousins."

Derian nodded. He tried to think how he would feel if for some unknown reason he was adopted out of his birth family and knew that there would be no way that he would feel that Damita and Brock were any less his siblings.

Nor, he thought, *would my parents seem any less my parents, not even if the king himself made me his son.*

Derian felt uncomfortable at this last thought, then soothed himself by remembering that Sapphire had grown to hate Melina long before the reputed sorceress had connived at theft and treason for her own mysterious ends. Surely the crown princess didn't think fondly of Melina—especially after what Melina had allowed to be done to Citrine.

At least he hoped she didn't.

The focus of Derian's musings entered the king's sitting room shortly thereafter. Crown Princess Sapphire—formerly Sapphire Shield—was a buxom young woman in her mid-twenties. Her pointed chin robbed her of classic beauty, but most were willing to overlook that defect in light of her lustrous blue-black hair, clear blue eyes, and graceful bearing. It didn't hurt that she knew how to dress to make the best of her assets—Melina had been a good mother in that matter at least.

Sapphire's husband, Crown Prince Shad, entered the king's sitting room with his wife. Shad wasn't as physically striking as Sapphire. Fair, with rounded lines that he had inherited from his mother, a noblewoman of Bright Bay's Great House Oyster, Shad was far more serious than someone in his early twenties should be, but then he'd trained at sea, fought in several major battles within the last year, and now was taking on the challenge of an arranged marriage with a very strong-willed woman.

Derian—his thoughts still fixed on family relationships—wondered how Shad felt about being away from his parents and siblings. He'd seemed particularly close to his father, the recently coronated King Allister of Bright Bay, but his relationship with his brother, Tavis, and twin sisters, Minnow and Anemone, had seemed free and easy, more like relationships in Derian's own family than what he'd observed in those noble families he'd been close enough to observe.

Maybe it's because Shad's siblings didn't really have prospects to compete over, Derian thought. *And maybe Shad's doing all right, here in an alien land. Those Bright Bay families can't feel the same about proximity as we do. They're always going off on sea voyages and things like that.*

Derian didn't really believe it. He'd spent a good deal of the last year away from his family, and he was aware of an almost physical tug of eagerness to be back among them.

All these thoughts darted through his mind as Derian rose, made his bows, answered a few polite inquires after his health, about travel conditions, and the health of Duchess Kestrel and her family. When such gossip was taken care of King Tedric brought matters around to business.

"We here are all aware," he said to Derian, "of the contents of the letters Firekeeper brought from House Kestrel—the information regarding Melina's remarriage and such. Do you have anything specific to add on that point?"

Derian shook his head.

"No, Your Majesty. Duchess and Earl Kestrel requested that I discreetly probe for rumors regarding Melina's doings as I made my journey here. I did my best—and without boasting I'll say I'm pretty good at gathering roadhouse gossip—and I heard nothing new, nor any indication that the news of Melina's remarriage is common gossip."

The king nodded gravely.

"That, at least, is good."

Derian continued, "If I had your permission to bring my parents—or at least my father—in on this matter, I could find out if he has heard anything. Lots of travelers come through our stables—and not just our stables here, but our affiliates as well. While we do have connections to the south, one of our busiest lines is between here and Port Haven. Rumor may have traveled by sea that has taken longer to cross the White Water River."

"By sea and over the Sword of Kelvin Mountains," Sapphire reminded him. "That would be a long haul, especially if the passes are closed by snow."

Derian acknowledge her words with a short bow.

"Yes, Princess. I wasn't saying that there *would* be any rumors from that direction, only that if there were any rumors my father and mother may well have heard them."

The king and his two heirs debated this point for a few minutes, reaching the conclusion that Colby and Vernita Carter were known to be loyal subjects and, as their interests were intertwined with those of their son, they would be certain not to begin rumors themselves.

Derian listened, evincing more patience than he felt. He couldn't help but feel that if he'd been dealing only with King Tedric the king would have given him a direct and decisive answer. This discussion, weighing and considering, seemed somehow to diminish the monarch.

Then again, Derian thought, *maybe I wouldn't feel that way if it wasn't my folks they were discussing.*

"Thank you for your patience," King Tedric said then, causing Derian to flush, suddenly terribly certain that the old king had seen how very impatient Derian had been. "Your parents' knowledge will be of value to us."

Shad leaned forward, his elbows on his knees.

"You see, Derian," he said, and Derian was reminded of the young man's earnest preparation in the days before he led a small group of which Derian had been part into the Smuggler's Light, "we've been a bit worried about what might be going on in New Kelvin, even before the Kestrels' report reached us."

Derian frowned. "I'm afraid I don't understand, Your Highness."

Shad waved the formalities aside with an impatient hand.

"There's no way you could, Derian. Sapphire and I didn't understand until King Tedric explained to us. New Kelvin has been an ally of Hawk

Haven for years—basically since borders stabilized after the Civil War. We've had an embassy there . . ."

Derian noted with approval how easily Shad spoke of Hawk Haven as "we." It reflected well the prince's identification with his new country.

". . . and a regular ambassador who attends their government sessions. Not only have we had an embassy there—mostly to facilitate trade—but we have had a handful of unofficial observers within the Earth Spires."

"Spies," Sapphire clarified bluntly. "Not to steal anything, just to provide information to balance against what we were being told through official channels."

A year before Derian would have pretended not to be shocked, but would have been. Now he wasn't precisely shocked, but he was curious, and he didn't hesitate to let his puzzlement show.

"How could we have spies inside Thendulla Lypella?" he asked, lapsing into the New Kelvinese name for their capital city. "The New Kelvinese are so *different*, their manners, their way of dressing, their face paints. . . . If my group hadn't gotten in and out as quickly as possible, and had the guidance of Grateful Peace, we would have been doomed."

King Tedric gave a dry chuckle that ended in a wet cough that made Derian worry that perhaps the old man should be joining his wife under the physicians' care.

"Most of our informants," the king said, "a term I prefer to 'spy' in this case, are New Kelvinese. Don't look so shocked, boy. They're not betraying anything, not as they see it. Trot out your lessons and tell me about how the New Kelvinese structure their government."

"It's a monarchy," Derian said, glad to still his confusion in recitation, "yet not like ours. Their king—the Healed One—doesn't seem to have much power."

"He must have some," Sapphire said dryly, "or Mother would never have married him."

Derian decided to overlook this statement.

"The real power seems to be held by someone called the Dragon Speaker. That's an elected position, like head of a society or guild, not an inherited one. The Dragon Speaker is the first among a group of counselors called Primes. He—or she, the Dragon Speaker can be either, though the Healed One is always male—rules only as long as he has the support of the other Primes. If they grow unsatisfied with the Dragon Speaker, a new one can be elected in his—their current one is male—place."

Derian took a deep breath.

"There's more," he said. "The Dragon Speaker has intimate counselors and the Primes are drawn from different sodalities—those are groups sort of like guilds, but not quite—but essentially those are the basics."

Derian paused, ready to add detail if King Tedric required. Before Derian had gone to New Kelvin he had studied only a little about the other land's weird government. After living there for several weeks and traveling with Grateful Peace—who had been a highly ranked member of the New Kelvinese government—he had learned a great deal more.

King Tedric, however, seemed satisfied.

"Now, Derian, you've mentioned how the Dragon Speaker can be voted in and out of office," he said, "but you don't seem to understand the implications of this. Our informants are members of what might be termed the opposition to the current Dragon Speaker—Apheros, I think his name is."

Derian nodded and the king went on.

"This opposition views it to be to their advantage to keep us informed about the intimate details of New Kelvin's governmental workings—hoping, doubtless, that we will become unhappy with some aspect of it and that our unhappiness will unsettle Apheros's government and ready the way for their own."

"Seems an odd way to run a nation," Shad commented, "until I think about what Father has been writing from Bright Bay. I think every government—except possibly the cruelest—relies on consensus and compromise . . . and on alliances."

Derian nodded. At any other time, he would have probed for more information on just how King Allister was doing with establishing his regime in Bright Bay, but right now he was more concerned about what King Tedric had said.

"Sire, Prince Shad said we 'have had' observers in New Kelvin. Don't we anymore?"

"Sharp as a sword that boy," the king chuckled. "Shad, now that Derian has finished proving he knows how New Kelvin's government works, why don't you return to the point you were about to raise."

Shad steepled his fingers and stared into them. Then, seeming to realize that this was a less than dignified posture, he straightened and looked Derian in the eye.

"You've hit the problem on the head, Counselor," he said. "We have had and maybe we still have an embassy in New Kelvin and observers within the

Earth Spires; the problem is, we haven't heard anything from them. News of Melina's remarriage should have reached us long before the White Water River subsided. It didn't. That raises concerns. If the news has been kept so quiet that not one among our spies—informants, I mean—heard of it, then how did the man who came to the Kestrels hear of it? If it has begun to leak out, then how have our observers failed to hear?"

"Twisty, huh?" Sapphire commented.

Derian nodded, wondering what they expected *him* to do. King Tedric coughed into his hand, looked suddenly weary, then pushed ahead.

"Since you're asking your parents for rumors, see if they have heard any about changes in the ranks of New Kelvin's Primes as well. I don't suppose you heard anything?"

"Nothing, Sire," Derian replied.

"That's worrisome," King Tedric said. "But perhaps we're troubling over nothing. Our ambassador could have caught pneumonia. The carrier pigeons could have all died from cold. Our informants—who tend to be among the more highly placed—might not have caught servants'-hall gossip."

The king tried to sound confident, but Derian wasn't fooled. Shad changed the subject then, so abruptly that Derian didn't have the nerve to press.

"There is another matter we'd like to raise with you—using you, as it were, as a touchstone for our common people."

Shad said that last without a trace of condescension or the faintest shadow of a sneer, simply with an acknowledgment that the people of Hawk Haven fell into two classes: those with titles and those without.

Derian nodded. "I would be honored, Prince Shad."

"Once again," the king added, rousing somewhat from his tiredness, a twinkle brightening his faded eyes, "we will be trusting you with a state secret, though this one, by its very nature, cannot be kept secret forever."

Derian nodded again, slightly puzzled. Then the king glanced over at Sapphire and Shad. Something in the young couple's bearing gave Derian a hint of what this secret must be.

By mutual consent, Shad spoke for them both.

"Sapphire is carrying our child," he said, managing to look both proud and embarrassed all at once. "She is two months in and thus far, according to the physicians, is doing just wonderfully."

"If throwing up one's insides every morning could be called wonderful," Sapphire added more mournfully than Derian would have expected from her.

Impulsively, Derian leapt to his feet, offering his hand in congratulations as he would have to far closer friends. He was just regretting his impulse when Shad's hand—rough and callused enough to show that all his time hadn't been spent in council chambers—met his own. The young prince's eyes were shining and Derian realized that this might be the first friendly— rather than formal—congratulations Shad had received on his news.

Derian wrung Shad's hand firmly, then turned to offer a more decorous bow to the princess. Sapphire, however, was holding out her hand, so he clasped it as well.

"That's just wonderful news!" Derian said. "Wonderful!"

Sapphire folded her hands complacently over her yet flat belly.

"We certainly think so," she said, resuming her seat and motioning Derian to his, "and we are wondering just when do you think it would be wise to share the news with our people."

She held up a hand to forestall Derian answering at once.

"Although I feel quite well," she said, "the midwives have been honest. A first pregnancy is a delicate thing. The baby may be taken by the ancestors. Would it be best to let the people know now, when there is still much risk, or would it be better to wait until I am more visibly ripening?"

"Tell them now," Derian said promptly. "No one loved Queen Elexa less for the babies who didn't make it."

He turned to King Tedric.

"I'm sorry to have to say such a painful thing, Sire, but it's a fact."

King Tedric nodded gravely.

"I know, son, I know. Our concern has come from Sapphire's rather unusual accession to her position. She was made crown princess because none of my own children lived to succeed me. She was chosen over other candidates for many reasons, but one of those reasons—to be completely honest—is that she is young and strong. Should we risk that perception of strength and of the perpetuity it will bring to the monarchy?"

"Absolutely," Derian said after a moment's careful consideration. "Sapphire and Shad have heroic battles to their credit—both in King Allister's War and during the quelling of the pirates last winter. Everyone knows they are brave. There's no chance that will be forgotten if they suffer the type of loss too many families know."

"Very good," King Tedric said. "Your thoughts match those of many of our counselors. Indeed, we have some small suspicion that those who argue in favor of silence seek to weaken, not strengthen, my heirs' position with their subjects."

The king nodded briskly, as if ticking off an item on a mental checklist.

"Very good. Thank you for both your report and your counsel. Tell me, what are your plans for the immediate future?"

Derian took a deep breath. He'd been dreading that this question might be asked. Prince Barden had been disowned by his father. Though the king had not censured Earl Kestrel for leading his expedition west the spring before, that expedition had not found the prince—or rather had found evidence of the prince's failure. Derian's self-imposed mission would, in its small, private way, honor a son King Tedric had disowned for his arrogant disobedience of the king's will.

However, Derian had resolved to answer honestly, no matter that he risked the king's ire. The king had too many ears and eyes. Moreover, there was the chance that Firekeeper, who worried far too little about incurring anyone's wrath, had already told the king their plans.

"I'm going west, Your Majesty," he said a touch stiffly, "to the place where we found Firekeeper. I made a vow after King Allister's War, a vow to mark the graves of those who died there. I plan to keep that vow."

King Tedric didn't look angry, but Derian felt as tight as a strung bow until the king actually spoke.

"Firekeeper said something of that, though in her case I have the impression that she is making a visit to family."

"That's pretty much the case for her, Sire," Derian replied.

King Tedric ran a finger along his jawline.

"Do you mean to mark all the graves?"

"There's only one grave, Sire," Derian hedged. Then he decided to continue to be direct. "But I mean to mark it with the names of all the members of the expedition. Lord Aksel Trueheart researched them for me and arranged for them to be cut into several stones I will carry with me."

Sapphire interrupted, "You're hauling grave markers?"

"Yes, Princess," Derian replied. "If I'm going to make the trip, I'd hardly like to leave wooden tablets. I'm sure my father will loan me two mules. I'll take them and a couple of mountain-bred ponies I brought from Norwood.

"They're a breed," he added somewhat inconsequentially, hearing himself the carter's son, "I'm interested in crossing with riding stock for use in some parts of the kingdom where the land is rough and hilly."

"I see," Sapphire said, looking a touch startled at the change of subject. "Well, I admire your thoroughness. I only wish I could go with you." She patted her belly ruefully. "But duty calls."

Shad folded his hand over hers. "And morning sickness would be a real problem on the road."

King Tedric shook his head at his heirs, an old dog watching puppies romp.

"Derian," he said, "kindly call on me before you and Firekeeper leave. I would like you to carry a few grave goods with you."

Derian tried not to let his astonishment show, but he knew his eyes had widened. It was one thing for Duchess Kestrel to wish to send something to her daughter's grave, but from King Tedric it was tantamount to rescinding Barden's disownment—to taking him back into the ancestry from which he had been exiled.

"Yes, Sire!" he said.

"And keep your eyes and ears open along the road," the old king said. "It may be you'll bring me home new rumors."

Derian nodded, but he sincerely doubted it. The road west should be quiet and deserted once they passed the outskirts of tilled lands. They might meet a trapper or a hunter, but otherwise he expected peace and quiet.

He didn't know just how wrong he was, or that the old king did indeed have ears and eyes in the most distant points of his realm.

III

FIREKEEPER MIGHT HAVE FIDGETED more during the days that passed as she waited for Derian to get ready to travel west with her except that she was enjoying visiting with friends she hadn't seen since late autumn.

King Tedric had invited her to stay at the castle and she had done so without hesitation. The castle backed onto considerable land—not enough to support Blind Seer were he to live there full-time, but enough to give both of them space to run.

Steward Silver had assigned them rooms in the same tower they had stayed in before, one with a staircase that opened into the grounds. The servants knew to let her come and go as she wished. She had permission to ask the head cook for food whenever she wanted it and abused the privilege for a day or two, until Blind Seer told her she was getting a belly like a pregnant doe.

Sapphire and Shad were pleasant to her, but Firekeeper didn't thrust herself upon them. They were busy making preparations for announcing that Sapphire was expecting. The news had come as no surprise to Firekeeper—pups were always whelped in the spring. What *had* been a surprise was learning that this human pup, though conceived in winter, would not be born until the following autumn.

Humans always make simple things hard, she said to Blind Seer.

Another simple thing made hard was the situation with Citrine Shield. The girl was apparently as unstable as a water-cut stream bank, though the instability was in her mind, rather than her body. Right now she was going through a phase where she wanted to see no one and so Firekeeper was kept away.

A friend who was always ready to see the wolf-woman was Queen Elexa. The queen was being kept in bed, but she was recovering and it amused her to have Firekeeper come and sit with her.

The wolf-woman had taken longer to warm to the queen than to the king, for Elexa's subtle ways of handling her myriad responsibilities had been more difficult to appreciate. Now, however, especially after seeing the very different ways in which Lady Luella and Duchess Kestrel managed their households, Firekeeper could appreciate how neatly Queen Elexa balanced the times she needed to intervene and when her best managing would be to step back and let those like Stewart Silver or the head cook or gardener run their parts of the castle without interference.

Queen Elexa liked asking Firekeeper for tales of the wolf-woman's adventures, sometimes about those things that had happened since Firekeeper came to the human lands west of the mountains, more frequently about Firekeeper's childhood among the wolves. Firekeeper was happy to tell the queen what she could and learned not to be astonished by what amazed the queen.

In return, especially as her cough began to heal and she could talk more easily, Queen Elexa would tell stories. She shared Firekeeper's fascination with the comet and told her stories that purported to explain its presence in the skies.

One story said a comet was a giant horse with a burning mane and tail that had broken from its place pulling the wagon that hauled the sun through the sky. It ran and ran, hoping to get free from the harness that still trailed behind. In another story, the comet was a dragon, breathing a steady stream of fire.

This last tale prompted a long discussion, for Firekeeper had never really thought about dragons, though she'd heard them mentioned frequently, especially in New Kelvin. She'd seen dragons depicted in heraldry, but had believed that they were just poorly drawn lizards. Queen Elexa told her otherwise, showing her brilliant paintings in bestiaries.

"But are these *real* things?" Firekeeper asked, looking at the drawings of dragons and other fantastic beasts.

"I never thought so," the queen admitted, "but then I never thought that there were wolves like Blind Seer."

The Royal Wolf woke from his drowse in front of the fire to comment:

"But what an impressive revelation I have been!"

Firekeeper must hide a grin then or explain. Months earlier she had decided—encouraged by the wolves themselves—that it was best that the humans believe simply that Blind Seer and Elation were fine animals, but animals nonetheless. Her early efforts to explain otherwise had mostly been frustrating. Now she didn't even try.

A few of her friends, Derian, certainly, and probably Elise and Doc, had their suspicions. Firekeeper didn't mind, but she no longer made any effort to represent Blind Seer as anything other than a wolf. She didn't even protest—though not long ago the thought would have sent her into furies—when some mistook the blue-eyed wolf for a dog.

ALTHOUGH FIREKEEPER ENJOYED HER VISITS with the king and queen—and with Citrine, when the girl was sane—first among her friends at the castle was Holly Gardener.

Holly was an older woman, retired from her position as head gardener of Eagle's Nest Castle. She had passed on the responsibilities of acting as head gardener to her son Timin, but she remained busy about the various gardens.

Even now, with spring providing more rain than warmth, Holly could usually be found outside, leaning on her stick as she moved from bedding area to bedding area, encouraging the young growing things—so at least it seemed to Firekeeper—with her very presence.

Gardening in all its forms impressed Firekeeper to no end. As a human art, it ranked right up with music and dancing in her estimation, and per-haps slightly above these, no matter how much she enjoyed them both. Music and dancing were, after all, entertainment only. Gardening was both entertainment and a means of providing food. The wolf-woman had lived through too many lean times to not be impressed by an art that guaranteed good things to eat, even in the leanest winter months.

"And you're not bored with potatoes and turnips," Holly said to her. "That's a good thing. Of course, most people don't have the option of broadening their cold cellar's contents with a duchess's venison."

Firekeeper overlooked the teasing and continued trying to get a feel for the spade she was using. Unlike the bow, which she had taken to with ease, or the sword—which she could use, but was less than adept with—or her beloved Fang, a shovel remained clumsy in her hands.

"That's because," Holly said with a great deal of insight, "you don't get immediate rewards from your work. A bow, now, that's very satisfying. 'Twang' and a goose-feathered shaft is sailing through the air. If you're lucky you even get something nice to eat. With a shovel, all you get is more dirt."

Firekeeper persisted in her efforts, though, and by the time they retired to Holly's cottage on the grounds she had turned over several rows and raked them ready for planting. She was muddy, too, but Holly had suggested she bring a change of clothing with her. By the time tea was ready Firekeeper was warm and dry.

Changes of clothes and hot baths are, Firekeeper thought, *two of the nicer things about how humans live.*

There was a knock at the door just as she was reaching for her first hot buttered biscuit. Holly called out:

"Come in!"

Firekeeper swiveled on her stool by the fire. She'd expected Robyn or Dan, Holly's grandsons. However, Derian was the guest who entered, ducking his tall form just a touch to get under the low lintel of the cottage door.

"Fox Hair!" she cried in delight.

She'd been hunting when Derian arrived from the North Woods and, though they'd met a time or two since, she'd seen little enough of him. He, of course, was staying with his family, while she remained at the castle. Although Derian had assured Firekeeper she would be welcome at the Carter house (if not at the stables) and Firekeeper believed him, the wolf-woman was unwilling to take Blind Seer through the city. They'd made the trip a time or two, and it had been stressful for both of them.

"Am I late?" Derian asked, bowing slightly to Holly. "Has Lady Voracious here eaten everything?"

Firekeeper looked at him in indignation.

"We have just started," she said. "Blind Seer hasn't even had his bone."

"A subtle reminder," Holly said with a smile.

She hobbled out to the kitchen, returning a moment later with a thick beef bone Firekeeper had brought over earlier. The wolf took it from the old woman with extreme delicacy, even resting the messy thing on the hearthstone rather than the rug.

Derian waited until Holly was settled before taking his own chair.

"Firekeeper, I hope you don't mind my inviting Derian," Holly said. "I'd meant to mention his coming earlier, but it quite slipped my mind. You with a shovel was something of a distraction."

Firekeeper wiped butter from her lips onto the back of her hand.

"I am not very good with a shovel," she admitted ruefully.

"And growing worse with a napkin," Derian replied sternly, handing her a square of cloth. "Good manners are for everywhere, not just for King Tedric's table."

Firekeeper submitted meekly, more because she didn't want Holly to think she valued her less than the king than because she felt particularly abashed.

"I can free up to leave town in a day or so," Derian said. "I've been waiting until the prince and princess make their announcement."

"That," Firekeeper said, "will be tomorrow. They have waited so that King Allister will hear first."

Holly, in whom Firekeeper had already confided the great news in order that she might quiz the older woman about just how humans went about having children and how long it took those children to mature to usefulness and such, looked pleased.

"I've been bursting at the seams," the elderly gardener admitted. "Just the other day Princess Sapphire's maid was giving herself such airs in the servants' hall. It was all I could do not to burst her bubble. Smug little minx—as if waiting on a princess makes her one herself!"

"Must run in the blood of those who wait on Shield-born," Derian said. "I recall that Melina's old confidential servant—Nanny, they called her—gave herself airs as well."

"After we have our tea, then," Holly said, "remind me that I have a packet for Derian."

"Packet?" Firekeeper asked.

Holly nodded, looking at that moment bent as much by sorrow as by age.

"Do you remember how once I told you that my daughter, her husband, and their little girl were among those who went with Prince Barden?"

Firekeeper nodded. She felt sad for the fine old lady. It was clear that over ten years might have blunted the intensity of Holly's loss, but had done nothing to diminish her grief.

"Well, I'm sending a few small grave goods for them. Derian and I spoke of this during one of his earlier visits. You, I think, were chasing rabbits."

Firekeeper frowned. "You and House Kestrel and the king and queen. Derian, we will need more than two mules and a few ponies!"

"They're all sending small things," the redhead replied with a chuckle. "Like the tokens that go into wedding pouches."

Firekeeper felt relieved.

"Good then."

DERIAN STUDIED FIREKEEPER as Holly spoke of her daughter's family, but no emotion but compassion crossed the young woman's features. He knew the names of Holly's family: Serena Gardener, Donal Hunter, and Tamara—this last the couple's daughter, still too young to have a use-name of her own. In any case, no other identification than a first name probably had been needed in Prince Barden's small colony.

What Derian was looking for on Firekeeper's face was recognition, for he knew—as perhaps no one other than King Tedric knew—that Firekeeper really was this lost Tamara, and that Holly, whom the wolf-woman had adopted from personal interest and fellow feeling, was her own grandmother.

But Firekeeper showed no signs of recognizing any connection between them other than fondness, and Derian was sworn to silence.

Besides, he thought, *aren't ties of love and friendship better than those of obligation?*

The truth of this stayed with him as he sat visiting with the old woman and the young, and his faint feeling that he should tell Firekeeper the full story of her relationship to Holly faded. Instead he thought over the past several days.

He'd enjoyed his visit home, would be sorry to be leaving again so soon, but Earl Kestrel had offered no difficulty with Derian living at home this summer while continuing in Kestrel employ. Derian could anticipate a long slow spring into summer, working part-time with his father, that routine enlivened by duties for the earl. A trip now would simply give him more stories to tell out under the peach tree in the garden as the family whiled away the hot summer evenings.

Derian considered telling Firekeeper some of the rumors he'd gathered at the stables, but held his tongue. This lighter conversation—Holly was chivying Firekeeper about the butter running down the young woman's chin—

was pleasant, and he would have time enough to bring Firekeeper up to date as they traveled west.

"Tell me, Derian," Holly asked, seeming to read his thoughts. "Are you and Firekeeper making this journey alone together?"

Derian shrugged and offered a rueful smile.

"There's no saving Firekeeper's reputation where I'm concerned, Holly. I was her body servant for too long. 'Round the North Woods we spread the rumor that Blind Seer will have the throat and heart of any man who so much as looks cross-eyed at her, and that stills most of the talk. I've no doubt the story will have come here with us."

"A wolf chaperon." Holly laughed. "That's rather unusual."

Yet true, Derian thought. *I wouldn't want to be the man who showed the wrong side of his hand to Firekeeper. Even if Blind Seer held himself back, she would not.*

THEY LEFT EAGLE'S NEST a few days later. Sapphire and Shad's announcement had been received with overwhelming delight by the residents of Eagle's Nest. There was dancing in the streets and the Festival of the Horse—which was in process already—took on the air of an impromptu congratulations party. Derian—who belonged to the Horse Society and so was already committed to attending the dancing and drinking—threw himself into the celebrations with double enthusiasm.

His head was still a bit heavy and felt about twice its usual size from overindulging the night before when Derian rose the next morning to saddle Roanne. The chestnut mare was skittish, dancing at her shadow, and unsettling the mixed string of mules and mountain horses Derian was taking along. His usual gift for handling horseflesh seemed to have vanished this morning and he found himself particularly glad that his younger brother Brock and old Toad were coming with him around the city and for a day's ride west.

Firekeeper would intercept him there. They had both agreed that while Roanne was accustomed to Blind Seer, and her habit of dominating any equine company in which she found herself would cause the other animals to eventually come around to tolerating the wolf, there was no need to start the introductions in a crowded urban area.

Rain fell fairly heavily all that morning and into the early afternoon, adding to Derian's misery. Even Brock's usual exuberance was quelled, though he bounced back easily enough when the sun came out during their lunch break. He was particularly excited about being taken along when their father made one of his annual buying trips to Hope, a town to the south on the border of Hawk Haven and Bright Bay. Colby Carter had promised his younger son his first horse if the boy selected well and wisely. Brock couldn't ask enough questions about conformation, gait, hidden flaws, and all the rest.

Eventually, Derian had sweated enough of the previous night's indulgence from his system to enjoy the conversation and found himself sorry to see Brock and Toad turn east the next morning while he took his pack string west.

Derian knew Firekeeper would meet him as planned. She'd come tapping at his window the night before while Toad was in the common room yarning with the other guests and Brock dead to the world, dreaming, doubtlessly, of horses.

Firekeeper had crouched out on the thatch, looking pleased with herself.

"I meet you where the near fields end," she had said, "and there are some little woods."

Derian had nodded. He thought he remembered the place from the year before. As if his nod had been all the acknowledgment she'd needed, Firekeeper had backed away. Although Derian tried to keep her in sight, he hadn't actually seen her depart.

Nor, the next morning, did he see her reappear. One moment he and his string were making fairly good time—given that the road was sticky with mud—and the next the lead mule was balking and Firekeeper was standing alongside the road.

She was dressed much as always: bare feet, leather trousers cut off below the knees, and a leather vest buttoned across small but definite breasts. Her hair was much grown out from the severe cutting she'd given it five or six moonspans before, and was just reaching the untidy stage where locks kept tumbling into her eyes. She'd clipped the most troublesome of these back with slim wire pins Duchess Kestrel had given her at that past winter's Wolf Moon festival, but this small effort at tidiness made Firekeeper look, somehow, all the more untamed.

A heavy leather belt held her sheathed knife on one side, a canteen on the other. An embroidered bag of fine white doeskin—a gift from Edlin Norwood—held her flint and steel for fire making. This meager equipment, Derian knew, was all she had brought for a journey that would take them outside of civilization and across mountains that would have barely shaken off winter's grip.

Blind Seer was nowhere to be seen and Derian, whacking the restive mule with his riding crop, was grateful. The pack animals were jumpy enough, just from catching Firekeeper's scent. He didn't doubt she smelled of wolf, of raw meat, and of other things equally unwholesome to a conservative herbivore's nose.

"Hi!" Firekeeper said by way of greeting, and Derian could hear the laughter in her voice.

She trotted across to the lead mule—apparently not minding the cold mud that stuck to her bare feet—pulled herself up onto the mule's back in one easy motion, leaned down, and growled into the beast's long ear.

The mule froze in place, then slowly, carefully, as if it had suddenly become aware of a stinging bee on its ear, it swiveled its head to get a look at the wolf-woman. She smiled and there was no doubt in Derian's mind that this smile was no friendly gesture but rather an arrogant baring of teeth.

The mule seemed to melt into itself, its muscles losing their tension all in an instant.

"There," Firekeeper said happily, moving down the line of pack animals and slapping each one heartily on the shoulder, "they should be good now. I not say they not go crazy if Blind Seer come out, but they have some idea. Not bad to start."

"Not bad," Derian agreed.

They moved along briskly after that, the pack animals frantically eager to please. Derian wondered what Firekeeper had said to them—for he had no doubt that she had said something that had put her on top of their little hierarchy. It didn't bother him. Out here, she was in charge and he was grateful for her expertise.

He also enjoyed the wolf-woman's high spirits. In many ways Firekeeper reminded him of a horse coming home to a familiar stable—not that he'd ever share the comparison with her. She just might find it a deadly insult. But her manner was much the same. He almost expected to see her ears prick forward.

Firekeeper's cheerfully arrogant queen-of-the-woodlands mood did not last for the entire journey. Horse Moon had died and Puma Moon was beginning to show when she grew somber, disappearing for long stretches both night and day. Derian didn't worry. He knew she was safer here than she was in any city in the land. Blind Seer was with her and he had caught glimpses of Elation from time to time, though the peregrine seemed to be attending to her own business rather than following Firekeeper.

For that matter, Derian himself felt fairly safe. As long as he didn't do anything stupid like lead the pack train onto a bad trail, he was unconcerned about the dangers of the wild. Firekeeper protected him, and every evening as he pitched his camp she brought him some sort of wild delicacy—rabbit or pheasant or fresh fish—for his meal. Often she added a handful of mushrooms or a bundle of spring greens to augment his supplies further. In some ways, Derian was more comfortable on this trip than he had been with Earl Kestrel's expedition, because his only concerns were for his immediate needs.

Puma Moon was rounding fat and full the night before they were to cross the gap in the Iron Mountains into the wild lands where Firekeeper had been brought up. The wolf-woman came into Derian's camp that night—an unusual thing, for she had been exploring most nights—and squatted with her back to the fire.

"Fox Hair," she said, "there are *humans* going this way."

The emphasis she put on the word made quite clear that she did not think this a good thing at all.

Derian nodded. The signs had been evident even to an indifferent woodsman like himself. Those who had come along this trail before them had made some effort to hide their signs farther back, but this close to the gap there was no such effort. Manure dried on the narrow trails, dead wood had been cut. He'd even seen the remnants of a fire circle or two.

He decided that now was the time to tell Firekeeper some of the rumors he'd gathered back in Eagle's Nest.

"I heard," he said, "around my father's stables, that the demand for mules and sturdy horseflesh is up. The buyers aren't who you'd think either, not some farmer getting a few extra head in now that planting and plowing has begun."

Firekeeper looked blank, but Derian continued:

"We get some of that market, you know. There are those who think it wiser to let someone else do the winter feeding for them. But these folks my father and the other livestock dealers—not only near the city, but their associates elsewhere—have been seeing aren't interested in that. Or, I should say to be fair, they aren't interested in *just* that."

Firekeeper gave a low, rumbling growl. Derian held up a hand.

"More haste, less waste, Firekeeper. I'm telling you all I know to spare questions later."

Firekeeper subsided, but Derian didn't need to know her as well as he did to tell she was as taut as a strung bow.

"These buyers wanted animals who could pull a plow—eventually—but they were looking for general-purpose animals, a horse or mule who could pull a wagon or plow, carry a rider, all the rest. They wanted well-broken animals, not raw youngsters. And there was one other element to the pattern. Often the buyers weren't one person or family, but a group."

"So?" Firekeeper asked, and while she didn't growl, her voice was rough.

"Firekeeper, you've figured it out already. You just might not know the word for it. These humans on the trail in front of us, they're not furriers or trappers. It's the wrong time of year for that even if they were. What we're seeing are the signs of . . ."

He shrugged, settling for a word that he himself didn't really use except in a historical context.

"They're colonists, like the people who came from the Old World to settle this land, except that they're not coming from across the sea. They're going across the Iron Mountains."

Firekeeper made a sound like several words trying to come out at once. The word that won through was "Why?"

"I don't know for sure," Derian said, "but I'll give you a guess. They want a place of their own."

Firekeeper stared at him. Then she nodded slowly and Derian realized that she was finding a correlation in her own knowledge. She didn't offer an explanation, so he went on.

"Since back before Queen Zorana the Great founded Hawk Haven," Derian said, "it's been traditional to stay east of the Iron Mountains. There were stories about horrible creatures that lived to the west, and there was land enough east, especially after the Plague killed so many.

"But ever since I can remember, well before Prince Barden took his expedition west of the mountains, there've been those who've grumbled that all the land Hawk Haven has is used up. We've never been a sea power—not like Bright Bay or Waterland. We've won a bit of land from time to time from Bright Bay, but they've always taken it back—sometimes taking a bit from us for a while."

Firekeeper nodded. She'd been drilled in the history of that conflict the summer before.

"When Prince Barden went west—I was six or seven at the time, old enough to remember the scandal perfectly—not everyone agreed with King

Tedric's anger. There were those who were ready to follow the prince, just as soon as the fuss died down. I'll tell you, most people thought that within a few moonspans—a year at most—the prince would have made peace with his father.

"But nothing was heard from Prince Barden, nothing at all, and the king didn't get any less angry. He got into a tremendous argument with Duchess Kestrel when she suggested that someone lead an expedition to check on Barden's group."

Firekeeper made a surprised sound.

"You didn't know that did you?" Derian's grin was a bit forced. "It's not common knowledge, but I heard about it out in the North Woods this year."

"Makes the earl brave," Firekeeper said thoughtfully. "Braver."

Derian was confused for a moment. Then he understood.

"You mean for going out there last year? That's true, but he didn't go without the king's permission. He brought his petition to the king at the end of autumn and worked on it all through the winter. I doubt King Tedric would have softened for anyone else, but the earl did have the excuse that his sister was Barden's wife—that he was going to find news of Eirene for his aging mother rather than to look for Barden."

"But he was looking for Barden," Firekeeper said, "and for Blysse."

"And all he found was you," Derian agreed. "Anyhow, as you might guess, both Barden's silence and the king's abiding anger made those people who thought that moving west would be a good idea think again. But I'd guess that when we went west and came back again, and the news got around that Barden's expedition had died in a fire, not by anything some mysterious monsters did, and that the king was taking as a favorite a girl most people thought was Barden's daughter . . ."

"Me," Firekeeper said.

"Right. Well, I'd guess those people who'd been chaffing for more land decided they should go get it now, before the king or his heirs got around to making a proclamation against it."

"Might they proclaim this?" Firekeeper asked.

"They might," Derian answered. "Or they might not. I don't know. The thing is, Hawk Haven is getting a little cramped."

Firekeeper looked at him incredulously. She waved her hand at the empty spaces around them.

"Cramped? We barely see anyone for days!"

Derian leaned back and checked the pot of tea hanging over the fire.

There was just enough for one more cup and he poured it before setting more water to warm.

"There's cramped and cramped," he explained, dreading that this would be beyond his ability to explain. "You understand that different people own different bits of land."

Firekeeper nodded. "Like the king owns the castle and the Kestrels the North Woods."

Derian felt relieved as he saw a good example.

"Right. Now, you know the North Woods have another name. They're also called the Norwood Grant."

"Yes."

"That word 'grant' means that the land was given to the Norwood family to own and administer . . . to manage. Now each of the Great Houses has their grant. The House of the Eagle—that's the king's house—owns more land than just the castle. They have a grant of their own."

And a few crown cities and other things like that, Derian thought, *but let's keep this simple.*

"Then the lesser houses—like Elise's," Derian felt an involuntary smile rise to his lips as he thought of their mutual friend, "they have grants of their own, smaller grants, but still grants."

Firekeeper nodded and Derian went on.

"That still leaves land, since Queen Zorana the Great didn't think it was a good idea to give the common folk nothing to call their own. The problem is that over a hundred years have passed since Queen Zorana's time. Just about all that unowned land has been claimed by someone. Sometimes the land has two owners—like in Doc's family. The Surcliffe land is actually part of the Norwood Grant, but Doc's family would have to do something pretty terrible . . ."

Firekeeper looked puzzled.

"Like help an enemy in a war," Derian explained. "Anyhow, they'd have to do something pretty terrible to give the Norwood family a reason to throw them off. That's good and that's bad."

"How? Sounds all good to me."

"It does, in theory," Derian admitted. "But what if the Norwoods want to reward one of their good retainers—like Wendee or Valet—or give land to one of their children. Remember, Earl Kestrel has four children. Only Edlin will inherit so Earl Kestrel has to find places for the others. That takes more land. Soon they don't have any more and need to buy more land."

"And," Firekeeper said, speaking so slowly that Derian knew she was reasoning it out, "that eats the land Queen Zorana left. Soon there is no more."

"You've got it," Derian said, more relieved than he could express. He'd thought he'd need to explain this far more carefully. Then he remembered something.

"Wolves are territorial," he said, "aren't they?"

"Very," Firekeeper said, and though she didn't turn to face him, he saw the edge of a scowl on her shadowed face. "And what these humans who want land don't seem to think is that this land they go to is claimed. It is claimed by my people—by the wolves and by the other Royal Beasts."

Derian swallowed hard. Even knowing Firekeeper, knowing Blind Seer and Elation, he hadn't ever thought about the western lands in that way. To him it was empty land, open for claiming. Now he saw that to Firekeeper, at least, that was far from the case.

"You say the wolves and the other Royal Beasts," he repeated. "They share?"

Firekeeper shrugged expressively.

"As beasts share. A wolf pack hunts larger game than do a raccoon. A raven eats the spoils of the wolf. A great cat, it may or may not share—so with the bear. Each lives in with the others or starves or dies. I not think humans is like this."

Derian bit into his lip. He thought of mousetraps and hound packs, fences and borders, and, of course, feuds and wars. Human culture seemed to have grown up around ways to keep from sharing with anyone other than those most important to you personally.

"No, I don't think so," he said.

They sat in uncomfortable silence for a time, then Derian asked:

"Firekeeper, do you think the beasts will harm these human colonists?"

Firekeeper shrugged.

"I don't know," she said.

Derian had the uncomfortable feeling that what she really meant was. "I won't say."

In that moment, he knew what side the wolf-woman would be on if a conflict came and the night which had seemed so safe and so friendly grew darker, and he shared with the mules and horses a restless unease.

IV

FIREKEEPER WAS THE FIRST TO SEE the small community that had been constructed over the ruins of Prince Barden's failed effort. Moments like this brought home to her more forcefully than anything else how much she had changed in a year.

A year ago she wouldn't have known what a horse was—much less how to differentiate it from a pony or a mule. She would have figured out that the oddly shaped things set about the cleared area were shelters, but she wouldn't have known how to see the difference between a tent and a cabin under construction, nor would she have recognized the purpose of the wall rising around the perimeter of the cleared area.

"Here," she said to Blind Seer. "They build their dens here!"

She was surprised at outrage rising within her. This place meant no more to her than any other section of the forest—or so she had thought. The wolf's reply was laconic.

"Not a bad idea, really," Blind Seer said. "The first to come here when you were small cut down the bigger trees. Even the many years that have turned since fire destroyed Barden's colony haven't been enough for those great trees to grow back. Earl Kestrel's venture last year cut down many of the saplings for corral and tent poles. They even cleared some of the rubble and vines. And this place was well chosen in the first place."

Firekeeper grunted irritably, but she understood what he meant, especially now that she had lived among humans and come to know what they needed and valued. The place Prince Barden had chosen was near to fresh running water. It was on fairly level ground, which humans liked not only for building their homes, but for planting their fields. Moreover, it was less than a day's easy journey from the gap through the Iron Mountains. Still, she felt offended, as if her own home had been invaded.

"Perhaps," she said to Blind Seer, "I didn't believe the humans had really come here to settle—no matter what Fox Hair said—until I saw this place. What are we going to do?"

Blind Seer rubbed his great head against her arm. In turn, she buried her hand in his fur and felt comforted.

"I think," the wolf said after some consideration, "that Derian must go to them. Humans are as territorial as a mother bird guarding her nest. They may already feel themselves owners of everything they touch. If they find Derian camping a distance from here, they may view him as an intruder."

Firekeeper nodded—a human gesture she had learned and that had become a habit. She'd been using it for moons past. Only now, here on the fringes of where she'd been only a wolf, did she feel herself use the gesture and think it odd.

"I agree," she replied. "Derian's purpose in coming west was to bring those stones and gifts to the ones who died here. He cannot avoid this place without failing."

She studied the human encampment, forcing herself to strip away the new construction and see the place as it had been when she had left it.

"These newcomers have left the place where the earl told his people to re-bury the bones and such they took from the Burnt Place," she said, feeling some relief. "They have some feelings then."

"Feelings for dried bones burnt beyond good eating," Blind Seer scoffed. "You are becoming very human, Firekeeper."

She caught him a sharp blow on one shoulder.

"Never say that!" she growled. "Never!"

Blind Seer's eyes narrowed and his lips curled back from his fangs in an ugly snarl. He glowered at her and she held his stare, her hand drifting in the direction of the garnet-hilted knife that hung at her belt.

Maybe it was this. Maybe it was that—despite the fact that he was younger than her in years—Blind Seer had been trained to view the wolf-woman as a pup, entitled to the forbearance the senior wolf gives the pup. For whatever the reason, Blind Seer's snarl melted to tongue-panting amiability and his tail gave a faint wag.

"I won't call you a human," he conceded. "Shall Fox Hair tell those there that you are with him?"

Firekeeper considered. Her first impulse was to deny her presence. She wanted nothing more than to flee humans and human things. Then her loyalty to and affection for Derian rose, reminding her just how vulnerable one human—especially one human possessed of what others might see as wealth—could be. She didn't know these humans. They might be as kind as Holly Gardener, but they could be closer kin to the bandits who had attacked them along the road in New Kelvin.

"I think," she said, "that I must let them see me. Fox Hair should not be thought alone. Where is Elation? That bird is always flapping about whenever one wants her least. Now that she could be useful, I haven't seen her since last sunrise."

"Elation flew west," Blind Seer replied. "I think she is as disturbed as you about this human settling—more, maybe, for the wingéd folk could have sent her word and forewarning and they did not."

Firekeeper considered that and the sour feeling in her gut grew stronger. She had grown accustomed to having little or no contact with the Royal Wolves. Blind Seer alone of all her pack had accompanied her east over the Iron Mountains when she departed with Earl Kestrel's expedition. There were Cousin Wolves in the Norwood Grant, but these were limited in their conversation. They might be bullied into telling where game could be found, but they no more offered friendly gossip than did a chattering brook.

For the first time she wondered why some member of her and Blind Seer's pack—for they had howled their coming—had not come to meet them and bring them this news.

"We go back to Fox Hair, then," she said with more confidence than she felt. "I will go with him to this denning of humans, see that they treat him well, and then go find our mother and father. They will know what is being done about this—if the Royal Beasts see it as invasion or as something to be tolerated as one tolerates fleas in the summer."

Blind Seer shook.

"Even with fleas," he reminded her, "one scratches."

⚜

DERIAN LISTENED TO FIREKEEPER'S report with mingled dismay and resignation.

Fleetingly, he wondered if King Tedric had known—if his request to Derian had been less a means of gathering information than a subtle warning that Derian and Firekeeper might not find the lands over the mountains as they had left them.

Then why didn't the king just tell me? Derian mused to himself. Immediately he answered his own question. *Because if he did so, he would have taken official notice of these adventurers and for some reason he doesn't wish to do so.*

Derian sighed. Not for the first time, he was very glad not to be the king. Sometimes it was hard enough being the king's most junior counselor.

He knew Firekeeper well enough to know that, although she was trying to keep her reaction to herself, she was very upset. He didn't need to ask why. This was the land in which she had grown up, the place where her parents had died, where her own ancestors were buried. To find that place defiled must be more upsetting that he could imagine.

However, since the wolf-woman was trying to hide her feelings, Derian decided not to comment. Instead he asked:

"Think we can get there today?"

"By twilight, yes," Firekeeper replied. "Maybe sooner, though parts of the trail are muddy and a creek so swollen we will need to take the pack animals around to a shallow place."

"The mules," Derian hinted, "will move faster if you and Blind Seer are with me."

Firekeeper nodded a touch grimly and fell into line next to the lead animal.

They arrived at the settlement shortly before dusk. The long rays of the setting sun filtering through the trees were more than enough for Derian to make his own assessment of the place. Firekeeper might have grown sophisticated enough to tell tents from cabins, but her counting still tended toward the "one, two, many" variety unless she felt numbers were important. Even then, she didn't bother much with numbers over ten. Privately, Derian suspected she continued to count on her fingers.

So I guess we'll need to get her using her toes. After all, she won't wear shoes.

He was still smiling slightly at his own joke when a man emerged from the settlement, walking through what would someday be a gate, though now it was only gateposts set in the framework of a partially built log palisade.

"Welcome to Bardenville," the man said, smiling widely. "I'm Ewen Brooks."

Ewen was shorter than Derian, but then most people were. By any other reckoning he would have been considered tall. There was no doubt he was strong. Even with the evening chill gathering, he wore nothing over his short-sleeved smock, exposing forearms rippling with muscle. His brown hair and beard were neatly trimmed, though the beard was worn somewhat longer than was typical in the city.

Fleetingly, Derian wondered if "Brooks" might be a newly chosen surname. It certainly didn't reflect a profession, as most did, and location names were more common in crowded areas where there might be more than one baker or carpenter. He filed that information away for future reference.

"I'm Derian Carter," he replied. Then, deciding that honesty was best, he continued, "I was out here a year or so ago with Earl Kestrel. I've come back with grave markers for . . ."

He paused, not certain if mentioning the failed first expedition might be taken as an insult to this new venture.

Ewen Brooks, however, didn't seem at all put out.

"For the prince's folks," he finished for Derian. "That's good. We found the burial plot and left it untouched. We'll be glad to have your markers. Kestrel's idea?"

"My own," Derian said. Realizing he sounded affronted, he quickly went on. "I was out by the battlefield at the end of King Allister's War, making markers for the dead. I kept thinking of these people, buried as best we could, but with their graves unmarked. It seemed their spirits would rest better for the remembrance."

"Quite a trip to make for spirits unrelated to you," Ewen said, and from his tone Derian couldn't tell whether the other man thought him foolish or honorable.

"I've brought someone who was related to them," Derian said. He glanced back and found Firekeeper standing alongside the lead mule, so still that she almost vanished in the dusk. "Firekeeper, come and meet our host."

He knew he was stretching the point. Ewen Brooks hadn't precisely invited them to stay, but he had greeted them and had said the grave markers would be welcome.

"Firekeeper . . . ," Ewen said almost under his breath. "That's the . . . the girl Kestrel adopted, isn't it?"

Firekeeper had advanced, walking a touch stiffly, like a dog—or a wolf, Derian thought with some shock—advancing on a stranger.

"Blysse," she said bluntly, and her refusal to use her wolf name, what she thought of as her personal name, told Derian that she was less than comfortable with this Ewen Brooks.

"Blysse," Ewen said. "Pleased to meet you."

Firekeeper nodded stiffly.

Derian glanced at her, but she didn't seem to be offering him any specific warning, so he decided to proceed.

"So," he said to Ewen, "I've been on the trail since dawn. Can I have shelter here or would you prefer me to bed down elsewhere?"

Ewen, who had been staring rather fixedly at Firekeeper, shook himself.

"Right! No, don't go. Come in. We don't have stabling yet, but there's corral space enough for your beasts. Nice stock you have there, by the way."

"Thanks," Derian said. "We're testing the mountain horses. They've some qualities my father finds promising."

"And the mules?"

"Tested and first-rate."

Derian spoke without thinking. He wasn't a stable owner's son for nothing. He could almost smell the other man's eagerness to own the mules himself.

Careful, Derian, he thought to himself. *These folks aren't in the city with tokens in their pockets or lines of credit to some Great House. They're out here without money and you're here with no one but Firekeeper to keep you safe.*

He smiled ingenuously and as he did so, somewhere out in the darkness a wolf—Blind Seer, he was almost certain—gave a long, plaintive howl.

The pack animals snorted and stamped. Derian was certain that if Firekeeper had not resumed her place by the lead animal a few might have bolted. Ewen Brooks started as well.

"Come ahead," he said. "It's getting dark and though the palisade isn't finished, it's better than nothing."

"Had much trouble with predators?" Derian asked, hearing the forced casualness in his own voice.

"Some," Ewen admitted. "Not wolves, though. They're too spooky of a big group like this. Don't like fire neither."

Derian knew better. He'd seen Blind Seer lounging in front of too many hearths, knew that Firekeeper had learned to use flint and steel from a wolf. If the Royal Wolves weren't bothering the settlement, they had their reason.

He wondered what it was and, glancing back at Firekeeper, felt certain that she knew the answer.

THE SETTLEMENT PROVED to be fairly large. Over forty men, women, and children lived in the small community, according to Ewen, and, as Derian quickly learned, more were expected before summer was fully under way.

"We decided," Ewen said when Derian commented, "that we would take our lead from the late prince—that's why we kept his name for the settlement. Prince Barden didn't come out here with just a couple of families. He came with those who could build, work wood, farm, handle animals, not just a few hunters and the like."

"You sound like you know a lot about his expedition," Derian said.

"I do after a fashion," Ewen replied. "Come this way. There's an old corral we've stopped using since we've built stronger. It'll do for your beasts for tonight at least."

Derian recognized the pole and lashing structure he'd built the spring before. It had been mended, but would serve at least as well now as it had then.

"My elder brother was one of Barden's followers," Ewen continued, helping Derian unload the mules. "He told me stories as I was begging to be taken along with him. I was sixteen, shy of my majority, but my parents were willing to let me go. I think Wythe would have taken me, too, but lung fever swept through our community that winter and I was too weak when early spring came. I meant to follow him out, but then King Tedric . . ."

Ewen looked as if he were about to spit at the mention of the king's name, but remembered himself in time.

"King Tedric made his proclamation disowning his own son and by association those who followed him. My parents would have nothing of my going then, and though I still thought of going, the same lung fever that had laid me low weakened my father. I didn't have the heart to leave my sisters alone to run the mill."

Miller, Derian thought. *I remember a Miller or so among the list that Lord Aksel made up for me. That must be Ewen's brother and maybe his family. I wonder why Ewen isn't using that name? He's clearly had the training. I wonder if his family wanted nothing to do with this expedition either?*

He put the thought aside for now. As if Ewen's leading Derian into the settlement proper had been a signal, people—mostly adults, though there were a few half-grown children among them—were filtering out of the houses and tents that clustered around the central square. Most watched silently, and Ewen didn't make introductions.

For the first time, Derian noticed that one edge of that square was a log-walled longhouse, sturdy and solid. It was large enough to serve as a stable at night, if the settlers didn't own too much livestock.

Sounds of babies wailing and small children fussing came from inside the longhouse.

That must be their fortress as well as stable, Derian thought. *Defensible in a pinch, especially against wild animals. They must not have thought me much of a threat, but figured to tuck the littler children away, just in case.*

By the time Derian's pack train was unloaded and he'd shown Ewen enough to reassure the man that he'd told the truth about the reason for his coming to Bardenville, Derian and Firekeeper were escorted to Ewen's own house.

They carried with them Derian's personal kit, his bedding, and, wrapped inside this, the small offerings with which Derian had been entrusted by the Kestrels, Holly Gardener, and the royal family. None of these were large and, as was the custom, sentiment was valued over costly materials, but still Derian thought it best to be careful.

Ewen Brooks's house was a log cabin like all the other buildings in the settlement, though larger than most. The one large central room and a sleeping loft above could have held a fair number of people in a pinch. Looking about, Derian guessed that Ewen's house must have been the first built and that it still sheltered more than his immediate family.

The floor was only packed dirt and the windows lacked even oiled cloth to cover them, just horizonal shutters made from boards and hinged with leather. These shutters, however, were sturdily functional and would, even when open, prevent all rain but that driven directly by the wind from coming into the house.

The furniture had clearly been made locally and consisted of three-legged stools and a couple of rough board tables. Sand-scoured pots and pans hung on the wall near the hearth, and a series of shelves held a few serving utensils.

Despite these rude accommodations, the house was comfortable. Some effort had been made to decorate it. Bed quilts hung along the walls like tapestries, and a family shrine held its position of honor in one back corner, a squat candle burning in a holder in front of it.

Remembering how fire had taken Barden's settlement, Derian found himself wondering if some similar homey touch had slain those first colonists.

He shivered at the thought and a pretty woman who Derian guessed was only slightly older than he was hurried over to him.

"Hello! I'm Dawn, Ewen's wife. Let me give you something hot to drink and a seat by the fire. I well remember how wearing a long day on the trail could be."

Derian let Dawn urge him into a seat, but insisted that Dawn make the tea from the supplies in his pack. It was too early in the spring for these people to have been able to much augment the stores they would have hauled across the mountains, and he wasn't about to take advantage of their generosity.

The eagerness with which Dawn accepted his gift confirmed Derian's guess that she was housekeeping on a slim margin. As she prepared the tea, she made introductions all around. Firekeeper was introduced as Blysse. Neither she nor Derian insisted on the title "Lady," a thing Derian thought wise given Ewen's disdain toward the king, a reaction that might extend to the Great Houses.

As Derian had guessed, the cabin was home to other than Dawn, Ewen, and their three small children. Five other adults and assorted children apparently took their meals in the cabin. All assisted with preparations for the evening meal and showered Derian with questions.

It was clear to him that although most had been out west only a few moonspans at most—and the majority for a moon or less—they viewed the land on the other side of the mountains as a foreign place, a curiosity. Ewen had chosen his fellow colonists well. At least in this sample, Derian saw no sign of homesickness, only excitement regarding their great adventure and, especially among the younger men, a slight condescension toward him as one who wasn't taking part.

I wonder how they'll feel when winter comes, Derian thought, irked by a particularly thoughtless comment regarding his own journey. *It'll be different when new supplies can't be gotten in by cutting back across the mountains, when the only faces they see are those in this small community, and when the snow is hip-deep. For them, this is springtime in more ways than one.*

Dinner when it was served was quite good. Indeed there was more meat in the stew than a city family might see in a week and broiled fish was included as a side dish. In contrast, for bread there was mounded journey cake, served dry but for a small pot of jam and smaller pats of strong-tasting soft cheese.

"We've a few cows," Ewen explained, "but they're nursing now. We chose breeds known for their hardiness rather than great givers of milk. Time enough when we've been longer settled to bring out finer stock."

Derian agreed. He knew little about cattle—Prancing Steed Stables had moved away even from draft oxen, except by contract.

"Feed must be a problem," he said, thinking of what he'd packed just for his own animals.

"Cows aren't as choosy as horses," Ewen replied, "and goats less than either. We opted for more goats than anything else. We're also planting oats for when winter comes and hope to import some. Oats are good for people as well as animals, as is corn. For a time, we'll be doubling up with the creatures, though we'll be eating mush and porridge rather than grain."

"Hunting's good, though," spoke up Hart, a youth a few years younger than Derian who was some sort of cousin of Dawn. "If it weren't for the wolves we could fair harvest the deer and elk like any other stock."

Ever since their arrival, Firekeeper had kept silent, looking about with interest, her dark eyes unreadable in a deliberately impassive face. Derian had done his best to help her, knowing that the wolf-woman was shy when confronted with strangers, leading the conversation, asking many questions, and hoping she would be forgotten.

From the silence that suddenly fell after Hart made his comment about the wolves, Firekeeper had not been forgotten—not at all. Derian held his breath, knowing how fiercely loyal Firekeeper was to the wolves. They, not any human living, were her family.

Firekeeper said nothing, however, affecting to look drowsy, and the comment passed without incident, though Dawn offered Derian some jam for his journey cake rather more quickly than would be usual manners. In a raised voice, she started telling him about her plans to start hives if she could find the bees. Honey, she said, would provide sweetener and sugar.

"Later," Ewen cut in, his enthusiasm for his projects robbing his words of the bragging note of some of the other men, "we'll tap trees for sugar or grow beets, but honey will do for now. I plan for us to be a self-sufficient community. Trade from the east will be welcome, but we've brought enough with us so that we shouldn't be dependent."

Derian wondered if Ewen had been as thorough as he believed. He might have been, if he'd been daydreaming about this project for more than ten years, ever since his brother planned to make a similar journey with Prince Barden.

Indeed, Derian thought that Ewen might have talked on into the next morning if Dawn had not hinted rather strongly that other members of the household needed their rest. A few of the young men, Hart among them, went out to sleep in the barn—apparently their usual place, Derian was glad to see, for he had no desire to displace a young buck and have him put out about it later.

Derian offered to go with them, but Ewen and Dawn would not hear of it. He was given a place in front of the hearth, where the coals, banked for the night, still gave off a pleasant glow of warmth.

Firekeeper would have been offered the same, but during the general confusion of comings and goings, she had slipped outside and did not return. Derian excused her, saying that she was woods wise and could take care of herself. However, he had a feeling that every word he said somehow damned his friend in his hosts' eyes. Silence seemed the better course of action and he adopted it, yawning broadly in a manner that wasn't entirely feigned.

As he drifted off to sleep he heard the distant howl of a wolf. Oddly enough, it comforted him.

FIREKEEPER FOUND THE EVENING SPENT with Ewen Brooks and his household incredibly disturbing. It was not just being closed into a small, somewhat smoky room with people she didn't know, nor was it that Blind Seer was not with her, nor even was it that she longed for the moment when she would be reunited with her family.

Memories surged beneath the surface of her thoughts, memories she hadn't even suspected she had and so were all the more disturbing for their gentle stirring.

Surely she had spent many hours in a room much like this one. Surely she had listened to similar conversations. There was a note in Ewen's voice as he spoke of his dreams that she had heard before, a barely suppressed passion so intense that she felt that the passion in and of itself should have been enough to make the dream come true.

Although the wolf-woman longed to flee, she made herself remain, listening, watching, learning.

She remembered all too well the stories she had heard from the Royal Beasts the previous autumn, stories that held their history of their encounters with humanity. She knew as none of these humans did that the Beasts had long memories and would resent this new settlement as they had resented little else.

As Ewen prosed on, almost worshipfully evoking images of hot bread baked in their own ovens, of tools crafted at their own forges, of mines dug in the western face of the mountain to supply iron, and of fields so bountiful that winter hunger would be laughable, Firekeeper found herself wondering for the first time why the Beasts had tolerated Prince Barden's settlement. Would they tolerate this one for the same reason? She resolved to ask the Ones just as soon as she could.

When Dawn Brooks began arranging for sleeping accommodations, Firekeeper slipped out the door. Only one of the long-bodied hound dogs drowsing in the yard noticed her going, and he swallowed his own baying alarm in response to her growled warning.

Shadows dark as puddled ink hid the wolf-woman as she raced toward the tree line. Once under the shelter of the trees she slowed, knowing that none in the human community had the eyes to see her. An owl hooted from a tree and she paused, wondering if it was speaking to her, but it proved only a Cousin, diving after mice foraging at the edges of the cleared field.

Once her eyes adjusted to the moonlight, Firekeeper easily found a game trail and paced along it. She didn't know yet where the wolves were denning, but they would find her. Blind Seer, at least, could be counted on to do so. Nor did he disappoint her. The wolf-woman was still breathing deeply to get the scent of smoke out from her nostrils when Blind Seer pounced at her from the shadow of a squat evergreen.

Quick as the wolf was, Firekeeper heard the sound as his paws pushed against the ground and was ready for him, bracing herself so that rather than knocking her flat as he had intended, he found himself caught in her arms. She couldn't hold him—he was too large for that—but it won her points in their undeclared game.

They wrestled for a bit until Blind Seer had pinned her against the duff and bracken, his paws planted on her chest, taking his penalty in sloppy licks across her face.

"Venison stew," he declared. "More heavily seasoned than is to my taste, but then I like my meat blood-hot."

"And from your sloppy bathing," Firekeeper said, shoving him back and tugging at a bit of matted blood his wade in a stream hadn't quite washed away, "I can tell you had it. Have you found the pack?"

"I have and they bid me bring you to them," the blue-eyed wolf replied. "They would have howled, but this year's pups are yet small and some of those young hunters—if what humans do can truly be called hunting—have shown too much interest in learning where we are staying these days."

Firekeeper held up a hand, again aware that this was a human gesture she would not have used a year before.

"This year's pups?" she asked. "When last we spoke with the One Female she said she did not intend a litter this year, that there were pups enough to rear."

Blind Seer's ears flattened slightly in an expression of confusion.

"I had forgotten that," he said, "and was simply pleased to see the fat fur-balls looking so healthy. There are four this litter: two males, two females."

Firekeeper put her question away as yet another one to ask the Ones and instead asked:

"You say the humans have been looking for where the pack dens. Have they found them?"

"Not yet," Blind Seer scoffed. "Those younglings are not as woods wise as they believe—not even as woods wise as Edlin and far from as expert as Race Forester. Nor has the pack made it easy for them. Some of our own yearlings have been going out to distant points and singing their own praises, leaving trampled paw prints in the mud where these trackers may find them, and otherwise confusing the signs."

"Wise," said Firekeeper, rising to her feet and brushing some of the mess from her clothes and hair, "for I do not think there is any great love for wolf-kind among those in the new Bardenville."

"So they remember the prince, then," Blind Seer said. "That's interesting."

"Their One," Firekeeper said, "this Ewen Brooks, has taken Barden's dream for his own. I think Derian was right. These people are like young wolves full of the urge to disperse. They saw nowhere to go until . . ."

She fell silent, her fingernails digging into her palms.

"Until?" Blind Seer prompted.

"Until my return showed them the trail."

"Don't blame yourself, dear heart," the wolf replied. "Even if you had not returned from here, Earl Kestrel and his folk would have done so. The end would have been the same."

Firekeeper nodded, but remained uncomforted.

Would the wolves have let Earl Kestrel return if they had not promised her mother—that forgotten human woman—that they would give Firekeeper a chance to know her human heritage? Kestrel's small company—Derian, Ox, Race, and Valet—would have been easy hunting even for her relatively small pack, and had Kestrel's expedition not returned, then the fear that had held the humans to their side of the mountain would have remained undiminished.

Such thoughts did nothing to assuage the unhappiness that had plagued Firekeeper since first she had realized that humans were moving west. As Blind Seer led her to this season's denning place, she felt like a young wolf who had been caught trying to steal a bone from a bigger, stronger wolf—certain she was about to get a drubbing.

But the only drubbing she received—initially at least—was the roisterous greeting of the wolf pack. The spring before, when Earl Kestrel had led his expedition west, the pack had consisted of eight adults, six pups, and Firekeeper. By the time she had visited the following autumn, two of the puppies had died, and an adult male had dispersed, ranging elsewhere, perhaps to find a mate of his own.

Nor had the internal dynamic of the pack remained unchanged between the autumn of her departure and the spring of her return. The Ones continued to reign unchallenged, but the younger ones had grown. The four surviving pups had become leggy wolflings. The Whiner—once the weakest yearling in the pack—had grown stronger and more confident. With the dispersal of the adult male, the hierarchy of the remaining adults had shifted.

Now, once the flying romp of fur slowed to a panting whirl, Firekeeper was surprised to see two strangers among the pack. These had not greeted her as the others had, but had hung back, neither unfriendly nor familiar.

Firekeeper stood, her hand still buried in the One Female's pale fur—for the One Female's coat was silvery, like new-fallen snow in the moonlight—and felt as shy before these lupine strangers as ever she did before humans. She felt more shy in a way, for among humans she entertained a vague sense of superiority that she did not feel when among wolves.

The One Female took mercy on her, saying:

"Firekeeper, this is Sharp Fang, who has come to us from further west and north. Since we now have our own Sharp Fang . . ." She indicated the Whiner with some pride. ". . . we call our visitor Northwest."

Northwest was a male, his fur white around jaw and muzzle, but mixed grey-brown around his eyes, over his ears, and down the back of his neck where the same grey-brown made a saddle over the lighter fur of his underbody. Her recent visit to New Kelvin had made Firekeeper all too aware of masks, and she couldn't help but think that this male looked as if he wore one.

Northwest's eyes were yellow-gold, their gaze so penetrating and analytical that Firekeeper felt like a bug on a rock. She locked her gaze with his, unwilling, even though Northwest was quite large and looked as if he could knock her down without half trying, to abase herself. She didn't know the stranger's standing in her pack and wasn't about to accord him the same automatic respect she had always given those who had cared for her.

The One Female did not demand she do so, but indicated the other newcomer.

"Do you remember Wind Whisper? She was with us many years ago, when you were very small."

Firekeeper studied the she-wolf. Wind Whisper's coat was equal parts silver-grey and charcoal black, the black clustering in the vicinity of her ears, muzzle, and legs, the grey blending in elsewhere, though the tip of her otherwise grey tail was black. Her eyes were the color of old pine-tree tears and her bearing was strong and lithe, with no trace of age.

For the first time, Firekeeper found herself wondering how old the Royal Wolves might grow to be. She had never much paid attention to the passage of time, but humans seemed to do little else. From them she had learned that her tenure among the wolves had probably been between ten and twelve years. She herself remembered no time she had not been a wolf, except sometimes, perhaps, in dreams.

A sudden panic squeezed her heart. She had heard Race Forester speak of one of his bird dogs as growing old at twelve years. Did Royal Wolves age at the same rate? She knew that Blind Seer had celebrated his fourth year early this spring. Numbers still were not her strong point, but she knew that twelve was just beyond two hands and that four filled one hand almost entirely.

There had been three One Males in her memory. Was this replacement a result of aging on the part of the wolves? Did they become unfit for their places just as age was rendering King Tedric unfit for elements of his? A human king might delegate others to lead in battle. Tedric had done just that last autumn—otherwise the war might have been called King Tedric's War rather than King Allister's.

A One never delegated another to lead. Either they were slain by a competitor or beaten so sorely that none doubted they were past their time.

Suddenly Firekeeper felt afraid of a human life, afraid that its length might take her beyond all those she loved. Then she shook herself. She herself was a wolf, no human to be coddled by servants in a castle as was King Tedric or by children and grandchildren in a cottage as was Holly Gardener. Death was more likely to find her than was old age.

And perhaps it was proof that she was a wolf at heart that this thought gave her comfort. Perhaps it was only proof that she was very young.

Firekeeper remembered her manners and recalled her attention to the One Female's question.

"I do not remember you," she said to Wind Whisper. "But puppies have no memory beyond their last meal and no dreams beyond the next."

Wind Whisper panted with laughter.

"True enough," she said, "and you were a very ill pup. How we struggled to make you to eat, but the fire had badly damaged you. If it had not been for . . ."

Wind Whisper stopped, snapping at her haunch as if after a fly. When she resumed, it was as if she had forgotten what she had been about to say.

"Well, you've grown into a fine young creature. Nicely spoken, too, and lighter on your feet than any of the two-legs I've seen over in that smoky nest they've built themselves."

Blind Seer wagged his great brush of a tail, pleased at this compliment to his friend.

"When did you leave this pack?" he asked Wind Whisper. "And where did you go?"

"Long before you were born, Blue-Eyes," she replied, "even before your mother came to rule this pack."

Again Firekeeper was struck by the difference between how she and the wolves grew and aged. She had known both the One Male and the One Female as pups. The One Female had been of this pack, the One Male of a neighboring pack with whom her own sometimes joined for winter hunts and summer romps.

To her, now, both wolves were adults, wise and strong, yet she could recall them as fat furballs like the four who even now romped with each other in a sheltered hollow, their mock battles indulgently supervised by a couple of the yearlings. How old were the Ones now? Eight? Ten?

The thought troubled her as never before. Citrine Shield was about that age and she was a child. Firekeeper knew that she herself was still growing. She'd grown taller even over the last year. With the bounty of human larders to augment her own hunting she'd put on weight, developed breasts, and, if Holly's comments were anything on which to judge, she had more changing yet to come.

Blind Seer had filled out some, grown a bit broader through the chest. Indeed, he promised to live up to the image of his father—the previous One Male, who had sired only one litter before dying in a winter hunting accident.

"You're distracted, Little Two-legs," the One Male commented.

Rip was a big silver-grey wolf with a dark streak running the length of his spine even to the tip of his tail and a broad, white ruff. He was the One Female's second mate, having won her against all comers. The Ones seemed well suited, but Firekeeper had the impression, as Northwest twitched an ear to attend to the One Male's comment, that Northwest thought that perhaps he himself would serve better as One.

Firekeeper shook herself from this uncomfortable thought by addressing the One Female.

"Mother," she said, gesturing toward the four romping pups who were now fiercely battling over a much-chewed tree branch, "when Blind Seer and I came home last you said that you didn't plan on pups this spring, yet here I see four as strong and healthy as any in the land."

Firekeeper knew from past experience that the One Female could decide not to bear pups. She wasn't certain of the mechanics of the choice, but recalled it happening several seasons over her life. Usually the reason was that enough young had survived the previous season, but that couldn't be the purpose here. The four yearlings were ample proof that the previous litter (numbering six initially) had done well.

The One Female swept her tail through the duff where she had reclined when her introductions were completed.

"Always full of questions, Little Two-legs," she said, amused. Then she grew serious.

"I had a dream," she went on, "a dream of flood. In it, a tree fell across a stream, damming it for a moment, but its trunk was too thin and the flood crashed over it and my pack was drowned. When I awoke, I felt stirring within me, stirring that had been quiet until that time, fed to fullness and settled into sleep by the growing pups. I might have fought them, I suppose, but my dream was warning and the One Male and I tied that very afternoon."

Firekeeper nodded, nor did she question the One Female's account of her dream. Its antecedents were apparent.

"Did you dream this," she asked, "before or after the humans came to the Burnt Place?"

"Before they came to settle," the One Female replied, "but over the autumn, before winter closed the gap in the mountains, a small group came and sniffed about. Perhaps these were the first trickle of the flood in my dream."

Blind Seer cut in.

"You never mentioned this to us!" he said indignantly.

The One Female growled softly.

"And since when is it my duty to inform wandering pups of the business of the pack?"

Blind Seer abased himself. His own status within the pack was ambiguous. He had left of his own desire, wishing to accompany Firekeeper. In this way he had separated himself from the pack. However, as he had never joined another pack, nor formed one of his own—unless his relationship with Firekeeper could be taken as a pack of sorts—Blind Seer could still be said to belong to this pack, even as Firekeeper was still welcome.

The One Female licked her son's nose, accepting his apology.

"You had worries enough last winter," she said. "The One Male and I decided that this human coming should not be added to them. Indeed, those first might have been trappers or furriers more daring than the usual run, brought across the mountains by curiosity and with that curiosity fed never to return."

"Are those who came last autumn among those who returned?" Firekeeper asked, never doubting the wolves would have noted the scents.

"Yes," the One Female replied. "The One Male has made a study of them, for he was here while I was away and took better note of them."

The One Male, who had been gnawing a thick bone much as a man might have smoked a pipe, cracked it along its length and licked out the marrow before speaking.

"Not only," he said, carefully arranging his thoughts, "are there those who are the same—though, of course there are more now—but the male who serves as One in their pack was the leader of those who scouted."

Firekeeper bit her lip.

"The humans call him Ewen Brooks," she said. Then she recounted Ewen's history as she had heard him tell it to Derian. Sensing the wolves' interest, she went on to detail Ewen's raptures about the potential of these western lands.

"So it is as we suspected," the One Male said, and he sounded not in the least surprised. "Human ways may be strange to us, but the wingéd folk who came to look at them said that the two-legs were showing denning behaviors. Indeed, we had thought so even before the birds offered their opinions, for why else would the humans fell trees to make sturdy places to live and bring their young with them if they didn't intend to stay?"

He rolled the shattered bone beneath his paw, but Firekeeper was certain his forlorn expression had nothing to do with having licked it clean of marrow.

"It is good," he said at last, "that you chose to come home. We were thinking about sending for you."

Firekeeper didn't need to ask why and didn't waste breath doing so.

The One Male went on. "There are many and mixed feelings regarding the coming here of these human folk. Do you remember the tales you were told last autumn, the tales of how the Royal Beasts first met two-legged kind?"

Firekeeper nodded. "At first there was some balance between the four-footed and two-legged kind. Then the humans became territorial. They fought themselves and they fought our people. In the end, because the humans had great powers we did not, we retreated across the mountains where they did not like to come. They did not follow us because they did not like the mountains. Also, a sickness came over the humans, burning to death those who had the most power. In the end, so many humans had died that they no longer had to fight each other for land. We in turn decided to stay where we had come and leave them the lands east of the Iron Mountains."

It was a short form of the elaborate tale she had been told, but served to demonstrate that she remembered the high points.

The One Male thumped his tail in approval.

"Good enough, Little Two-legs, though you condense the time over which events occurred. Remember that this rivalry and fighting and the time of the sickness happened over many long years."

"I," snapped Northwest, "do not see why how much time it took matters at all! What is important is that these humans now are different from those humans then. Those humans then had great powers. The Ones of my pack tell of lightning drawn from the sky, of fire burning through the air and catching onto fur and flesh, of senses so acute that not even the stealthiest among us could go unnoticed.

"These humans have none of these powers. Two nights ago I crept into their settlement, ate one of their foolish birds as she slept on her nest, pissed on their doorposts, and the only ones among them who noticed my coming were their silky-haired foxes and these cringed from my least growl. They at least knew their master."

"Dogs," Firekeeper said inconsequentially. "The humans raise them as they raise their horses and mules. They come in many sizes and shapes. Some of the larger, indeed, might give a wolf second pause."

"But not these," Northwest challenged.

"No," Firekeeper agreed. "These have been bred for tracking by scent and for bringing back prey felled by arrows. Hunt more often in their chicken coops and Ewen Brooks might bring from the east dogs meant for the hunting of bear and wolves."

"Cousin-kind," Northwest sneered.

"True," Firekeeper said, "but enough of these Cousin-kind hunting dogs might give even a sharp fang like yourself trouble."

Northwest grumbled, but did not debate the point further. Instead he said:

"But you agree that these humans have none of the great powers that eventually drove the Beasts of old to flee west of the Iron Mountains?"

Firekeeper frowned. "Most do not, but last winter Blind Seer and I went into New Kelvin—the human land north of the White Water River—and there we saw things that make me think we cannot dismiss human powers so easily."

"You wish to protect them!" Northwest snarled. "They are naked, hairless beasts like yourself. You think if we take them as our prey you will no longer be safe among us, no longer safe to swagger beneath your pack's protection. That is why you speak of them as if we, the greatest hunters in all the forests of all the world, should fear them."

Firekeeper jumped to her feet, her Fang in her hand. In a single leap, Blind Seer was at her side, crouched to spring.

Sharp Fang—as Firekeeper must grow used to thinking of the Whiner—joined them. Apparently, she felt more fondness for her two-legged sister than Firekeeper might have imagined.

"Stop!" barked the One Female, surging to her feet, her fangs bared at all. "Stop this nonsense!"

Everyone cringed back, for the One Female did not lead the pack owing to the glossiness of her gleaming silver coat. Indeed, everyone knew that though she had but one mouth to bite with, the One Male would be as her second and two such bites would take a season to heal—if the victim did not die at once.

"Stop," the One Female repeated. "Little Two-legs, curl away your Fang. Northwest, stop taunting Firekeeper. You are a guest here and she is my pup."

Obediently, Firekeeper eased her Fang back into its Mouth. Blind Seer and Sharp Fang ranged back onto their haunches, but their lips didn't quite hide their snarls nor their posture their smugness. They were one with the pack. Northwest was outside it and in anything but a leadership challenge he would fight one to many.

No fool, Northwest flung himself down and rolled onto his back, exposing his throat to the Ones and whimpering in proper apology. The Ones accepted this and only when all were restored to harmony again—a romping and playing that involved all the pack, even the puppies and the guests—only then did the discussion resume.

"So," Firekeeper said, keeping her comments neutral and nonjudgmental, "I take it that Northwest believes the humans should be killed or driven away, not allowed to take root here. I can't say I disagree with him."

Northwest perked his ears in surprise.

"Nor can I say I agree," Firekeeper continued. "The matter is complex. Fear kept the humans from west of the Iron Mountains once, but it may not again. I have seen humans flee what they fear. I have seen them seek it out and kill it. What I do not understand is when they choose to run and when they choose to kill."

"You are saying that the humans might try to kill all of us if we kill these invaders?" Wind Whisper asked, the first thing she had said in a long time.

"I don't know," Firekeeper replied honestly. "There are many of us, but there are many of them, too, and if what Derian—that is my human friend with fur the color of a fox's—if what Derian says is true, many humans feel there is no longer land enough for them all in the east. Many years have passed since the Fire Plague and territories have been sectioned out among the humans as birds section out nesting grounds in the spring. Some feel—like this Ewen Brooks—that they need new nesting lands and these are easiest to take."

"Then we shouldn't make the taking easy," Northwest replied, his ears canted and mouth open to indicate the utter simplicity of the concept. "If they find that those who come here die, then no more will come. We will be a fur plague to them, even as once we were.

"And this time," he reminded them all, "they will not have the great powers."

This time Firekeeper did not challenge Northwest on that point. She herself wasn't sure just what powers did rest among the humans. She knew they had lesser talents, such as Doc's for healing or Holly's for raising plants. These did not seem akin to the ability to make lightning strike or fire rage through empty air.

"I have a question," Firekeeper said, turning to Wind Whisper, "if you will forgive me if what I ask is somehow rude."

Wind Whisper wagged her tail. "Ask and I will forgive if you give insult unknowing."

"You were of this pack when Prince Barden came and founded the first human settlement. If I understand rightly, the wolves did not chase these humans away. Indeed, my human mother apparently had friends among the wolves who would take in her orphaned child and raise it as one of the pack."

Those words were harder to say than Firekeeper had believed possible. She hated with every pulse of her blood to admit she had ever existed as other than a wolf.

"Why didn't the wolves then chase away the humans? Why did they even make friends with them?"

From the stirring of the other wolves, Firekeeper realized that the rest of the pack—except for possibly the One Male and the One Female—did not know the answer any more than she did.

Wind Whisper glanced at the Ones and held their gazes a long moment.

"I do know," she replied at last. "Now, remember. I was but a junior pack member, maybe of the age of your Blind Seer, here. Indeed, I came here as part of my own dispersal journey. I do not know the full counsels of my elders."

Firekeeper grunted her understanding and Wind Whisper continued:

"Those who crossed the mountains when you were small did much as this group has done. First they sent scouts. Only after these had found a good place for the rest to den did they go back and bring their mates and young. Because of this, we had a good deal of time to consider what to do.

"Many felt as Northwest does, that the humans should be slain, but there was one great difference between our knowing now and our knowing then. Then we did not know that the humans were without the great powers of which our legends still tell."

"So!" began Northwest triumphantly, but the One Female growled him to cringing silence.

Wind Whisper went on. "The wingéd folk had maintained spies among humankind, but these were few and could only learn so much by watching and listening from without. Their observations seemed to confirm that the great powers were gone, but there were evidences here and there of talents that made us wonder if the Fire Plague had completely burned sorcery from human blood."

She paused and thumped behind her ear with a hind foot, though it was early for fleas.

"I speak, you understand, of the humans of those lands directly east of this part of the mountains. In other areas such as the lands farther north— New Kelvin, I think you called it—the wingéd folk were less certain. That uncertainty was why the humans who came were let live and indeed somewhat courted by our pack. The wise ones decided that we must learn more about them before we hunted. What if the great powers had grown again into their blood? Then we might be bringing the old wars into this new refuge."

Firekeeper leaned forward, her posture imitating the pricked-eared interest of the wolves.

"And what did you learn?"

"We saw no lightning drawn from the skies," Wind Whisper replied, "but we saw evidence of strong talents. There was one among them who could influence the growth of plants, another who understood those of other bloods so well that almost could he speak to us. There was one who could tell what the weather would be with near impossible precision and one who could not become lost, no matter how far from her den she wandered.

"These," Wind Whisper said, "were the talents we observed. There may have been others. The blood speaker gave us to understand that their leader had gathered to himself those with talents in order that those talents could help his outlier pack to survive."

Humans might have broken into one of their babbling debates at this point, but the wolves were a hierarchical folk and so all eyes now turned to the Ones, mutely requesting confirmation of this outlandish tale.

" 'Tis true," the One Male said, "as much as I was ever told. This was long ago, though, before either of us were born, and so we cannot confirm from our own knowledge."

Firekeeper stirred.

"What Wind Whisper says," she offered hesitantly, "mates with something I once heard a human who had kin among that group say. It seems reasonable that had there been humans with great powers, Prince Barden would have gathered them to him. If this is so, he was a rebel against more than his father's will."

Northwest clearly thought such discussion of long-dead people a waste of time.

"But there was no clear evidence that these humans had great powers?" he pressed Wind Whisper.

"No clear evidence," she said.

"And they dwelt here for the turnings of several season cycles," Northwest went on.

"True."

"So surely you would have seen great powers if they possessed them."

Wind Whisper curled her lip at him.

"Puppy wise to say that what you have not seen must not be."

Northwest snarled and there might have been a scrap between the two visitors, but the One Female intervened.

"Be still," she commanded and stillness there was. "Wind Whisper has told us all she knows. The humans were permitted to live here so that we could watch them and learn. It is not for any of us to attack her for the wisdom of a decision that was not hers to make."

Firekeeper nodded, and since the question had been hers, it was her place to offer thanks.

"I have heard enough," she said, "and I thank Wind Whisper for offering her wisdom."

Wind Whisper swung her tail in acknowledgment, but her hackles didn't quite smooth when she looked over at Northwest.

Firekeeper dismissed their dispute, relaxed in the knowledge that such things were for the Ones to deal with. Instead she let herself consider what she had learned.

Had Prince Barden known that his colonists lived in the western lands on suffrage? Had he suspected why? Most humans might have forgotten that the Royal Beasts even existed, but the more she learned of this long-dead prince the more she respected him.

Derian had once told her that Prince Barden was more like his father than either of his siblings had been. Would King Tedric have mounted such an expedition without learning everything he could about the lands in which he planned to go? Firekeeper thought not.

She recalled the old tales that Lord Aksel Trueheart had drawn out of musty tomes in the libraries of Eagle's Nest Castle and elsewhere—tales that told of long-ago conflicts and hinted at the existence of the Royal Beasts. Until her coming with Blind Seer and Elation, these had been dismissed as bragging exaggerations as were the right of every storyteller. Then she and her companions had come, and such old tales were beginning to be reconsidered as fact.

What if Barden had taken those tales for fact? Might he have taken care that his people hide any great powers they had among them—if indeed they had possessed such? Humans lied far more easily than did wolves, though she was learning that wolves, too, could lie—especially by not telling the full tale.

Could Wind Whisper herself be believed? Had the Royal Beasts seen some evidence of great powers among Barden's people? And if they had, would that evidence have been reason enough to execute the humans? Had the fire that came that fatal night been an accident or, perhaps, had it been set?

V

DERIAN DIDN'T PLAN TO turn around immediately after his arrival in Bardenville. The journey west had taken the better part of a moonspan and he and the animals certainly deserved a rest. Moreover, Firekeeper wouldn't want to visit with her pack for only a few days and then leave again. Indeed, Derian had wondered if she would return with him at all. Perhaps she would prefer to escort him into safer areas east of the mountains and then return to summer with her family.

Now Derian was glad that he hadn't given any of those at home any reason to expect him before several moonspans had passed. He knew that he must report what he had found here to King Tedric, and he hoped to have full and accurate details. Moreover, Derian wanted to be very careful not to give Ewen Brooks any reason to worry that Derian was a potential enemy of their venture. A quick departure might make Ewen worry about what Derian would say when he got home. Better to stay and make some friends among the settlers. It might make them less likely to decide to detain him forcibly—or worse.

Derian had no illusions that Firekeeper's influence made him immune to harm. Indeed, his friendship with her might add to his danger. The settlers clearly viewed all the large carnivores in the area as their rivals for local game, and were ready and eager to exterminate them. Already a magnificent puma pelt was drying on the side of a shed, and a bear hide was spread before Ewen's fire. Derian had stared at its empty eye sockets his first night in the cabin, wondering if it might have been someone Firekeeper knew.

The wolf-woman played a more dangerous game than she knew where the colonists were concerned. Not a day passed that she didn't visit the settlement, but not a night passed that she didn't leave to be with the wolves. Moreover, as had been the case with Race Forester a year before, her incredible skills as a hunter and tracker made some of the young bucks in Ewen's group quite resent her. Every deer or brace of rabbits she brought to augment the supper kettle made them resent her more.

Indeed, the fact that the deerskin was rarely wounded with more than a single arrow shot—adding to the value of the gift while silently flaunting Firekeeper's skill—did not add to the wolf-woman's popularity with those who had, before her coming, fancied themselves the lords of the forest.

And it doesn't help, Derian thought ruefully, *that Ewen is forcing these same young men to put their hands to the plow and saw rather than encouraging them to roam the forest as he did when they first arrived, when the need for food and a knowledge of the territory was more important than such work. My arriving here when I did with extra mules to help with the plowing and hauling has made Ewen all the more eager to get crops in, stumps pulled, wood hauled, and all manner of exhausting menial tasks done before I—and my livestock—take our leave.*

Derian had already resolved that he'd be wise to make a gift of at least one of the mules to the colony. The horses, even lovely Roanne, were safe enough. Their more delicate constitutions made them less attractive than the hardy mules, but he was coming to wonder if he would get away with either of the mules. Ewen's initial covetousness had become nearly proprietorial.

Oh, well, Derian thought, *if I must, I'll leave the mules here and have Father take the cost out of my earnings. Maybe I can get Earl Kestrel to advance me some of my commission for the beasts I'm purchasing for his stable.*

If both Derian and Firekeeper were less than popular with the young men of the colony, both of them had made friends with other members. Dawn Brooks appreciated Firekeeper's help in finding bees to populate her much coveted hives. When the wolf-woman brought Dawn a double handful of quail eggs, suggesting that Dawn incubate them under her hens, Dawn had been delighted. Much of her domestic poultry had fallen prey to foxes and weasels, and this opportunity to augment her flock had been a matter for rejoicing.

Only to Derian did Firekeeper confess that at least some of the poultry had fallen prey to resentful wolves and he suspected that the quail eggs were the wolf-woman's unspoken restitution.

Derian's willingness to plow, chop wood, and otherwise make himself useful had won him friends among the older colonists—many of whom he came to know during the late-afternoon wall-building sessions, where the logs that had been hauled and trimmed during the day were added to the palisade surrounding the settlement.

Never mind that about half the settlers were still sleeping in tents. Ewen had decided that a solid wall would serve them all far better than cabins. Derian, knowing far better than Ewen what lived in the forest, had to agree.

Although many of the settlers were quite young—even leaving out the children, the majority were rarely into their third decade—Ewen had recruited some older couples. These were usually masters of those skills the colony would need to flourish—carpentry, blacksmithing, medicine. They had cultivated these skills working for others, but had nearly given up hope of setting up where they could be more than another's assistant.

These craft masters held a more realistic view of what the coming winter would bring and how close it was, never mind that the trees were just now unfolding their pale green leaves. They knew that having friends back east might make all the difference to their venture. Indeed, theirs were the most serious faces when the stones for Prince Barden and his people were set in place.

They're wondering, Derian thought as he looked at them, *how soon they will take their places next to these long dead, and if anyone will have survived to put a stone with their name in place and to commend them to the ancestors.*

It was during this ceremony for the dead that Derian learned that Ewen's colonists had found the remnants of another cemetery off in the woods. It held markers for at least seven of those on Derian's list and for a few who were not on his list at all. Some of these—judging from the dates inscribed— were apparently children born to the colonists after their arrival, children who had not survived the harsh conditions. A few were adults, probably late arrivals who had risked—as Ewen's parents had not let him do—King Tedric's wrath in order to join the colony.

Most of the deaths seemed to have been due to illness or accident, but a few of the inscriptions were ambiguous. These were ascribed by the new-comers to the actions of predators and were used to fuel the "get them before they get us" philosophy of Hart and his fellows.

Another portion of the population with which Derian could have made himself quite popular was the young ladies, for not all were married and not all of those who were married seemed completely happy in this small com-munity. Flirtation—a mere game in a populous city or town—was not viewed as an acceptable pastime here where everyone knew everyone else all too well. Although he was aware of several women giving him welcoming glances, Derian kept himself under a tight rein. It wasn't that he didn't long for female companionship, but he knew there were those among the men who would welcome any excuse to pick a fight with him.

Even without flirtation, there was much to do around Bardenville, and Derian was quite willing to do whatever was needed for as long as was needed, provided he was still welcome. If asked, he responded that he hoped to leave for home sometime around the end of Bear Moon. Thus he was greatly surprised when as Bear Moon was hardly showing a sliver against the night sky Firekeeper came to him, every line in her slim body eloquent with tension.

The labor of the day was winding down into evening's routine chores and Derian was in the process of grooming his mules when Firekeeper arrived.

"Can't we talk here?" he asked in response to her request.

Firekeeper bit her lip.

"Only if none come," she said.

Derian forced a laugh.

"I doubt any will. The lazy ones won't want to risk my asking them to help, and the hardworking have jobs of their own."

Firekeeper nodded solemnly.

"How soon you can leave?"

"After I've finished the grooming."

Firekeeper snorted in impatience.

"Not this place." She gestured widely, encompassing the settlement in the sweep of her arm. "This place."

Derian understood her, though he made a mental note that her time with the wolves had done nothing good for the wolf-woman's command of human speech.

"Bardenville," he said. "A day or two, I suppose."

She tugged at her earlobe.

"Not tonight?"

Derian stared at her, his hands still automatically continuing with their work.

"Tonight?"

Firekeeper growled low in her throat.

"Tonight. Am worried. There is much unhappiness with the Beasts to this place. I have tried to stop it—though my heart does not know if I am right—but I have done all I can. Maybe, I think, if King Tedric tell these to go away they go . . ."

Derian digested this.

"And if they don't?"

Firekeeper frowned, looking across to where a small girl was toddling to her mother.

"I think they then die."

FIREKEEPER'S HOMECOMING HAD NOT BEEN at all as she had imagined. She had dreamed of lazy afternoons sleeping in the sun, of hunting with Blind Seer. Of showing off how her newly won skill with a long bow made her more of a match for her seniors—at least where game like deer was concerned. She still didn't think she could take an elk without help.

Instead there were all the complications brought on by the presence of Ewen Brooks and his people at Bardenville. The council held the night of her arrival was only one of many such. Others of the Royal Beasts came to scout the humans and to discuss what should be done with them.

From any and all of these—even from those who should perhaps feel some gratitude to Firekeeper for her service to them the winter before—the wolf-woman met the same mixture of hostility and guarded acceptance that had been her portion from Northwest. That these conferences were held under the lowering eye of the comet made Firekeeper feel no better about them or about how quick the Beasts were to see her as a human now, and not as one of their own.

Despite her unease, Firekeeper helped the visitors wherever she could. She answered their questions about humans, and reminded the Beasts of what she herself had once forgotten, that the humans tracked by eye more than by nose. Often she went with various of these four-legged ambassadors when they spied on the humans. Following behind, she took care to wipe away any incriminating tracks as Race Forester had taught her to do back when she scouted for King Tedric on the eve of King Allister's War. Thus the humans were kept in ignorance of just how closely they were watched.

Arguing this same need to preserve secrecy, Firekeeper convinced the

Ones to forbid hunting of the humans' domestic animals. Scorn had been her greatest ally in this matter, and soon not one of the young wolves would have been caught with even a whiff of chicken or beef upon their breath. Such hunting, so the Ones declared, was for the toothless and the stupid, not for strong, fine wolves. The visitors from other packs or even from other bloods within the Royal Beasts respected the Ones in this matter.

Firekeeper suspected that Northwest still slunk within the human camp, searching, most likely, for evidence of those great powers the Beasts all feared. If he took a chicken or duck then, he was careful to wash thoroughly before returning to the pack, and her nose, at least, was not sensitive enough to know if the poultry that Dawn regularly missed—no matter how tightly sealed the carpenter made his coops—fell to Northwest or to another.

But from some of Blind Seer's sly comments, Firekeeper suspected that foxes and weasels did not hold all the blame.

So Firekeeper made her mute apology to Dawn and the other farmers in the form of wild bird eggs. The chicks and ducklings that hatched—being more stupid than rocks, in her opinion—gazed upon the creature that had hatched it and thought they were looking upon their mother. So it was that mallard ducklings waddled after chickens and quail trailed in their busy way after confused ducks. Eventually, Dawn took care to foster like with like, but the initial errors remained.

Among the humans, Firekeeper made few friends, but both Dawn and Ewen went out of their way to show her welcome, and their community at least gave lip service to that welcome.

Firekeeper liked Dawn far more than she liked Ewen. Ewen was what Derian called a man of vision. That meant, as Firekeeper understood it, that Ewen saw as much the image of how things would be as he did the place before him. Thus, even as he walked rutted muddy paths, he saw tightly cobbled streets. Even as he perched on a stool, he felt himself in a high-backed chair.

Or perhaps a throne? Firekeeper didn't care for that image at all.

Dawn was like a young tree trying hard to drive deep roots to hold her for the winter. Before coming west with Ewen she had been a miller's wife, for Ewen had followed in his parents' craft. She had learned something of the art, but her three children—the eldest barely six—had been her main occupation. What energy she had left went to tending to her household and small garden.

Ewen had refused to have his old mother live with them—planning as he did to leave and not being willing to abandon a dependent—so Dawn had all the labor to herself. She knew much about the basics of cooking, sewing, cleaning, child-rearing, but she was equipped only with theory in matters such as beekeeping, farming, and all the myriad tasks that fell to her now. True, there were others in the community with those skills, but since Ewen was the One among them, he insisted that his wife lead as well.

Firekeeper admired Dawn's tenacity and helped with her efforts, often tending to the little ones—Dawn's and others—so the women would be free to do other tasks. The one thing the colony was sorely lacking were the children of middle years who would usually do such tasks. Most of the colonists' children were much younger.

"In a year or two," Dawn would say, brushing her pale hair from her face. "Then we will have children grown enough to tend the smaller ones, for now . . ."

"In a year or two . . ." That was Dawn's constant refrain, usually said bravely, but sometimes Firekeeper heard the weariness in her voice.

So she watched the squalling brats. The job was not unlike what she had done with litter after litter of new emerged pups—for such nursemaiding always fell to the younger wolves, so the wiser and stronger would be free to hunt. However, always Firekeeper must remember how fragile these little humans were and how dependent.

Gradually, this nursemaiding made Firekeeper friends among the parents, but it increased the resentment the young hunters—mostly male, rarely parents themselves—felt for her. They reminded her so much of young bucks with the velvet barely off their first set of antlers that Firekeeper had no problem understanding why Derian named them so. Proud in the flush of their first strength, these bucks thought they should do little but flaunt it. They liked not at all that Firekeeper—who was as strong as most of them—should humble herself to child-rearing.

Nor were the bucks flattered that she was indifferent to their charms. She could smell the sexuality of them in their sweat as they strutted by her, and so was careful with them as she had not had the wisdom to be careful with Derian a year before. Her Fang never left her in any case, but she bid Blind Seer to take his rest within call, and never did she casually remove either vest or trousers lest her nakedness be taken as invitation.

I have learned more of humans, she thought, *but I do not care for what I am learning.*

Yet she knew that wasn't true. For every annoying young male there was someone like Dawn, and so, when she felt the mood of the Beasts' councils shifting from curiosity and fear toward violence, she knew she must act.

Now she struggled to explain why they must leave to a clearly puzzled Derian.

"These days since we come and before, the Beasts have watched this place. They know the humans stay, and they think that more come to stay. They think before the log wall is strong, before there are many within with bows, make them go."

Derian frowned. "You said that the people here might die if you can't get King Tedric to make them go. Do you mean the Beasts might kill them?"

Firekeeper nodded.

"It would be easy and if they no come back, then . . ."

Derian stared at her, horrified at the thought of such slaughter.

"We must warn them!"

"That would be their dying," Firekeeper said, shaking her head, "for if the Beasts found themselves hunted, they would surely attack. For now there is still fighting among the leaders as to if this killing is the thing to do."

Derian frowned. "But if we don't warn them, then Ewen and his people will die without a chance to defend themselves. This way they'd at least finish the walls and set defenders on them."

Firekeeper knew Derian was thinking of human tactics and felt her heart flood with pride for her people and scorn for human limitations.

"The Royal Beasts are no fools," she said. "Why should they do armies fight or battles? By night the wingéd folk could carry and drop hot coals, then tents and straw would burn. Is there any wall to defend from fire from the sky? When the fires burn, those who flee into the dark night will meet the owners of this land."

She was careful not to share her own suspicion, never confirmed, that something like this might have been the end of Prince Barden's colony. Only the fact that the wolves had saved her gave her hope that her suspicion was not valid.

Derian looked narrowly at her.

"Has this been done before?" he asked bluntly.

Firekeeper shrugged, deliberately ambivalent.

"Not in my knowing."

Derian bit into his lip.

"Anyhow," he said slowly, "where would birds get fire? I don't suppose you would be here kindling it for them."

Firekeeper waited until he met her gaze.

"I won't," she said, "but they get fire if they need it. They steal it from the humans if they must."

Derian nodded.

"I see why you want to leave now, but I don't think that's wise. How about this? I'd indicated that I didn't plan to leave before the end of this moonspan so I'll need to make some excuse . . ."

He finished currying the mule he'd been working on when she arrived, moved to the next.

"I think I'll tell Ewen that I need to leave because his young bucks don't like me and I'm afraid that if I stay much longer there'll be trouble. He has to have seen the tension and I think he'll accept it. I'll sweeten the pot with a gift of both mules. The mountain horses can carry my gear and provide me with remounts."

Firekeeper nodded.

"That is good," she replied, relieved. She'd been worried that she might need to leave Derian behind. "Tonight you tell?"

"Tonight," Derian promised.

DERIAN'S PROMISE GIVEN, Firekeeper next sought counsel with the Ones. At first they were indignant, even angry, when they learned she had confided so much to Derian, but they calmed when Firekeeper explained why she could trust him to keep a still tongue.

"Derian will not say of what I told him," she said, "except maybe to warn Ewen of the danger of hunting wolves and Ewen will think this simply Derian's indulgence of me. I told Fox Hair that if the humans hunted us, then that hunting would unleash the very killing he fears. He knows me. He knows Blind Seer and Elation, and has the wisdom to know this is true."

"You know this Fox Hair best," the One Male said, "and we will take your promise for him, but I assure you, you did not exaggerate the humans' peril. Already there are many of the Royal Beasts who follow Northwest's trail and would exterminate the humans before they become too numerous or too strong. Though you run quick foot to try to enlist this human One in our cause, you may still be too slow."

"Have you any thoughts, Little Two-legs," asked the One Female, "on how we might stem the slaughter? Much as I have no desire to have humans dwelling within my lands and ruining my hunting, I would be content to see them leave of their own accord. Is there anything in human ways that might drive them back to their own lands so we do not need to kill them?"

Firekeeper paused, considering everything she had learned about humans and their needs.

"My great wish," she began, wishing to emphasize her point, "is to make these humans see and obey the will of their One, and so go from here for now and for ever. If we drive them away in any other fashion there is nothing to stop them from returning in another season."

"We understand," the One Female assured her, "but if the choice comes to rest between slaughter or some other method, what do you advise?"

Firekeeper framed her thoughts carefully, knowing that what she was about to suggest might still lead to deaths, especially among the young and fragile, but knowing that any other course of action would be fatal to all.

"Take away their foodstuffs," she said. "These humans have more than game to sustain them, but game augments what they can grow and what they have brought with them. Start by driving the game animals to distant pastures. It will make leaner hunting for us, true, but wolves can range farther than humans and even the bravest of the human bucks will hesitate to travel abroad when wolves sing in the night."

The One Male snapped his teeth gleefully.

"That could be fun," he admitted. "We had considered moving the pups in any case. For now we can split the pack. One part will stay here and sing to the humans. The others will drive away the game and provide for our little ones."

The One Female huffed her agreement.

"With all those who come to see the humans," she said, "there will be no end of voices for the chorus. Tell on, for I think this is not the end of your plotting."

Firekeeper nodded. "If still the Beasts worry, then have the browsers and the grazers come by night and eat the young plants as they grow in the fields. The humans rely on these as squirrels do their stored nuts, to feed not only themselves, but their livestock.

"It will be dangerous work," Firekeeper warned, "for the humans have bows and can shoot from the cover of their walls. Still, taking away the growing stuff will force them to consider leaving when autumn comes, even if they are brave through the summer. With no game to eat and no fresh growing things, they should have dipped deeply into those supplies they brought from the east."

The One Male flattened his ears.

"But what if others come, bringing supplies with them, as your Fox Hair did?"

"Don't let them get here!" Firekeeper replied, a trace exasperated. "Drive them back as they mount the trail. Terrify their beasts. If these stupid creatures run away the humans alone will not haul the sacks and bags. Humans are weak in all but their ability to harness others to be their strength."

"That will take many wolves," the One Male said doubtfully. "Some to drive away the browsers and grazers, some to haunt the gap in the mountains and maybe some ways east, some to tend our young . . ."

"There have been enough not of our pack or our blood coming here to look and then to brag of their prowess as those who would slaughter naked, hairless, fangless humans," Firekeeper said, some of her indignation at the insults she had suffered rising forth. "Let them test their mettle on more delicate work."

"Firekeeper has a point," Blind Seer commented from where he had been silent witness to this small conference. "If the Beasts are given tasks, then the ones with the hottest blood may find it cooled enough for thought."

"We can but try to get them to help," the One Female agreed, "and we did ask for you to tell how the humans might be beaten. I can see how this trail runs from here. If loss of game, grain, and growing things is not enough, then we must hunt their foolish animals. That will not be easy, for the humans are sure to keep them locked within that wall of tree trunks they have been raising."

"Only," Firekeeper said, "until they must let them out to graze. It is a shame that we have not Royal songbirds and other little creatures here."

She thought of the tale she had heard the autumn before—a tale that gave reason why such creatures were nearly unknown. She wondered if any but her saw in it a warning against past pride and impetuosity.

"The songbirds could have sneaked within and ruined the stored grain and such. Still, we should have opportunity to go after the goats and cows and mules if the need arises. If nothing else, your singing should dry the udders of even the calmest cow."

"Your plan is good," the One Male said after considering its details and ramifications. "I hope only that we can convince the others to adopt it. Quick slaughter would be easier to manage and lend less risk to ourselves as well."

"True," Firekeeper replied, "but if we slaughter these humans, others may come to avenge them. Certainly, I have heard no proof of great powers among humankind, but we cannot be certain they do not exist. Think of those things you sent me to hunt last autumn. What else might come out from hiding places if we give the humans cause?"

"A wise argument," the One Female said, "and one we shall use in our turn. However," she continued, and her entire mien was solemn, "if the One of the humans does not do as you wish, I do not think the Beasts will tolerate this intrusion or others like it. This land is ours and ours it must remain."

"Even," the One Male added, "if many of us must die to preserve it."

VI

THE BOWSTRING SNAPPED BACK, stinging Elise across her cheek so sharply that she knew there would be a welt. Tears flooded her eyes, temporarily turning the landscape into wobbly pale green shapes. When she dashed them away, she saw her father, Baron Ivon Archer, glaring at her, disapproval in every line of his black-bearded face.

"I don't ask much," he said, "but can't you at least keep the bow held straight and strung?"

Elise felt a momentary desire to burst into tears and run back into the house, but she fought it down.

"Can't you," she replied sourly, "accept that I'm simply not cut out for archery?"

"No," Baron Archer answered. "I cannot. Your grandfather won this land for us with his bow. I have upheld the tradition. My sister Zorana is a fine enough archer that she was welcomed in the ranks during the last war. I will not have the heir to this grant unable to even shoot."

"I can shoot!" Elise protested, but even she knew her protest was weak. Her training to this point had been with a target bow so light and with such an easy draw that a child of eight could manage it. Baron Archer wanted her pulling a bow proper to her weight and strength.

Her father's only reply to her protest was to extend her bow—somehow dropped when the string had slapped up against her cheek—in mute command that she restring it and they continue.

Elise obeyed, leaning with her full weight on the bow to string it, then putting arrow to string and pulling it back. Her arm shook slightly and she could feel sweat beading down her temple from the effort. When she loosed the arrow, the string snapped against her wrist guard, not her face, but the arrow went wide, burying itself for a moment in the outermost ring of the target before gravity pulled it loose and it toppled to the ground.

Baron Archer handed her another arrow. Elise fit it to the string. So it went, sometimes the arrow flying wide, sometimes hitting the target, rarely placing anywhere near the center. Still, Elise didn't injure herself again and she counted that as a small victory. What Baron Archer thought, she didn't know, for he rarely said anything and when he did it was always to remind her to adjust her stance or posture or some such thing.

If Elise hadn't known that her father mostly approved of her, the entire process might have made her furious, for, despite her fair-haired loveliness and the sea green eyes about which had been written several poems, she was neither weak-willed nor a fool. She simply wasn't a warrior and that was something Baron Archer could not understand.

Previously, Baron Archer had concentrated his efforts at military training on his nephew Purcel, but Purcel had died in King Allister's War and his younger brother, Kenre, was only eight years old. Perhaps, even if Purcel had been alive, Ivon's attentions would still have shifted to his daughter. Events over the past year had forced Ivon to think much more about the reality that Elise would be his heir.

The sun had shifted so that the target had to be moved at least once, and it might have had to be moved again before Baron Archer relented, but Ninette, Elise's confidential maid, came hurrying down the path.

"A messenger has arrived, Baron," she said. "Lady Aurella thinks you and Elise both need to come and read what he has brought."

Elise lowered the bow, grateful for the respite. She didn't doubt that her mother had asked Ninette to come down rather than one of the other servants because she was one of the baron's cousins and he always treated her with family courtesy he sometimes forgot with his servants.

Or with his daughter, she thought, reaching up to finger the welt on her cheek when the baron's back was turned.

Aurella Wellward knew perfectly well that her husband hated to be interrupted, but that he wouldn't take his pique out on Ninette. Indeed, he was quite courteous.

"Thank you, Ninette," he said, glancing up at the sun as if he'd just noticed it had moved—though he himself had been the one to shift the target. "Perhaps we have been at this long enough. Is the news so urgent that we need attend immediately, or does Elise have time to change?"

"I believe the news can wait at least that long," Ninette said, knowing that Elise would prefer a chance to get clean.

"Very well." Baron Archer took his daughter's bow. "I'll put this up for you, Elise, and we'll see what news awaits us. Meet us in our sitting room. By the way, not too bad at the end there."

Elise smiled, knowing this was all the praise she was likely to get and grateful for it. As she and Ninette hurried up the path to the house, Ninette fussed over her mistress's cut cheek.

"Does it hurt terribly?"

"It stings," Elise admitted. "Is it likely to leave a mark?"

"Not if we clean it well and put some of that salve Hazel Healer sold us. What is your father thinking? Doesn't he value his heir's beauty? He's lucky to have you, himself such a dour sort!"

Elise wanted to fall in with Ninette's condemnation, but she was no child anymore and felt she had to be fair.

"He knows my inheritance is dowry enough that I could look like a tracking hound with bloodshot eyes and giant nose, and it would be no matter. Why he doesn't understand that just because my grandfather won this land with a bow doesn't mean that I need to hold it with one . . ."

She let her words trail off.

"Anyhow," Ninette added in wry agreement. "He probably looked at the welt himself and saw it wasn't a maiming injury. Ivon's not a cruel man, just hard."

Elise nodded and shifted to other matters.

"Any idea what the news might be?"

Ninette glanced around, pausing to make certain they were alone.

"The letter bears the royal seal," she said softly.

"I hope nothing has happened to Sapphire's baby!" Elise exclaimed.

The two women hurried inside and up to Elise's rooms before continuing the conversation. As Ninette dabbed at Elise's face with a cloth dipped in warm water—sent up ahead doubtless by Aurella, who was very good at anticipating her household's needs—she continued:

"I don't know if it has to do with Princess Sapphire or some other matter. Had Lady Aurella not sent me to get you, I would have slipped by the servants' hall to gather any gossip."

"Do," Elise said, "when I go to my parents. The messenger may have details that won't be included in any official document."

Ninette nodded, her eyes shining. She rather enjoyed ferreting out gossip.

Sponge-clean, her pale golden hair combed out and then rebraided and fastened in a neat coil at the nape of her neck, Elise hurried down to her parents' sitting room. Baron Archer was there before her and must have told Aurella about the incident with the bowstring, for though Aurella's gaze went to the welt and her gaze was sympathetic, she asked no questions.

"I've waited for you before opening the packet," Baron Archer said. Such courtesies were among those he had started to extend Elise over the past winter, little acknowledgments of her right as his heir to be fully involved in the business of the estate. They made up a great deal for his impatience with her in other areas.

Elise nodded and seated herself, folding her hands in her lap and trying to look attentive, not eager. A maid entered, carrying a pitcher of spring water flavored with strawberry juice and a tray of glasses. Baron Archer waited until everyone had been served and the maid had departed before breaking the seal and unfolding the several heavy sheets contained within. He glanced over them for a moment, his eyes darting across the document, gathering the gist.

"It opens with the usual string of formalities and wishes for health and the like," he said, "which I will skip if that suits you ladies."

Aurella and Elise nodded, and Ivon continued:

> *Certain rumors may have reached your ears regarding the situation of certain people with a presumed relation to the throne. However, given the far southern location of the Archer Barony, and its relative isolation at this season when spring rains contribute to flooding and marshy ground, we take it upon ourselves to inform you how matters stand in full.*
>
> *If any rumors have reached your ears, we ask that you recall them and compare them to the facts as we know them at this time. Possibly they may contain kernels of truth unknown to us. More probably, they will contain distortion of the truth. Either will be useful to us.*

Ivon paused to drink, and Aurella commented:

"Cryptic and portentous, not at all like King Tedric's style. I see the hand of the heirs in this."

Ivon nodded, setting down his glass and lifting the missive once again.

"Perhaps, my lady. However, King Tedric can be quite cryptic when he wishes. I wouldn't lay the blame entirely at the young couple's door." He read on:

> In the early days of Horse Moon, confidential messengers arrived to us from House Kestrel bearing information just arrived from New Kelvin. As you know, last autumn, Melina, once the bearer of both the title 'Lady' and affiliation with House Gyrfalcon, traveled across the White Water River into our neighboring country of New Kelvin in company with Baron Waln Endbrook of the Kingdom of the Isles. Her actions both there and in this country before her departure were such that we were forced to renounce her relation to our kingdom and to exile her from our land.
>
> House Kestrel sent the first information we have had of her since last Wolf Moon. Melina has apparently made an advantageous marriage for herself, becoming the bride of the Healed One of New Kelvin. There is evidence that the marriage was kept secret, at least for a time, giving rise to speculations that perhaps this marriage was thought to be no more welcome to some of New Kelvin's citizens than it was to ourselves.
>
> Although the title of Healed One is often equated with that of reigning king or queen within our own land, we have been advised that the Healed One is less of an absolute monarch than we are. His role is mostly ceremonial, the actual business of government residing in a body called the Primes, headed by an elected representative called the Dragon Speaker.
>
> We apologize for repeating information that is known well to at least Lady Elise, she being one of our own most recent sources of information about New Kelvin, but we wish you to understand exactly how and where Melina's new alliance fits into the power structure.
>
> Horse Moon has waned and Puma shows her waxing edge since House Kestrel sent its initial information. However the passage of time has permitted us to confirm House Kestrel's news from at least two reliable sources. Moreover, as the White Water ceases its spate, trade has resumed between our lands and along with goods have come such rumors that we are certain that not much time can pass before the information—doubtless distorted and misunderstood by the bulk of the hearers—spreads to our people. These, lacking specialized knowledge of the New Kelvinese's peculiar government, will believe that this potentially dangerous exile from our own land has made herself queen of another.
>
> We have several charges to lay upon you as loyal servants of this

*throne. First, call your household to you and tell them the gist of this let-
ter. Make certain all understand that although Melina has made herself
a marriage, she has not made herself queen.*

*Second, send messengers to the extent of your grant with the same
news. If your resources permit, spread the news to the outlying freeholds
as well. Give these messengers whatever information you can so that they
will be able to answer any and all questions that are put to them. Rumor
is our great enemy in this potentially delicate matter. We wish to smother
it with truth.*

*Third, we request that Lady Archer come to the castle at Eagle's Nest
at her earliest convenience. We have no wish to create new rumors by having her speed to our side, but her knowledge of New Kelvin will be of great
use to us as we seek to shape policy for handling this matter. There is no
need to hide the reason for Lady Archer's coming to us. Indeed, there may
be those among our subjects who will take comfort in knowing that we are
consulting with our noble counselors.*

Baron Archer looked up, folding the missive and setting it on the table.

"That's about all," he said, endeavoring to keep his tones even, though
Elise had no trouble recognizing his pride at his daughter and heir being
summoned to the royal presence. "There are the usual closing wishes, confirmation that despite morning sickness Princess Sapphire continues well
and the pregnancy strong, and the like."

Elise smoothed her skirt, trying to still her own rapidly beating heart
before answering. She knew King Tedric well. Lady Aurella was one of
Queen Elexa's most trusted companions and when the Archer family
resided in the capital city, Elise spent much time at the castle. She knew
Princess Sapphire as well—they were second cousins and had been playmates, rivals, and, more recently, friends.

It wasn't fear of her rulers that made Elise's heart beat so hard. It was
awareness that this was her first summons before them as one of their own—
as an advisor to the Crown. She thought how she had teased Derian Carter
for his awe when King Tedric had given him a counselor's ring. She hadn't
understood then what an awesome and thrilling thing such a responsibility
could be. When she spoke, she tried to be worthy both of it and of her
responsibility to the Archer Grant.

"I should leave tomorrow," she said, "or perhaps the day after if you think
tomorrow would show undue haste. Along the way I can stop and speak to

our landholders and to the freeholders to the north, passing on the news as King Tedric wished."

Ivon Archer nodded, and the very matter-of-factness of that gesture made Elise glad she had weighed her words before speaking.

"Good," he said. "If the roads permit, you can leave tomorrow. The very fact that you will make stops along the way will balance the fact that you depart so soon after the arrival of the messenger. The one will show your awareness of your duty to the Crown, the other your duty to our holdings."

Aurella, who had been embroidering while her husband read, now rested her hoop in her lap.

"I wonder if I should go with Elise. It is nearly time for me to wait upon Aunt Elexa in any case and we would be company for each other on the road."

"That's a thought," Ivon replied. "Let us see how our people react and what rumors we hear before deciding if you should take your leave with Elise. It may be you will be needed here."

Aurella rose. "Shall we do our monarch's bidding, then? The longer we wait, the more time our people will have to build new conjectures that might muddy the old."

Elise cleared her throat, slightly embarrassed to admit her own initiative.

"As I was preparing to join you," she said, rising and smoothing her dress, "Ninette and I agreed that it might be wise to have some idea of what the messenger might say that wouldn't be included in the king's letter. Ninette has a steady mind and I don't doubt that she'll be able to remember what was being said before and what after."

Ivon guffawed, much as he might with one of his militia captains, and clapped his daughter on one shoulder.

"You may not be able to shoot an arrow straight," he said, "but I begin think there's a field commander in you nonetheless."

THERE WERE RUMORS, Ninette reported to the Archers.

"First, the messenger coyly let on that he thought the king's letter might have something to say about doings in New Kelvin. Then Cook said she'd heard from her sister who lives west of Port Haven something about how Melina had joined some sorcerous cabal in New Kelvin—for everyone knows that those New Kelvinese are crazy for magic."

She stopped, glancing at Elise as if hoping Elise would deny the common belief, but Elise only nodded.

"They are indeed," she said, "hard as it is for those of us raised in a more civilized tradition to believe. Their love for magic gave Melina her welcome there."

Ninette shuddered. She had seen real evidence of Melina's power and feared it with all her devout soul. She steeled herself and continued her report.

"Then the butler said that he didn't wonder if this hadn't been planned for a long time past, that wasn't it too neat that Sapphire takes the crown and her mother goes and makes alliances with a nest of sorcerers. It couldn't be coincidence, he said, and everyone nodded."

"That's not good," Ivon muttered.

"And it's completely untrue!" Elise said defiantly. "Sapphire broke with her mother—everyone knows that. Melina did what she did in spite of the injury it would cause her children, certainly not to help them. Look to Citrine if you doubt it!"

Lady Aurella smiled at her.

"Easy for you to say, Elise, for you know more of the inner workings of those lives than most, but to commoners who hold their first alliance to their families, their second to their societies and guilds, and only their third to those of us who rule them, well . . . who can blame them for thinking that we place our priorities in some similar fashion?"

And who's to say we don't? Elise thought, remembering the intricate maneuverings that the struggle for the throne had engendered only a year before. As a noble raised to inherit she belonged to no guild, but she did have something similar in the alliance of noble houses, nor was her society essential to her advancement as it might have been, but she never missed a meeting of the Lynx Society when she might attend.

"Should I tell them what I know?" Elise asked.

"Tell them some," Ivon said, "but they will remember how you stood for Sapphire at her wedding and though some will heed you, some will think 'Lady Archer looks to advance herself and her family through keeping in good with the future queen' and so disregard your words."

"It's maddening!" Elise exclaimed.

"It is no different than how we would think in similar circumstances," Aurella replied, "and don't think that our people will think ill of you for it. On the contrary, they will brag of your intimacy with Sapphire and Shad from one side of their mouths, even as they trade scandal about that same young couple from the other. Only if you seem to be trading your honor—and ours—to gain royal goodwill shall you diminish in the eyes of your people."

"And that's what they fear, isn't it?" Elise asked. "That Sapphire has traded her honor, by remaining secretly allied with her mother, and so dishonored her adoption by the king."

Ninette interjected, "That's about it, at least from what the worst of the doomsayers offer. They don't really believe it, I think, not yet, not now, but if anything gives proof, well, the doomsayers will be delighted and others will be convinced."

"Anything else, Ninette?" Ivon asked.

"Just a small thing," she answered. "Princess Sapphire has not been much seen and people are using that as evidence against her."

"She has morning sickness," Elise said indignantly, "and is throwing up her meals. Her last letter complained about it quite bitterly. No wonder she isn't out and about."

"But it hurts her," Ninette persisted, "because she was so strong before. Folk don't want to think a princess is a normal woman—a warrior princess like Sapphire least of all. She's to be prancing about on her armored steed thrilling their souls with her power and warming them with her implied protection."

"That's a lot to ask of a newlywed woman whose father died not half a year ago, whose mother abandoned her after leaving her little sister to be driven mad . . ." Elise trailed off, sputtering.

"But," Aurella replied, "that is what is expected of a princess. Just wait until Sapphire is queen. Hawk Haven's last queen was our founder, Zorana the Great. Sapphire will have to live up to a hundred years and more of exaggeration and legend."

"I am so glad," Elise said, "that King Tedric didn't choose me."

Ivon surprised her with his reply.

"And I am glad he didn't choose me, either."

ELISE'S DEPARTURE WAS DELAYED a full day owing to rain that began that evening and continued through the next morning. Baron Archer ruled that giving the roads a day to drink the water was only wise.

For the same reason, she didn't take a carriage when she left, riding instead on Cream Delight, the elegant golden-coated, silver-maned mare that had been her parents' gift the autumn before. Baron Archer delegated trusted attendants to manage the remounts and the pack animals, and to protect Elise and Ninette on their journey.

Having judged that the level of local rumor was verging on dangerous, Aurella elected to remain behind for a few days, employing her time regulating the mood of the estate while Baron Archer himself rode about his lands, spreading the king's news.

Elise reached Eagle's Nest six wet and muddy days later. In good weather the trip might have been made in half the time, but the roads were sticky and the people she met along the way so eager for news and reassurance that Elise felt herself honor bound to remain longer than planned at her various stops.

Indeed, rumor was so pervasive and so colorful that Elise wondered if, secrecy being no longer possible, Melina might have viewed the opposite as her best servant.

It was certainly possible.

ELISE WAS INVITED to Eagle's Nest Castle the very day of her arrival, but the invitation was for the following day, "in order that you have opportunity to recover from the rigors of your journey."

In truth, she was glad for that opportunity. Although Baron Archer had taken care that Elise not lose the hardiness she had developed during her journey to New Kelvin, the fact was this was the first multiday ride she had taken since the previous Wolf Moon. The journey to Eagle's Nest had been easy enough. They had slept at inns or at the residences of families proud and honored to have the heir of the Archer Barony under their roof. Still, Elise was tender in muscles she had forgotten existed.

Ninette, for whom a far greater time had passed since she had made such a trip—winter journeys were commonly by sled or sleigh and summer made in carriages—was in visible pain. Elise insisted that one of the resident maids in the Archer manse in Eagle's Nest be assigned to Ninette and that she could take care of herself.

Ninette protested, but weakly, and since the staff of the Archer manse would no more let their young lady wait upon herself than run naked through the streets, the matter was settled by the housekeeper delegating herself to attend on Elise.

This proved opportune. Although Steward Dayle wasn't precisely a scandalmonger, her interpretation of her duties did involve mingling with many levels of society. This might not have been the case. Many stewards would have decided dealing with merchants and menials beneath them, but Steward Dayle's kingdom was a small one and so nothing escaped her notice.

Technically, Dayle shared her administration with the butler, who in addition to the wine cellar was responsible for matters of protocol and such. However, as this worthy traveled back and forth between the Archer Grant and Eagle's Nest, usually in company with either the baron or his lady wife, Dayle's authority was absolute among those who must cater to her whims, no matter where the owners of the property might be residing.

Elise decided to find out if the rumors here in the capital were as vicious as in the provinces or if the relative sophistication of Eagle's Nest's residents had moderated their views. She didn't open with that subject, of course. Indirection and playing at politics were far more natural to her than riding a horse or shooting a bow.

Instead they chatted for a while about local news: this one's new baby, that one's engagement, another's marriage celebration. This last topic was arrived at naturally enough. Spring began the new year in the calendar used by Hawk Haven and Bright Bay alike, and weddings were traditionally celebrated then—especially among the upper classes, who didn't need to worry that a spring wedding might mean a bride heavy with child during the lean months of winter.

"And what a tale," Elise said, "this is about what Melina once of Shield has done! Do you really believe that she could have married a foreign king?"

Dayle was clearly torn between a desire to speak her mind and the respect accorded to the doings of the upper class. She gave into the former notion, doubtless encouraged by the fact that Melina was exiled both from her homeland and from her family, and so not due any deference at all.

"I think it's frightening," she said bluntly. "I never liked that woman, didn't care for it at all when you were engaged to that son of hers."

Elise reflected and decided that Dayle was being honest. There had been a certain degree of stiffness in the congratulations she had offered and in the hospitality that she had offered Jet when he came by the Archer home. At the time, blinded by her own infatuation, Elise had dismissed this—if she had noticed at all—as the older woman's awkwardness in acknowledging that a girl she had known since infancy was grown into a young lady.

"I'm glad to be free of Melina, too," Elise said, "but what is there to fear now? She's across the White Water River and miles further inland. The rulers of New Kelvin live in a city in the foothills of the Sword of Kelvin Mountains, far from us."

"And wouldn't you just know that, lamb," Dayle said, her fingers lightly stroking the front of Elise's head, where the hair was still markedly shorter than the long, pale gold curtain that fell to the middle of her back. "Having gone among those barbarians and even taken on their strange ways. I nearly wept when I saw you when your family came here for Winter Fest, I don't mind saying."

Elise didn't bother correcting the steward. The fact was that no one in New Kelvin had made her cut her hair. She had done it herself in order to go disguised into Thendulla Lypella, the Earth Spires, where the rulers of New Kelvin lived and worked.

As the fashion in New Kelvin was to shave the front portion of the head and wear a long braid behind, there had been no other way to pass. Elise understood that the custom had grown up in order to permit the wild face paints favored by the New Kelvinese—paints worn in addition to numerous tattoos—to be seen. More practically, it meant that the wearer's hair did not become streaked and matted with paint.

Instead of correcting Dayle's impression, Elise decided to probe the steward's evident aversion to the New Kelvinese—an aversion Elise did not recall encountering during the family's winter visit.

"Barbarians?" she asked, careful to sound curious rather than critical. "Surely people who have the skills of the New Kelvinese can't be called barbarians."

"Well, maybe that's not the right word," Dayle replied, doing up Elise's braid rather more tightly than was comfortable. "But I don't care how fine their glasswork is nor how lovely their carpets, a people who worship the magical arts like they do—well, I call that barbaric."

"I see." Elise nodded, pretended to study her reflection. "Dayle, would you mind undoing my hair? I think I'd like a ribbon or two worked into the braid."

Dayle complied cheerfully enough, and when she went to work again she didn't pull nearly as hard. However, clearly her thoughts were running on the same track.

"This ribbon," she said, "New Kelvinese silk it is. Tell me, Lady Elise, do they really raise the silk by natural means? Recently, I heard someone say that it's woven by monstrous spiders that they feed on human blood."

"The truth's hardly prettier," Elise said with a laugh. "I did learn a bit about the art—they call it sericulture—while we were there. Our landlady, Hasamemorri, had done something related to the work."

"No giant spiders, then?" Dayle sounded almost disappointed.

"No, rather caterpillars. The silkworm, as they call it, spins the thread for its cocoon. The humans harvest them. It's fairly difficult. Apparently, the silkworm loves a warmer climate from somewhere in the Old Country, but the New Kelvinese use their glass houses and the heat from underground fires . . ."

Elise frowned, "Remember, I'm not sure just how they do it, only what Hasamemorri told us."

"Quite right," Dayle said encouragingly. "So they use these glass houses and the underground fires . . ."

"To make a place warm enough that the silkworms think they're at home. They grow plants to feed the caterpillars, too, special ones. Silk is a major industry for the New Kelvinese in all its parts, from the glass and plants, to the caring for the silkworms, and then the actual dying and weaving of the silk."

"But no giant spiders," Dayle said. She sounded almost sad. "I guess that there's no truth to the stories that New Kelvin is making closer trade with Waterland then."

"With Waterland?" Elise tried not to sound too eager.

"That's what I heard," Dayle said, almost embarrassed. "The one who told me said it was on account of the spiders, you see. Those Waterlanders keep slaves, you know."

Elise nodded.

"And from what I heard, the New Kelvinese were going to raise their silk production and for that they needed more blood for the spiders so they were making trade overtures to Waterland."

"That's interesting," Elise said. "Who told you about the spiders?"

"Well . . ." Dayle considered. "I've heard that tale since I was small. My mother used to ask me why I wanted silk, given how it was grown."

Elise raised her eyebrows.

"I never heard such stories!"

"Well"—Dayle smiled indulgently—"maybe now your lady mother didn't need to persuade you that you didn't want silk ribbons and maybe she didn't want you refusing to wear them if you did know, given how much some noble folk judge by a dress or the like."

There was a certain logic in that, but Elise didn't pursue it. After all, she knew—or at least she thought she knew—that silk didn't come from giant spiders that fed on human blood.

"But Waterland," Elise persisted. "Did your mother tell you about that?"

"Gracious, no!" Dayle said. "Mother has been with the ancestors three years now. Summer fever took her. I heard about the trade with Waterland just a few market days ago from the fishmonger."

"The fishmonger?"

"That's right. He was saying that it should be a good year for saltwater fish if the Waterlanders were going to be selling their slaves to New Kelvin. It would mean they wouldn't be building so many ships and such to put to sea.

"Wishful thinking, I thought," Dayle continued, finishing Elise's coiffure. "After all, if they're making money selling slaves to New Kelvin, wouldn't they have more money for buying ships?"

Depends on who's building them and where they get their timber and a dozen other factors, Elise thought.

The economics of international trade was something of a hobby with her, but she didn't plan to get into a discussion of its complexity with Dayle. Enough that here was a new rumor. She stored it away to bring to King Tedric.

She didn't have much time to brood. Soon after Elise was finished with her breakfast, Dayle arrived to announce that Elise's grandmother Grand Duchess Rosene wanted to see her.

"She's in the front parlor," Dayle said nervously.

"I will see her immediately, Steward," Elise replied. "Send in a maid with cool drinks. There will be no need for her to remain. I will wait on my grandmother."

Grand Duchess Rosene was the younger sister of King Tedric, a haughty lady, who never let anyone forget her birth. Sometimes Elise wondered how Rosene had become this way, for once she had been so young and romantic and indifferent to place and title that she had married a man commoner-born, though elevated by his deeds to the rank of baron by King Chalmer, Rosene's father.

But that girl was long gone and the seemingly frail white-haired woman of seventy who waited for Elise in the parlor bore no trace of her. Indeed, she seemed to have no desire to recall those days and rather than residing with either of her children and their families, she lived in the suite of rooms in Eagle's Nest Castle which had been given to her upon her marriage.

Elise made a deep curtsy to her grandmother, then knelt for the old woman's embrace. Grand Duchess Rosene smelled of the rose sachet tucked in her bodice and of peppermint. From the latter, Elise deduced that her grandmother's indigestion had been acting up again, and readied herself for a lecture. Nor was she disappointed.

"I understand that you have been summoned to the castle tomorrow," the grand duchess began, "and thought to see you before Tedric could fill your head with foolish notions."

"Ma'am," Elise murmured, at a loss how to respond.

"I can't imagine that Tedric wants to talk to you about playing nursemaid to that child his heir is bearing," Rosene said. "Even if he considered it, you can't imagine the number of well-born young ladies who seem to think—or whose parents seem to think—that they are just perfect for the post. Why choose them or you? Better some big-breasted country wench with milk, I say. Benefit the child and make the common folk preen."

Elise sat mute. All she could gather from this was that the grand duchess had no notion why her granddaughter was summoned before the king and that she was burning to know. Surely she would have tried King Tedric first. Rosene was no respecter of her brother's august position. Therefore, if he hadn't told his sister, it was up to Elise to do so.

After all, hadn't the king's letter said she wasn't to hide her reason for coming to him? He must have some reason for wanting Elise to do the telling. Maybe he thought it would gain her respect in her grandmother's eyes. Maybe he was just fed up with his sister's nagging and prying.

"Well, Grandmother," Elise replied, "the king's letter said that he wished to ask me about New Kelvin. That's all I know."

Grandmother Rosene snorted, quite unladylike.

"New Kelvin!" she said. "As if he doesn't have advisors who could tell him better than some chit of a girl."

Elise bit the inside of her lip to keep from an unladylike retort. After all, she did speak the New Kelvinese language—as most Hawk Havenese did not. She had been to New Kelvin as recently as the previous winter. She had met one of the advisors to the Dragon Speaker, and had even been within Thendulla Lypella itself.

The grand duchess was having nothing of meek silence, however.

"Well?" Rosene said in a way that demanded a response of some kind, even if Elise wasn't quite certain of the question.

"I did visit New Kelvin," Elise began.

"You did indeed," Grand Duchess Rosene retorted as if Elise had said something rude. "As I see it, child, you are getting completely out of hand. First you finagle that engagement to that utterly unsuitable Jet Shield."

Elise forbore from saying that for a time that engagement had definitely made her Grandmother Rosene's favorite among her five grandchildren.

"Then you go tearing off to war, hanging about the soldiers like some camp follower."

That accusation was harder to swallow. Elise, like Ivon, his sister Zorana, and her son Purcel, had accompanied King Tedric at Rosene's express command—no matter that Ivon and Purcel, at least, would have gone anyway, holding as they did commissions in the army. Everyone had resided in the camps except for the king himself.

"Then last winter you shame both your own family and Duchess Norwood by forsaking her hospitality and gallivanting off to a foreign country without your chaperon and with several unmarried men."

Elise refrained from biting her lip, but she did grind her teeth, just a little. Rosene was completely accurate in what she said. It was just *how* she said it. For a moment Elise thought about mentioning that there had been a perfectly respectable chaperon along, then surrendered the point unspoken. None of this was what bothered the grand duchess. What bothered Rosene was that she sensed she was losing control of her family.

"Yes, Grandmother?" was all Elise could think to say when the grand duchess paused and sat, obviously waiting for a response.

"What do you mean, 'Yes, Grandmother'? Yes, Grandmother, I've gotten completely out of hand?"

"If you say I have," Elise replied with a slight shrug, "I must have done so. My parents seem resigned to me, however."

"Your parents," Rosene said, "have resigned themselves to the fact that you are their only child. Well, I plan to do something about that."

Elise blinked. This last was beyond her. Aurella was sterile. Ivon was too much a gentleman to divorce his wife—especially since she had produced a living heir. Besides that, Elise thought that in his formal way Ivon was fond of Aurella.

"Yes," Rosene continued. "I have been thinking. Your father and mother have only one child—you—and you have taken to doing dangerous and unpredictable things. Therefore, I am going to insist that your parents adopt one of your aunt Zorana's children. With Purcel's death, Nydia is now the heir. That leaves Deste and Kenre. It would be too much to ask Zorana to surrender both of her sons. Therefore, it will have to be Deste. She's young . . ."

"Thirteen," Elise supplied automatically.

"But her youth is in her favor. Ivon will have a chance to undertake her training. I understand Deste takes after her mother in her use of a bow . . ."

This last was said slyly, so that Elise knew it was meant—as it did—to sting. It also told her that this entire conversation was meant to sting, meant to warn Elise that she was not irreplaceable.

Instead of reacting as she suspected Grandmother Rosene intended, by angrily attacking her right to meddle with her son's family, Elise managed a calm smile. It took almost more strength than she possessed to keep her voice level as well.

"You have a good point, Grandmother," she said. "I had always thought that if something happened to me, then Aunt Zorana's eldest would take my place if she did not herself, but you are right. After all, are you not merely following your brother's example by securing the line through adoption?"

That hit home, Elise thought as Grandmother Rosene blinked. *She doesn't want to be thought of as imitating King Tedric.*

Elise pretended not to notice and continued on.

"Better my parents formally adopt Deste than to continue in uncertainty, I think. I only hope Aunt Zorana agrees without a fuss. After all, having Father adopt Deste will set Aunt Zorana further out of the line as Baroness Archer, if anything should happen to both Father and myself, that is."

"Ancestors forfend," the grand duchess muttered automatically.

"And being a confidant of the crown princess is dangerous," Elise said with a sigh. "Certainly I have been on the knife's edge more than once this last year. Better that Deste live a quiet life, away from court and its problems . . ."

And its influence, she though maliciously, knowing that Rosene would be thinking something similar.

". . . Than have her take similar risks."

Elise's polite defiance, for defiance it was no matter how agreeable her words sounded, seemed, oddly, to do her good in her grandmother's eyes. The faded blue gaze that studied her now held a trace of respect.

"You've thought the matter through so quickly," Grand Duchess Rosene said. "It must come from all your royal friends. Or maybe," and the sneer was back in her voice, "you just want to be disinherited so you will be free to marry your common-born lover."

Elise flushed. She had no doubt who Grandmother Rosene meant.

"I have no lover," she said stiffly, "nor any serious suitors."

"Then why is your cheek so red where it is not pale?"

The old woman chuckled, pleased now that she felt she had regained the upper hand.

"Very well, Granddaughter. So the king wishes to consult you about New Kelvin—wishes to consult you so urgently that he has summoned you to the capital when the mud is deep on the roads. Very well. Just remember what I have said, and don't forget to visit your granny when you next come to the castle."

Later, Elise remembered little of the polite conversation that had followed, only vague notions that she had answered questions about her parents' health and about the prospects for the coming year. She sat alone in the parlor long after the grand duchess had taken her leave, but she was not thinking of the grand duchess. Instead she was thinking about a man she had not seen since the previous Wolf Moon, and whom she wondered when—and if—she would see again.

VII

THE NEXT DAY, Elise kept her appointment with the king. She chose her attire carefully, knowing she would be observed by dozens of jealous pairs of eyes.

Let them think I'm going to a garden party, not a meeting, she thought, having Steward Dayle lace her into a becoming gown of ivory cotton printed with tiny blue forget-me-nots with hearts of gold. Ribbons in matching shades were woven into her hair when Dayle put it up, and Elise threaded a cameo on a braided choker in the same three shades and fastened it around her throat.

The end result was becoming while remaining maidenly and perfectly proper. Elise nodded to her reflection in the mirror, well pleased.

Today she didn't ride, but told Steward Dayle to have a light carriage readied. Traffic in the city streets was becoming so congested that there was talk of forbidding horses and vehicles during daylight hours. So far, nobles protesting their privilege had halted such a drastic move, but Elise felt it wasn't far away.

And then what will we do? she thought. *Entertain only at night? Certainly foot travel is out of the question. My slippers wouldn't hold up to such abuse.*

With such thoughts, Elise distracted herself from her budding nervousness at the coming meeting. She did such a good job that by the time she'd arrived at the castle she'd pretty much decided to suggest to her father that if such a law was passed the noble houses should donate a sum toward the founding of a new trade, one in people-drawn vehicles or perhaps fancy litters.

I'm certain that I saw something along that line in New Kelvin, she thought. *And in the long run it would be less expensive than every House making up their own litter. The operators could be part of the guild that deals with livery stables and carters. Derian Carter would be just the person to consult.*

The sound of the castle gates opening to admit her carriage roused Elise from her thoughts. She straightened, resisted an impulse to pull a mirror from her small handbag, and concentrated instead on appearing more confident than she felt.

Why am I so nervous? Elise scolded herself. *I've been here hundreds, if not thousands of times. I know Great Uncle Tedric well. He has always been kind to me. Queen Elexa is far sweeter than Grandmother Rosene.*

But such assurances did no good. Elise knew why she was nervous. All those other times she had been here as a child. This was her first attendance upon the king as an adult, her presence desired for herself and what she could offer rather than out of kindness to her parents or respect due to her birth.

And what if I disappoint?

On that terrifying note, Elise let herself be handed down from the carriage. Then she politely asked the coachman to wait for her—a formality, for he certainly would have done so in any case—and made her way into the central keep.

The interior of the castle was cool, almost chilly after the warmth of the sunshine without, for the weather had made one of those rapid springtime transformations, as if apologizing for the rain that had plagued Elise during her days of travel.

Elise shivered and wished she had brought a shawl. The room to which she was taken for her meeting with the king was markedly warmer, sunlight pouring through windows and even—wonder of wonders—a fire burning on the hearth. King Tedric was sitting near the fire, a rug over his knees, a bit more bent than she recalled from her last visit.

She made a deep curtsy. When Elise rose, the king smiled at her and she saw that his gaze had lost nothing of its sharpness.

"Give your old uncle a hug," he said, "and forgive me for not rising when you entered, as one should for a lady. I caught a cough this winter that will not leave no matter how many foul-tasting syrups I drink."

Elise complied gladly with the king's request and was shocked despite herself to feel how frail he was. Even the jacket he wore over waistcoat and shirt did not provide enough padding to conceal how wasted he had become.

The king coughed slightly as she released him. Elise hastened to apologize, but the king waved the words away, sipping on a cup of tea ready at his elbow. Elise had some training in medicine—mostly of the first-aid variety, but she had some knowledge of more practical herbalism—and she recognized the scents of hyssop and wild cherry. That confirmed the king's story about his cold.

Why should I expect him to lie? she thought.

She had no chance to consider this further, for King Tedric was gesturing her to a chair.

"Don't feel you must seat yourself by the fire out of courtesy," he said. "I can see you wherever you place yourself."

So Elise chose a chair near to a window that stood ajar enough to admit fresh air without creating a draft.

"Sapphire and Shad should join us quite soon," the king continued. "Sapphire had an appointment with a midwife—no troubles, just checking on the pregnancy—and Shad wanted to be with her.

"Sapphire's impatient these days," Tedric went on, and Elise heard the implied warning in his words, "with herself for not being stronger and with . . . other things."

Elise nodded. She might have hazarded a question, but the king asked after her parents and her journey. Then she asked after Queen Elexa—who she knew from the queen's letters to Lady Aurella was also suffering from the same winter chill. So the time was spent until the arrival of the heirs to the throne.

When she arrived, Princess Sapphire looked quite good for someone who was still regularly throwing up her breakfast. It was impossible to tell if she was rounding out yet. Fashions in Hawk Haven varied with the seasons and if the gown Sapphire had worn for her autumn wedding had been quite trim to the waist, it was not unreasonable for her summer gown to fall less closely from beneath her breasts.

The embrace Sapphire gave Elise was warm and genuinely affectionate, from which Elise guessed that the midwife's news had been positive.

"She says," Sapphire replied in response to Elise's question, "that the signs are all good. She even said that I may stop vomiting soon. I am past the first third of the pregnancy and my body should be growing accustomed to its new tenant."

She patted her abdomen when she spoke with such genuine affection for the little life within that Elise found herself beaming. It was delightful to see Sapphire, so long a fighter, mellowing into motherhood. Within a few minutes, however, Elise would learn that the fighter had not vanished, but had merely moved to other tactics and other battlefields.

"Shad," Sapphire continued, "will join us soon. He needed to attend to some of yesterday's business."

The king nodded and as this was obviously routine, Elise did not question further. Instead, as Sapphire bent to embrace the king—an automatic gesture so relaxed that it said everything Elise needed to know about how successful the adoption had been—she took the opportunity to study her cousin.

The blue-black hair was bound in a loose braid threaded with a gold cord, a hairstyle that left the princess's forehead open to view. With anyone else, this would hardly matter, but for Sapphire it was a statement.

Since she was an infant, Sapphire had worn a resplendent blue sapphire on the center of her forehead. Her attire was always dominated by shades of blue. Her toys were blue. Even her horse was dyed blue.

Similar themes were followed for each of the children of Lady Melina Shield and Lord Rolfston Redbriar. Black for Jet, the current head of the household and once Elise's betrothed. Swirling sheens of red and orange sparked with gold for Opal. Deep, shining red, rich as freshly drawn blood, for Ruby. Reddish orange, vibrant as a good cognac, for Citrine.

Although Lady Melina was gone, dishonored, exiled, and disowned, Elise had heard that all her children continued the pattern set out for them by their mother. All of them except, that is, for Sapphire.

On Sapphire's forehead there was no glittering gemstone, only its absence, marked by a white oval the precise size and shape of the gem, which remained even after the mark left by the cornet had faded to match the surrounding skin. It seemed to Elise as she studied what remained of that oval mark that it, too, had faded so that if she hadn't known what to look for she might have missed it entirely.

Elise was one of the few people who knew just how difficult it had been for Sapphire to throw off her mother's bond. Even as she rejoiced in this further evidence that Melina's influence was completely gone, she felt a tremor of concern.

Melina's hold was gone, but Melina herself was not. She was showing herself a power in a much more important arena than merely her own family politics. Whatever that might mean for Sapphire, it wouldn't be good.

Prince Shad entered then. Elise thought he had lost a bit of weight since his wedding, but otherwise he looked good. His bearing was martial, the relic of training in the navy since he was young, and his manners were courtly.

After making his bow to the king, Shad came and gave Elise a cousin's embrace. Elise stole a glance toward Sapphire, but the princess only looked pleased. Knowing her cousin's capacity for envy, Elise thought this augured well for the marriage.

Or that Sapphire's got Shad so snugly under her thumb that she doesn't worry about him being unfaithful.

Even as she tried to dismiss the thought as unworthy of Sapphire, Elise felt a thread of concern. The arrangement for the inheritance of Hawk Haven was peculiar—unique to her knowledge. Shad was the eldest son of Allister of the Pledge, ruler of the neighboring kingdom of Bright Bay. Shad remained his father's heir, even after his marriage to Sapphire. Moreover, he was King Tedric's heir as well.

That in itself was not too odd. Households had been known to make similar arrangements in order to merge lands or assets. What was odd was that Sapphire had not renounced her right to inherit in Hawk Haven. At the arrangement of King Tedric with King Allister, she shared it. Equally, Shad shared the inheritance of Bright Bay with Sapphire.

Therefore, ideally, they would rule in both lands and the lands would merge into a single kingdom already named Bright Haven in anticipation. If one or the other died, the remaining partner did not lose the inheritance. In theory, this was meant to stop any bickering or hope that assassination would end the union of the monarchies.

In reality, it meant that everyone watched each of the heirs apparent with double the care, looking for any sign that one ruled the other—and thus that one land might be favored over the other.

No, it would not be a good thing if Sapphire came to dominate Shad. Or Melina to dominate Sapphire.

That last thought made Elise shiver, but she thought that no one noticed until Shad, a slightly concerned smile on his lips, handed her a cup of tea from the fresh tray the servant had just brought in and offered to close a window.

Elise smiled, "No, the fresh air is lovely, that is, if the king isn't cold."

"I'm well enough," King Tedric grumbled. "Now . . ."

He waited until the maid had left and his personal guard, Sir Dirkin East-branch, had signaled that he would assure their privacy, and then he went on:

"Queen Elexa wished to join us, but her cough is troubling her and the physician refused permission. However, she had certain things she insisted that I say to you, Elise, and I promise to do so at the appropriate time."

Elise nodded, thoroughly confused, and sipped her tea.

"As my letter noted," the king said, "the matter at hand is the marriage of Melina to the Healed One of New Kelvin. Do you have any questions about that matter?"

"I don't think so, Sire," Elise said, "unless there have been new developments."

"None," Tedric said, "unless the burgeoning of rumor could be considered a development. As we feared, the populace widely believes that Melina has made herself queen and the fear that a sorceress is queen in our neighboring land is spreading, especially in the towns and cities, where the people trust more to their societies and guilds than they do to the landholders who rule over them."

"My father and mother," Elise hastened to assure him, "are doing their best, both with our own people and the freeholders near by."

"I have no doubt of that," the king said. "Aurella and Ivon have always been faithful servants to the Crown. I only hope that their diligence will not be turned against them."

"Your Majesty?" Elise asked.

"He means," Sapphire said, the tense note in her voice not for Elise, but for the subject, "that there are those who will believe that the need to spread reassurance is in itself proof that there is something to fear."

Elise nodded. "Like a child who fears a spook in the cupboard, nothing but a candle held within to chase away all the shadows will do any good."

"And even then," Shad said, the laughter in his voice suggesting he knew the situation all too well, "there is the fear that the spook returns when the candle is withdrawn."

King Tedric set down his cup—having taken advantage of the interlude to drain nearly an entire cupful of his medicinal brew—and continued:

"Sapphire, tell Elise some of the rumors. I wish to know if she has heard any we have not."

Sapphire nodded and it was proof of her strong will that she did not protest reporting on such a personally unpleasant subject.

"Happily, King Tedric's informers are not reluctant to bring ugly news," she said, the corner of her mouth twisting in a wry expression that was meant to be a grin. "Most of the rumors we have heard involve Melina's plans to reign here through me. Distance has not diminished the reputed power of her sorcery. Where she was once merely a harridan who used her powers to demand docile obedience from her spouse and children, now it is said she is capable of wonders.

"Take any marvel performed by an Old World sorcerer from the days of colonization and Melina has been witnessed performing it. Usually the witness is a friend of a friend of the trader who sells to a friend of the teller's favorite innkeeper, but that hasn't reduced interest—or belief—in the tales.

"When folk believe a sorceress can summon lightning from the sky or cause plague among the cattle, then it seems little enough to believe that she still rules a daughter who she ruled for the first twenty-odd years of her life."

Shad cut in, not so much interrupting as taking up the thread.

"To make matters worse, Sapphire's pregnancy has made her less able to show herself to the populace. Indeed, she wanted to do so, but the healers would not consider themselves responsible for the consequences. I have done my best in her place, but . . ."

He shrugged. "I am an outlander, the son of an alien king. For every one who has forgiven me my heritage and who tries to forget the years of war between Hawk Haven and Bright Bay, there are three who think me a conqueror who is merely waiting to make conquest through inheritance.

"I can only do so much, but I am bound. If I ride about the countryside, making myself known to the people, then it is said that I am sizing up the land for my own greedy interests—or, worse, given the current situation, that I am avoiding Sapphire lest she swallow my will as her mother has her own, making both of us her foils."

Elise frowned. "I doubt this is any comfort, but most of these rumors are far worse than any I or Ninette heard at my parents' home or along our road here. However, have you heard the tale about increased trade between Waterland and New Kelvin because of Melina?"

"We have heard some," King Tedric said, "but share your story with us."

So Elise told them Steward Dayle's story about the giant spiders who spun New Kelvin's treasured silk and how they fed upon human blood, how New Kelvin now desired greater wealth and so was prepared to make trade concessions to their slaveholding neighbors to acquire fodder for these spiders.

"Of course I told her," Elise concluded, "that New Kelvinese silk comes from caterpillars, not from spiders, and that the caterpillars eat exotic plants, not blood, but I don't know if even Dayle believed me."

Shad laughed harshly.

"Still, that's better than the version of the tale we have heard," he said. "What we've heard is that the New Kelvinese want the slaves in order that Melina might sacrifice them to some dark end."

King Tedric raised a hand to halt further discussion.

"What this does tell us is that there is increased trade between New Kelvin and Waterland. That in itself is interesting. New Kelvin has always feared Waterland's greed would extend to taking over the farm, rather than buying the cattle. Thus, she has done much of her trade through us, rather than give Waterland too great a foothold. However, there have always been such signal differences between those lands that direct trade was restricted."

"Signal differences?" Sapphire asked with a sigh. "Father Tedric, I must admit—again—my ignorance. I know they are different, but we trade with both, how could they not trade with each other?"

King Tedric started to answer, began to cough, and when the coughing was under control said in a slightly weaker voice than previously.

"Elise, answer Sapphire for me. You have always loved foreign lands."

Blushing slightly, Elise turned to Sapphire, fearing that Sapphire would be offended. Indeed, once she would have been, but apparently several moonspans as crown princess had proven to Sapphire how little she knew and how much she needed advisors. All Elise saw on either of the heirs apparent's faces was studious interest.

Still, she stammered as she began, unused to being an authority.

"Everyone knows . . . I mean, you know that New Kelvin is ruled by those who practice, or believe they practice . . . The thaumaturges, that is . . ."

Sapphire leaned forward and put a hand on her arm.

"Relax, Elise. Yes, we know that New Kelvin is ruled by people who call themselves thaumaturges and are dedicated to restoring magic. We know that Waterland is ruled by an oligarchy of its wealthiest citizens, and that they have very complicated ways of assessing who is the richest and such. What we don't know is why these things would put them at odds."

Shad nodded. "That's it in a nutshell."

Elise closed her eyes, trying to find words for something she herself understood almost more intuitively than rationally.

"It's a question of values," she said at last. "New Kelvin values old ways and old things because those things come from before the Plague—they call it the Burning Death—caused the Old Countries to withdraw from the New World. Their Healed One is supposed to be a descendant of the last of their Old Country mages, one who survived the Plague and, though weakened, helped them preserve their lore until his death.

"Waterland doesn't value much that's old. Maybe it's because so much of their land is at sea level and is subjected to storms and hurricanes. Maybe it's just that most old things aren't worth as much as new. However, they do respect old things that are worth something because of their artistry or materials. New Kelvin just has to have hoards of such things."

Shad interjected, "More than anywhere else, probably, because most countries destroyed the relics of the original settlers, either out of malice or out of fear that they might hold magical powers. So New Kelvin doesn't just have industries—like their glassworks and silk—that Waterland would like to have. They'd love a chance to plunder the New Kelvinese treasuries. There are those in many lands who would welcome that—especially if the Water-landers melted everything down for raw materials."

Elise nodded. "That's how I see it. After last winter's events, I'm not certain the New Kelvinese even know how to use what potentially magical things they still have. It seems that their own original settlers were treated much as our own were. Colonials with magical talent were trained across the sea and bound against telling how to train others in their lore. When the Plague came and the rulers retreated to the Old Country, they took their magical things with them. This doesn't change that the New Kelvinese have lots of old things left, however. And far from making them a less tempting target for Waterland's greedy oligarchs, it makes them more tempting."

"Because," Sapphire said, "they need not fear they'll stumble on too much dangerous magic."

"That's right," Elise said. A thought came to her. "You know, the ban against teaching magic here in the New World seems to have been followed by several different Old World nations. Our founders had it, so did the New Kelvinese's, the Waterlanders' and the Stoneholders'. I wonder if they made some sort of compact to keep our ancestors in ignorance?"

"It makes sense," Shad said. "I haven't sailed much beyond the Isles, but those who have—mostly meeting small settlements south down the coast, there isn't much north—report that similar beliefs are held, and a similar aversion to magic. New Kelvin's attitude may not be unique, but it's very rare."

"The Isles," King Tedric said, changing the subject with those two words. "Have you heard any rumors about them?"

Elise shook her head. "But then the Archer Grant is well inland."

"I thought traffic along the Barren River might have brought some news," the king said.

"Father has heard nothing important from the Isles," Shad offered, "and he would tell you, you know."

"I know," King Tedric assured him. "I trust Allister as I trust myself—and maybe more so. He is young and strong whereas I am old and suspicious. So maybe Valora is lying low and licking her wounds. Your defeat," his nod included all three of those present, "of the pirates last winter may have robbed her of a good part of her army."

Sapphire crooked her arms behind her head and stretched.

"I certainly hope so. May I suggest that we take a recess? I am growing stiff and hungry. The rest of you must be too."

The king concurred. "Elise will, of course, remain for lunch and perhaps for dinner as well. Yes, that would be best. Send a message to the Archer manse and tell them not to expect you. Have your maid bring your dinner gown and plan to remain."

Elise agreed. Hearing that she had a small amount of time before the meal and sensing that the young married couple wanted some time to themselves, she excused herself to go off to the gardens and visit Holly Gardener.

She spent a happy half hour there, nearly ruining her taste for lunch with strawberries and fresh cream, made richer by the news that Firekeeper and Derian had been through back in mid–Horse Moon before heading west so that Firekeeper might visit her wolves and Derian keep his vow to place markers on the graves of Prince Barden's expedition.

Before the meeting resumed after lunch, Elise took an opportunity to visit Queen Elexa. Elise was pleased to see that while Elexa was frail, she seemed no more in danger than she had a score of times before.

"It is simply that," the queen said, "when you are my age and have my history of ill health, the doctors grow more and more careful with every illness."

They chatted until a messenger came, saying that Elise was needed by the king.

As Elise rose to go, Queen Elexa motioned her close and, under the cover of their parting embrace, said, "Don't let Tedric talk you into anything you think unwise, child. There are things in this world just as important as international politics."

When Elise, surprised, would have asked for clarification, the queen waved her away.

"They're waiting, dear, and Tedric has promised to be fair with you."

More mystified than ever, Elise left, wondering what else there was to discuss. Certainly, as Grandmother Rosene had said, there were others who could advise the king about New Kelvin. She had just about concluded that King Tedric wanted her to become a tutor to Sapphire and Shad, and that Queen Elexa didn't think it was right to so demean the heir to a barony, when King Tedric opened the discussion.

"I suppose you have heard about young Citrine?"

Elise nodded. "I know what Queen Elexa told my mother in a letter, that Citrine's spirit was badly wounded by the time she spent among the pirates at Smuggler's Light, and that, despite best attempts to heal her, Citrine has become worse, rather than better."

"So much," the king said, "is fairly common knowledge. You know that Citrine was given by her mother to Baron Waln Endbrook of the Isles . . ."

"Formerly of the Isles," Sapphire hissed, and there was angry satisfaction in her voice. "Queen Valora has disowned him."

"As an assurance that Melina would not act against either him or the Isles," the king continued as if he had not heard. "As you know, Melina violated that assurance. It is likely that she planned to do so from the start. Certain things reported by Grateful Peace, once of the Dragon Speaker's Three, make clear she had laid the foundations for her treachery well in advance.

"Baron Endbrook did not know this, of course, and in a rather crude attempt to remind Melina of the hold he had over her, he sent her two of Citrine's fingers. We now know that he cut them from the child without offering her anything to dull the pain, nor did he see that she was given any treatment other than what was needed to make certain that she did not die from contamination of the wound.

"The injury itself would have been horrible to a child of eight. What aggravated it was Citrine's gradual realization that her mother must know what had been done to her and did nothing to avenge it. To make matters even worse . . ."

Shad muttered, "If that is at all possible."

"Citrine apparently kept the pirates at a distance by invoking the specter of her mother's sorcery. Early in her days in the Smuggler's Light, someone tried to steal her gemstone headband. Her reaction was so extreme that most kept at a distance after that. Their cruelties were verbal rather than physical.

"Still, it was enough. Some of the time, Citrine is quite herself. Others she is smothered in a terror so acute that she cannot bear any companionship; others she clings to whoever she trusts. Yet others, more disturbing still, she babbles oddly, saying things that contain some kernel of truth but strangely twisted. There are those among the servants who say her mind has been pushed so hard that she now sees the future mingled with the past and present.

"I think," the king continued, "that Citrine merely hears more than people think and in these moods sends it out again. I am continually astonished by what people will say in front of the ill."

Sapphire, seeing the king was looking a bit drawn and coughing again after his long recital, poured him more tea and, as she spooned in a generous amount of honey, took up the story.

"You may believe that we have tried everything we could imagine. We have summoned healers and physicians—even Sir Jared Surcliffe from the North Woods. All concur, the damage is not organic. It is to Citrine's mind."

Elise tried not to color when Sir Jared's name was mentioned. She knew perfectly well that Sapphire knew of their mutual attraction and thought sometimes that the princess was trying to make a match—an unusual and uncomfortable thought, for Elise had had it repeatedly drummed into her that she must think of the Archer Barony as much as herself when considering marriage. The idea that the future monarchs of Hawk Haven might consider Jared suitable was very tempting indeed.

She found it easy to push such thoughts from her mind, however. Citrine was one of her favorite cousins and the idea that the once cheerful child was so tormented was almost more than she could bear.

"Can I help?" she asked.

Sapphire gave a thin-lipped, worried smile.

"We hope so, but let me finish."

Elise nodded.

"As you can imagine, we tried everything. When Hazel Healer was here . . ."

Sapphire shrugged at Elise's small exclamation of surprise. Hazel lived far south of Eagle's Nest, in the border town of Hope.

"I told you we tried everyone. Perhaps we should say everyone proven both skilled and discreet. Hazel is certainly both of those."

"I'm sorry," Elise said. "I didn't mean to interrupt. Please go on."

"When Hazel was here, we tried a similar ceremony to the one that freed me of the bond Melina put on me. We had no success. There are so many reasons why this might have been the case that I can hardly offer a single guess. Perhaps Citrine depended on her mother's protection for so long that she could not bear to break the thread, even when it was proven untrustworthy. Perhaps she, like me, had come to equate herself with the stone she wears. For whatever reason, nothing we did sufficed. Citrine remains bound."

"Hazel believes," Shad added, "and as she is as much of an expert as we know in such matters, we must place some weight on her words, that even if we did succeed in removing the stone from Citrine, it would not cure her. Citrine has been driven mad by her mother's betrayal and by the cruelties done to her in that mother's cause. Hazel thinks that the only chance there is of returning Citrine to herself is to allow her to confront Melina. The girl may not even need to speak with her mother, just see her, transform her from a powerful specter into a living woman once more."

"I wish," the king said, "I thought it would be so easy."

He sounded hoarse and he looked tired. Elise realized how grueling today had been for him and felt suddenly frightened. A year ago—less than a year ago—King Tedric had been strong enough to travel to Hope in order to negotiate with his nephew Allister. Only this past autumn he had been strong enough to travel to Silver Whale Cove for Sapphire and Shad's wedding. Today she knew that if she were one of his doctors she wouldn't let him travel beyond the castle.

With a sudden burst of insight, Elise realized that if either King Tedric or Queen Elexa were to die, their deaths would be blamed on Sapphire, used as proof of her mother's evil influence on her.

And never mind that a year ago every noble in the land was after the king to name an heir lest he die and leave the kingdom in confusion. They'll forget that easily enough—at least the ambitious will.

Elise could not see her parents acting to undermine Sapphire and Shad, but then they had little to gain if the crown heirs fell from grace and much to gain if they did well. But there were others, in both Bright Bay and Hawk Haven, who would all too much enjoy a new scramble for the throne. And there were neighboring countries who would do anything to halt the projected union of Hawk Haven and Bright Bay.

Suddenly, Elise was very glad for the silent, hovering figure of Sir Dirkin Eastbranch, for her knowledge that the Royal Physician was a very good, very skilled healer—even if he lacked Sir Jared's talent.

"Don't take King Tedric and Queen Elexa quite yet," she silently pleaded with the ancestors. *"We still need them."*

Sapphire had risen and tended to the king, for all the world as if he really were her father, not merely an honored and often distant great-uncle. Now she returned her attention to Elise.

"We want you to take charge of a group that will escort Citrine into New Kelvin, somehow get access to her mother, and do whatever you can to heal her. If we can break Melina's hold on Citrine and heal her madness, then we will be able to answer those who claim I am under her influence."

Elise wanted very much to yelp "Me?" but she swallowed the word and managed a serious nod. Shad gave a tired grin.

"And, Lady Archer," he said, "as if that isn't enough, we want you and your companions to find out exactly what is Melina's position within the New Kelvinese government. We need to know how much influence she has. Moreover, we need to know how much truth there is to these rumors about increased trade in slaves with Waterland. If it is true, we need to know why New Kelvin needs more slaves. Is it merely for increased industrial capacity or is there any truth to the rumors that they are wanted for their blood?"

Elise stared at her rulers.

"And you want *me* to do this," she said.

"You and a few others," Sapphire replied. "Elise, except for a few diplomats mostly interested in trade concessions and keeping New Kelvin sweet while we fought with Bright Bay, Hawk Haven really hasn't bothered with New Kelvin. They were a small power with no real military strength, though able to offer unique and interesting trade. New Kelvin wasn't interested in us except for sending the occasional tattooed, pointy-shoe-wearing representative to some major event.

"We don't just want you for your knowledge of foreign languages and customs—though I'll admit right out and up front that those are rare enough. We want you because you are one of about a dozen people who know the truth about what my mother did to me and to Citrine. Do you want the full list?"

Elise said nothing, but Sapphire continued on, nearly raging.

"There's you, Ninette, Derian Carter, Firekeeper, Sir Jared, Hazel Healer, King Tedric, Queen Elexa, King Allister, and Queen Pearl. Sir Dirkin probably has guessed, but he's as trustworthy as an oak. Then, of course, there are my esteemed birth-siblings who cannot speak of the matter and would not do anything if they could."

Elise wondered if perhaps Sapphire was being too harsh on her siblings, but knowing what she did of Jet and thinking of the apparently frivolous young ladies Opal and Ruby were becoming, she could not be certain.

"Now," Shad said, laying a settling hand on his wife's arm, "you see why we need you—and some of those others—so much. This would be the absolutely worst time I can imagine for taking someone else into the secret. A wink or a nod from the wrong person—and diplomats who make their living trading secrets are very much the wrong people—and suddenly there would be confirmation."

"But," Elise burst out, "Melina no longer has any hold on Sapphire!"

The look of pure gratitude Sapphire turned on her made Elise color.

"Well, it's true," Elise repeated, "and you defied her when she could have done terrible things to you. I have not forgotten your courage."

"And I haven't forgotten your part in setting me free," Sapphire replied. "The sad thing is, the only reward I can offer you is asking you to put your hand in the mad dog's mouth again."

Elise nodded, thinking that this sounded very much like something she had heard her father say once.

"Can I guess," she said, "who you suggest my companions should be?"

Sapphire grinned. "Try."

"Firekeeper, Derian, Doc—that is, Sir Jared. Essentially, the people you mentioned already, those who are in on your secret. I don't know if I could ask Ninette. She's a good woman and I trust her with my life, but the road to Dragon's Breath is a hard one and she isn't up to it."

"That is true," Sapphire said, "and while my secret does matter, we don't want to put you in too much danger. Even with Firekeeper and Blind Seer accompanying you—trusting that they will go, which we are not yet certain about since we haven't had a chance to ask them—that is a very small group. Why not take the other two who went with you into New Kelvin? Take this Wendee Jay about whom we've heard such good things. See if Earl Kestrel will let Edlin go with you. Both of them learned something of the language and customs of New Kelvin before. They could be useful now."

Elise nodded. "That's a good idea. I'm certain that House Kestrel could be easily convinced. Edlin would be harder to stop from coming than to get to join us. Wendee . . . Well, we'll have to see. Maybe I can convince her to come by appealing to her good heart. She's a mother, you know, and Citrine will need care."

"Wendee Jay can also act as a chaperon for you and Firekeeper," Sapphire said. "In reality, Firekeeper's honor may be beyond saving—though oddly enough, she's probably a virgin. I've certainly never seen her look at a man in anything but friendship. You, however, still have a reputation to guard."

King Tedric spoke. "That's what Elexa wanted me to remind you, Elise. She was very unhappy at the thought that you would sacrifice your reputation—not your honor, mind, we know you'll guard that as you see fit—but your reputation to our needs. Traveling about with a group of unmarried men—one of whom anyone with two eyes can see is in love with you—will make some people talk, no matter how many chaperons you take."

Elise took a deep breath. "Sire, given what is at stake here—Citrine's sanity, my future queen's reputation, maybe my homeland's safety—I don't see how I could refuse and still respect myself. I'm certain my parents will understand, especially if you and your heirs explain at least a little."

"Very well," the king said with a dry cough. "Consider that we will."

Elise turned to face Sapphire and Shad.

"Now I've agreed and you've agreed. Edlin will be no problem, nor Sir Jared. But Derian and Firekeeper? Holly Gardener told me that they have gone west."

The king interrupted. "I expect to see them back before the end of Bear Moon."

Elise wheeled to stare at him. She noticed that Sapphire and Shad looked equally surprised.

"Both?"

"Both," the king said. "Trust an old man a few secrets. Not even that—a hunch. I think they will be back and I think that the first thing Firekeeper will do is come here and request an interview with me. But speak on, Lady Elise. I believe you had another matter to raise."

Elise returned to her original thoughts with an effort.

"Yes," she said, "I wanted to know how you thought we should handle our return to New Kelvin. You see, the last time we were there we left as hunted fugitives with soldiers at our heels."

VIII

HAVING EXPECTED AN IMMEDIATE ANSWER to the question she put to the king, Elise was almost shocked when King Tedric replied.

"I don't have an answer for you, Lady Archer, but I do agree that this will prove a problem. Moreover, it is a problem we have anticipated, and we are working on solutions. Are you still willing to undertake the task?"

"Yes," she agreed a touch hesitantly.

After all, it was one thing to agree that something needed to be done while in the back of your head you expect that someone else will have come up with the brilliant plan that will make the task possible. It was quite another to find that the plan was still under development.

King Tedric leaned forward and patted Elise's hand.

"My dear, none of us would sacrifice you or your comrades lightly. We hope not to sacrifice you at all. Finding an excuse to send you into New Kelvin may be quite simple. We are not at war. Indeed, our lands are actively trading. That may provide excuse enough. Baron Archer is known to have ambitions for his family. Perhaps he will seek to exploit his daughter's fascination with strange lands and cultures in a venture into trade."

Elise thought this unlikely, given the geographic location of New Kelvin relative to the Archer Grant, and said so. The king waved his hand lightly, dismissing her protest.

"You worry too much about little things. Perhaps the venture would be undertaken in partnership with House Kestrel. After all, young Edlin is to be one of your companions. In any case, no matter what excuse is created for your making the journey, we . . ." King Tedric's gesture included Sapphire and Shad. ". . . feel that it would be best if more of your companions were skilled in the language of New Kelvin."

Elise nodded. It had been a nuisance last time that only she and Wendee Jay spoke the language at all well.

"Grateful Peace has agreed to tutor your entire group."

This didn't really surprise Elise. Peace must be grateful to them for saving his life and be eager to pay back the debt.

"Moreover . . ."

A fit of coughing interrupted whatever the king was about to say.

"Moreover," Sapphire said, handing King Tedric yet another cup of medicinal tea, "if Citrine is to make the journey under your care, you and she must have time to become reacquainted. More importantly, there must be time for her to learn to trust you and the others. Any plan we devise to ensure your safe return could be seriously jeopardized if one of her fits caught you unawares."

Again Elise nodded. She didn't know whether Sapphire was hinting that they were considering sending the team in disguise or that there would be those prepared to help if they were forced to make a rapid retreat. Either would be jeopardized by a small girl acting up. Elise considered asking just what form Citrine's episodes took, but Sapphire was continuing on.

"We would like you to escort Citrine to the Norwood Grant. We have already been in contact with Duchess Kestrel and she is preparing a private house where Citrine can live with you and at least some of your companions." Sapphire added quickly, "She is also arranging for proper servants and chaperonage. Grateful Peace can teach you there. Also, when Citrine has bad days—and it is too much to hope she will not—you will have privacy."

Sapphire sighed heavily and Shad unobtrusively slipped his hand around hers in comfort. Elise swallowed hard. A private house somewhere in the vast reaches of the North Woods. Her companions. That meant Edlin and Wendee. That meant Jared.

The others pretended not to notice her discomfort.

Shad spoke. "When either Firekeeper or Derian Carter return, you shall be notified by pigeon. If they do not return or we need you to go ahead without them, you will also be notified."

"And," Sapphire continued, "you don't need to leave this moment. I suggest that we send a message to your parents informing them that it might not be a bad idea for them to come to Eagle's Nest in a few days. I believe it is about time for Lady Aurella to attend upon the queen in any case, so it shouldn't raise too much gossip. This way, we can explain to them in person."

"You seem to have thought of everything," Elise said gratefully.

Except just how we can be sure we will leave New Kelvin—or at least that we will leave there alive.

THE NEXT HANDFUL OF DAYS passed far more quickly than Elise could have hoped. She and Ninette were fully occupied with shopping and making calls. Not many of her Wellward relations had come up from their holdings yet, but there was a cousin or so around upon whom she was required to call. Then there were those who hoped she would call on *them*.

Elise's recent interview with the king and his heirs—already common gossip among those with connections in the castle—had raised her social allure greatly. Some wanted to see if they could pry details of the meeting from her. For this, Elise found that the best thing to do was to start chattering at length about meaningless intricacies of New Kelvinese culture. She managed to sound quite informed—informed enough that it was reasonable that the king might have wished to consult her—but so dull and caught up in minutiae that she left the majority of her audience suspecting that the king regretted giving her his time.

Most of those who sent her invitations, however, were not interested in what Elise had done and said, but in what she had seen. How did the crown princess look? Was it true that Crown Prince Shad was trying to make over the Royal Guard after the fashion of Bright Bay? Did Elise think the Bright Bay custom of assigning new posts and titles would find favor in the court? Had she seen young Citrine? Was it true she raved constantly and had torn out most of her hair? Were the king and queen as ill as everyone said?

The last was the only question Elise had any difficulty answering. For most of the rest a little consideration let her find the answer that would do the royal family the least damage.

One person who markedly refused to see Elise, though Elise faithfully offered to attend upon her daily, was Grand Duchess Rosene. The day following Elise's long conference with the king, Grandmother Rosene had commanded Elise to attend on her in her apartments at the castle. When Elise told her only what she was telling everyone else, Rosene flew into a rage, and from that point on Elise's notes, sent faithfully every morning by special messenger, were returned with "Not In" printed across the fold.

Elise tried not to worry, but she wasn't completely successful.

Five days after Elise's audience with King Tedric, Lady Aurella and Baron Archer arrived in Eagle's Nest. They were barely settled when Grand Duchess Rosene swept in. She closeted herself with her son, pointedly leaving Elise out—though she was at home. Later, Lady Aurella was summoned to join them and soon after Lady Aurella's confidential maid came bearing a note from her mistress.

"*Elise*," it said, "*I suggest you find an excuse to leave the house. Surely you have calls to make. Your grandmother is behaving shamefully and I have no desire for you to suffer while her tongue is dripping venom.*"

Since Elise already knew she had her parents' support for her participation in King Tedric's plan, she took her mother's advice and left the Archer manse as quickly as was reasonable. She had been invited to tea with some of the young ladies of her generation and had accepted tentatively, not being certain whether or not her parents would need her. Now she had a fit excuse both to attend and to leave the house.

Still, as Elise sipped tea and chattered about the most fashionable styles for the coming summer and the most eligible of the young men, she wondered what the grand duchess was saying. Elise had not told her parents of Rosene's plan to insist that they adopt Deste Trueheart, feeling that for better or worse, it was wisest to have it come from its source. Now she wondered what they would think and what they would do.

And maybe, Elise thought, even as she giggled over someone's description of someone else's flirtation, *it wouldn't be a bad idea to have them adopt Deste, not a bad idea at all.*

WHEN ELISE RETURNED home she saw the grand duchess's carriage still parked around the side. This surprised her. On the whole, a visit from Grand Duchess Rosene was like a sudden windstorm, tearing through, upsetting everything, and leaving disruption, if not devastation, in its wake.

Rosene preferred to hold longer conferences in her own rooms at the castle, where she could conveniently forget to have windows opened or closed, or refreshments served, or play whatever little games she deemed necessary to keep her audience off balance.

Feeling rather apprehensive, Elise went inside. She hardly had time to hand her light shawl to the downstairs maid when Lady Aurella emerged from the parlor.

"Elise," Aurella said with a slightly apologetic smile, "your grandmother has waited expressly to see you. Would you come with me?"

Elise could imagine the scene that had preceded this quiet request and reached out to squeeze her mother's hand before following. She fought down her resentment that Rosene would use Aurella as an errand girl. If Lady Aurella could take such treatment in her own house so calmly then Elise resolved to model her own behavior on her mother's.

Grand Duchess Rosene was seated in a high-backed chair upholstered in floral print fabric—an heirloom of her own days as mistress of this house. Gowned in pale pink, her white hair piled high on her head, her fair skin flushed, she did not rise when Elise entered. Such a gesture would have been wasted, for they both knew that her remaining had nothing to do with affection and everything to do with power.

And it's very strange, Elise thought as she bent to properly embrace the old woman, *because she is fond of me—loves me dearly in her own way. Just because that way is rather after the fashion a spoiled girl loves her dolls doesn't change that the love is there.*

Rosene did not soften under her granddaughter's embrace, remaining as stiff and brittle as a porcelain doll. Nor did she wait to get to the point.

"Your parents told me that you have agreed to some madcap scheme of Tedric's," she said sharply. "Something that involves your taking off for the North Woods."

Elise nodded, thinking how interesting it was that when Rosene was angry with her brother he was "Tedric," but when she was playing on her relation to him he was always "the king" or even "His Royal Majesty."

"Yes, Grandmother," she said softly.

"Have you thought what this will mean to your House?" the old woman continued. "Already scandalmongers retail accounts of your adventures last winter. This will surely destroy what rags of a reputation remain to you as thoroughly as if you were to dance naked in the market square."

Elise couldn't help but smile at the image. It was so like something Fire-keeper might have done early after her return from living among the wolves.

Grand Duchess Rosene chose to interpret the smile—with some justification—as impudence.

"So you think that's funny!" she said. "Well, I do not find it at all funny. To
think that the house my dear Purcel founded at the price of his blood and
that we thought to perpetuate through our children should have come down
to a single silly chit with no sense of self-respect. It makes me want to weep!"

Grandmother Rosene didn't look in the least like she was about to weep.
Her eyes were bright, not with tears but with fury. Elise thought about offer-
ing her a handkerchief, then wondered where such impulses came from.
Surely she would never have entertained such a thought before. Maybe
Rosene was right. Maybe she had changed and not for the better.

So Elise bowed her head and listened with a meekness she didn't feel.
Underneath the curtain of her hair, she sneaked a glance at her parents.

Baron Archer sat bolt upright in his chair, restlessly twirling a brandy
snifter—though it was a touch early in the day for brandy—between his fingers. Otherwise he revealed no sign of agitation. Lady Aurella had picked up
her omnipresent embroidery hoop and was stitching away with mechanical
regularity. If anyone was to look, they might have seen she was drawing the
stitches rather more tightly than was necessary.

Grandmother has said something to force them to school their tongues to
silence, Elise thought, *and they are not terribly happy about it either.*

"I'm sorry, Grandmother," Elise offered when Rosene ceased her indignant though wordless huffing.

"Then you will tell the king you have consulted with your parents and
thought it wiser to refuse?"

"No, Grandmother," Elise said stiffly. She suspected that if she did as her
grandmother said, then before the end of the conversation Rosene would
have come up with some reason that she should, after all, comply. That,
however, would not do, not if Elise was to keep her own self-respect.

She wondered if her father would have recommended such a tactical
retreat, but Baron Archer was not saying anything and she read no portents
in the restless spinning of the snifter between his fingers.

"You will *not?*" the grand duchess said.

"No, Grandmother. I have given my word to the king. Moreover, care has
been taken that I will be chaperoned—Ninette is coming with me as far as
the Norwood Grant . . ."

"And what good did that do last winter?" Rosene interrupted. "None.
You ran off, unchaperoned."

"No, Grandmother, I did not. There was a respectable married woman—a retainer of Duchess Kestrel—who was with me at all times."

Elise decided not to mention Firekeeper. Sapphire was right. In circles such as those her grandmother frequented, Firekeeper's reputation was not even in rags; it simply didn't exist. For those people it was not chastity, but the appearance of chastity that mattered.

"A retainer of Duchess Kestrel," Grand Duchess Rosene sneered, "as if that is any recommendation. It's no longer spoken of, but Saedee Norwood isn't one to whom I'd trust a young girl's honor. If you think I'm just being a sour-tongued old woman, ask your mother who fathered Saedee's son and daughter."

Elise turned wordlessly to Lady Aurella.

"No one knows," Aurella answered.

Despite her desire to keep impassive no matter what she heard, Elise felt her eyebrows shoot up in surprise.

"No one?"

"No one," Grand Duchess Rosene repeated with savage satisfaction. "And this is the woman to whom I am to entrust the honor of the House I helped to found."

"The story was more current," Lady Aurella went on as if the interruption had not occurred, "years ago when Norvin and Eirene were seeking to wed. When Eirene wed Prince Barden, well, that was both the height of the fury and its end. Most people felt that if King Tedric didn't care who the father of his future daughter-in-law had been, then the rest of us didn't have any reason to bother either."

"Nor do I bother," Rosene replied haughtily, "except where there is the matter of considering such a scandalous woman as a guardian for my granddaughter. I fought back my doubts last year when you decided to let Elise make a winter visit to House Kestrel, but what happened then . . ."

She let the words trail off, quite satisfied.

Elise straightened in her chair.

"Well, Grandmother, this is interesting, but old gossip does not alter the obligation I have to His Royal Majesty. Nor," she hurried on before Rosene could interrupt, "does it alter the obligation I have to my House. I suppose you have told my parents of your thoughts regarding my cousin Deste?"

Grand Duchess Rosene nodded, for once too surprised, or perhaps merely too upset, to reply.

Elise turned to her parents, leaving Rosene out of the matter.

"The grand duchess does have a point," she said seriously. "I am the sole heir to the Archer Barony. If something happened to me, there would be chaos and scrambling for position. We all saw how that upset the kingdom last year when the issue was who would inherit from King Tedric. I think we owe our tenants the assurance that they will not suffer similar unrest on our account."

Baron Archer's nod seemed casual, but he was clearly interested. Elise noticed that the brandy had stopped its restless swirling.

"My hope and dream is to inherit our land and to administer it as I have been trained to do since birth," Elise went on. "The same sense of responsibility, however, makes me realize how foolish it is to leave me without an heir. I dearly hope the ancestors can do without you, Father, for a long time to come, and I hope that even if they should call you, Mother would continue in her place aiding me as I adjust to my new role."

This last was a less than subtle jab at Grand Duchess Rosene herself. Rosene had relinquished to her son all practical administrative work within the Archer Grant almost the moment Purcel had died. Rosene had claimed that her grief made her unfit, that her son was more able than she, but Elise had always felt that Rosene's real reason was that she preferred to be thought of as the king's sister rather than the baron's widow.

Baron Archer gave a wry smile.

"I am glad to hear you are not eager to have me join the ancestors," he said. "I have felt myself dead and buried at times during today's discussion."

Grand Duchess Rosene was not enjoying this turn of the conversation at all. Elise had a sudden insight why. All her childhood, Rosene had been an heir in waiting to the royal throne. True, she had been at the end of a long line, but the sense that she was somehow special had been there. As her actions the summer before had shown, any means, no matter how tenuous, to get her blood on the throne was to be seized.

Now here was Elise offering, in effect, to weaken her own claim to her own—admittedly lesser—inheritance. For all the grand duchess's threats, she clearly had never expected this response. Elise seized hold of her grandmother's temporary confusion to keep control of the conversation.

"Of course, Aunt Zorana may not like this plan at all," she said. "If something happened to both you and me, Father, the law would make her Baroness Archer and her children would follow after in turn."

Ivon nodded.

"However," he said, "Zorana would be less than perfectly trained for the position. Deste is young enough to be malleable—I hope."

He grinned at his daughter. "I understand she's pretty good with a bow, at least."

Elise answered his grin with one of her own.

"We could promise that no matter what happened, we would dower Deste. Aunt Zorana's resources are stretched rather thin—even with Purcel's death."

"What do you think about Kenre?" Ivon asked.

"From the point of view of teaching him his new duties and responsibilities," Elise said, "Kenre would be even better than Deste, since he is quite a bit younger, but Aunt Zorana has lost one son. It would be too much to expect her to give up the other."

"Still," Ivon said, glancing over at Aurella to gage her reaction, "I believe I will offer Zorana the choice of either child. She may have thoughts we have not considered. After all, she is their mother and knows them best."

Aurella nodded her agreement. Interestingly, given that she had initiated this discussion, it was Rosene who raised a protest.

"And if Zorana will not agree at all?" she asked, her voice a bit shrill.

"Well," Ivon replied, "we will have time to discuss the matter, to bring her to our way of seeing things. However, if Zorana cannot be convinced, I am certain I could get the Crown's permission to adopt from another family. I would simply prefer to keep the land within the blood descendants of Purcel Archer. However, Mother, you have been wise in pointing out how tenuous that line is, especially with both Elise and myself devoted to the service of our monarchs, no matter how dangerous that service may prove to be."

Rosene sputtered something wordless, but Elise ignored her, rising and embracing each of her parents in turn.

"In any case, Father, Mother, I hope that this safeguard will be unnecessary. No matter what some may think," and she could not keep her gaze from straying to Rosene, "I will not behave in any fashion that will make the question of my reputation a matter for the gossips. If the scandalmongers talk, well, at least you will have the assurance that there is no truth to the scandal."

Baron Archer managed to look both stiff and pleased. Lady Aurella reached up and touched Elise lightly on one cheek.

"We knew that already, dear," she said.

❧

DERIAN WONDERED at Firekeeper's silence and evident unhappiness as they journeyed back east. At first he thought she was suffering from homesickness—after all, her visit had been cut short and distorted by the need to deal with the colonists.

When Firekeeper's moodiness persisted beyond a few days, Derian wondered if she was worried about the colonists. Surely, she couldn't care so much about the fate of a group of humans. He knew that Firekeeper thought of herself as a wolf so completely that there were times when *he* thought of her as a wolf.

Could it be that memories from her childhood were reawakening? Firekeeper had always claimed to remember nothing other than living as a wolf. Sometimes Derian suspected she remembered more than she even realized. She had acquired a command of Pellish, the language of both Hawk Haven and Bright Bay, rather more quickly than even her talent for mimicry could account for. Occasionally, an odd word or gesture hinted at memories buried beneath what she admitted to knowing.

Yet Derian didn't think the wolf-woman a liar. He didn't remember much from when he was small, so why should she? If she chose to deny that those memories were there, then what harm did she cause?

Two days after they had crossed the gap through the Iron Mountains and successfully negotiated the worst of the descent, Derian learned that neither homesickness nor concern for the colonists was behind Firekeeper's bleak mood.

Daylight was fading into evening when she melted out of the brush. Derian had been expecting this. It had become the wolf-woman's usual custom to arrive and inform him that she had selected a place for him to camp. She often brought something she had caught for his dinner at the same time, or told him that she had already built a sheltered fire and that his meal was cooking under Blind Seer's watchful gaze. It was a luxury that Derian knew he would miss when he went back to traveling with humans—almost as good as having an inn waiting.

On this evening, Firekeeper walked along with him, chivying the tired mountain horses into new energy, and annoying Roanne. When they arrived at the designated spot, she helped him pitch his tent—an unusual gesture. Usually she sprawled comfortably on the ground, teasing him about his dependence on such things. This evening, however, Derian had the impression that she wanted him quickly settled.

Tonight, his meal was a duck wrapped in clay and baked in the fire. Race Forester had taught Firekeeper the trick—one that eliminated the need for removing the feathers before cooking. She liked things that saved time and effort, and if she was a bit forgetful about spices and tended to ignore flourishes like side dishes Derian wasn't about to complain. He'd taken to foraging along the trail, filling a small canvas sack with greens or mushrooms that cooked quickly when he made his camp.

Tonight, as always, Firekeeper refused to eat with him. Derian tried not to think about what she did eat and just how long she bothered to cook it. She'd survived for ten years without his nursemaiding. He'd just have to trust her to continue now.

Derian's impression that something was up increased when Firekeeper hunkered down at the edge of his camp where the firelight would not ruin her night vision, her arm flung around Blind Seer. The wolf's remaining, despite the nervousness he created among the horses, said louder than words that Firekeeper was tense and needed his support.

Derian didn't press her, going about the routine of cooking his mushrooms, checking the duck for doneness, heating a few potatoes he'd roasted in last night's fire, and waiting for her to get around to whatever was troubling her. He'd cracked the mud from around the duck and found the meat well cooked when she finally spoke.

"Fox Hair," Firekeeper said, and her voice was hoarse, as if she was feeling her way into the words, "I need to tell you something."

Derian pulled a bit of meat from the duck, sucked on his fingers when he burnt them, and nodded encouragement.

"You don't mind if I eat while I listen, do you?"

Firekeeper seemed startled by the routine courtesy. Derian had gotten the impression that wolves let very little get in the way of their meals. It was an indication of how very much a wolf she was this evening that she had apparently forgotten that humans were different.

"No, go, eat," she replied.

She was silent for so long that Derian wondered if she was waiting until he finished before continuing with whatever was so obviously bothering her. Then she spoke:

"Fox Hair, I tell you part of why I need to go from my wolves. Is true part," she hastened to add, "but only part. Part I not tell you then for I not want you tell Ewen and his people."

"But you're telling me now?" Derian clarified.

"Yes."

He saw her nod, a motion of dark against gathering darkness. It wouldn't be long before, to his fire-blinded eyes, she and Blind Seer would be nearly invisible. Firekeeper had a way of sitting that hid her bare arms so they didn't catch the light and her face, of course, was averted.

Firekeeper went on. "I not want you to tell anyone, but I need tell you. If I not make it to king, someone should know."

"Is it likely," Derian asked, feeling a sudden thrill of fear, "that you won't make it back to the capital?"

He sensed her shrug.

"I think I make, but . . ." She paused as if listening, then went on. "There are those who are not happy with humans and these are less happy with me. The road to Eagle's Nest is long and I might not come back."

"And I would?" Derian blurted out.

"Maybe not," Firekeeper admitted. "But they not angry with you."

"I think," Derian said, the greasy savor of the duck suddenly less tasty than it had been a moment before, "that you'd better start at the beginning. Right now, I'm only confused—and scared."

"Yes," Firekeeper said with a deep sigh. "I try. Words are so slow and need to march in a narrow line."

This was not the first indication she'd given that the manner in which the wolves—maybe all the Beasts—spoke was different from human style. Normally, Derian would have probed for more, but this time he remained silent, unwilling to distract Firekeeper from the subject she was circling around, as deliberate yet hesitant as a wolf pack selecting which member of a herd to pursue.

"I tell you," Firekeeper began again, "that the Beasts are not happy with Ewen and his people, that if Ewen and his not leave, then the Beasts may kill them. What I not tell you is that . . ."

She stopped again and Derian nearly threw a duck bone at her.

"I not tell you then, but I tell you now and I go to tell King Tedric," she went on, "that the Beasts maybe not stop with killing Ewen. Some Beasts think that killing all the humans is a good thing, a thing to be done now, that this was a thing that should have been done when the Fire Plague started the hunt, but was not."

Derian took advantage of her pause to sort through this. He'd heard her refer to the Fire Plague once or twice before and the reference had stayed with him. In both Hawk Haven and Bright Bay, the illness that had devastated all the colonies and had sent the Old Country rulers back to their homelands was referred to simply as the Plague. The New Kelvinese, he had learned, called the same event by a phrase that translated roughly as "the Burning Times."

Not for the first time, Derian wondered if Firekeeper was simply merging those terms or if she was making something of a literal translation of what the Beasts called the Plague. That, of course, implied not only intelligence, but some sort of history that went back for well over a hundred years. He was ready to accept intelligent animals—he had the evidence of his own experience on that matter—but facing that those animals had history, recorded in some fashion, was a leap he was not quite ready to take.

Hesitantly, Derian asked, "You are saying that the Royal Beasts once made a choice not to kill all the humans, that they thought about doing so at the time of the Plague?"

Momentarily, Firekeeper turned to face him and Derian saw the watchful expression on her face. Apparently, however, she thought his question reasonable.

"So my parents say," she replied, "as their parents did to them. The Beasts have many stories and though I am but a pup in their eyes, they are teaching me some."

So this is new to her, too, Derian thought. *No wonder she's so tense.*

Firekeeper went on, speaking a bit more quickly now.

"They tell me that long ago before humans come from Old World, all this land was for the Beasts. When humans come, first there is . . ." She paused, obviously seeking a word. "If not peace, not war, and even borders. Humans break this as there are more humans and humans have more need for space."

Derian swallowed a groan. Humans needing space sounded far too much like what had pushed Ewen across the mountains.

"Humans have power then," Firekeeper went on, "the great magic that Queen Zorana the Great hate so much and try to destroy. Humans tell how this power is used on humans. Humans not tell how it is used on Beasts. In time, Beasts go west, leave humans behind. Iron Mountains become new border. When Fire Plague come and humans die too little, then Beasts think to finish what Plague do. They not do, now some are sorry."

Derian wasn't an idiot. He had been spending much of the last year immersed in political game playing. He also understood Firekeeper's choppy, abbreviated speech better than anyone else.

"So," he said, choosing his words very carefully, "now the Beasts see the humans coming across the mountains and don't like it. They also realize that humans no longer have the 'great powers'—the strong old magic—and some Beasts are no longer content to let humans live on this land, even east of the mountains. They think to kill all the humans."

"Yes," Firekeeper said, gratitude and dismay equally mingled in her tone. "That is how it is. Many Beasts would die, I think. Many Beasts, especially four-footers, not know how really dangerous humans is. Wingéd folk know better, but even they think that without great powers humans can be killed so easily."

"And you?" Derian asked. "What do you think?"

"Maybe so," Firekeeper replied. "Maybe so, but many Beasts die and for what? Land we not use from time my pack leaders' own pack leaders not even fat pups? I tell King Tedric, tell him he must make humans stay east."

Derian rubbed his hands across his face.

"I wonder if he can make them," he said.

"If he not," Firekeeper said, "then the humans die and someday the Beasts die."

"I believe you," Derian said. "I think King Tedric will believe you. I just wonder if that one tired old man can make a difference. Sometimes people are pretty stubborn. Even if our people don't go west, what's to stop people in other countries?"

"For now," Firekeeper said, "I have heared nothing of that. True, maybe I not get told. Still, even if fighting must start, maybe it can start in other places."

Her tone became pleading.

"Derian, no you see? If Beasts fight humans then it is my pack, my family who is first to die. Wolves have ever held the land for the Beasts. We watch it as we hunt it, as we raise our pups. My family . . ."

She obviously could not find the words to clarify what she was trying to explain. Derian wanted to walk over to her, to hold her even as she was holding Blind Seer, but he knew she would not welcome such comfort. He settled instead for words.

"And you want me to tell this to King Tedric if for some reason you aren't able to do so."

Firekeeper perked up at this.

"Yes. Do. Some of the Beasts not think I am Beast since the last year and the magical things." Her voice dropped. "I was to bring those things to them. I not obey to word, though I think I do to heart . . . to spirit. Still, that I not obey as pup to One, this for some is reason not to trust that I am of heart with my people."

Derian actually understood. "So you think that some Beast—one of those who wants war with the humans—might come after you."

Firekeeper nodded. "That is it. And I am small to even the smallest hunter. Even with Blind Seer to help, I might not win. You say war, but from what I learn of human war, war is agreed to like a dance. What Beasts would do would be no war. There would be no dance, no counsel. There would just be deaths, many deaths, and someday humans would understand who is doing the killing, then Beasts would learn of arrows and spears and armor and poison and other horrible human killing things."

From the length of this speech, Derian knew how upset she was, and guessed that some of her silence over the past several days had been her studying on what words to use.

"I understand," he said, hesitated, then spoke his own fear. "But if they kill you, won't they kill me? I'm a human. I'm one of the enemy."

"Yes, they might," Firekeeper said as she had before, not soothing him a whit. "But you have gift of making letters that others read. You can write this story over and over and over. We will hide it on the horses in their bags. Maybe Elation, who is not of this thinking, would carry a message. The words will speak when we cannot. It is worth the trying."

Derian nodded, but as he pulled out paper, quill, and ink, determined to write at least one version of this incredible tale before he went to sleep that night, he thought that Firekeeper might be overestimating the power of her story—whether written or told—to prevent this strange and terrible unde-clared war.

IX

THUNDER WAS SHAKING the canvas walls of the pavilion tent, thunder so loud and pervasive that it was omnipresent, unlike the eye-searing flashes of lightning that periodically lit the interior of the tent. Those washed out the lantern light so effectively that between bolts Elise always felt vaguely surprised to find the lanterns—they'd lit several both for light and warmth—still burning.

She stepped out of her wet riding clothes, cold to the bone, and hastened to draw on a heavy flannel nightdress that was only vaguely damp. Ninette had already done the same for herself and for Citrine, and was now warming water over the lamp.

It was a terrible night to be on the road. A storm had arisen when their small group traveling to the Norwood Grant was in between settled areas where they might have found shelter. There had been nothing to do but pitch the tents on the nearest rise of high ground and huddle within, soaked to the skin, but at least with a dream of getting dry. Elise thanked the Lynx—who as a cat must set some value on being warm and dry—that the escort her father had sent with her was so skilled.

She hoped that they were comfortable and in their own tents. The horses, who could not be put in a tent but had to settle for the shelter offered by a copse of trees, must be miserable.

There was something about the beating of the thunder, about the hard pounding of the rain against the canvas, that made anything outside of the pavilion seem less than real. Elise, Ninette, and Citrine might have been on some island in the middle of the ocean, cut off from everyone and everything.

Citrine, praise every ancestor in their shared lines, had not gone into one of her wild fits when the storm hit. Instead she had sat her pony like a doll, not even raising a hand to wipe the water from her face. Elise had set Ninette to mind the child while she did her best to help with pitching the tents and strapping covers over what remained in their wagon. The skills she'd acquired during last winter's journey into New Kelvin had been of some use, but she realized oddly that the greatest assistance she had given was by being willing to help. It had put heart in the baron's men to have their young mistress struggling with them against the elements.

And they needed heart, for Citrine's odd moods had sucked the spirit out of them far more than any attack by bandits or wild beasts would have done.

Superficially, Citrine was the same sweet-faced little girl she had been the year before, a touch thinner certainly, but that could be explained by a growth spurt, though at nine she was young for such. Yet more had changed than the acquisition of maybe an inch of height and a slimming of build. Even when Citrine was at her most peaceful there was a brooding cynicism in her blue-eyed gaze that should not reside in a child so young. At her wildest she was a screaming terror, flailing out at enemies that dwelled mostly within her own mind. Worse, however, than these screaming fits were the times Citrine turned weird and fey, saying things that almost made sense, couched so that the mind worried over them long after their speaker seemed to have forgotten what she'd said.

Thunder shook the pavilion once more, a basso rumble accompanied by a tattoo of hail beating the canvas. The baron's men had avoided the child, obeying his orders that she not be troubled so punctiliously that not one had as much as spoken a word to her. Elise had seen more than one touch their amulet bags when Citrine's oddly vacant blue-eyed gaze had turned their way—a superstitious gesture Elise couldn't bring herself to rebuke.

Tonight's storm, so curiously violent, would not help morale. Elise resolved that when the rain let up some she would check on their escort, and began laying out a fresh set of traveling clothes in preparation.

Ninette looked up from adding tea leaves to the water heating over the lamp. She frowned slightly when she saw what Elise was doing, but didn't protest. Instead, she glanced up at the pavilion roof.

"If that hail keeps up, we'll have holes through for sure."

Elise nodded. There wasn't any use in pretending she hadn't had the same thought. The pavilion was one of the best in her father's store, the one he used himself, but even the thickest canvas couldn't take such punishment forever. Had their roof been of solider stuff, it might have already been pierced, but the canvas gave just enough.

"At least it's still watertight," Elise offered by way of consolation. "Freshly treated before we left, and to think I was muttering over my father's insistence. I didn't even think we'd need half the gear he insisted we take."

"Good thing he wouldn't give in," Ninette said, even managing a smile, "and that he insisted we lay in such varied stores. I'm glad we won't need to do without a solid meal."

Elise nodded. Citrine was sitting on a campstool, a blanket wrapped around her for added warmth, as blank-eyed as a doll. Half a moonspan ago, Elise would have felt pity and a touch of impotent fury. Now she was only glad not to have any additional trouble.

None of the nurses, maids, guards, or other attendants Princess Sapphire had hired to take care of Citrine had volunteered to make the trip to the Norwood Grant—not even when the princess had hinted strongly that she thought this would be a very good idea. Elise had stopped Sapphire from making her hint a direct command.

"After all," she had said, "when we go into New Kelvin, we will need to leave all those people behind. Best we begin getting used to each other right away."

And Elise and Ninette had done fairly well, but the reality was, Elise had never been a mother. Moreover, she was an only child, a rather privileged only child. She was not accustomed to having someone depend on her every hour of the day. Ninette was only slightly better prepared for the responsibility. She had siblings, but they were all older than her. She had never had to look out for them. It had been their place to look out for her.

A narrow trickle of water was working its way between the side of the pavilion and the ground cloth. Without really thinking about it, Elise set the wet blouse from her riding habit to sop up the flow and hopefully discourage it from going elsewhere. The hail shifted back to rain, then to hail once more, then back to rain. There seemed no indication that it ever intended to let up.

Elise ate the meal Ninette had prepared for them, a sort of porridge with dried meat suspended in it, this last adding flavor but rather too chewy to be good. The food was warm, though, and filling. As she ate, Elise alternated her own bites with spoonfuls for Citrine. The little girl ate automatically, showing no awareness of her surroundings.

I suppose it's one way to deal with the situation, Elise thought. *I wonder if I need check on the men. It's still raining so hard.*

She didn't want to go out in the rain, but she knew what was expected of her, what her father would think if she didn't go. Ninette didn't comment when Elise started changing out of her now warm and comfortable flannel nightdress into her spare riding clothes, so she must have arrived at the same conclusion.

The fabric of Elise's clothes was just slightly damp and extraordinarily clammy. It seemed to have acquired extra folds, all striving with great vigor and enthusiasm to get as close to her warm skin as possible. She could have sworn the damp chill had a life of its own and in contrast the rain outside—now driving down harder than ever—seemed almost welcoming.

She draped an oilskin cape over the entire ensemble and stuffed her feet into her boots. Neither she nor Ninette had taken the time to scrape the mud off of them and they felt as if lead anchors had been sewn into the soles and hung around the ankles. Elise was raising the flap to duck outside when Citrine spoke:

"There's an ocean behind the wagon. Give heed or else you'll drown for sure."

Elise glanced at the girl. Her face was as wooden as before, but for her eyes, which moved to follow Elise's movement.

"An ocean?" Elise repeated. "Right. I'll keep clear of it."

"Mind you do," Citrine said in that same odd, almost inflection-free tone of voice, as if in spite of the caution she was offering, she didn't care one way or another.

Ninette shrugged.

"I'll make more tea," she offered, "and set your gown by the lamp to warm it."

With this comfort and Citrine's strange words still echoing in her mind, Elise ducked out.

The rain came down as if it had an intelligent desire to conduct an experiment as to whether a human being could really be soaked to the bones. Elise declined to participate. Wrapping her cloak more carefully about her, she made her way to where the other tents—rounded structures, not as fancy as the pavilion, but comfortable enough—had been erected. If she went out of her way to avoid the area behind the wagon, she tried hard not to think about it.

Most of the men of her escort were crowded into one tent, playing cards—a thing made rather difficult in that they were sitting so close to each other that honor alone kept them from reading each other's hands.

When Elise pushed the flap aside, the man nearest started to curse, thinking her one of his fellows who'd chosen to bed down in the other tent rather than play. He stopped in midword, seeing the pale face framed in its wisps of fair hair beneath the dripping hood.

"Just came to make certain," Elise said hesitantly, squeezing inside, careful not to touch the sides of the tent and give the water a way through, "that you all are all right."

Heads bobbed and even the man near the tent flap, on whom she was unavoidably dripping, grinned.

"Well enough, Lady Archer," their leader said. "Fairly dry, at least."

Now that Elise was inside, she could smell a thick, beery reek. Oddly, she felt relieved. If they had drink as well as something to eat—and she could see heels of bread and rinds of cheese from completed meals shoved here and there—then they should be content.

"Then I'll just leave you to your game," she said, ducking out once more. She didn't stop to listen to what they might say about her. Lady Aurella had taught her that what one overhears is rarely pleasant.

BY THE NEXT MORNING, the storm had spent its fury, leaving a muddy road partially obscured by large spreading puddles. The woods and fields within sight were sopping, but the trees were unfolding new leaves as if encouraged by all the wetness.

Elise imagined that the sky looked vaguely embarrassed for having made such a fuss.

What she didn't imagine was an especially broad pool—nearly an ocean if one was feeling poetic—that spread from beneath the wagon to its rear and across the road. It was so wide that there was no easy way to avoid it unless they wished to abandon the wagon entirely.

Elise warned her escort to be particularly careful about this puddle, suffering slightly under their condescension as they obeyed. She knew they were humoring her. However, her care was repaid when one of the less perfectly obedient decided to lead one of the horses through the edge of the pool.

The murky water proved deceptively deep and the horse sank nearly to its chest in the clingy, clay-suffused mud. They lost a fair amount of time getting the horse out without injury, and then Elise suggested that they take shovels and dig a few channels to divert most of the water.

"This pool could prove a hazard to other travelers as well," she said. "We owe their care to the king."

There were no condescending glances this time, and the men—all but the driver and one delegated to continue the packing—dug with a will. The majority of the water drained away readily, revealing a deep hole, far deeper than any of the road ruts they'd seen thus far.

The leader of Elise's escort poked down into the remaining water with his shovel, three-quarters of its length vanishing before the blade rang against stone.

"I recall there was a big rock flush with the surface of the road just where we pulled the wagon off," he said. "Must have been loosened by all the water last night and fell down into some animal den or such. Good thing you told us to be careful, my lady. We could have lost a man down there."

Elise nodded polite acceptance of his praise, but her gaze shifted to Citrine. The little girl sat her pony, almost as motionless as she had been the day before. Today, however, her gaze was animated, and she looked faintly amused and quite superior.

The expression was familiar and Elise struggled to place it. After a moment she did so, but she felt no pleasure in the memory. Citrine's expression was a perfect match for that of her mother, Melina, the sorceress.

THEY ARRIVED at the Kestrel estate on the Norwood Grant a few days later than expected, but, given how wet the weather had been, the duchess had not yet ordered search parties to find them.

However, Elise did not think it was a complete coincidence that Edlin Norwood, the earl's eldest son, had chosen to take his afternoon ride down the road along which they could be expected to arrive.

Edlin was in his very early twenties, a handsome enough youth if one liked loose limbs, and a somewhat rangy bearing, accompanied by a beaming smile. There had been a time when Elise had quite liked all those things, enough to overlook how unfashionably short Edlin wore his curly black hair and the cheerful irreverence in his laughing grey eyes. Elise's fancy had passed, but had left her with a fondness for Edlin that had been intensified by their shared trials in New Kelvin.

Accompanied by a half-dozen of the red-spotted white hunting dogs that were one of his great enthusiasms, Edlin rode forward. The horse he was mounted on was a rather flashy liver chestnut with a flaxen mane and tail. Elise felt certain she would have remembered the horse if it had been part of the Kestrel stables the previous winter and decided that here, as with her own Cream Delight, she was seeing the end result of doing business with Prancing Steed Stables.

Fleetingly, she wondered where Derian Carter and Firekeeper were now. Had they even turned back from the western lands? What if King Tedric was wrong and Firekeeper intended to winter there? Could Elise manage this proposed expedition without their aid?

Edlin reined in, swiveling the liver chestnut around so that they were all headed in the same direction. He shouted commands at the dogs—each of which seemed to find the wagon endlessly fascinating, though they took care to avoid the horses.

"Ho, you pack of worthless dogs! Away from there, Dancer. You'll have a hoof through your head! Back, Spangles!"

Despite Edlin's flurry of commands, the dogs were actually fairly well behaved and fell to sniffing along the side of the road or—in the case of a particularly serious-seeming pair—setting themselves to lead the procession toward the house.

Edlin wiped his arm across his forehead. His tricorn was set at a jaunty angle rather far back on his head, doubtless to permit just this. Elise couldn't help compare Edlin with his far more serious father and wondered, not for the first time, how well they got along. Nor was Edlin terribly like his mother, Lady Luella Kite.

A cuckoo's chick, she thought, meaning no disrespect to either of Edlin's parents, for though he lacked the distinctive hawklike nose, Edlin was clearly Kestrel.

Edlin bobbed something like a bow from the saddle.

"Greetings, Lady Archer! Wet road, what? Guessed as much from all the mud on the wagon. No real trouble though, right?"

"Not much, Lord Edlin," she replied. It occurred to her that Edlin had as much right to be called Lord Kestrel as she did to be called Lady Archer. Both of them were past their minority. However, on Edlin the youthful form of address seemed to have stuck.

"Wonderful! Wonderful!" he replied happily. He maneuvered his horse so that it drew alongside Citrine's pony. "And how are you, cousin?"

Elise held her breath, her hands tight on Cream Delight's reins. Citrine had adjusted to the presence of the men in the escort by refusing to acknowledge their existence. However, one of the worst moments along the road had come when a fellow traveler had offered the child a cheerful greeting. Citrine had screamed so that it had been a blessing when the man's horse had bolted.

After that, Elise had tried to get Citrine to ride in the wagon, where she could be screened from casual observation. The child's tantrums at that suggestion had been so violent that Elise had never dared make it again.

Citrine, however, took no offense at Edlin's words, nor at his proximity. She bobbed her head in a shy, childish fashion and positively twinkled at him.

"I'm well, cousin," she answered softly, offering her hand. "That's a pretty horse you have."

"Name's Moonkissed," Edlin replied. "New come to our stables. I like her too. Want to ride with me?"

In reply Citrine held up her arms and, to the unconcealed amazement of all, permitted Edlin to lift her from her pony's saddle to sit in front of him.

"Make Moonkissed go fast!" the little girl giggled, and Edlin, always impulsive, obliged, urging the mare into a gentle canter.

His dogs ran after, a few barking as if on the chase.

Elise stared after them, amazed and yet curiously unsettled. As far as she knew, Citrine and Edlin were mere acquaintances. Certainly, they knew each other, but over ten years separated them and so those social occasions when they would mix would have been rare. Citrine had only been permitted to attend adult gatherings maybe the last two years and at those her family's seat would have been lower than the Kestrels'.

Yet here was Citrine treating Edlin as if he were her dearest friend. From the muttering of the rider who came forward to gather up the pony's reins, Elise wasn't the only one unsettled by the girl's spontaneous friendliness.

I should be happy, Elise thought. *Relieved. Surely if Citrine has taken to Edlin it will make our journey easier.*

She remained unsettled, though, and tried to make herself believe that all she was experiencing was a spate of petty jealousy at being replaced as "best cousin." Try as she might, in her heart of hearts, Elise was not reassured.

"WE'RE PUTTING YOU in a nice house about an hour's walk from this one," Duchess Kestrel said. "It has been a dower house in its time, also a place where more than one young couple of the family has first set up. It's large enough for you and Citrine, your maid, Wendee Jay, and some servants.

"I've handpicked those," the duchess went on, "for their skill and discretion. You won't be entertaining, so I didn't bother with a butler, but you'll have a housekeeper, cook, several maids, a gardener, groundkeeper, groom, boot boy . . ."

"So many!" Elise gasped. "You won't have any servants left for your own household."

"Nonsense. We have more than enough to go around and a few who will be happy to prove their worth in a new establishment. Laundry, however, will need to be sent here. I have been informed that the tubs at your house are in need of repair and scouring before they will suit."

For a moment, Duchess Norwood looked like any housekeeper informed of such an annoyance, then her pale eyes became serious.

"In any case, the more servants I send you, the more eyes there will be to see that your behavior is perfectly respectable. The more tongues to confirm it, too, if the gossips get started."

Elise blushed, but the duchess pretended not to notice and went on with her description.

"There is a gatekeeper's house on the grounds, quite large enough for a bachelor establishment. That is where Grateful Peace will stay, and the other gentlemen when they come for their lessons. There will be no question of lack of propriety."

Elise smiled in gratitude at the old woman. It was very hard to believe Duchess Kestrel the scandalous creature of Grand Duchess Rosene's acid-tongued memories, but when Elise had questioned Lady Aurella her mother had confirmed that no one knew the name of the man who had fathered Norvin and Eirene.

"You have gone to a great deal of trouble, Duchess."

"Not too much when it's to fulfill the king's own request," came the bland reply. "In any case, the house needed to be opened, aired, and put into order. No one has lived in it for several years. Eventually, we will need it for Edlin and his wife . . ."

"Is he planning to marry?" Elise asked, realizing too late that she had interrupted.

"Not that I've been told," Saedee Norwood replied with a laugh, "but he's of an age and even if he is not ready to marry, it might not be unwise for him to learn how to manage his own household—perhaps when he returns from New Kelvin. In the meantime, this gives a good excuse to learn what drains aren't working and just where the roof has begun to leak."

They shared a laugh over this; then Elise grew serious.

"You do know that the king wishes to keep gossip to a minimum," she said.

"I do," the duchess replied, "but the easiest way to start gossip is to tell the servants not to talk. Everyone knows that the crown princess's sister is touched in her mind. I have given out that she has been brought here to get away from things that will awaken bad memories. You have come as a confidant of the queen. As to your language lessons, well, that was a bit of a puzzler. Norvin suggested that it was reasonable to give Citrine something new to concentrate on—that perhaps she had been left too much to herself and to familiar things."

"Clever," Elise said, and meant it.

"Norvin is that," his mother agreed a touch complacently. "You are known to have interest in foreign things, so the material that was chosen to distract Citrine was also chosen so as not to bore you. What do you think?"

"It will do," Elise said, and her smile made the simple words into praise, "at least until we vanish off into New Kelvin."

"Time enough to worry about that when you are ready to go," the duchess said calmly. "Happily, the child's instability provides ample reason for Sir Jared Surcliffe to call. The crown princess requested he come all the way to the capital this past winter. It would seem odd if he not call on her here. Grateful Peace has been Jared's patient as well. If the doctor should get interested in the lessons and choose to stay . . . well, that won't seem odd at all."

Something in the duchess's tone caused Elise to blush once more, this time more deeply. She was certain that Duchess Norwood was teasing her, but the lined old face looked so completely innocent that Elise didn't dare comment.

"Will that serve?" the duchess asked.

"Admirably," Elise replied. "It is easy to see that you were once a soldier. You plan just like my father does."

Duchess Kestrel accepted the compliment with a gracious nod.

"Now, I think it best that you and your entourage relocate as quickly as possible. Luella agreed to take Agneta and Lillis away for a few days so that they would not be here when Citrine arrived. Tait was not a problem, but the girls are so much of an age that it would be awkward keeping them apart—that is, it would emphasize Citrine's instability. However, the delay in your arrival means that Luella may return before you can leave. Will you be insulted if I send you off tomorrow morning?"

Elise shook her head.

"Not at all, Your Grace. Quite honestly, I have been relieved at the level of composure Citrine has maintained thus far. Her friendly greeting of Edlin was quite a bit more than we dared hope; she has been rather apprehensive of men to this point. Tell me, were they ever particular friends?"

"Not that I recall," the duchess replied. "Ask Edlin, though. He has a playful streak and may have involved himself with the children at some point or in some fashion that I am unaware. I rarely travel to Eagle's Nest now that Norvin is available to serve as my representative. I could have missed something. Is it important?"

Elise started to shrug, realized that was an ungraceful motion, and settled for a shake of her head.

"I don't know, Duchess. It is simply that I am trying to understand anything that will make it easier to help Citrine. Her reaction toward Edlin was unusual, therefore, I thought it worth examining."

"Wise," Saedee Norwood replied. "Very wise. Well, don't forget to ask Edlin when you get a chance. Would you mind writing me every few days and keeping me current on the situation? I think it best that we not have unwarranted comings and goings between our houses lest it be difficult to keep visitors away. However, I would like to know how things develop. My grandson can bring your letters to me. An hour's walk is nothing to him and doubtless he will have a horse or two with him. The boy acquires pets like a dog acquires fleas."

"Writing you will be no problem at all," Elise said, wondering if, for all her courtesy, the duchess saw her as a girl, even as she saw Edlin as a boy.

Elise decided that the duchess could hardly avoid doing so. After all, it had not been many years ago that Elise and Edlin both had run about these grounds, pulling each other's hair and shouting insults. She would take the duchess's courtesy as it was offered—freely and with no condescension. In return, she would seek to do nothing that would make the duchess regret her courtesy and trust.

After taking her leave, Elise went to inform Ninette of their plans and to make ready for the next—though thankfully very short—leg of their journey.

ꙮ

ON THE ROAD WEST, Firekeeper hadn't much minded her pace being tied to that of Derian and his horses. On the return trip she came to resent it greatly. She longed to push to her limits, walking only when she could not run, sleeping without regard as to whether it was night or day and then only for as long as her body demanded. The plodding steadiness of the string of horses, the need to seek a campground as soon as night approached, the loss of all the good night became almost more than she could bear.

Blind Seer, catching fire from her own impatience, took to ranging on his own, sometimes sleeping for part of the day and then running to catch up. Firekeeper missed the blue-eyed wolf more than she cared to admit, but she couldn't blame him for his choice. In any case, the horses had learned to tolerate his scent, but they did not like it and their edginess slowed what progress they did make.

More than once Firekeeper considered hurrying on ahead, leaving Derian to follow at his own pace. Elation, traveling with them for some inscrutable purpose of her wingéd-folk mothers, dissuaded her.

"There are predators who would find him all too tasty," the peregrine falcon warned, "and not all of these are to be found in the wild lands. Derian will be in different danger when we reach the lands where humans are thicker. Even I could not protect him by myself. If I were so inclined," she added rather hastily.

Firekeeper could not disagree, no matter how much she wished to do so. Derian had made the journey west with no other human companion but herself because he trusted in her protection. To abandon him now would be as bad as leaving a puppy to starve.

Derian himself was aware of her impatience—he would have been hard-pressed not to, with her readying the horses for the road in the dank bleakness of false dawn and pressing them down the trail into twilight, urging him just a little farther with a promise of a campfire ready at the trail's end.

One night after particularly grueling travel through heavy rain, Derian sat drying his boots over a sheltered fire in a deserted shack no one but Firekeeper would have found, so overgrown was it with vines and close set with young saplings. He was thoughtful and without his usual quips or conversation.

"Firekeeper," he said at last, "if you're so worried about getting this news quickly to the king, why not have Elation carry him a message?"

The wolf-woman snarled, less at Derian's suggestion than because his words spoke a private war she had been fighting with herself.

"I cannot," she replied stiffly. "I refuse to have Kestrel words carried to king by Elation. I cannot make . . ."

She paused, hunting for a word.

"Exception?"

"Yes, that. I cannot do for me except as I do for them. Otherwise, I do become what the Beasts fear, one who will betray them to the humans."

Firekeeper didn't tell Derian that Elation had already made a similar suggestion and that she had refused the falcon for the same reason.

Derian nodded. Rain, lighter than what had plagued them during the day, pattered against the layer of pine boughs with which Firekeeper had temporarily restored the roof. The horses were visible through a gap in one side of the shack, shifting uncomfortably against their pickets when the wind changed, bringing the rain their way. Mostly they were content, pleased enough not to be moving. The warm mash Derian had insisted on preparing hadn't hurt either.

"In a few days," Derian said, "we'll be in more civilized lands. I was thinking. I could leave the mountain ponies with some farmer, promise to pay him for keeping them until my father can claim them—or even to reward him if he brings them to Eagle's Nest for me. Roanne's faster than they are. We might make better time."

Firekeeper felt a warm flush of gratitude. She knew something of human values now and knew that Derian already stood to be in great trouble with his father over the mules he wasn't bringing back. Now he was offering to leave the mountain ponies as well.

"No," she said. "Is kind of you, but Roanne cannot go so fast on roads of mud. We may as well bring the ponies. We are as far behind if she is hurt going fast."

Derian nodded. "True enough. Weather's foul."

Firekeeper understood with that split perspective that was so useful—and so uncomfortable. On the one hand, she could see how the weather was unpleasant for human-style travel. It wasn't great for wolf travel, either, but a wolf would have borne whatever the weather had to give, driven by hunger or by need. If there was no need, the wolf would lie low until the weather was better. Wishing for the world to be what it was not wasn't usually an option.

In the distance, a wolf howled. Not Blind Seer, a Cousin probably. They would be ranging out, hunting to feed their pups, enjoying the warmer days.

She wasn't afraid of them. Even if they were attracted by the scent of the horses, she felt certain she could drive them back. Cousins were timid creatures unless pressed and she had many ways to convince them that easier game lay elsewhere.

Once Derian had banked the fire and settled into his bedroll for the night, Firekeeper went outside for a final patrol. The rain had abated and the skies were clearing, clouds breaking up into thin white wisps that showed the stars behind.

The comet was up there, too, coldly burning against the black. It had changed little in size or shape though the moon had waxed and waned and waxed again since its appearance. Firekeeper found its constancy unsettling, seeming a reminder that no matter how those beneath the moon's sphere changed their lives, some things were unchanging.

"Ever wonder where it was before it came here?" Blind Seer asked, stepping silently over the damp bracken to lean against her leg.

"Often," Firekeeper replied. "Humans have stories of this, or of ones like it. Queen Elexa wasn't certain whether all the stories were about one or about many. Still, comets are rare. I wonder when this one will migrate to its other hunting grounds."

"A Waterlander might know," Blind Seer said, surprising her greatly. "I have heard tell that they look to the stars as the humans of Bright Bay and Hawk Haven look to their ancestors."

"I think I may have heard that, too," she said. "I hadn't realized you cared about such things."

"I care about anything that might touch you, dear heart. Even lights in the sky that do nothing but distress you."

"Maybe someday we will go to Waterland and ask them about the stars," Firekeeper said. "Maybe someday we can go many places. I still would like to find where the songbirds went."

"Curiosity," the wolf said, "Little Two-legs."

"I know," she replied, hearing the implied criticism but not stung by it.

Blind Seer was nearly as curious as she was or he would never have left the ordered patterns of the wolf packs to accompany her east. He would have dispersed, roamed for a time, fought his fights, perhaps won a mate. Certainly won a mate. Firekeeper couldn't imagine Blind Seer as one of the lesser males, valued for his strength and hunting prowess, but content to settle in a lesser role and never build a pack of his own.

She wondered why the thought of Blind Seer as a leader of his own pack made her so sad and knew in her heart that she was perfectly aware why. For now, for all her professed curiosity, she decided not to pursue it. Time enough, always time enough.

When Firekeeper finally slept, she dreamed she rode astride the comet—or was it Blind Seer whose tail streamed out so broad and bright behind?—and that they traveled to places where time and earthly limitations mattered not at all.

X

THE HOUSE WAS as comfortable as Duchess Kestrel had promised. Indeed, it was nearly the equivalent in size and elaborate appointments of the family residence on the Archer Barony lands. The comparison brought home to Elise that the difference between a Great House and a lesser one went far beyond titles and wealth, but into their relative places in history as well.

Not only had the Great Houses been in place since the creation of the kingdom, but their founders had often held lands—or claimed them after the departure of the Old Country rulers—before the kingdom's creation. Queen Zorana the First had less granted land as much as confirmed those holdings, and provided the Crown's tacit support in maintaining that holding.

Idly, Elise wondered how matters of property and precedence were handled in New Kelvin and resolved to ask Grateful Peace. It might help her understand this strange land into which Melina had now inserted herself so successfully.

The thaumaturge—or Illuminator, as Peace preferred to be termed now that he was in exile—had taken up residence in the gatehouse a few days after Elise's own arrival. He looked more frail than she recalled, doubtless in part because of the physical struggles related to his healing from the amputation of his arm, but more—at least so Elise thought on later consideration—because he had been robbed of the trappings of office and position that had been such a part of him.

The ornate silk robes and curly-toed slippers were gone, replaced by shirt, waistcoat, knee-breeches, and buckled shoes after the fashion of a

Hawk Haven gentleman. His facial tattoos remained, but seemed disfigurement rather than adornment in a land where they marked him a stranger. In New Kelvin even the youngest child would have known at a glance the things Peace considered important about himself: his place as a member of the Sodality of Illuminators, his personal vow not to remarry, his promotion to a counselor to the Dragon Speaker.

In Hawk Haven all that anyone saw were stylized patterns that rather than clarifying who Grateful Peace was seemed to set him apart. The untrained eye flitted between the tattoos and the face beneath, uncertain which to focus upon and, inevitably, coming up with a confused image that muddled both into one useless mess.

Peace's myopia didn't help matters, the spectacles through which he surveyed everyone and everything providing yet another means of distancing himself from his surroundings. All in all, he was not an easy man to like, yet Elise did like him at least a little—a liking that was two-quarters pity, one-quarter admiration, and one-quarter curiosity.

Citrine had not warmed to Grateful Peace as she had to Edlin, but that would have been rather much for which to hope. At least she had not started screaming or having nightmares after their initial introduction. That was a start.

Elise began Citrine's initiation into New Kelvinese language and custom with costumes and makeup. Elise had yet to meet a child who didn't like playing dress-up and Citrine was no exception. This could provide a bridge to more complicated things.

Elise also realized she needed to polish her own command of the language. Last winter she had developed a good enough accent to be able to pass almost as a native—all other things considered. She wanted to achieve that again and to add to it the myriad details of body language and mannerism that would further help.

"I don't see why, what?" Edlin said, when Elise pressed him to practice his own New Kelvinese.

The young lord's tones were somewhat more peevish than usual. Grateful Peace had suggested that Edlin grow his hair longer since almost no one wore it short in New Kelvin and Edlin complained about how heavy his hair felt. Spring had become summer when no one was looking. The days were longer and the nights hotter. Even here in the northern reaches of Hawk Haven there were ripe fruit and fresh salads on the table. The cook Duchess Kestrel had loaned them made a fruit tart Elise was ready to die for.

Elise knew these culinary flourishes interested Edlin less than the fact that two litters of puppies were toddling around. There were also some promising foals—fruits of Derian's initial purchases for the stables—to be checked over lest the grooms be less than perfect in their training.

Especially when the days were hot, Elise felt something of the same desire to avoid study. It would be much nicer to sip cool drinks on the terrace over at the Kestrel manse and gossip about fashion with Lady Luella and her attendants. She knew her relatively fresh arrival from the capital would make her quite popular in such discussions. However, duty called—duty assigned by the king himself—so Elise was a bit strict with Edlin when he whined.

"I mean, we can't hope to pass over there, can we?"

Elise frowned.

"We may need to, cousin. In any case, even if we do not disguise ourselves, learning New Kelvinese language gives us an amazing advantage in any circumstance. The New Kelvinese are not accustomed to foreigners who can understand their language. They tend to speak about us to our faces, trusting in the language barrier to hide their meaning."

Edlin saw humor in this and grinned.

"But we would understand them, what? I say, what fun! And maybe it wouldn't be a bad idea to be able to speak the stuff anyhow. I mean, what if we need directions or something?"

Elise didn't comment further, pleased enough that Edlin was willing to add to the couple dozen memorized words and phrases he'd acquired the winter before.

She turned her attention to Wendee Jay. Full-figured, with rich dark blond hair that Elise secretly envied, Wendee was a fascinating person—especially to Elise, who had made few friends outside of Hawk Haven's nobility and "better" families until the previous year.

A former actress, Wendee was now a full-time retainer with Duchess Kestrel, a patronage she had accepted because of the security it offered her immediate family—two daughters and her mother, who cared for the girls when Wendee needed to travel on the duchess's business.

Wendee was something Elise had never before met—a divorced woman who didn't even pretend she had anything to be ashamed about. Indeed, her opinion was she would have been far more worthy of censure if she had stayed in her destructive marriage.

Duchess Kestrel had been far too clever to restrict this free-spirited woman to boring routine and when Firekeeper had come to winter in the

North Woods, the duchess had offered Wendee the challenge of serving as the wolf-woman's personal attendant. Wendee had courage and enthusiasm enough for three—just the things needed by a personal attendant who was going to face the duty of forcing Firekeeper into her despised formal attire.

Wendee Jay provided no problem when it came to learning the New Kelvinese language. She already possessed a fairly large vocabulary, acquired when performing New Kelvinese dramas, for which there was an enthusiastic audience in northern Hawk Haven. Mostly the plays were performed in translation, but the translators always left in a seasoning of the New Kelvinese language. From that basis, Wendee had gone on to build her command of the language, both through study and on occasional trips into New Kelvin.

The problem was that Wendee needed to unlearn much of what she knew. The dramas, in some cases hundreds of years old and dating to the days when the Old Country still ruled, were filled with archaic terminology and idioms. These, mingled with the market argot Wendee had rapidly acquired during their last stay in New Kelvin, led to some unforgettable combinations that left Grateful Peace—though long trained to impassivity—with a smile twitching his thin lips.

However, Wendee was ahead of Elise when it came to adapting her body language and intuitively grasping the reasons for certain gestures or mannerisms. In matters of custom, New Kelvin was so traditional as to be nearly stagnant. The working classes reserved these formal manners for holidays, but the ruling classes at all times mimicked behaviors passed down for generations.

"I shall admit," Peace said once, "that those very plays Goody Wendee has committed to memory are—in their unadulterated form—sources for protocol. They are deferred to when such matters are not covered in the traditional works on manners."

Wendee nodded. "I thought so. There was a part in one of the more modern works—*Butterfly Meets the Glass Trader*—that seemed to hint at just that."

Peace nodded agreement, but Elise thought it was unlikely that he was familiar with modern New Kelvinese drama. Surely the ruling class—in which he had been preeminent—reserved their interest for the antique plays.

Later Elise would find that she was both right and wrong in this assumption. The ruling class did tend to favor the older works, but Grateful Peace had been a very special person in that elite group. As the Dragon's Eye—one of the exalted group of advisors known as the Dragon's Three—Peace had been responsible for watching anything and everything that might affect the stability of the government he served.

Since the Dragon Speaker could be voted down by the Primes, the Dragon's Eye was alert to those things that revealed the mood of the country and its people. Dramas, with their ability to sway hearts even more than minds, were key and Peace had been very much and very secretly a patron of the theater.

So the days passed, full and busy. Even when amply distracted, Elise found herself hoping for news of Firekeeper and Derian—though it was still too early, even by King Tedric's odd estimate. And she watched for someone else, too.

Jared Surcliffe had not arrived, though the duchess had expected him to reach the Norwood estate at around the same time as had Elise's party. Not even a note came and Elise found herself worried—unduly, she tried to tell herself. Nevertheless, she had to restrain herself from running to the window every time hooves sounded in the yard or from rooting through her letters looking for a certain hand and a certain seal.

Elise wondered what was keeping Doc away, worried that despite their seeming accord upon parting last winter maybe he was avoiding her.

FIREKEEPER, DERIAN, and the mountain horses made the trip to Eagle's Nest in what, if anyone had been measuring, would have been considered record time. However, Derian was far too worn out from riding dawn to dusk, from attending to the needs of his string—not to mention staying alert for signs that Firekeeper's impatience was going to transform into abandonment—to notice just how many sunrises and sunsets had passed.

Firekeeper, never much of one for keeping time, only felt the pressure to get somewhere faster than she possibly could. This was a relatively new sensation and one she did not like at all. There were nights when, lying awake on the fringes of Derian's latest encampment and invigorated by the coolness that came with the dark, she fought back the urge to get up and go just a bit farther.

When the wolf-woman slept, she dreamed of her impatience. She wondered how the situation was developing between the new Bardenville and her pack. She wondered if the wolves had already begun their campaign of unwelcome. She wondered if the humans realized there was intelligent malice behind the eating of their crops and trampling of their fields. She wondered if anyone had died.

She hoped that if anyone had died, that someone was human.

This last would have greatly shocked Derian, who, without knowing quite as much as Firekeeper did about the situation, entertained similar musings. While he sympathized with the Beasts, his was an abstract sympathy born mostly of his fondness for Firekeeper and her friends.

The human colonists, among whom he had lived and worked for all those days, were real to him. Derian hoped Firekeeper could work out something that would enable Ewen and his settlers to come to terms with the Beasts. He never really thought that the Beasts would win and drive the humans away.

After all, througout human history, humans had always won. Sometimes lots of humans died to attain the victory, but they always won. It was just the way things were.

Derian never thought about the logic behind this assumption, just as he never thought about just how limited was his grasp of human history. In destroying the books left by the Old Country rulers of the former colony of Gildcrest, Zorana the Great and her followers had destroyed a great deal more. Even for one like himself who had seen things that most would dismiss as myth, it was hard to abandon gut-level assumptions. The thing about gut-level assumptions is that you don't think about them.

Firekeeper and Derian separated one evening, with Derian headed for a post-house a day's ride outside the city. Derian had sent a message ahead by one of the king's fast post-riders Blind Seer happened to get wind of—and stop.

Brock and old Toad should be at the post-house to meet Derian. Colby would also know about the mules ahead of time, a matter that Derian had mulled over, weighed, and considered, deciding it was better to give Colby time to think than to have to tell his father what he'd done to his face.

Derian had done many brave things in the last year or so—some of them even heroic—but he'd still rather climb a rope ladder into a pirates' den than face the uncertainty of his father's wrath at the loss of two good mules.

Disregarding the gathering darkness, Firekeeper cut north and east across the fields—doing her best to remember not to trample the young plants that were greening the cultivated plots. She rested occasionally, but didn't bother with sleep, pressing on with the relentlessness of water spilling over a dam.

By midmorning, when Derian was jogging down the road with Brock and Toad, being reassured once again that Colby wasn't going to have his ears over the mules—though it might be a good thing that Derian could count on Earl Kestrel's patronage for the occasional suit of new clothes—Firekeeper was crossing the almost impassable ravine west of the castle, hauling Blind Seer up after her, the wolf complaining about the uncomfortable rope harness, then trotting across the semi-wild hunting preserve.

No one saw them but a gamekeeper who wisely went about his business. Once they were in the more formal gardens, several gardeners shouted greetings, but only Elation, soaring overhead, replied.

The head cook was just rising from her morning cup of tea and plate of biscuits—well earned after preparing breakfast for the hundred or so full-time inhabitants of the castle—and was considering where to start with the midday meal.

Firekeeper trotted through the kitchen door, mud-smeared and tired, grabbed half a loaf of bread off the sideboard, and, Blind Seer at her heels, headed up the servants' stairs to the next floor.

"Lady Blysse has come back," the cook said to a rather pale scullery maid who had all but dropped her bucket when the wolf came through the door. "The king'll be pleased. He's been asking every morning if anyone's seen her."

"Yes, m'm."

The maid, new to the castle and only acquainted by rumor with its odder denizens, hurried out and poured her bucket onto the compost bin, then leaned against a wall until her hands stopped trembling.

In the kitchen, the cook gave the orders that would start preparation of the next major meal. She herself went into the cool room and pulled out the roast from the night before. There had been some rare pieces near the center, and she suspected that someone would be ringing for a tray. There should even be a bone.

FIREKEEPER WAS LUCKY. The king was not only willing to see her, he was immediately available, the meeting he was supposed to be in that morning having been canceled on account of several of the counselors having severe colds. The Royal Physician had insisted that the king was not to be exposed to such.

"So," Tedric said, accepting Firekeeper's embrace with a pat on her back, "Sapphire and Shad are attending for me. It's rather delightful in a way. I never much cared for routine business. Now it's laudatory for me to let someone else deal with it."

Firekeeper didn't understand words like "laudatory," but she had a fair idea of what routine business was and shared the king's distaste for it. She settled onto the floor, looking up at him.

"Now, Firekeeper," the king said, leaning back in his chair and raising a tall glass of something that smelled of crushed strawberries to his lips. "What is the emergency?"

The wolf-woman didn't bother to ask how he knew her business was urgent. The old man was wise, and even a fool would know that she wouldn't come before him unwashed and weary from the trail without reason.

"It is your people," she said. "Some have gone west of the Iron Mountains."

King Tedric nodded.

"I suspected something like that. Go on."

"My people do not like this," Firekeeper continued, wondering what signs the old king had used to know that his people were dispersing. "They will hurt your people if they stay. I come to beg . . ."

If Tedric had been a One, she would have literally done so, pressing her belly to the ground and fawning. She settled for pressing her hands together and looking up pleadingly.

"I come to beg that you make them come back."

"You do?" he said. "They're far away. How can I do that?"

"Not too far away," she said, "for some of your people to go. Derian could show them where."

"I may have other uses for Derian," the king said mysteriously. "You are right. I could send some of my troops to order these people back. Tell me what you saw there."

Firekeeper did so, beginning with the traces along the trail, moving through their first meeting with Ewen Brooks, and how the colonists had given them cautious welcome. From there she went into the composition of the group. Derian would have been surprised how much she had noticed, how much detail absorbed and committed to memory.

Partway into her account, a tray laden with meat and bread and cheeses along with a pitcher of chilled well-water came up from the kitchen. Firekeeper set to, trying to remember to talk as she ate—a thing alien to her wolfish nature. For once, however, she had a driving impulse in her as fierce as her hunger, and Blind Seer got the majority of the cook's offerings.

King Tedric asked few questions, but those he did ask drew out details Firekeeper would have neglected. She told him about how Ewen Brooks considered himself heir to Barden's dream, about the hunger in his eyes when he described how close he had come to being part of that earlier expedition. How he had fed those dreams for ten long years.

"And I am to blame," she ended sourly, "for if I had not lived, if I had not come from west lands, then there be no tinder for his flint. Ewen would dream and dream, but never would he go west."

"That is possible," the king agreed, "though not definite. However, it is certain that he would not have found so many eager followers if they had not felt they were relatively safe."

"But they are not!" she cried. "They are not! The Beasts will not keep their staying. You must make the humans leave or the Beasts will make them—and many may die."

"Many humans," King Tedric asked, "or many Beasts?"

"Many both," Firekeeper replied levelly, "but I think more humans. There are more Beasts and that is their land."

"Then why are you worried?" the king asked. "Surely, a few Beasts dead is a small price to regain their land."

"Human counting," she said, "not mine. If my mother die or my father, then that is too many already. Yet they would die to keep their pups from dying."

"A willing sacrifice," the king said. "Yet I sense this possibility of loss is not what troubles you so."

Firekeeper nodded, wiping her greasy fingers on her trouser leg and sinking back from the well-stripped tray.

"I think if these die, it might not be the end," she said.

"I could decree that humans not cross the mountains again," the king said.

"But can you stop the Beasts from crossing?" she asked. "I think not. If the hunting fire rises in the Beasts, I am not thinking they will stop at the few in Bardenville. Some already . . ."

She was frustrated by her lack of words, but Tedric was patient.

"This is important," she said, "and to be kept secret."

"I shall," the king promised.

Firekeeper asked for no more solemn promise. How could she enforce it if the king chose to break his word? She wouldn't kill him. In any case, killing him would only worsen the situation.

"Some Beasts," she said, "hate being only west. They want back east, too."

Tedric cocked an eyebrow.

"Back?"

"Back."

It took her a long time and much retracing of her thoughts, but Firekeeper found the words to explain the complicated history and politics that made many of the Beasts feel that the time had come to drive humans from the land.

Several times she thought she would have been wiser to wait for Derian to arrive, to have schooled her steps to his so that his tongue and greater powers of speech would have been hers to use. Yet she felt this was her petition— her plea that the humans give the Beasts no incentive to follow the way of their more fanatical fellows.

Tedric listened, speaking only to ask for clarification. When Firekeeper finished, he frowned.

"This is a serious matter," he said, "and not one to be settled lightly. Go. Get some sleep, have a wash. I will have the staff warned of your return."

"Some see me already," Firekeeper said, almost apologetically.

"Even so," the king replied. "There are those who are reassured to know the wolf is a guest."

Firekeeper rose a trace unsteadily.

"And you will do as I say?" she asked.

"I will think on it," the king replied.

And from the firmness of his tone, Firekeeper knew she had no choice but to wait.

WHEN HE ARRIVED home that evening, Derian learned why his father hadn't been more upset over the mules. Derian had barely finished greeting his mother and sister when Vernita handed him a folded sheet of heavy writing paper. It was addressed to The Family of Counselor Derian and bore the royal seal.

"The king has sent a message," Vernita reported, trying hard to sound businesslike rather than impressed and almost succeeding, "requesting that you notify the castle upon your return so that a meeting with you can be arranged."

Derian blinked, then nodded. He wondered if there had been further developments in the Melina situation. He knew that if there had been, the letter wouldn't say. Perhaps he was worrying too much. For all he knew, the king might want the common opinion on possible names for Sapphire's impending baby.

Vernita was continuing, the rapidity of her speech an indication that she was slightly nervous.

"When we got your letter saying where you were and asking to have someone meet you, I sent a message to the castle saying when we expected you. This came today."

She held out another letter, this one addressed to Counselor Derian and still sealed.

Derian accepted it and paused before opening it to give Vernita a hug, noting as he did so a few strands of grey among the vibrant red of her hair. It made him feel oddly old.

"Thanks, Mom," he said. "When I'm dreadfully important, I'll steal you from Prancing Steed Stables and keep you to do all my paperwork and handle my social obligations."

Vernita laughed.

"And who would keep your father in line?"

"Let Dami," Derian suggested, breaking the red wax seal with its imprint of an eagle inside an eight-pointed star. "She's smart enough, when she isn't being useless."

Damita stuck her tongue out at him, but she was too interested in what the royal missive might contain to sass him as she might have at another time.

After the usual formalities and greetings, the letter was brief:

Firekeeper has returned and we know something of your journey west. We had wished in any case to consult you on other matters. Could you call on the afternoon following the date of your arrival to discuss these and other matters?

It was signed by the king himself, though the rest of it was written in another hand, probably that of Farand Briarcott, the king's confidential secretary.

Derian showed the letter to Vernita—Dami dancing up to look when he didn't tell her not to—and asked:

"Should I send an acceptance, or would that be ridiculous? I mean, does anyone turn down an invitation from the king?"

Vernita glanced up from the letter, a hundred questions about everything it didn't say in her eyes.

"It never hurts to be polite," she replied, "even with a king. I don't know how nobles handle such things. Answer according to the manners of your class and while some self-important person might fault you for ignorance, no one will fault you for rudeness."

Derian smiled his thanks.

"Can I borrow your desk and writing materials? I'd better answer right away if they want me by tomorrow afternoon."

Vernita waved in the direction of her office.

"Help yourself, but don't smear dirt all over the contracts. Damita, put on shoes and a nice frock. You can run your brother's letter up to the castle. Get Brock to walk with you."

Damita, comfortable in open sandals and a loose smock, looked as if she might protest, thought better of it, and ran upstairs. By the time Derian had finished sanding the wet ink, she was down again. She'd even taken the time to twist her brilliant red-gold hair up and fasten it with the doe clasp that had been her mother's gift on her last birthday.

Derian gave his sister a courtly bow, aware of his own road dirt, but relieved to have this responsibility dealt with.

"You look lovelier than ever, Dami," he said. "I am delighted to have you as my courier. The guards at the gate won't be able to say they forgot your coming and so fail in their duties."

Damita turned bright red, snatched the sealed letter from his hand, and scurried out without another word.

Derian looked after her with fondness.

"She's really getting pretty," he said to his mother. "Is she still in love with Uncle Jeweler's apprentice?"

"I'm not sure," Vernita said. "She's not at an age to confide in her mother. Maybe you could learn something before you vanish once more."

Derian stared at her.

"Do you know something about my plans that I don't?"

"Many things," Vernita said, a trace of Derian's own flippancy in her tone. "But in this case, no. Just a suspicion."

THE NEXT AFTERNOON, Derian headed up to the castle, determined to be on time. He'd dressed up for the appointment and was stifling in the vest and jacket. He found himself wishing that his best shoes were better broken in—especially after weeks wearing nothing but his more comfortable old boots.

Since Derian knew what a nuisance navigating a horse through the streets could be he'd waved off his father's offer of a riding horse from the stables. Even so, as Derian made his way up the hill he found himself wishing for a mount or better yet, a carriage.

He wondered if some sort of hired service could be contracted for and distracted himself from the pinching of his shoes by working out some of the details for such a business. It interested him more than he thought it would, and when he arrived he filed the matter away for discussion with his parents at some later time.

A runner escorted Derian through the corridors despite Derian's mild protest that he knew his way perfectly well. Derian knew that such an escort was a matter of protocol and that whether or not he thought himself worthy of such treatment didn't matter a whit if Steward Silver decided that he did. The castle staff would more willingly cross the king than his steward over such matters.

The king's private receiving room had been moved to another location in the two moonspans' length that had passed since Derian had last attended on Tedric. In this room, no fire burned. Vases of cut roses filled the hearth instead, their red, yellow, and orange making a glow of their own. Windows were wide open, curtained with muslin that let in the breeze while keeping out most of the insects. The stone floors and walls that had seemed so dank before now seemed welcomingly cool.

Blind Seer evidently thought so. The wolf lay flat on the floor near one of the open windows, his belly and chin pressed against the stone. Last winter Derian had envied the wolf his thick fur. He didn't this afternoon.

Firekeeper, sitting on the floor next to the wolf, wore her usual combination of vest and knee-length trousers as if the weather were no warmer than before. This set was cleaner than the ones he'd last seen her in, so Derian guessed that someone in the castle had been assigned to maintain a wardrobe for the wolf-woman. It might be unusual, given Firekeeper's comparatively low rank, but it certainly beat having her grubby and smelling of sweat during her unanticipated visits.

Princess Sapphire, gowned in something loose and flowing, didn't seem any happier than Blind Seer about the summer heat. She might have been a bit rounder through the middle, but Derian wasn't going to look closely enough to be certain; Sapphire didn't look like she was in the most affable of moods.

Otherwise, the crown princess looked very well indeed. Vernita had told Derian that the castle had given out that the princess was over her morning sickness. Derian had wondered if the announcement was merely good politics. Looking at Sapphire he was certain that it was true.

King Tedric also seemed somewhat better. His cough was gone and his color stronger. However, the weight he had lost over the winter had not returned. The skin around his neck and under his eyes hung loose. Derian had a rather better look at the king than he had anticipated, for Tedric had forgone the formality of wearing a wig. His close-cut white hair showed his scalp at points, vaguely embarrassing Derian. It seemed like he was seeing the king naked rather than merely unwigged.

Prince Shad, rising to greet Derian when he entered, was as informal as the king. He was young enough that he didn't bother with a wig, but he was in shirtsleeves and his trousers were loosely tailored. He looked more like the sailor he'd been a year ago than a prince.

"Thank you for coming, Counselor," said Shad, "when you must be longing to rest from the road. The kitchen has sent up a variety of cool drinks. What would you like?"

Derian accepted both a glass of tea heavily infused with mint and Shad's insistence that he put aside both jacket and vest. So eased, he seated himself and answered questions about the journey over the mountains and back again—moderating himself more than he had with his family last night. It wouldn't do to criticize Firekeeper for the pace she'd set, not when her need was so real and urgent.

He wondered what the king's need was. The letter that had been sent to Derian's family had been dated before Firekeeper arrived back in Eagle's Nest—indeed, from a few days after their departure from Bardenville. King Tedric couldn't have known what they'd find and how Firekeeper would react.

Could he?

Derian recalled the king's cryptic speech before their departure and wondered. However, he schooled himself to patience. One thing he'd learned about dealing with royalty was that they got around to business in their own time—and sometimes that was a lot faster than the common man was ready to deal with.

"Lady Archer," the king said, something in the shift of his tone or posture signaling that the time for visiting was over, "asked us to give you her greetings. She arrived in Eagle's Nest some days after your departure, in response to a summons we sent regarding the Melina question."

Derian knew some of how the Melina question had developed since their departure. For one thing, knowledge of her remarriage was now general gossip. Opinions varied along much the range he had anticipated, though the level of fear and resentment was rather higher than he had imagined. Even his own family—as sane and loyal supporters of the Crown as could be desired—had expressed some fear that Melina's influence would reach the castle. Derian had done his best to dissuade them, but he hadn't been happy about the need to do so. He also hadn't liked the rumors he'd heard about what Melina was doing with slaves and human sacrifice.

"Lady Archer is in Eagle's Nest then?" he asked, feeling on more comfortable ground there.

"No," the king replied. "She has gone to the Norwood Grant to prepare an expedition into New Kelvin."

Derian straightened in his seat, sensing why that letter had been sent to his parents' house half a moonspan before. King Tedric seemed once again like a ruler with his own and his country's interests at heart rather than a seer.

"We need a chosen few to go into New Kelvin," King Tedric continued. "There are two reasons. One, we need inside information as to how much truth there is behind the rumors. Two, it may be our only hope for saving Citrine's sanity."

He went into detail then on the first matter. When he had finished, Sapphire spoke about Citrine's situation, the tears pooling in her blue eyes eloquent of the sorrow and fear she would not let into her words.

Derian listened to both speeches without asking a single question, already knowing that he would do as King Tedric desired. Even if the politics of New Kelvin didn't interest him—and they did, especially now that Melina was involved—he would have risked himself for Citrine alone. It wasn't that he valued her life more than he did his own—and he had no illusions that he'd be risking his life if he returned to New Kelvin, especially with Melina in a position of influence—it was that he didn't think he could face himself if he let Citrine suffer, knowing there was something he might have done to heal her.

Firekeeper was less altruistic—or perhaps merely differently so. Her first words when Sapphire ended her recitation were:

"And my people and your people? What do this going to New Kelvin do for them?"

If Derian had not sat through some of the king's counsel meetings, he would have thought the wolf-woman impossibly rude. Now he recognized the note in her voice as akin to that he'd heard in the voices of the heads of Great Houses. She might see that she could be of use to the king, but her own interests must be dealt with first.

King Tedric didn't look surprised at Firekeeper's question. Indeed, he may have been watching her fidget as Sapphire spoke.

"Indirectly, your going to New Kelvin may do a great deal for your people, Firekeeper."

He held up a hand when the wolf-woman looked as if she might interrupt.

"I have considered the matter you brought to me and have discussed it with my heirs. They agree with me that what you have told us is indeed serious. They also agree that it is a matter to be dealt with in secrecy and with great care."

Firekeeper frowned, but King Tedric had kept his words fairly simple and it was clear to Derian that she had mostly understood.

"The reality is," the king continued, "that the concept—the idea—of the Royal Beasts is a difficult one for us humans to grasp. Even those of us who have met Blind Seer and Elation, who have heard reports of messages relayed by crows and seagulls, must make a great effort to accept that these are other intelligent people."

Firekeeper made a noise like a kettle coming onto a boil, but said nothing. Shad, who had been quietly holding Sapphire's hand, now spoke:

"Firekeeper, try to imagine what it would be like if you had grown up with wolves—only wolves—as the only people to whom you could talk. Now suddenly someone is telling you, offering proof even, that the rabbits and the deer and the elk and the bear are all just as smart as the wolves, different, but just as smart."

Firekeeper nodded, her head tilted to one side in a fashion that made Derian think that she had possibly entertained just such thoughts at one time or another.

"Now, to make that matter more difficult," Shad went on, "you're being told that it's not every rabbit or deer or elk or bear who is as smart as your wolves, just some, and those all live far away, across the mountains. That's how it is for us. We can see Blind Seer and Elation, but it's hard to imagine a whole pack of Blind Seers, a whole flock of Elations. Do you understand?"

Firekeeper said "Yes," but from her tone the word hurt her. Shad went on.

"Now, we here believe you, but getting the rest of our people to believe is going to be very hard to do. Some will refuse to believe in any case. They will say that you have trained a handful of animals and are running a scam . . ."

Firekeeper tilted her head interrogatively.

"A trick," Shad clarified. "That you're trying to fool us for some gain of your own."

"Why I do this?" Firekeeper asked.

"Maybe to get control of all the lands west of the Iron Mountains," Shad offered. "People will remember that Earl Kestrel was the one who found you and they will remember that he holds much land bordering the mountains. They might decide that the earl was lying after all, that he was playing a far deeper game . . . more complicated," Shad clarified, "trickier . . . than he ever let on."

Firekeeper snorted.

"That stupid! Not even Norvin Norwood could manage that!"

King Tedric spoke, "People believe what they want to believe and many would find it easier to believe that Norvin would go to that much trouble to create an interesting heir to the throne and then, when that gambit—trick—failed, come up with something else."

Firekeeper chewed her lower lip for a moment.

"Humans have," she said thoughtfully, "so many words for 'trick' that they must use many, many of them. Wolves," she continued proudly, "do not lie."

Blind Seer raised his head and stared at her.

"Not often," she added, clearly in self-correction.

Derian swallowed a smile. Shad and Sapphire traded a glance that held a lingering trace of disbelief. Then Sapphire took over.

"There will be those people who will believe," she said. "Some of these will be more open-minded than most. Others will be dreamers. Others will be those who have seen you and Blind Seer at work—soldiers during King Allister's War, members of the Kestrel household, people here at the castle. However, most of these are not going to be decision makers. Moreover, just because they believe won't mean they'll like what they're learning."

"Because humans believe," Firekeeper said scornfully, "that they are the Ones and the rest are tail-dragging followers."

"That will be true for some," Sapphire admitted with more patience—or perhaps more personal insight than Derian would have given her credit for. "However, others will simply be afraid."

"So they should be," Firekeeper said smugly. "That is what I warn you." Smugness melted from Firekeeper's features to be replaced by fear.

"And that is what I am warning Beasts, too. Humans afraid are very dangerous. Even without old magics humans have once I think many Beasts would die and many, many Cousins. There would be sickness from dead and dying. In the end, I think Beasts would win, but they would not like what is left when they are finished."

Derian thought he understood what she was imagining. He'd seen the battlefields following both the Battle on the Banks and King Allister's War. He'd smelled the sickly sweet smell of rotting corpses, the odor of gangrene in the field hospitals, the vomit and diarrhea from those who fell ill with fever and infection when there were too few hands to clean up the mess. And those had been small wars.

What Firekeeper had sketched out for him along the trail home had been a long campaign, one side fighting from cover. No farmer would be safe in his fields, no hunter would dare go out alone. Domestic animals would be stolen from their barns and coops. Fields would be stripped. Orchards would be covered with flocks of birds set not on gorging but on ruining.

With a sudden shock, Derian realized what Ewen Brooks and his colonists would be up against, even if they weren't killed outright. What could they do in return?

They could burn huge swaths of forest land so that the Beasts would lack cover to approach them. They could poison their fields or bury traps or dig pitfalls. Sickness would come, for they would try to kill any animal who came close—without bothering to learn if it was enemy Royal or uninvolved Cousin. Thus the scavengers would be unable to perform their role in the natural order.

Mind, none of this would save Ewen's colony, but he and his people might get revenge for the ruin of their dreams. If they were among those who accepted that the Royal Beasts were as clever as humans, then they might figure that their opponents would be clever enough to assess loss and make a truce. Given this thought, Ewen and his people might destroy all the more, hoping to force that unwilling accord.

And would the Beasts make a truce? Looking at Firekeeper, sitting there on the floor, her arms wrapped around her knees, her dark eyes as unreadable as a cloudless night sky, Derian wasn't certain they would. They might just prefer to fight until their enemy was destroyed and trust the land to heal after the battle was ended. And if the war of Beasts and humans crossed the Iron Mountains, then the same scenario would be repeated over and over again—even to the walls of this city and these quiet castle gardens.

After a pause, clearly offered to provide a chance for the king or his heirs to reply, Firekeeper went on:

"But even if they not like what would come, I think there will be those who will start the fight unless they are given reason not to fight. My people will be dying, my pack nearest to the front. Why would I wish to go to New Kelvin?"

There, as clear as the sunlight on water, was Firekeeper's declaration of what side she would join. A potential enemy—all the more deadly for the knowledge she had gained over the past year—she sat there upon the king's floor, waiting for him to offer her an answer.

"If I promise to send troops to make Ewen Brooks and his colonists leave," the king said. "If I promise to declare that venturing beyond the Iron Mountains is forbidden on pain of death. If I dig into my treasuries to build a keep on the eastern side of the gap through the mountains, will that be enough to free you to go to New Kelvin?"

Firekeeper visibly relaxed, but her dark eyes remained watchful. Obviously, she suspected a trick, making Derian, at least, think that her upbringing among the wolves must not have been as straightforward as she claimed.

"For me, yes."

She frowned, freeing her legs from the circle of her arms and rolling onto her belly on the floor, rather like Blind Seer—until, that is, she propped her elbows on the floor and her chin in her hands.

"Maybe it not enough for the Beasts, though, those who are most angry and most afraid. They may still wish to prey on humankind."

Sapphire drew in her breath rather sharply. Derian had the impression she was annoyed by Firekeeper's informality, even in this most informal of councils.

"Why should they?" Sapphire said. "Wouldn't we be keeping to our side of the mountains?"

Firekeeper looked at her, somber and sad.

"They not see it that way, Princess. To them there is no human side. Our tales tell when all sides were for Beasts and humans lived in humans lands."

Sapphire snorted, quite unladylike.

"That was long ago. My people don't remember a time when we didn't live here. Where would we go? Back to the Old Country? We don't even know where it is or if anyone is alive there."

Firekeeper shrugged, pivoting around to sit upright again.

"I not know. I not even know if the Beasts know."

"I wonder," Shad said softly, "if they do. Birds can fly, can't they? I wonder if the bigger ones fly across the oceans and know what is on the other side?"

Firekeeper looked surprised.

"I not know. No one ever told me."

"Told," Derian murmured under his breath.

Firekeeper glowered at him.

King Tedric cleared his throat.

"Speculation must wait until later," he said. "Unfortunately, there is a formal banquet tonight, and soon we will need to go and prepare."

"Not me!" Firekeeper exclaimed.

"No, not you," the king said. "That would be showing you rather too much favor, I fear. Firekeeper, the truth of the matter is, I don't want you to get hurt."

"At dinner?"

"No." King Tedric smiled. "No, if matters between humans and Beasts become as ugly as you think they might, I don't want you hurt by humans who will see you as an instigator."

"A what?"

"A troublemaker," the king clarified, "a problem, a starter of bad things. They won't see you as a friend of humanity—which I think you are, or you wouldn't bother to give me this warning. They would see you as an enemy. I would like to send you somewhere far away, yet somewhere where there will be no doubt of your presence for others will be able to swear to it.

"Then, if indeed there are those among the Beasts who will not accept Ewen Brooks's departure as our acknowledgment of the Beasts' sovereignty to the west, then you at least will not be blamed."

Firekeeper nodded.

"I see and I am happy that you protect me. Is kind."

"Kind, but self-serving, too," Tedric said bluntly. "Not only will you serve me by putting your singular talents at Lady Archer's disposal, but you will serve me by staying alive. Someday we may need you to help us treat with the Beasts."

"Treat?"

"To talk to them for us, for Hawk Haven and Bright Bay, maybe for all humankind."

A strange look passed over Firekeeper's face. For a moment she looked so distant and so disoriented that Derian thought she was about to be sick.

"Need me to talk . . . ," she muttered almost inaudibly.

The wolf-woman shook her head.

"I have heared that thought before," she said, "but I not remember where. No matter. It is wise. I will go to New Kelvin."

She directed her dark gaze to Sapphire.

"I promise to help your sister, Princess," she said, "but I not promise to help your mother."

Sapphire straightened and not all the flush in her cheeks was from the heat.

"My mother is Queen Elexa," she said proudly. "This other woman only gave me birth."

"And I," Firekeeper replied thoughtfully, "think I give her death."

Derian didn't know what unsettled him more: Firekeeper's statement or the fact that none of the other three so much as raised an eyebrow in reproof.

XI

ELISE BALANCED THE PAINTBRUSH in the join between thumb and forefinger and leaned back on her heels to inspect her work. Satisfied, she held up a hand mirror so Citrine could see the stylized drawing now adorning one cheek—two slanting eyes, a hint of whiskers, and an outline of pricked ears.

"That's the mark of the Sodality of Beast Lorists," Elise explained. "Grateful Peace says that they study many animals. They also raise some exotics kept from the days before the Plague and brought here from other lands."

"Neat!" Citrine said, raising her hand to touch the design then lowering it, clearly remembering just in time that this one gesture was the most to be avoided if an outlander wished to pass as New Kelvinese. They never touched their faces if it could be avoided lest they smear the elaborate designs almost everyone wore.

"Now if you were raised to the highest rank, like Peace was in the Illuminators," Elise went on, "then you could have the design tattooed on. Until then, you'd need to paint it on every day."

"*Every* day?" Citrine asked.

"I think so," Elise said, "at least if you were going out of your house. Peace says that a New Kelvinese would no more go out without at least some basic designs in place than we would go out without clothes."

Citrine giggled and Elise gave her an impulsive hug.

The little girl was doing much better since their arrival in the North Woods. Her sense of humor had returned and she hadn't had a screaming fit for days. Elise wondered if the very delicacy with which Citrine had been handled since her rescue had contributed to her moodiness. Maybe if she had been thrown in with a bunch of children her own age and left to fend for herself she would have done better.

Maybe not, though. Children could be quite cruel, especially to someone who was different, and Citrine with her maimed left hand and her exiled mother was different indeed.

"What's a sodality?" Citrine asked.

Elise ran her hand through her hair trying to find the best way to answer.

"It's sort of a very important guild," she said. "The sodalities do what our guilds do—monitor quality of work, set rules for educating apprentices, punish bad work. That sort of stuff."

Citrine nodded. She seemed genuinely interested and for the first time Elise wondered how much Citrine knew about things like guilds. Elise herself had learned about them quite young, since a grant holder often had to work with the local guild representatives. Citrine, however, had neither that reason to learn, nor the reason most common folk would—the fact that future employment and education lay within the guilds.

How many are there like Citrine? Elise thought. *Too related to the noble class to bother with education and employment, too unconnected to the responsibilities of running a grant or House to need to bother with much at all. I wonder if this is precisely what Queen Zorana the Great was trying to avoid when she refused to allow a proliferation of titles?*

Elise made a mental note to share her insight with Sapphire and Shad—preferably by letter in case she accidently offended one of them. She knew that many of the Hawk Haven nobles had started gently agitating for more titles so they could compete with their Bright Bay neighbors. If those titles came with responsibilities—real ones, not created—then maybe they would be a good idea. If they did not, however, they would just add to the proliferation of useless semi-nobility.

Shifting to a low chair, Elise motioned Citrine over and went back to work on her facial ornamentation, continuing her explanation at the same time.

"But the sodalities don't match our guilds. There are sodalities for things we don't have at all, like sericulture, which is the art of growing silk. And there are sodalities for things that we deal with much more informally, like these Beast lore people.

"And the sodalities have a lot more power than our guilds do because even though the guilds are very important to trade, they have no say in how the kingdom is governed. That is left to our monarch in consultation with the royal advisors, many of whom are nobles."

Citrine piped up, "But not all! Derian isn't a noble. Neither is Firekeeper."

"Firekeeper isn't a royal advisor," Elise corrected, but even as she spoke she wondered if that was true.

Certainly the wolf-woman had a great deal more access to the Crown than many of the lower-ranked nobility. She was allowed a lot more leniency in matters of decorum and etiquette, too. Was this another of Citrine's oddly incisive insights?

"Maybe you're right," Elise said. "Maybe Firekeeper just doesn't have the ring."

"She'd lose it anyhow." Citrine giggled, then became more serious. "So are the sodalities more important than the king of New Kelvin?"

Elise licked her lips, aware that she was treading close to sensitive matters.

"I'm not sure," she hedged. "However, they are very important to the running of the government. The Primes are elected from the most important members of the sodalities, and they in turn elect the Dragon Speaker, who takes care of all the day-to-day business of government."

"Does that mean the king doesn't have to go to meetings?" Citrine asked. "I know that Sapphire hates going to meetings. She told me that if she knew that she'd need to go to so many meetings and receptions and things she wouldn't have wanted to be queen nearly so much."

Elise smiled. "I don't know if the king—the New Kelvinese call him the Healed One—has to go to meetings, Citrine. I know he has duties dating back to the days before the Plague. Maybe those keep him quite busy."

"And his wife?" Citrine asked, a guarded glitter in her eyes. "What does she do?"

Elise tried to be casual, but feared that she failed completely.

"I don't know, cousin. I guess that's one of the things we'll be going to New Kelvin to find out."

FIREKEEPER SLEPT OUT on the castle grounds that night, in a broad meadow beyond the first wall.

Ever since the wolf-woman's meeting with the king and his heirs, the castle walls had seemed to close in on her. Firekeeper was smart enough to know that the walls were not the problem. The press she felt was that of obligation and duty—not to one group, but to many.

Sensing her mood—or perhaps responding to a similar sense of pressure on his own behalf—Blind Seer took himself off to hunt. Maybe his sense of bondage was even worse, for he, unlike her, could not pass in human society.

Alone, Firekeeper lay on the grass staring up at the sky. For the first time the comet didn't seem like an ominous intrusion against the star field. Its glowing white head and streaming tail seemed friendly, familiar—and very free.

Firekeeper remembered her recent dream and wished that she were indeed riding on the comet's shoulders. They would be rounded, she thought, deliberately building up a picture in her mind, and very warm, for anything that gave so much light must give heat as well. They might even be furry.

The comet was becoming a wolf again when she drifted off to sleep.

Again, she dreamed.

Small. Looking up at everything, even into the faces of the Royal Wolves. Sometimes the One Male crouches and lets her ride on his back. She grips hard onto his neck ruff and crouches low to keep her balance.

They are running, running hard and fast. Their goal is not a hunting ground, not a broad river meadow where the elk graze or a grove where the deer browse on the young foliage. They are running through the night, leaping from bright star to bright star, sometimes wading through the blackness as they might through a stream or a summer shallow river.

Firekeeper feels the blackness snowmelt frosty against her toes. She pulls them up, tucks them under the One Male's belly. His heartbeat is rapid and strong, counterpoint to a faint singing that seems to come from all around.

Do stars sing?

Firekeeper wants to ask, but her throat is full of smoke. She can't speak for the choking, she can't see for the burning in her eyes. The fire roars. Its sound drowns out the singing that might have been the voices of the stars. Sometimes the wind adds its howling voice to the fire's roar and the two together are terrible.

Distantly, she seems to hear warning cries. Without understanding a single syllable, she understands that there is fear that the fire will leap onto the wind's shoulders, that the wind will carry the fire into the trees, that the trees will be reduced to ash and ash to earth.

Something must be done to still the wind. The girl—not yet Firekeeper, someone else whose name she almost knows—huddles near the ground, listening. The stars are singing again. The wind's howling is growing quieter, though it mutters unhappily as it stills. The fire continues to roar defiantly. It will burn the earth if that is the only way it can reach the trees.

The girl has never heard anything so angry, so hungry. It frightens her and she feels her own tears wet against her cheeks. They are warm, warm as the fire, warm as wolf-breath. Suddenly, they become like ice and the girl is frightened. How can her tears be cold? Life is warm, not cold. If her tears are cold, is she then dead?

She is trying to move her hand to find her heartbeat, when she hears the fire's angry hissing. In its profanities, the girl knows the truth. Her tears have not transformed to ice, rain is falling, rain that will swallow the fire as the fire swallowed . . .

Everything . . . The scream rising in her throat is clamped off by teeth at her throat. A growl vibrates against her skin and warns, "Make no noise or it will be your last noise."

Heart pounding, Firekeeper forced herself out of her nightmare, emerging to find waking life as horrible.

She was no longer trapped in that faintly remembered girl child. The air no longer stank of burning and of smoke. She was lying on her back in the soft summer grass of the castle grounds.

But there were fangs at her throat and a furred head hovering over her own, its shape blocking out all the stars as the comet glow haloed it from behind.

Firekeeper's sense of smell, doubly precious after its loss in her dream, knew this wolf was not Blind Seer. Memory identified her enemy a moment later. Northwest, the outlier wolf, called Sharp Fang by his own pack. Even in her fear, Firekeeper felt a flash of humor when she realized that the name was apt indeed.

Blood warm against her skin trickled from where Northwest's fangs had pierced her throat. Firekeeper was very afraid, and in fear, rather than in thought, she acted.

Two arms came up, one on either side of the looming wolf's head. Two hands clapped down upon its ears, thudding hard against the skull. Fingers slid and pinched, twisting the soft-furred, outward-flaring ears, biting them harder than would any summer fly.

Yelping in astonishment and pain, Northwest released her throat. Firekeeper rolled from his reach, bounding to her feet and pulling her Fang from its sheath. She snarled, glowering down at the wolf, her dark, dark eyes grabbing his amber gaze and holding it fast.

Her own blood was flowing down her front now, trickling between her small round breasts and pooling in her navel. Northwest's bite had not been deep, would not have done more than dent a wolf's hide, but Firekeeper's skin was human: soft and easily broken.

Northwest crouched, vulnerable belly and throat low to the ground, but Firekeeper held the Fang in front of her, lightly circling the point. It was not for nothing that she had learned to fight from wolves, with wolves.

She knew that Northwest could not leap at her without exposing himself to her blade. He might bring her down, might even kill her, but he himself would find her Fang slashing deep into his belly and mixing up the soft parts there. From such a wound none ever recovered.

Yes, Firekeeper knew this. The question was, did Northwest? He had not grown from pup to wolf in her company as had Blind Seer. He might not realize just how deadly that slim metal blade could be. He might yet risk the leap.

So the wolf-woman stood, poised on the balls of her feet, feeling the warm blood cool as it trickled down her front, unable, unwilling to go off her guard to check the severity of her wound, trusting that it was slight.

Northwest held his crouch, but he did not spring. Instead he accused her:

"You have betrayed us! How can you hold your head so proud and defy me? If I were such as you, I would welcome the killing bite."

"Betrayed you?" asked Firekeeper, though in truth she thought she knew what Northwest meant.

"Aye! Betrayed us to your human kin, run fast on two legs to tell them of our presence and so rob us of the night-swift secrecy that is one of our powers."

Firekeeper could not deny Northwest's accusation, for she *had* told King Tedric of the Royal Beasts' anger, but she could rob it of its bitter bite.

"I spoke, yes," she said, never lowering the knife tip nor flagging in her watchfulness, "but I no more betrayed my people than does a mother who knocks a pup from its feet lest it walk off a ledge and tumble to its death."

"So you, pup," Northwest sneered, "still so weak you lick your parents' jaws for food, so you are suddenly wise mother to us all?"

Firekeeper felt very tired and her throat was beginning to ache as if terribly bruised. Every sound she made caused the wound to throb and she knew she could not howl, even if she were sure Blind Seer would hear. Worse, yet, if her cries brought humans, for she did not think Northwest would show them any mercy.

"I know that the course you would have the Beasts follow would be bloody disaster for many," she replied, concealing her pain as best she could, "and who made you judge of my actions?"

"You have fooled those who fostered you," Northwest snapped, "but you have not fooled me. I see you for what you are. You are the thorn that remains buried under the skin, festering, breeding heat and infection until you kill your host. You are the sickness that spreads and carries off the pack. You are no friend to us. You must be destroyed lest you bring us harm. I would have killed you as you slept, but I would first know what you told your kin."

"You heard what I told my kin," Firekeeper replied, "for you were there. As for what I told the humans, that is my business and maybe my family's business, but certainly no matter for a sneaking coward who can only bring himself to kill when his prey is asleep."

Firekeeper lashed out with her words as she longed to do with her blade, but secretly she was harboring a new fear. Where was Blind Seer? Had Northwest found him and harmed him? She could not let herself believe that Northwest had killed Blind Seer, for if she did she would lose all her strength.

Even as her worry threatened to weaken her arm, the wolf-woman strengthened herself with the thought that Northwest's fur was without bite mark or blood splatter. Surely he could not have slain Blind Seer and come away unmarred. And if Blind Seer lived, eventually he would return. She would have help dealing with this mad creature.

Wolf-like, Firekeeper took strength in the knowledge of her pack mate. She needed that strength, for her knife arm was growing tired as the slow drain of blood from the untamped wound in her throat weakened her. Northwest must know she could not stand strong forever. He crouched, resting and waiting for the first sign of weakness.

Then shadows and moonlight shifted and from a scrubby cluster of oak, Wind Whisper stepped forth. The she-wolf was all silent scorn, her hackles raised, and her lips curling back from clean, white fangs. Firekeeper stiffened, for though she could hold off one wolf—more by threat of the wolf's own death should it kill her—she could not hope to hold off two.

More than ever, she wished for Blind Seer, wished that her throat were not so bruised. Should she risk a howl, even if the sound was a poor choked-off thing? No. She would not bring Blind Seer here to face these two alone and surely if she did howl, she would not live long thereafter.

But even in her aching weariness, Firekeeper became aware of a strange thing. Northwest was not welcoming Wind Whisper. His tail was not wagging a slow arc of greeting, nor were his ears perking. If anything, they were flattening further, slicking themselves to his skull. He had been belly-close to the ground, now he was belly-flat to the ground.

Hope came fresh to the wolf-woman. Hope that Wind Whisper might be here on some business of her own, rather than as Northwest's ally. Firekeeper did not lower her blade, did not relax her guard, but she did dare dream she might live to see the sunrise.

Wind Whisper yawned, her teeth strong and healthy for one who had been grown when Firekeeper first had been taken in by the wolves. They looked well for any wolf, come to that. The elder wolf stretched out her scornful gesture until Northwest nearly peed himself.

"I was," said Wind Whisper, speaking to no one in particular, "one of the council who met and discussed what was to be done about the humans. So was this one here—this Sharp Fang, brave hunter of sleeping furless beasts. There was much arguing and even a little blood spilled, but in the end it was thought that there had been wisdom in the warnings of one naked wolfling, one Firekeeper.

"Drive the humans away, the council decided. Try to keep them away. Even let Little Two-legs speak for us, if she speaks wisely. All there agreed to bide by this, for a time, unless the humans gave us cause to do more than drive them away. Even this Northwest Sharp Fang, hunter of stupid chickens and stupider ducks, even he agreed, though his breath was sour upon his promise.

"Some days after, this Northwest took his leave, saying he had no wish to spoil crops and frighten cattle. We saw him depart with no great sorrow for he had been poor company indeed. But I remembered the sourness of his breath as he swore to abide by the council's wisdom, and when he struck out for his home pack, I decided to follow. After all, such sour breath might mean an ill stomach and it would not do to have him fall sick on the trail.

"He jogged north and west for a night, but the next night his trail turned. Soon even an old wolf like myself could tell the trail he cast about for was that of the little Firekeeper and her human companion. I said to myself, 'Surely Northwest is ill. He is so ill he cannot even hunt rabbits but must take the stupid horses for his meat. I must go with him and hunt for him in his illness.'

"But this Northwest surprised me. He hunted well, taking rabbits and fish and even, once, a deer. Still, though, he tracked those horses. I, unwilling to show myself unless he needed my aid, for I did not wish to embarrass him with my knowledge of his sour belly, I trailed him.

"And this Northwest took his time following the horses. In truth, I think he was a bit in terror of the human lands, for he traveled slowly and then only in the darkest night. Then came the night when the scent trails of the Firekeeper and her human companion parted. The human continued on the slow road east while Firekeeper took off with her pack mate north, across fields and through forests.

"Here came the strange part. Sour Belly Northwest didn't follow the horses, that easy game, he followed Firekeeper. I said to myself, 'Poor wolf! He must be very ill. He follows them so as to eat at their leavings.' I followed, too, to succor Northwest when his illness took him. Always I hid myself and made sure that the wind did not carry my scent to him, for I did not wish this Northwest, or Young Sour Belly as I thought him in my affection for him, to know I pitied him his illness.

"When the trail of Firekeeper and Blind Seer vanished at the edge of a ravine, Northwest prowled until he found a place where he could scrabble across on a heap of deadfall and winter tangle. I followed, grateful for this bridge, for indeed the humans had protected themselves quite well from unwanted visitors.

"And so I was here when Northwest would have eased his sour belly on the soft meat of Firekeeper's throat and I would have leapt in sooner, but . . ."

Northwest snarled interruption.

"Stop your idiot tale-telling, old one! So you followed me! So you caught me! So you will preserve this human. Tell me why if you can."

Wind Whisper looked at him and her disdain was cruel to see, but her reply was mockingly gentle.

"I saw Little Two-legs brought into the world of the Beasts. Maybe I wish to see what she will do now that two worlds beckon her."

"Destroy one or both," Northwest sneered. "That is the human way. They cannot live without reshaping the world into their image."

Firekeeper actually agreed—at least somewhat—with Northwest's assessment of humanity, but she deeply resented having the same criteria applied to her. She also didn't much care for being ignored while these two argued.

During Wind Whisper's narration the wolf-woman had checked her wounded throat. A shallow slash proved to be the source of most of the blood. She was more concerned about the bruising, which made it difficult for her to raise her voice above soft tones.

Once again she wondered where Blind Seer was. Wind Whisper had protected Firekeeper, but would she have extended the same protection to Blind Seer? She struggled to think of a way to ask after the blue-eyed wolf without implying that he was unable to watch after himself. Happily, circumstances made this unnecessary.

Head held low, nose to the ground, so absorbed in a scent trail that he was otherwise unaware of his surroundings, Blind Seer loped into the far end of the clearing. He brought himself up short when he noticed the three clustered across from him.

His ears flickered back and he panted in foolish surprise. Then he looked at Firekeeper.

"I was hunting near the ravine," the blue-eyed wolf explained rather lamely, "when I caught an odd scent trail. I was nearly certain it belonged to our outlier kin, but some effort had been made to muddle the scents and though they ran parallel, they did not seem to run together. I followed the trails and, well . . ."

He stopped, sat, scratched vigorously behind one ear. Firekeeper thought with sudden amusement that if he had been human he would have shrugged.

Then Blind Seer raised his head and scented the air sharply. In two enormous bounds he was at her side, hackles raised.

"Who has shed your blood?" he demanded, but his glare was fixed on Northwest as if he suspected the answer to his query.

"Easy, dear heart," Firekeeper said, curling her fingers in his ruff. "A misunderstanding, I think. Northwest wished to question me about my doings with King Tedric and forgot when he sought to wake me how fragile is my naked human hide."

Blind Seer didn't look convinced, but he seemed willing to accept this half-truth, especially since Northwest seemed quite contrite and Wind Whisper amused. Still, Blind Seer did not miss that Firekeeper's Fang rested bare-bladed in her hand. Firekeeper knew she would need to give him a fuller account when such telling would not precipitate a brawl.

"And did you tell him what you have done?" Blind Seer asked.

"I hadn't yet found the time," Firekeeper replied. "Aunt Wind Whisper arrived and told us of her coming just at Northwest's heels. Perhaps she would care to hear my tale."

"I would," the older wolf agreed, "since we have settled matters of rude awakenings, perhaps you should begin."

"Let me go and wash this blood from my skin," Firekeeper said, "and then I will tell."

Leaving the three wolves to sniff tails and go through whatever posturing was needed to settle them into accord with each other, Firekeeper ran to a nearby brook. She was accustomed to always being at the bottom of any wolf hierarchy and so when she returned, bare from the waist up so that her vest might soak off the worst of the blood in the water, she was surprised to find that in ways subtle but unmistakable, Northwest deferred to her.

It was a new experience, as stimulating as her dip in the cool water had been. Firekeeper seated herself on the grass, head held high and proud, and began:

"Humans are not as wise as wolves, and so they do not always listen to their Ones. With this in mind, listen to my tale."

She told them then of how she had implored Tedric to order Ewen Brooks and his settlers to leave the land west of the Iron Mountains, how Tedric had not only agreed to do so, but to issue a declaration making such settlements illegal.

"How can he do this?" Wind Whisper asked. "The land is not his to govern."

Firekeeper twisted uncomfortably.

"Humans do not see it so," she admitted. "They draw lines on paper and declare that all within those lines, whether or not they have walked that land, is their own. It is a custom," she added, trying to make some excuse, "that they inherited from those who founded these colonies and one that helps them keep some peace among themselves."

Northwest looked as if he wanted to say something rather nasty, but when Firekeeper caught his eye he humbled himself and only muttered:

"It seems foolish to claim what is not yours, but if it keeps them from fighting each other, I suppose the custom is of some use."

"I think it is foolish also," Firekeeper said, not willing to press her advantage to condescension. "I do not say I agree with them, only report how it is among humankind."

Northwest swished his tail once to acknowledge her wisdom, and then Firekeeper went on:

"Now Tedric will need to send humans west in order that they may order the colonists to leave. If these humans do not make the crossing safely, then Ewen and his people will not know they have incurred their One's wrath."

Wind Whisper gave a lazy stretch and looked at Northwest.

"It might be possible to see that these messengers arrive safely—and without doing further harm."

Northwest looked rebellious, so Firekeeper hastened on.

"Now Tedric has made another promise. He will command his people to build a small den—like this great one here in that it will have high and powerful walls—in which some of his soldiers will stay and turn back those who would cross the gap in defiance of his commands."

"You did say," Wind Whisper said, "that humans would not obey their Ones when they were out of sight. In that way," and she looked slyly at Northwest, "they are not too unlike some wolves."

"But," Northwest retorted defiantly, "might not such a place be turned against us?"

Firekeeper hadn't thought of this, but she tried to answer smoothly.

"It might," she replied, "but what limits us to crossing the mountains through the gap? Humans need such wide breaches in the mountain wall for, as you have said, they cannot survive without many aids. Their horses and mules could not climb where wolf or bear or puma would go lightly."

Northwest acknowledged her point but persisted in his criticism.

"Yet this is not the only such crossing point, only the easiest."

"Is that so?" Firekeeper said. "Well, that is new to me and may be new to the humans. Once again, we know much more than they do. If there is worry that the humans will come through these other points, then we can set our own guards upon them. Surely," she added, and her dark-eyed gaze was hard, "my pack should not bear the entire weight of protecting the west."

Northwest swished his tail low in apology, but Firekeeper was not completely at ease with this persistent show of humility. She might have beaten him in a fight—but it was a victory assured because of Wind Whisper's intervention. Firekeeper understood now why Wind Whisper had waited so long to show herself. Had she not, Northwest would have continued to think of Firekeeper as easy game. Now he would be more careful in his dealing with her—and that care would not always work in the wolf-woman's favor.

"There is a price for King Tedric's cooperation," Firekeeper went on, knowing that the wolves would trust the king's actions more fully if they had not emerged simply out of goodwill or prudence. Wolves fought their own both for precedence and respect. Something freely given was a sign of weakness—a puppy piddling on its belly out of fear of those larger and stronger.

"King Tedric would have me and Blind Seer join with some of his pack who are set to hunt down a renegade. This renegade is the same woman who stole the magical artifacts from Bright Bay last winter and from whom we ultimately stole them back."

Firekeeper could tell from the differences in the two wolves' postures that they had each heard the tale, but she thought that Wind Whisper knew more than did Northwest.

"This renegade has allied herself with another pack, the humans of New Kelvin. They are a pack which has much interest in magical lore. My sense of these New Kelvinese is that where magic is concerned they are like young bucks growing their first rack. They have sharp points, but not many and they have yet to learn how to make those points truly dangerous. If this human woman—Melina—has her way with them, she may transform them into lords of the forest with racks of many sharp points and the skill to make them pierce deep."

Wind Whisper licked her nose nervously.

"Can one do this?"

"A strong leader makes a strong pack," Firekeeper quoted from wolf lore. "And whatever else is said of Melina, she is a strong leader and has ways of making even the reluctant grovel before her and obey her will.

"It is for our people," Firekeeper went on, "as much as for the humans that I agreed to hunt Melina. New Kelvin is a small land, much walled in stone. I think she might encourage a western press, for it would be far easier to go that direction—even with the mountains barring her route—than taking her neighbor's lands."

Blind Seer added, "And if Melina goes west, then she has also gained a route by which she can slip her hunters into her neighbor's lands undetected, rather like a large pack that leaves a few strong hunters to spring out from where they will not be expected and where they will do more damage."

Firekeeper thought about adding King Tedric's concern for Firekeeper herself, his desire to get her away from this area at a time when her loyalty to the Beasts might be misinterpreted by humans. She decided that this would be unwise. Northwest, at least, already thought her capable of speaking from head and tail at once. No need to remind him—or to show him that humans distrusted her as well.

Wind Whisper and Northwest discussed what Firekeeper and Blind Seer had told them at some length, enough so that Firekeeper began to feel the weight of her interrupted sleep, heaped on top of the ebbing tide of fear and fighting, pressing down on her eyelids. She stifled a yawn with one hand.

"So you go north to hunt at the behest of this human king," Northwest said, adding quickly when Firekeeper shifted her knife in her free hand, "and for our own people's good as well. What should we do in turn?"

"Wind Whisper spoke well and wisely," Firekeeper said, still startled to have the outlier look to her for wisdom. "Escort the human messengers— tracking them unseen and silent, as you have shown so well you can do. Thus the king's word will reach his people and make their punishment or defiance a matter between humans, not between humans and Beasts."

She ticked her tongue against the roof of her mouth as she puzzled out a thought.

"If some of the wingéd folk were near," she continued, "I would beg them to carry word to the Beasts of what King Tedric has agreed to do. Best that we do not give the humans any cause to change their minds regarding leaving our lands to us."

"The peregrine Elation came east with you," Wind Whisper said. "Where is she?"

"Ask the wind," Firekeeper replied, quoting a proverb that ran, "Ask the wind, ask the rain. Empty howling and wet fur are all you earn for your pain."

Blind Seer said, "Elation came with us, but flies her own course. She separated from us some days past. Perhaps she is with Derian. I think she has a fondness for him."

"Perhaps," Firekeeper agreed. "In any case, she is not the only of the wingéd folk who nest east of the Iron Mountains. My guess is that others are nearby. Surely we can seek out one or more of these and make them understand the need is not ours alone but of all Beasts."

Wind Whisper puffed a bit of laughter.

"I think we can. I seem to recall hearing that a raven or two was considering nesting in these very castle towers."

Firekeeper was not surprised—though she would have been a year before.

"The humans call the place Eagle's Nest" was all she said, "but it would make a fitting rookery."

She yawned, this time not bothering to smother it in her hand, though among wolves such could be taken as insult. Still, she thought that they must smell her exhaustion in her sweat and breath alike.

"Northwest interrupted my rest," Firekeeper apologized, "and I am weary from all this talk. Humans do business by daylight and I must be rested if I am to speak well for us."

She didn't mention her throbbing throat. The ointment she had rubbed on it, part of a little jar she had from Doc, had helped, but she knew it would be days before the bruises healed. Idly, she considered how she would explain them to the humans. The truth wouldn't do.

Blind Seer settled himself beside her. During all the talk he had remained bolt upright, and even now there was something of a guard in his posture. Firekeeper hid a smile. Northwest would hesitate to come within ten paces of her now.

"Sleep," Wind Whisper agreed. "I am for hunting. This travel is tiring. Surely Blind Seer has left something for us."

She gathered Northwest to her and they left.

Firekeeper pillowed her head on Blind Seer's flank. She was considering telling him how things were with Northwest, but even as she was framing the words, she was asleep.

XII

THE DAY FOLLOWING her rather uncomfortable discussion with Citrine, Elise took advantage of a cool afternoon following a thunderstorm to practice her archery. She'd promised Baron Archer she wouldn't completely ignore her work with the heavier bow, but in truth she had let it slide.

This afternoon, however, Elise could find no excuse to avoid practicing any longer. Race Forester had come by to consult with Edlin regarding some puppies. The sight of the bow he wore slung from his shoulder had awakened all Elise's latent guilt. Citrine was working on her elementary New Kelvinese vocabulary with Grateful Peace. Wendee was with them, having decided that the best way to polish her own command of the language was to relearn the basics.

Sighing slightly—for she'd much rather have curled up with the book of New Kelvinese verse she'd been working through—Elise had one of the manservants set up a straw-backed target in a little-used alley alongside the house. The enclosing walls would serve two purposes: Her arrows couldn't go too far astray on a wild shot and no one was likely to cross her field of fire.

Dutifully, Elise plunked her way through her first quiver, missing the target entirely as often as she hit. Ninette insisted on gathering up the arrows while Elise manufactured a makeshift headband from her spare handkerchief, then drank sparingly from the pitcher of chilled fruit juice the cook had supplied.

When Ninette was safely back in her seat well behind the line of fire, Elise set arrow to string once more. She tried to remember her father's instructions, tried to forget the budding throb in her shoulders and arms. The first arrow flew fairly true, coming within a finger's breadth of the dark spot at the target's center. The second arrow went so badly astray that the shaft shattered against the alley's stone wall.

Elise gave a ladylike stamp of her foot and muttered a very unladylike curse. The third arrow flew true, burying itself in the target's heart. She was setting a fourth to the string when the clatter of horse hooves in the courtyard distracted her.

She lowered the bow, listening as the deep voice of the head groom addressed someone who—maddeningly—replied in a voice too soft for her to recognize. That is, her ears could not claim to recognize it, but her inner self knew the cadence and her heart started pounding far too hard.

Idiot! Elise chided herself. *What are you so excited about? So it's Doc, at last. So what? Didn't you tell him yourself just last winter that there could be nothing between you?*

It seemed, though, that the well-thought-out words of last winter meant nothing to this summer's heart. Elise started to put another arrow to her bowstring, then realized she was being a fool. She would go to welcome any other new arrival, so why not this one?

Because no other new arrival would be Doc.

For a moment Elise regretted her sweaty face, her hands reddened despite the archer's gloves she wore in obedience to her father's instructions. Then she gave an inner shrug. Sir Jared Surcliffe had seen her exhausted, blood-smeared, terrified, and even with her head shaved in the very unflattering New Kelvinese style. Through it all he had persisted in his fondness for her. Besides, didn't she want to discourage him in what was probably a vain hope?

Elise told herself that she did, but she didn't believe herself. Last winter she had told Doc that he could hope for nothing more than her affection. Her duties to the rank she would inherit meant that she must carefully consider any marital alliance. Even so, Elise knew she would be irrationally heartbroken if Jared took a second wife. Indeed, Elise knew herself to be vaguely jealous of Jared's first wife, a woman who had died years before in childbirth.

It's all impossibly stupid! Elise told herself as she unstrung her bow, leaned it against the alley wall, and went out to meet the new arrival.

Ninette followed, a trace anxious. Normal and usual protocols fell apart when the people meeting were, effectively, comrades-in-arms, due to serve together again soon. What was a chaperon to do? Insist on keeping form or skip the fuss?

Elise, knowing exactly what had drawn those worry lines on her companion's face, smiled reassuringly and was rewarded by seeing Ninette relax and offer, if somewhat tentatively, an answering smile.

As the two young women rounded the side of the building, Doc was handing the reins of a rather nondescript grey riding horse to the groom. Sir Jared Surcliffe was a man of middle height and middle build. His black hair was drawn back into a queue from which a few wisps had escaped. His features, like those of his cousin Norvin Norwood, were aquiline rather than handsome, but unlike Norvin, whose grey eyes seemed to hold something of a raptor's fierceness, Jared's similar visage was mild.

Yet Doc was not a soft man, nor a cowardly one. He had earned his knighthood on the battlefield, and possessed more than most men's fair acquaintance with bloodshed and pain. These were his enemies, more so than for most. A talent for healing had repeatedly brought Sir Jared into conflict with death and suffering. Elise suspected that she was one of the few outside his circle of colleagues who realized how much using his gift for healing drained Jared.

They had known each other since Elise was a girl, but then Jared—some eight years her senior—had seemed a distant, very grownup figure. Later their paths had crossed and recrossed, for Earl Kestrel was a good patron to his cousin and frequently made him one of his party on visits to the capital. However, not until both had become friends of Firekeeper had they been much thrown together.

And even then I was betrothed to Jet Shield, Elise thought. *Jared's has always been an impossible fondness.*

As they drew closer, Elise noted the saddlebags resting on the flagstones near Doc's feet. He himself was attired for travel rather than a social visit, no waistcoat over his shirt, his hat a worn, slouch-brimmed item of stained felt that had clearly seen more than its share of weather, but if Doc felt at any loss he didn't show it.

"Lady Archer. Mistress Ninette," he said, bowing over each of their hands in turn while the groom led the grey off to the stables. I am delighted to see you both."

He seemed to be, too. Elise saw none of her own fluttering feelings on Jared's composed features.

Then again, he knew he was coming here and that when he arrived he would see me again. There is none of my being caught unawares.

She took some small comfort in the realization. The housekeeper had emerged by now and was calling for someone to come and take the doctor's luggage.

"I believe I'm staying at the gatehouse," Doc said to the housekeeper, "but my horse was so tired I thought to relieve him of his burdens."

The housekeeper looked unconvinced. Elise suspected she thought Doc had been trying to thrust himself unwanted into Duchess Kestrel's carefully arranged establishment. Meanwhile, Elise realized she'd done nothing but murmur some vague response to Jared's greeting.

Knowing the housekeeper would be scandalized if she invited Doc inside while he was still covered in road dust, Elise said, "Perhaps when you've had a chance to change your clothes, you would come up to the house and have some refreshments."

Oh, no! she thought. *I hope he doesn't think I'm condescending.*

Doc's smile was comfortingly casual.

"I'd like that," he said. "I have apologies to offer for being so late on my arrival."

"What happened?" Elise asked.

"I was on my way from my family's lands . . ." The Surcliffes owned some rocky land somewhat to the south that they were turning into a winery. ". . . when a boy came from Widow Chandler's holding. It appears his mother had fallen. The boy was frantic. He recalled I was at my parents' and took the initiative to come after me, leaving his little sister—only six, I think—to look after their mother."

"Oh?"

Elise found she was thinking very ungenerous things about this Widow Chandler and her enterprising son.

"Turns out," Doc went on cheerfully, "that the widow had broken a leg. Clean break, thankfully, and I was able to urge it to mend more quickly. Still, I couldn't very well leave them without a fit adult around the place. We sent a message off to Widow Chandler's brother and when he came I took the road here."

Elise was fighting down images of Doc handling this unknown woman's leg. A lower-leg break, surely. And she must be fairly old if she had a six-year-old daughter and a son older than that. Couples weren't encouraged to marry until they reached at least their majority at nineteen. That means this widow was at least twenty-seven. . . .

"I'd have sent a message," Doc said, apparently aware of something odd in Elise's expression, "but I thought that the boy—he's only nine—had taken enough risks."

Twenty-nine! crowed the uncharitable part of Elise's mind. *That means this widow was at least twenty-nine.*

Elise shoved these thoughts aside.

"Very reasonable," she replied. "Will you stay for dinner? Grateful Peace has been dining with us most nights rather than putting the staff to the trouble of preparing separate meals."

"If that's the case," Doc said, "I would be honored."

He looked slightly puzzled as he took his leave and Elise didn't blame him. Her attitude had been completely out of line. One moment she was greeting him informally as an old friend, then she was tongue-tied as a chit at her first dance, next she was getting frosty when all he'd done was his duty as a doctor.

I really have to get myself in line, Elise scolded herself. *I'm the one who told him I can offer him nothing. It's not right for me to act like a flirt.*

Elise and Ninette retired upstairs so that Elise could change into something other than her archery habit. By the time Elise had washed off most of the grime and put on a clean summer frock, she thought she had her emotions under control.

Ninette had gone to tell Citrine that they had a guest and brought the child back with her. The girl's hands were smudged with ink from her efforts at writing New Kelvinese and she willingly scrubbed them in a basin, turning the water bluish black.

"I like Doc," Citrine confided, letting Elise button her into a clean frock while Ninette brushed out her mistress's hair.

Elise hid a sigh of relief. Citrine was reacting to the news of their guest's arrival far better than Elise had dared hope.

"Doc helped me when my hand was hurt," Citrine went on, pausing for a moment to stare at the maimed member. "He helped Peace, too. Peace says Doc saved his life.

"You know," the girl added thoughtfully, "I don't think I was hurt too bad. I lost only two fingers. Peace lost a whole arm, his right one, from the shoulder down. He was an artist before. Now he's learning to write all over again, like he's a baby."

Elise hugged her.

"You're very brave, Citrine."

Citrine frowned.

"I don't know if I am. I've cried a whole lot and I still hate Baron End-brook."

"I would, too," Elise replied, taking Citrine's maimed hand in her own. "Let's go down and see Doc."

"I'll come down a bit later," Ninette said, taking advantage of Citrine as a replacement chaperon. "I'd like a moment to put on a clean dress."

Elise nodded, knowing that even sitting and watching was sweaty work in this oppressive summer heat.

"Take your time," she said. "Citrine and I will guard each other's honor."

Citrine giggled at the idea and nearly skipped down the hallway.

Jared was chatting with Edlin when they entered the parlor. Edlin wore his kennel clothes, which were covered with a wealth of fine white hairs.

"We're bottle-feeding the pups cow's milk," the young lord was saying, "since the bitch's milk dried up, but I think we need to get them on something more solid. The pups are shitting . . ."

Edlin stopped in midphrase when he heard them enter, coloring slightly. Elise noted once again that when Edlin was talking about something he was passionate about—like his dogs—he lost some of his verbal ticks.

He recovered quickly from his momentary embarrassment and beamed at them.

"I say, pretty ladies, all dressed in flowers! Here I am in my grubbies. The housekeeper's been glowering at me since I came to give the glad cry to Cousin Jared here. Excuse me while I go make myself respectable, what?"

He bowed his way out and Elise gave a fond shake of her head.

"He's hopeless," she said with a sigh. "I wonder if we'd do better to leave him here."

"Maybe so," Doc replied ambivalently. "Is that Citrine hiding behind your skirts? Come out and say hello—or don't you remember me?"

He looked so hurt that Citrine giggled.

"I remember you, silly," she said, advancing and offering an embrace.

Once again, Elise noted that lately the girl seemed more ready to trust men than women—though earlier the opposite had been true. Was it because though Citrine claimed to hate Baron Endbrook—who was a man—in her heart of hearts she was coming to terms with the fact that her mother's indifference had been the real reason for her injury? Elise didn't know and she wasn't about to ask lest she trigger another of the hysterical fits that, thankfully, were becoming less and less frequent.

The housekeeper brought in the refreshment tray herself, doubtless so she could get a look at how much dirt and dog hair Edlin had tracked into her spotless parlor. Elise dismissed the woman with thanks but did not accept her broad hints that she could send a maid in with a broom. If Elise could live with dog hair and a bit of mud, so could the housekeeper. For now, Elise wanted to learn how much Doc knew about the situation.

She asked directly, feeling some anxiety about how Citrine might react. Sometimes the girl took the hints that they might be going into New Kelvin quite calmly. Other times she grew hysterical or creepily silent. This time Citrine only bit into an oatmeal-raisin cookie.

Doc's reply was equally frank.

"I know everything Norvin did when he wrote me. The king wants some of us to return to New Kelvin to check out which of these rumors are rumors and which hold some truth. I am glad to go—eager even. Given the injuries some of us suffered last time, I would not wish you to be without my talent."

"Thank you," Elise said with honest fervor. "You've taught me a great deal about treating injuries, but I have no talent for healing."

Citrine grinned and there was something unsettling about the way she drew her lips back from all her teeth as she did so.

"Doc doesn't have talent enough to heal me," she commented, her words underlaid with a ripple of shrill laughter. "No one does. My fingers are gone, gone forever and ever and ever."

Elise stiffened. On some inner level she felt responsible for Citrine's injury, as if she should have foreseen all the details of Melina's plan instead of just grasping the barest outlines.

Doc, however, seemed to bear no similar burden. Kneeling without regard for what Elise knew must be one of his few pairs of good trousers, he tilted Citrine's chin so that she must meet his calm grey gaze.

"Now why do you say that?" he asked steadily. "Are you trying to make Lady Archer and me feel bad?"

Citrine wrinkled up her nose and jerked back a step, but she neither ran and hid, nor fell to screaming, nor withdrew into one of those impenetrable silences.

"I just said it," the girl replied sulkily.

"You must have had a reason," Doc pressed.

"I just said it," she repeated stubbornly.

"Well," Doc said, straightening. "I think you should think about why you said it. Your sister is almost a queen now. That makes you—no matter what titles you don't have—almost a duchess. People will expect more of you than when you were the youngest and least useful daughter of Rolfston Redbriar and Melina Shield."

Citrine looked shocked. She rolled her wide blue eyes and for a moment Elise thought she was about to crumple into one of her fits. Elise stepped forward, ready to catch or restrain the child as needed, but a small motion of Doc's hand halted her in mid-motion.

There was a moment of tense silence so absolute that Elise could hear the settling of the ice in the pitcher on the tray. Then Citrine gave a great, shuddering sigh and sobbed:

"I want my mama! I want my daddy!"

These had been her two high cards, the exclamations certain to elicit sympathy from whoever heard them. Doc, however, merely brushed a bit of dog hair off his trouser legs.

"Do you really? I can understand wanting your father. Rolfston was a nice enough man, even if your mother did crush his spirit. But why would you want your mother, especially after what she did to you?"

Citrine gulped silent in mid-sob.

"Well?" Doc prompted.

Elise had never seen Sir Jared so coolly critical, not even with patients who were clearly feigning illness to gain a few days' holiday. Citrine screwed up her face for another sob.

"I don't have a daddy or a mama!"

"You and lots of other people," Doc said bluntly. "It happens to all of us. That's why we honor our ancestors."

Elise couldn't bear it. She knelt and squashed Citrine to her, glowering up at Doc.

"How can you be so cold! The child has suffered so much!"

"And is likely to suffer more," Doc said, pouring fruit juice into three glasses, "unless she accepts that all this sobbing and whining and making people feel guilty and miserable on her behalf isn't going to change a thing."

With Citrine pressed against her, Elise felt the girl tense, then push away from her comforting embrace. The nine-year-old looked up at Doc and stamped her foot angrily.

"What do you know?" she said cruelly. "Your parents are still alive. You just came from seeing them. Your biggest sister isn't someone else's family now. Your brother isn't all taken with being an almost lord. Your other sisters haven't left you and run off to a foreign court!"

"No," Doc replied. "That's true. In fact, I doubt there's anyone else in the entire world who shares exactly your burden. Does that make you so special?"

Citrine pouted with her lower lip outthrust. She didn't reply, so Doc went on.

"You can't change any of those things. No matter how you fuss, your father will not return from the dead. Ruby and Opal will still be in Bright Bay. Sapphire will still be crown princess.

"Your mother is another matter. I notice you didn't include her in your lament of woes. Or is it you like to think of her as dead? I have news for you, Citrine Shield, Melina isn't dead. She is an exile by her own will. She abandoned you. She knew what Baron Endbrook had done to you and didn't come to your rescue."

"My mama is a queen," Citrine replied with perverse pride.

"Is she?" Doc shrugged. "That's one of the things we are going to New Kelvin to learn."

"She married a king!" Citrine protested.

"Is that excuse enough for what she did to you?" Doc asked. "Is that why you still wear so proudly the stone she put on you? Do you think that she'll have you back? Maybe that she'll make you a princess as King Tedric has made Sapphire a princess?"

Citrine said nothing, but there was a fierce, guarded look in her eyes that reminded Elise of when a falcon was prepared to bolt to freedom, to refuse the fowler's glove.

Elise held her breath, wondering if Doc was close to the truth. Certainly, at least in her hearing, no one had spoken so harshly to the child, no one had done anything but offer her pity and sympathy.

The silence stretched, became impenetrable, but this time Citrine was clearly willing it. There was no emptiness behind the girl's eyes. She was refusing to reply, trembling with the effort. Doc studied her for a moment more, then offered Elise the tray holding the chilled juice.

"Lady Archer?" he queried and, after Elise had accepted the tall glass nearest her, he offered one to Citrine, "Mistress Citrine?"

His emphasis, ever so slight on the courtesy title with its denial of any nobility at all, was too much for the girl. With a shrill, almost soundless, shriek she dashed from the room, slamming the heavy door behind her. Elise made as if to follow, but Doc restrained her with a hand on her arm.

"Let her go," he said. "She can't do herself any more harm than has been done already."

"She might injure herself—jump from a window or something."

"She won't," Doc said, letting his hand drop, "or if she does, she will make certain that what harm she does to herself is treatable, though I, for one, would be tempted to refuse my aid."

Elise's eyes widened in shock, and Doc laughed dryly.

"Not really, but Citrine is clever enough to calculate my presence and my talent into her actions."

Elise sipped from her juice, taking the moment to think how to phrase her question.

"You were so harsh with her."

"Everything else had been tried," Doc said. "You must remember, I saw her this winter. I saw how she was coddled and pitied. Such indulgence would turn the head of a much less wronged child."

"Then you do think Citrine has suffered?" Elise asked, obscurely relieved.

"I do, but we all suffer. Sometimes I think the pity we offer a suffering child is really the pity we wish someone would lavish on us when we're hurt. Not every child who loses a father receives such attention. Many a widow or widower has remarried, leaving his or her children to wonder just where they fit into the new family."

"But not under quite such spectacular circumstances!" Elise protested.

Doc grinned.

"No, but I'm not sure Citrine would have been so aware of how spectacular the circumstances were if everyone hadn't gone out of their way to let her know. When you're that young, loss and grief is a private, intimate thing. Indeed, somewhere deep inside, Citrine probably blames herself for both her father's death and her mother's exile."

"Not really!"

"Oh, yes. If only she'd been a better daughter Rolfston would have taken more care on the battlefield, Melina wouldn't have left . . ."

"You've become quite wise all of a sudden," Elise said, regretting instantly the mocking note that underlay the words.

Doc seemed not to hear it.

"Not really. After my trip to the capital I took every opportunity I could to talk to people with children, people who had lost parents when they were young, even those whose parents had divorced. Since the injury to Citrine was no longer organic—I could feel that when I tried to treat her—it must originate in her mind.

"And maybe," he added sadly, "I know something of assuming guilt. After all, despite my much praised talent for healing, I couldn't save my wife or our baby."

There was a quick knock on the door and Ninette, ever faithful to her duties as chaperon, came in without waiting for reply. Evidently, she was relieved to find them so decorously positioned.

"Citrine is in her nursery," Ninette said, not commenting on what might have driven the child away, "and the second housemaid is going to give her supper there."

Elise smiled thanks and offered Ninette the remaining glass of juice.

"Has anything been heard from Firekeeper and Derian?" Doc asked, hastening to change the subject.

"Not that I know," Elise replied, "but it is early days yet. The king did not expect them until the end of Bear Moon. It is only that now."

"I wonder how he thought he could expect them—or at least Firekeeper—at all," Doc said, voicing a question over which Elise herself had puzzled a great deal. "I'd have thought we wouldn't see her until the first snowfall—and maybe not even then."

Elise raised her hands in a gesture of confusion.

"Who knows how the king knows what he knows? I only hope King Tedric can teach Sapphire and Shad some small portion of his wisdom before he goes to join the ancestors."

"Or share his spy network with them," Doc added with a cynicism that surprised Elise, though she knew it shouldn't.

She considered whether in the half-year or so that had passed since she had last seen Doc she might have idealized him a bit. It was quite possible. Their contacts had been brief and utterly unromantic, mostly the exchange of a few letters containing pamphlets on medical subjects. Once she had sent him pressed and dried samples of a river herb that a local wise woman swore brought down swelling and fever.

The correspondence between them had been so proper and correct Elise would not have hesitated to let her parents see the letters if they had asked. Neither did, though. She wondered if this indicated approval, disapproval, or merely indifference to her friendship with Sir Jared. Or maybe it was none of these things. Maybe they simply trusted her to make the best choice with the barony in mind.

Elise gave herself a mental shake and returned her full attention to Ninette and Doc.

"Sorry," she apologized somewhat lamely, unable for a moment to recall what they had been conversing about. Then she remembered.

"Another thing I wonder," she said quickly, "is under what guise the king will have us go into New Kelvin. He promised us some guidance on that matter, but thus far we have heard nothing."

Doc raised his hand in an involuntary motion toward his forehead.

"I only hope that His Majesty does not expect us to pretend to be New Kelvinese," he said. "I might manage to pretend to be someone other than myself, but I do not think I could sustain the deception."

Elise recalled how strange she had felt for those brief hours when she had acted the part. Her hair was finally recovering some from having been shaved after the New Kelvinese fashion. Indeed, making certain it grew quickly and strong had been a matter of much concern that winter. She'd spent more hours than she cared to recall with her head smeared with some odorous paste of artemisia and rosemary, then wrapped in warm cloths, the procedure culminating in a vigorous scalp massage. It would be hard to sacrifice that hard-won golden fringe once more.

"You could if you must," she scolded with mock severity. "Simply act the part of the silent and somber male, and leave the talking to facile females like Wendee and myself."

"I usually do," Doc laughed.

Elise made as if to tap him across the knuckles with an imaginary fan.

"In any case," she went on, "you are much behind the rest of us in your studies of New Kelvinese. We must ask Grateful Peace to give you intense tutelage."

"Not that!" Doc said, stretching his accents into those of a country man. "Don't you know ma'am that I'm just a poor healer from the backwoods?"

The soft ringing of a bell announced that dinner was ready. Elise rose and Doc, with natural courtesy, offered his escort to both her and Ninette.

"I've brought some wine," Doc said, "from my family's vineyards. It's a newish vintage, but we're pleased with it. I understand that Race Forester brought partridges in addition to puppies. I think they shall go well together."

Elise made some proper answer, but she couldn't help thinking: *As well as you and me?*

XIII

DERIAN SOUGHT Firekeeper two days after their meeting with the king and his heirs. When Firekeeper emerged from the trees toward which a lazily circling Elation had directed him, Derian found the wolf-woman edgy and tense, but as she was often this way when delayed in her course, he thought nothing much of it.

He did think something of purpling bruises on her throat, but seeing her glower when his gaze rested on them, he decided that it would be wisest not to ask her about them. Doubtless she'd gotten the worse side in one of her wrestling matches with Blind Seer and was still sore—in more ways than one—about it.

"I had a letter today," Derian began, relaxing onto a rock that bordered one of the streams. "It came under a cover addressed to my mother as if routine business for the stables, but the contents were for me—for both of us."

Firekeeper looked unsurprised by this evidence of court intrigue, standing with her back against a young oak, tossing her knife restlessly into a log several yards away. Derian was impressed when he realized that she was targeting a knot no bigger than a human eye and hitting it every time.

"Read letter?" she suggested, pulling the knife from the wood and stepping back to her place again.

Derian pulled the missive out, unfolded it, and then paused.

"We're alone?"

"But for those little wild things," Firekeeper assured him, "too stupid to fear a wolf. No human is near."

Derian began without further delay, " 'From His Most Gracious Majesty, King Tedric . . . ' "

"Yes, yes," Firekeeper said. "We know who from! What it say?"

Derian, who had deliberately not skipped the formal opening in order to tease her, grinned and moved ahead to the text.

> *As previously agreed upon, you and Firekeeper shall proceed to the Norwood Grant, there meeting with Lady Archer and the other members of your expedition. After long and careful consideration, it has been decided that you may best serve our purposes by entering New Kelvin—at least initially—as yourselves and in your own form and guise.*
>
> *The reason to be given for your traveling there will be that you go as agents for the Kestrel Duchy and the Archer Barony, both of which are interested in entering into a joint agreement wherein goods shall be imported from New Kelvin and sold not only in Hawk Haven, but also in Bright Bay. Baron Archer has been consulted on this matter and has given his enthusiastic approval. We expect equal cooperation from Duchess Kestrel and are writing to request such.*
>
> *This explanation shall provide ample reason for nearly all members of your party to make the journey. Lady Archer and Lord Kestrel represent the interests of the Houses they will someday inherit. Lady Blysse is a member of House Kestrel. Derian Carter is not only favored by the patronage of Earl Kestrel, but is a representative of one of the most prominent firms offering transportation of goods and persons within the realm. Sir Jared Surcliffe is a healer, known for his interest in all types of medical lore. He would make a good advisor on the types and quality of medicinal herbs for which this consortium might trade. It goes without saying that a chaperon must be provided for the two young ladies. Wendee Jay not only serves admirably in that capacity, but also as a representative of Duchess Kestrel.*

Derian stopped in his reading and grinned. "I bet that last paragraph was Sapphire's doing. King Tedric would expect us to figure out the excuses for our going ourselves."

Firekeeper flashed him an answering grin and nodded.

"Read!"

Derian complied.

Given your prior journey into New Kelvin and despite that journey's rather sensational conclusion, not many should question any of those mentioned above being chosen for the task.

The attendance of Citrine Shield could raise some small question. We suggest that her presence, if at all possible, be downplayed. Wendee Jay has two young daughters; perhaps Citrine could be represented as one of these. However, whatever excuse you choose to manufacture, none of those with whom you do business should take much note of a child of nine.

Enclosed in this packet are letters of introduction to the staff of our embassy in New Kelvin. That Lady Archer and Lord Kestrel would call upon the ambassador and make their presence in the city known should raise no questions. Indeed, their failure to do so last winter could have raised more. Also included are documents for lines of credit that House Kestrel may convert into appropriate currency to fund your expedition.

Needless to say, there will be those who will wonder at your presence in Dragon's Breath and who will suspect that you are interested in more than silk, glass, and medicinal herbs. However, their very interest in you may provide opportunities to learn some of those things we desire to know.

Derian concluded his reading and looked up to find Firekeeper poised, knife in hand. She threw it as his gaze rested upon her.

"When we go?" she asked, retrieving the knife and checking the blade for nicks.

"Tomorrow morning," he said, "if you can hold on that long."

Firekeeper nodded.

"I can wait—till tomorrow. Others know we come?"

"I sent a pigeon the very day of our meeting with the king," Derian agreed, "giving my guess as to when we could depart."

"Then they be ready to go when we get there?"

"Probably not immediately," Derian said. "There will be packing and other preparation to make. Still, I doubt whether we'll be delayed more than a day or two. Why are you so impatient?"

Firekeeper shrugged.

"Every day my feet wish to go west to my pack. The sooner they are tired from going other the best."

Derian nodded. In many ways, he felt the same—though in his case his impulse was to drag his heels. He had spent much of the winter away from his family, and much of the spring and autumn before that. Now summer was being taken as well. It wasn't so much that he liked the drudgery or the routine of Prancing Steed Stables, but that it was the one place he still felt he belonged.

Even there, though, he was being displaced. Damita and Brock were being trained to take over Derian's routine. The stables themselves were changing in character, cartage being replaced by boarding other's animals and by the sale of fine beasts. Still, home was home and if his own was threatened as Firekeeper so clearly felt hers was, Derian didn't know how he'd feel about being told that the best thing he could do for those he loved was to leave them to their fate.

"We go in the morning," Derian said. "I'll meet you along the north road."

Firekeeper nodded.

"Good then. Tomorrow."

She turned, stepped into the forest's edge, waved once, and, although it was broad daylight and Derian could have sworn he never took his gaze from her, was gone.

AS SOON AS the carrier pigeon arrived bearing the news that Derian and Firekeeper would leave Eagle's Nest on or about the twenty-sixth day of Bear Moon, Elise started getting her band ready for their departure into New Kelvin.

Wendee Jay, a traveling player in her youth, was of considerable assistance. Indeed, within a day of the message's arrival, Wendee had taken over the preparations. Elise had other things demanding her attention.

Duchess Kestrel came to call, Edlin trailing at her heels. The young lord's expression and the dusting of dog hair on his clothing eloquently showed that he'd been called from the kennels.

Elise sighed. She knew she would be glad to have Edlin along once they were on the road, but he was taking his preparation for the trip far less seriously than was Citrine. The little girl had acquired a good smattering of functional phrases and an even better vocabulary. She could identify the marks for the thirteen sodalities at a glance, even in their abbreviated form. All Elise could hope was that Grateful Peace was managing to tutor Edlin when the men retired to the gatehouse in the evening.

As soon as they were settled in the parlor and refreshments had been served, Duchess Kestrel produced a letter bearing, Elise saw to some surprise, the seal of House Archer. She experienced a momentary flurry of fear. Had something happened to one of her parents? Had Baron Archer withdrawn his permission for her to go into New Kelvin?

The last seemed all too possible. Although the common people thought of the nobility as solidly supporting the king and his policies, Elise knew how much jockeying for position and precedence went on behind the scenes. House Wellward and House Kite, for example, had long been rivals. No matter how much they smiled and exchanged cordial words in public, the bite of that rivalry was there. Had something happened to make Baron Archer decide he needed to show his own House's strength?

Duchess Kestrel's initial words relieved Elise of her fear.

"It seems," she said, her inflection holding a touch of humor, "that after long negotiations carried on this winter, the Barony of Archer and the Duchy of Kestrel are entering into a joint trade venture."

Edlin looked completely confused.

"I say!" he said. "What?"

Momentarily, Elise felt as flabbergasted, though she fancied she hid it better. Then revelation dawned.

"Our reason for going to New Kelvin!" she said. "That's marvelous."

She felt a touch of chagrin as she realized that part of her enthusiasm for the plan was that she needn't chop off her hair—at least not yet.

"That is so," Saedee Norwood replied, looking at her grandson with some resignation. "Baron Archer has written me on the king's behalf. Although the plan originates in a need for subterfuge, Baron Archer is actually quite enthusiastic about it. He points out that as the Barony of Archer shares a river border with Bright Bay we could set up a trading post there without needing to bring in other interests, as we would if we were to use the established crossings at Hope or Broadview."

Elise smiled, knowing her father's ambitions for their land and pleased that she would be serving them along with the king's interests.

"And you, Your Grace," she asked politely. "Are you interested?"

"Very much so," the duchess replied. "We have been less able to exploit the White Water River crossing at Stilled than we might since the one at Plum Orchard, being farther east and so closer to both Port Haven and Broadview, has dominated trade. This could work to our great advantage, especially with Bright Bay opening up as a market.

"However," the duchess continued, "this does create a small difficulty. We will be giving out that this is a plan that had been in the making since you, Elise, so kindly agreed to stay with our family this last winter—a visit that was interrupted by events of which we all are too aware. That means that both you and Edlin should be well acquainted with the exports of New Kelvin. You should be able to judge the quality of both glass and silk with some ease, and to handle bartering and related negotiations."

A look of pure loathing was spreading over Edlin's features.

"Grandmother!" he said. "I say, that's a bit much!"

"It is indeed," Duchess Kestrel agreed. "However, Derian Carter and Firekeeper should not arrive here for at least another six or seven days. Much can be done in that time. I took the opportunity to speak with Grateful Peace regarding his knowledge of these things and he says that his education is limited, his service first being as an Illuminator and then as a member of government.

"There are, however, members of my own household who have handled such trade for us, admittedly on a smaller scale and only in the Gateway to Enchantment. I will delegate one of these to teach you what he can and to supply you with texts that you can study as you travel. The tutor I have in mind is closemouthed and quite willing to imply—if asked—that the education has been under way since last winter."

Edlin didn't protest further. He must have known that there was no way—short of his being eliminated from the expedition—to escape. Elise, while dreading the intensity of the projected course of study, actually found herself looking forward to it. She had always enjoyed tales of foreign lands and foreign doings, and this promised her more of both.

SEVERAL DAYS into this tutorial, when Elise's mind was spinning with information on dyes and weights, weaves and tensile strengths, Grateful Peace made a formal call on her in her private chambers.

Unusually, the slim, somber man radiated tension. Elise was reminded of a bow strung too tightly and hoped that she would do nothing to make that string snap.

"Lady Archer," Grateful Peace began, "if I might have some of your time . . ."

Elise gestured him to a chair.

"Please, be seated. I've been going over what I'll need to know in order to trade for silk and my head is spinning. I thought I knew quite a bit—my mother and I prefer to shop for our own fabrics when possible—but I find I know nothing at all."

Peace smiled, but his expression remained strained.

"Perhaps I can aid you in this matter," he said. "I know little about fabric, but I know much about people."

He took a deep breath and continued, "I want to go with you into New Kelvin. I know that King Tedric did not include me in the plans you and he initially designed. At first this seemed wise. However, much of this last moonspan I have spent talking about my homeland, teaching its language, dwelling there in spirit if not in body. I am . . ."

He faltered and Elise spoke:

"Homesick?"

"I believe that is the term," Peace agreed a touch ruefully. "Although my dear wife is long dead and we had no children, I did leave siblings behind. I would see them and my nieces and nephews. Duchess Kestrel and the family Surcliffe have been kindness itself, but I desire to see the multihued attire of those who throng the streets of Dragon's Breath, to see faces decently adorned in paint and tattoos, to eat food spiced after the manner of my land."

Confronted with Peace's passion, Elise oddly felt herself the older, though the New Kelvinese must be her senior by more than thirty years.

"You do realize that you will be in tremendous danger," she said, adding, though she felt herself cruel to do so, "and so a danger to us. What news we have gathered from New Kelvin marks you a traitor, more despised than any of us. What we did cannot be declared openly without bringing shame to the Dragon Speaker and his allies. Your desertion of your place is excuse enough to revile you."

Grateful Peace winced under the force of her words, but persisted.

"What you say is true, Lady Archer. However, I could accompany you in disguise."

Elise, looking at his tattooed features, his distinctive bearing, his missing arm, raised her brows in disbelief. Peace leaned forward in his chair, forgetting dignity in his eagerness to explain.

"You are looking at my tattoos. I can hide them. There are stains—available just over the river in the Gateway to Enchantment—that I could apply to my face. These would darken the skin enough to significantly hide what is written there. Then I could apply paint over what is still visible. My darker skin would let me pass for a laborer. Moreover, no one knows that I lost my arm."

"And so?" Elise prompted.

"I could act in the role of a guide hired by your people. Such is not considered very honorable employment. However, it would be an acceptable alternative for someone who had been maimed."

Elise nodded. The New Kelvinese were arrogant about the superiority of their culture, an arrogance that could verge on xenophobia.

"Therefore," Peace continued, "no one would look too closely at me. If any suspected I hid the original markings on my face they would think it had been done because I was embarrassed about my current work."

"Flattering," Elise said dryly, "but honest. Do you think such a disguise would fool your former associates? After all, we left New Kelvin with you. Wouldn't it be reasonable to assume that the New Kelvinese we returned with might be you?"

"Some may suspect," Peace admitted. "Most likely would be Xarxius, the member of the Dragon's Three who works most frequently with foreigners. He is a suspicious soul. However, I have good hope that Xarxius would not share such thoughts. He, too, disliked the influence Melina had upon those who associated with her overlong. I doubt that her current marriage will have changed his opinions. Indeed, that may be the case with many of my associates. If they think I have returned to right what has gone so drastically wrong, they may say nothing."

"Possible," Elise admitted. "Still, it is a great risk, both for us and for you."

"Think of the advantages to be gained," Peace countered, restraining his eagerness with effort. "I know Thendulla Lypella as few do. I know hidden entrances. I can tell you the histories of many who may seek you out, helping you to better judge their reliability."

"True," Elise said, "and tempting."

"I have one more idea," Peace said. "Citrine is a difficulty for you. Isn't that so?"

Elise nodded. The matter had been discussed so frequently and so openly within their inner group that she could not deny it. Simply put, everyone else had ample reason for making the journey. Citrine's only reason would be to see her mother. Such an open declaration of their intent was not wise.

"What if we disguise her as a New Kelvinese?" Peace offered. "She could pose as my child. Variations in New Kelvinese attire would permit us to conceal the stone on her forehead far more easily than if she continued as a native from your land. Moreover, we would be protection for each other. My associates might not see the former Dragon's Eye in a crippled laborer with a small child. Equally, a New Kelvinese child—perhaps a bit mentally infirm—would not immediately seem to be the daughter of Melina."

Elise frowned thoughtfully. There was something to the plan. It would solve many of their problems and provide them with a valued advisor. She hoped that she could trust Peace. Where Melina was concerned, they were bound by mutual dislike. However, if they were to endanger the Dragon Speaker . . .

She shook off the thought. They had no intentions against the Dragon Speaker. Worrying about such was as foolish as buying a saddle for an unborn foal.

"Son," Elise said, speaking an evolving thought aloud. "Citrine is young enough to pass for either girl or boy. Let her pass as your son."

"Then you will let me accompany you?"

"Let us say that I will consider your proposal and put it to Duchess Kestrel and my companions."

Peace looked pleased. He rose.

"Thank you, Lady Archer. I promise that you will not regret having me with you."

Watching him depart, Elise wished that she were equally certain.

DESPITE FIREKEEPER'S URGING, Derian refused to push Roanne.

"We wore her out on the road back from New Bardenville," he said, "and she has only had a few days' rest. If you get your way, we will be leaving the North Woods as soon as possible for another long trek. Roanne is an excellent horse, but I will not exhaust her without reason."

Firekeeper wanted to sulk, knew that was a puppyish thing to do, and forced herself to consider the concessions Derian had already made. He could have insisted on traveling with a trade caravan as he had done before but, knowing that a group would invariably move more slowly than he could alone, he had agreed to take the—perceived—risks of solitary travel.

And Roanne *had* been rather hard used.

If Firekeeper felt herself abused, well, wasn't that a wolf's life? The rain didn't stop just because the pack was hungry and needed to hunt. The snow didn't sculpt its drifts to a wolf's comfort. The winds kept their vagaries and the sun its heat.

So, though Firekeeper would have liked to explore more, she and Blind Seer traveled by day, stayed in Derian's vicinity, and, as before, hunted for him and selected his campsites. All the while the comet, growing somewhat fainter now as it turned to adventure into new parts of the night sky, seemed to mock her.

Blind Seer, overheated although he had shed his heavy winter coat and many of the roads they traveled were through forested areas that offered much shade, found the going difficult. Within a few days, the blue-eyed wolf was seeking out somewhere to rest during the worst of the day's heat, catching up later.

Firekeeper missed the wolf desperately, but she reminded herself that she would miss him far more if he was killed in fighting between humans and Beasts. Nor did she doubt that if such came to pass Blind Seer would place himself in the forefront. He had learned much of human tactics and habits during his sojourn east, and would feel he must share that knowledge with his pack mates.

Wolves, unlike human generals, did not lead from behind.

WHEN DERIAN AND FIREKEEPER ARRIVED at the Norwood estates, some eight days after their departure from Eagle's Nest, they found that some of their news had traveled ahead of them. Elise was glad to get King Tedric's letter and, even as she read the contents, she offered Derian the letters that had arrived before him.

"So we'll all know everything," she explained.

Firekeeper, who still hadn't learned to read, fidgeted some as Derian read her the various letters. What pleased her was learning that preparations for departure were further along than either she or Derian had dared hope.

Firekeeper clearly felt that quartermastering details were no concern of hers. After asking for an estimate as to when the expedition would be ready to depart, she headed off to the deep forests with Blind Seer. Derian watched her go with mingled exasperation and sympathy.

Elise caught his expression and laughed.

"Well, she does deserve some reward for patiently guarding you all those days," she said.

"I suppose," Derian admitted grudgingly. "Still, you'd think she'd give this up. It's not like she's fresh from the forest anymore. She's lived among humans for over a year now."

Elise frowned.

"I think," she said slowly, "it would be a mistake to think that proximity has changed Firekeeper's underlying self. She is more at ease with you than with any other human—and you have spent more time with her than has anyone else. I think you overlook how very strange she is."

Derian forced himself to grin, though he wasn't at all certain he agreed. Firekeeper, he thought, considered herself a person of privilege and took advantage of her perceived status. Not wanting to discuss his mixed reactions to a person he, after all, essentially liked and valued a great deal, Derian changed the subject.

"You've done a tremendous amount to get us ready," he said.

"As soon as your letter arrived," Elise said, "we started. Later, the letter from my father to Duchess Kestrel gave us a fair idea of what King Tedric had in mind. Wendee mentioned this morning that she'd like you to review her preparations."

"Happily," Derian said, "though I doubt she needs my help."

"Even so," Elise replied, "it cannot hurt to have two sets of eyes review our plans."

She looked around the tidy parlor as if suddenly dissatisfied.

"Come outside into the garden with me," she said. "It's pleasant this time of day and we can talk there."

Derian had spent far too much time on the road to find the idea of strolling appealing, but he wasn't about to question a noblewoman's request.

"I was thinking," Elise said once they were out in the coolness of the dower house's immaculate garden, "that there is no reason for us to wait to secure a dwelling in Dragon's Breath until our arrival. Do you think Hasamemorri's house would serve again?"

Derian considered.

"It would," he said, "though there is no need for you to stay in such mean quarters. I'm certain the embassy could arrange for a house where you wouldn't need to share a room."

Elise laughed.

"You have odd ideas, Derian Carter. I think you imagine that those of noble birth live in some splendid isolation. Surely you've seen enough to know otherwise."

Feeling his face blush hot—a habit he had been certain he had overcome—Derian answered more sharply than he intended.

"Well, you do have fine houses and great suites within them."

"And we share them with chaperons, maids, and servants of all sorts. They're in and out constantly, putting away linens or clothes, opening and shutting curtains, dusting, sweeping, laying fires. You probably have more privacy in your parents' house than I do in mine. Even now the only reason Ninette isn't here is that she doesn't know that Firekeeper has left us alone. If she did, she'd be here arrow swift and arrow straight."

Derian thought about the truth in Elise's statement, remembered the constant comings and goings of disregarded servants, and he nodded a touch grudgingly.

"Still," he said, "Hasamemorri's is a very common house."

"But," Elise replied, "its very commonness is to our advantage. Our movements will be less remarked."

Derian nodded, but found another protest almost at once.

"Won't that in itself be a problem? Won't people wonder why we want such freedom?"

"And you the son of a horse trader! Merchants don't wish to make all their contacts in the open."

Elise laughed, and Derian had to concede her the point. The noblewoman went on.

"If we are too closely questioned, we can use Firekeeper and Blind Seer as our excuse. Hasamemorri does have stables for the wolf and none of her neighbors offered complaint last time."

"Fair enough," Derian said. "Shall I write?"

"Let me," Elise said. "I will write both to Hasamemorri and to the ambassador."

She lowered her voice and Derian realized that she had had more reason than the pleasant coolness of the garden for inviting him outside.

"There is one other advantage."

"Oh?"

"I told you that I have agreed to let Grateful Peace accompany us."

Derian nodded.

"If we were to take a great house with many servants," Elise went on, "it might seem odd that we keep on our guide. Also," she paused, seeming uncomfortable, "it will be more difficult for Grateful Peace to make contacts without our knowing. In a house with many servants, any one might be an agent of the Dragon Speaker—and at least one would surely be. We know Hasamemorri and her maids are not so allied and can request the dismissal of any too newly come."

"You don't trust Grateful Peace then?" Derian asked, both apprehensive and weirdly relieved.

"No more than I must," Elise replied firmly. "He could find contacts out in the streets if he is minded to betray us. However, we do not need to make it easy for him. He may think twice if he needs take risks with his own life."

Derian once again envied Firekeeper for not needing to worry about intrigues within intrigues. The sound of distant laughter from an open window reminded him of something he had been meaning to ask.

"And Citrine? How is she and how does she take being asked to disguise herself as a New Kelvinese?"

A strange look passed over Elise's pretty features.

"She is doing well, far better than she did either in her brother's care or in her sister's."

"A compliment to you," Derian offered gallantly when Elise seemed reluctant to continue.

"I wish I were so certain," Elise replied. "Certainly she weeps less and has nearly given up her hysterical fits—including those where she draws so deeply into herself that it is as if she sees or hears nothing. Only occasionally does she make one of those odd comments."

"Odd comments?"

Elise laughed a trifle uneasily.

"I forgot, you haven't seen her. Citrine has been given to making comments that on face value seem to mean nothing. Later, however, they almost always prove to mean something."

She told him about the hole in the road.

"There were other such comments as well," she continued. "At Eagle's Nest Castle, Citrine kept some of her regular attendants quite on edge.

Ninette learned from a rather indiscreet bit of gossip that it was being put about that Citrine had inherited some sorcerous talent from her mother."

Despite himself, Derian felt uneasy.

"But you say Citrine is all right now?" he asked, and hated himself for sounding so in need of reassurance.

Elise didn't appear to notice.

"Maybe not 'all right,'" she replied, "but at least much better. Citrine says she likes the idea of disguising herself as a New Kelvinese child. She even said she hopes to help us, that 'No one notices a child or watches what they say around one.'"

"It sounds as if you have done well by her," Derian said, feeling Elise needed reassurance.

"Not me so much as Doc," Elise replied with a smile that was momentarily so unguarded and so warm that Derian was assured that, whatever else had passed between these two the winter before, Elise's feelings had not much changed.

"At first Citrine was furious at Doc," Elise continued. "Then she underwent a gradual change of humor, as if seeking to prove Doc wrong. Today she is hard at work with Wendee and Grateful Peace, designing her costume."

"Have they found a way to deal with that gemstone?" Derian asked, thinking that it would little matter how they disguised Citrine if her identity was proclaimed by the presence of the gleaming gem, especially since the New Kelvinese practice of shaving the front several inches of hair meant that the forehead was more than usually visible.

"Wendee did," Elise replied, admiration in her voice. "She discovered that the band that holds the gem has some play in it—as it must for matters of hygiene. She experimented while tending to Citrine and discovered that Citrine is not at all upset if the stone is worn front to back or side to side, just as long as it is there.

"Headbands are not uncommon in New Kelvin, especially for those whose hair is not long enough to braid behind. One idea is to turn the stone to the side where it can be concealed in a variety of fashions. Or they may make a sheath for the entire band—though the difficulty there is making one that does not show so clearly that it covers a thicker, heavier portion. What is important is that Citrine will be disguised and in a fashion that will arouse no comment."

Derian was satisfied—and relieved.

"I'll just go look up Wendee, then," he said, "and offer to take over the packing and quartermastering so she will be free to work with Citrine."

"Do," Elise agreed. "You will be staying with the other young men in the gatehouse. It must be getting quite crowded by now."

"Not really," said Derian, who had already been by. "Lord Edlin is staying there only part-time. I hear that he is splitting the rest between the other house and his kennels."

Elise shook her head but didn't voice the disapproval so evident on her features.

"I appreciate your willingness to take over as quartermaster," she said, "but you also need to talk with Grateful Peace about improving your New Kelvinese. I see it as essential to the success of our story that everyone— other than Firekeeper, who hardly speaks Pellish—shows some comfort with the language. After all, this is a trip we are supposed to have been contemplating since last autumn."

"Yes, my lady," Derian said, startled slightly by the commanding tone in her voice. They had been talking so easily that he'd almost forgotten that Elise was the daughter of a baron. "I'll look Peace up right away."

"You may find both him and Wendee in the same place," Elise said, softening slightly, "since they are preparing Citrine for her new role. If you see Ninette, tell her I will be in my rooms reviewing the trade reports and she need not stop her work with Citrine to come to me."

Elise sighed slightly. Derian, remembering her outburst on how little privacy she possessed, thought he understood. Daughter of a baron or not, he pitied her.

BOOK

TWO

XIV

IF THERE WAS ONE THING that amazed Melina about the New Kelvinese it was that a land so obsessed with the past could be so immune to curiosity.

Even during her first visit to the country, back when she was fifteen, Melina's awe and wonder had rapidly been followed by a flood of questions.

What did the symbols that adorned everything from skin to fabric to the walls of buildings mean? (For she rapidly deduced that they were more than merely alphabetic signs.) Why was the ruler of the land called the Healed One? Why was his elected administrator called the Dragon Speaker? What purpose did the sodalities serve? Was there any truth to the hundreds of legends that were repeated in so many different contexts?

Melina wasn't interested in the more practical elements of international trade or city management or local economics. However, the heritage that underlay these things and shaped them either explicitly or covertly rapidly became an obsession.

Was it really necessary that a special dance be performed every time a new glass furnace was opened? What purpose was served by the elegant rituals that began and ended each session of the Primes? What would happen if these things were not done?

This last she even asked, shocking her New Kelvinese hosts. Her mother, who she had accompanied on this journey, had been mortified and forbade Melina to ask anything else.

From this incident Melina came to believe that the New Kelvinese did possess magic. Why else be reluctant to answer questions about the fashion in which things were done? Why else be so steadfast in refusing to change even the smallest detail?

Melina had seen paintings of the first Primes—old paintings, contemporary to that revered body—and the clothing the members wore, the manner in which they styled their hair, even the way they folded their hands or positioned their feet in their awkward, curly-toed slippers, remained essentially unaltered all these years later.

The attempts to awaken the magic within the three artifacts that Melina had contrived to have enter New Kelvin's hands had proven a great shock to Melina. Watching the thaumaturges she had heretofore revered as wise mystics and faultless keepers of knowledge bumble and argue their way toward a solution had nearly shattered her reverence for the New Kelvinese.

Nearly. The experience did teach Melina to view the thaumaturges' claims to magical knowledge with less confidence, but it confirmed her certainty of their devotion to the magical arts. Therefore, even after the catastrophic end of that venture, Melina had resolved to remain in New Kelvin.

Political connections were not enough to assure Melina the place she desired among the thaumaturges. She must have a more solid link.

After some observation, Melina decided that there was nothing more solid in all New Kelvin than the respect in which the Healed One was held. At first she thought about simply making Toriovico her advocate, but when she got to know the young man better and learned enough of New Kelvinese manners to recognize the lithe strong body beneath the heavy robes, she could not resist making him her husband.

Melina's desire was not solely based on sexual attraction. The Healed One was unmarried, but would not remain so for long. There was a resistance bordering on insanity to having the Healed One succeeded in his office by anyone but a male of his own begetting.

Childless and with no brother or even uncle to follow him, Toriovico must marry. A wife—no matter how docile a broodmare Melina might use her connections to arrange—would insert herself between Melina and her chosen anchor in her new homeland. Therefore, there was no choice but for Melina herself to become Toriovico's new wife.

Not that she found this prospect at all repulsive. The Healed One was younger than herself, his dancer's body strong and virile. Rolfston Redbriar, Melina's late husband, had long ceased to pleasure her when she permitted him into her bed. However, Melina had been too interested in perpetuating her family's connections to risk the stain of infidelity. Celibacy had been a deliberate choice, reluctantly accepted.

It was to the comet that glowed through the night skies late that winter that Melina owed the successful approval of her marriage to the Healed One. In Hawk Haven an astronomical phenomenon of that order awakened responses ranging from the passive interest with which sunsets and newborn babies are viewed through superstitious fear.

In New Kelvin the comet was an event to celebrate, proof that magic had not gone entirely out of reach. The Sodality of Stargazers was particularly voluble, explaining that the comet was a star come free from its place in the heavens. This was an event regularly witnessed in the fall of shooting stars and always indicated change.

Dropping a few hints into sympathetic ears, Melina suggested that the comet was absolute proof that Toriovico was meant to marry her—that she was the shooting star and that her marriage to the Healed One was indicative of great events to come.

Melina knew that this was true, but doubted that those who so blithely spread the word of this good omen realized just how much change she meant to engender.

After Melina had placed her mark on him, the Healed One became the perfect lover, interested only in his wife's pleasure. Moreover, outside the bedchamber, Melina discovered a void of intense loneliness within her young husband, a void that cried out with flattering intensity for her to fill it. There were times when Toriovico turned those blue-green eyes of his on her, their expression intense with many levels of longing, that Melina could have begun to love him.

Love, however, was a weakness in which Melina did not plan to indulge. Her woman's cycles still followed their lunar order, but they did have their irregularities, and Citrine's birth had been nine years before. Time would show whether or not Melina was still capable of bearing a child.

In order to secure her hold on the Healed One and, through him, upon her newly acquired homeland, Melina must not only bear a child, but a healthy male child—and preferably more than one such son. Having already borne five living children, Melina found that prospect exhausting even to contemplate.

Thus, although she consulted a discreet (and controllable) member of the

Sodality of Herbalists, and faithfully swallowed powders and potions meant to enhance her fertility and ability to bear a healthy child, Melina delved into more definite ways of securing her rule in New Kelvin.

⚜

SOMEHOW TORIOVICO HAD THOUGHT that being married would mean the end of being alone, but he was married now, had been for several moons past, and now he knew. Marriage wasn't an end to loneliness. Right now it seemed to be a door wide open into more loneliness.

He should have known that no other person could end the loneliness. That was his to bear, one and the same with the title he bore.

Healed One.

Toriovico thought it rather amusing that the title he had borne these five years assured all his subjects that he was healed, whole, one, while he himself knew just how empty and fragmented he was.

Toriovico knew that anyone who saw him saw him first as the Healed One, only after as an individual. His natural hair color was an unremarkable brown, but tradition required that the Healed One tint it to represent each season. Currently, it was a dark green. His eyes were a blue-green blend that his cosmetic artists loved to enhance appropriately. Today, of course, they shone like emeralds. His strong, lithe body, flexible as a reed from years of study as a dancer, was routinely swathed in heavy robes that made him look remarkably solid, less a man than a monolith.

Toriovico had lived for twenty-seven years, but he had lived within the isolation of the Healed One for only the past five.

Before that he had been part of something larger, like a kitten tumbling about with the rest of its litter. In Toriovico's case that litter had consisted mostly of sisters. He'd had six older sisters, still did, but now that he was the Healed One he didn't see them very often.

He'd had a brother, too, an older brother. Not the oldest of them all. That place belonged to one of the many sisters. Vanviko was the third born, but from the start he had been special. He was the one who had been destined to be the Healed One after their father died.

Toriovico sometimes wondered if Vanviko had ever felt this same piercing loneliness. He doubted it. Unlike Toriovico, Vanviko had been isolated from birth, proud of his privilege, of the special lessons he attended, of his place in his father's shadow—literally, for custom dictated that this was where the Healed One's heir stood during ceremonies.

Although he had been the Healed One for five years, as of yet Toriovico had no one to stand in his shadow. He had been unmarried when his elevation had come. Indeed, he had even been encouraged *not* to marry, since his father lived, his brother lived, and his brother's wife was expecting. Why rush to create children?

Toriovico wondered if his new wife, Melina, was capable of bearing children. He was certain that she could. Hadn't she already borne five healthy children? Wasn't she a wonderful woman?

He felt reassured, but still some part of him wondered. It was very important that there be an heir to the Healed One. Sometimes it was easier not to wonder. Sometimes it was easier to remember.

Even when that remembering was painful.

Toriovico recalled the day his brother had died as clearly as if it had just happened, rather than being an event years gone. A minstrel had come to Thendulla Lypella, filling every ear that would listen with tales of the wonderful mountain sheep he had seen on his journey to Dragon's Breath. The minstrel sang eloquently of how its horns shone like gold and hooves sparkled as if cut from solid diamonds.

Winter had been slow to depart, storm-filled, and damply cold. Vanviko had been glad to have an excuse to leave the confines of Thendulla Lypella and the endless cycle of ceremony. The occurrence of such a miraculous beast needed to be investigated.

Even then Toriovico had his own interests and had not cared for the idea of a midwinter hunt. Thus he had avoided the avalanche that had wiped all but three members of the hunting party from the mountainside.

Vanviko was not one of those who staggered back into Dragon's Breath. For days there had been hope that he and some of his companions still lived, perhaps trapped in a cave or hollow in the snow. After a week's digging, searchers brought the bodies home. All of them, even Vanviko's.

The mountain sheep the hunting party had been pursuing had escaped. Some of the rescuers said it had stood on a nearby mountain crest as they went about their ugly work, bleating with laughter. Most dismissed this as the hallucinations of their tortured minds.

Vanviko's death had been a great tragedy for all the kingdom of New

Kelvin, but for no one more than Toriovico. From his quiet artistic seclusion, he found himself promoted to the place in his father's shadow. He barely knew the most common rituals. Now he had to learn them all and as quickly as possible.

The Healed One had not been young when his eldest son had died. However, he took to the task of educating his new heir with the energy of a much younger man. His burden burned him out like a candle with too long a wick. He died when Toriovico was twenty-two and Toriovico stepped from the shadow into the light, in the difference between one breath and one never taken becoming the ruler of a kingdom.

But before that final breath had been taken, Toriovico's father had sent all his advisors, doctors, nurses, even his grieving wife, from the room. In rasping whispers he made Toriovico swear never to speak a word of what he would now hear except to his own son, and never then but on his own deathbed. Then the Healed One told his heir the truth, the truth that transformed everything Toriovico knew into a lie.

STILLED IN SUMMER, with trade thriving and vigorous, differed from the town that it had been in early winter. By contrast, the town in winter had been a dead place. Then the majority of the goods that had come across the river had been consigned to warehouses, awaiting the snow-packed roads of later winter to be hauled away.

Stilled in summer was a busy place, full of noisy bustle and shoving people. In it Elise Archer saw a shadow of what her father envisioned for the Archer Grant should he establish a trading station along the Barren River.

Brightly curtained stalls lined the crowded streets, the merchants within selling goods from both Hawk Haven and New Kelvin. Their customers wore the costumes of both nations, the bright robes of the New Kelvinese contrasting with the open-necked shirts and practical smocks worn by the residents of Hawk Haven.

Minstrels set up impromptu pitches wherever they could, often in association with a food vendor who profited from those who dallied to watch the performance. A juggler clad in long robes and face paint—though Elise would have sworn he was of Hawk Haven rather than New Kelvin—was pulling quite a fine crowd.

Viewing this colorful chaos, Elise felt a twinge of nostalgia for her family's land as she had left it, completely foolish since the change of which Baron Archer dreamed had not yet come, nor might it ever.

They were leading their horses now, all but Derian, who was driving their baggage wagon while Doc had charge of Derian's mare, Roanne.

The wagon had been the only way they could think to get Grateful Peace and Citrine into New Kelvin unseen. It would not have done for their party to set out with two comrades who vanished and were replaced by two simi- lar yet different ones on the other side of the river, so the man and the girl traveled rather uncomfortably secreted in an ingenious smuggling hold within the wagon's cargo. Duchess Kestrel's prestige promised to get them through customs with the most cursory of inspections.

The trip from the Norwood estate to Stilled had been stretched out over two days rather than exhaust the animals with one very long push. Jostled from all sides as they worked their way through the crowded streets, Elise wondered rather woefully if it might take them as long just to get to the Long Trail Winding, their chosen inn.

A scream and a shout jerked her from her musing. Grasping Cream Delight's bridle tightly, Elise turned to find Firekeeper, her blade pressed against the throat of a man easily two heads taller than herself, but frozen with fear nonetheless.

The surrounding crowd dropped back from them, leaving a wide border as if this was simply another entertainment. Indeed, on the fringes of the group Elise glimpsed an opportunistic sweets seller trotting over to offer her goods to the bystanders.

Firekeeper looked wild-eyed and a trace anxious. She hadn't wanted to come into the town by daylight—wanting to join Blind Seer, who would be staying outside and crossing the river on his own. Elise and Derian had insisted, warning Firekeeper that she must begin to accustom herself to large groups of people and that she must cross with them so that all the customs formalities could be handled appropriately.

Now Elise hoped that she wouldn't regret her insistence.

Edlin, nearest to Firekeeper, grabbed the reins of grey Patience, the horse that came closest to being Firekeeper's own.

"I say!" he said. "What's going on?"

"This," Firekeeper said, gesturing at the man she still held, "was taking things from the saddlebags. I not think you want."

"I say not!" Edlin replied. "Good going!"

Firekeeper's prisoner looked as if he was about to protest, but a glimpse of the wolf-woman's dark eyes as she glowered up at him and his resistance melted.

"I did!" he squealed. "But you can't let her kill me for taking a few little things? Not since you'll have them back."

"No?" Firekeeper asked with a soft growl.

Elise tossed Cream Delight's reins to Wendee and hurried back. Events were starting to get out of hand. Firekeeper had been taught not to kill humans—at least not without cause—but she had a wolf's territoriality. Stealing, therefore, might well seem just cause.

"What's the law on the matter, Lord Kestrel?" Elise said to Edlin.

"What?" Edlin said. "I say, let me think. Just a moment. Trade tables, not law in my head right now."

The thief, realizing who he had been foolish enough to rob, gave a low moan.

"We don't usually kill minor thieves," Edlin said at last. Then he brightened, remembering something else. "But the penalties for assaulting one of the ruling house can get rather nasty. Grandmother, you know, had to assert her prerogatives."

"Spare me, young lord!" the thief wailed. "Mercy to a poor starving man!"

Edlin, who wasn't nearly as stupid as he sounded, Elise knew, looked at the thief. The man might be thin, but there was a wiry strength to him.

"Good meat on you for all that," Edlin commented doubtfully.

"Really, lord. I am perishing hungry," the thief quavered. "I lost my job on the waterfront and haven't eaten for two days."

Edlin looked as if he might be softening, and Elise thought the mood of the crowd was shifting slightly in favor of clemency.

Firekeeper, however, was having none of this. She sniffed at the man's lips.

"Lies," she commented coolly. "Beef pasty. Spiced. Too much garlic. Ale, too."

The crowd murmured with one astonished voice. Edlin beamed.

"I say, really?" he asked.

When Firekeeper nodded, Edlin turned to the thief.

"My sister," Edlin clarified. "Adopted, what? Lady Blysse, you know."

The thief, who hadn't looked particularly happy before this, now looked completely terrified. Firekeeper was also getting increasingly edgy.

"His pockets?" she suggested.

"Right-oh," Edlin agreed.

Under the view of numerous witnesses, Edlin removed an choice array of small goods, most of which, to the thief's evident dismay, had come from Edlin's own saddlebags.

"My tortoiseshell comb!" Edlin exclaimed. "I say, Grandmother gave that to me last Lynx Moon, wouldn't want to lose it. My soap! My spare handkerchiefs. Agneta put my initials on them. She's not very good with her needle yet, but she means well."

The crowd's mood had shifted from tense to positively delighted. Edlin had assumed the air of a conjurer's straight man and Firekeeper had put away her knife, though she kept a firm grip on the thief's arm.

"Now, this is interesting," Edlin said, trying another of the thief's pockets. "This purse isn't mine, but I'd bet my left eyebrow it isn't yours either, what?"

The thief could hardly protest. The item in question was a rather dainty drawstring affair, embroidered with flowers. Its strap had been cut through. Edlin discovered a second and third purse on the thief before he finished, along with a small fortune in loose trade tokens.

"I say, you were having a good day," Edlin said. "Let this be a lesson to you, what? Don't get greedy. Now," he said, restoring his own property to his saddlebags, "I think you and these things should go to the local law. Anyone care to point the way?"

"I will, Lord Kestrel!" came the prompt response from several different throats.

With more judgment than Elise had expected, Edlin selected a steady-looking young fellow and thanked the others with a winning smile.

"We'll just trot along there," he said, turning to Elise. "Me and Lady Blysse and this fine fellow. Meet you at the Long Trail Winding, what?"

Elise agreed. Edlin dispersed the crowd with a wave of his hand.

"Off to your business, good people. Let this be a lesson to you as well. Watch your pockets in a crowd. Think of what an ass I'd have felt when I went to comb my hair this evening. Would have cursed my valet's forgetfulness for no good reason at all!"

Laughing, the crowd did part, a few of the children forming an informal escort for Edlin and Firekeeper. Elise noted to her amusement that several people were patting their pockets as they went on their way.

Once they had taken their rooms at the Long Trail Winding and reacquainted themselves with the establishment's friendly owner, Derian sneaked Citrine and Grateful Peace in via a back stair. He reported them comfortable in the room he was sharing with Edlin and Doc.

"Glad to stretch," Derian added. "I'll arrange for a bite for them later. Happily, young men have hollow legs, so no one will think it odd if Edlin and I eat more than one meal."

Soon after the rest had assembled in the public room for a glass of something cool, Edlin rejoined them.

"Firekeeper's off," he said matter-of-factly. "Stuck by me until we had the thief under lock and key. He's a known man hereabouts it seems, so there was no trouble about it. She stayed long enough to ask a few questions about when a man is a thief and when a bandit, then headed for the hills. Says she'll meet us at the docks come morning."

Wendee shook her head.

"More than she could take, poor girl."

"Nearly more than I could take," Derian commented. "I thought Firekeeper would cut the man's throat then and there. I'm not at all surprised she asked about bandits—not after last year. How'd you explain the difference, Lord Edlin?"

Edlin grinned reminiscently.

"Took some doing, what? Basically, though, I told her that a thief just stole, but a bandit threatened violence and when that happened, well . . ."

He blithely mimed a knife blade across his own throat.

"I suppose it will answer," Elise said, a trace uneasily.

Suddenly she was reminded of the journey ahead of them, a journey where the threat of bandits was all too real. Last winter she had been more innocent—or at least more ignorant. Now she lacked the comfort of illusion. She shivered, wishing that the road ahead didn't seem so long or so dangerous.

Across the table, she saw Doc was watching her, his own gaze mirroring her fears.

FIREKEEPER HAD ENJOYED her tangle with the thief in Stilled. It was about the only thing she did enjoy for the next several days.

The river crossing the next morning wasn't much fun. The wolf-woman had yet to grow accustomed to the feeling of a boat deck moving under her feet, but would have died rather than let anyone know how miserable she was.

She would have been happier if their group had immediately struck out from Gateway, but this, too, proved unexpectedly complicated. It seemed that Peace and Citrine could not simply emerge from their hiding places, put on their New Kelvinese clothing, and become the party's guides.

No, this, too, must be made unexpectedly complex. Derian tried to explain.

"It's like this, Firekeeper," he said, "people are going to be watching us when we get to Dragon's Breath, quite possibly before. It would look pretty strange if we suddenly had a guide—a guide no one remembered meeting before."

"Big place," Firekeeper protested. "Many people. Not everyone know everyone."

Derian sighed.

"Right," he said, "but wrong. We want people to have seen Peace—or his new self, Jalarios. Remember to call him that, right?"

Firekeeper nodded curtly.

"Peace says," Derian went on, breaking his own admonition with that inconsistency that Firekeeper found so maddening, "that no one will look too closely at him—not with the makeup he's wearing—because they'll know he has something to hide."

"So then they look to see what hiding is!" Firekeeper said.

"No," Derian said in a way that made Firekeeper positive that he was less certain than he seemed. "Peace says they'll think he's a rich man grown poor or something like that, that people don't like looking too closely at failure or defeat because they're not sure it won't rub off on them."

Firekeeper didn't understand this at all, but didn't bother saying so. She suspected it was another of those human traits that made no sense.

"So we wait," she replied, "and you play these games. I wonder what games Melina play while we wait?"

Derian didn't answer, but he looked very unhappy as he walked away.

However, neither the delay nor the discomfort of staying at a New Kelvinese inn were the worst things to happen over the next few days. The worst thing was when Elation announced she was leaving.

Firekeeper was moodily practicing archery with Edlin at a vacant range near the edge of town when Elation came slowly circling in from the direction of the river. A smaller hawk was with her, and before the pair had landed, Firekeeper was certain she knew Elation's companion.

Unstringing her bow, she strode over to meet the two hawks, leaving Edlin to gape wide-eyed and openmouthed after her.

"Go on shooting," she called to him. "I be back."

Elation shrieked greeting to Firekeeper, her cry cutting the humid stillness of the afternoon.

"This is Bee Biter," she went on. *"I am sure you remember him."*

Firekeeper nodded. She did indeed remember the brightly colored Royal kestrel, and she felt a surge of apprehension.

"I do," she said. *"What brings him from the lands west of the mountains?"*

"As before," Elation replied, *"he comes to tell me that the Mothers of our people have need of me."*

Firekeeper knew that among the wingéd folk the females were larger than the males and by extension more usually their rulers. A wave of dismay washed over her.

"Just like that?" she cried. *"You are leaving?"*

Elation beat her wings as if unsettled, but her reply was uncompromising.

"Bee Biter will stay with you," the peregrine said evasively, *"and he will contact those of our people who have gone ahead to Dragon's Breath. I am needed elsewhere."*

Firekeeper thought of the reasons the Mothers of the wingéd folk would call back their wandering daughter and liked none of them. Peregrines were large and agile, fine fighters, far better than a little bug-eater like a kestrel. Did that mean warriors were needed, that the situation with Ewen Brooks and his settlement had gone rotten?

Then again Elation was wise in the ways of humankind. Indeed, a year and a half ago she had understood more Pellish than had Firekeeper herself. Firekeeper suspected that the falcon still understood some subtleties that escaped her. Was Elation then needed to interpret and advise on human behavior?

Or were the wingéd folk—perhaps having heard Wind Whisper and Northwest's report—removing their support from Firekeeper's venture? Firekeeper tried to dismiss that thought, recalling that Bee Biter was to stay with her and help her make contact with the wingéd folk in Dragon's Breath, but she was all too aware how easy it would be for the kestrel to take wing one day and never return. Perhaps the promise of his assistance was more a sop to ease Elation's departure.

But the wolf-woman tried to let none of this flood of worry color her reply:

"Why must you go?" she asked as casually as she could.

Elation puffed out her feathers.

"There is no law that says I must justify my actions to little wolflings," she squawked angrily.

"None," Firekeeper agreed. *"I only wonder, friend to friend. Weasels might have climbed into your aerie or perhaps the humans have found the Brooding Cliffs?"*

"Nothing so terrible," Elation replied, softening slightly, but still she offered nothing more and Firekeeper must be content. She turned to Bee Biter.

"We thank you for coming with us," she said.

The brilliant blue and red hawk preened his satisfaction. Although much smaller than Elation, like all Royal Beasts he was larger than the Cousin kind. Indeed, Firekeeper thought sardonically, Bee Biter might be able to slay a robin rather than merely a sparrow or a bee.

She couldn't help but feel they were getting the worst part of the trade. Bee Biter might be able to make introductions, but there was no way that he would be the fighter Elation was, nor that he would be able to scout as far.

Blind Seer, who had been asleep in a shady copse of trees some distance away, came ambling up now.

"And what is the news from home?" he asked.

Bee Biter nervously twisted his head side to side.

"News?" he repeated shrilly.

"News," replied the wolf, gaping his jaws in a yawn so cavernous that the kestrel could have perched on his tongue.

"All is well," Bee Biter said, recovering somewhat. *"The humans are yet in their village, but something has stirred them like a hive of hornets."*

"King Tedric's men?" Firekeeper mused thoughtfully. *"I would not have thought they would have had time."*

Blind Seer sat and scratched hard behind one ear.

"Perhaps it is our own people who have done the stirring," he said.

Bee Biter said nothing more and with this the wolves had to be, if not content, at least satisfied.

THE MAGICAL LORE OF THE NEW KELVINESE, Melina felt certain, held the answer to what she desired. Even before the disaster of the artifacts she had begun reading text after text, trying to find secreted within the epics, songs, and stories some hint as to how magic had worked in the days of the Founders.

The Sodality of Songweavers grew accustomed to sending over their members to recite for her. The Illuminators grew resigned—if not enthusiastic—about lending her copies of their precious texts.

Melina found the attitude of the Illuminators particularly hard to bear. She thought that if they had their way not a single book or scroll would ever be read. The precious texts would only be copied, embellished, and admired as if they were mere paintings, not things of sense and meaning. Their libraries were maintained, Melina noted with disdain, not by librarians, but by custodians whose only interest was in assuring that insects and molds did nothing to damage their charges.

After the disaster of the artifacts, Melina redoubled her efforts to learn about how magic might once have worked. She even incorporated her research into her courtship of Toriovico. The Sodality of Dancers and Choreographers, in which Toriovico would have enrolled had not his brother's death elevated him to the place of heir apparent, was custodian of a great deal of lore about the past. Indeed, a sequence of dances contained as much knowledge as did any book or treatise.

Toriovico knew many of the dances by heart. Those dances he did not know well enough to perform for her himself, he was familiar with. He sincerely enjoyed escorting her to scheduled events and later sponsored performances so that she could see some obscure pieces that might otherwise be celebrated only under very special circumstances.

Eventually, Melina narrowed the focus of her research to those events that had occurred here in the New World during the days before the Burning Times had ended the easy practice of magic and sent the Founders back to the Old Country.

No longer did she settle for stories of what might or might not have been. She wanted absolute, provable evidence of miracles. There was no doubt that these had been commonly performed once. Buildings Melina had seen both here and in Hawk Haven held evidence enough. However, the hundred years and some that had passed since the Plague was enough time for stories to build up, distorting fact, shading it with fancy.

She visited Urnacia, the Sand Melter, where some of New Kelvin's finest glass was made, and convinced herself that though there was tremendous art and craft beyond the knowledge of the simple glassblowers of Hawk

Haven, there was no magic in the crafting of even the most beautifully hued glass.

Another trip to the steaming mountains north and west of Dragon's Breath convinced her similarly that there was no magic in sericulture. The Sericulturalists did wonders in keeping their delicate charges alive, in growing the specialized plants needed for them to thrive, and in collecting the silk thread, but unless in the original creation of the silkworm long ago, here again there was no magic.

Other visits, mostly to places within a few days' journey of Dragon's Breath—for she would not risk that her hold on the government might have opportunity to weaken—proved to Melina beyond a doubt that much of what the residents of Hawk Haven took for magic was merely specialized art and craft.

These disappointments did not weaken Melina's resolve any more than a mother who knows her child must be somewhere within the house stops looking simply because the first few rooms are empty. In her mental floor plan she simply closed a few doors and moved on. In this way, at last, Melina focused upon the tale of the Star Wizard and the Dragon of Despair.

This time, to her excitement and even to her amazement, research did not eliminate the legend from consideration. Instead it led her more and more deeply toward something that looked rather like truth.

MELINA'S RESEARCH into the tale of the Star Wizard and the Dragon of Despair fell into two separate but connected channels. One was hunting for the places mentioned with such exasperating obliqueness in the story. The other was searching for the spell by which the Star Wizard had bound the dragon and by which, so the tales said, it could be again set free.

True, all the tales said that the holds that bound the dragon could not be released without terrible cost, but Melina was not afraid of cost. Hadn't she already given up her homeland and proximity to her children? Hadn't she given up property and the respect of her brothers? Hadn't she accepted that she was spoken of in the same breath as her brother Newell—and she as the worse of the two, though Newell had sought to murder King Tedric?

Cost frightened Melina little enough, and if she succeeded in this venture she would take back much of what had been stolen from her. She would reclaim her obedient children and punish that traitorous bitch Sapphire. She would have property enough—kingdoms' worth.

As for slander on her name, none would dare speak of Melina with other than perfect respect. The New Kelvinese would give her honors easily, for their awe of magical power was universal. The Hawk Havenese would struggle, but fear was a powerful force, as Melina had learned in educating her children. There would come a time when no one spoke of Melina with anything but wonder, awe, and respect.

She would be like her ancestress, Zorana Shield, now called the Great, but where Zorana had been merely the queen of one small, constantly embattled kingdom, Melina planned to rule all this region. The New Kelvinese had waited too long for their Founders. It was time they acquired the ability to go looking for their absent landlords—and to demand an accounting.

The first step in that journey was solidifying the region and its resources behind one leader. Realistically, New Kelvin was a small kingdom. It needed harbors and fleets, land more fertile than its own rocky soil to support such an effort.

To the north New Kelvin was bordered by mountains, inhabited, as far as Melina knew, by nothing but a few isolated communities. To the west were the Death Touch Mountains, known as the Iron Mountains in Melina's natal land. There was nothing but wilderness in those western lands, and although someday the raw resources of that wilderness might prove useful, for now the west could be ignored.

South and east were where Melina looked to find what she desired. In the south lay Hawk Haven and beyond it its new ally, Bright Bay. Hawk Haven would provide a source for rich agricultural resources as well as laborers and skilled crafters. Bright Bay would serve as a buffer against potentially aggressive neighbors farther south. Its navy would be sent to conquer the Isles and bring them back under mainland control.

For her exploratory navy, Melina planned to go into Waterland. Conquest there would be interesting, for the only thing that the Waterlanders valued—as far as Melina could tell—was money. She had several plans she might employ in her conquest, one of which simply involved using the hoarded treasury of New Kelvin—backed by sufficient force of arms—to buy herself into the place of the Supreme Affluent. There might be laws forbidding such, but Melina planned to find that which would make laws a formality—at least where she was concerned.

Such were the dreams and visions that kept Melina at her research long after Toriovico had slipped into sated slumber, that kept her at them when even Apheros the Dragon Speaker relaxed and took time for some light entertainment. Such were the researches that led her at last to the tunnels beneath Thendulla Lypella, hunting for where the Dragon of Despair was imprisoned.

XV

FOUR TIMES A MOON PHASE the Healed One met with the Dragon
Speaker in a very private meeting. Ideally these meetings should occur
at neat, astronomically defined times, but the responsibilities of being
joint heads of government meant that the current Dragon Speaker and
Healed One met when convenient, usually on a date as close as possible to that which had been the appointed.

Toriovico knew this casualness regarding date had not always been the
case. During the reign of the second Healed One the Stargazers had gained
great prominence by dictating the precise hour at which the moon was full
or at her first quarter or whatever—and dictating when meetings should be
held thereby.

The Stargazers had abused their power, though, often calling for meet-
ings at odd hours of the night, or hauling the Dragon Speaker from other
duties at the whim of the heavens. When the insanity of the third Healed
One had meant that meetings were held when possible rather than when the
Stargazers ordained, and when no great catastrophe had befallen New
Kelvin, then the Stargazers had fallen from glory.

They never had recovered.

Or rather, Toriovico thought, observing who Apheros had admitted at
the end of today's briefing, *they have never recovered until today.*

The man and woman Apheros had begged permission to admit so that
they might advise on an order of new business were the two most prominent
Stargazers in the kingdom: Dimiria and Xarxius.

Technically, Dimiria was merely one of the three Primes elected from within her sodality. In reality, she was the driving force within her triad. It was widely—if quietly—said that the other two did not dare vote contrary to her wishes.

For eighty years the stars had looked down upon Dimiria and the brave jested that for at least seventy-five of those years she had been ordering them about their business.

Dimiria wore her eighty years neither well nor with any attempt to disguise what they had done to her. When her hair had thinned, she had adopted a hooded robe rather than a wig or weaving hair in to thicken her queue.

When the majority of her teeth had fallen out, Dimiria had ordered the remainder pulled. The dentures she now wore were as much statement of identity as her tattoos or the patterns of her face paint. Each ivory tooth was incised with an astrological symbol from her personal horoscope. As if this wasn't enough to draw attention, the set had an idiosyncratic fit so that Dimiria's speech was underlaid with a certain hollowness.

Superficially, Xarxius could not be more different from his colleague. Indeed, although his training had been among the Stargazers, for the last decade or so he had been a member of Apheros's Dragon's Three—appointed as the Dragon's Claw, whose specialty was interaction with foreign peoples.

Xarxius reminded most people of a hound dog, both because of his general friendliness and because of the bags under his eyes. People tended to get lost in his amiable personality—a mistake that Toriovico, who was himself often misjudged, did not make.

Xarxius had become interested in foreigners and their customs during a tour in Waterland as a member of the New Kelvinese embassy. This, because of the Waterlanders' superstitious regard for the stars, always included several promising Stargazers.

Apheros said that it was as an expert on Waterland and an expert on trade, rather than as a Stargazer, that Xarxius had been asked to attend today's meeting. Still, Toriovico did not forget Xarxius's training and his probable bias.

After the new arrivals had supplicated themselves before their Healed One and offered less humble but equally formal greetings to the Dragon Speaker, Apheros moved to the business that had brought them together.

"The most important matter of new business is a proposal from certain Waterland business interests that will increase trade between our countries. In short, these interests wish an exclusive contract to handle foreign sales of certain types of glassware, silk, and pharmaceutical products."

Toriovico raised an eyebrow.

"And in return?" he asked. "What do we get?"

Apheros went on as placidly as if he had not just presented a proposal that would put the majority of New Kelvin's foreign trade—and profit—into another country's hands.

"In return the Waterland interests have offered to reduce the prices we will pay for slaves, for goods of their own manufacture, and . . ." The Dragon Speaker cleared his throat. "And to give into our hands a certain number of artifacts dating from before the Burning Times—artifacts that hold great promise of being magical."

No one made a sound, so Toriovico was certain that the other two had been briefed in advance. Certainly Dimiria would not have kept silent otherwise. He glanced at her now and noticed an odd vacancy about her expression.

"Dimiria," he said, "what do you think about this offer?"

"It is very generous," the Stargazer said immediately. "I have examined a few of the artifacts in question, both some years ago when I served as part of our embassy in Waterland and more recently when I traveled there as an honored guest for their major planting festival. They seem to hold potential, at least as much potential as did the three artifacts that were in our possession last winter."

Silence fell again as everyone remembered those events and their disastrous conclusion.

"Moreover," Dimiria continued, "it has been hinted to me by several of my Waterland contacts that these are not the only advantages we could gain through this trade agreement. One of the Opulences with whom we would be doing business has told me that he is willing to lease to us—for a token fee—a small harbor and the surrounding land."

This was an offer nearly as stunning as the one to supply New Kelvin with potentially magical artifacts. One of New Kelvin's great shortcomings was that it lacked an ocean port. This would answer that need, even if the New Kelvinese would be forced to travel a great distance to use the promised harbor.

Toriovico could not believe what he was hearing.

"How certain was that 'hint'?" he asked.

"Quite," Dimiria said blandly. "The merchant in question is among the top-ranking members of the Waterland oligarchy. I think he believes that securing an exclusive trade contract with our country would be sufficient to raise him to the Supreme Affluent."

The Supreme Affluent was a post similar to that of the Dragon Speaker, the first among a larger ruling body. Unlike the Dragon Speaker, however, the Supreme Affluent held the post by merit of wealth alone, wealth calculated and assessed by a complicated formula that only the Waterlanders themselves understood.

Internally, Toriovico shook himself. Something was very odd about all of this. This type of meeting was a dance he knew quite well, but something was off in the cadence of the steps.

He turned to Xarxius. The Dragon's Claw had been unusually quiet during the presentation—unusually not because he was a particularly talkative man, but because this was his area of expertise and he was permitting others to present the proposal. Moreover, although Apheros had included Xarxius in the meeting, he had not once asked him to speak. Indeed, now that Toriovico had been given an opportunity to observe them, it seemed to him that all was not well between the Speaker and his Claw.

"What do you think, Xarxius? You've been remarkably quiet."

Toriovico regretted the last phrase as soon as he said it. He didn't want to draw attention to the oddness he sensed until he had a chance to figure out its source.

Xarxius, however, appeared to notice nothing. He smiled apologetically in response to the Healed One's rebuke.

"The Dragon Speaker and Prime Dimiria have made such an excellent presentation," Xarxius said, "that I had felt my words unneeded. However, may I suggest that we proceed with some caution? A Waterlander thinks first of his own profit, then of others."

The phrase was such a commonplace as to nearly be proverbial. Despite this, both Dimiria and Apheros glared at Xarxius as if he had suggested refusing the proposal out of hand.

This is more the dance I know, Toriovico thought. *There should be more debate, more flow of ideas. Why are both Dimiria and Apheros so in favor of making this deal? Is it the lure of the artifacts? Before the others were stolen we were close to unraveling their secrets. Melina's fresh point of view was a great help.*

As always when Toriovico thought of his newlywed wife he felt a mingling of wonder and awe, a rosy haze that made him smile warmly—rather like an idiot, he feared.

Toriovico shook the feeling from him, aware that he had fallen into a completely inappropriate daze. He succeeded in pulling himself into the present, though the warm feeling lingered caressingly at the back of his mind.

Toriovico looked sharply at his three advisors, but none of them looked as if they had noticed his lapse. Apheros and Dimiria still glowered angrily at the Dragon's Claw, while Xarxius waited patiently for the Healed One's comment.

"Certainly Xarxius has a point," Toriovico said with a slight effort. "We do not wish to make such a monumental decision in haste. For example, we must make certain the promised artifacts are indeed from the days before the Burning Times, not manufactured 'antiques.' I suggest that the Sodality of Artificers could give us assistance there."

Dimiria didn't look pleased at Toriovico's suggestion. After all, she had already offered her opinion as to the authenticity of at least some of the artifacts, but, oddly, she spared them her acid comments.

It's as if Dimiria is waiting for something, Toriovico thought. *A cue? Are she and Apheros working on this together? Are the Waterlanders paying them some bribe? Has Xarxius refused to be bribed and so finds himself on the opposite side from his usual ally?*

Apheros's expression showed that he also was less than pleased with Toriovico's caution. His reaction confirmed the Healed One's evolving theory that the Waterlanders must have bribed the Dragon Speaker.

Normally, Apheros was the representative type of the isolationist New Kelvinese, often refusing to meet even prominent ambassadors. One reason that Xarxius was so valuable to Apheros was that he spared the Dragon Speaker such distasteful inconveniences.

Had this been a more usual quarter-moon meeting, Toriovico would have been inclined to let himself be persuaded by the mere sign of the Dragon Speaker's displeasure. This, however, had not been a normal meeting, nor was this routine business. As Torio saw it, it amounted to signing away a good portion of New Kelvin's trade income in return for these nebulous artifacts and the unseen harbor—and for preferential trade options on goods they could do without.

"No decision will be made at this time," the Healed One stated firmly. "That is my final judgment."

At his words, Dimiria and Apheros rose from their seats almost as one and began their part of the departure ritual. Xarxius moved a bit more slowly. When the other two marched from the room, their disappointment evident despite their formal and ceremonial farewells, the Dragon's Claw lingered.

"A good decision," Xarxius said softly, "and thank you for your hospitality."

"Oh?"

Toriovico was puzzled.

"Yes, Apheros didn't really want me to attend, you see." The hound dog face gave a wry smile. "I pointed out to him that you were certain to want my advice on such an important matter of trade. Your questions, as well as your support of my opinion, justified my insistence."

Xarxius bowed himself from the room before Toriovico had an opportunity to ask more. That didn't stop the Healed One from wondering. Usually, he was content to leave governing to the Dragon Speaker and to restrict himself to the secret duties of the Healed One. After today's meeting, however, Toriovico thought he had better pay more attention to less esoteric matters for a time.

After all, last winter he had overlooked the machinations that had brought both Lady Melina and three magical artifacts into New Kelvin. He smiled as he considered how those events had changed his life. It wouldn't do to miss anything that had the potential to transform it once more.

DESPITE DERIAN'S CONCERNS that Peace—or Jalarios, as he must remember to think of the Illuminator—and his young "son" would be immediately discovered, the deception survived their stay in the Gateway to Enchantment. Derian was somewhat surprised that Peace insisted that he and Citrine remain in character once the group had left Gateway and the roads seemed empty of any travelers but themselves.

"I was the Dragon's Eye," Peace reminded them when Elise expressed the discomfort they all felt at treating the other two as servants. "That meant I learned to watch people, to see what they gave away when they thought themselves unobserved. I have learned more from a fist clenched in anger by a man who believed his action hidden within the cuff of his sleeve than from any smiling face and sweet words."

Doc looked up from sorting through the additional medicinal herbs and ointments he'd purchased in Gateway.

"How'd you manage to see it if the man's fist was hidden within his sleeve?"

"Simple, Doctor," Peace replied. "You of all men know how the muscles and sinews are connected. I saw the sinews along the man's neck tighten slightly on one side and wondered why. Then I saw that his hand was withdrawn and guessed the rest."

"Clever," Doc said with a grin. "I guess much isn't hidden from you."

Peace only smiled, too polite to agree.

Derian, however, thought that Doc's observation was probably only the truth and he wished that he felt happier about it.

For this trip, Peace had chosen a different route than the one they had taken to Dragon's Breath the first time. It was a longer route, but then, as Peace pointed out, speed was not the important thing—at least not at this point.

"King Tedric wishes you to gather information," he reminded them. "You will not learn much from farmers in the high country. Better to travel the more usual trade routes, stopping at the public houses, pausing to buy a bit of fabric or glassware.

"Besides, we are traveling in summer with good horses to pull the wagons. In the winter you would be lucky to have light for a third of the day on the road. In summer we can travel for half the day or even longer."

Derian agreed. As Peace had noted, they were well prepared to follow this course. The wagon gave them room to pack away their purchases. In the high country, they would have had to abandon the wagon completely—an unrealistic decision for those who were coming to trade.

Moreover, Citrine could ride in the wagon when she grew tired of walking or of riding one of the spare horses. They'd felt they could bring a few extra mounts from Hawk Haven without arousing comment, but a pony comfortable for one her size would have been too unlikely.

In this fashion, they made their slow but deliberate way through the more settled portions of New Kelvin. In some ways what they saw was not unlike what they knew in Hawk Haven. Many of the same crops grew in the fields, though the ones that throve in the warmer, wetter reaches did not. The birds and animals were similar, too, though Derian noted that the horses tended toward stockiness and strength rather than grace and elegance, and Edlin commented that the dogs were more often bred for herding than for the chase.

The people, though, they were different. It was hard to tell how many of those differences were bred in the bone, for the long robes—worn even by the field-workers, though these kilted them up—and the omnipresent facial decorations obscured much.

From what Derian could see the New Kelvinese tended toward leaner, finer builds. Not that they were fragile or frail—far from it—but it was the strength of the willow rather than the oak. And who could tell fair or dark when hair and skin alike was dyed and painted in hues that would make a field of spring flowers envious?

Wherever the people touched their land, the land was different again. The houses—even of the poor—wore gaudy hues. The poor were limited to adorning doorways or windows, but the wealthier washed their entire homes in color. A few towns had ordinances that coordinated shades and tones, but many followed no law but the whims of individual owners.

And the architectural styles differed as well. Much of what was built in Hawk Haven—and in her sister Bright Bay as well—was built for use first with considerations of art second. In New Kelvin art often won over practicality, so Derian found himself stabling horses in miniature palaces delightful to look upon, but where the hay was stored in some inconvenient outbuilding since a loft would have distorted the dreamer's lines.

The inns they stayed in were the same, each rivaling the other to invoke some old story or legend, even if it meant that the rooms had ceilings that canted at odd angles or the dining area was halfway across the structure from the kitchen.

Citrine's favorite was an inn built in the shape of a fat, red dragon. The kitchens were positioned so that the smoke from their fires eddied out the dragon's nostrils.

The visitors were told that the Red Dragon Inn was bitter cold in winter, for the landlord disliked lighting fires elsewhere lest the smoke from other chimneys ruin his effect. His devotion to his art was why they were welcomed to stay at such a fabulous place at all, for even outlander money was welcome at a place that needed to do much business in summer to survive winter.

As their road took them farther inland, angling to intersect the long turnpike that ran along the base of the Sword of Kelvin Mountains, they found fewer inns that welcomed outlanders. Derian thought this shortsighted of the innkeepers, since Dragon's Breath was the capital city and any foreigners who wished to do business with the rulers of the land must come there.

However, the xenophobia of the New Kelvinese was such that most foreigner traders chose to come no farther than Zodara in the east or the Gateway to Enchantment in the west. Since the New Kelvinese desired to keep secret the making of silk and the cultivating of the medicinal plants that were their most valuable exports, they were willing to bear the expense and trouble of hauling their goods to the border. Therefore, the inland New Kelvin-ese, even those along the roads, could maintain their splendid isolation and feel that it was at very little cost to themselves.

Grateful Peace nearly glowed with joy to be in his homeland once more, and for the first time in a long while Derian contemplated the sacrifice the man had made in the hope of improving his land's future prospects. As Jalarios, Peace could talk unguardedly about the history of a certain region or press them to try a certain dish or liquor. No one thought it at all odd that a guide should turn loquacious for his employers' benefit and Peace took full advantage of this.

Nor did any of the Hawk Havenese particularly mind. Although they were held to a wagon's pace, the group traveled on as long as light and weather would permit. Peace's stories livened the hours of plodding travel that—even with marvels of architecture and dress to liven the view—would have grown monotonous.

Peace told them tales of the White Sorcerers of the Eversnow Mountains who had performed miracles in the days of the Founders, of the Star Wizard, and of the First Healed One's tragic love for a maiden made from moon dust and ice crystals. Many of Peace's tales went back to the Old World. New Kelvin's Founders had not been the same as those of Hawk Haven and while some of the stories had a similar tone, being heavily freighted with won-drous enchantments and marvelous beasts, they differed, too.

Derian could not help but note that whereas the tales he had heard as a child were cautionary in nature, Peace's made one want to reach out and embrace magic. No wonder the New Kelvinese had been willing to risk an international incident to lay their hands on magical artifacts.

He wondered if Melina, coming to New Kelvin as a girl right about Damita's age and similarly restless, had heard some of the same stories and if they had awakened in her a hunger for forbidden magic.

Could a story change a life?

MELINA MIGHT HAVE BEEN AMBITIOUS, but she was not such a fool as to believe that she could conquer an entire kingdom single-handedly—not even with the assistance of those members of the government who were conditioned to follow whatever course of action she might suggest.

She had slaves, far more than either Toriovico or Apheros realized, for starting with the winter moons of her arrival she had begun her purchasing. Later, when she became Consolor, she did her buying through private agents. The wife of the Healed One was given gifts by almost anyone who wanted the ruler's favor, so she wasn't hurting for funds.

In the course of her researches into New Kelvin's history and lore Melina learned there were caverns beneath Thendulla Lypella. Almost as soon as she had wed Toriovico, she found reasons to explore beneath the city, following ancient maps to dusty, unused tunnels that led to complexes abandoned and forgotten since the Burning Times. Here her purchases could be imprisoned, kept tame by promises of eventual liberty and by living conditions more comfortable than they could expect elsewhere.

However, even the most reliable slaves needed to be supervised and directed. For this Melina needed a few agents who were free and who could be convinced to join their cause to her own. From her own experience of politics within Hawk Haven, Melina knew that the best lever in such cases was some private cause or vendetta. Hadn't her own brother Newell been driven to astonishing extremes by the simple flaw in his personal logic that told him that since he had been an honorary prince he should be an anointed king?

New Kelvinese politics were at least as complex and vigorous as those of Hawk Haven, but Melina hesitated to choose her tools from among one of the political groups anxious to replace the current government. She liked Apheros's government—indeed had gone to great lengths to secure its actions so they favored herself. Therefore she did not need some ambitious would-be Dragon Speaker for her ally. Nor did she want a foreigner, for there were times she needed counsel from someone who understood the intricacies of New Kelvin from the gut rather than from study.

But Melina did not despair. She put out feelers through the spies she had borrowed from the Healed One's network, even dropped a few very discreet hints. Therefore, she was alert to opportunity when Idalia, mother of Kistlio, sister of Grateful Peace, begged audience with the Consolor of the Healed One.

Ostensibly, Idalia was seeking a pension to compensate for the financial loss accrued on the death of her son, but the fact that she came to Melina directly rather than going through the usual channels whispered to the Consolor that here was someone who sought a private compensation, something more than mere money or advantage.

Idalia was elegantly formal and fair like her brother. She rather resembled him, Melina thought, but that was hardly remarkable. What made Idalia remarkable was the fierce hatred that burned in her eyes, a hatred so intense that her eyes seemed to lack color or dimension, serving only as hooded caverns to shelter their fire.

At first Melina thought that hatred was directed toward herself. After all, Kistlio had been her clerk, her devoted admirer. He had met his death while defending his mistress from what he perceived as an attack. There was good reason for his mother to blame Melina for her loss.

However, even after Melina had said all the right things and had even employed a touch of her ability to suggest to Idalia that she should accept Melina's version of events, the inner burning in the other woman's gaze did not diminish.

Clutching in one hand the silken pouch of coins that Melina had given her, Idalia refused to accept the Consolor's gentle hints that she should depart. Instead she blurted out,

"Kistlio loved you. He told me he did. I don't blame you for my son's death. I think Kistlio would have committed suicide if you had been slain through his inaction."

Melina nodded gentle understanding she did not feel. In truth she was deeply puzzled, but in Idalia's words she sensed an intensity that prompted her to stay the hand that had been about to rise in order to ring for a guard.

"My son," Idalia continued impassioned, "was betrayed not by you, Consolor, but by my brother Grateful Peace. Had Grateful Peace not conducted those thieves into the Granite Tower then there would have been no monster present to slay my son. The wolf's fangs may have killed my boy, but I don't even blame the wolf—that dumb beast may have been as innocent as a bow hanging on a wall is innocent until someone takes it down and strings it. I tell you, I blame my brother. Peace was the traitor who carried the bow. His was the hand that loosed the arrow that slew my son."

Feigning a maternal grief she did not feel, Melina curled an arm around Idalia. She soothed the other woman into a chair, sent Tipi for spiced wine. Then through gentle questions and skillful probing she learned the entire twisted story of Idalia's resentment of her younger brother's advancement. Idalia told how she had been forced to take charity from her brother—charity that had led to Kistlio's death.

Immediately, Melina recognized that the true source of Idalia's rage at her brother was the woman's own guilt. Had Idalia and her husband provided better training and opportunities for Kistlio's advancement the boy would never have taken his uncle's offer of patronage. Without that patronage, he never would have been in a position to be killed.

Unable to face her own complicity, Idalia had displaced her personal guilt, transforming it into rage at Grateful Peace, a rage all the more ferocious because it was so utterly unreasonable—and because the focus of her rage was out of reach, unable to answer for himself and so all the more easily transformed into a monster.

Melina could have shared her insights with Idalia, but what would have been the use? Idalia might not have believed her, and even if Idalia had she might have been overwhelmed to the point of suicide if she accepted her own role in her son's death. Better to preserve the woman's life and through skillful manipulation of the impulses that were already there turn her into Melina's faithful sycophant.

For this reason Melina mentioned the rumor that Grateful Peace had escaped with his life and was now dwelling in luxury just over the border in Hawk Haven. Idalia had heard some hints of this, news brought to her by well-meaning friends who had thought the information would be a comfort. Hearing confirmation that Peace lived and even thrived sealed Idalia to Melina's cause, especially when Melina offered her the means to be on hand if and when Grateful Peace returned.

"Be my secret hand, even as your brother was once the Dragon's Speaker's watchful Eye," Melina said. "I am certain his sister shares his talents for organization and alertness."

"I do, Consolor," Idalia responded eagerly. "Indeed, I am his better at organization, for Peace was the spoiled youngest while as one of the elder children my place was never easy."

"Very good," Melina said, though part of her resented the implication that younger children were spoiled. Surely she hadn't been! Duchess Pola had been hard on her daughter. After rearing four sons Pola had lost the softer touch.

"I have a husband," Idalia said eagerly, "and several grown children who could assist me. Will you have me move into Thendulla Lypella?"

"To someplace more interesting than that," Melina answered teasingly.

She wished to check Idalia's story before confiding more. Happily, given Idalia's brother's prominence, the information should be near at hand. For now Melina urged caution.

"Say nothing of this to anyone," Melina went on, "not even to your husband or other family members. I shall summon you when a place is made ready."

"My silence," Idalia vowed, never realizing how true were her words, "is your wish."

Melina's research into Idalia's history revealed that the other woman had a browbeaten husband and several adult children who were kept snugly under her thumb. Moreover, her resentment of her brother was both well known and long-standing, ruling out that Idalia might have put on the guise of resentment for some reason of her own.

Their pact was made and Melina sealed it with only the lightest touch of her power, for she needed Idalia clear-thinking and capable of initiative. In any case, there was no need to bind Idalia other than by offering trust and feeding her obsessions.

Grateful Peace, Melina thought, *may have forged the weapon best used against him.*

Once Melina was sure of Idalia, she told her of the hidden magical force beneath Thendulla Lypella and relocated the woman and her family to a comfortable residence set up in a large cavern. To those who expressed curiosity, it was given out that Idalia and her immediate family had accepted a compassionate relocation to a town in the far northwestern edge of New Kelvin. However, no one—not even Idalia's own siblings—seemed to much regret the family's going.

Indeed, though moons had waxed and waned since their departure no one sought to take advantage of spring moving into summer to make a friendly visit to Idalia's family, and the contingency plans made for just such a purpose moldered.

With her subterranean coordinator in place and proving herself more and more reliable as time passed, Melina could concentrate on other matters. As her research progressed she gave Idalia hints as to what landmarks might be significant and had her keep the slaves busy by organizing searches. However, never did Melina tell her ally precisely what she sought.

After all, it wouldn't do to risk frightening Idalia away.

XVI

IN HIS PRIVATE STUDIO, Toriovico was dancing. He danced very
well. Before his elevation to Healed One he had been training to
become a member of the Sodality of Dancers and Choreographers. It
had been a matter of pride for him to be superb at his chosen occupation so that no one would doubt his eventual elevation from apprentice
to master and, maybe, someday to thaumaturge.

If he hadn't felt such a fierce desire to prove himself, Toriovico could have
sought out the Herbalists or the Divinators. Their knowledge was hard to
test except by other experts. Even the Artificers and the Smiths could conceal an unskilled apprentice within their ranks, though such an apprentice
would never rise to great prominence. So, if the matter was pushed, could
most of the other sodalities.

Dancing, however, was something that even the meanest eye could assess,
though it might take an expert to judge. Dancing never fully came to life
without someone to observe the dance.

From his earliest days toddling around after his sisters Toriovico had
desired to possess at least one thing that no one could say he owed to his
birth. Dancing became that thing.

If anything, Toriovico's passion for dancing grew after he became the
Healed One. Some of his subjects whispered that he was feeling his way to
the heart of the ancient rituals. Toriovico could have told them that there
were no ancient rituals—at least no more ancient than a few centuries old.

For Toriovico knew what no one but the Healed One ever knew—that the
lore of the Healed One and indeed everything upon which New Kelvinese

culture was founded was lies. Toriovico often meditated upon this as he danced, his knowledge the undercurrent that made even the most joyful dance subtly sorrowful when he was at its heart.

As he leapt and spun Toriovico remembered the day his father had called for his heir to attend upon his deathbed. Past became present, present past, what had been became more real than the cool marble tiles beneath his feet or the thudding of his heart beneath his breastbone.

"WE ARE ALONE, son?" Father asked.

Toriovico looked about, even darted to check behind the curtains hung upon the wall. As always, he felt very young in the old man's presence, far younger than his twenty-two years. When he was sure, he returned to Father's side.

"We are alone," he answered. "Absolutely."

"Even so . . ."

Father coughed, cleared his throat, accepted a swallow of water from a cut-crystal goblet, then began again.

"Even so, it is good that illness has so thinned my voice. None but you could hear me, even if they stood directly outside the window."

Toriovico nodded.

"I am sorry to leave you, Torio," Father continued. "You have learned many of the duties of the Healed One, yet there is much more for you to learn. Your tutors will continue to work with you. You have a gift for ceremony and I think will learn quickly."

"Thank you, Father."

The dying man pulled himself up in the bed, propping himself on the pillow. With one hand he touched the tumor that was sucking away his life.

"Heed me, Toriovico," Father said, and in that moment he was the Healed One and not Toriovico's much loved if somewhat distant father, "and swear unto me that you will never repeat what I tell you, not to your dearest friend, sweetest lover, or most trusted confidant. Swear!"

"I swear on the sacred name of the First Healed One!" Toriovico said, twisting his fingers through the appropriate, complicated gesture.

"Even as I did," Father said, and his expression was both wry and sad. "Now I shall reveal unto you the truth. That first Healed One was a liar and a conniver. Our heritage is as false as the painted mountains on a stage set."

"What!"

Even as Toriovico uttered his startled exclamation, he glanced at the swelling just visible through the light blankets. Had the tumor driven his father mad?

Father saw his son's expression and shook his head.

"No, Torio, it is not the illness making me talk this way. You can find the same information written down in a locked and sealed book—a book that will not open for you until you are confirmed as Healed One, a book whose pages will be blank for any but you. Ironically, that book may be the only true magical artifact in all of New Kelvin. It began its life as the First Healed One's book of spells, but he blotted out the spells and employed it for this purpose instead.

"My last duty as Healed One is to tell you first what you will find there so the shock will not be too great. There have been newly anointed Healed Ones who have learned the truth only from the book. In at least one case the knowledge drove the reader insane."

Toriovico knew the list of past Healed Ones and thought he knew to whom his father referred. Happily, or unhappily, the Third Healed One had not died until several years after his mind broke. There had been no provision—even within the complexities of the New Kelvinese code of protocol—for replacing him. Much knowledge had been lost before the Third Healed One had died in an attempt to take flight from one of the highest towers of Thendulla Lypella.

Toriovico wanted to ask questions, but Father was clearly tired and in pain. With his dancer's eye for the body and its pulses, Torio saw that this conversation was costing the old man a significant segment of his remaining life.

"Tell on, Father," Toriovico said, squaring his shoulders and trying hard to look braver than he felt. "I'm listening."

"It begins with the Burning Death, Torio. You've heard the stories, of course."

"A terrible plague," Toriovico said, saving the old man's breath. "No one was safe from its touch, but some scholars say that it burned more heatedly in those who possessed skill or talent in the magical arts."

"That is why," Toriovico volunteered, eager suddenly to show his father that the position of Healed One would be filled by one who had attended to his lore, "the Founders left. They sought to escape the plague so that their knowledge and power would not be lost to us. Before they left, they set a seal against magic over the land so that the Burning Death would find nothing upon which to feed.

"Of course," Toriovico went on somberly, "the Founders never returned, so the plague may have been worse in the Old Country. Neither our Founders, nor any of their kin, nor any of the Founders of any of the colonies have ever returned, and we, who have the desire to seek them out, lack the harbors we would need for a fleet.

"The First Healed One was too ill to depart with his kin," Toriovico continued in response to his father's encouraging nod, "so ill that his death was watched for by those who attended him, dreading the event, for when he breathed his last, so would the magical arts vanish."

"But he didn't die," Father prompted.

"No," Toriovico said, slightly puzzled that his father wanted him to continue with a tale as familiar to all New Kelvinese as their own names. "He didn't. He recovered, though he remained weak and fragile. Still, he was not too weak to father a son—the son who is our own direct ancestor. Moreover, he dictated the tomes of lore that we rely upon to this day. He established the thirteen sodalities, designed the arrangement of our current government, and instigated many of our most valuable rituals and customs."

"And why did the First Healed One do this?" Father asked.

"Because he wished us to remain faithful to the magical arts," Toriovico replied, astonished. This was something the smallest child knew. "Even in the earliest years of the Burning Death reports reached our land about how our neighbors were reacting to the departure of their own founders. We heard how those books and artifacts that had not been taken by their owners were being wantonly destroyed. We heard how surviving practitioners of the sorcerous arts were being slain.

"The First Healed One wanted us to possess an advantage when his associates returned from the Old Country. He felt that if we trained and practiced the forms of magic, we would be readier to use them. Therefore, we would have the advantage over our neighbors and become a great empire."

Father sighed and shifted uncomfortably in his bed. Again Toriovico held the goblet for him, wiping away the little drops that dribbled unnoticed down the sick man's chin. When he had swallowed enough, Father said:

"That was a good account, Toriovico, free of much of the embroidery and fancy that has sprung up in the last centuries. However, much of it is as false as a Waterlander's word."

Prepared as he was for this, Toriovico still felt a chill. Protest would be foolish—Father would not waste his dying breaths on a lie.

"The First Healed One, according to his own accounts, which you will be able to read when I am dead," said the Healed One with brutal bluntness, "was a sorcerer of the lowest rank, not a great power as he has been represented since. Doubtless this is why he survived the Burning Death. The disease did, however, maim him as history has it and what talent remained to him was quite small.

"The Healed One," and Toriovico knew his father now spoke of this long-ago sorcerer, not himself, "despite some of the stories about him, was a practical man. He firmly believed that his associates would return, probably in no more than a decade. He saw the chaos that was springing up around our borders and resolved that he would preserve our kingdom intact. This meant giving the survivors a reason to bind together.

"Magic had always been important in New Kelvin, more so than in many of our neighbors' lands, for the soil here is poor, though the mining is good. In all the colonies, magic was used to support the rulers—even as armies and navies are used today—but in New Kelvin, magic was even more important. The Founders were all mages, their government was structured around magic. Therefore, the common folk were conditioned to obey, honor, and respect the magical arts."

Toriovico marveled how his father seemed to grow stronger as he related the tale. He coughed hardly at all and his eyes shone with a strength that had been gone for many moons past.

"You have related how the Healed One established our government, our lore, our rituals and traditions. All of that is true—all but his reason for doing so. He did not wish to make us strong; he wished to make us weak."

Toriovico couldn't stop himself.

"What!"

"Weak." Father smiled dryly. "That's right. He believed that his fellows would return and he wished to present them a kingdom intact and obedient. This would not be the case if we had reason to merge with another land— Waterland, for example. As long as we believed ourselves special, wedded to a destiny no other could share, that would create a border as real as any mountain or river.

"Our government was set up in the same way. The sodalities serve a good purpose in keeping the arts and crafts alive. Indeed, many foreigners perceive them as little more than trade guilds encumbered by useless ritual and elaborate titles. In many ways, the Primes are as good a governmental system as any. The First Healed one knew he lacked the strength and energy to rule as an absolute monarch, so he established a government where his lackeys would take care of routine, but he and his descendants would remain the supreme authority.

"However, not wishing the Primes to become too powerful, the Healed One made certain that each sodality would have one vote but three representatives, thus ensuring deadlocks and debates. The Dragon Speaker would be drawn from the Primes, assuring even more competition within those ranks. The establishment of the Dragon's Three meant there would be further maneuvering for position."

Toriovico was shocked, as horrified as if his father had told him to slice his own throat. He no longer wondered that at least one of his predecessors had been driven mad upon learning this version of history. It was akin to knowing you stood upon stone only to learn that you stood upon air.

"And my place in this?" Toriovico said, ashamed that he could not keep a quaver from his voice.

"Is to maintain the lie," Father said bluntly. "Any who get close to the truth, you must divert. The First Healed One suggested many strategies for doing this. Other of our ancestors have added to his list.

"That's something I forgot to tell you," Father went on. "The book I told you about—the one only you will be able to read? You will also be able to write in it and your words will be safe from prying eyes. In this way generations of Healed Ones have been able to share their experiences with those who will follow. It is some comfort in a lonely task."

For the first time then, Toriovico experienced pure and absolute isolation—a sense of being alone that had not left him since.

FIREKEEPER ENJOYED LISTENING to Grateful Peace's stories, even though she frequently found parts quite difficult to understand. Wolves were storytellers by nature, a thing, she guessed, that must come from not having a way to write down their history and teaching. She wondered if some of her reluctance to learn to read and write came from this. Not liking the flavor of that bite, she spat it out and considered it no more.

Wolves were listeners, too. As the perpetual pup in her pack she had heard some of the same tales over and over again. Warning stories about flooding streams or poisonous snakes, boastful ones about hunts that went right and hunts that went wrong. Stories of the past and of interactions with other packs and other Beasts.

Peace's stories, with their sorcerers and magical artifacts, strange beasts and stranger battles, were of things so alien to the wolf-woman that sometimes she could not even shape her mind around them. She had seen ships—though never traveled on more than a barge—but ships that sailed through the air? What, when one came down to facts, was a griffin or a wyvern or a basilisk?

Things with these names were depicted sometimes in paintings or tapestry, but she had noticed that artists never seemed to agree on the details. A wolf was a wolf was a wolf, but a dragon was not always recognizable as a dragon.

Firekeeper might have asked Bee Biter, who was far more well traveled than either herself or Blind Seer, but the kestrel had vanished one morning and had not yet returned. Firekeeper wasn't worried. The kestrel was inclined to get impatient about the slow speed of human travel.

Quibbles about the reality of Peace's various monsters did not stop Firekeeper from enjoying his stories, nor from discussing them at length with Blind Seer, who enjoyed them as much as she did. They both decided that hunting a griffin might be interesting, if one could get around the fact that the puma/eagle hybrid flew, but that many of the others sounded as if they were better avoided.

"Why bother when there are deer in the forests and elk on the plains?" Blind Seer yawned.

Firekeeper thought this question good enough to ask, and put it to Grateful Peace.

"Why in so many stories," she said, "people go after monsters? Surely there were deer and rabbits then."

Peace looked slightly surprised.

"I had never thought about the matter," he admitted. "It is simply the way of the stories. I suppose it is because great heroes need great challenges. Since many of these are stories from the days of the Founders, who were far more powerful than we are today, I suppose they needed bigger challenges. And in some cases, the monsters were a threat to the homes of those who fought them."

Firekeeper nodded, willing to accept this as yet another incomprehensible human prejudice, but Blind Seer was less willing.

"I still think it odd," he said, *"that they simply didn't have the wisdom to leave such creatures alone. And the monsters weren't always a threat."*

"Maybe." Firekeeper offered, running her hands through his fur, *"it is because these Founders were more like regular humans than Peace wishes to believe. I have seen how human hunters brag after taking a deer or even a pheasant, game no wolf would brag on. Maybe these Founders hunted to brag, not to eat."*

"If they hunted these griffins and dragons," Blind Seer said, *"then they had earned the right to brag indeed."*

Traveling north had been good for Blind Seer, shaking the heat-borne laziness from his brain. Still, like most wolves, he preferred to rest when the day was hottest. Last time he had traveled through New Kelvin he had taken to lying up during the day and catching up with them at his leisure. Here in more populated lands, with the party often staying in towns or villages at night, this had proven more difficult.

Now when Blind Seer grew weary of the plodding pace he rode in the wagon, at first encouraging the horses pulling it to new enthusiasm for their task, though later, like all the party's mounts, they became resigned to—if never pleased with—their burden. Sometimes Firekeeper joined him, putting up with the jolts for the pleasure of sleeping with her arms buried in his fur.

The horses weren't the only ones who were less than delighted by Blind Seer's presence. The New Kelvinese humans were unhappy, too. However, between them, Firekeeper and Blind Seer had evolved a plan to cope with this that, even many days into the journey, left them both shaking with laughter.

Once or twice before, Blind Seer had posed as an enormous dog. Now, with Wendee's assistance, they constructed an impressively heavy-looking collar. At need, the collar could be attached to a leash of triple-braided leather.

What no observer realized was that the buckle that fastened the collar was tacked into place with the lightest of stitches. Indeed, the collar itself was loose enough about Blind Seer's neck that he could paw it off over his head. The density of Blind Seer's neck ruff—and the fact that no one was interested in getting too close to him—made the deception good.

Firekeeper took delight in strutting about with the wolf "safe" on his leash. Blind Seer also enjoyed the game until one evening it turned ugly.

The party had paused along the turnpike at a place that was too small to even be called a village, but was too large to be merely a coach stop. It boasted a large and elegant inn called the Mushroom Stanza, several stables and storage buildings, a station for a local branch of the New Kelvinese militia, and even a few shops.

Peace explained that the location was fortuitously placed, a good stopping-off point for those traveling to many destinations within the kingdom. All the structures were of fairly recent construction, but like everything in New Kelvin the place sought to seem old and freighted with history.

Had the weather been less foul, their party might have passed the inn by in favor of some other place or even camping in the open, but a summer thunderstorm had broken out that afternoon, turning even the well-tended New Kelvinese roads to shallow streams bottomed in slick mud.

Moreover, Elise was sniffling and sneezing, possibly in reaction to some rather pretty yellow-orange flowers that grew profusely on the neatly tended verges of the turnpike. She rode on gamely, but her misery was evident.

So was Doc's, especially since his healing talent seemed unable to do anything for this particular affliction except relieve Elise's misery a bit—and Firekeeper cynically thought this relief might have more to do with Doc himself than whatever magical gift he offered.

Peace bullied the innkeeper into giving two rooms to the group. Had they not been foreigners, latecomers as they were they probably would have been expected to settle for blanket rolls in the common room, but that would have sent the rest of the custom scattering. Indeed, there were a few grumbles when the Hawk Havenese came out to dine, but no one actually insisted that they leave.

Firekeeper didn't join the rest. Wet weather and all, she preferred to stay outside with Blind Seer. They'd been given a stable—really more of a glorified shed—for their horses and in that hay and manure-scented refuge Blind Seer bolted down a large haunch of venison. He was cracking the bone so they could share the marrow when the bullies and their dogs came upon them.

Firekeeper didn't much bother to count above ten, but she didn't need to here. There were six men and more than that in dogs. The dogs were ugly creatures with short dung-colored coats, thick skins, and heavy, blunt muzzles. They wore collars adorned with long spikes. Their masters were even uglier.

Like all New Kelvinese these men wore some form of facial adornment. However, wet weather and general personal sloppiness had not been kind to their paint. Firekeeper thought that it had begun in strong colors: red, black, white, and yellow. Now it had all run together, the worst aspects of a puddled rainbow.

The bullies wore their hair in the usual New Kelvinese queue, but where Grateful Peace's braid was as smooth as a coil of silk, these men's were ratty, bits of scruffy hair sticking out around the edges. Their robes were more of the same. About half of the group wore them kilted up, as if they'd forgotten to let them down after a day in the fields. These were the neater ones. The others hadn't even bothered to kilt their robes up at all and the hems were bordered inches deep in caked-on mud and manure.

Firekeeper recognized the men and their dogs. She'd seen them several days before at a low inn, one so slovenly that Peace had refused even to check if it would grant foreigners shelter, though they had stopped long enough to draw water from the well to refresh both humans and horses.

And wolves.

The bullies had seen Blind Seer when he'd leapt from the wagon to drink at the horse trough. Even worse, their dogs had seen him and the dogs had been wise. They had cowered back.

The men had not liked this at all. Firekeeper had met this type of human before. Whether it was title or weapon or some animal they owned, they thought themselves better than other people because they possessed something they could use to intimidate. They mistook cringing before that tool as a sign of quality in themselves. Lack of respect to the tool was seen as lack of respect to themselves.

To be honest, Blind Seer hadn't improved the situation by pissing on the edge of the horse trough, marking the dogs' territory for his own with his arrogant stream. The dogs hadn't made it any better for themselves by cringing away from the wolf without even a token snarl or snap.

At the time, Firekeeper had been proud of her pack mate. They'd laughed over the incident, entertaining themselves by recalling every aspect of the event, shaping it so that it would make a good tale for the story circles when they next went home.

Tonight the dogs were not cringing. Firekeeper scented something in the air, a sharpness like liquor or like blood. She wondered if the men had given something to their dogs so that the dogs wouldn't feel fear or if the dogs had been beaten.

There were many dogs, more than there were men. Their eyes were muddy brown in the shifting lantern light and their teeth were the color of old ivory, not white like Blind Seer's. But there were many mouths filled with many teeth and all of them were bared.

At the first sound of the approaching group, the wolf-woman had risen to her feet in a single lithe motion so natural that it didn't seem motion at all. Blind Seer had also eased to his feet and stood beside her, enormous in the confined space. His silver-grey fur caught the lamplight and gave it back. There was a sound like distant thunder.

The Royal Wolf was growling.

A dog shrank back and tried to run, but a man booted him in the ribs. The dog froze, caught between pain he knew and a fear so visceral that he could not deny it.

A man said something to Firekeeper. He spoke New Kelvinese. Firekeeper, who had not been present for Grateful Peace's language lessons and probably wouldn't have paid attention even if she had been, didn't understand.

"I not know that talk," she said, haughty as Earl Kestrel.

Another man spoke in Pellish as broken as her own, though the fractures ran along different lines.

"You have a big dog there, girl," he said, and she understood his mocking tone better than any of his words. "We have dogs, too. We don't like your dog. We think he make a good rug or maybe a cloak. What you think?"

Firekeeper's answer was to lunge. Her logic was simple wolf logic that answered threat with either an answering threat—if one felt the opponent could be so intimidated—or with surrender or with attack. She did not think she could threaten these men. They would not see their danger until too late. Nor did it occur to her to surrender. That left only attack.

Besides, the difference between thieves and bandits was the level of threat they offered. These had said they would kill Blind Seer and make him into a cloak or rug. That meant they were bandits, not thieves. Edlin had said that it was permissible to kill bandits.

The bullies' spokesman was dead before he hit the dirt. There was a distinct chance that his severed head watched the action a bit after his body had stopped breathing, for his eyes were wide in shock.

Blind Seer acted as if linked in thought with his pack mate. At his slightest movement, some of the dogs ran. Others leapt at him, maddened by the smell of blood and by the conflicting fears that coursed through their veins. The wolf snapped at these as he might have at flies. Two dropped dead, one with a broken back, the other with a broken neck.

Then did the other dogs turn, tails between their legs, their yelping cries warning the night.

Blind Seer paid them no heed. He lunged at a man who was slashing at Firekeeper. The man's arm was crushed just below the elbow. His knife fell to the muddy ground. The man's screams blended with those of the dogs. He backed off a few steps, then crumpled in a faint.

Four men armed with knives or swords or, in one case, a long spear now faced a solitary young woman armed only with a hunting knife, a wolf poised at her side. The men had strapped on leather wrist braces and donned heavy boots of the type favored by people who enjoy kicking other people in the ribs. The girl wore a fine leather vest and trousers cut off beneath the knee. Her feet were bare.

It wasn't anything like a fair match and the men knew it. Turning, they ran. There's a problem about running from wolves. Wolves like to give chase—and Firekeeper and Blind Seer were wolves.

By the time people had streamed out of the inn, responding to the commotion as humans do, first with confused discussion, then with action, the hunt was over.

Firekeeper and Blind Seer weren't hungry, though, only upset, which is why the four men lived. They lay unconscious in the muddy fields just beyond the shed and if they bled a bit, well, one does after falling . . . or being knocked down rather hard.

It took Firekeeper several minutes to realize that she and Blind Seer were in big trouble.

First the horses had to be calmed. Spattered with blood as she was, Firekeeper knew she wouldn't be much help with that, but it did mean that Derian wasn't there to explain things to her. Edlin was helping him. Doc and Elise were checking the man whose arm had been crushed. Nothing could be done, of course, for the one she had decapitated.

Firekeeper drifted back to the edge of the circle of light created by the emergence of numerous lantern-bearing people from the inn. She was watchful, for Firekeeper was always watchful, but she wasn't particularly apprehensive. Well, maybe a little about the human she had killed, for humans were odd about the killing of humans.

But why should she be nervous? She had been attacked. She had defended herself. Blind Seer, who she was learning to protect from human fear, hadn't even killed a human, just a couple of dogs.

Ugly dogs, too, belonging to low-status humans. Bandits. Did that make the dogs bandits, too? Could dogs be bandits or did the human tendency to assume that all animals were stupid absolve the dogs from guilt? Perhaps there would be trouble over the dogs after all.

Firekeeper was chewing over this when she heard Wendee calling for her. There was an odd note in Wendee's voice, so Firekeeper paused rather than heading directly over.

Wendee was not alone. She had come about halfway across the inn's courtyard. Behind her paced six or seven armed guards.

"Wait here," Firekeeper said to Blind Seer. *"I don't like this."*

The wolf's reply was to fade further into the darkness. Then Firekeeper came forward, moving easily as if she had seen nothing to cause concern.

"Firekeeper!" Wendee said, and there were emotions in her voice Firekeeper couldn't quite place, but the wolf-woman was willing to bet that they had something to do with those armed guards. "These men want to talk with you."

"So," Firekeeper said, stopping in midstride. "Talk."

Instantly, she knew that she had done something—she wasn't sure what— wrong. Several of the guards shifted their grips on their weapons as if readying them. Their leader, a big, thickset man who reminded Firekeeper of a tree trunk, stepped alongside Wendee.

"Not here," he said in Pellish, his accent heavy. "Inside."

"Why?" Firekeeper asked, thinking her query completely reasonable.

The guard captain apparently didn't share her opinion. He started to say something in Pellish, then shifted to New Kelvinese, directing his remarks at Wendee.

Wendee translated, evidently quite unhappy.

"He says that he doesn't see why he should stand out in the mud to interrogate a murderer."

Firekeeper frowned. She knew the word, but didn't think it applied to her. Perhaps Wendee had mistranslated.

"Me?"

"You," Wendee replied, "at least as he sees it. From what I can gather, they see you as a killer in possession of a dangerous animal. They thought it was Blind Seer who had killed the man, but Doc assured them that even a wolf as big as Blind Seer couldn't have taken off a man's head—at least not while leaving it intact."

"Good," Firekeeper said. She wouldn't want Blind Seer to get either blame or credit for her actions.

Wendee nodded, but it was clear she misunderstood the wolf-woman.

"Yes, at least you'll have a chance to argue for Blind Seer's life—and for your own. Won't you come inside? Making them come after you or remain standing in the mud and wet isn't going to help."

Firekeeper had numerous questions. Why should she need argue at all? The bandits had needed killing. Maybe these guards wondered why she hadn't killed all six. She doubted it, though. The use of the word "murderer" was not a good sign.

She also saw the wisdom in Wendee's suggestion.

"I go inside," she agreed, "but tell them no to touch me."

Wendee took a deep breath.

"They want you to hand over your knife."

Firekeeper shook her head.

"No."

The manner in which she said the word gave it the force of a blunt weapon. The guard captain needed no translation. He said something to his men. Two unslung bows and began to string them. Firekeeper considered for barely a breath, weighing the options. As she saw things, there was only one wise course of action.

These men were not bandits, only guards doing their duty. She had known many such and would not harm them for so slight a reason. Equally, she would not surrender her Fang. She had always refused, at first out of prudence, but the concessions she had gained now made it a matter of pride as well.

The bows were hardly bent, the stings not even tight before Firekeeper made her decision. She dove for the shelter of a nearby wagon parked in the courtyard. From there she had her choice of many shadows. Once within their embrace, she was gone into the friendly darkness.

XVII

TORIOVICO SPUN, balancing less around his physical center than around his loneliness. It was a more perfect center than anything else could be. Weight and muscle might shift and change, but never this.

As the Healed One came to a halt and was about to go into a new move, one that involved reclining in a split on the cool marble floor followed by motions recalling a willow in the wind, he heard a sound from the open archway. He looked up.

Melina stood in the doorway, a heavy book tucked under her arm. Her pale blond hair had been dressed in the New Kelvinese fashion and she had taken to New Kelvinese styles as if they had been designed for her, wearing the long embroidered robes with grace, tripping along in shoes with the longest and curliest of toes.

Although Melina had not resisted cutting her hair—indeed, she had been pleased that New Kelvinese style and dyes hid its silvering—she had been slow to adopt tattooing on her face, not wishing, Toriovico thought, to mar her elegant if rather severe features with the puffing and scabbing that followed the procedure.

However, Melina loved elaborate face paints, especially those that emphasized her startlingly clear blue-grey eyes. In this way, she did not embarrass anyone by exposing her naked face.

Today her eyes were the centers of wispy flowers that also evoked the wide-awake look of owls. Her drawn-in eyebrows were set slightly higher than her natural ones, enhancing the impression of startled alertness and inviting the trained eye to study the contrast.

Toriovico felt his gaze drawn into hers and saw Melina's smile turn slightly lascivious. Since today's dance was for practice rather than performance, he wore little more than a loin wrap. Melina, rather than being offended by his lack of formality as many highborn New Kelvinese would at least pretend to be, seemed to enjoy her husband's undress.

She motioned for him to come closer, and Toriovico rose as if a puppet on strings. No longer did he wonder at the wisdom of his marriage to her. She was the heart and soul of his universe, a warm caress that blunted the pang of his solitary state.

Melina kissed him, warm and lingering.

"After you bathe and cool yourself," she said, "come and sit with me in the gardens. I've hardly seen you today."

Toriovico obeyed. It never occurred to him to do otherwise.

YET WHEN TORIOVICO CAME TO MELINA IN THE GARDENS, she hardly seemed to notice his approach. The large book she had been carrying earlier was open across her lap and she looked up from its ornately calligraphied pages only reluctantly. Even after she had turned her face up to accept his kiss and patted the bench beside her as an invitation for Toriovico to come and sit beside her, she still seemed distracted.

Torio, basking in the warm glow he felt only when Melina was near, was only slightly miffed at his wife's inattention. Idly, he glanced at his rival's spine, unsurprised to find it a scholarly compendium of folklore and legend. Melina was always reading one of these. She said she'd never understand her adopted people if she didn't study the type of things they imbibed with their mother's milk.

"I had a nurse," Toriovico had replied, a thing that had seemed quite witty at the time. Now, fresh from immersion in the dance, the statement seemed both flat and stupid.

He put the memory from him, not wanting anything to ruin his comfortable mood. Melina, too, made an effort to put aside her distraction, honoring him with a particularly warm smile and slipping her slender hand into his own larger, heavier one.

"You wanted to see me, my dear?" Toriovico asked, not really because he cared about anything but this moment, but because he would not leave undone anything Melina desired.

"Who wouldn't want to see you?" Melina said playfully, inserting two fingers under the collar of his robe and stroking his skin. "You keep yourself in such wonderful form."

"I must," he said matter-of-factly, "for the dance."

"Did I take you from your practice too soon?" Melina asked with that thoughtful attention to his needs that was mysteriously unlike the flattery of courtiers and servants.

"Never too soon," he said, "if my lady can spare me her time."

His words sounded like a rather trite line from a play. Indeed, a few seconds later Toriovico had placed them *as* a line from a play, one of those romantic melodramas his sisters had sighed over when they were girls.

Melina continued to stroke the skin just beneath Torio's collar with a repetitious, soothing motion that relaxed him completely. Indeed, Toriovico had to struggle not to drift of to sleep.

"I saw Apheros today," Melina said idly. "The poor man seems quite put out."

Torio thought it rather odd to hear the formidable Dragon Speaker described in a fashion that would be more appropriate for a small boy.

"Oh," he said drowsily.

He must not yawn. Melina would be terribly offended. Put out, even.

"Yes," Melina said, shifting her caress to the base of his neck and massaging the muscles in slow circles. "I asked what was troubling him and he finally admitted that he'd brought a proposal to you some days ago—something to do with Waterland trade—and he felt you'd been less than enthusiastic."

Toriovico struggled for a moment, then recalled the Waterland trade packet.

"I told you about the meeting at the time," he reminded her, "that same evening. I rather thought the Waterland business representatives wanted quite a lot for far too little."

"Magical artifacts are too little?" Melina said, surprised.

"Potential magical artifacts," he countered, sitting up a bit straighter. "Dearest, you're going to have to stop rubbing my neck if you want me to think straight."

Obediently, Melina dropped her hands into her lap. Toriovico took the opportunity to put two fingers under her chin and tilt her face up for a kiss. Then, with an effort—for those lips were powerfully distracting—he returned to business.

"The Sodality of Artificers will send someone into Waterland to make a preliminary inspection when—and if—the Waterlanders agree. They've been rather uncooperative to this point—as if they'd expect us to buy a horse without checking its teeth!"

Melina chuckled softly.

"Perhaps I am to blame, beloved," she said. "After all, didn't you accept me and those artifacts I brought without prior inspection?"

"True," Toriovico said.

Or rather Apheros did. I think I might have hesitated. Yet Apheros was right in his judgment. Those artifacts—well, at least the mirror—were magical.

"But those had a provenance," he said. "These artifacts have been rather conveniently discovered. Prime Dimiria claims to have seen some of them years ago during her residence abroad, but she's not an Artificer. Indeed, her vision has dimmed over the years—not that she'd appear in public wearing spectacles!—and I doubt she'd be able to detect a substitution."

Melina snuggled against him and he encircled her slender body with one arm.

"You seem to have thought a great deal about this, Torio."

"I *am* the Healed One," he reminded her gently, "and the welfare of my people, especially in regards to magic, is my special duty."

I wonder what she would say, he thought, *if she knew that my most sacred duty is to forbid magic rather than to encourage it?*

He didn't need to think hard to find the answer to that question. Melina was the most devoted magical scholar in Thendulla Lypella, for she alone was undistracted by any duty to a sodality. Indeed, some had suggested creating a title and post for her, perhaps giving her a staff to facilitate her research. The matter was being debated in the Primes this session.

However, such thoughts drifted away even as he grasped at them. How long they sat in the shaded nook in the flower-scented bower, he didn't know. What he was next aware of was Melina pulling away from his loose embrace.

"Where are you going?" he said.

"Inside. It's getting rather chilly."

Torio didn't think so, but perhaps his southern bride felt such things differently. He rose as she did.

"Torio," Melina said, her tone subtly commanding. "You will think about giving Apheros his way in this Waterland matter."

"Yes, my dear," he said obediently.

She smiled then and kissed him lightly. Then, gathering her book, she hurried from the garden.

Toriovico watched her until she was out of sight, mindless of anything but her departing admonition.

⚜

"THEY SEE LADY BLYSSE'S FLIGHT as an admission of guilt," Grateful Peace explained to Derian after a harrowing few hours during which the Hawk Havenese had not been certain how much of the anger and fear directed at Firekeeper would rebound upon them.

Peace had done wonders, never abandoning his guise as Jalarios, humble guide and translator, but somehow managing to keep his charges free. It hadn't hurt that Doc had immediately offered his services to tend the wounded man. Indeed, Doc had insisted. Even now Elise, Wendee, and Doc remained with the patient and the word had just been sent down that he was expected to live.

"I don't understand," Derian said stubbornly, though in his heart of hearts he did.

Peace explained patiently. "As the guards see it, if Lady Firekeeper had nothing to fear, why then would she run?"

Derian and Peace were sitting in the inn's common room at a table by themselves. They weren't quite under arrest, but the guards had made clear that they would be happier if they didn't go anywhere out of sight. Citrine had been permitted to go to bed. Edlin was out with some of the guards, helping track down the dogs that had been set on Firekeeper.

"Firekeeper didn't run," Derian explained wearily.

He was amazingly fuddleheaded. They'd been on the move since dawn in lousy weather and he'd been just about to retire to his bed—after too much to drink, he had to admit, but the inn's wine had been very good and there hadn't been any trouble for so long—when Firekeeper had to stir up a fuss.

Then Edlin's Moonkissed had kicked him a glancing blow just above the knee. Normally, Doc could have set such right with just a touch of his talent, but he and Elise were desperately trying to save the life of the man Blind Seer had attacked, a man who anyone could see was gutter scum.

"Firekeeper just left," Derian went on. "They wouldn't talk with her without taking her knife. She hasn't let King Tedric—who I think she reveres about as much as she does any human—take that knife away. She didn't run, she . . ."

His wine-fogged head couldn't find the words. Grateful Peace took mercy on him.

"Made a tactical retreat," he suggested.

"That's about it," Derian agreed. "I'd bet my . . ."

He'd been about to say "right hand" then caught himself. That wouldn't be the right thing to say, not to Peace, not after he'd seen the expression on the New Kelvinese's face when they'd brought in the man Blind Seer had mauled. The way Peace had glanced at the bloody ruin of the man's arm and then at his own empty sleeve had been as eloquent as volumes of some epic. It had all been there: loss, grief, adjustment, the wondering if the man might be better off dead.

Derian wondered just how much they could trust this already chancy ally. Might Peace's sympathies be with the wounded rather than with Firekeeper and Blind Seer?

"I'd bet anything," Derian went on, "that she's somewhere nearby."

Peace leaned forward and lowered his voice.

"I wouldn't make statements like that if I were you," he said. "Right now the guards are convinced that she's fled to the hills. They're talking about setting hounds on her trail . . ."

"Fat lot of good that would do," Derian murmured.

"No matter," Peace said. "If they thought she was near enough to learn what was going on here, they might try other forms of persuasion."

Derian's eyes narrowed and his head cleared with amazing, unsettling speed.

"Are you saying they might use torture?"

"Let us just say," Peace replied smoothly, "that they might decide that stronger methods of questioning than those to which they have resorted thus far might be in order, especially if the questioned person was then permitted a turn or two about the stable yard for fresh air."

Derian shuddered. He didn't want to, but he did. Peace's next words didn't do anything to restore his confidence.

"Lady Archer should be safe from such treatment, as should Lord Kestrel. The guards would not wish to cause an international incident. Sir Jared should also be safe. Not only would they respect his title, but he has shown evidence of being able to do magical healing. That grants him near reverence in their eyes—especially with how freely he uses his gift for others. You and Goody Wendee, however . . ."

Peace shrugged.

"Which . . . ," Derian asked, croaking on the first word. "Which would they think a more useful victim?"

Peace gave an eloquent lift of his brows.

"Difficult to say. I suppose it would depend on whether the guards think that Lady Blysse would feel more pity for one of her own gender or for her oldest friend."

Derian didn't doubt that the guards could learn about his relationship with Firekeeper. They might know already. The New Kelvinese had a strong spy network. They kept dossiers on interesting foreigners. Like him. Like Firekeeper.

"But they don't know she's likely to be near," he said after a moment.

"No," Peace agreed, "and I will not tell them."

Derian wished he believed Peace, but why shouldn't Peace tell the guards if he could turn the information to his own advantage? Might such an act not be the first step toward Peace's own rehabilitation into New Kelvinese society?

The guard captain stomped into the inn's public room at that moment. He was a big man just going soft about the middle, with thick iron grey hair plaited long down his back. Given the hot, sticky weather, he wasn't affecting elaborate face paint, but he had something that looked like a stylized mountain range tattooed along one prominent cheekbone.

The captain kicked his feet against the doorpost to knock the worst of the mud free before entering the room and scattering more mud over the fine carpets. The innkeeper looked as if he wanted to protest but didn't dare. The outpost guards weren't in his employ but were part of the contingent maintained by the New Kelvinese government.

Normally, Derian guessed, the guards' presence suited the innkeeper just fine, given that their being so near must just about eliminate theft, but tonight with his establishment turned head over heels and the guards sticking their noses into what could have been dismissed as a brawl that turned out badly, the innkeeper clearly was regretting the arrangement.

You and me both, buddy, Derian thought wryly. Then he turned his attention to the guard captain with what he hoped was the correct mixture of interest and concern.

The guard began by giving Grateful Peace a look that said without the need for translation that he considered the guide one of the lowest of the low. Indeed, he seemed about to send the other New Kelvinese away, but halted.

"Do you speak New Kelvinese?" he asked in that language.

"Not very well," Derian admitted, following this with the phrase he'd learned from Peace early in his instruction that meant the same thing.

The guard captain grimaced, but he didn't send Peace away.

"Who speak us good?" he asked in Pellish.

"Lady Archer," Derian said, figuring that it would never be too late to start throwing around titles, "speaks your language best of us, but she's with the doctor."

Peace said something that sounded like water running over rocks with a few interesting boulders formed by familiar names.

"Doctor. Sir Jared Surcliffe," said the guard captain.

Peace is right, Derian thought, assessing the guard captain's expression. *They are in awe of Doc. Good. Anything that slows down their search for Firekeeper.*

"With Sir Jared," Derian agreed, "and he needs Lady Archer to help him."

He made motions of someone handing things to someone else. The guard captain seemed to understand. Sighing gustily, he hooked out a chair with the toe of his still muddied boot and took a seat.

"We talk," he said. "Me to you, you to me. He," this last with a jerk of his head toward Peace, "help."

"Sounds good," Derian said. He remembered a polite formal expression Peace had told him meant something like "Thank you very much" and decided that it couldn't hurt to throw it in.

The guard captain looked confused, then smiled, recognizing the intent and clearly deciding to forgive Derian's limitations.

"I am Brotius," he said, jerking a thumb toward his chest. "You Derian Carter?"

"I am Derian Carter," Derian agreed. Then he remembered what Peace had said about titles and, though he felt like he might be throwing Wendee into the bear pit, he added, "Also called Derian Counselor."

Brotius glanced at Peace who said something fluid-sounding and multi-syllabic. When Peace finished, Brotius glanced at Derian's hand.

"Where?" he said, tapping a broad signet ring on his own hand.

Derian was getting into this abbreviated manner of speech. It really wasn't much different from talking to Firekeeper. He pulled from around his neck the embroidered amulet bag his sister Damita had given him as a birthday gift and spilled the ruby counselor's ring into his cupped hand.

"I don't wear it for everyday," he said. "It's a very special ring."

Peace translated and Brotius nodded. From a leather wallet on his belt he produced a pad of the excellent paper the New Kelvinese made, along with one of the writing sticks Edlin had so envied their last visit. He made a quick, recognizable sketch of the ring and the emblem incised into the stone, then gestured that Derian could restore the ring to its carrying bag.

"Where go girl?"

Derian looked at Peace, pretending to be more confused than he really was. "Could you ask him to explain more fully?"

Peace did and Brotius rattled off his question in a fashion that made Derian think that perhaps he'd better be a bit more careful when he played dumb.

"Captain Brotius says," Peace translated, " 'Where is the girl, the one with the knife and the big dog? She's a killer'—actually the word he used could mean murderer in that context—'and I don't want her running around where she might harm someone else.' "

"I don't know," Derian replied, looking Brotius straight in the eyes. "Jalarios," he barely remembered to use Peace's adopted name, "ask Captain Brotius why he calls Lady Blysse a murderer."

Peace did—or at least he said something. Brotius's reply was prefaced with what Derian recognized as a minor profanity, which Peace did not translate.

"Because she killed a man and would have killed more if we had not come out."

"That's not how I see it," Derian retorted, looking at Brotius, trusting Peace would translate without direct order. "As I see it she was attacked by six grown men and showed remarkable restraint. Only one died and one was injured. She could have killed the other four but only knocked them down."

Too late did Derian realize that he might have said too much. He was accustomed to how dangerous Firekeeper was. Admitting openly that she could have killed all six men might not have been wise, but the words were out of his mouth and he could only hope that Peace would moderate what he said.

Apparently, Peace did not, for the next thing Brotius, speaking in his own broken Pellish, said was:

"Girl kill one. You say kill six?"

Derian shrugged, throwing caution to the winds.

"She's a trained warrior or hunter or whatever a human wolf is. I don't know if she could, but she and Blind Seer could. She saved King Tedric from an assassin last year—and that was after someone had shot her in the leg."

Peace translated, then listened as Brotius positively fountained speech. What Peace gave Derian had to be only the smallest fragment.

"Are you saying this girl is important to your king?"

"Very," Derian said. When Peace didn't add more, he asked, "That isn't all he said, is it?"

"No," Peace admitted. "He hadn't heard about the assassination attempt and wanted to know if I had. I had to admit that I had heard something of the sort."

Brotius was looking suspicious. He frowned at Peace and Peace said something to him that had to be "I was just clarifying a point for the outlander" because Brotius stopped frowning. He turned to Derian.

"Girl like doctor?" he made a sweeping gesture with his hands.

Derian was completely confused and looked at Peace.

"He wants to know if Lady Blysse is like Sir Jared—possibly magical."

Remembering the New Kelvinese reverence for magic, Derian nodded enthusiastically.

"Yes. She is. Very much."

Only after he saw the unwilling awe spreading over Brotius's rugged features did Derian realize that he had probably spoken no more than the truth. Someone—Hazel Healer, he thought—had once speculated that Firekeeper had inherited talents that made her communication with animals easier, more natural for her, though Hazel had also thought that Firekeeper's upbringing among the wolves had contributed a great deal.

Derian wasn't about to go into those particulars now. If Brotius wanted to think that Firekeeper was some wonderful magical being, and that would make him treat her with more respect, then that was all for the best.

Or was it? Derian remembered how many of Peace's stories along the trail had dealt with brave heroes going after magical beasts and he sincerely hoped that Brotius didn't see himself in that role.

Brotius's next words didn't give Derian any comfort on that point.

"Girl . . ." Brotius frowned, his ability in Pellish, which to his credit was better than Derian's in New Kelvinese, failing him again. He snapped a command at Peace, and Peace politely translated:

"Captain Brotius says, 'You called her a warrior, a hunter, a human wolf. Do you mean that?' "

Derian answered carefully, now all too aware that Peace would not cover for him.

"Lady Blysse is certainly a fighter, but maybe not yet a warrior. She is one of the best hunters I've ever seen. As for her being a human wolf, well, she thinks she's a wolf, but we can see that she's human, so I was just trying to find a way to explain why she's the way she is."

Ancestors, please! Derian pleaded mentally. *Don't let Brotius decide this means she's some storyteller's fancy of a shape-shifting creature!*

Perhaps the ancestors listened, for Brotius's next query was prosaic.

"Why do you think she killed that man rather than yelling for help?" Peace translated.

"She wouldn't think to," Derian said honestly. "Where she grew up there wasn't anyone who could help. Anyhow, there were six men with weapons and all those dogs. I don't think any help could have arrived in time."

"In time for what?" came the translated reply, snapped out in tones so like Brotius's own that Derian nearly forgot the intermediary.

"For whatever they had in mind for her," Derian replied impatiently. "You don't think that six armed men went after a solitary girl with anything good in mind, do you?"

Brotius's reply was a guffaw of laughter as unwilling as it was spontaneous. He immediately sobered, but Derian liked him better for the slip.

"Captain Brotius would still be happier if Lady Blysse could be called in," Peace said.

"So would I," Derian agreed, "but that's beyond me. Try to see the situation from her point of view. She's out in the stable minding her own business when six men come at her and Blind Seer. The two of them can't run so they fight. When the fight's over instead of being thanked or apologized to, more men with even bigger weapons and wearing armor come at her and demand she hand over herself and her knife. This time she could run, so she did."

It took a while for this to be translated, but when Peace was finished, Brotius asked through him:

"You think she would have run the first time?"

"I do," Derian agreed. "We have taught her not to kill humans if she has a choice."

Again he wondered if he had said too much. If Brotius sent men to chase down Firekeeper then they could use this against her. On the other hand, maybe something was to be earned from showing her as civilized—at least after a fashion—and as respecting the rules of civilization. After all, a hunting party would be armed with bows as well as swords and spears.

And anyhow, if Firekeeper's cornered, she's quite likely to decide that in a case of her life or theirs that theirs can go out with the trash.

Brotius looked thoughtful and Derian didn't doubt that their thoughts were running along parallel lines. The rain would wash out a scent trail, so tracking the fugitive wolf-woman with dogs would be difficult. The guards might be counting on her and Blind Seer to leave tracks, but Derian knew that the wolf-woman had learned a considerable amount about avoiding leaving tracks since one errant footprint had revealed her existence to Earl Kestrel's party a year and a half before. Blind Seer might prove a bit more difficult to hide, but there was much uninhabited country in these mountainous reaches and Derian had learned that wolves were far better climbers than he would have imagined.

"Girl no come," Brotius said heavily, "you no go."

Derian nodded. He understood that statement well enough. They—and their secret mission for King Tedric—would be held hostage against Firekeeper.

He didn't blame Brotius. The man was only trying to contain what he must see as dangerous and unpredictable foreigners, but Derian also knew he couldn't let Brotius hold them for long.

THINGS WERE NOT GOING WELL.

With the first rays of dawn, men emerged from the militia headquarters. They reminded Firekeeper somewhat of ants trailing each other, dressed so alike, the sunlight reflecting off the polished leather and metal of their armor as it would off an insect's carapace. They spread out in an even line and waited.

A big man Firekeeper thought might have been the one who told her to hand over her knife the night before was leading them. From his hand gestures he was separating the guards into groups, having one group go this way, another the opposite. It didn't take her long to guess they might be coming to search for her.

She turned to Blind Seer.

"Shall we away, dear heart?"

The wolf looked north.

"If we go that way, we will see if our friends travel the turnpike to Dragon's Breath today."

"Good."

They stayed away until after noon and the disgruntled guards had long returned to their stony lair. The rest of their companions did not come out though, so wolf and woman found themselves a good place to rest and settled in to wait. Perhaps their friends were waiting until the cool of the afternoon to leave.

Afternoon did not bring their friends, but it did bring another search party. This one added dogs to their number: low-bodied, nose-sniffy hounds. These were given something Firekeeper could have sworn was one of her spare vests and a hank of Blind Seer's shed fur to sniff. Then they set their wide noses to the damp ground.

Once or twice the dogs caught a scent trail. Firekeeper—and even Blind Seer—was impressed. However, each time the trail ended in a muddy patch or a shelf of rock washed clean.

Their friends didn't leave that afternoon either.

The wolf-woman had glimpsed each of the others about the grounds, usually going and to and from the place where the horses were kept or to one of the shops, so she knew they were alive and well.

She'd even seen the man Blind Seer had maimed, his arm carefully wrapped, sitting in a chair where he could get some fresh air. Of the other four bandits she'd seen nothing, but that didn't bother her. Perhaps the guards were keeping them locked up just as their dogs were locked in a pen alongside the guardhouse.

The failure of Firekeeper's companions to leave the inn and journey on did, however, play havoc with the wolf-woman's intentions. She had planned on following them when they left, rejoining them when they were some distance from this place. She knew their final destination was Hasamemorri's house in Dragon's Breath. She figured that her friends knew she knew this and would count on her joining them.

But they didn't leave.

The first full day since her escape passed and turned into a new day. Firekeeper watched carefully whenever one of her friends came outside, hoping for a signal. She saw none, but she realized that the guards were keeping a close watch on her companions. Never did one leave the inn but a guard or two emerged at the same time. Her friends were not imprisoned, but certainly they were being restricted.

Firekeeper cursed the kestrel Bee Biter, who was still absent. If Bee Biter were near, Firekeeper could have begged him to gather information. It would be humiliating, but better than this nervous not knowing.

On this second day of watching, armored guards and the sniffing dogs came out again. Firekeeper praised herself for having not given into an urge to sneak down to the grounds the night before. Had she done so, the dogs would have gotten her trail. As things were, they failed again. Several troops of men tromped through the surrounding area, but Firekeeper and Blind Seer found them easy enough to avoid.

By the third day, what game there was started growing wary and though Blind Seer did not need to eat every day, when he did eat he needed to eat heartily, not the little fish and squirrels on which Firekeeper could subsist. With these complications in mind, Firekeeper decided that the only solution was to sneak down by night and find out why her companions were being delayed.

Blind Seer wanted to come with her, but Firekeeper refused.

"You will frighten all the animals, sweet hunter," she said, embracing him, "and their noise will alert the guards. Wait for me."

"And if you do not return," the wolf growled, "as the others have not?"

"Then," the wolf-woman said, "do come, but come when the wind and the night both are with you. Slay a creature or two, perhaps those sniffing dogs would do for starters. I think we can put such fear into these foolish ones that they will be glad to see the back of us."

Laughing, his teeth white in the light of the waning moon, Blind Seer agreed.

"You have only this night," he warned her. "Tomorrow I strike."

"I would not have it other, dear heart," she assured him, and kissing him on the damp leather of his nose, she slipped down into the grounds.

There were human guards posted, but Firekeeper had watched them these last several nights and she knew that they were past that tense alertness that had marked their first night's watching. Even so, her heart pounded a little faster than usual, but she knew that was good. Were she not to feel the thrill of the hunt, then she might grow careless.

Dodging into the darker shadows where the torchlight didn't fall, Firekeeper made her way to the side of the inn. She had already noted which

rooms her companions had been given. They were on the third story, back
in a corner, doubtless so that the locals need not get too close to the foreign
taint. There was an outside stair near them, but Firekeeper disdained it.
Besides, if there was a watch on her friends, a guard would surely be set in
that close stair.

The inn was built from stone, rough chunks probably cleared from the
local fields and in the building of the turnpike. They were mortared together
in the form of a small castle complete with turrets. Much art had gone into
the design, but the stones had not been dressed smooth and they provided
ample toe and finger holds for her.

She swarmed up and sniffed at the open window. The air smelled of male
sweat, not unclean, simply the body cooling from summer heat. Had there
not been so much at stake, Firekeeper would have slipped in then and there,
trusting her own speed and agility to get her away if she was detected by the
wrong person. Because she could not take that risk, she crouched on the
windowsill, wishing for a proper wolf's nose so that she could be absolutely
certain—as she was almost certain—that one of the scents was Derian's.

She crouched there a long time, until one of the men shifted in his sleep
and began to snore. A slow smile spread over her face. That was Edlin, sure
as rain makes wet.

Dropping from the windowsill into the room, Firekeeper took a moment
to assure herself that Edlin, Doc, and Derian were alone. She knew from earlier travel that Peace, in his role as servant, must sleep elsewhere, just as the
women must have their own room. The women had arranged to keep
Peace's "darling little boy" with them, thus sparing Citrine some potentially
awkward encounters.

None of the New Kelvinese apparently thought this last at all odd. Doubtless they dismissed it as another foreign peculiarity.

Firekeeper debated only a moment on who to wake first. Doc always slept
lightly and seemed used to keeping his tongue when awakened from a sound
sleep. She padded over to where he slept and, crouching next to him so that
her mouth was near his ear, spoke softly.

"Doc," she said, touching him lightly on the arm. "Is Firekeeper."

Doc did not disappoint her. He blinked to full wakefulness as easily as she
had climbed the side of the building.

"Firekeeper? Ah, good. We thought you had stayed in the area."

He glanced over at his snoring cousin and poked him in the side.

"Ed! You're snoring!"

"I say!" Edlin muttered sleepily. "So sorry, really."

He rolled onto his side and started to snuggle back into his pillow.

"Edlin," Doc said holding his hand ready to clap over the younger man's mouth. "We have a visitor. Firekeeper is here."

Edlin blinked blearily.

"What? I say, did you say?"

"Keep your voice down," Doc urged. "Firekeeper has come here at great risk to herself."

By now Derian was stirring. He didn't seem to be as muzzy-headed as Edlin and had apparently gathered something of what was going on. He propped himself up on one elbow and looked around the dark room, eventually identifying the darker blot next to Doc as their visitor.

"We thought you would stay close," Derian said, his voice soft but choked with emotions Firekeeper couldn't begin to define. "We're in a bit of a bind. The guards won't let us leave until you're found. Elise has done the ruptured-dignity thing and appealed to our embassy—I know we didn't want to draw a lot of attention, but it would have seemed odder if we hadn't."

Firekeeper nodded, realized Derian couldn't see her, and said, "What is 'ruptured dignity'?"

Derian laughed softly. He reached for the lantern near his bed and lit it, bathing the room in a pale yellow glow.

"You've seen it. When a noble gets all formal about privilege and proper treatment and all."

Firekeeper had indeed seen such behavior, many times—but rarely from Elise. She thought, however, that Elise could rupture her dignity very well if she chose.

"And what has happened?" the wolf-woman prompted.

"It will be days before we hear anything from the ambassador," Derian said, "and it's quite likely the ambassador won't be able to get us out right away. You see, it's not any of us the guards want."

"It's me," Firekeeper said.

"Right."

There was a span of silence during which Edlin finally woke up all the way. Then he had to be forestalled from making a great commotion in his joy at seeing his "dear sister."

Firekeeper sighed. Edlin wasn't an idiot. She knew that, would even defend him against those who misjudged him. However, there were times this was hard to remember.

"You not come out window and go?" she asked wistfully.

"No," Derian replied, a touch of admonishment in his tone. "That would make nearly impossible the task for which we were sent here."

"I know," Firekeeper sighed. "You cannot go. I cannot . . ."

She stopped, chewing over the beginnings of a plan.

"Give me a knife," she said.

"What?" Doc asked, apparently speaking for all three men, judging from their wordless exclamations.

"You give me knife," Firekeeper said. "I give this knife to guards. I hide *my* knife. Like Elise I rupture my dignity if they say they search me. I also rupture dignity if they try to hurt me. Am I not daughter of Earl Kestrel?"

"I say!" Edlin said. "That's not bad at all!"

"No it isn't," Derian agreed, "and it goes well with what we have told them already. I've seen their attitude toward us shift over the last few days. They're less confident than they were the night you fled."

"I wouldn't be surprised," Doc added in the tone of one who knew more than he was saying, "if my patient has talked a bit about the intent with which he and his companions went after Firekeeper and Blind Seer."

"You wouldn't have had anything to do with that, would you, Doc?" Edlin said with a delighted chuckle. "Just like I didn't point out how those dogs were all fighting animals, not some farmer's herd dogs, what?"

"Right," Doc agreed.

He turned to Firekeeper.

"It's a good plan," he said to her, "but there is a chance that they will attack you or lock you up. They've had several days to get worried and tense."

Firekeeper shrugged, though in truth she didn't feel nearly as easy as she pretended.

"True," she said. "That is why I keep my Fang."

XVIII

AT DAWN, the wolf-woman padded into the Mushroom Stanza Inn's central stable yard. Blind Seer, pacing at her side, seemed twice his usual size with his hackles raised, but she took no comfort in this. Rather she wished he were smaller than the smallest mouse so that no arrow might hit him.

So that none of the New Kelvinese humans could claim to have been surprised by their coming, Firekeeper and Blind Seer had howled to signal their approach—an act that, while eliminating surprise, set the resident livestock into a panic. However, even that warning might not be enough to keep them safe from a nervous bowman.

Some of Firekeeper's companions—most importantly Doc, for whom the New Kelvinese held deep, superstitious respect—were waiting outside when the two wolves descended from the rocky high ground into the stable yard.

Edlin ran forward to greet them, an action that must have looked spontaneous to any who had spent time with him these last few days but was calculated to insure that any guard would think twice before loosing an arrow or throwing a spear.

"Sister Blysse! Good to see you, what?" Edlin said, his joy so sincere that Firekeeper felt a twinge of guilt that she could not feel for Edlin what he did for her.

"And you, Edlin," Firekeeper said, giving the young man's lanky torso a quick embrace. "I waited for you and for others to go on the road, but you no go, so I come back for you."

"I say," Edlin replied, his tone slightly stagy even to Firekeeper's ears.

"These New Kelvinese won't let us go, you know. Captain Brotius wants a word or two with you about the other night, what?

"I have words," Firekeeper growled, unable to control a momentary flash of anger that some stranger would expect her to answer to him. "Where is this Brotius that he might give me his?"

Edlin looked around and there was Brotius crossing the yard from the militia guardhouse, a severe and angry expression on his face. Today his face bore a few lines of red and white like a reversed widow's peak descending his shaved forehead. Firekeeper matched them to the device on the guard post's flag and thought she understood their meaning.

"Are you ready to surrender?" Brotius demanded as soon as he was close enough not to shout.

Firekeeper had been trying to prepare herself for this moment—surrender was, after all, considered a viable option between wolves—but Brotius's arrogance made her unwilling to back down without question.

"I still not know why I do this thing," she said, her hand moving to the knife she had borrowed the night before. She had hidden her Fang—after some consideration of the limitations of her usual costume for hiding much of anything—strapped close to Blind Seer's belly where his thick fur hid both sheathed blade and the light thong that bound it to him.

Brotius replied, "Because you kill a man and your dog arm bit another."

"I could have killed all," the wolf-woman reminded Brotius, locking her gaze with his, "but only took life to keep my own. You should give me thanks for having taken away such ugly ones."

Off to one side Firekeeper heard Derian swear softly. She knew she had departed from the script they had worked out the night before, but she couldn't help herself. Surrender was a serious matter among wolves.

Brotius looked angrier than ever.

"I the guard, not you," he said stiffly. "I deal with 'ugly ones.' "

From somewhere on the fringes of a gathering crowd, Grateful Peace glided smoothly forward.

"If my services as a translator may be of help," he offered. He spoke first in Pellish, then said something in New Kelvinese that Firekeeper figured must be about the same thing.

Brotius grunted, then spoke at such a rapid spate that his native language's liquid sounds flowed in an uninterrupted torrent.

Grateful Peace translated blandly, "He wants to know why you came back if you didn't plan to surrender."

"I come back," Firekeeper said, "so he let my friends and you go. I do nothing wrong. The men I kill were bandits."

Peace translated. Brotius snarled something, a fairly long speech this time, which Peace must have shortened in translation.

"Captain Brotius wishes to know if you think that your being a noblewoman in your own land makes you immune to New Kelvinese law."

Firekeeper shook her head, addressing Brotius while trusting Peace to give her words sense.

"No. I think that because I try to keep my life hot in me that is the first law."

"The men didn't want your life," Peace translated for Brotius. "They wanted to have their dogs fight your dog."

"Blind Seer is my life," Firekeeper said simply, "and the bandits not just want fight. They say they make carpet or cloak of him. They follow us here from other place to fight."

Peace finished speaking, listened while Brotius spoke, then waved for Elise, who had pushed her way through the throng.

"Lady Archer," Peace said, addressing her with a formal note to his words that had not been present when he translated for Brotius, "you speak our tongue best of your group. Captain Brotius wishes to know whether you think that Lady Blysse could have mistaken bluster for an actual threat."

"I do," Elise said, crossing the stable yard at such a pace that Firekeeper knew she had been longing to do so ever since the conflict began.

Once she was close enough that her words could be kept private, Elise spoke earnestly to Captain Brotius in his own language. He replied with what Firekeeper thought was at least a little courtesy. The wolf-woman was getting tired of being discussed as though she were a piece of furniture, but given the alternative she thought she could bear it.

Idly, she reached and rubbed behind Blind Seer's ears.

"You are as impulsive as a pup with a butterfly. See what trouble it causes?" the wolf said affectionately. He shifted his huge head under her hand, *"A little to the side there."*

Eventually, Brotius and Elise stopped speaking. Elise's expression was tight around the mouth and eyes, and Firekeeper braced herself for bad news.

"Brotius wants Blind Seer caged," Elise said shortly.

"No."

"He says Blind Seer is a dangerous animal."

"He is," Firekeeper said proudly. "I will not make Blind Seer like dead meat to make Brotius feel he can pee farther than anyone else."

Elise pressed her lips together, whether to swallow a giggle or a snort of disapproval Firekeeper couldn't guess. Before Elise could speak further, Firekeeper offered:

"I put Blind Seer on leash and collar."

Elise translated the offer. Brotius shook his head. Firekeeper had another idea.

"Ask why he want this. I have come. Now we can go."

Elise replied woodenly, "Captain Brotius says he is not the one who can judge whether or not what you have done was murder. Therefore, he is not qualified to let you free."

Firekeeper snorted.

"Easy, dear heart," Blind Seer cautioned.

Firekeeper held her temper with difficulty.

"Who is this qualified?"

"Brotius has sent for a judge. The judge should be here within a few days."

"Then we go?"

"If the judge says that you are not guilty of murder."

For the first time Firekeeper considered that someone might be stupid enough not to see things her way.

"And what happen then?"

"At the best they would send you home."

"And at worst?"

"They would kill you."

"They not do that to Earl Kestrel's daughter," Firekeeper stated confidently.

Elise bit her lip.

"No, I don't think they would, but Firekeeper . . ."

"Yes?"

"They might kill Blind Seer."

"WHERE'S CONSOLOR MELINA?" Toriovico asked Tipi.

Melina's maid gave him a saucy look.

Tipi was a slave, probably—judging from her upward tilting slanting dark eyes, but light brown hair and pale skin—originally from Stonehold, where children from mixed-race matings were still considered shameful in some social circles.

The slave had been purchased as a novelty when she was a girl of fifteen some thirty years before, but her novelty had vanished along with whatever peculiar beauty she had possessed. The thoughtful administration of Thendulla Lypella had seen her retrained as a domestic. Until recently, Tipi had been considered so inefficient that she had been assigned to the service of foreign visitors—among them the visiting Melina Shield.

Now Tipi's fortunes had risen along with her new mistress's and she treated everyone—even the Healed One—as if she herself was a greatly privileged person.

"I couldn't say," Tipi replied. Then offering a modicum of helpfulness, she gestured back into the roomy suite that was her mistress's private domain. "She's not here."

Toriovico leaned against the doorframe. He had come to his wife's suite from his own half of the complex. All afternoon he had been sweating over a new routine for this year's harvest festival. He had been hoping to get Melina's opinion on a particularly difficult segment—one over which he and his Choreographer had been in fairly heated disagreement.

The Cloud Touching Spire had been arranged with the understanding that sometimes married couples got along better if each member had his or her own space. Melina shared a bed with Toriovico, but otherwise occupied her own elaborate suite. The arrangement had worked well, thus far. However, for the last several days Toriovico had not been finding Melina in when he sought her. More and more often Tipi didn't seem to know where to direct him.

Toriovico felt a surge of anger, the first he had ever felt toward his wife. Immediately, he felt guilty. Mingled guilt and anger roughened his words.

"Tipi," he said, stalking a few steps into the room, "I am not pleased with your attitude. Do you remember who I am?"

The woman immediately looked frightened.

"You are the Healed One."

"That's right. You, on the other hand, are a crossbreed slave, a discarded sex toy, and—if the condition of your mistress's footwear lately is any indication—a less than attentive domestic."

Tipi fell to her knees and bent over, exposing her back while veiling her face in the cascade of her grey-streaked hair.

"Don't beat me, Master!"

For a confusing moment, Toriovico felt certain that Tipi *wanted* him to beat her. Why? Because she could then complain to Melina? Because she was genuinely contrite? Or—he struggled to hold on to the thought—because she wanted to distract him?

What had he last said? Footwear. He'd commented on the condition of Melina's footwear.

As always, when Toriovico thought of his sweet and lovely wife, he found it difficult not to become distracted by a catalogue of Melina's many charms. This time an image of some of the astonishingly wonderful things she had insisted on doing to him last night in the privacy of their bedchamber threatened to lull him, but his anger, fading ember that it was, burned through.

Toriovico pushed pleasure away and found the memory he sought.

He had come to find Melina. She had been in her bath. On his way to her (he fought down images of her reclining in the scented water, of how she had opened her arms to him) Toriovico had passed a heap of discarded robes. Next to them had been shoes. Serviceable leather shoes, not the curly-toed slippers Melina usually wore. Even though the shoes had been cursorily scraped, he could see mud clinging to the instep and along the edges.

The robes hadn't been Melina's usual attire either. With summer Melina had discovered the joy of embroidered silks. Her coloring was such that she could wear anything but the most brilliant shades. Neither pastels nor jewel tones were barred to her and she had greedily accepted lavish gifts of robes, cloaks, and stockings.

No, the robes Toriovico had seen piled for the cleaners had been of utilitarian cotton dyed the same neutral tone that was worn by the Alchemists when they puttered about with some noxious blend that would ruin better fabrics. He knew Melina possessed a few sets of such robes—relics of the aborted investigation of the artifacts last winter—but why would she be wearing them now?

Toriovico stared down at Tipi's bent back, almost certain now that the maid wanted him to beat her, wanted to infuriate him so that he would forget his queries after her mistress. He was astonished that she would think it would be so easy. Then, uneasily, he wondered if she might have had reason.

He had been rather scatterbrained lately, but he'd put it down to adjusting to marriage.

He didn't want to think about that either. Instead he looked at the still-crouching Tipi. Resisting an urge to boot her in her spreading fundament, he strode past her into Melina's dressing room.

He had no idea just how many robes Melina possessed. Such were considered gifts in good taste, even to a woman of her unique status. What he was looking for were those cotton work robes and what he found quickly confirmed his vague conclusions.

There was only one such robe hanging in her wardrobe. Another, quite possibly the very one he had seen last night, was crumpled in the wicker laundry basket. Melina could well be wearing a third.

He heard a sound behind him and wheeled. Tipi had risen from her abasement and stood timidly in the doorway to the dressing room.

"Where is your mistress?" Toriovico demanded and his tone brooked no evasion.

"I don't know!" Tipi wailed. "The revered Consolor does not tell me, her most humble slave, where she goes. All I know is that for several days she has dressed herself in those ugly robes and ugly shoes, covered this with a light outer robe, and gone from here commanding me to await her and keep ready warm water so that she might bathe upon her return."

"That is all?"

"Yes, gracious Healed One."

Toriovico wasn't certain. There was a knowing glint in Tipi's eye, but he didn't care to beat her. He might learn some small detail more, but not enough to merit having to explain to Melina that he had beaten her slave because she didn't keep close enough tabs on her mistress. That wouldn't do at all.

From the first, Melina had demanded a certain degree of autonomy, explaining that she had been accustomed to such for many years now and was reluctant to change. Toriovico had been content to give her what she wished. Not only did he wish time for himself—time he would not have if a wife clung to him at every step—but he was not brother to six sisters for nothing. An unhappy woman could make a man consider the most horrible torments ever devised a welcome relief.

Instead of questioning Tipi further, Torio took the dirty robe from the laundry hamper. Mud clung to its hem, carrying with it a slight sewer stench.

The Healed One pursed his lips thoughtfully and wished that Grateful Peace, the Dragon's Eye, had not turned traitor. Although his post was within the administration of the Dragon Speaker, he had always been a good servant to both aspects of the government. He would know where this mud came from—or if he didn't, he would have a fair idea where to inquire.

But Grateful Peace was far away and his post had not been filled. Instead, Apheros had appointed Siyago of the Artificers into his Three, naming him the Dragon's Fire. For the first time, Toriovico wondered at this. The Dragon's Fire was usually a war leader and New Kelvin was at peace with all her neighbors. Did Apheros think it might soon be otherwise? Perhaps such concerns were wise when one so trusted as Grateful Peace defected to another kingdom.

Toriovico asked no more after Melina's whereabouts, but left, taking with him the dirty robe. He didn't bother to order Tipi to say nothing of his actions. She would disobey him if she feared her mistress more, and such an order would only make her sneaky.

He resolved to make some inquiries after what might be behind Melina's actions. Perhaps Xarxius would know something. He knew about foreigners. Maybe there was some odd ritual that Melina needed to attend to at this time of year, some Pellish thing that she was ashamed to mention.

The idea comforted the Healed One as he made his way back to his studio and to the still unresolved dispute with his personal Choreographer.

ELISE COULD SEE that it took every bit of courage that Firekeeper possessed to restrain herself from bolting when she realized the threat her surrender offered Blind Seer. Elise laid her hand protectively on the younger woman's arm, then turned to Captain Brotius.

"Lady Blysse will not permit Blind Seer to be locked up," Elise said in New Kelvinese, "and if you value your life I would not press her on this matter. In any case, do you really want to risk harming the chosen daughter of a noble house?"

Captain Brotius snorted as if unwilling to admit that he would defer to any foreign noble, but Elise saw the worry in his eyes.

"We would not harm even the dog," he replied stubbornly, "if it cooperates."

"Blind Seer will not cooperate," Elise said. "It is against his training. The only one he obeys is Lady Blysse and she will not give the orders."

"Then what harm comes to the dog is on her head," Brotius said triumphantly. "Tell her that."

Elise nodded. "I will, but first let me warn you that any harm that comes to your men will be on your head."

She spoke loudly enough that she was certain the captain's men could hear. Brotius scowled at her.

"We will restrain the dog with nets. Perhaps we will set dogs on him."

"I was not talking about any injury Blind Seer might give you," Elise said with false sweetness, "but what Lady Blysse will do if you attack her pet. As you have said over and over again these last few days, she did kill a man for threatening her dog. Why do you think she will not do the same again?"

Brotius gaped at Elise, his glance flicking over to where Firekeeper stood tense and alert, her hand curled in the thick fur of Blind Seer's ruff, her dark gaze unreadable.

Perhaps he realized that Elise's warning was not without reason. Perhaps he feared his own men might mutiny. In the end, Brotius accepted Firekeeper's surrender of the knife in her sheath along with her promise to keep Blind Seer on collar and leash at all times. Then the two groups settled into an uneasy stalemate, waiting for the arrival of the judge.

For the better health of all their sanities, the judge arrived the next day. Judge Ulia was a tall woman past middle years but very fit. She sat her dapple grey with the posture of one who spent much time in the saddle. Her hair was the color of cold ash and her eyes a neutral brown. Her long, oval face was divided down the middle by a solid black bar, symbolizing—so Peace told them—the balance of justice.

This bar was a tattoo, not face paint as Elise had initially thought. Judges, Peace explained, were elected for life. If they were proven corrupt or impulsive, then they were executed, the axe brought down to meet that black line and slice the skull in two. Condemned judges were restrained so that they could not move their heads and drops were put in their eyes so they could not blink.

It was an ugly death and the incidence of corruption among judges was quite low.

As unsettled as Elise was by this evidence of the brutal side of New

Kelvinese law, she was also comforted by it. Surely Judge Ulia would be very careful in whatever decision she made.

Judge Ulia spoke Pellish fairly well, a necessity given that her jurisdiction contained numerous traders. In answer to Elise's rather anxious inquiries, Ulia explained the procedure she would follow.

In private Judge Ulia would talk to the prisoners, both Firekeeper and the surviving bandits. Then she would question any associated with the incident.

"Given," Ulia said, her accent giving the words an odd music, "that you are foreigners and that Lady Blysse is odd even for a citizen of Hawk Haven I may have many questions."

The formal hearing would be very limited. There would be no jury, and the judge would be the only one to ask for testimony. After offering what evidence she thought was important, Judge Ulia would then publicly give her decision on the matter. If there was disagreement from any in the audience, she would defend her judgment immediately. Once that was done, sentence would be passed and any punishment carried out as soon as was reasonably possible.

The entire procedure seemed a bit abrupt to Elise, to give too much power to one person's judgment, but when she remembered that tattooed black line and what it symbolized she allowed herself to hope.

Judge Ulia spent the full day following her arrival interviewing prisoners and witnesses. Of Firekeeper's friends she spoke longest to Elise and Wendee since they could answer her in New Kelvinese, thus eliminating at least some misunderstandings that might arise from the different values each language gave to words. Ulia even spent a fairly long time talking with Edlin about dogs. On the morning following her arrival, she convened her court in the public room of the inn.

By now Elise was aware that more than Firekeeper were on trial. The bandits were as well, and even Captain Brotius stood to be censured if Judge Ulia thought he had acted outside his area of responsibility.

First called forth was Firekeeper, who tersely reported what had led her to kill the one man and to Blind Seer's maiming of the other.

Next called was Lucho, the man whose arm had been maimed. In assisting Doc to save Lucho's life, if not his arm, Elise had spent a great deal of time with Lucho and she had seen the near worship with which he now regarded the healer.

Lucho's testimony confirmed the truth of Firekeeper's version of the story. Judge Ulia asked him if his version of events had been in any way coerced, "even by kindness."

Lucho shook his head.

"No, Judge. That's how it happened. Nobody made me tell it that way."

Lucho's fellows looked at him with such hatred that Elise feared for the man's life if they were set free.

Judge Ulia then called on Captain Brotius. He reported what they had encountered.

"You saw Lady Blysse and her dog running after the fleeing men?"

"Yes, Judge."

"Was she aware you were there?"

"I think so, Judge, but I can't be certain."

"Did she have the opportunity to kill or harm the remaining four men?"

"Yes, Judge."

"But they were not harmed beyond the bruises and scrapes that occurred when they were prevented from fleeing."

"Yes, Judge."

"Thank you, Captain."

Those flat brown eyes surveyed the gathered people, stilling with a glance those observers who had begun to whisper.

"I am prepared to pass judgment," Judge Ulia said. "As is only right, the New Kelvinese should be judged first. All evidence agrees that Lady Blysse and her dog were attacked. The men who came upon her possessed dogs which were trained fighters, and show the scars of pit fights and bear baiting. Moreover, I have discovered that several of these men have been before a judge for other infractions of the peace.

"Therefore, I rule that all five of these men shall work a term of hard labor in the glass foundries of Urnacia, their services to be bid upon by appropriate persons. Until that bidding can take place, they are to be kept in the custody of Captain Brotius, who will arrange for their transfer. They may be worked sufficiently to cover the expense of their care, but should not be exhausted or underfed."

The New Kelvinese bullies did not look happy. Knowing a little about the heat at which glass was made, Elise did not fancy that their work would be at all pleasant. She wondered how Lucho would manage with his maimed arm. From the look on his face, he was wondering this as well.

"Lucho," the judge continued, motioning him forward. "You have already been at least somewhat punished for your role in this assault. More-over, your testimony gave me information that I was able to use to break down the lies told by some of your former associates. Therefore, I offer you a different sentence.

"If you so choose, you may work your term here as a servant of the guard under the supervision of Captain Brotius. Understand that any further trou-ble from you will lead to you being given not one but two terms at a glass foundry.

"Are you interested in accepting this alternate sentence?"

"Yes, Judge Ulia," Lucho said, stepping sideways to avoid a sharp kick from one of his former associates. "I won't cause any trouble and I'll work as hard as I can with this arm."

Judge Ulia made a note, then looked up.

"Don't use that arm as an excuse for shirking, Lucho. I pass through this area regularly and I'll be checking on your behavior with Captain Brotius."

Lucho nodded and, in response to her gesture, stepped back, careful to take up a stand nearer to the guards, who had now become his protectors instead of his enemies.

Judge Ulia now turned her attention on Captain Brotius.

"Captain, it has come to my notice that in your eagerness to make certain that these foreigners did not defy our law with impunity you nearly—very nearly—created an international diplomatic incident. This will go on your permanent record and will be considered in your next posting. Careful han-dling of the prisoner Lucho and any other foreign travelers might well miti-gate any charges that you were imprudent. Do you understand me?"

"Yes, Judge Ulia."

The look Captain Brotius turned on the Hawk Havenese when he was certain the judge's attention was back on her notes was not at all kind.

I don't think we've made a friend there, Elise thought despairingly.

Looking up from her papers, Judge Ulia continued:

"Lord Edlin Kestrel has advised me that the dogs owned by these men are all fighting animals. It is his expert opinion, supported by local authori-ties, that these dogs cannot be retrained for another type of work. Since they are apparently accustomed to being set on humans, they must be destroyed lest they do injury to an innocent."

"I say!" Edlin began, but he was silenced by a single look from the judge. No one else felt moved to protest.

Elise felt a cold twist in her belly at what this last judgment foreshadowed for Blind Seer, but she knew she must not say anything until the judge was done speaking.

"Lady Blysse Kestrel," Judge Ulia said.

Firekeeper stepped forward and curtsied. She was wearing a gown today out of deference to the formal occasion and had, after great resistance, agreed to leave Blind Seer outside. She had only made this concession after Doc had offered to stay with Blind Seer so that no harm could come to the wolf unwitnessed.

Judge Ulia studied Firekeeper for a moment, then said:

"All the evidence says that you are innocent of anything but being somewhat beforehand in your self-defense. Since you could have disabled the man who threatened you and your pet or even screamed for help, my belief is that you overreacted."

Firekeeper said nothing, only held her head high and fixed her gaze on the judge.

"However, I have spoken to many people and have heard from them the story of your peculiar childhood. Indeed, I had even heard some tales of you before this meeting—though I must admit I did not believe them until we met. Given your upbringing, I can see how it would be natural for you both to kill rather than disable and to value human life rather more lightly than I would like.

"Because of these circumstances, I am releasing you without penalty into the custody of your older brother, Lord Kestrel. Understand, however, that I will send a letter to be circulated to all those responsible for enforcing the law in this land. They will be told that you have been warned that killing when disabling will serve is against our law. Next time—if there is a next time—you will not get away so lightly. Do you understand?"

Firekeeper tilted her head to one side in consideration.

"I think so," she replied, "but I will ask Derian and Elise to tell me again so I am sure."

"Wise," the judge said with the faintest of smiles. "However, I cannot permit your dog—or wolf, as I now realize him to be—to go free. He has shown himself more restrained than you, but clearly as fearless as any fighting dog when it comes to attacking humans. As they are to be destroyed, so he will be destroyed."

"No," Firekeeper stated. "He will not be."

Judge Ulia did not look surprised either at the interruption to formal procedure or at Firekeeper's response.

"I say he will be destroyed," the judge replied coolly. "It is only right and harmonious. Moreover, there is none to answer for him as your brother must answer for you."

"I answer for him," Firekeeper growled.

Her hand drifted toward the folds of her dress and with a sudden tingle of fear Elise realized why the wolf-woman had been so willing to wear a dress. She could conceal her Fang in the folds of a skirt as she could not in trousers.

Elise bit her lip, willing herself not to scream or give warning, trying to remember if Firekeeper could accurately throw her Fang, wondering what she would do if the wolf-woman fled again.

Judge Ulia looked at Firekeeper, flat brown eyes meeting those so dark that they seemed almost without color, and found no retreat.

"You say you will answer for him," the judge said, "but you yourself have already proven to be too dangerous to be trusted with control of such a deadly beast. There is no other answer. The wolf must be destroyed."

Firekeeper howled, a single long, shrill note that Elise didn't doubt contained a wealth of meaning for the right ears. Then she bared her teeth at the judge.

"I tell Brotius," Firekeeper said, "what happens if Blind Seer is hurt. You are as warned as he."

Shouts came from outside the inn and the whinny of a horse in panic. Elise thought she heard Edlin's "I say!" above the other voices and wondered just when he'd slipped outside. Doubtless as soon as he recognized the threat to the wolf. If he'd risk trouble for fighting dogs, he'd risk more for a companion.

"Grab Lady Blysse!" Captain Brotius shouted to his men, even as Wendee and Derian moved toward the wolf-woman, obviously hoping she would not harm them as she would a stranger.

Then the door into the inn's common room opened and a man in traveling clothes stepped through. His amiable features were illuminated by the outside light and Elise thought she saw several people in the room—Captain Brotius among them—stiffen.

"I've been listening from outside," the newcomer said, in New Kelvinese, "and it has been very interesting. Lord Kestrel has a hold on the wolf, but no one will harm it without killing the young lord—a thing his grandmother the duchess would not like at all."

Elise quickly translated the gist of this speech.

"Firekeeper, Blind Seer is safe. Edlin is protecting him."

Firekeeper relaxed marginally, but her hand remained in the vicinity of what Elise was now certain was her Fang.

"Judge Ulia, you have really done very well," the newcomer said, "but perhaps you and I should adjourn and discuss this last sentence further."

Judge Ulia dismounted the high seat from which she had passed her rulings with alacrity, ordering that the New Kelvinese bullies be taken away, and for everyone else to settle down. The pair were gone for a far shorter period of time than Elise would have thought possible to sort out such an intricate problem.

The newcomer took a stand at the front of the room alongside the judge. Although he did not wear the black stripe, it was evident that Ulia respected him as a peer—or at least that she feared him enough to defer her authority. Elise wasn't certain which was true.

Judge Ulia spoke in New Kelvinese. The newcomer, speaking in very good Pellish, offered a summary immediately after.

"Judge Ulia has agreed," he said, fixing his gaze on Firekeeper, "to accept Lady Blysse's decision to answer for the wolf, Blind Seer's, actions. After all, the wolf only acted in defense of his mistress and with more restraint than did she herself. He should not be killed for that."

Firekeeper listened and though her tension did not leave her, Elise no longer feared the wolf-woman would spring upon the next New Kelvinese to step near her.

"Then we can go?" Firekeeper said when the newcomer paused.

"You can go," the newcomer replied.

He motioned for Judge Ulia to precede him, and they led a general exodus of chattering New Kelvinese from the room. Elise and her party followed more slowly.

"What a good man," she said, overcome by relief, "and what good luck that he arrived when he did."

Grateful Peace turned toward her, his expression somber.

"I don't doubt that he is a good man—in his way and when it serves him, but as for it being luck that brought him here at this time . . ."

Peace trailed off, shaking his head slowly.

Elise stared at him, suddenly afraid again.

"What do you mean?"

"I mean," Peace replied, "that the newcomer who so easily overruled Judge Ulia was none other than Xarxius, a member of the Dragon's Three, and a very powerful person indeed."

XIX

WITH THE SOILED ROBE wrapped into a neat square package, Toriovico went searching for help.

The Dragon Speaker and the Healed One maintained separate staffs for many things. Ostensibly the reason for this was that while whoever held the post of Dragon Speaker could—theoretically—change on a regular basis, the Healed One reigned for life. It would not do for his administration to be disrupted whenever a Dragon Speaker lost the confidence of the Primes.

This was a good reason, but as Toriovico alone knew, it was not the real reason. The real reason was that the First Healed One had been a cynic and had desired to set up a government that would devour as many resources as possible—human and otherwise. Two sets of clerks, two sets of spies, two sets, even, of purely mundane things like stationery and pens.

So although the Dragon Speaker's spy network had been disrupted by the defection of Grateful Peace, the Healed One's had not.

Apheros was clearly Melina's creature—as indeed he should be, Toriovico thought, nearly drowning in a wave of guilt, for was she not the wife of the Healed One? But this meant that Toriovico could not risk that word would reach Melina through Apheros or one of his lackeys that her husband was looking into her activities. Just the thought of her displeasure were she to know chilled his bones.

Therefore, Toriovico did not go to where his watchers maintained their offices or to where Apheros's maintained theirs. Instead, he went to the little museum within the Earth Spires kept by the Sodality of Lapidaries. It was not a grand place compared with their own museum in their Hall of Minerals in the city proper, but it had one resource that the grand museum lacked—Columi, emeritus Prime, and currently retired to the token job of custodian.

When seeking to have the dirt clinging to the hem of Melina's robe identified, Toriovico could have tried several of the sodalities.

The Lapidaries concerned themselves with gems and all manner of minerals, but the Smiths also knew much of what came out of the earth. The Illuminators, too, had much curious knowledge, garnered in their perpetual quest for new, brighter, and more vivid pigments. Finally, the Alchemists had burned, boiled, or exploded at least one of everything that they could lay hands on. They were quite likely to have someone who was a specialist on dirt.

But it was Columi himself who had tilted the balance in favor of the Lapidaries. Indeed, though Toriovico tried to hide the thought from himself, the Healed One was planning on consulting the old man not merely as an honored and wise member of his order and as someone he had known from childhood—but as someone he knew did not at all like Melina.

Columi and Melina had disputed last winter during the analysis of the artifacts brought from Bright Bay. Toriovico didn't know the details. Their mutual dislike was a thing more sensed than known, something read in the intricate dance of human relations.

Toriovico skipped a few steps of a favorite folk reel to calm his nerves. Let any who watched him think he was going to the museum for something to do with the upcoming harvest celebration. Besides, dancing seemed to clear his head.

An elaborate chime made from elongated splinters of some shining dark rock—Toriovico thought it might be obsidian—made a delicate, glassy clangor as he opened the door. The museum occupied the base of a tower whose other functions Toriovico could not remember—if indeed he had ever known. Some days it was a busy place, but this afternoon it drowsed in cool, mineral-scented, just faintly dusty stillness.

The museum was not the only thing drowsing. Seated in a comfortably padded chair, his feet up on an equally padded footrest, the museum's custodian was blinking himself awake.

Columi was a man of moderate height who looked smaller than he was. Much of this illusion was due to the fact that he seemed built from a series of spheres. A remarkably round head was set almost directly onto a plump torso. Robes, of course, hid the details, but short pudgy fingers extending from well-cushioned palms enhanced the impression.

Although barely awake, Columi struggled to stand as soon as he recognized his caller. Once he was upright, he immediately worked his way awkwardly to the floor to make the necessary obeisances, pressing his forehead to the floor in abject apology for having been caught less than fully alert for his sovereign's visit.

Had the matter been left to him, Toriovico would have excused the old man. Indeed, his own joints ached in sympathy as he watched Columi bobbing away. The problem was, the matter was not up to him. His role in these rituals had been dictated long ago. He could not change it without offending not only the living but the dead.

So Toriovico bore the bobbing and formal greetings stoically, not even extending a hand to help Columi to his feet. Columi might have remained on the floor, but happily, there was a cane near at hand. He grasped it and used it to push himself up.

To Toriovico, who knew something of the internal rituals of the Sodality of Lapidaries, the ruddy brown of the cane's polished wooden length, inlaid with a small fortune in precious and semiprecious stones, spoke of a lifetime of meritorious service by Columi to both his organization and to his kingdom. To a less well educated eye, the cane looked remarkably like the popular conception of a wizard's staff—a bit shorter perhaps, but evocative nonetheless, right down to the polished rock-crystal sphere set in a stylized eagle's claw at the top.

"Honored One," Columi wheezed, surreptitiously patting his midsection to encourage his breathing to slow while leaning heavily on his cane. "I am honored by your presence in this temple dedicated to knowledge. Our hard-earned learning is enhanced threefold and more by your crossing the threshold."

Now Toriovico could offer a bow—brief and without the apologies, but an honor to any who merited it.

"Although I bring with me the accumulated wisdom of the ages," the Healed One replied, knowing how very minimal that knowledge was, "I am honored to have such a wise and ancient teacher ready at my disposal."

"Not quite as ready as I should be," Columi replied a touch ruefully, his manner becoming easier now that the formalities were over and there were none to observe them, "but ever ready to serve the Healed One."

Had there been a slight hint of emphasis on the term "Healed One"? Toriovico wondered. Who else had been inquiring after Columi's services?

"Has the museum been busy?" he asked.

There was the slightest of pauses, and then Columi replied, "About usual for the season, I believe. The Illuminators brought by a group of apprentices for a test on raw mineral identification. They like to do it here rather than at the Scriptorium lest some enterprising soul get a gander in advance at their collection and so identify a specific piece rather than a mineral type."

Toriovico grinned. He'd heard similar tales from each and every sodality. Sometimes he thought that if students put half the energy and ingenuity into learning their subjects as they did to trying to outwit their instructors they would do far better. On the other hand, that was a test in itself. Rarely did the cheats rise high, and those who did had wit and cleverness to offer in lieu of perfect knowledge.

"And that's all who have graced these halls?" Toriovico prompted.

Again Columi paused, but that might simply have been an effort to gather his still ragged breathing.

"A few have come by to ask specific questions or even to enjoy the quiet and the coolness." The Lapidary's round face grew rounder as he chuckled. "I've compared notes with other museum custodians. All the museums seem more popular in the heat of summer or the cold of winter when they offer relief from the elements. Spring and autumn see a distinct falling off of custom."

Toriovico decided to leave this matter, though he remained curious as to what Columi might be hiding. Did he perhaps have a lover with whom he lightened his hours? Or was he playing politics still and wanted to conceal who might come to use this unfrequented spot for a meeting or as a place to pass messages?

"If the museum has not been too busy," Toriovico said, "then I would not be inconveniencing any scholars if I asked you to close the doors and meet in private with me? I am correct in guessing that we are alone, am I not?"

A blush reddened Columi's face, quite visible as he wore nothing but his accumulated tattoos and a bit of emphasis about his eyes. Clearly he was still embarrassed about being caught napping.

"We are alone, Healed One," he said formally, "and if you will bide a few moments, I shall take precautions to assure that we will remain so."

The Lapidary returned before Toriovico had time to do much more than study the nearest case of specimens, which contained some very nice fossils, including creatures he was certain no longer walked the earth. Then again, he could be wrong.

Do the horns of a wondrous mountain sheep remain golden after the creature is fossilized? he wondered. *They would if they were really metal, wouldn't they?*

"Come this way, Honored One," Columi said, gesturing to a room deeper in the tower. "I've some apricot nectar on ice that would taste just fine right now."

The room into which they settled had been furnished like a cozy little parlor, complete with a sleeping sofa tucked along one wall. Toriovico accepted a seat in a comfortable armchair rather like the one in which he'd caught Columi dozing.

"Sometimes it just seems too much effort to go all the way back to the Hall of Minerals," Columi said by way of explanation for the informal decor. "Then I stay here. Now, Toriovico, about what do you wish to consult me? I'd word it more prettily, but you might not have all day."

Toriovico nodded. It was a relief to be able to shed some of the cumbersome formalities. He set the package containing the soiled robe on the table alongside his chair.

"It is this robe," he said, "or more specifically, the stain on the hem. I wish to have it identified. Quietly, without a fuss, preferably without anyone but you and me knowing either my request or your conclusions."

Columi hadn't spent years as a member of the Primes without knowing how to keep his mouth shut. He accepted the charge without comment and reached for the robe, carefully not disturbing the stain.

He raised the hem to his nose and gave a sniff.

"Hm. A trace of sewer filth. A touch of sulphur. Quite a bit more there though. The old nose is still pretty good, but it can't do the job alone."

The glance Columi gave Toriovico was sharp and canny, worlds away from the doddering old fellow he'd seemed when first awakened.

"Mind if I take some samples? A precipitant would tell me a good deal. Separate the material into component elements, all that."

Toriovico nodded his permission.

"Do whatever you wish. Destroy the entire robe if you must. What is important is that no one knows what you are studying. Will this be possible or will you need an assistant?"

Columi considered.

"I might need an assistant for collecting samples, but he won't need to know why I want those samples. Research is reason enough, especially for someone with my seniority. Age helps, you know. Half the time you get dismissed as a bit daft anyhow. Might as well use it to your advantage."

"Indeed," Toriovico forced a grin, wondering if he himself had fallen for an act a bit earlier. "I shall remember that . . . when I'm older, of course, and it will be useful to me."

"Do," Columi said companionably. "Be my guest."

He was holding up the robe now, inspecting it minutely, perhaps for other stains. Perhaps not.

"Tell no one," he said, looking quizzically at Toriovico, then back at the robe, "not even the Honored One's bride?"

"No one," Torio replied, though his stomach fluttered as he said the words.

"That's all right then," Columi answered. "That's quite all right."

"NO, FIREKEEPER," Derian said firmly. "We cannot leave right away."

The redhead folded his arms across his chest and accepted the wolf-woman's glowering unhappiness with a greater appearance of equanimity than he felt. It wasn't easy to defy Firekeeper after seeing her cold fury at Judge Ulia's decision. He had really believed she would start killing people if anyone had moved to harm Blind Seer.

He still believed she would have, but it would do no one any good to let Firekeeper know how easily she could terrify even those closest to her. Such a way of sorting out power might work in wolf society, but it would not work among humans.

At least, Derian thought a trace sardonically, *not among humans who possess less power than do kings and queens.*

"Why we not go?" Firekeeper argued. "Is much hours in the day yet, much light in the sky."

"There may well be," Derian agreed, "but there won't be after we've packed all our gear, topped off our supplies, and all the rest. We'd barely make it a few feet down the turnpike."

"Good! Even a small way is better than no," Firekeeper said. "I hate this place."

"You shouldn't," Derian countered. "It's probably the only place in New Kelvin where Blind Seer is perfectly safe."

Derian left Firekeeper to chew over that, and went to dicker with the stable manager for oats. It was familiar work and he was comforted by the odors of hay, manure, and horse sweat.

Derian needed comforting. Not only was Firekeeper agitating to leave, Edlin was in a funk over the planned destruction of the fighting dogs. He would have tried to buy them and take them with him if Firekeeper had not flatly promised to kill them herself. Edlin might be infatuated with his adopted sister, but he wasn't fool enough not to believe the sincerity of her threat.

Inside the Mushroom Stanza, Derian knew there would be the chaos associated with hurried packing. Doubtless Citrine would be whining, for it had been decided that lest she give the secrets away she spend much of the last several days "in bed" with a summer ague. At first the girl had enjoyed being pampered, but now that the danger was assumed to be ended she wanted to be up and about.

Thank the ancestors for Wendee! Derian thought. *None of us would have the least idea how to deal with a cranky child.*

After a long and leisurely haggle with the stable manager, Derian went back to the inn. Edlin and Doc were seated at a corner table in the public room near the door. Even as they waved Derian over, Elise descended from the stairway and came to join them.

"Wendee is with Citrine," she reported. "Jalarios is lying low. Any idea where Firekeeper is?"

"Probably somewhere with Blind Seer," Derian said. "She's miffed that we aren't moving on already."

"Well, if she hadn't been so impulsive," Elise said with a supreme lack of sympathy, "we wouldn't have been delayed at all."

A serving maid came over with tankards of ale for Edlin and Doc. Elise ordered some of the local wine. Derian vacillated, then went with the ale.

"I seem to recall that Dragon's Breath favors wine over ale," he said by way of explanation.

"It does indeed," a new voice commented, "though beer and ale can be found if one knows where to shop. Shall I give you an address of a reputable brewer?"

Derian looked over his shoulder to find that the mysterious judge from earlier that day had just entered the public room. He rose and gestured the man toward a seat. The judge accepted readily enough.

"Certainly we'd enjoy knowing about a reputable brewer," Derian said, "but we're already in your debt. Your arrival was fortuitous to say the least."

The man smiled.

"I am Xarxius," he said, "an official involved with trade. When I heard that there were foreigners staying at the Mushroom Stanza and that they had come into difficulty with the local law, I decided to interrupt my journey to Zodara. As you say, my arrival was fortuitous for us all."

Derian decided to leave that last hanging, wondering if Xarxius was referring to Firekeeper's potential for violence or hinting that he hoped for some trade concessions.

"Whatever," he said, "the least we can do is buy you a drink."

Xarxius ordered a goblet of the same wine Elise was drinking, and for a time the conversation centered on the local grape harvest and the promising earlier vintages that were just now being sampled.

"Are you planning to trade in wine?" Xarxius asked. "I perceive that Lady Archer has good taste and that Sir Jared is quite knowledgeable in such matters."

"Perhaps," Elise replied evasively, "in the future. Our immediate interest is in the more exotic goods for which New Kelvin is famous."

"The bane and the blessing of our trade," Xarxius said with a laugh. "Everyone wants silk, rare herbs, and colored glass. A few are interested in our art and cosmetics. Fewer, however, look to our other riches. I was hoping that you young people would have a wider view."

Elise raised her brows.

"Edlin and I are only agents for our parents' interests," she informed him. "However, if you can convince us to look into some of these other assets, perhaps we can influence the ones with the money."

Derian was tickled to see this evidence of practical manipulation on Elise's part. He wondered if it was an old skill or one she had acquired more recently.

Xarxius took Elise's words as a challenge and began what was obviously a practiced spiel. Derian listened attentively, but given his role as an advisor rather than a actual purchaser he restricted his contributions to questions about transportation and how it might add to cost.

Eventually, Xarxius thanked them for the pleasure of their time and for the wine. He invited them to look him up in Dragon's Breath, saying that the Hawk Haven ambassador could direct them to his offices. He departed, leaving Derian with a comfortable, relaxed feeling that was not entirely due to the ale he had consumed.

"Nice fellow," he said. Then he caught the guarded expression on Elise's face, so unlike her enthusiasm of a moment before.

"Maybe," she said. Then she explained what Peace had told her at the end of the trial.

"Therefore, I'm not surprised," Elise went on, "that Xarxius stopped to talk. What I wonder at is that he didn't let us know exactly who he is. After all, his importance couldn't help but influence our decisions, especially when we were talking possible price concessions and such."

"Xarxius told us his name, what?" said Edlin, obviously trying to calm his own uneasiness. "I mean, King Tedric doesn't need to say 'I'm the king, don't you know.' Maybe this Xarxius thought we did know who he is."

"Maybe," Elise said. "Maybe. Nevertheless, I'm looking forward to asking Peace a few questions."

HART BROUGHT THE WORD to New Bardenville, running through the gates as if all the wild wolves of the wild wood were at his soft-booted heels.

Ewen Brooks, standing guard at that gate, swung open the heavy iron-bound wooden structure to let the youth through, slamming the gate shut and swinging home the heavy wooden bolt in one practiced motion. Only then did Ewen look out through one of the many spy holes in the wall, expecting to see nothing.

They never saw anything of their enemies. This was one of the terrifying things about the not quite siege under which they had been living since Bear Moon was a slim sliver against the night.

The trouble had started soon after—though Ewen didn't like to think on it—that fellow Derian Carter and his Lady Blysse had left for back east.

Ewen didn't like to think about the possible connection between the two events, because he was one of those men who throve on being in control of his environment. It was bad enough that his settlement was under attack. It was worse that they were slowly losing the war to those unseen forces. Worse yet to believe that someone—Lady Blysse, perhaps—had such control over what Ewen thought of as *his* land that she could turn it against him.

So Ewen looked out through the spy hole, expecting to see nothing, and nearly shouted aloud at what he did see. He looked again for good measure, all the while listening to what Hart was saying.

"I was checkin' my snares, Ewen," Hart babbled, transformed into a scared green boy from the solid young man he'd been when he left the settlement that morning. "I was checkin' them just like always, and what do I see but a file of soldiers, soldiers on horses with bows and swords, armor and everything!"

Ewen turned. He had himself under control now. Control was important. Control was everything. Without control he might think. He might remember.

"I have two good eyes, Hart," Ewen said coolly. "Tell me something I can't see. Did these men come through the gap?"

Hart nodded, then he whitened. Ewen had forbidden any of his people to go near the gap. Too easy to slip away to the safer civilized lands. So tempting, too, with the gap only a day's travel away.

"The squirrel I was hunting darted that way," Hart said lamely, "and then it scared up a bunch of ducks. I thought to myself . . ."

Ewen made an impatient silencing gesture. The file of men on horseback was close enough now that he could make out the device on the shield of the man in the lead.

Yellow field with a black border that was squared off and indented, like castle battlements. In the middle of the yellow field there was a hand, palm outward, also painted in black.

Before he'd become Ewen Brooks, Ewen had been a miller, a country miller at that. He'd been to Eagle's Nest once and his family holdings were in Kite lands. Still, he wasn't ignorant. After a moment, he placed the device. Shield.

That meant that the man bearing that device was in service of House Gyrfalcon. It wasn't likely the duke himself, but judging from the cost of the man's gear he was probably a ranking member of the House.

All this went through Ewen's mind in the time it took for him to decide not to wallop Hart across the side of his face for disobeying orders. If trouble was coming—and that line of armed soldiers sure looked like trouble—then Ewen Brooks needed all the members of the Bardenville settlement on his side.

It'd be easier to get them to cooperate with whatever trouble those soldiers represented if Dawn were still here. Dawn was good at getting people to work together. But Dawn wasn't here. Wouldn't ever be here again. Another way of looking at it, though Ewen didn't like that way of thinking at all, was that Dawn was here, for now and for ever.

In a misery of loss, Ewen thrust away from him that thought and the attendant image of the grave marker in the little yard, searching for something that would make him strong to balance what threatened to melt him into tears.

Hadn't he founded this settlement? Hadn't the men and women followed him across the Iron Mountains and built this village from nothing? That was truth, a truth that no one could take from him, not even armed soldiers on horseback.

Ewen concentrated on his achievements, putting from him the gradual dissolution of that unity of purpose since the siege had begun. Then indeed had Dawn's gentler way of leading become important, and then indeed had Ewen begun to resent his wife's influence.

How he regretted that resentment now. If he hadn't resented her, she might still be alive.

The sound of the approaching troop brought Ewen from his reverie. Abruptly, Ewen realized that he and Hart were no longer alone at the gate. The settlers were emerging from the houses and workshops, crossing from the small gardens they so carefully tended within the palisade.

Nearly all the residents of New Bardenville now stayed inside those sturdy log walls. Only a few brave youths like Hart ventured abroad by daylight to see what they could garner from hunting and fishing.

Going outside the palisade had become too chancy. Bad things had a way of happening if you went very far in any direction at all but east. Branches fell from the green tangle above. Strange howls and yelps echoed and reverberated in the thick green tangle.

Just a few days ago, Garrik the carpenter had gone abroad seeking some green wood he needed to bend into shape before letting it season. Once he was out of sight of the settlement a flock of crows had descended on him, driving him hither and yon until he abandoned his search and ran back through the palisade gates.

The crows had been as thick as swarming bees and Ewen could have sworn the crows—who carefully stayed just out of bow shot—laughed at the humans before wheeling back into the forest.

Such attacks had been worse earlier. Several of those who had gone out hunting and trapping had never returned. Based on the few mangled bodies that had been found, all were presumed dead.

Those losses had hit the community hard, but even worse from the standpoint of long-term survival had been the morning the settlers had awakened to find that overnight the lovingly plowed fields outside the walls had been stripped of their young greenery. Deer and elk prints dimpled the soft earth in such numbers that entire herds must have descended to feast.

However, when the bravest hunters ventured out that very day, hoping to make up the community's losses in meat and hides, they saw not so much as a fleeing hind or hart. Nor had they since. Squirrels and rabbits didn't go very far when split among so many. With supplies of feed running thin and no grazing available, the settlers had been forced to slaughter some of the livestock—including those two new mules Ewen had been so happy to acquire just a short time before.

Even the fish traps set in the nearby streams were repeatedly found broken and emptied. Raccoons were the likely culprits, but some whispered that the tiny foot- and handprints were those of ghost babies—the returned spirits of the dead children of the first Bardenville, unhappy to have their birthplace taken over by others.

Dawn Brooks had been good at stopping such talk, pointing out that the newcomers had adopted the first settlers as ancestors, that their ghosts were more likely to defend the settlers than to bring harm. Even her reasonableness hadn't mattered, though, when weird hoots and yowls jolted the settlers from their already restless sleep.

But Ewen didn't want to think about Dawn and what she might have achieved. Without waiting to take opinions from the loosely gathered settlers, Ewen went out to meet the soldiers.

"Be ready to open the gate for me," he said to Hart as he reached for the latch, "but keep it closed until then."

The youth, eager to make amends for his not quite confessed infraction, nodded. Ewen thought he could trust Hart even to hold the gate against those who might have different ideas.

He strode out, holding his head high. Immediately, he noticed the guarded look the man riding in the lead gave him. What was his problem? Didn't he like having to deal with someone not of noble birth?

"Welcome to New Bardenville," Ewen declaimed, as if this mob of armed soldiers were no different from any of the other visitors the settlers had entertained thus far.

They were different, of course. Except for Derian Carter and Firekeeper, all the others had been coming to join the settlement or had been bringing welcome supplies. Then his greeting had truly been a welcome. Today he was aware of a certain ring of defiance to it.

Indeed, he realized that on some level he felt much as he had when his father had stumbled on the fort he and his buddies had built at the edge of some scrubland upstream from the mill. Then as now, what he had thought of as so grand suddenly looked rather shabby and makeshift.

"I'm Ewen Brooks," he went on. "Who do I have the pleasure of addressing?"

The leader of the riders straightened slightly in his saddle.

"I am Lord Polr Shield. I have come here from the king."

"King Tedric?"

Ewen kept his expression as innocent as possible.

"Of course!" Lord Polr didn't look at all pleased. "Who else?"

"My companions and I have been out of touch with Hawk Haven for some time now. It was possible that old King Tedric no longer sat his throne. When we departed the king was elderly and reported ill."

Actually, Ewen was fairly certain that the king had not gone to explain himself to his ancestors. Two groups of settlers had come to join New Bardenville since Derian Carter's departure and both had reported the royal situation unchanged. What Ewen had intended was to move Lord Polr away from whatever prepared speech he had ready—and to emphasize that the settlement had been in place for some time.

Lord Polr regained his poise with regrettable ease.

"I am happy to report that King Tedric is alive and well. My officers and I received our orders from him personally."

Ewen stood and stared rather blankly, doing his best impression of a simple yokel. He wasn't going to help Lord Polr along by asking "And just what were those orders?" or anything like that, though he was itching to know.

During the longish pause that ensued, Ewen made some estimates as to the disposition of Lord Polr's command. Only ten soldiers. That meant *his* group outnumbered them three or four to one. Of course, that was only if you counted the children and the malcontents.

Lord Polr's group was well armed, too. Every soldier wore a sword and most also carried bows. They were lightly armored in leather with metal reinforcements, good armor for the summer weather, when heavier mail might lead to problems with the heat.

The thing that really impressed Ewen was that the upper right-hand corner of every shield bore a small insignia—a wavy line flanked by two squares. It wasn't much, wouldn't even show from a distance, but it indicated that the bearer had fought in King Allister's War. Fought, not just served. Ewen felt chilled. Veterans, then. He reestimated his odds.

Lord Polr grew tired of waiting.

"I bring an announcement for all of those who dwell west of the Iron Mountains. Is this the only community here?"

"Only one I know of," Ewen said laconically. As if he'd rat on someone else! He was genuinely insulted.

"It would be easier to be certain the announcement was heard," Lord Polr pressed, "if you would let me come into your settlement. What was it you called it? New Bardenville. And read it in your public square."

"If you read it from where you are it should be just fine," Ewen said. "Out here to the west of the Iron Mountains we hear with our ears, not our eyes."

There were a few smothered chuckles at this sally, but Ewen didn't dare look around to see if they were from Lord Polr's troops or from inside his palisade. It was important he seem unmoved by such considerations.

"Very well," Lord Polr replied stiffly.

He reached into his saddlebags, pulled out a stiff roll of parchment, and read from it without further preamble.

"Let it be known," he read, his voice ringing out with practiced ease, "that by order of King Tedric, monarch of Bright Bay, and with the full support of his heirs and nobles, the lands west of the Iron Mountains have been closed to any settlement or colonization.

"Moreover, as a means of enforcing this commandment, a guard post is being established at the gap in the Iron Mountains, where, in time, a full keep will be built to enforce our royal will. Any who violate this commandment will be punished to the extent of their voluntary participation in the venture."

That leaves a loophole for the children to slip through, Ewen thought idly, *and maybe a spouse or so, but no escape for me.*

"This order," Lord Polr continued, "shall be enforced seven days following the publication of this commandment. Any who wish to avoid being in violation of this commandment and so risk full displeasure of the law shall by that time remove themselves and their persons to the lands east of the Iron Mountains."

Lord Polr finished by declaiming a proper listing of the king's titles and honors. Busy planning his response, Ewen hardly heard the words, instead hearing the silence when Lord Polr's declamation ceased.

"And when," Ewen asked, hoping he sounded casual, "was this commandment publicized?"

Lord Polr's aristocratic mouth shaped a thin smile.

"Why this very moment, Ewen Brooks. In seven days you and your followers will be in violation of the king's will for the disposition of his lands."

"And if we resist?" Ewen asked.

Lord Polr gestured to his soldiers.

"These are not my only troops. There are others a day away, preparing the guard post mentioned in His Royal Majesty's proclamation. However, if you or your followers resist, I shall command them to stop building and assist me in rooting you out."

Ewen said nothing, only wheeled on his heel and gestured to those within the palisade. In obedience to his signal, Hart swung open the gate and Ewen strode inside.

He slammed the gate behind him. Somewhere in the trees he could swear he heard the harsh, mocking laughter of crows.

XX

ON THE NIGHT following the trial's end Firekeeper sat with Blind Seer upon one of the many hills that had so recently been their refuge.

Wolf and woman sat with their backs against a wall of stone. Although Firekeeper knew they were nearly invisible, she felt exposed. The tensions of the last several days, when they had been hunted by Captain Brotius and his men and then forced to surrender, were still fresh.

"I wonder," Firekeeper said, leaning into Blind Seer for comfort, "how does our pack back home? Elation has not come back and Bee Biter has less than nothing to say on that run."

The wolf's reply was a deep, shuddering sigh that commented far more eloquently than mere words that he, too, had been worrying about both their wingéd friend and the pack they had left behind.

"I thought that any wolf, even any Beast," Firekeeper went on, "would be more than a match for mere humans, but Brotius and his men, they pressed you and me hard."

Blind Seer lapped her forehead reassuringly.

"But we," the wolf replied, "were trying to stay near our friends. The pack will have no such constraints. They can move wherever they wish."

"There are," Firekeeper reminded him, "the new pups to slow them."

"The pups will be running by now," Blind Seer said, "not very fast, true, or very surefooted, but no longer burdens to be carried dangling from their mother's mouth."

"I hope so."

Firekeeper found herself looking up into the night sky. The comet was still visible, but it was much fainter. Soon it would be gone. She wondered where it was going and once again wished that wherever that was she was going with it.

Blind Seer mouthed her arm.

"Well," he said, astonishing her by his perspicacity, "I'm glad you're down here with me."

"Do you read minds now, hunter?" she asked, almost believing this must be so.

The wolf snorted dry laughter.

"Not a bit," he said, "but I know my Firekeeper and I know her sighs and how she has watched that comet, first with fear, later with longing."

Firekeeper hugged him.

"I want to *do* something," she admitted.

"I know."

The wolf sat straighter, his blue eyes twinkling merrily.

"I don't like the idea of those dogs being killed by the humans."

"You pity dogs?" Firekeeper was astonished.

"No." The wolf rose and gave a lazy stretch. "I don't like the idea of the humans getting target practice. Let's go free the dogs. You can slip down there easily enough."

Firekeeper nodded agreement.

"And then? Judge Ulia was right. They are a danger to humans and beasts alike."

"Then," the wolf said, barring his teeth, "we will hunt them down."

The wolf-woman laughed, liking her pack mate's idea of a joke.

"Away then, sweet hunter," she said. "I'll let the dogs out to run. Even if the humans hear barking, they will think nothing of it."

When morning came and the men Brotius had delegated to shoot the fighting dogs went to the pen they found it empty. However, they soon learned that not one of the dogs had escaped their promised execution.

In the rocky hills surrounding the inn, Brotius's men found the dogs' stiffening bodies, the fattest of which showed signs of having been dined on by wolves.

❦

ONLY AFTER they had returned to the turnpike toward Dragon's Breath with Mushroom Stanza Inn and its environs far behind them could Elise convince Peace to speak again of his former associate.

"Xarxius began his career as a Stargazer," Peace began inconsequentially, as if feeling his way into the subject, "but his greatest talent is seeming less than he is. Whereas my role as Dragon's Eye mostly involved internal affairs, as the Dragon's Claw Xarxius works with foreigners. Therefore, I cannot overlook the possibility that he was present by deliberate design rather than chance."

"Wait," Elise interrupted, seeing a flaw in this division of duties, "you said this Xarxius was in charge of dealing with foreigners but, from what you've told us, you not he went to meet Lady Melina when she first arrived in New Kelvin with the artifacts."

Peace's smile was exquisitely dry.

"Yes, but then she was not arriving as a foreigner. She was a dissident seeking sanctuary. Moreover, there was the awkward problem of disposing of Baron Endbrook."

Elise glanced around to check if Citrine was in earshot, and felt a certain degree of relief that the girl was riding ahead with Edlin. Hopefully, she hadn't heard this painful reminder of how her mother had abandoned her.

"Very well," Elise said quickly. "So you think Xarxius might have wanted to take a look at us?"

"That was my first thought when I realized who had entered the inn," Peace admitted. "Remember, Lady Archer, you had sent a message to Hawk Haven's ambassador in the capital. Word of such could have reached Xarxius. Indeed, if the service I established during my tenure as the Dragon's Eye has not disintegrated into uselessness, it *would* have reached him."

Elise looked thoughtfully at Peace.

"And so," she said slowly, "hearing we were come again to New Kelvin, Xarxius raced from the city to make certain nothing happened to us. He just happened to arrive before the axe fell or Firekeeper did something that would get us all thrown out of the country. Nice. Then he says a few cordial words before going on with his business. What about that makes you so tense?"

At that moment, Edlin proved both that he wasn't always slow on the uptake and that he and Citrine were within earshot of the conversation.

"I say," he called back, "I wonder if this Xarxius recognized our guide? Is that's what's bothering you, Jalarios?"

Edlin enunciated the alias carefully, as if someone might be close enough to hear.

Peace nodded.

"I feel that Xarxius must have done so," he said. "We were close associates and Xarxius is skilled at seeing through others' masks."

"You did stay in the background," Derian reminded Peace, his tones offering comfort, "and you don't look much like you did."

"True," Peace agreed with a quiet smile for the redhead, "and that may have been enough. However, let us consider for a moment that Xarxius did know me. Does it mean ill or good that he did not act against me? If he knew who I was, he could have had me arrested and even executed on the spot. It is within his rights. Why then did he not?"

"Perhaps," Wendee offered, her voice thrilling with enthusiasm, "he's on our side! He knows we're not friends of Melina and he wants her out of there as much as we do."

Peace nodded.

"That is possible. However, Xarxius is a subtle soul. It is equally possible that having now assured himself that I am indeed one of your number, he is going to let us ensnare ourselves before showing his strength. Even if Firekeeper might have acted in a fashion that would have been considered unfriendly if Blind Seer had been harmed . . ."

The wolf-woman snorted in a fashion that left no doubt on that matter. Peace ignored her.

"That would not have been sufficient reason for your entire party to be sent from the kingdom. Xarxius may have wanted to implicate all of us."

"Or," Doc said, surprising Elise by entering into the conversation, "a combination may be possible. Xarxius may be against Melina and may want to use us as the means of eliminating her. Then he can offer his regrets to her new husband and get rid of us—by one means or another."

"Or," Elise said, finally getting into the spirit of this particularly unsettling game, "Xarxius might want us to go after Melina so that—after she has some narrow escape—she will become more popular. Look how the risks Shad and Sapphire have taken in battle have made them heroes with people who were previously unhappy about the idea of them eventually inheriting from King Tedric."

"I say!" Edlin exclaimed. "It is a pretty tangle, isn't it?"

"It is indeed, young lord," Peace agreed. "Though I fear I would not call it pretty at all."

ojo

A DAY AND A HALF after his initial meeting with Columi, Toriovico received a note that—beneath a barrage of flowery apologies and humble declarations that being of service to the honored ruler was the sole desire of the writer—boiled down to being a request that the Healed One call upon the emeritus Prime at the museum.

The hour Columi suggested meant that Toriovico had to cut one of his practices short, but he brushed away his Choreographer's protests and went. Melina had disappeared twice more in just the short interval that had passed. When she was available, he almost always found her surrounded by books. When he once commanded her into his presence—ostensibly to review a new dance—she toted an enormous tome along with her, "for something to read in case you couldn't see me right away, dear."

He'd even caught her sneaking a look at the magical book that held the First Healed One's history and the commentaries of his successors. That at least had disappointed her, and Torio evaded her coy efforts to get him to read to her from it.

What terrified Toriovico was that he had nearly betrayed this most secret and vital trust. He'd found himself thinking that it would be nice to have someone with whom to share the burden of his knowledge, that being foreign-born Melina wouldn't be shocked, that surely the other Healed Ones had told *someone* else. Why shouldn't he?

But ingrained conditioning to respect the office of the Healed One—a conditioning that might perhaps be even deeper in Torio than in most who had inherited the office, because some part of him still thought of the office as he had before he knew it would be his—enabled him to remain true to his responsibilities.

Melina sulked, though, and refused to sleep in his bed that night. Her rejection more than any enforced sexual abstinence hurt Toriovico deeply.

So he hastened to Columi's summons, hoping that the Lapidary would have an answer for Melina's curious behavior.

The museum was deserted when Toriovico arrived, and the round-bodied Lapidary wide awake and eager. Columi even seemed to bounce more easily through his obeisances, though he did pant upon rising.

"I have the information you requested," Columi said once greetings were concluded, "waiting in my office. If you would deign attend upon my humble hospitality . . ."

Toriovico nodded. Once settled into a chair, he eagerly accepted the tray of nut bread and sweet drinks Columi had prepared. He had come directly from his postpractice bath and was voracious.

Columi looked at him seriously as the Healed One wolfed down a third slice of the sweet, dense bread.

"You should take more care, Honored One," he said.

"That I don't get indigestion?" Toriovico laughed. "I never do. It makes my Choreographer crazy."

"I was thinking more about the risk of poison," Columi said, and went in on response to Toriovico's shocked look, "No, I am not taunting you, Honored One. That food is as safe as I could make it and I have eaten from the same loaf and drunk from the same pitcher. It just strikes me that your dancer's appetite makes you vulnerable—and that you do not yet have an heir."

Torio felt his appetite vanish, but he forced himself to eat a few bites more, just to prove that he didn't distrust his host.

"I have a food taster," he said, "but you are right. It is a custom I do not like and I tend to avoid calling on him."

"Yet these are unsettled times," Columi said, "and you would be wise to take precautions."

"Unsettled?" Toriovico asked. "Are the Defeatists agitating for a vote against Apheros? Has some new faction arisen?"

"No," Columi replied, "and yes. Or rather, to most the answers would be no and no. Apheros is more secure than he has been for years—this even with the defection of his Dragon's Eye. Yet to me—watching from the outside as it were—there does seem to be a new faction."

"Who?"

"First," the Lapidary said, maddeningly evasive, "let me supply the answer to the task you put to me a few days ago."

That was the only thing that could distract Toriovico from Columi's hints about a new faction and he felt an irritable certainty that the Lapidary knew this perfectly well.

"Yes," he said. "Have you located the origin of that dirt?"

"Within limits, yes, I have."

Columi steepled his fingers, consulted a page of notes to one side of his chair, and went on:

"I narrowed my search to the immediate vicinity for two reasons. First, in portions where it was thickest, the dirt remained slightly damp. Even in our current rather humid weather, this would not be the case if the garment had been transported a great distance. Secondly, to the best of my knowledge, you had not been away from Thendulla Lypella for at least a moonspan. True, the garment could have been brought to you from elsewhere, but I had the impression you had acquired it yourself."

"That is so," Toriovico said curtly.

"Very well. That confirmation does help. I made a precipitant from some of the dirt. This revealed trace organic material. Interestingly, there was no fresh grass or seeds such as there might be if the wearer of the garment had been out-of-doors. Rather what was present was dry and old. Much of it was, well, slightly fecal."

"Sewer dirt?" Toriovico prompted.

"Yes," Columi agreed, "and that predisposed me to think that the wearer had been roaming the tunnels beneath Dragon's Breath. I then set out to try to narrow the range.

"One thing that interested me was the amount of sulphur and certain other minerals in the samples I took. Although hot springs are not uncommon in New Kelvin—our sericulture could not survive without them, nor could our more exotic horticulture—within Dragon's Breath they are largely limited to the vicinity of Thendulla Lypella.

"Moreover, the places where underground tunnels and geothermic activity coexist are again mostly within—or rather beneath—Thendulla Lypella. The hot springs and baths in the city, the specialized greenhouses maintained by a few sodalities, are all separate from tunnels, both as a safety measure and as a means of channeling the waters more efficiently.

"Thendulla Lypella, however, was built over caverns, some of which were cut—depending on whether you are being metaphoric or literal—by the presence of dragons in early days or by latent volcanic action."

Columi stopped speaking and looked quizzically at Toriovico.

"I could not restrict the area further without bringing in apprentices to do some field research and I thought I should consult you first, given what else they might learn."

Toriovico asked mechanically, his mind still whirling through a wide variety of possibilities, "And that is?"

"That your lady wife is prowling the bowels of Thendulla Lypella— searching for who knows what."

For a moment, Toriovico thought about denying that Melina had been the wearer of the garment. Indeed, he felt an almost physical compulsion to protect her name and honor from any scandal at all. However, he was suddenly weary and shocked. Columi's report matched too well with Melina's sudden interest in old tomes, many of them faithfully copied histories and records from before the Founders' departure.

Toriovico knew—though Melina did not—how the First Healed One had carefully made certain these records were distorted and twisted. Still, there was some truth left in them. The First Healed One could not do otherwise given how many New Kelvinese had survived the Burning Times and knew the truth.

Instead of denying, feeling far older than the old man, Toriovico looked at Columi and said: "Tell me about this new faction."

Columi looked suddenly unhappy, as if he regretted his earlier impulse, but he did not resist.

"It is evident to me that the newest faction in court is no faction at all in that it does not agitate to displace Apheros or any Prime. Indeed, as you yourself noticed, the Dragon Speaker has not been so secure for years.

"However, to one who watches from the outside, it seems to me that there is a new motive power nonetheless. There is talk of trade with Waterland—of granting enormous concessions that we never would have given before."

Toriovico heard himself speaking without conscious volition.

"But we must. It is terribly important. You may not know this, but Waterland has offered magical artifacts in return for merely commercial concessions—and they've offered a good rate on slaves and a possible harbor . . ."

Torio stopped speaking, feeling oddly as if he'd wound down, like one of the string spinner toys made for holidays.

"So you agree?" Columi asked, a suggestion of doubt in his voice, though Torio wasn't certain whether the doubt was at his own wisdom for speaking or at Toriovico's belief in what he'd just said.

Torio decided to reply to the latter.

"I don't entirely agree," he said. "Indeed, I insisted that we check into the authenticity of these artifacts. However, Melina says there are advantages and I must agree."

" 'Melina says,' " Columi repeated and his voice was tight. "Honored One, surely you don't need me to spell this out further. Melina is the heart and soul of this new faction. She has strengthened Apheros's power but only because he is unable to do other than what she wishes. There are others within the

Primes—ones who would normally be obstructive and cantankerous if for no other reason than the joy of it—who are now amiable companions."

Toriovico nodded, though his head was pounding as if a drummer beat upon it. He thought of Dimiria, of the Defeatists, so suddenly placid.

"Think!" Columi pleaded. "Think on what she is doing . . . and wonder why on top of it all Consolor Melina has taken to prowling beneath the ancient towers of Thendulla Lypella."

"I DON'T RECALL this being a toll road last year," Derian commented after they were waved through yet another checkpoint.

"It wasn't," Peace replied making certain they were well out of earshot of any other traveler. "You and your friends should be honored. The change is due to you."

"Us?"

Peace pulled a weary, thin-lipped smile.

"You recall your departure from Dragon's Breath last year?"

"Of course."

"As I understand it—and you must understand that my information is secondhand," Peace looked momentarily sad, "your ability to avoid those sent out to search for you was much discussed, as was Baron Endbrook's similar departure somewhat earlier that season. There was great unhappiness over the ease with which the two groups of foreigners had departed when those involved in the national interest were hoping to speak with them."

Derian remembered that freezing journey with a shiver.

"Getting away wasn't easy," he protested. "You know that. If the weather hadn't been so horrible—and without Firekeeper's help finding food and shelter—I doubt we would have made it to the border."

"So it may be," Peace said with a noncommittal shrug. "I was too discommoded to remember much of that journey. In any case, as I understand it, it was universally agreed that the Sword of Kelvin Turnpike, at least within a few days of the capital, needed to be guarded. Such installations as the guard post we just passed cost money."

Derian nodded. "I'd say so. The horses I saw in the corral were superlative, bred for speed."

"Better to catch us with, what?" Edlin commented with interest.

"Something like that," Peace agreed. "An ingenious member of some committee came up with the idea that the guards might as well collect tolls to cover the expense. After all, travelers of all kinds benefit from the greater security on the roads and the guards need to be kept alert. Indeed, this road began as a toll road—a thing that is recalled in its name. My people are always quick to return to tradition."

Derian shook his head. There were toll roads in Hawk Haven, mostly roads that crossed private estates, but they weren't either common or popular. He didn't imagine the case would be otherwise here. The New Kelvinese were weird, but they weren't crazy. Then Edlin's words came home to him.

"I just hope," Derian said, the thought making him quite uncomfortable, "that we don't need to work a quick departure this time."

"I doubt," Peace agreed, "such would be nearly as easy. I wonder if it would be possible at all."

POLR SHIELD HAD a tremendous amount to prove. His brother Newell had been a traitor—an assassin who had tried to kill the king. His sister Melina had been exiled for plotting with the Isles against Hawk Haven and Bright Bay.

Polr didn't know the precise details of what Melina had done. Those were being kept very, very quiet, but his brother Tab's expression when he had returned from meeting with King Tedric had been eloquent. Young Jet Shield, now officially head of what had been his mother's household, had looked shocked.

No, Tab wouldn't say what the king had confided in him, and Jet was acting as if he'd forgotten he ever had a mother. Then again, Polr wasn't inclined to probe. He really didn't want to hear the details. Melina's flight into New Kelvin and her recent marriage to the king of that very weird land seemed to confirm her guilt.

Two traitors out of the Shield family would be enough even if the pair's deeds had been stretched out over the history of the kingdom. Two within a year was a shame the family might never live down, not even—or maybe because of—their descent from the near kin of Queen Zorana the Great herself.

The Shields knew better than anyone, maybe better even than the Eagles, Zorana's own immediate descendants, that Zorana Shield hadn't been quite the upright and stainless ruler everyone portrayed her as these days. You'd think that the story of how she won the castle now known as Eagle's Nest would be hint enough, but no one seemed to take it.

Polr had thought about what hints other people might take from recent actions, though. He knew that if his family didn't straighten up and do something notable then they were destined to be looked at slantwise by everyone. There'd been a rumor going around the House that when Sapphire ascended to the throne she was planning to displace Tab's heir and put one of her siblings in as duke or duchess. They were Shields, after all, merely a cadet branch.

It wouldn't be like the current House was being displaced, just shuffled around a bit.

So Polr felt that the honor of his house and continued dominance of his immediate line rested on his shoulders as he rode out on this mission for the king. He suspected that King Tedric knew just badly House Gyrfalcon needed to prove itself. Polr just hoped that the whole escapade wasn't meant to provide yet another example of his family's disgrace. It would be so easy, after all, to send him on a task in which he was destined to fail.

Polr resolved to succeed and studied the situation to find his best advantage. He and his immediate band had camped outside of New Bardenville for several days now, and if Lord Polr Shield was certain of one thing it was that Ewen Brooks was an odd one.

Commoner-born Ewen might be, but he didn't act it. From the records Polr had been invited to inspect before leaving Eagle's Nest, he knew that Ewen was a miller's son, nothing more. Ewen carried himself like he thought he was king or at least the mayor of some great city rather than an unofficial leader of a settlement whose proudest boast was a collection of half-built cabins.

Ewen had all but ordered them to camp outside the palisade—this when he should have been falling all over himself to welcome a noble to stay beneath his roof.

He'd told them where there was a stream with good water, but when Polr had offered to pay a few of the settlers to carry water and help with camp chores—a friendly gesture, he'd thought, given that they'd all be heading back east, where a few Gyrfalcon tokens could go a long way toward helping the former settlers set up housekeeping again—Ewen hadn't only refused to send anyone, he'd seemed insulted.

At his royal briefing, Polr had been warned to expect some resistance on the part of the settlers. That was the reason for the seven-day waiting period, to give them a chance to adjust to the idea of leaving. However, Polr hadn't seriously thought they'd resist, not once they had a chance to mull over what they were up against. He'd thought resistance even less likely after he'd gotten a look at the interior of their rude fortification.

Though the settlers had cleared a good bit of land around the palisade, they hadn't come close to getting rid of all the trees surrounding them. Numerous sturdy oaks and maples offered safe vantage points from which Polr and his scouts could inspect the interior of the palisade.

New Bardenville appeared to consist of a dozen or so structures grouped around a central square. One log longhouse looked quite solid—Polr would have bet anything that it had been the settlers' first fort, before the exterior wall was built. The other sides of the square were flanked with a mixture of tents and log cabins. A couple of the cabins weren't even roofed yet, relying on canvas tops, doubtlessly scavenged from former tents.

The settlers kept goats and hens, a few dogs and cats, but there were no horses or mules, and only a few cows. This was odd, because Derian Counselor had reported precise numbers and types of livestock present in the settlement and there had definitely been more domestic animals than they could now account for.

The size of the population seemed about what had been reported, but the balance had shifted. Polr saw no one who matched the description of Ewen's wife, Dawn—a person who he had been told might be convinced to be on the side of reason if some within the settlement chose to resist the king's will. A few other town leaders seemed to be missing as well.

Then there was the matter of the fields outside the walls. Derian Counselor's report had described tended areas prepared for a variety of grains and other staples. The open fields were there, the plow ridges still discernible, but there were no crops. The only gardens were comparatively small patches within the palisade.

So the settlers had met trouble, possibly from deer or rabbits, which—so said one of Polr's soldiers with the relish of a man who had escaped a farmer's life—could strip a field of young crops overnight. The settlers had to be short of food, perhaps of other necessities. If they were hoping for supplies from the east they now knew they weren't coming.

So why didn't Ewen make arrangements for his people's departure? Why didn't he invite Polr and his troops in so they could lend a hand? Surely he didn't mean to fight.

Lord Polr seriously considered this last possibility for the first time since his initial briefing. Well, if they wanted a fight, he'd give them a fight, for the good of king and country—and for the honor of the Shields.

SETTLING INTO HASAMEMORRI'S HOUSE should have been easy and peaceful.

Their enormously fat landlady, dressed as ever in something floating and pink, her facial ornamentation in shades of the same color, was delighted to see them. Clearly, as far as Hasamemorri was concerned, they were not foreigners of questionable character who had been forced to flee the city on rather short notice. They were valued clients.

I wonder if Hasamemorri ever figured out that Edlin and Derian doped her and her maids the night we left, Elise thought, recalling the tea Doc had blended. *Probably not, judging from this welcome. And, of course, that welcome has more to do with Doc than with all the rest of us combined.*

Indeed, they had barely finished dinner their first evening in Dragon's Breath before Hasamemorri had plunked down in a chair in their former consulting room, propping her plump leg up on a footstool so Doc could check on her perpetually aching knees.

Doc had just knelt to examine the tormented joint when a loud scream of raw, unornamented terror came from the backyard.

Elise bolted from her place at Doc's side and dashed down the center corridor to the kitchen. She arrived just as Wendee pulled open the door into the yard. The action admitted a thunderingly angry Firekeeper, who was alternately kicking and shoving in front of her a New Kelvinese in kilted robes. Although he was at least half again as tall as Firekeeper—and apparently in the prime of life—the wolf-woman was having no trouble herding him as she wished.

"Thief or bandit?" Firekeeper demanded sharply. "What is it when a man is in the dark listening at windows? Do I cut his throat or not?"

The man wailed in such wordless terror that Elise felt a sudden wash of pity for him. Thief or not, meeting Firekeeper in the dark was not something she would wish on anyone.

"Let's ask him," Elise suggested. "Is he armed?"

"Two arms," Firekeeper said, contemptuously letting go of her captive, her Fang blossoming in her hand as she did so. "You see if more."

"Don't do anything threatening," Elise advised the man in her most formal New Kelvinese. "I won't answer for my companion otherwise."

The man turned his face up to her imploringly and Elise saw clearly defined on his right cheek the stylized spindle that was the mark of the Sodality of Sericulturalists. Otherwise, he wore minimal paint—just a few dark lines defining brow and jaw. Elise recalled that the Sericulturalists usually wore less paint than the majority of New Kelvinese, lest they mar the exquisite fabrics that were their pride and their responsibility.

Certainly the man's robes seemed to confirm him as a member of the Sericulturalists. Elise couldn't recall when she'd seen such magnificent silk. Its dark blue dyes were deceptively simple, doubtless to show off the quality of the weave.

"I am," the man replied, also in New Kelvinese, his voice trembling, "Nstasius, least Prime of the Sodality of Sericulturalists. I beg you, do not let that mad creature kill me!"

"Lady Blysse," Elise said slowly, "has had a very difficult visit here in New Kelvin. She did not expect to find such an honored personage prowling in our back garden. Neither, for that matter, did I. Do you wish to explain yourself?"

Elise was aware that the rest of their company had joined them, even Peace, who hovered almost unseen in the partially open kitchen door, Citrine clinging to his robes.

Demonstrating the tact and prudence that had made her such a fine landlady during their former visit, Hasamemorri was lumbering up the stair to her own apartments. In a few moments, the door that separated the two portions of the house was heard to firmly shut.

Elise felt vaguely strange when she realized that no one was going to take over interrogating Firekeeper's catch, but she pressed on.

"And what, Nstasius of the Sericulturalists, were you doing in our back garden?"

"Actually," he said, looking a trace calmer, "I was around the side of the house when this . . . Lady Blysse took exception to my presence. She brought me around to the back."

Elise repeated the gist of this to Firekeeper, who nodded.

"That is so," Firekeeper said, grinning wickedly. "I think it not good for Hasamemorri if I bring this in front door. Blind Seer," she added apparently as an afterthought, "is seeing if there is more."

"Nstasius," Elise said, "tell me quickly. Did you have any companions in your spying?"

"Spying!" he protested indignantly. "I was not . . ."

"Later," Elise interrupted. "Answer my question. Any companion of yours may be in grave danger."

Nstasius shook his head.

"I was alone," he replied, "but I was not spying. I was trying to learn if you had retired for the evening. I had no wish to draw your landlady's attention if you had done so."

Derian, his New Kelvinese understandable if unpolished, interjected, "Well, you've failed there, and I hope you've told the truth about companions. Lady Blysse isn't the most formidable of our guards."

Nstasius looked unbelieving, but reasserted that he had been alone. Shaking down his kilted robes, he added, "I wished to speak with you of Hawk Haven about matters that would benefit us both, but I wished that our audience be private."

"Wait a moment," Elise said, "while I translate your request for those of my companions who do not speak your language."

She did so. When she had concluded Doc spoke for the company.

"I don't see what harm listening will do. Does our visitor speak Pellish?"

"A little," Nstasius answered when Elise put the question to him, "but for such complex matters I would be happier speaking my own language— especially since this lady speaks it so well."

No one argued that this should be otherwise and so everyone except for Grateful Peace and Citrine adjourned to the consulting room. The kitchen was public space shared with Hasamemorri and even the most tactful of landladies should not be tempted beyond reason.

Elise wished they had reason to include Peace in the conference, but prudence dictated that no undue attention be drawn to one who was—after all— simply a hired guide.

"I represent," Nstasius began when all of them were settled, "a group

vitally interested in better, more open relations with those lands that neighbor our own. My associates and myself hold progressive views regarding
how New Kelvin should best advance. For too long have resources been
diverted to antiquated and arcane interests that benefit none but a few
researchers. We would see that change. We see Hawk Haven as a strong ally
in our cause."

One of those, then, Elise thought as she translated for the others, *who
oppose the policies of the current Dragon Speaker. King Tedric spoke of such.*

"This is interesting," she said aloud. "Why do you bring this matter to
us? If you have heard rumors that Lord Kestrel and myself represent a
potential market for your country's goods, you are correct, but our finances
are not vast."

Nstasius did not look disappointed. Indeed, he looked rather pleased.

"You might find that your resources buy more than you had imagined
possible," he said delicately, "if you were to make your purchases through
those with whom you have established friendly ties."

"Isn't that always the case?" Elise replied blandly, being deliberately
obtuse.

Nstasius looked momentarily frustrated, then said, "Let us say, then, if
your friends were in positions of power within the government and so able
to grant trade concessions."

"I begin to understand," Elise said. From the look in Derian's eyes, the
horse trader's son did too. "That would be very nice, but how could we
assist you to promote yourselves and your allies into those positions?"

Nstasius tugged sharply at the end of his braid, twisting the coordinated
blue ribbon around the end of his finger.

"Consolor Melina," he said abruptly. "She is a new power among us. She
is your countrywoman. Our hope is that you can help us to understand her."

Understand? Elise thought. *You would not like at all what we could help
you to understand, Prime Nstasius.*

Aloud she said, "Lord Kestrel and I are not close associates of the lady.
She is of our parents' generation. Still, if you tell us what you know of her
and what she has done to make herself a power here—for we understand
that a Consolor is not the same as a queen in our own land—then perhaps
we can be of some assistance. Surely, there can be nothing wrong with promoting understanding between such different cultures."

Nstasius managed to look relieved, sly, and eager all at once. Elise rattled off a rapid translation of what had passed. When she had finished, Fire-keeper rose and stretched.

"I go see if Blind Seer find anyone else," she suggested, sheathing her Fang.

"I'll walk you out," Wendee said, clearly determined that neither Fire-keeper nor Blind Seer be given excuse to rough up other visitors, "and see if there's enough warm water for tea. We could be talking for a while."

Elise appreciated Wendee's simple practicality—and the insight to the more complicated problem that it demonstrated.

They had been several hours on the road that morning, spent much of the day unpacking, and every bone in her body longed for bed, but this Nstasius wouldn't have come so soon after their arrival or so secretly if he didn't think that his business was urgent.

Prime Nstasius, too, would probably have preferred a meeting where they would have been more awake, more alert. Or would he?

Her own head spinning with possibilities, Elise prompted, "You were about to tell us what Consolor Melina has done to make herself such an influence in the nine moonspans in which she has dwelt in New Kelvin. We are especially curious how a foreigner could have so deeply involved herself in a land that so values tradition."

"Consolor Melina has deeply embraced New Kelvinese manners and customs," Nstasius began slowly. "Indeed there are those who say she shames those of us who desire change. Consolor Melina soaks up information about our past as a towel does water. There is no legend so obscure that she will not listen to it, no dance or ritual so arcane that she will not observe it. For those of us who had hoped to see such nonprofitable rites take a background to forward-minded production and trade, this is disquieting."

Derian leaned forward and asked in his awkward but serviceable New Kelvinese, "Do you and your associates then hope to become another Waterland?"

Nstasius looked appalled, almost angry, then thoughtful.

"I can see how a foreigner might so perceive it. No, we do not. We would simply see some resources allocated in directions other than those that are chosen by Apheros and his cronies."

Derian nodded and sat back, but Elise was certain that he—like her—suspected that Nstasius was not telling them everything. Therefore, she felt quite comfortable being less than complete in her report on Melina.

Elise spoke at some length about the woman: her late husband, her children, her family estate. She mentioned the importance of House Gyrfalcon, into which Melina had been born, and explained in greater detail than she would have thought necessary about inherited positions.

However, neither Elise nor any of her companions said anything about Melina's singular hold over her children or how Sapphire had broken that hold. To do so would cast doubt on the crown princess, and this foreigner had not proven himself trustworthy.

By then the hour was so advanced that Elise must smother yawn after yawn behind her palm. At last, Nstasius apologized:

"I fear I have been untactful and unkind, but I wished to make this contact before your arrival was widely known. May we meet again?"

Elise considered.

"Perhaps it would be better if arrangements were made through the Hawk Haven ambassador. Lord Kestrel and I are meeting with her tomorrow."

Nstasius neither agreed nor disagreed with this suggestion, but nodded thoughtfully.

"I shall consider your suggestion," he said.

Firekeeper had not reentered the consulting room after her departure, but she was waiting in the central hall when they exited. Blind Seer was with her and Nstasius poorly concealed his shock.

Firekeeper bared her teeth, and the expression was not quite a smile.

"This was the only one this close," she reported, "but I think some wait for him. We did not frighten them."

Elise nodded.

"Thank you for your visit, Prime Nstasius," she said. "If you have questions more precise—or perhaps specific actions of your Healed One's Consolor you wish interpreted—please do not hesitate to contact us."

Nstasius sketched a brief but respectful departure ritual that included them all.

"Thank you," he said.

When he was gone and the door secured Firekeeper said, "Bee Biter will follow him to his nest, just to see if his pack is as he says."

"Good," Elise said.

Firekeeper wasn't done with the matter.

"Now," she said, her posture indicating that she, at least, was willing to sit up all night until the matter was resolved to her satisfaction, "was this a thief or a bandit?"

Elise considered.

"Neither," she replied, remembering how literal Firekeeper could be. "Prime Nstasius was a spy—and perhaps a future ally."

Firekeeper frowned.

"I don't understand 'spy,'" she admitted.

Derian cut in, shoving Firekeeper toward the kitchen.

"We can worry about fine tuning later," he said, winning Elise's gratitude. "Not all of us slept throughout the afternoon while others worked."

Firekeeper had the grace to look shamefaced, for honestly she had done little of the unpacking, considering such beneath her.

"But I must know," she protested with a touch of a whine.

Grateful Peace turned from where he had been tending the kitchen fire.

"A spy," he said, "is like a scout—but a scout for another pack and one who may steal your game from you."

Firekeeper nodded.

"I understand that," she said. "Are spies for killing?"

Peace—once spy-master for a kingdom—smiled, a touch sadly, Elise thought.

"Often," he said, "but never without talking to them first."

The answer might have satisfied the wolf-woman, for Firekeeper gave a brief bow of thanks and slipped out into the night, but Elise found that it unsettled her, chasing through her dreams and tainting her rest so that sleep offered no refreshment.

XXI

TORIOVICO WAS DANCING. Toriovico was.

Toriovico was dancing. Dancing. He was.

Toriovico was the Healed One.

Was? Is! Was.

Toriovico was Dancing. Only when dancing was he—

Toriovico.

Toriovico, the healed one, ruler of New Kelvin, struggled to hold on to a single, elusive thought. His feet were still moving, arms still pumping, working their way almost independently through the series of choreographed motions that made up his part in the Harvest Joy dance.

It was a dance he had first performed as a small boy. He'd been a minor vegetable then, a yellow squash. Now, of course, he danced the Harvest Lord's part. It was only right. He was the Healed One. He was also a fine dancer in his own right.

Flautist and drummer noticed a faltering in Toriovico's steps, faltered themselves, anticipating a command to begin the section over again. Toriovico shook his head at them, the gesture so fiercely contained it was terrifying.

Toriovico was dancing. Toriovico was . . .

Dancing? Was he? Dancing? Who was he?

He felt himself losing the familiar sequence of steps, fumbling, losing with the dance the momentary clarity of thought that had nearly led to revelation. Toriovico sank himself in the simple repetition of the dance, forced himself not to think, and in not thinking Found.

What had he been doing? What had he been thinking? Had he been thinking? Had he?

Maybe just a little. Feet still moving, arms tracking their way through his interpretation of the traditional gestures, Toriovico recalled his recent visit to Columi, this time without the surge of guilt that had accompanied such thoughts before. He had been thinking then.

Dancing. That was the key. It was while he had been immersed in dancing he had first felt angry about Melina's recent disappearances. He had not been actively dancing, but he had gone to find her directly from a practice, the steps he wanted her opinion on still occupying most of his attention.

His anger had carried him through his encounter with Tipi and through his meetings with Columi, though in that latter case guilt had nearly made him abandon his purpose. He had hardly comprehended the old Lapidary's warnings, his hints that Melina had become the force behind much of the court's actions.

Anger was not something Toriovico could hold on to, not for long, but dancing . . . Dancing might just be enough to . . .

Toriovico struggled again, working his way toward a thought that was there, but so walled behind barriers that he felt as if his thoughts were within the dense threads of a silkworm's cocoon. He grasped the image, worked it into his dance, transforming the rhythmic motions of the Harvest Lord's labors among symbolic fields into the unraveling of silk.

Silk is spun in a single thread. Toriovico made a spindle of one hand, held the cocoon in his other. Unwrapped, unbound, removing the bonds, finding within . . . Clarity.

The barriers tumbled down. He saw a pair of oddly crystalline blue-grey eyes, heard lips admonishing him to trust, to love, to obey, to forget, to adore, to forget, to obey, and above all to forget.

Toriovico stopped dancing, aware for the first time of the awed murmurs from his musicians, of the expression of mingled astonishment and annoyance on his Choreographer's face.

"What do you think you were doing?" the Choreographer asked, his astonishment robbing him of the usual ritual courtesies. "That wasn't part of the dance!"

The flautist, revered for her art by two sodalities, and therefore intimidated by neither the Choreographer nor the Healed One, interjected:

"But it was magnificent!"

"I was dancing," Toriovico replied woodenly, his tongue numbed by revelation. "Dancing."

"WHERE DOES THE HEALED ONE LIVE?" Citrine asked Firekeeper as they wandered the streets of Dragon's Breath.

Ostensibly, the "boy" was serving as Firekeeper's guide and translator, but Firekeeper was the more knowledgeable about the city and with occasional whispered commands she kept Citrine on course.

"You not ask that so loud," Firekeeper chided her, "and not in so good Pellish. You should call Healed One by New Kelvinese name, I think. They do this with many places and people to make us feel small."

Citrine accepted the reprimand gracefully enough, but she didn't forget her question.

"Where is Thendulla Lypella?" she asked. "That's the name of his castle, isn't it?"

In a softer voice Citrine added, "I think I can ask that, Firekeeper. After all, I might be a country boy, right?"

"Not if you guide," Firekeeper reminded her.

"My father is the guide," Citrine answered. "Our story is that this is my first time to this city. I'm just with you to translate, right?"

Firekeeper sighed and shrugged. She had trouble keeping these layers upon layers of deceptions straight. She was also edgy because there were so many strangers around. Had Blind Seer not been at her side, she would have been quite tempted to go hide in Hasamemorri's stable.

Unlike in Eagle's Nest, here in Dragon's Breath the Royal Wolf could walk the streets openly. Indeed sometimes he was not even noticed by the humans amid the panorama of odd costumes and odder vehicles that filled the New Kelvinese city. The animals, however, had no doubt what he was. Beasts of burden sometimes panicked. Dogs barked. Cats snarled.

That didn't bother Firekeeper a bit. The dogs and cats knew to keep their distance. If the occasional horse or ox grew nervous, that wasn't her problem.

Knotting her fingers in Blind Seer's fur, Firekeeper considered Citrine's question.

"Thendulla Lypella," she said, "is over there."

The wolf-woman gestured roughly north with a toss of her head.

"Where those towers is," Firekeeper continued.

"Are," Citrine murmured, but her correction was automatic and she stared at the towers with raw hunger in her eyes. "It's a really big castle, isn't it?"

"Is not so much castle," Firekeeper replied. "Is a city in a city. Is very big and confusing."

Citrine didn't seem convinced. She fidgeted, shifting from foot to foot, and tugging at the long skirt of her New Kelvinese robe.

"Can we take a closer look?"

Firekeeper shrugged. She wasn't quite certain what it was the others expected her to do out here in any case, and humoring Citrine had become habit. The girl had fewer fits these days, but when her eyes shone with that particular feverish light it was not a good time to defy her.

"We go," Firekeeper said.

She led the way to where a large main street dead-ended against a huge wrought-iron gate that they had learned during their previous visit was opened only when some elaborate ceremony demanded it.

Wordlessly, the friends stopped across the street from the gate. For a moment, Firekeeper thought that Citrine might run over and press her face against the cunningly crafted vines and flowers that intertwined into a deceptively solid iron barrier, perhaps try to worm her way inside. The girl held her ground, however, her stillness a marked contrast to the intensity of a few minutes before.

"You're right," Citrine said after a long pause. "It's a city, not a castle."

Then, to Firekeeper's utter confusion, she began to sob uncontrollably.

EWEN BROOKS didn't need the notched stick on which he'd marked the days since Lord Polr had read that thrice-cursed proclamation to know that time was up for New Bardenville.

He'd have known it from the phase of the moon if nothing else, for chance had ordained that the first day of Hummingbird Moon was the day they must decide whether to resist the king's will or to move on.

Some of Ewen's people took the moon as a bad omen. The dog, whose moon had just passed, was a creature who lived side by side with humans, who guarded and protected them, who made one family with them. When Dog Moon shone it had seemed only right to resist the forces that would move them from the settlement. Now, though . . .

The hummingbird was a fierce creature, one who could never be tamed, who might sup on the nectar of a human garden, but who never offered anything but a flash of brilliant color in return. Some saw the fact that King Tedric's proclamation took effect at the very start of Hummingbird Moon as an omen that they, too, were expected to move on. Others, Ewen foremost among them, saw it as an omen that they were meant to fight.

He told the doubters so on their last meeting come dawn of the dreaded day.

"The hummingbird is small," he said, "possesses neither talons nor cruelly curved beak, yet when it comes to fighting spirit it would combat eagles. So we are called to fight this House of the Eagle and its predator herald. The ancestors will it and have shown their will by the day on which we must decide our fate."

That speech swayed them, though a few, like Garrik Carpenter, murmured that it was wrong to resist the king's will. Not many wanted to listen to him. They'd held their ground when their crops had been eaten, when they'd been made prisoners in their own hard-built fortification. It was almost a relief to have something visible and tangible to fight.

The majority of the settlers also thought—and Ewen was foremost among those who held this opinion—that in the end Lord Polr wouldn't order his men to attack those who honored the same ancestors. Hadn't King Tedric only disowned Prince Barden, not brought any harm to him or to his followers?

Surely the new settlers would be left to struggle as they might rather than risk the spilling of familial blood. Being disowned would be hard, but they would adjust.

New Bardenville's struggle for survival might be very difficult indeed without the promise of fresh supplies from the east and the very land seeming to fight the residents, but Ewen was confident that the settlers would win.

After a few seasons had passed, the settlers might even strike up trade with the soldiers assigned to the new garrison at the gap. That would be nice. And the wild creatures who had been harassing them certainly wouldn't be so fierce and bold with armed men patrolling the forest.

Indeed, by the day that Ewen climbed to the walkway from which one could see over the top of the palisade, some of the settlers were beginning to view the soldiers with a certain fondness—as a future lifeline, rather than as potential enemies.

Lord Polr alone, armed and armored, wearing a helmet, his shield slung over his arm, strode to within twenty long paces of New Bardenville's eastern gate.

"The sun has risen on the first day of King Tedric's new law," the lord cried, his voice strong and fierce. "Will you come forth and let us escort you to the gap?"

"No," Ewen called in return, enjoying the steady ring of his own voice. "My friends and I have made a home here. In this home we will stay. Let King Tedric know that in all things but this new proclamation we will remain faithful to him and his descendants, but that wasteland should not remain unused when there are farmers to farm it and crafters to tame it for the use of civilization and the king's own greater glory."

Ewen was proud of his speech. He'd sat up the night before going over it again and again until he could say the words naturally. Lord Polr did not look impressed, but then Ewen had not thought that a few words—no matter how well chosen—would end it. They must debate until Lord Polr saw how determined the settlers were to remain.

Lord Polr made a dismissive gesture with one hand, then called out:

"I ask again. Will you not come forth and obey the wishes of your king? We have observed how pressed you are, how your fields are stripped of all grain, how your livestock has died. We have even found fresh graves in the plot by the forest edge. You have lost many of your number. You will lose more before winter releases her grip. Come and we will escort you to safety."

Ewen was aware of the stirring from below and behind him, where the majority of the settlers stood in a tight cluster, listening intently to the exchange. Even without turning to look he could tell that they were remembering what this new threat had made them almost forget—the fear under which they had been living even before Lord Polr arrived.

Without glancing down lest someone catch his eye and gain excuse to interrupt, Ewen shouted his defiance again.

"No! We will not return to the east, to a life as little better than slaves to large landholders such as yourselves. In a realm where you begin to outstrip the generous holdings granted to you by Zorana the Great what room is there for us to grow?"

Ewen knew that he spoke as much to his own followers as he did to Lord

Polr, standing there so arrogant in his strength and the implied power of his distant monarch that he had not even bothered to bring his soldiers up with him. Doubtless they lounged in their comfortable camp having a last cup of tea before escorting the settlers away from their hard-earned home.

Lord Polr shook his head, though whether in pity for the smallholders' plight or in annoyance at Ewen's continued defiance, Ewen could not tell.

"There are other solutions to your difficulties," Lord Polr responded. "New lands are opening to settlement in Bright Bay. Skilled crafters are always welcome. If land is what you desire, then petition those who hold the grants on which you reside or move to lands that are open for settlement."

"We did move to such open lands," Ewen replied, and this time his voice was raw with anger. "We moved to lands empty of all but beasts. We made a place that would have extended our monarch's holdings. This being chased away like children out of their mother's garden, is this is our reward?"

Lord Polr gave no answer to Ewen's question. Perhaps he had none. Instead he called,

"A third and final time I ask you, Ewen Brooks—and all those who have followed him here—will you obey your king's command and come east again?"

"No!" shouted Ewen, and a few other voices—but only a few—answered with him.

Lord Polr raised his hand once again, and this time Ewen recognized the seeming gesture of dismissal for what it was—a signal.

From the cover of the brush the rest of Lord Polr's soldiers stepped forward. With a single motion, each nocked an arrow, angling it so that it would clear the palisade and fall within.

The archers were firing blind—or so Ewen thought until he caught a glimpse of motion in a high, broad-limbed oak, and realized that another soldier was poised on a branch there, elevated sufficiently to see over the palisade and so direct his fellows' firing that it might fall where the greatest concentration of inhabitants stood.

Lord Polr glanced to the man in the tree, took his direction, and dropped his hand like a band leader.

As one the archers fired, the arrows rushing through the air with a hiss that sounded rather like hard-falling rain. The first flight was followed by another almost before the first shafts cleared the palisade.

Ewen spun even as the bows were drawn, hollering for his people to scatter, to get to cover. Some did, reacting on the same visceral level that makes rabbits flee when their sentry stomps warning. The rest reacted more humanly, staring up at Ewen in confusion. A few even shouted questions.

Or began to do so. When the arrows struck, all questions were answered. For two of the settlers there were no questions remaining but to wonder from whence came this sudden pain. One of those hit was Garrik Carpenter, the same who had protested against resisting the king's will. Another was a woman bending to shelter the babe in her arms and so moving less rapidly than the others.

Ewen turned away from the bloody scene in dismay, red flooding his vision. It was always the same. The powerful had their way whether they were the monsters of the dark forest or their seeming civilized kin in the cities and villages. Before them fell the wondering and the weak.

Ewen saw Lord Polr signal his archers to hold their fire. Then Lord Polr called out:

"Now, Ewen Brooks, do you understand that we will enforce our king's wishes? We have more arrows in our quivers, and have already marked a fit ram with which to batter down your gates. There is fire, too, the very element which cleansed the earth of a son who disobeyed his royal father and which could render you and your rebels into ash. Will you surrender now?"

Ewen felt the walkway beneath his feet shudder as someone ran along it. He was heartened when a quick glance showed him several of the other settlers coming to join him.

A sneer twisted Ewen's upper lip as he drew breath to shout defiance. Then, astonishingly, a blow fell upon his head and another upon his back. Ewen crumpled to his knees, his words choked to a cough within his throat, his throbbing head barely managing to hold consciousness.

With the last thread of sense he heard Hart crying out in a thin boy's voice. "We surrender, lord! We surrender! Just don't send any more arrows."

Darkness came and took Ewen away, and in his bitter fashion he was glad.

DERIAN CAME IN from checking if the hired carriage was ready, to find Elise and Edlin waiting in the hall.

After weeks in riding gear, to Derian's eyes Elise almost seemed oddly dressed in the pretty but formal summer frock she'd packed along in anticipation of just such occasions. Edlin, in turn, looked mildly miserable in his knee-breeches, waistcoat, and jacket.

"I say, it's just so hot, what?" he protested. "Can't I at least do without the coat?"

"Sorry," Elise said, though she didn't look at all sorry. "We must make the right impression."

"I'll make an impression all right," Edlin muttered, "in sweat on brocade."

Elise wasted no sympathy on him but turned to Derian.

"Is our coach here?"

"It is," Derian assured her. "Brace yourself. Oculios sent along one of those pulled by people rather than horses. He said it's the only way to navigate the streets with any speed at the busiest times of day."

"If he says so," Elise replied doubtfully. "I certainly can't hope to arrive at the ambassador's residence at all clean if we walk."

Edlin had strode to the doorway, his complaints about his clothing forgotten in the novelty of the forthcoming experience.

"I say!" he called back. "Why are they dressed like that? I mean, I can see the loincloth and harness routine, rather practical in the heat, don't you know? But why are they wearing wings on their shoulders?"

Derian shrugged.

"To show they're fast?"

Edlin grinned.

"I say! Come along, Lady Archer. Our vehicle awaits."

Elise colored slightly when she saw the state of undress affected by their "steeds" but sallied forth with style, letting Edlin hand her up into the seat slung on the light carriage frame.

"We should be back for dinner," she said. "If our plans change, we'll send word."

Derian waved.

"Have a good time!"

As he watched them clatter down the street, Derian became aware that Doc had emerged from his office/consulting room. Doubtless he'd been watching from the window the entire time.

Derian couldn't resist teasing.

"Elise looked awfully pretty, didn't she?"

Doc made a rude gesture.

"She is never less," he said with dignity, "than perfectly lovely. Now, if you will excuse me, I'll step across the hall and check how my convalescents are doing."

Derian felt a little bad about teasing Doc, but for himself, Derian felt decidedly restless. It had been a long time since he'd been with a woman. He didn't want to count back and figure out just *how* long, but he realized that face paint, tattoos, and all Hasamemorri's maids were looking pretty good.

It's when Hasamemorri herself starts looking good, Derian thought wryly, *that I really need to worry.*

That thought shook him out of his self-pity and with a whistle on his lips he went looking for Wendee. They'd both been collecting information in the various business centers and it was time they compared it.

Wendee was in the kitchen, hanging a market basket over her arm.

"Are Lady Archer and Lord Edlin on their way?" she asked.

"Off and running," Derian assured her. "Or at least their bearers were. I'm not sure I can get used to the idea of grown adults being hauled around by other people."

"Seems odd to me, too," Wendee agree, "but it does work nicely in these narrow streets where a horse and carriage would have trouble. I suppose the New Kelvinese had to come up with something if they were going to keep all their old buildings."

She shrugged.

"Want to come to market with me? Jalarios isn't around and Doc just brought me two sacks of the local tokens and suggested I go shopping. I know Jalarios didn't want me going on my own, but you should do."

Derian took the market basket from Wendee's arm by way of accepting her offer.

"Why wouldn't Jalarios want you going alone?" he asked. "You did last time we were here. It seems to me that you and Elise—because you were the only ones who had at least some command of the language—went out more than the rest of us did."

Wendee frowned.

"I'm not exactly sure why," she admitted, "but in the few days we have been here Jalarios has been as close as a burr on a bear's behind. Today's the first day that he's gone off on his own, and before he did he asked me if I would be going out."

"And?"

"And I said I didn't plan to," Wendee said, "but then Doc gave me the tokens and the kitchen was feeling rather close, so . . ."

She gave another of those so eloquent shrugs that managed to say more than someone else could put into words. Derian remained troubled.

"It must be nice," he said as they traced their way along one of the twisting streets toward the nearest market square, "for Doc to have money to spend. I know it was for me when I actually earned some for myself rather than taking what my parents gave me. It felt even better to give them some back."

Wendee nodded.

"I think Doc is putting some by to send home, but mostly types of currency that will transfer well."

"I'm a bit surprised," Derian said, feeling his way to an idea, "that Doc isn't putting something by for himself."

"Why should he?" Wendee said, cutting to the heart of the matter as if she'd read Derian's mind. "What he wants most he can't buy—and if you'll forgive me, Lady Archer isn't being encouraging—so why should Doc be putting by for her? He may as well enjoy having a bit to spend."

The tall redhead nodded. He dodged a tall, skinny man dressed like a crane, complete with a gaping bill that so dominated his head that his face— painted in a pinkish red that matched the interior of the bill—looked out through the open mouth.

Derian looked after the fellow, wondering how well he could see, and then returned to the conversation. He was in midphrase before he realized how much he was starting to take New Kelvinese oddities for granted. It unsettled him more than the crane-man had.

"I wish we could help advance Doc's suit," he said lamely.

"So does Firekeeper," Wendee replied with a laugh. "She was asking me about human courting customs this morning and was appalled when I assured her that the matter wasn't going to be resolved as simply as she imagined.

"Mind," Wendee continued, squeezing close to Derian to avoid a parade of women in elaborate floral robes who strolled down the middle of the street as if no one else were about, "I think Firekeeper isn't as ignorant as that. I think she was hoping that I'd find her a loophole. She's frustrated by something—and I think it's more than our current situation. What's going on with her?"

Derian hesitated. Matters west of the Iron Mountains, especially the remarkable news that the Royal Beasts were prepared to defend their lands, might just be a state secret. On the other hand, Firekeeper had been edgy lately, and telling Wendee something of what was troubling the wolf-woman might prevent disaster later.

"She's worried about her family—wolf family," he began. "When we went west earlier this spring we discovered some people had taken over the site of Prince Barden's old settlement. They weren't particularly sympathetic to the claims of those who were already living there."

"By which you mean wolves," Wendee said, obviously trying to wrap her mind around the concept. She nodded crisply, clearly having succeeded. "No wonder Firekeeper's in a snit. Why isn't she back with her pack?"

"King Tedric told her he wanted her out of there," Derian replied honestly, "that if she started trouble it wouldn't do any good for the wolves or for her or for the Kestrels. He promised to send representatives to evict the settlers if she'd come along on this trip. Firekeeper agreed, but it's eating her alive, not knowing how her family is doing."

Wendee nodded.

"It would me, too," she said sympathetically. "We need to find things for her to do to keep her busy. Right now while we're feeling our way into the local situation she's too much idle."

"Any ideas?" Derian asked.

"Let me think," Wendee replied. "In any case, we shouldn't be discussing such things in the middle of the market."

The last turn of the street had brought them into Aswatano, the Fountain Court, their local market square. Like similar open spaces in Eagle's Nest, Aswatano had at its heart a fountain supplying fresh water to the local residents.

Unlike the ones in Eagle's Nest, however, which were attractive but fairly utilitarian structures, this New Kelvinese fountain was an ornate sculpture depicting a group of robed figures apparently trying to rope a storm cloud. The water falling from the cloud gave the impression that the scene was alive and moving.

"I'm glad Hasamemorri's house has its own well," Wendee said, glancing at the sculpture. "That gives me the creeps. Jalarios told me that it depicts a scene from one of their legends of the Founders, something to do with subduing some monster."

Derian took a second look at the sculpture and saw hints of claws and fangs in the cloud, and maybe a long, serpentine tail.

Wendee defiantly turned her back on the fountain and began inspecting fat, round yellow squash in such a fashion that Derian knew further discussion of that matter would be unwelcome.

To distract himself, Derian went a few stalls away and began fingering some long, thin peppers that burned his mouth just to look at them. The vegetable seller gave Derian a rather nasty look for which translation was unnecessary, and Derian managed an apology in his halting New Kelvinese that only slightly mollified the . . . man? Woman?

Derian couldn't really tell and a wave of disorientation came over him, strong enough to wash away his previous smug sense of being acclimated to this foreign land.

Shopping took longer than it would have in Eagle's Nest. Wendee wasn't about to be taken just because she was a foreigner, but her awkward version of the language with its persistent threads of archaic expressions didn't help matters much.

A butcher, his face and upper body stained in wild patterns as if to compensate for the clothing his trade made impractical, started hooting in laughter when Wendee called him something that Derian understood translated as "Thou callow fool!" Such expressions might sear the malefactor to the bone in a play three hundred years old, but clearly they didn't have the same impact on a modern listener.

When he could stop hooting with laughter, the butcher said to Wendee: "You Hawkus?"

His Pellish was worse than Wendee's New Kelvinese, but clearly he thought he'd done something clever by showing he knew a smattering of their language.

Wendee replied with icy precision in his own language:

"Yes. I am from Hawk Haven."

The man replied with a long, deliberately slow statement from which Derian caught only the most simple words. That it was insulting, he had no doubt, given the rise of color to Wendee's fair cheek. Seeing her blush, the butcher laughed again, pointing and adding some comment that the bystanders seemed to find even funnier than his previous effort.

Derian hated putting himself to the fore, but he couldn't leave Wendee to face this alone.

"What did the butcher say?" he hissed at her under the cover of the crowd's laughter and a few shouts that only raised the level of hilarity.

"It was very rude," Wendee said stiffly, "a comparison of unpainted faces and nakedness. I'd rather not repeat it, but it implied that I was a prostitute. When I blushed, he said that it was too late to cover myself with such thin paint."

Derian felt his own color rising, but with anger rather than embarrassment. His right fist balled of its own accord. He might not be a soldier, but years of handling horses had given him impressive upper-body strength. He glowered at the butcher, wishing he had the words to tell the man what he thought of him.

He might have tried, but at that moment an angry shout from the back of the crowd cut through the laughter. It was a statement of some sort, and whatever the speaker said brought silence where there had been crude humor a moment before. The only sound was the splash of the fountain.

Then Wendee squared her shoulders.

"That's cut it," she said.

"What?" Derian asked.

Wendee didn't reply directly, but instead began inspecting bags of pungent dried herbs and spices at the stall directly next to the butcher's.

Derian found himself thinking inanely that the placement probably wasn't completely fortuitous, since spices could be used to preserve meat. He was aware that every eye in the immediate vicinity remained fastened on them.

"What did that last person shout?" he persisted in Pellish, keeping his voice so low and level that they might—though he doubted anyone was fooled—have been discussing whether to buy sea salt or rock salt.

Wendee responded in kind, hefting a small cloth pouch of something that made Derian want to sneeze, apparently checking to see how well it was filled.

"He said, 'Go home and take your whoring-spy-bride'—that's the best translation I can come up with, but it implies a great deal more, all of the ugliest type of behavior—'with you.' "

She put the pouch in their market basket and looked inquiringly at the stall tender. The spice vendor was a young woman—at least, Derian was fairly sure was a woman; it could have been a rather effeminate boy under all the cosmetics—who looked decidedly uncomfortable at being the center of so much attention.

Wendee picked up another pouch of the same spice, studied it consideringly, and placed it in the basket. Again she looked at the spice vendor.

This time the young woman—Derian felt pretty sure it was a woman once he heard her voice—stammered out a price.

With a coolness Derian was pretty sure she did not feel, Wendee countered with a lower offer. The crowd, which to that moment had remained almost completely silent, stirred. There were a few murmurs, which Derian was certain were admiring.

Taking his cue from Wendee, Derian sniffed a bunch of dried flowers as if trying to decide whether they were worth purchasing.

Wendee grinned at him.

"Those are marigolds," she said, "used for making a nice golden-yellow dye. I doubt you'd like if we cooked with them. Too strong a flavor."

Derian almost forgot the crowd, which was, in fact, beginning to forget them—or if not to forget, to ignore.

"And these?" he asked, pointing to some purple flowers.

"Asters," Wendee said, "though you'll never guess what color you get from them."

"Not purple?" Derian asked. "Or blue?"

"Shades of green, gold, or brown," Wendee said, putting the asters back, "depending on what you mix them with."

"Mix," Derian said, glad to play student to Wendee's impromptu lesson if it would give the crowd a chance to decide not to bother them. "With what?"

"Oddly enough," Wendee said, pointing to some medium-sized wooden boxes set near to where the stall tender could lay hand on them, "often powdered metals. They help the dyes to set and affect the colors."

"Interesting," Derian replied, "but we won't be dying cloth, will we?"

"No," Wendee said, glancing surreptitiously around. "However, I don't think it's quite safe to venture in to the thick of the market yet. Cooking spices are always useful . . .

"For many reasons," she added rather mysteriously.

Derian was distinctly puzzled, right up until they had finished their purchases and Wendee slipped him a packet of the strong-scented spice she had first selected.

"Put it in a pocket where you can easily lay hands on it," she instructed. "If there's trouble, a pinch or two in the face will stop someone as well as a fist in the jaw."

Derian accepted Wendee's gift, giving the older woman an admiring glance.

"Cool head and hot eyes," he said, trying to make a proverb of it.

"Something like that," Wendee agreed. "Just be certain you loosen the tie so you can get to the powder if needed."

"Needed?" Derian asked. "Surely you're not staying out here!"

Wendee squared her jaw.

"We certainly are," she said. "We've already learned something about local feelings for Melina that we didn't know before. Let's see what else we can learn."

XXII

THE AMBASSADOR welcomed Elise and Edlin with a courtesy that could not completely hide that she was a very worried woman.

Ambassador Violet Redbriar was the younger sibling of the current Duchess Goshawk, an able woman in her own right who had transformed a formidable talent for languages into a diplomatic career.

In her mid-sixties, with iron grey hair and skin like fine leather, Violet Redbriar had taken, Elise noted with some surprise, to wearing New Kelvinese cosmetics. She didn't wear them in any great quantities, true, but the blush on her lips and cheeks, the foundation covering the worst of the sun damage to her skin, were as startling on a woman of Violet Redbriar's birth as a tattoo would have been.

Perhaps this is what happens when you live among foreigners for too long, Elise thought. *You begin to see the world through their eyes.*

It was an uncomfortable thought, especially about a person Elise had been counting on for—if not help, at least understanding.

After the usual greetings and offering of refreshments, Ambassador Redbriar withdrew with them into a book-lined room that was clearly an office, not a parlor or drawing room.

Elise found this choice rather ominous and her sense of foreboding was not lightened by the ambassador's first words.

"Things have changed in New Kelvin," Violet Redbriar said, "and not at all for the good."

"I say," Edlin replied, leaning rather stiffly back in his chair as if his buttoned waistcoat was too tight, "that's what I've thought, what?"

Elise frowned him to silence, then turned her attention to the ambassador.

"Lord Kestrel may have noticed, Ambassador Redbriar, but I fear I have not. Of course," Elise gave a small, self-deprecating shrug, "I have not been much away from our house since we arrived."

"Has the mood in the street been so bad that you have feared to go out?" Ambassador Redbriar asked.

Elise was puzzled.

"Not at all," she explained. "Far from it, really. We've had numerous patients calling for Doc's—that is, Sir Jared Surcliffe's—services. Their mood has seemed fine, enthusiastic even."

Edlin tried to interject something, but Ambassador Redbriar spoke right through him.

"You haven't sensed any odd moods," she persisted. "Urgency, perhaps? Guardedness?"

Elise frowned.

"Anyone who seeks out a doctor seems rather urgent," she replied, made hesitant by the ambassador's own intentness, "and all but the patients we see regularly are a bit aloof. We *are* foreigners, after all, even if the locals do believe Doc has magic."

"I had heard something of Sir Jared's reputation," Ambassador Redbriar admitted. "Healing talent, is it?"

Elise nodded reassuringly. "That's all. He's a good doctor without it, but it does give him an edge."

"Well, I find it hopeful that your patients have returned," Ambassador Redbriar said. "They must have come fairly soon upon your return."

"Even before we were settled," Elise said. "We were a bit surprised by how soon they heard of our arrival, actually."

"I," the ambassador said, "am not. Anything from Hawk Haven is big news now, because, you see, of Consolor Melina."

"They like their new queen so much then?" Elise asked.

"Some may," the ambassador said rather evasively.

"But most don't!" Edlin blurted out. "I say! Elise may have been busy healing the sick and all, don't you know, but I've been out on the streets—went to the apothecary a few times, once to the market with our guide. I don't speak the lingo well, but I can read an expression with the best of them. Some of the folks don't like us, not half."

Elise stared at him.

"Edlin, why haven't you said anything before?"

The young lord shrugged, almost embarrassed.

"No one much to talk with, what? You've been busy, so's Doc. Fire-keeper's off wherever Firekeeper goes. Citrine's hardly a confidant. Derian and Wendee, they've had things of their own to do."

Elise felt suddenly sorry for Edlin. They had rather left him out of things since their arrival in Dragon's Breath. After all, the young lord's main reason for being along had been a combination of security on the road and offering the excuse that House Kestrel was interested in starting up trade with New Kelvin. Edlin's good-naturedly playing at doorman or performing whatever odd jobs were needed had disguised what was evidently growing discontent and restlessness.

"Lord Kestrel is correct in his impressions," the ambassador said, giving Edlin a more respectful look than she had accorded him thus far. "Many of my contacts within the current government do not like Consolor Melina. They resent her as a usurper of a place that should have gone to one of their own. Recent shifts in policy from the Dragon Speaker have not made things any better."

"Shifts?" Elise asked.

"The Dragon Speaker has become markedly more aggressive in pursuing magical lore," Violet Redbriar said, "despite the 'disappointments' of last winter. This has put a real crimp on one group—call them the Progressives, though their enemies call them the Defeatists—who have been trying for years to get New Kelvin to base its economy on something more tangible than magic and antiquities."

"Surely that's not enough reason for Edlin to be scowled at in the streets," Elise protested. "After all, New Kelvin has always been devoted to old things almost to the exclusion of good sense."

"Good sense was beginning to get the upper hand," the ambassador said, "or at least what you and I would term good sense. Indeed, it is not telling tales out of turn to say that Hawk Haven rather hoped for a Progressive coup next election. This is unlikely now."

Violet Redbriar gave Elise a meaningful look and Elise answered with a slight smile.

"I believe we've spoken with one of these Progressives. Least Prime Nstasius of the Sericulturalists visited us upon our arrival."

"He has spoken with me as well," Ambassador Redbriar said.

"Is Prime Nstasius your only source for these indications of unhappiness among the New Kelvinese?"

"No." Violet toyed with the fringe on her sleeve as if considering how much to say. "I have heard from other than him about Melina's politicking. It is widely agreed that she is in favor of granting trade concessions to Waterland in exchange for things—rumor is not consistent on what these are—that will benefit her. This has not made either the merchants or the lesser members of the sodalities very happy."

Edlin nodded enthusiastically.

"I can see why not," he said. "They set up their trade, then some overruler messes with the balance, what? I think anything like that would make Grandmother furious, don't you know, and she likes King Tedric. Calls him Teddy when she forgets."

There was a slightly stunned pause at this last inconsequential bit of information, then Ambassador Redbriar cleared her throat and went on.

"Perhaps the least popular of the Dragon Speaker's recent decisions has been the appointment of a Dragon's Fire to replace Grateful Peace, the former Dragon's Eye."

Elise chewed on her lower lip, realized this was undignified, and sipped from her cup of rather tepid and overly sweet tea.

"Dragon's Fire," she said after sorting through her memory for the various New Kelvinese titles, "that's a war leader, right?"

"Absolutely," Ambassador Redbriar replied approvingly. "The problem with a war leader is that there must be something to lead—an army to be precise. You young people may not realize this, but New Kelvin has not had a standing army for many years. Local militia companies deal with bandits."

"I say!" Edlin commented. "They don't deal with them too well, either. From what we've seen, I mean. Been attacked both this trip and last. Last time was understandable, but this time we were staying at an inn along a major public road, don't you know. No excuse for such sloppiness."

Violet Redbriar looked rather more thoughtful than Elise thought Edlin's latest diversion merited, but she replied without directly addressing his point.

"This may be, but with the exception of the local militia, New Kelvin has no army. It has not had a standing army since the time of the First Healed One—that is, in the time of the Plague. There isn't even a provision in the rather complex New Kelvinese legal code for an army to be raised."

"Impossible!" Elise said, thinking of her own family's contract with the throne of Hawk Haven to raise a certain number of soldiers in time of war.

"Not at all," the ambassador said. "In the past, when New Kelvin has been forced to fight, an army has been raised by the simple expedient of requesting volunteers. If this does not garner sufficient warm bodies, then a nonvolunteer army is formed."

"Nonvolunteer?" Elise queried, not believing her own ears. "Isn't that dangerous? For the commanders I mean."

"Sometimes," Violet Redbriar agreed, "but there are penalties for resisting service—and not all of them are applied just to the rebel. Families, sometimes extended groups, pay the price."

They all thought about this for a long moment. Elise made a mental note to ask Hasamemorri for more details.

"I say," Edlin said, irrepressible as always. "I can see why the locals are unhappy, but why take it out on us?"

"Because they think that Consolor Melina is responsible for the creation of the Dragon's Fire," Elise offered slowly. "Is that the case, Ambassador?"

Violet Redbriar nodded. "And they may not be incorrect. My sources say that Consolor Melina has considerable influence over Apheros—that is the current Dragon Speaker—as well as over her husband, the Healed One."

"Do you think Consolor Melina is really so influential?" Elise asked. "And, if I may be forward, have you reported your thoughts to our king?"

Ambassador Redbriar frowned. Clearly she *did* think Elise was being rather forward, but she was too polite to say so.

"I have told the king something of this," she said, "but Consolor Melina is no longer his charge. He himself has declared her exiled."

"Easy enough to do," Elise said with a cynicism that she was surprised to find in herself, "when the woman is unlikely to return of her own accord and it is even more unlikely that she would be extradited—given her intimacy with the local government."

"With the Healed One," Violet Redbriar said. "Toriovico, the Healed One, is not all the government. Indeed, he is hardly concerned with its routine business."

Elise let the comment with its undertone of schoolroom correction pass, though she didn't much care to be spoken to in such a manner, especially after King Tedric himself had consulted her on the matter of international policy not so long ago.

"I understand," Elise said. "You have given us much to think on. Certainly, we will take care with our ventures into the city."

"You have a guide?" the ambassador asked.

Was her question a touch too casual? Elise couldn't be certain.

"A crippled fellow we hired in Gateway," Elise replied airily. "He and his young son are staying with us. In a pinch we can borrow one or more of our landlady's maids. Hasamemorri is devoted to Doc—Sir Jared—or rather to what his healing arts do for her abused knees, and will gladly aid us."

Elise was aware that her last sentence was less than eloquent, but talking about Grateful Peace was unsettling, and Sir Jared was hardly the distraction to still her soul. Violet Redbriar, however, seemed satisfied.

"Very good. I think it would be better for all concerned if we left our associations fairly general. This embassy has already attracted unwelcome attention from those who are certain Consolor Melina spies for her birth land. Let them think this a courtesy call and nothing else."

Elise was pleased. She had been dreading an invitation to remain for dinner, especially now when she had news she wanted to get back to the others.

They parted soon after. So absorbed was Elise in her thoughts and in the ramifications of what the ambassador had told them that she didn't even notice the sullen glares, like rapidly concealed ripples in a formerly still pond, that their passage generated in the crowd.

Beside her, Edlin did, and it might well have been his forester's watchfulness—usually so out of place in the city—that kept them safe to the tidy door of Hasamemorri's house.

EWEN BROOKS lay on the soft earth, swallowing hate more bitter than the bile that surged from his unsettled gut. A long while seemed to pass before he could do more.

At first, he thought the pounding that made thinking or moving so difficult was all inside his throbbing head, but when he managed to open his aching eyes, he realized that the pounding had an external source as well—rather, several external sources.

Back and forth, back and forth, in their steadiness more like ants than people, the settlers were moving between the cabins and a line of rough but serviceable wagons that stretched across what had once been a village square. Ewen wondered where the wagons had come from. Then, looking from side to side—the space behind his eyes flashing ruddy-colored lights as he moved his head—he understood.

Lord Polr must have brought the wheels and axles with him, but the bodies of the wagons were being built from timber salvaged from the cabins. The outer structure of the cabins had been made from logs, but lofts and furniture had demanded planks. Garrik Carpenter had proven he deserved his place in the community by locating seasoned wood, then showing them how to split it into planks.

Ewen had been a miller's son, so he was accustomed to sawing wood, not splitting it. Garrik's transformation of downed trees—some of which they had speculated might even have been felled by Prince Barden's settlers ten years earlier—into handy boards had seemed like magic. It also had given them a level of luxury Ewen had thought they must do without until they had a mill of their own.

Now, through open doors—indeed, through gaping door holes, for the doors themselves were gone—Ewen watched as lofts were torn up, their boards handed down to cheerful hands reaching from below.

The town square within the palisade of which Ewen had been so proud seemed emptier now. The tents that had been pitched in the intervals between the cabins, waiting their turn to be replaced by tidy log structures, had been dismantled. Even as he watched, a few of the remaining domestic fowl were carried by, their legs trussed, their necks craning at ridiculous angles as they sought to make sense of their predicament.

"We'll pay for any beast or fowl you don't wish to carry back," said a firm voice that Ewen placed in a moment as that of Lord Polr. "Remember that!"

Lord Polr's voice sounded different somehow, robbed of the tension that had echoed beneath its every word or statement, no matter how innocuous.

Ewen struggled to pull himself upright. He didn't have much luck, but his motion brought a shadowy figure that had a tendency to split into multiples hunkering down beside him.

"Easy," Lord Polr said. "You took a nasty wallop, then went down off the walkway. They tried to catch you, but . . ."

His shrug made his image fragment. Ewen squeezed his eyes shut for a moment. When he opened them again, things seemed to have stabilized. Again he tried to struggle upright and he felt Polr's firm hands assisting him to sit and lean back against something solid—the palisade, Ewen realized. They hadn't moved him far from where he fell. They'd made him a thick pallet on which to rest, brought him a pillow. When he glanced up—a thing that hurt more than he could have imagined—he saw that a bit of canvas had been strung over him as a roof.

How long had he been out?

"Water?" Lord Polr asked.

Ewen tried to nod, then decided that was a bad idea. His "yes" came out more as a grunt, but Lord Polr apparently took it as assent.

A canteen was held to his lips, the well water within it still cool. Ewen swallowed greedily, making some infantile noise in protest when the water was pulled away from him.

"Sorry, but the company doctor says we have to be careful, can't have you retching it all up again. See how that sits and we'll try more in a bit."

Ewen acceded. His stomach was turning from the few swallows and he didn't want to humiliate himself further by puking.

Polr bent closer, studying Ewen with a clinical efficiency that spoke of training in the medical arts. He peeled back one of Ewen's eyelids, nodding with satisfaction.

"I think you're with us again," he said. "You've been out for a day's turning and some."

Ewen grunted astonishment.

"You fell hard," Lord Polr said, "and though you've made sounds enough that we thought there was sense left, you didn't seem to know what we said to you. Do you understand me now?"

"Yes," Ewen said or tried to say, but the sound was more a croak than a reply.

"That's fine," Lord Polr replied. "You take it easy."

He waved his arm, gave orders that the doctor be found and brought over.

"You'll be pleased to know," Lord Polr continued, carrying on their one-sided conversation with a certain ease that recalled to Ewen his idea of what the social gatherings of the nobility must be like, "that you have no broken bones—not even in your skull, thanks to the giving of the earth on which you fell. The doctor wants to watch you carefully for the next several days. There remains a danger you bruised your brain, but even that swelling should recede if we treat you with sufficient care."

Will you? Ewen thought.

"And we will," Polr answered, anticipating Ewen's obvious concern. "Look, man, we're not enemies, not unless you insist on being so. You and your followers overstepped what the king wished. We have been sent to rein you in. You and your people will be relocated with no stigma, no punishment. If you don't make a fuss about it, I don't even plan to report our little disagreement of the other morning.

"If you don't want to return to the town you left, well, I'll help you relocate. I have some land. My brother, Duke Gyrfalcon, can always use skilled crafters—and you people have shown both your skill and your willingness to work hard."

Ewen wanted to spit on Lord Polr's charity, but his mouth was too dry.

"I've heard from your companions a bit of what you all have faced these last moonspans," Polr went on, wonder shading his aristocratic accents. "Crows attacking, wolves and bears as large as horses stalking your walls, fields stripped by deer and elk who held their ground against arrow fire as if they were soldiers! It's like a story from the days of colonization. I'd think you'd be glad to get away from here."

You have land, Ewen thought, glad his mouth and throat would not cooperate with his will. He was afraid of the things he wanted to say. *You have prospects. You have title. I can go back to swallowing other people's chaff and sawdust and bowing to your kind. I'd rather deal with the bears and pumas. They at least were honest. They don't "good fellow" you out of one side of their mouths, but expect you to scrape in the mud when they pass you in the street. Give me honest hate any day.*

Lord Polr, of course, knew nothing of Ewen's thoughts, but went on talking as calmly as if they were seated in some parlor.

"We move out in the morning," he said. "My soldiers have worked side by side with your people . . ."

Stop calling them "my" people! Ewen thought furiously, though all that came from his lips was a strangled grunt that Lord Polr took as a request for water. He carefully tilted the canteen against Ewen's lips, still talking.

"And the progress has been amazing. His Majesty insisted that we bring the wheels and axles. They were a heavy load, but worth it. No one need leave anything they wish to take."

Except for dreams and hopes and pride, Ewen thought.

"We're also going to pay for the fowl, a litter of kittens, and probably the dairy goats. From what I understand, they were owned by the community as a whole, so the money will give everyone a start-up. I've also been authorized to pay for those materials you'll be leaving behind: the logs from the cabins and palisades, for example. Again, the funds will be split among the adults.

"We'll use the building materials," Lord Polr said, interpreting Ewen's dismayed cry that soon nothing but a barren meadow would remain of their hard labor as a request for explanation, "to construct the rough beginnings of what will eventually be a stone keep at the gap. Even with having to haul the timber—and we've enough wheels to make logging carts— the materials should save us considerable time."

I hope the wolves eat you! Ewen cursed him. *I hope the crows pluck out your eyes and feast on their softness! I hope the pumas bite through the throats of your horses!*

But he knew they wouldn't. The beasts would be glad to see the settlers leave. They would be glad to see any return west by humans prevented by their own kind.

How would dumb beasts know what is happening? a mocking voice that sounded remarkably like his own asked. *How would beasts know what Lord Polr intends?*

A memory swam before Ewen's eyes, a sharp-featured young woman with dark, haunted eyes—too scarred and silent to seem even human. She had sat by his fire, eaten his food, played with his children, and all the while she had nursed his destruction in her animal heart. Lady Blysse, that wolf-suckled wench—she would be the one to tell the beasts even, as Ewen now realized, as she must have told the king.

A chill shook him, followed by a tremendous wash of heat. Lady Blysse was his enemy, not this prattling noble idiot with his well-meaning words and utterly hollow heart. Lord Polr might not even know that he'd been a lackey not of his king or his own noble family, but of a flea-bitten traitor to the people who bore her.

But there was no touching Lady Blysse—at least not now. Instead Ewen struggled to find some way to save his role as leader and the dignity of this venture. If that last was lost, all hope that they might someday be permitted to settle the western lands was lost.

He cleared his throat and found that his voice was with him.

"Our dead," Ewen said softly. "My wife . . . the others. We cannot leave them."

Lord Polr's eyes widened as he considered a new contingency—and recognized that here Ewen had found the means to disrupt this orderly retreat.

"The soldiers at the garrison can make the appropriate offerings," he said, but it was clear from his inflection that Lord Polr knew this battle was lost even before it was joined.

The people of Hawk Haven revered their ancestors, saw them as their continuity with the past, their protection for the future. If anything, the nobles were more devout in this respect than the commoners.

They have to be, Ewen thought bitterly. *Everything they have rests upon the deeds of those who bore them.*

He didn't say this. He didn't need to. All he did was moan, softly, persuasively, his voice as loud as he could make it:

"Dawn."

THE SETTLERS FELL in so rapidly with Ewen's muttered exhortations that he realized how almost by accident he had tapped into their own sense of failure and betrayal.

Yes, they wanted to leave this besieged place, especially now that a new and more direct opponent had entered the field. Yet to go like a cowed apprentice beneath the master's whip—they who had dared so much to make a place for themselves where they might prosper by their own work—that hadn't pleased the bolder of New Bardenville's settlers one bit, especially when the soldiers' bows were unstrung and the immediate threat of attack removed.

Ewen's plea had found a way for the settlers to regain their lost self-respect, a way they could retreat with dignity, if not triumph.

Before long the word had gone round, and the settlers were dragging their heels, no longer so hard at work destroying what they had built. One by one, sometimes in little clusters of two or three, they came to visit Ewen, to tell him how glad they were that he was looking so well, telling him that they had heard about his hope to bring Dawn and the rest of their dead home with them and that they approved.

Some bright mind had carried the matter one step further and now it seemed that the remains of Prince Barden's people must also come home again. Never mind that the grave was communal—for the members of Earl Kestrel's expedition had found only scattered bones—and therefore none could be returned to specific families. The settlers had adopted these forerunners as their own ancestors, and as such must bring them home.

Many looked to Ewen for direction, but though he was feeling much stronger, he stayed meek and docile, directing each to Lord Polr as the one in charge.

By midday, Lord Polr had capitulated. The boards that had not yet been hauled away were set aside to be transformed into rough coffins. A few of the more hearty men went willingly to work disinterring the dead.

Courteously, Lord Polr tried to salvage some of his dignity by offering a few of his own soldiers as laborers, but that offer was curtly refused. This task, ugly as it was, belonged to the people of New Bardenville.

Ewen Brooks lay on his pallet, sipping spring water freshened with mint, and felt well pleased.

MELINA LOOKED at the letter, at the blocky childish print so unlike the graceful New Kelvinese script that had been her reading matter of late, yet she couldn't escape the feeling that this was the most important thing she had ever read.

> *Dear Mother,*
>
> *I am here in Dragon's Breath. I am living with Lady Archer, Lord Kestrel, Lady Blysse, and some people I don't think you know. They are very nice to me, but I can't wait to see you. I hope you will let me come visit.*
>
> *Your obedient daughter,*
>
> *Citrine Shield*

The news of this little group's arrival was not new to Melina, for Melina had spies posted at the major crossing points between Hawk Haven and New Kelvin.

Indeed, one of these, Kiero, had sent an express message announcing the company's arrival to her—and had taken it upon himself to arrange an incident that should have removed that nauseating Lady Blysse from the country. Kiero's plan had failed, and Melina thought his removal to Urnacia was only fit. She really couldn't understand why he kept sneaking messages out to her. Did he expect her to reward failure?

No. The group's arrival was not news, but Citrine's membership within it was news indeed. Why had her spies not mentioned this?

Melina unlocked the carved wooden box where she kept her more private correspondence and checked the appropriate missive.

No, Kiero had said nothing of Citrine being part of the group. Had the girl been kept hidden? That was likely or could she be . . .

Melina reviewed the list of those included in the expedition, pausing to dwell on a single sentence.

"Hired as guide is one Jalarios, a cripple with a small son, also called Jalarios or, more usually, Rios."

Small. How small? Small enough to be a nine-year-old girl in disguise? Now that she knew to look, Melina thought this might indeed be the case. This Jalarios merited attention as well. Either the Hawk Havenese were paying the man a considerable fee to insure his silence or they knew something about him that would guarantee his cooperation or . . .

Something touched the edge of her mind, and she reached to make it solidify. A New Kelvinese . . . associated with . . . a man who would be an ideal guide . . .

Grateful Peace?

It was too likely a possibility to ignore. Kiero had seen this Jalarios. Easier to ask him what he thought than to raise suspicions. He would be eager to prove himself after his time at the glass furnaces.

Melina reached for pen and paper.

It looked as if Kiero would be getting out of Urnacia, and Idalia might be getting a surprise.

Melina looked down at her daughter's letter again. Could she use Citrine against her annoying associates? It was certainly a possibility.

There were other possibilities, though, ones that didn't rely upon a nine-year-old. Melina had met with what seemed to her an astonishing amount of resentment from some sectors of the New Kelvinese population. Perhaps she could turn this to her advantage.

Ink blotted outward from the tip of her quill while she plotted. Then Melina swept the stained paper to the floor and, placing a fresh sheet before her, began very rapidly to write.

BEE BITER CAME darting to Firekeeper, his blue and red feathers with their black barring quite dramatic in the late-summer light. The little kestrel might lack the peregrine's dramatic stoop, but he possessed a trick as wonderful, for he could hover in the air almost like a hummingbird, a great advantage in hunting his much smaller prey.

The wolf-woman was drowsing in a tree near Hasamemorri's stable. She had tried the hayloft in the stable, but the flies had been too much. Blind Seer was in the tree with her, having accepted her assistance in making his way to a limb strong enough to take his weight. The pair made a startling sight, or would have had the tree's thick leaves not hidden them from everyone but members of the household. Even Hasamemorri's maids were becoming quite accustomed to oddities—a thing that, in any case, they accepted as normal from foreigners.

Firekeeper awoke instantly, inspecting the kestrel through slitted eyes.

"You've been gone long enough," she said lazily, enjoying a good yawn. "We were beginning to think that someone had drawn you down from the air and we were going to need to rescue you."

Bee Biter fluffed indignantly and Firekeeper laughed.

"Don't be so hurt. At least we would have come and found you. That's some comfort surely. So where have you been?"

"Scouting," the little hawk replied sharply. "Not lolling idle in the trees."

"And what has your scouting found?" Firekeeper rolled slightly, bracing her back against the tree trunk and shifting her position as effortlessly as she would have on the ground.

"At last," the kestrel said, calming as he grew interested in his subject, "I have found the wingéd folk who dwell in this place. It wasn't easy, nor were they happy to learn you are here and meddling again."

"Who would dream that it would be easy to find them?" Firekeeper replied, deciding to ignore the latter comment, though Blind Seer growled. "The wise riders of the winds would not make their presence too easily known, especially in a city where there are those who pride themselves on their beast lore."

She snorted slightly to herself as she recalled that particular New Kelvinese sodality. She had been in and out of their walled gardens repeatedly, Blind Seer with her, and the so-called masters of those places had never spotted either of them. Grudgingly, though, she had to admit admiration for the wide variety of beasts they kept. All were Cousins, at least as far as she had been able to tell, else she would have freed them, but each and every one was healthy and unbroken in spirit.

Surely the Beast Lorists would love to have Royal Beasts for their collection—and the wingéd folk who risked themselves keeping watch on the humans for all their people would be particularly vulnerable.

"So you found your brothers and sisters," Blind Seer said from where he sprawled on a broad limb, paws dangling down on either side as if he were some great cat. "What news had they?"

"Not as much as I could wish," Bee Biter replied, turning his head to clean between his sharp curving talons where pink fleshy evidence remained that he had stopped to eat before finding them. "They have watched but have little to report. Melina goes nowhere but within Thendulla Lypella. At first she traveled some, but moons have waxed and waned since last she crossed the gates. The Granite Tower from which you stole the artifacts remains quiet and unused."

Firekeeper hadn't expected otherwise. If Melina had done something noticeable from the outside then surely someone would have reported before this. She sighed.

This was no good news, especially in light of her friends' reports the previous day from both the embassy and the marketplace. The wolf-woman hadn't understood all the fine details, but she had understood enough.

Melina was becoming important and influential—with more people than her new mate. The New Kelvinese did not uniformly like her, but she had control over many of those well-placed in the pack. The anger of the lesser ones, rather than helping Firekeeper and her associates, was more likely to give them difficulties as the lesser ones turned their fury with their new queen on those from her homeland, much as a low-ranking wolf might beat up one still lower in the hierarchy.

It all made perfect sense, and made Firekeeper all the more certain that delaying a move against Melina was as foolish as letting a herd of elk form a defensive circle.

"If there is no news from the wingéd folk," she said, "who must by their nature watch from outside, then we must go inside."

"Inside?" asked Bee Biter. "Inside Thendulla Lypella? How? You lack wings and, forgive me, wolf-child, but humans' walls are high and well guarded."

"I know," Firekeeper replied. "Had there not been confusion and had I not had Elation and Bold to watch for me, I doubt I would have escaped last winter. I do not plan on going over the walls. I plan on going under."

Blind Seer snorted softly.

"As we did last time?" he inquired. "Those tunnels reeked then and it was the cold season. They may be choking now. And remember, dear heart, then we had a guide."

"I think," Firekeeper said, "that it is time we had a guide once more."

SOME HOURS LATER Firekeeper succeeded in hunting out Grateful Peace—Jalarios, as she must remember to call him—finding him resting from the heat of the day in the relative coolness of the stone-flagged kitchen. He was alone, and to make certain they were not surprised Firekeeper set Blind Seer and Bee Biter to guard. In as few words as possible, the wolf-woman outlined her need.

"We not learn from outside," she concluded bluntly. "Walls hide too much. Last time you is inside. Now . . ."

She shrugged. Her point was clear and logical, and she saw no reason to belabor it.

"So you want me to take you into the sewers," Grateful Peace said, "and through them into the areas beneath Thendulla Lypella."

"Yes."

Peace could be as still as stone when he wished, but Firekeeper had noticed that he tapped his fingers together when thinking about something that agitated him, a restlessness he was indulging in now.

"They know we escaped that way last time," he said. "It is unlikely that the ways are as open."

Firekeeper merely cocked a eyebrow at him.

"And it's going to reek. Last time there was some ice."

Firekeeper, though the wolves teased her about being nose-dead, actually had an acute sense of smell for a human. She didn't like the idea of subjecting herself to the contained scent of subterranean filth, but she saw no way around it.

"You have another way in?" she asked, trying not to sound hopeful.

"If I were still the Dragon's Eye," Peace said, "yes, I would, but I am not and I do not. At least for now the sewers are our best way to penetrate Thendulla Lypella."

"Then we do this thing," Firekeeper said, "tonight or tomorrow—soon."

Peace stared at her, then shrugged.

"I did force myself on your company by offering myself as a guide," he said, "and I suppose this is guiding. You and I alone?"

"And Blind Seer," Firekeeper said.

"But of course," Peace said. "We will need lanterns. I think it would be best if we didn't disturb the workers' caches."

"As you say," Firekeeper replied, trusting Peace to prepare properly. "I speak with others. They have thoughts, too."

"Let us keep our group small," Peace interjected quickly, "at least initially."

"Very," Firekeeper said. "I have thought for one to bring. Edlin."

"Lord Kestrel?" Peace looked surprised.

"Edlin is great mapmaker," Firekeeper said. "Even Shad say so."

Grateful Peace blinked at this last, an apparent non sequitur worthy of Edlin himself, but he didn't comment.

"A mapmaker would be useful," he admitted. "I will be occupied working out our trail, and you do not write, do you?"

Firekeeper shook her head fiercely, feeling once again her inferiority in this area.

"Since will stink," she said, "I not be sure Blind Seer and I sniff our trail back. Best to have map."

Grateful Peace nodded.

"Good tactics, Lady Firekeeper. You are thinking like a general."

Firekeeper wasn't sure she liked this comparison. From what she'd seen, generals were involved in getting large numbers of people killed. However, perhaps good planning got few killed. That had been the case in King Allister's War.

She swelled a bit at the compliment, wolf-like, thriving on admiration and praise.

"I speak Edlin and others. You get lantern. Maybe," Firekeeper added hopefully, "sewers not stink so much. Rain has been in the mountains and even in city. Maybe it wash stink away."

XXIII

SAFELY IN HIS SIDE of the Cloud Touching Spire, Toriovico removed the First Healed One's book from its locked chest. The chest—its exterior intricately carved and polished ruddy oak, its interior lined in exotic aromatic woods and padded in shining midnight blue satin—was far more lovely than the book. The book was thick and solid, its covers bound in age-darkened leather, its pages heavy vellum, peculiarly unyellowed by age.

Indeed, the book's very unremarkableness was one of the remarkable things about it. Several former Healed Ones had attempted to make the tome more remarkable—to inscribe legends on the front cover in gold or to adorn the plain binding with costly gems. Their efforts had met with spectacular failure. Not the greatest Illuminator nor the most skilled Lapidary could anchor anything at all on the book's dull exterior.

Except for the occasional slipcover ordered by those who could not accept that a tome so extraordinary remain so superficially ordinary, the book remained as it was, protected from and isolated by time.

There was one exception to the now universally acknowledged rule that the book could not be changed. Whatever the current Healed One chose to write upon those pristine vellum pages remained—at least, it remained to his eyes and to those of his successors. No one else could see anything written there at all.

A corollary oddity to this was that the book never ran short of pages. Toriovico had tried to count those remaining, but he never came up with the same number twice. Finally, he gave up, contenting himself with the knowledge that there always was enough blank space for whatever he cared to write.

As a small boy, Toriovico had sat in his father's lap when his father wrote in the book. He had been fascinated by the way the dark ink would flow from the quill and vanish on the yellow-white of the page. Sometimes he had insisted on poking his finger under the quill, just to make sure the ink was real. It always was and the bluish black stains had sometimes lasted for days, much to the dismay of his nurses.

When Toriovico had been anointed the Healed One, he had opened the book and been startled to see writing on what had always been an infinity of blank pages. On that first opening, he had been compelled to turn the pages to the beginning and there had read the words that had transformed his universe.

Later there was no such compulsion and Torio had browsed, randomly, fascinated by this tangible link to his predecessors. Their handwritings had varied from spidery to bold, from neatly formed letters that could almost pass for printing to cryptic shapes that had to be stared at for a long while before their similarities to recognizable letters became clear.

One hand had been heartbreakingly familiar, and this was the one section of the book Toriovico never read. His father had written for himself, and for Vanviko, the son who had not lived to succeed him. Toriovico had no desire to see what that Father had written about him, secure in his knowledge that little Torio would never read those words.

Therefore, when he had first grown lonely in the burden of his terrible secret Toriovico had left several pages between his father's words and his own creamily pristine. Only then had he felt comfortable in setting his own quill to the page. He'd half expected the words to vanish before his eyes as they had when his father had done the writing, but they had remained, crisp and clear, and sadly saying less in their tidy little symbols than what he had hoped to express.

Despite his dissatisfaction with his own prose, the book had become friend and confidant, and though Toriovico continued to express himself best in dance, he found some contentment in this outlet.

This afternoon, however, Toriovico did not turn to where he recorded his own journal. Instead he turned to the very beginning, where the First Healed One had written. Skipping over the initial pages with their disturbing revelations, Torio moved to where the First Healed One, like his sons and grandsons and great-grandsons to follow, had recorded his most private thoughts.

Toriovico was seeking some mention, any mention, of what lay beneath Thendulla Lypella. The First Healed One seemed obsessed with the small details of life.

> *We must have silk. There is no way we can prosper without it. How to keep the growing rooms the correct temperature without recourse to regulating spells?*

> *Agitation today to tear down Ashnernon's old palace. I realize the people need building materials, but I am reluctant to face my fellows when they return and find their houses in ruins—or worse— vanished altogether.*

> *Herbalists report disturbing die-off of some medicinal plants. Mold seems likely culprit. What do they expect me to do? Botany wasn't my line!*

> *Sat through the dullest ritual imaginable, all the while my mind was spinning through how to deal with the Primes. Some members are showing disturbing initiative. This cannot be. We don't want a repetition of what's going on over south of the White Water.*

Years later, as the First Healed One had come to realize that his fellow Founders were unlikely to return, the entries became filled with deeply sorrowful recollections of the homeland he would never again see. Even as he clung to those memories, the Healed One became more determined that the colony would not lose sight of its heritage.

Those were the years in which the ritual dances and choral performances were instituted, in which the cult for preservation of original architecture had become entrenched. Now the Healed One sought to establish a dynasty that could carry on his self-imposed deceptions. Soon, the reason for maintaining those deceptions became intertwined with the simple need for establishing an unbreakable hold on rulership.

He must have gone a little mad, Toriovico thought sadly. *No wonder with his health so poor and his hope all but gone.*

Whether for these reasons or others not mentioned in the portions of the First Healed One's journal Toriovico had read, the First Healed One did not appear to have often ventured beyond a few sections of Thendulla Lypella. Certainly, he had not gone beneath the Earth Spires.

Toriovico placed more hope in the sections of the book written by the Second Healed One, a man popularly remembered as the Restorer.

In any other culture, the Restorer probably would have been known as "the Builder," for he authorized the building of more structures in his comparatively short reign than did any other Healed One. However, the Restorer was his father's son to the core. New buildings were constructed under his aegis, but they were built along old patterns—even to the perpetuation of design elements that Toriovico suspected had been practical when magic existed to whisk one up and down great heights or to provide light to secluded interior chambers.

It was during the Restorer's tenure that Thendulla Lypella had gone from being a hodgepodge of related buildings to the dramatic Earth Spires, that Thendulla Lypella had become a living maze, that the scattered walls between structures had been connected into one inviolable fortification.

It was in the Restorer's writings that Toriovico hoped to find some hint of what Melina had located beneath the city.

His hopes were not merely based on the Restorer's reputation. He had noticed that the books Melina had been so absorbed with had been older volumes and had been naively pleased that she took such an interest in her adopted county.

After he had danced the curious swaddling from his mind, Torio had gone to Melina's suite and noted as many of the titles as he could. Lest Tipi report his interest to her mistress, Toriovico had locked the maid in the bathroom and had dropped a few jealous comments that would make her think that what he searched for was evidence that his wife had taken lovers.

A large number of the books on Melina's shelves were from the time of the Restorer. Rather than duplicate her labor and risk that the key volume or volumes were secreted elsewhere, Torio placed his faith in his predecessor.

It was a shaky foundation on which to build his own tower. The Restorer had been a practical man, even to his ink, which was a pedestrian brown rather than the more exotic blue preferred by his father.

After his initial shocked reaction to learning the truth about the Healed One's plans for the kingdom, the Restorer had almost pointedly eschewed recording his personal reactions to events. Instead he had noted page after page of measurements and formulae for estimating stress, torque, and other such arcane engineering problems.

In the early days of his reign, the Restorer had recorded what was in essence his manifesto:

> *To build and preserve a city—a kingdom—so fine that when the mages from across the sea shall return, they shall see our wit and wisdom, and so rule us fit inheritors for those arts that have been taken from us.*

Almost pathetically, the Restorer's desire had been the same as that of the father he never mentioned in all his writings—to make of New Kelvin a place worthy of those who had abandoned both the land and her people.

Toriovico continued reading, skimming over charts and diagrams that were alien and incomprehensible to his way of thinking. It was not until Torio reached the later entries that the Restorer began to include text explaining what his current batch of sketches meant.

On a hunch, Torio looked at the dates and did some counting. Yes, these explanatory notes began to appear after the Restorer had contracted the cancer that would cut his life comparatively short. Although this dry engineering mind did not overtly state that this was the case—or maybe he had spoken of the matter more in person—he was no longer writing for himself but for the son who would succeed him.

Had Toriovico's father done the same? Like the Restorer, he had known that his death was looming. Like the Restorer he had not avoided facing the reality. Torio put the thought from his mind as an unwelcome distraction. It did not matter what his father had done. What mattered was the current crisis.

It was among the Restorer's notes that Toriovico found the first hint of what might have drawn Melina into the tunnels beneath Thendulla Lypella.

The words were cryptic and brief, not as if the Restorer were hiding anything, but as if he was writing about something he expected his reader would understand, and therefore he need not employ his flagging energy to explain. Even so, there were tantalizing fragments, a bit here and there from which Torio thought he could piece something together.

He reached for a stack of the paper he kept near for the sketching out of choreographic routines, hesitated, and then instead turned to the end of the book to the portion where he had been keeping his own journal.

Poking his finger between the pages, Torio took up a pen. Awkwardly flipping between the sections, he started taking notes, slowly building from the Restorer's fragmented references a picture he found in equal parts intriguing and horrifying.

ॐ

CITRINE SHIELD VENTURED from Hasamemorri's house with the hesitation of one who moves into utterly unknown territory. For her, the unknown territory was not the city of Dragon's Breath, but the going out on her own.

The woman once called Melina Shield might not have been a good mother—a concept with which Citrine was still struggling—but even at her most confused Citrine had no problem admitting that Melina had been addicted to control.

There were few places that Melina's children were permitted to go unsupervised. Jet, as a boy and his mother's favorite, and Sapphire, as the heir apparent to the family estates, had been granted a bit more freedom, but the younger three—all girls and all most useful in their mother's eyes as potential marriage alliances—had been carefully supervised.

Indeed, the only reason Citrine had been permitted to roam in the gardens of Eagle's Nest Castle with no more supervision than the omnipresent gardeners and guards had been because Melina took great pride in this expression of the king's favor. Even so, Citrine suspected that if she had been a few years older that privilege would have been denied her. However, she had not yet "come out" as a marriageable prospect and children are permitted some indulgences.

That indulgence had led to Citrine's friendship with Firekeeper—a friendship that had, Citrine thought, struggling with a complex web of cause and effect, led to her mother's dishonor and eventual exile.

Blame as hot and heavy as the summer weather lay on Citrine's heart, dragging her down, splitting her into fragments that argued with each other. One of these fragments took the blame for her mother's fall. One—a thin, indignant voice—insisted that this was ridiculous. No one had forced Melina to enter into the intrigues that had led to her downfall. Only Melina herself was to blame.

But the blame voice, shame voice couldn't agree. Certainly if Citrine had been a better daughter her mother would have been happier. Melina wouldn't have needed the wonder and enchantment the artifacts promised. She would have been happy at home working, as her husband had done, for the betterment of her children.

Didn't Citrine have proof enough that she had been a disappointment? Hadn't her mother punished her by sending her to stay with the pirates? If she had been a better daughter, Mother would have taken Citrine with her when she went to New Kelvin. She would have taught her magic. They would have been together.

But Citrine had been a failure and a disappointment, good only to be used and discarded. The stumps where the two smallest fingers on her left hand had been cut off stung as if salt had been rubbed into them when Citrine tried to resist such thoughts. They were reminder enough that Citrine had ceased to matter to her mother.

Once she had sobbed when such thoughts filled her mind, but now Citrine let her heart weep quietly, imagining tears of blood leaking out and puddling in her body. Certainly she felt heavy and slow, wishing for sleep but unable to sleep when she tried. The oppression had become worse once they arrived in Dragon's Breath. Everyone else had things to do. Citrine had nothing to do but occasionally run an errand to Oculios the pharmacist or go for walks about the city with one of the others.

Sometimes the arguing of the voices in her head made Citrine stand outside of herself, yet another person, witness to what went on around her. Those were the times she tended to say things that disturbed people—like her remembering the rut in the road and realizing that it must have filled with water.

Elise had been disturbed by that incident, as Citrine's nurses and family members had been disturbed by similar incidents.

(Another voice—a hard, cynical one—laughed mockingly.)

Citrine hadn't been able to explain, not even to Elise, whom she loved with an unguarded affection that she had never been able to feel for any of her blood sisters. The words came from the dull, watchful Citrine when they would. Afterward their content and form seemed to have come from someone entirely other than herself.

Citrine knew she had been brought to Dragon's Breath in the hope that confronting her mother would make her realize how horrible Melina had been to her. It seemed impossible. The closer she drew, the more she longed to see her mama, to be cuddled up in those shapely, elegant arms, to hear Mother sing the lilting chants she had used for lullabies on those nights she was home to tuck her daughter into bed.

That longing was why Citrine had written her mother almost immediately after their arrival in Dragon's Breath. Citrine had only blotted the ink a little, smeared it hardly at all. Later, Citrine had taken some of her own money—money she'd been given back in Hawk Haven by Sapphire and others who wanted her to feel less sad—and had paid one of Hasamemorri's maids to post the letter for her.

But Mother hadn't come to fetch her off to the palace, hadn't even asked after her as far as Citrine knew. That had hurt and Citrine had almost believed that Melina was as bad as everyone said.

Then, like a cool wind blowing through her overheated brain, Citrine had learned how Thendulla Lypella was a city within a city, cut off from the residents of Dragon's Breath.

Hope rode that discovery. Mother might not know about things happening in the city outside the Earth Spires. Hadn't everyone else been worried that now that Elise and Edlin had gone to see Ambassador Redbriar Melina would know that they were here? Didn't that mean they didn't think she had known before?

Citrine knew this must be so, and that it was her duty to let Mother know that her very own Citrine was with Elise and Edlin and what her address was—just in case she didn't see past the New Kelvinese boy-robe and the name Rios. She'd written another note. Today she hoped to send it.

The words played through her mind as she walked, going as briskly as her curly-toed slippers would permit.

> *Dear Mother,*
>
> *I am here in Dragon's Breath and staying at a house owned by a big woman named Hasamemorri. I think I have spelled her name right, but if I have not, she is very large and wears lots of pink. Ask for Jalarios's son, Rios, there and you will have me.*
>
> *I would very much like to come and visit you and see your new palace.*
> *Your obedient daughter,*
>
> *Citrine Shield*

When Citrine could stop thinking about the letter and wondering if she had said the right things, she concentrated on trying to look like she was on an errand so no one on the street would stop her. Amidst all these distractions, her heart beat very fast.

No one stopped her. No one even looked at her much. She hurried up to the message drop-off, a building that looked like a sculpted pillar except that it was hollow inside. It stood alone at the edge of Aswatano. Inside, a bored-looking clerk stood stiff and straight, as if he was a pillar himself. He—Citrine felt fairly certain it was a he—looked at the carefully printed routing instructions: Consolor of the Healed One Melina, Thendulla Lypella, Urgent. He frowned, the expression creasing the lines on his face.

"Why is the address written in these alien characters, boy?"

Heartened by being taken for a boy, Citrine responded as she had planned.

"My father works for foreigners. The message is theirs. I am only the runner, great lord."

She knew that calling the clerk a great lord was overdoing, but she also knew that few people minded being praised above their station.

The clerk continued to frown, staring at the routing instructions, then at Citrine. For a moment, she felt that his gaze saw far too much. Then he shook his head dismissively.

"For the Consolor Melina," he snorted. "Foreigners wouldn't know that such missives are to go directly to the post station at Thendulla Lypella."

Citrine felt a flare of anxiety. She didn't think she could get away from Hasamemorri's unnoticed long enough to make her way to the opposite end of the city. Would Firekeeper notice if she dropped something off? Probably. The real question was would the wolf-woman fasten any importance to the action.

"Still," said the clerk, dropping the letter into one of the baskets that surrounded him, "they are foreigners. There will be an extra charge for delivery."

Uncertain whether the charge was for taking the letter to Thendulla Lypella or because the senders were foreign, Citrine obediently paid the amount asked. Then she stopped at a sweets stand and bought some brightly colored rock candy and sweetened dry ginger—her excuse if anyone noticed her absence.

Wendee Jay had, and though she scolded Citrine mildly for taking off without telling anyone, she didn't seem at all angry. Citrine smiled sweetly at the woman and offered her a few rock crystals.

Wendee was really very nice. Maybe Citrine would ask her mother if they could keep Wendee for a servant when Citrine came to live in Thendulla Lypella.

Ignoring the laughter that echoed between her ears, Citrine wandered off to the kitchen to see if she could help by chopping vegetables for dinner.

⚛

"WHAT ARE THEY DOING?" growled Northwest, his hackles raised. "Why are they rooting about in the earth like that?"

Initially, the falcon Elation had been equally confused, but she had an advantage over the wolf. She had flown over and taken a look.

"They are digging up the dead two-legs that are buried there," she replied.

"Surely, they're not so very hungry," Northwest replied, his hackles smoothing flat, so complete was his astonishment. "These new ones have brought food with them and are sharing it. In any case, we haven't killed anyone for these long nights past. The meat must be spoiled beyond what even a two-legs would eat."

"I think," Elation replied, though she was not completely certain this was the case, "they intend to take the dead ones away with them. This would make their retreat entire, and show their willingness to keep their One's promise to Firekeeper."

Northwest's hackles rose again at the mention of the wolf-woman. Pressured by Wind Whisper, he might have carried Firekeeper's message west, but his defeat had made him dislike her even more.

Elation tightened one foot's grip on the branch on which she perched, cutting through the bark into the living wood. There were times she grew very tired of wolves. They were impulsive, limited—as were all the ground-bound—by their inability to see things from more than one elevation. Firekeeper's pack valued the wolf-woman, but other than Wind Whisper—who was after all an offshoot of that same pack—the remainder of the wolves, indeed, the remainder of the Beasts, seemed to view the wolf-woman as a thing to be used when useful and to be scorned the rest of the time.

"We don't care about rotting carcasses," Northwest said, sniffing the air to confirm Elation's report. "We should give them a scare so they'll know."

He tilted back his head as if to howl, but a decisive growl from behind them stilled the sound in his throat.

"We commanded," said Shining Coat, the One Female of Firekeeper's pack, "that as long as the two-legs were working as if they would depart then they were not to be troubled."

"But they aren't departing," Northwest whined, cringing a bit in what Elation knew was good manners, junior to senior, among the wolves.

"Oh?" Shining Coat studied the situation, sniffing the air and reading more from those scents than she did from what she saw. "What are they doing?"

Elation repeated, "They are digging up the dead two-legs who are buried there."

"Hard labor for little good meat," Shining Coat replied. "They buried the bodies deeply and set large stones and sections of tree trunks on top. Only the littlest diggers could get to the carcasses."

Elation fluffed her feathers at the provinciality of wolves.

"Two-legs value their dead," she replied. "At least this breed does. In their own lands they have fields where they plant them. Some even build them houses. Have you forgotten how Fox Hair came all this way simply to carry marked stones with which to do honor to Firekeeper's dead?"

"I had," Shining Coat said with the simple humility that was the only good thing Elation saw in the continuous precedence games all wolves played. "I wonder why these bring their dead away with them? The hawk-nosed One who led those with whom Firekeeper departed two springs ago found dead but left them behind."

"But he did bury them neatly," Elation reminded her, "and showed the bones great respect."

"True," Shining Coat agreed. "Like knows like best, and these two-legs are unlike anything I know—even our Little Two-legs might be puzzled."

"Might," Elation said, "though Firekeeper has learned much. If she were here, she would know the answer to give us."

Northwest had been ignoring the byplay between senior wolf and pere-grine, his attention returned to the humans and their strange digging. Per-haps the smell of meat, no matter how rotted, excited his senses, for he wheeled on Shining Coat almost as if he would attack her.

"Let us kill them all now!" he said. "They have taken down the close ranks of dead trees behind which they hid. There are holes now big enough to admit us—and the bears and pumas. We could eliminate them all in a few fast strokes."

"Have you forgotten the ones to the east?" Shining Coat countered.

"I did," Northwest said, "but what does that matter? They don't yet have this strong den they are to build. They are easy now, relaxed that they have won the fight with these here and certain that we will give them none."

Shining Coat leapt on the wild-eyed young male, knocking him to the ground with a thud so solid that Elation was certain that even the humans must have heard it. They did not seem to, however, and by the time her quick glance had darted between the humans and the struggling wolves, Shining Coat had subdued Northwest.

Moreover, her pack, more sensitive than the busy humans, was emerging from the cover from which many of them had been watching the activity at New Bardenville.

"We will not kill these humans, Northwest," Shining Coat growled. "Do you forget how many there are across the mountains?"

"They seemed thin spread to me," Northwest said with remarkable defiance.

Shining Coat shook him and Elation saw the blood well up through the younger wolf's fur.

"Two eyes, one nose, no sense," she snarled in a reproof that Elation knew was more commonly applied to pups rather than grown adults. "You run a few days' distance—mostly by night— and by this journey you will judge all of two-legged kind."

"A further run than you have taken!" Northwest persisted with incredible defiance.

"A hunter doesn't need to see the size of the herd," Shining Coat replied, "when a good scout howls back the count. You reason like a late-autumn pup." That was one born when the winter is coming, and so stupid and weak. "It is no wonder your pack sent you away."

"Gently, Shining Coat," warned Rip, her mate. "No need to direct your anger to Northwest's kin. They are not here to answer for themselves."

The One Male turned his attention to the bloodied, cringing, but still somehow defiant young wolf.

"You may be willing to defy me and mine," Rip growled, "but are you also willing to defy all those of the Beasts who have agreed that for now we are to be careful in our dealings with the two-legs?"

Reminded thus, Northwest went limp.

Shining Coat accepted his surrender, releasing his ruff and licking her bloodied muzzle, but she still eyed him with dislike.

"We let these two-legs go," she said, "even if they take time to dig up old bones. Only if they make a move to replant their dead trees or dig some other secure den do we remind them whose will is law here in the west."

Her pronouncement was a reminder not only to the quelled rebel, but to anyone in hearing. Elation knew how many listened from the surrounding trees and knew that the news of this confrontation would be everywhere before the humans stilled their labors with the coming of night.

The peregrine was not surprised to see a raven winging east toward the gap in the mountains, doubtless to assure himself—and them all—that the humans were not readying there a den from which they could defy the Beasts, rather than the promised watch post.

How long though, Elation thought, *does it take for one to become the other?*

Holding this uncomfortable thought, the peregrine resumed waiting, wishing that Firekeeper were there to explain how a human might answer that question.

XXIV

PURE DARKNESS didn't come for many hours, but Firekeeper—possessed of a wolf's patience now that the hunt was impending—didn't fret.

At dinner she ate her share of the roast joint and vegetables, actually enjoying the potatoes roasted crisp in beef fat. Then she and Blind Seer went outside and dozed, awakening in the small hours when even Dragon's Breath had stilled to sleep.

In the kitchen, Grateful Peace and Edlin were readying themselves. Peace, sorting through his gear, was as alert as the wolf-woman herself. Edlin reeked of a frantic excitement, reminding Firekeeper irresistibly of a puppy grown nearly into adult size and so included in the hunt.

Still, Lord Kestrel managed a façade of calm, and neither Firekeeper nor Blind Seer felt a need to scrape through it to the truth.

"I've pencils," Edlin said, holding them up for inspection. "Better than ink, won't smear if we get wet, what?"

Firekeeper nodded approval.

"And you have light?" she asked Peace.

"Light for me and for Lord Kestrel," the thaumaturge replied. "I thought you would do without."

Firekeeper smiled, pleased that Peace remembered. "I see enough with what you have."

She glanced to where Edlin was busily belting on a long hunting knife and noted that Peace, too, was armed, though his choice of blade was somewhat smaller. Knowing of what her Fang was capable, Firekeeper didn't fault the men for their choices. Indeed, remembering how close the sewer tunnels could be, she thought them wise.

"I try to get Bee Biter come with," she said, "but he will not. Too close for him beneath the ground, though I tell him it as wide as sky for a tiny creature like himself."

Edlin shrugged philosophically. The matter—and Bee Biter's probable refusal—had already been raised in their earlier conference.

"I say, shall we go, then?"

Firekeeper nodded. She could hear stirring from the rooms where the others slept, but knew that though they were nervous about this expedition they would not emerge to offer wishes for luck and success. Such activity had been ruled out as possibly drawing unnecessary attention from the New Kelvinese inhabitants of the house.

Doc had protested that he should go with them in case a doctor was needed, but his offer had been refused.

"You have teached me and Edlin both," Firekeeper had told him firmly. "No need."

She hoped she was right.

They emerged from the back door and side yard into the dark alley that ran along the rear of this row of houses. Although some areas of Dragon's Breath had streetlamps, this neighborhood did not. It might be within the main wall and so superior to the areas without, but it did not merit such flourishes.

Firekeeper was glad. Dark streets did not encourage night traffic. Moreover, she and Blind Seer would be aware of any potential thieves long before the thieves were aware of them.

A small corner of her mind remained troubled over the distinction between thief and bandit, between necessary self-defense and what humans saw as excessive violence. She understood surrender—indeed, her honoring of such had been her weakness—but such fine lines made her restless and unhappy.

They turned on to a side street where a heavy stone capped an entrance into the sewer. Not wishing her human companions to strain themselves, Firekeeper lifted the stone, tilting it against its iron hinges without the lever Peace produced.

The New Kelvinese raised his eyebrows, but said nothing, merely tucking the implement back where he had extracted it. Firekeeper motioned to the ladder.

"Go. I come last with Blind Seer."

She knew she should go first and so scout the area and avoid being blinded by the light from the lanterns her companions carried. Either Edlin or Peace could close the hatch with little difficulty, but the sewer stench was more powerful than she had imagined.

Peace's slight grin before he clambered down awoke a momentary flare of anger in the wolf-woman, but she recognized that this wasn't really anger, but shame at her own delaying, and so hung her head in mute apology.

When the two men were below, Firekeeper took a few steps down the ladder, then Blind Seer—complaining vigorously about the omnipresent reek of human shit—backed into her grasp and let her carry him down. In an emergency the wolf could have leapt, but neither of them particularly wanted to risk his slipping from the comparatively narrow walkway into the filth that flowed alongside.

Taking one last breath of the good night air, Firekeeper pulled the hatch closed after her and felt her way down the rungs to the tunnel floor. The stones beneath her feet were cool and damp, but not wet enough to be treacherous. After a few deliberately deep breaths, she could even sort the difference between the smell of the sewer flow and the air in the tunnel, tasting even the scent of burning lantern oil. Whether she would be able to make any finer distinctions waited to be learned.

Blind Seer was also making every effort to translate the scent of the sewage into the olfactory equivalent of background noise. Grumbling slightly, but admitting that he was less overwhelmed than he had been initially, he shook to announce his readiness to go on.

"As I expected from a creature who will perfume himself in the reek of rotting carrion," Firekeeper teased. *"You can revel in any stench."*

Blind Seer bumped his head against her in a wolf's equivalent of an embrace.

"If the others are done choking at the smell," he said cheerfully, *"let us move ahead. Ask Peace what we should watch for. I know he has some concern that the humans will have taken precautions against the easy use of this trail."*

Firekeeper nodded.

"Ready?" she asked Edlin and Peace, keeping her voice low but not whispering, for Peace had warned them that the sibilance of whispered talk would carry through the tunnels.

"I say!" Edlin replied, also guarding his tone. "A bit strong, what?"

Peace, carefully holding his dark lantern so that the small light he let through the shield illuminated only the stones at his feet, said nothing, but Firekeeper saw his curt nod.

"What should we look for," Firekeeper asked, "to know if there are traps?"

Peace considered.

"Wire or string stretched at any level where a trespasser might touch it unaware. I think that we need not fear more complex pressure traps, at least here. They have not had time to do such engineering. Initially, there should not be many traps. The sewers must be serviced and killing workers would not serve at all. The Artificers will have kept their finer work for nearer to the Earth Spires."

Firekeeper nodded. Then, letting Blind Seer go a few paces in front of her, she led the way. The wolf was to give his full attention to the way ahead while she split her attention between their path and any word from their companions. This much the men who followed her knew.

What she hadn't bothered to tell Edlin—and of course would not tell Peace—was that she did not completely trust their New Kelvinese companion, and was ready for the slightest indication of betrayal on his part. It would have been too easy for him to get word to allies in the city and prepare an ambush.

Not one of their group had overlooked Grateful Peace's delight at returning to New Kelvin. Firekeeper's own strong feeling that she should be at home with her pack made her ever conscious that Peace could not be trusted. King Tedric had been righter than she had realized. She could not have stood neutral or even merely defensive if her people went to war. Why should any of them expect Grateful Peace to act differently?

If truly he saw Melina as a threat to his homeland, then they stood together. What if Peace thought that he might make amends for his earlier transgressions by offering the new queen something she wanted? A daughter and the very people who had ruined her earlier plans might be as tempting to Melina as a wolf would find a marrow-filled bone or a chunk of still-hot liver.

For a long while they paced in near silence. The two men had worn soft-soled shoes, so they made no noise that the moving of the filthy river did not cover. Firekeeper and Blind Seer made no sound at all.

Occasionally, Peace would tell them to take one turn or another. At these times Edlin would halt to make notes for his eventual map. Firekeeper felt acutely aware of the weight of stone surrounding her, of the closeness of the walls, but she didn't complain. After all, hadn't she been the one to suggest this expedition?

To distract herself, Firekeeper concentrated on the map Edlin was drawing. She was quite impressed with how Edlin was measuring by counting his paces. It spoke of a coolness of mind and self-discipline that she admired. She was also secretly impressed that Edlin found a use for such large numbers. Once again it seemed Derian and Wendee were right when they pressed her to acquire a human education to complement her wolf one.

The tunnel in which they had begun had been comparatively narrow, hardly more than a channel to carry local sewage to the main "river." Eventually, the tunnels into which Peace directed them became progressively wider, the walkways large enough that a wheeled cart could be rolled along. They encountered no workers, but this was no real surprise. There had been sufficient rain that the sewer was flowing steadily and no one who was not desperate would descend into the filth and stench.

Despite a growing desire to be anywhere but in this close, stinking place, Firekeeper forced herself to remain alert, but she located nothing out of the ordinary. The failure to find a trick, trap, or guard became an obstacle of its own. Firekeeper found herself moving more and more slowly lest she miss anything significant.

When they encountered the gate that blocked the walkway it was almost a relief.

"This no here last time," Firekeeper said softly.

"No," Peace agreed. "It is new. See where the rivets were driven into the stone to hold it?"

Firekeeper looked. The tool marks from cutting and grinding in the rock were still pale against the dirtier stone. Cautiously, Peace raised the shield on his lantern so that they might better inspect the obstacle.

"Ceiling to floor," he murmured. "That's to be expected, but the gate extends out into the channel, too. Someone has been careful."

Firekeeper looked to where Peace indicated. The gate did not cross the flow—with insight born of too great proximity to this place she realized that was to keep debris from becoming hung up and creating a blockage point. However, the fence did extend far enough that intruders would not be tempted to hang themselves around the edge and so swing to the other side. With a further bit of genius, the fence did not suddenly end, but instead tapered. Anyone climbing that would take a dip in the sewer.

She heard Edlin abort a whistle of admiration in midbreath.

"I say," he commented hopefully, "I don't suppose it's unlocked."

Peace gave the obstruction a careful inspection before touching it. When he did touch it, he used the end of the lever he still carried. Nothing happened, so he placed a hand on the gate and softly pressed the latch.

"Locked," he said, but there was a note of satisfaction in his voice. "But I never did turn in my keys."

Firekeeper held the lantern for Grateful Peace while he inspected the bunch of keys he drew from a pouch on his belt. He was very careful in how he handled them, making sure he did not rattle them in the slightest. Indeed, Edlin taking advantage of this stop to update his notes and make a rough sketch of the gate made more noise with the scratching of his pencil across the paper.

Peace chose one key, identical in Firekeeper's opinion to at least three others in the bunch, and once again subjected the lock to a close inspection. When he was satisfied, he inserted the key, working it slightly, as if it were a very small lever. The end result was a satisfying click, loud only because of the comparative silence.

"Siyago," Peace said in satisfaction. "I thought I recognized his work."

He put the keys away before again pressing down on the lever. The gate opened without even a squeak of hinges.

Again Firekeeper and Blind Seer took point. She vaguely recognized the section of tunnels they came to next as a central area at which a large number of tunnels converged. It was not so much a hub as a confluence, smaller stinking streams joining a main river.

Walkways such as the one they had made their way along were linked in a ring by a system of small bridges that could be dropped over the stream or drawn back so that they would not provide the least obstacle to anything that needed to flow through. The bridges were cleverly made, each going back into a recess in the wall. The walkways were solid masonry, much wider than those elsewhere. She assumed that this was because greater labors must be carried out here where several streams joined the main and more than one man needed to have room to easily pass.

Even as Firekeeper committed the place to her memory, she marveled at the care taken to first bury a river, then give it a place of its own. She thought that the river had become rather like a horse, bridled and saddled so that it could be put to human service.

Edlin insisted on pausing long enough to sketch this complex and to clearly label both the tunnel from which they had emerged and the one toward which Peace was leading them.

"Good place to get confused, what?" he explained. "Bet my inheritance that if we went a bit down each of those tunnels we'd find a gate like the one we came through. Good security. Only wonder why it wasn't done sooner."

Peace stiffened a touch defensively.

"Because sewers are made to facilitate the disposal of waste. Anything that blocks the flow could have serious consequences."

Edlin looked up from his drawing to favor the other with one of his ingenuous grins.

"So you're not taking my bet?"

Peace sighed. "What would I have to match your stake?"

Hearing this byplay, Firekeeper grinned. Blind Seer, leaping carefully over one of the narrower feeder streams, had already confirmed that Edlin was right. She wondered if Peace's pique came from the fact that he had not taken similar precautions when he had been the Dragon's Eye.

Despite her amusement, the wolf-woman felt edgy. This complex was the last landmark she recalled from their first journey. Unlike her companions, she had been through the tunnels only once. Her own escape from Thendulla Lypella had been overland.

In the first tunnel away from the confluence, they encountered the expected barrier. Once again Peace subjected the gate to a careful inspection before opening the lock—with a different key, Firekeeper noted. Then they went on. Their path was now taking them up a slight incline. After a few more turns and several more gates, the four intruders left the sewer entirely. Its channels served Thendulla Lypella, but Peace had a different route in mind, tunnels intended for humans, not for their waste.

He was also taking them beneath a different part of Thendulla Lypella. The Granite Spire, which had been their goal on their last venture, had been reported nearly empty by Bee Biter and his wingéd allies. Going there would get them no closer to Melina.

The Illuminator looked soberly at his companions as he pulled the latest gate closed behind them so that their passage would not be noted by sewer workers going about their duties.

"Now we must be more careful than ever," Grateful Peace said, "for in these tunnels there need be no consideration of hapless sewer workers. The Artificers will not have constrained their cleverness. Perhaps I should take the lead?"

Firekeeper refused with a quick shake of her head. There was a different feel in the air now. When questioned, the two men said they sensed nothing—Edlin even attributed her response to nervousness—but Blind Seer agreed with her.

"The scent in the air is altered," the wolf clarified, lifting his head and sniffing. *"Not only fresher, but something . . ."*

He growled, frustrated by his inability to place something apparently outside his experience. Desperate for Blind Seer to pin down her own vague awareness, Firekeeper forced herself to remember that the wolf was only four years old. Even in the forests in which he had been born much might still be new to him.

Here traveling alongside caged rivers beneath an artificial mountain range—for so Firekeeper couldn't help but think of Dragon's Breath's towering buildings—even a Royal Wolf could be excused for not knowing everything.

Firekeeper gave Blind Seer a reassuring stroke along one shoulder.

"We go even more slowly, then," she decided, *"until we find what it is that troubles us both."*

Neither Grateful Peace nor Edlin questioned the wolf-woman's decision when she repeated it to them. As they made their slow way forward Peace more frequently sent a ray from his lantern to course the floor ahead of them. Firekeeper nearly told him to stop but decided not to. The amount of light wasn't sufficient to ruin her vision and it might indeed reveal a trip wire or some other small trap.

And since there was no doing without light it might as well be useful, yet she was all too aware that even these pale beams could be fatal.

As they padded upward, Firekeeper became aware that Blind Seer was sniffing the air so vigorously that his action was audible. She tried to detect what had him so distracted, but other than burning lantern oil and the latent sewer scent clinging to their clothing, she could smell nothing significant.

Or could she? A musky scent, somehow familiar, somehow out of place.

"Blind Seer, what is it?" she asked.

The wolf's reply was a low, rumbling growl before he stopped in his tracks and shook as if he'd been soaked by a cloudburst.

Peace and Edlin, who had drawn up short when the wolf stopped, were obviously confused.

"I say!" Edlin said, keeping his voice low with an effort. "What's wrong?"

As to Peace there was only a faint metallic chink as he drew his knife from its sheath.

Firekeeper ignored them both—a foolish thing, for that knife could have been meant for her. However, Blind Seer's suddenly odd behavior drove any other consideration from her mind.

"What is wrong?"

She touched the wolf and found that his hackles were raised and he was shuddering, a bone-deep vibration that rippled over his increased heart rate. Had he been poisoned? She cast her gaze over the stone floor of the tunnel but there were no spikes or caltrops, not even a suspicious sheen.

"Blind Seer!" she cried, so frantic that even the humans were aware of her low howl.

"I am," the wolf wheezed, panting, *"here. Hush, dear heart. Ah, the smell!"*

Firekeeper acted at once. If a smell was what was troubling him . . .

Darting out her hand, she grabbed the spirit flask from Edlin's belt. Doc had insisted they carry brandy in case a wound needed to be sterilized or someone needed a quick jolt to a shocked system. Now she was glad.

Firekeeper opened the flask and held it beneath Blind Seer's nose, sloshing a little of the liquor onto her palm for good measure. The strong fumes welled up, so powerful that at this proximity they even overwhelmed the sewer stench.

Blind Seer breathed in through both mouth and nose, coughed, and seemed to be choking. Firekeeper thumped him on the flank with her free hand, amazed when she felt the wolf plunge his nose into her brandy-dampened palm.

Once again he shook, rather like a human trying to clear his head.

"I have . . . ," he said. *"I can think again, but the smell!"*

"What smell?"

The wolf hesitated.

"Like a thousand bitches in heat," he said at last, clearly somewhat uncomfortable. *"It took the thought from my mind and put it in my loins. If it had not been Cousins . . ."*

"Cousins?" Firekeeper repeated, appalled, though she wasn't quite sure by what. Blind Seer had explained to her that the Royal Wolves did not mate with the Cousins, so the very thought that he was attracted by their bitch scent was bad, but there was something else, something that made her uncomfortable and angry all at once.

She pushed this last from her mind, focusing on the immediate problem.

Edlin, too, was meeping at her, making sounds that it took her a moment to translate into words.

"I say! I would have just handed the flask to you? What's wrong? Something bite him on the nose?"

Firekeeper considered lying and didn't know why. She shook her head.

"No, not bite him. A smell like a bitch in heat. It makes him not think clear."

To her complete surprise, Edlin appeared to understand.

"Lure," he said. Then, when she blinked at him uncomprehendingly, he went on. "You've told me humans are nose-dead, what? But that doesn't mean we've not noticed that others are not. Hunters make lures to attract creatures they want to hunt, to make them, well, stop being cautious, don't you know. . . ."

"Humans do this?" she asked, appalled.

"That's right," Edlin agreed. He shuffled his feet. "Usually trappers use lures. Make them out of urine and such. Keep females for it."

Firekeeper understood. Animals—people, too, though they'd forgotten how to read the signs—told a great deal through their urine. A pregnant female advertised her situation; so did one in heat. Urine from a bitch in heat, especially if concentrated . . .

Blind Seer was right. If whoever had blended this lure had not used urine from Cousin wolves, then the Royal Wolf might not have been able to control himself.

Again Firekeeper felt that strange emotion. Protectiveness? Possessiveness? She put it from her, but she couldn't put the growl from her voice.

"Lure. I must find and kill."

Edlin put a restraining hand on her arm. A very brave thing to do given her sudden anger. She barely resisted snapping at him.

"Let me," he suggested. "I know what to look for, what? And no matter what you think, you are not nose-dead. The scent could be affecting you as well."

Firekeeper stopped, considering. Edlin might be speaking the truth. It would explain her anger—rather as if she'd found other wolves peeing their marks in her territory.

She nodded stiffly.

"Be careful."

Edlin went without further comment, holding his lantern, but not encumbering himself in any other fashion. The others waited in silence. Indeed, Peace was so still that Firekeeper must look to confirm his presence. There he stood, a robed pillar, just visible in the dim light.

Beneath the hand she kept on his back, she could feel that Blind Seer was growing calmer.

"It's not just the brandy scent," he explained. *"It's knowing what's happened. I can work against my reaction."*

Firekeeper wrapped her arm around the wolf's shoulder and hugged him. Then they awaited Edlin's return—or for the least indication that he had met with trouble.

Firekeeper was considering going after the young man when Edlin returned. He ghosted over the stone pavement, waiting to give his report until he was closer. Then he hunkered down on his heels and displayed a small bundle which reeked of a mixture of brandy and other, less definable, scents.

"Gave it a splash, what?" he commented. "This is the worst of it. I think the floor had been dabbed, but lure doesn't last long, not convincingly. Trappers reanoint their traps regularly."

Beneath Firekeeper's hand Blind Seer remained calm, though he gave the lure an inquisitive sniff.

"With the brandy mixed in," he said, *"it's not even interesting. Like an image in a mirror. It bears a resemblance but does not fool upon closer inspection."*

Firekeeper did her best to translate.

"I found it hung over a rather nasty pit trap," Edlin went on. "Pit must have been there for ages. Spikes at the bottom, what? If Blind Seer had rushed out unheeding . . ."

He shrugged, then looked increasingly uncomfortable.

"There were other things, too," he said. "Loose stones near the pit edge. Caltrops that matched the stone. Wouldn't fool someone careful, but someone who might be running full tilt would have been in trouble. The designers were probably limited by how they could adapt that bit of tunnel. Couldn't be too subtle."

"Other than the lure," Peace interjected. "That lure is very subtle, indeed."

"Other than that," Edlin agreed.

Although Blind Seer claimed that the lure no longer touched his mind, Firekeeper insisted on running the bundle back to the nearest sewer channel and dropping it in. Distances so laboriously traversed when every step needed to be checked for traps or trip wires proved ridiculously short on the return.

She came back to find Peace and Edlin discussing this latest development.

"You do realize," Peace said to her, "that this means someone expects your return—and quite possibly my assistance?"

Firekeeper nodded. The thought had occurred to her. Why else would they set a trap meant to befuddle a wolf if they hadn't expected her and Blind Seer? And Peace was one who knew these under roads and had last been seen in the company of her associates.

"I know," she said. "Yet this only tells us what we feared was true. A good thing as I see it."

From the flicker of expression that crossed Peace's normally impassive features, she thought he was amused—but not necessarily at her expense.

"Very true," he said. "It is better to know than not. Do we go on from here or do we take what we have learned to the others?"

"Go on," Firekeeper said firmly. "We may not have two chances to scout."

As they progressed, the tunnels through which Peace guided them varied wildly in width and height. Firekeeper found herself balking when the passages they must travel grew narrow, but as both her companions were larger than her, she didn't care to lessen herself in either man's eyes by complaining.

Along the way Peace taught Edlin and Firekeeper something of disarming the traps that were set with increasing cunning along their path. There were alarms as well, and Peace expressed the concern that sometimes the trap was no trap at all, but merely an excuse to conceal an alarm. As there was no choice except to turn back, they attended to these as they had the others.

Edlin proved more adept at these lessons, but Firekeeper's strong fingers and acute sense of hearing gave her an edge that her general unfamiliarity with things mechanical did not.

The tunnels branched off many times. Each time before they took a turn, Peace would give Edlin an idea of what the alternative route would hold. His memory for small detail seemed inexhaustible—so much so that Firekeeper doubted his veracity. Once, however, a caved-in ceiling forced them back to the alternative tunnel and they found everything much as Peace had described it. After that, Firekeeper felt more confident.

The cave-in was not the only obstacle they met. Indeed, each branching could be counted on to hold its deterrent—and all of them, complex or simple, Peace stated were new since his time. Many of the traps were simple:

trip wires that triggered spills of rock or released a hidden bow. More than once they encountered use of wolf lure, but Blind Seer was wise to that game and held himself firm while they dismantled and disarmed it as best they could.

"Taking a toll on the brandy, what?" Edlin commented as he dribbled the last of his flask on a scented bundle.

Firekeeper agreed, but her private concern was deeper. She knew that because of the lures Blind Seer was using his sense of smell in as limited a fashion as possible—rather like a human squinting against a too bright light. What might he miss under these circumstances?

At last their route leveled somewhat and Peace told them that they had arrived beneath Thendulla Lypella proper. Here Firekeeper noticed that many of the tunnels were natural, connected and enhanced by tools. Eventually, they came to an open space as large as a great hall in a castle. After the tunnels, the feeling of open surroundings was very agreeable. Indeed, Firekeeper hadn't realized how trapped she had felt until she was so no longer.

Peace, too, seemed glad of a chance to stand straight and stretch. Edlin, however, was aware of their surroundings only as some new challenge for his mapmaking skills. Firekeeper didn't know whether to admire him or think him mad.

Grateful Peace was looking around the open area with such care that Firekeeper frowned, fearing again the possibility of betrayal.

"What you looking for?" she asked.

"I thought," the Illuminator said slowly, "to find more here. In the tunnels the wit of the artificers was retrained by confided space and solid rock walls. Here . . ."

He trailed off and Firekeeper understood. The open space was deceptive. Their way might be narrowly constrained by hidden trip wires and pitfalls. She found herself thinking how an apparently wide-open swamp could be crossed only by leaping onto certain solid hummocks and eyed the apparently solid black vault above, wondering if there were nets of rock or flights of spears hidden in the darkness.

Edlin squinted into the gloom.

"I say. What about letting up the lantern sides for a bit more light? I can hardly tell what's a shadow and what's a rock, don't you know?"

Peace was about to reply when a clear, almost shrill, female voice spoke in heavily accented Pellish from the concealing shadows on the opposite side of the cavern:

"He wants light. Give it to him."

They were dazzled, nearly blinded, by the light that flooded over them. Her right arm flying up involuntarily to cover her eyes, Firekeeper took a step back, ready to retreat into the tunnel mouth. An arrow shaft shattering on the rock wall near her shoulder caused her to freeze in her tracks.

"Don't move!" commanded the same shrill voice again.

Firekeeper didn't. She was relieved to see that Blind Seer had hunkered close to the ground, where he was somewhat protected by the unevenness of the cavern's floor and clustered boulders that at some time, probably decades ago, had been dragged away from the center.

The reason for all this effort was clear as soon as her vision adjusted enough to see. In the light of a score or more open lanterns, the cavern was revealed as a place of beauty.

It looked as if the earth itself had taken a deep breath then blown it out to create a long, elongated bubble of iridescent black stone, honeycombed with countless tiny holes. The floor possessed a slight curve, but rubble and time filled it with a gravel carpet. Larger rocks, cut in severe blocks that made elegant contrast to the smooth lines of the cavern, were piled in what Firekeeper was sure was a deliberate attempt to make a human reply to nature's breath.

The wolf-woman heard Edlin give an involuntary gasp of surprise and a wondering "I say!" but she was more interested in blinking tears from her light-tortured eyes than in any array of rocks and in getting a clearer look at their enemy. Enemy this must be, waiting for them here at a place where she knew from Peace's descriptions to Edlin that many of the tunnels beneath Thendulla Lypella came together.

"Trausholo," came the woman's voice again, her tone mocking. Apparently wishing Edlin and Firekeeper to understand her words, the speaker switched back into Pellish. "Grateful Peace. So you've come home again. I wonder that you can show your face."

Firekeeper actually heard Peace stagger, as if physically shocked or stunned, but she smelled no blood.

"Idalia!" he said. "Idalia! Is that you?"

"Me myself," the woman said. "Your own sister."

She spat.

"Kistlio's mother. You murdered my son, Grateful Peace. Did you think I would forget that? Forgive that? Never."

"Idalia . . ." Peace was pleading, a thing Firekeeper had never thought she would hear.

She thought the accusation terribly unfair. Peace had not killed his nephew. The responsibility for that rested with Blind Seer, and the wolf had not wanted to hurt the youth—his target had been Lady Melina, but Kistlio had intervened to defend the woman he worshipped.

Idalia had now switched back to New Kelvinese to better gloat over her brother—Firekeeper might only have a few dozen words of the language, but the tone was universal—and Peace continued to flinch as if her words were blows to his body. Definitely unfair.

However, the wolf-woman did not expect fairness from life. Nor did she see how defending Peace's honor at the expense of Blind Seer would help. She knew enough of humans now to know that this Idalia would only see the wolf as the weapon with her brother as the wielder, since without Grateful Peace none of them would have been in the Granite Tower on that fateful night.

Instead Firekeeper stood poised to flee or fight, whichever was needed, trying to figure out what Idalia intended for them.

Now that Firekeeper's eyes had adjusted to the light she could see that Idalia was not alone. Ranks of armed and armored figures stood behind her, spreading out behind their leader so that they could bring their weapons into play. A few carried short bows, compact but easily possessing enough range to span the cavern. Most bore only hand weapons—a practical consideration in tight spaces where spears and longer weapons would need to be abandoned.

To one side, Firekeeper glimpsed Edlin doing something, his hands held carefully at waist level. There was a muted crackling sound that she identified after a moment as the sound of paper being folded. Seeing he had her attention, he twisted his hand to extend something to her.

"The map," he said softly. "Take it!"

Firekeeper frowned.

"Take it!"

The wolf-woman obeyed, slowly sliding the map inside her vest, where it rested stiff and unpleasant against her skin.

Edlin looked both relieved and unwontedly serious.

"Get ready to run," he said in the same low tones, barely moving his lips. "I learned more of the language than you. We've been taken prisoner. If Peace's sis wasn't having such fun, we'd have been hauled off already. I'm going to give you a chance to get away."

Firekeeper didn't want to believe him, but a glance at the armored contingent now beginning to approach them, at the readying of bows done ever so casually, confirmed his words.

"I leave you?" she asked.

"I'm afraid so," Edlin said conversationally. "You and him"—he gave a faint toss of his head toward Blind Seer—"have the best chance of getting away. Don't want them to get all of us, what? Afraid . . ."

Whatever he'd been about to explain, Edlin stopped in midphrase, apparently alert to some change in the New Kelvinese conversation that tone alone would not reveal.

"I say!" he called out loudly in Pellish, then more softly to Firekeeper. "Go!"

"I say," Edlin said, striding forward. "I am Lord Kestrel and I don't take kindly to this, what?"

Idalia sneered at him.

"The idiot," she said. "I've heard about you."

Firekeeper understood that Edlin was providing a diversion—even if she wasn't quite certain why. She halted for a moment, reluctant to leave her friends.

Blind Seer was already belly-creeping toward the welcome darkness.

"Dear heart, come away."

"I am no idiot!" Edlin proclaimed, looking around the cavern in wonder. "Fine place this, what? Wanted to see it for a long while, don't you know."

Every head, armored or otherwise, turned toward him in wonder.

And Firekeeper, feeling as if somehow she was a worse traitor than Peace had ever been, took advantage of this moment when all eyes were on Edlin and slipped back one step, two, then melted into the shadows.

XXV

AFTER FIREKEEPER, Peace, and Edlin departed, Derian found he could not sleep. He lay on his cot in the room he shared with Doc and Edlin, trying to keep his restlessness to himself.

Finally Doc's voice, low and holding a certain ironic resignation, spoke from the other side of the room.

"I could brew you some chamomile tea," he said, "blended with other herbs to help you sleep. Or mint if your gut is troubling you."

"No thanks," Derian said. "Sorry if I woke you."

"You didn't."

There was a rustle of movement; then a candle flared, its light just enough for Derian to see the highlights of his friend's face.

"I've been trying to tell myself," Doc said, "that I'm worrying about that broken arm we set earlier, but that's nonsense. I'm worried about my cousins."

Derian was momentarily puzzled, then he realized that if Edlin was Doc's cousin, so was Firekeeper—even if the link was made even more tenuous by adoption.

Hoping to distract them both, Derian asked, "What exactly is your relation to Edlin?"

Doc chuckled.

"Distant. Saedee Norwood had a brother. He married a Surcliffe. They had children, the eldest of whom was my father. Father inherited the Surcliffe name and holdings. So my father is Norvin's first cousin. That makes

Norvin and me second cousins, and his children my third cousins or second cousins once removed or something like that."

Doc sighed.

"But Norvin has always been very good to me. My father is younger than Saedee, but had children sooner, so my siblings and I are older than Norvin's children. I suppose Norvin's interest could have originated in keeping a close eye on those he could adopt to follow him should he fail to have children, but I think it is genuine family feeling."

"You've known Edlin a long time, then?" Derian asked.

Even idle chatter was better than imagining Firekeeper and the others stalking through sewer tunnels, being assaulted by who knew what horrors.

"Since we were both children. I'm only a few years older and we played together."

"Edlin seems much younger than you," Derian said, realizing only after the words were out of his mouth that they could be taken as an insult.

"That's Norvin's fault, I think," Doc replied, overlooking the flub. "He wanted a son who was just like him in every way. Edlin isn't at all. He's more like Eirene in personality—and she was so unlike a typical Norwood that gossip said she must take after her father."

"And that was?" Derian asked, daring a question in the single-candle privacy that he never would have asked in daylight.

He could see the outline of Doc's shrug.

"A mystery. No one, as far as I know, knows who he was except Saedee."

"Ah."

Derian felt himself blushing. He had overstepped that time. He could hear it in the faint note of rebuke in Doc's tone. Such speculations would be reserved for longtime retainers or family. To cover, he spoke what was on his mind—the very thoughts he had been avoiding.

"I wonder how the others are doing."

"So do I," Doc answered.

Hours before dawn, the two men surrendered any pretense of sleeping and pulled out a deck of cards. When they gave up on this, Derian put on boots and outdoor clothes to tend the horses. Doc crossed over to his patients. There were always a few in the infirmary. He found Elise there before him, but Derian, hearing their voices, only made sure that any of their scouts were not among those speaking and went out to the stables.

Firekeeper did not return until after dawn and when she did push through the back gate she was far from the proud figure Derian knew so well. It wasn't just that the wolf-woman was filthy enough to cause notice even among Dragon's Breath's motley population. It was that her spirit was in rags. Blind Seer leaned against her, clearly worried.

"I leave them," Firekeeper told Derian without preamble. "Peace and Edlin. I leave them behind."

Derian stared, then ran to get the others.

Upon seeing Firekeeper, Wendee insisted on immediate baths for both the wolf-woman and Blind Seer. Firekeeper did not protest, but she insisted that her companions join her so she could report while she washed.

"In the stables," she suggested, "so no one overhear."

Derian could tell that both Wendee and Elise had to fight down their social conditioning, but that both were possessed of enough common sense not to protest. After all, Derian had seen Firekeeper naked. Doc had been her physician following the terrible injuries inflicted by Prince Newell.

Citrine, hauled from her porridge, seemed to think the entire occasion quite amusing. The manic look had come back into her eyes over the last few days and she was losing ground rapidly. Derian wondered if Citrine had come to think that Peace in his Jalarios role really was her father and if she was now orphaned anew.

Derian made the situation easier for the ladies' modesty by suggesting that he and Doc help Blind Seer with the wolf's own bath. They found the wolf eager for a good scrubbing—even if he did have to stand in a deep trough used to water the horses and be sluiced down with buckets.

Firekeeper started talking as soon as they were alone and Bee Biter was sitting perched where he could see any who might come to spy.

"I leave them," she said, repeating what she had said the moment she had come in through the gate. Even though it was old news, her voice was still raw with pain. "I leave Peace and Edlin behind."

She went on to tell them about the journey through the tunnels, praising both guide and cartographer with such fervor that Derian knew she already dreaded that they were dead. When she came to the caverns, she slowed her narrative, making the excuse of dunking her already rinsed hair.

"I not trust Peace, not even then," she said at last. "When first the woman Idalia speak, I think he has betrayed us and am wondering how to get away. Then I smell his fear and his unhappiness. Blind Seer smell it, too," she added, as if wondering if they thought her words mere rhetoric.

"Then I am very afraid, for I think of patience waiting for us beneath the earth. Idalia's soldiers have bows and arrows. We would be dead if we flee, and I hear such hate in her voice that I know she not stop saying to shoot. Then Edlin give me map."

Derian nodded, seeing her sudden anxious expression.

"It's safe, Firekeeper," he said. "I have it right here."

He tapped his trouser pocket. Firekeeper nodded and went on.

"And Edlin tell me something I still not understand. He say 'Don't want them getting all of us. Afraid . . . ' "

Firekeeper mimicked Edlin's intonation's so flawlessly that Derian could imagine the young lord speaking. Resuming her own voice she went on.

"Then Edlin stop talking, seeing that guards is so close that if he not make fuss now, it not be soon enough. What he mean he afraid? He was very brave."

Elise replied, couching her words in unwontedly gentle tones. Derian knew she was remembering Edlin not just as their recent companion but as the boy she had played with when they were both children.

"Firekeeper, I think Edlin wanted to make certain that someone escaped to tell what happened. If no one got away, then the New Kelvinese could deny any complicity in your disappearance. How could our ambassador protest if they denied all knowledge of you? Edlin is not known for his brilliance and street crime does exist. You, dear, are known for disappearing at a moment's notice.

"This way, however, you have returned as a witness. True, if we are to ask after them through public channels, we will have to admit to lurking where we should not have been. Even so, the New Kelvinese would find it more difficult to deny that Edlin was last seen in the custody of one of their own. When Edlin sent you away, he might have been aware that his life could still be forfeit for spying, but he did not need to worry that he would simply disappear without a trace."

Firekeeper looked puzzled by many of Elise's words, but she did not ask for clarification. Doubtless she'd grown very good at sorting out the basic meaning.

"So Edlin not afraid," she said, "except of dying and no one knowing."

"That's about it," Elise concurred, "and he probably thought there was no reason his little sister should die, too."

Firekeeper growled and stepped from the tub, shaking water everywhere as if she had forgotten there were such things as towels.

"I not want him to die," she protested. "I go find him and Peace. I owe Peace, too, for not being traitor."

"We aren't giving up on them," Derian said. "Edlin didn't send the map because he figured our cause was hopeless. We just need to regroup."

He spoke bravely, but he didn't know if he believed his own words. So much depended on who had taken Peace and Edlin, and for whom they were working. From what Elise and Edlin had learned at the embassy, not all the New Kelvinese supported Melina. Was this Idalia, Peace's sister, on Melina's side or against her?

"Xarxius," he said aloud.

"Xarxius?" Elise echoed, looking at him as if he'd gone insane.

"Xarxius," Derian repeated. "Peace told us that he and Xarxius had worked together. I got the feeling they'd been more than business associates, that they'd been friends. Maybe Xarxius could help us."

Mingled hope and worry showed on his companions' faces.

"We could contact him through Ambassador Redbriar," Elise offered somewhat hesitantly. "His post is as liaison with foreign interests. Contact between them must be fairly regular."

"I like it," Firekeeper said decisively. "It is something. Otherwise I must go under the earth again, and without Peace and Edlin—I try to see traps, but I may not."

"Before we run off to Ambassador Redbriar," Doc said, "we should give time for Edlin—and Peace—to be returned to us."

"Returned?" Firekeeper looked at him with undisguised confusion. "I tell you, Doc. This Idalia woman take them. She very angry. I not think she let them go."

"Maybe so, maybe not," Doc said, unshaken by the disbelief in the wolf-woman's dark eyes. "Haven't you ever caught something bigger than you planned?"

Firekeeper looked about to deny it, but Derian saw her gaze flicker to Blind Seer. The wolf, his fur spiky from his bath, was looking at her, his mouth gaping in what even unenlightened humans recognized as a canine laugh.

"Once," she said. "Twice. What does that matter?"

Wendee, who had been toweling off her charge, now handed Firekeeper undergarments in a pointed if silent command.

"I think," Wendee said, when Firekeeper began dressing, "that what Doc means is that this Idalia may find that capturing Lord Edlin Kestrel, heir to that duchy, has more ramifications than she had originally thought. You said she recognized him."

"She said he was idiot and that she'd heard of him," Firekeeper corrected.

"Interesting," Wendee said. "That may mean she had heard more of Edlin's peculiarities than of his position. Don't make faces at me! I'm not talking in riddles. From how Peace talked about his family, this Idalia is of the same general social class as Derian or myself. She is not involved in trade—at least Peace never mentioned any of his family in that line.

"That means that Idalia, unlike her brother, unlike Lady Archer, has had no reason to learn the details of our culture and government. To her the relative importance of a 'lord'—especially since it's a title used for many low ranking nobles, even those with no inheritance prospects . . ."

"Like Lady Melina," Firekeeper said, nodding her understanding as she slipped into her vest and twisted the toggles shut, "or Lady Blysse."

"Right," Wendee said, taking out a comb. "Now, this Idalia may not realize that she has caught herself not just any lord but a lord heir—and that idiot or not, Edlin is not to be lightly disposed of."

Derian felt hope for the first time since Firekeeper's return home.

"And Edlin should be taken even less lightly than any other lord heir. His grandmother's lands are directly across the White Water. She controls one of the major trade crossings."

"Xarxius's purview again," said Elise with a wry grin. "Even if for no other reason, he should be involved because of that."

"But I wonder," Firekeeper said, dressed now and strapping her Fang to its accustomed place at her side, "whose side is Xarxius on?"

And no one, of course, had an answer for that.

TO TORIOVICO IT SEEMED as if the entirety of Thendulla Lypella must know what he had learned in his readings the day before. From the moment he awoke and called for his body servant to fetch his dressing gown he felt aware of a suppressed tension in the air.

He knew it was his imagination. No one could have read what he had and, of course, no one could read his own notes. The excitement and trepidation he sensed were his own, no other's.

Thankfully, Melina was not beside him this morning. She had dined with him and gone to bed with him, but in the dark hours of the night he had awakened to an awareness of her departing his side. When he had called after her, she had said that something she had eaten must have disagreed with her, that she would return when she felt better or else rest in her own suite.

Torio had thought he had glimpsed Tipi and wondered if some message the maid had brought was the cause of Melina's going, but he had not pursued the matter. Indeed, he was glad to have Melina gone from him.

The evening meal had been a nightmare. He had feared Melina would see his new knowledge in his eyes, but she had not, perhaps too distracted by her own thoughts—perhaps believing him so lulled by her powers that she need but give him some small attention.

Still clad only in his dressing gown, hurrying lest Melina return, Toriovico penned a brief note to Columi requesting another private meeting. He knew he was taking a risk accepting the Lapidary into his confidence, but he also knew that someone other than himself must share his knowledge. Sharing was both danger—for Columi might betray him—and insurance, for should something happen to him Columi would know enough to act.

This was not an idle dread. Toriovico realized that Melina had gulled him once, even as she still held many of his key counselors in thrall. He had been fortunate that her intense interest in her new discoveries had distracted her from him, fortunate, too, that his dancing had provided its own charm. One or the other might not have been enough to break her hold. Together, both had succeeded.

Lest someone note a difference in his manner, Toriovico forced himself to hold to his usual routine. He ate heartily, though his tongue scarcely tasted the food. He attended several meetings and spoke the ceremonial words required of him with so much intensity that several of the other participants looked at him rather strangely. Though his ears could hardly hear the music for the pounding of his heart, he went to his morning practice and danced the part of the Harvest Lord.

Only after lunch did he excuse himself and head for the museum.

When Torio arrived, Columi was waiting and whisked him away to the private office at the core of his tower.

"There was an urgency to your note, Healed One," he said. "Have you discovered something?"

Toriovico found his tongue resisted talking about any of the secrets from the book, but he forced himself on by reminding himself that the knowledge was available from other sources—hadn't Melina learned it?

At least he thought she had. . . .

"I think I have," he said slowly, "but nothing of what I tell you must go beyond we two unless . . ."

He swallowed hard.

"Unless you have reason to believe that I have taken leave of either my senses or my life."

Columi looked at him with an understanding that was worse than the disbelief Toriovico had inwardly feared.

"Tell me, Honored One."

"It begins," Toriovico said, "in the earliest days of the Founders. They came here from the Old Country and settled more land than is commonly known—all the way from the shores where Waterland now holds sway to these mountain fastnesses.

"Eventually, others came and wanted that land for themselves. There were terrible battles and—I am ashamed to say—our ancestors lost. Yet they did not lose entirely. They forfeited the coastal lands, but they held the mountains—and made a new one."

Columi cleared his throat.

"That was in the days of the wizard Kelvin," he commented almost diffidently. "As the tale is told within our sodality, the mountain range that now bears the name Sword of Kelvin was raised at the end of those wars. Our lore relates how the Founders made the unquiet rock come to life and raised a barrier between the remnants of our people and the invaders."

Toriovico's lips curved in the smallest of smiles.

"That is a tale not often told these days," he said, "for the First Healed One felt that accounts of heroism rather than defeat would keep our kingdom strong after the Burning Times. It is interesting that your sodality still tells it."

"We study rock and how it lives and grows," said the emeritus with a slight shrug. "The tale must stay alive or be rediscovered in some version by every bright young Lapidary. And I notice you do not tell it as if it was new knowledge, so it was not completely lost."

"No," Toriovico said, aware of how many secrets he still kept. "Much of the Healed One's education is in tales and legends that otherwise might be lost."

"How true," Columi said, and there seemed to be a double meaning in his inflection.

Toriovico wondered just what the old man might have learned or guessed in his long life, but decided that this was not the time to ask.

"Tell me," Columi went on, "what this raising of a mountain hundreds of years ago has to do with the actions of a foreign-born sorceress today?"

"Since you know stones," Torio acceded, "you must also know the legends that dragons are creatures of the elements, some say children of the elements."

"I have heard these tales," Columi admitted, "but never in all my delvings beneath the earth, even in volcanoes where I have seen the pumping of the earth's own blood, have I seen a dragon. I have been to the crests of the Eversnow Mountains where the stone blends with ice and the wind screams its secret name and there, too, I have never glimpsed even the claw print of a dragon."

"I am sure that the hero Kelvin felt as you do," Toriovico said, "for if he believed the tales, I doubt he would have done what he did. You see, it seems that when Kelvin raised the Sword Mountains, he also raised a dragon."

Columi leaned forward, his eyes glittering, but he made no sound.

"Some sources insist that Kelvin created the dragon," Torio went on, "with the power he channeled through that unquiet rock. Some say he merely summoned it. Others that the dragon was there already, nascent, a spirit of the place without a body—that the magic gave it a body.

"Whatever the truth—and personally I favor the last—a dragon surged into being even as the mountains rose. At first our people cheered and laughed for they saw the monster as a new weapon to turn against the invaders. Indeed, so the Waterlanders saw it as well, for they fled and not even their deep and abiding greed has made them attempt to claim as much as an inch of the foothills.

"Yet this was not the case. The dragon seemed to know from where had come the power that had raised it and, rather than being pleased, it was filled with fury. It descended on the sorcerers. Several died. Among these was Kelvin himself, dying, not beneath an onslaught of enemy magic as our tales now tell, but from the result of a magic he himself had caused to be summoned."

Now Columi could be silent no longer.

"I wonder that we have no tales of this!" he exclaimed. "Surely hundreds if not thousands saw the dragon and witnessed these battles."

"But we do," Toriovico replied with a sad smile. "Every child knows the story of the Star Wizard and the Dragon of Despair. It is part of the same tale, separated from its beginning because it holds no shame."

"Truly?"

"Truly," Toriovico assured him. "The Star Wizard was the first among those sorcerers that the hero Kelvin marshaled in order to raise the Sword Mountains. He was a more powerful wizard than Kelvin, but not as great a warrior. Circumstances forced him to become one. The Star Wizard's circle of allies lay broken and bleeding. Kelvin was dead. The city—not yet named Dragon's Breath—was burning from the monster's fire.

"The Star Wizard used a magical mirror, so the tales say, one that magnified the light of the sun until it became a solid beam. Wielding that light as a sword, he drove the Dragon of Despair into the caverns beneath Thendulla Lypella. Then he dissolved it once again into the elements, so successfully that its energy fed the latent volcanic activity.

"Some say that the dragon attempted its revenge once or twice, seeking to store its power and release it all in a rush, but the Star Wizard and those who became his apprentices quieted it until it merely sulked and steamed. Eventually, its consciousness faded and it slept.

"Other tales relate how rival wizards sought to awaken the dragon, promising it freedom in return for its power in their fights. The Star Wizard balked them, for the spells by which he had bound the monster were so potent that only the most horrible magical rites would set it free. And so the Dragon of Despair was bound and so it remains bound to this day."

Columi had been listening, nodding almost like a child listening to a familiar tale. Now, as Toriovico stopped speaking and poured himself a cup from the pitcher that rested between them, the old man's smile faded.

"Good tales, old tales, but surely you do not think that Consolor Melina believes them?"

"You believe the story of how the Sword of Kelvin Mountains were raised, O wise Lapidary," said Toriovico. "That is why I began there—with the origin of the dragon. I think that not only does my wife believe the tale, she believes that she can achieve what even the great wizards of the Founders' time did not dare to do. She plans to awaken the Dragon of Despair and make it her weapon against her enemies."

Columi gasped.

"And I am not entirely certain," Toriovico concluded, "that she will not succeed."

Although Toriovico succeeded in convincing Columi of the validity of his theory, showing him various sections from old books and scrolls and even quoting him portions of the Restorer's journal, he could not convince the Lapidary that he knew enough.

"You need to know precisely where Melina is going when she ventures on one of these subterranean jaunts," Columi said stubbornly. "As I see it, there are two ways in which we can manage this. She can be physically tracked—preferably by some agent other than yourself—or you can continue to trace her through books and records."

Torio nodded, though he liked neither option. The one meant more people entering into his secret. The other was slow and tedious. It might also attract unwanted attention, especially if Melina had allies among the Illuminators who provided librarians for Thendulla Lypella.

He shared his concern with Columi, who nodded and looked distinctly unhappy.

"I, too, had considered those problems," he said, "but I feel it is essential that you know more precisely what she has discovered before you act against her. What if Melina has found someone who could do the rite in her stead? Restricting her actions might precipitate disaster rather than preventing it."

The image that arose then was so horrible Torio put it from his mind immediately, but he did not disregard his counselor's words.

"Very well. We shall pursue both courses of action," he said. "You shall be my agent among the books. I will have a parcel delivered to you here."

Columi looked both alarmed and gratified.

"My vision, Healed One," he said hesitantly, "is not what it was. . . ."

"You have spectacles," Toriovico replied brusquely. "Use them. If our concerns are correct, this is no time for one who has aroused Melina's ire to be careful with his vision. You might lack life soon enough."

Columi realized the truth in this and offered no protest.

"And as to tracking Melina?" he asked cautiously, as if he feared that task would be put on him as well.

"Your words about regarding what allies Melina may have gave me an idea," Toriovico said. "One of her closest confidants is her maid, Tipi. I shall convince her to be my informant."

Columi looked dubious, but offered no objection.

"If that does not work," Torio went on, "I shall speak to someone on my staff of watchers. Surely not all of them have been suborned."

Columi nodded.

"You will not trail her yourself?" he asked, clearly wishing reassurance.

"I did not promise that," Torio said, a trace bitterly, "only that I shall not go alone."

With that, Columi had to be content.

KICKS AND BLOWS herded Grateful Peace and Edlin from the sewer tunnels, up and into rougher tubes of fire-melted stone. From the change in the surrounding construction, Peace deduced that he and Edlin were being taken into the little-used natural caverns beneath the northern edge of Thendulla Lypella.

The odor of sulphur and the rough, jagged basalt that tore boots and clothing alike made these regions supremely unpleasant. Indeed, Peace doubted that any but advanced members of the Sodality of Lapidaries ever descended to these regions—any but they and a thoroughly inquisitive Dragon's Eye, and none of them had dared penetrate too deeply.

Idalia stalked ahead of her prisoners, seemingly unaware of their harsh treatment by her servants, yet Peace didn't doubt that she was aware of every kick, every blow, and that in some perverse way she gloried in each one.

He had never realized how much his sister hated him, and her hatred bruised and battered his soul. Had Idalia always hated him or had Kistlio's death been what pushed her from resentment—he had been aware of her resentment—into hatred?

Peace wanted to ask, but feared that his words would emerge in the piping voice of the little brother rather than the sardonic inquiry of the man. With his mind fragmented through the dozens of throbbing hurts upon his exhausted frame, he believed in the possibility of that transformation. The terror that somehow he could be forced into that younger self kept him mute.

Beside Peace, Edlin staggered forward, head bent, blood dripping from the corner of his mouth. Once the crossbows had been lowered, he had made some effort to fight free. Edlin's valor or idiocy—Peace was really not certain which—had resulted in his being beaten nearly unconscious. Only later, when Idalia delegated some of her servants to go out and bring Fire-keeper back, did Peace wonder if Edlin had once again sacrificed himself to gain his adopted sister time to escape.

Yet for all his greater injuries, Edlin did not labor under such strain as did his companion. The pride the young man felt in having helped Firekeeper escape was visible even in his bowed shoulders. Yet neither this nor Edlin's immunity to Idalia's particular scorn were his greatest protection.

Ignorance was Edlin's armor and shield while knowledge blew into Peace's face as might a high wind. With every step, the onetime Illuminator must struggle against what he knew—and what he feared.

Peace knew that these fire-sculpted caverns had been the conjuring place for the earliest magics of the Founders. The caverns had been abandoned by the First Healed One, and all but forgotten by successive generations. Peace possessed no superstitious fear of magic as did the Hawk Havenese. His fear was real, rooted in belief, respect, and trembling awe. To be taken into these reaches, to be shut into a side cave, and see it sealed from without against his escape, these shattered his nerve as physical torment and psychological quandary had not.

The former Dragon's Eye collapsed onto hands and knees and took no comfort that the floor had been polished to some smoothness so the basalt did not abrade his palms. That smoothness meant this cave was among those the Founders had turned to their use and the proximity to such mysteries made him tremble and sink into black nightmare.

Grateful Peace came to himself to find Edlin crouched beside him, dabbing a rag dipped in water onto the worst of his cuts.

"How long?" he whispered.

"A bit," Edlin replied, his voice soft and the words distorted by his swollen lips. "Hard to say, really. They left us lanterns and there's water from a seep, even a clay cup. Here . . ."

Peace felt his head gently tilted and a cup placed against his mouth. Obediently, still trying to sort nightmare from truth, he drank. Edlin brought him more water and he drank again. The water tasted strongly of various minerals, but was no more unpleasant than some of the draughts offered by various baths throughout New Kelvin.

His thoughts cleared somewhat, and he struggled to sit up. Edlin assisted him and in the pale light Peace saw the youth wince as pressure was put on his arm.

"Is it broken?" Peace asked.

"I don't think so," Edlin replied. "Throbs every time my heart beats. Wish Cousin Jared were with us."

He paused, glanced about their prison, and amended.

"Then again, maybe I'm gladder he's not."

Peace found himself admiring the irrepressible spirit that wouldn't stop chattering even through broken lips. He fought to rise to Edlin's example.

"We're somewhere beneath the northern portion of Thendulla Lypella," he said. "How are we guarded?"

"Pretty well," Edlin replied. "The cave has a door, hinges and everything. Old-looking. I don't think we're the first to stay here. I listened at it and there's at least two men out there. Heard them talking—not New Kelvinese or Pellish, though."

"I understand several languages," Peace said. "Let me listen."

Stiffly, every limb aching as if he'd aged years with the passing of a few hours, Peace moved over to the door. The planks, he saw, were old, showing evidence of having warped and bent so that there were cracks between them. He didn't doubt that the planks themselves were solid and didn't waste precious strength testing them.

Although he heard some sound without—the squeak of leather, a damped clanking of metal, a guttural cough—the guards were not conversing. Peace thought about calling out to attract the guards' attention, but decided against this. He and Edlin had at least the illusion of privacy, and should use it to their best advantage.

Most important, perhaps, would be to learn just how real that privacy was. The cave seemed solid, but spy holes could have been drilled in any number of places. The presence of the lanterns also argued that they were being watched. Darkness would have been a fine tool to use against them, making it impossible for them to investigate their prison, even for them to find the water that had provided such a distinct comfort. His aching injuries reminded him that if their enemies were granting them light, it was not out of the goodness of their hearts but because they had some advantage to gain.

Limping over to the seep, Peace tore a rag from his robe and began systematically to wash his various cuts and scrapes. While attempting to seem completely distracted by this, he let his gaze rove. A crack in the door would offer the most obvious peephole, but its very obviousness would prove a disadvantage. Ideally, a second vantage, one that overlooked the back of the cave, would be ideal.

He was only partway through his examination, accepting Edlin's help in treating those injuries that were out of reach, when muffled sounds from the corridor drew their attention.

Holding up a finger for silence, Peace limped over to the door. Its thickness muffled what he could make out but he distinctly heard several voices, two of which, at least, were female. He felt a chill down his spine, for he knew to whom at least one of those voices belonged. There was no mistaking that cadence, silky yet commanding.

He turned to Edlin and hissed, "Melina!"

There was no time for more before a snapping and clattering of metal announced that the door was being opened. With the creaking of unoiled hinges as herald, Consolor Melina swept into the cell.

Marriage—or at least New Kelvinese styles in clothing, Peace thought cynically—apparently agreed with Melina, for she seemed taller, more slender, and even more commanding than he recalled. The dark green robe the new Consolor of the Healed One wore made her silvery blond hair seem to glow with a faint inner light, and her facial ornamentation served to emphasize her crystalline blue eyes.

Peace knew enough to avoid the direct gaze of those eyes, no matter how compelling they might seem. So, though he longed to glower at Melina, he only gave a perfectly correct bow, then focused his gaze over her shoulder.

Prudent as this tactic was, it meant that Peace could not avoid the smoldering gaze of the person who stood directly behind and slightly to one side of Melina. There Idalia waited, her expression mingling restrained fury and anticipation in equal parts. When her gaze met his own, Idalia's lips parted in an involuntary hiss of pure hatred.

Edlin had taken part in numerous discussions over just how Melina managed her particular form of magic. There had been differences of opinion on the fine points, but all had agreed that Melina's eyes were central to her control of another person. Therefore Peace was not worried that Edlin would make some careless mistake. However, he wasn't certain how the young man would react when at last confronted with the woman who had been responsible for so much in so little time.

Indeed, Peace thought it completely possible that the youth would say something like, "I say! Sacrificed any children to the silk spider gods? What?"

Edlin surprised him, however. From the corner of his eye, Peace saw Lord Kestrel give the Hawk Haven equivalent of a courtly bow—one nearly as deep as he would have given his own queen. After in this way acknowledging Melina's elevated status, Edlin said in a fairly good approximation of his usual breezy tones:

"I say. You're looking fine, Consolor Melina. Those robes really look classy. You'll be the envy of all the ladies when you make the diplomatic rounds."

Apparently, Melina was as surprised as Peace by this greeting, for she paused before replying.

"Thank you, Lord Kestrel, but I do not think the other ladies will be as quick to change their established fashions as you might believe."

Edlin responded with an easy, drawing-room laugh.

"If you were doing the convincing, Consolor Melina," he said, "it might be different."

Be careful, you young fool! Peace thought, momentarily panicked that Edlin might decide to push his teasing further.

Melina said nothing for a long moment. One did not need to be Grateful Peace and possess his long education in the interactions of men and women to realize that the Consolor was adjusting to their apparent composure.

I wonder what she expected? Peace thought. *To find us cringing? Threatening? Demanding our freedom? Whatever she expected it wasn't Lord Edlin's casual insouciance.*

He felt a flood of completely unheralded fondness for this young man with his foolish ways and—just maybe—wise heart.

But Melina was not one to be put off her stride indefinitely. She stepped into the cave, Idalia and two of the guards, each carrying a lantern, following. Six in the makeshift room made for rather cramped quarters but Peace immediately understood the reason.

She cannot risk either herself or Idalia being overpowered by us, yet she does not wish to let us out. Interesting. I wonder how far her control within Thendulla Lypella has spread—and just who she feels she still must be careful around.

Continuing in his role as genteel guest rather than prisoner, Edlin made a sweeping gesture with one hand.

"Ladies? I'd offer you a chair, don't you know, but I'm afraid we're rather short."

Idalia gave an indignant sniff, but Melina summoned a smile.

"Thank you, Lord Kestrel, but we won't be staying long."

"Right-o," Edlin said, leaning back against the wall in a relaxed attitude that had to hurt his tortured limbs. "Delighted to have such charming company, what?"

Melina gave a rather icy smile.

"I am sorry I cannot invite you into my tower, Lord Kestrel, but it really wouldn't be convenient. However, if you cooperate with me, I can make your stay more comfortable."

Edlin said nothing, only tilted his head in a fashion that rather reminded Peace of Firekeeper—or of her wolf.

Melina went on.

"Your greatest use to me would be as a hostage. At this point, however, I am not certain what price I would take for your return. I have so much, you see. . . ."

Again Edlin resisted the obvious prompt and Peace, aware that he himself was being deliberately snubbed, had to stifle a completely inappropriate chuckle. Once again he felt certain that this interview was not going as Consolor Melina had anticipated.

"What would make your stay more comfortable?" she asked.

Edlin looked around the cave, which, other than the lanterns and the clay cup, was completely unfurnished.

"Your hospitality has been even greater than I expected," he said smoothly. "I could not ask for more."

Peace saw Melina stiffen as the insult went home, but she refused to show her anger—perhaps because of the presence of the guards. These were clearly foreigners—Waterlanders, Peace thought, perhaps purchased from the debtors market. Debtors made among the most tractable of slaves because by Waterland law they were stripped of any place within their own society and so they were determined to make the most of their new life.

Debtors were also among the most expensive of slaves. Peace wondered just how high the ransom for Edlin might be set. No matter what gifts Melina had managed to extract from her besotted spouse and his associates, here was evidence that she was spending amply as well.

As for himself, Peace had no illusions that ransom would be an option. Idalia's gaze, unwaveringly fixed on him no matter what her mistress said, told him that he was the price for another's service. He only wondered how long he had until that price was exacted and how painful the ultimate paying out would be.

"Well," Melina said to Edlin after a long pause, "I can only say that my hospitality can be greater than you imagine. I hope you do not mind sharing your quarters?"

Edlin gave a casual shrug.

"It matters not. What are your plans for Grateful Peace?"

Melina's smile turned momentarily cruel.

"Eventually, he will be reunited with his older sister. I believe she wishes to have a long . . . discussion with him regarding her late son. However, that joyful reunion will be somewhat delayed."

Peace heard the "can be" in her inflection. He was being offered a chance to buy a few more days of life. What would the cost be? As he had not yet been addressed directly, he forbore from asking. Edlin, however, had no such restraints.

"Really? It must be something very important to delay such a reunion."

"Important?" Melina made a dismissive gesture. "Let us rather say help-ful. I am eager to learn about my new homeland yet find surprisingly few people knowledgeable about the more obscure geographies of Dragon's Breath—especially of the subterranean city. Repeatedly, I have heard 'If only Grateful Peace had not turned dirty, stinking traitor. He would know what you wish to learn.' "

Peace schooled himself to impassivity, but the taunt went home, even more as he didn't doubt the words were perfectly accurate, even mild.

Within New Kelvinese society, where merit overwhelmed all other con-siderations for promotion, slandering the competition was common. Com-plete character destruction was usual in cases of overwhelming failure—as Peace had failed his Dragon Speaker and his kingdom.

Edlin didn't know this, of course, and had the grace to look offended, but the wisdom not to comment.

"What would you want him to do?" he asked instead.

"Recite at length and in full the details of the hidden ways above and below Thendulla Lypella," Melina said promptly. "That will do for a start. If he can prove to me he knows more of value relating to other areas of the kingdom, he may preserve himself longer."

Idalia gave a small, indignant squeak of protest.

Melina laid a hand on Idalia's arm.

"Of course, maybe he can attend a family gathering or two," she said silkily. "As a reward."

Peace knew that the reward was Idalia's, for her patience, and he knew, too, who would supply the punishment if the information he gave was less than correct. From the fashion Idalia's fevered gaze rested on the limp sleeve over his amputated arm, he didn't doubt that she was contemplating more of the same.

He strove not to vomit, not to scream, not to rush forward in a desperate dash for freedom. Surely one of the guards might cut him down? Perhaps if he attacked Melina herself . . .

But such impulses died even as they rose. Melina had too much self-control to let herself lose such a valuable tool. All he would do would be to put himself in Idalia's hands the sooner.

Instead Peace said in a rusty voice he hardly recognized as his own:

"I would be honored to see my humble knowledge preserved so that it might serve the Healed One and his wife. If you would do us the great kindness of returning to Lord Kestrel his drawing materials, he might be willing to make maps of what I recall."

"I say!" Edlin said. "That might be fun."

"Fun," Melina echoed flatly. "Perhaps. But certainly useful."

She signed that the audience was ended and her entourage filed from the cave. The last look she gave them was cold and judgmental. It left no doubts that her cordiality had been feigned, nor that she had forgotten the one of their company who had escaped—and what the wolf-woman had likely borne away with her.

XXVI

THEY WERE IGNORING HER and that was the last insult. She'd been hauled halfway across two countries, dressed as a foreign boy, treated as a servant all for a single reason—so that she could see her mother. Now no one was making any effort to bring them together.

They'd set up a hospital. They'd bought cloth and funny-smelling herbs. They'd talked and talked and talked and talked, and none of that talk had brought her to Mother.

Now they were all worrying about Edlin—and even about Peace, even though he was just a servant and a traitor whom they admitted they hadn't even trusted—and worrying about them meant that they weren't thinking about her.

Citrine's fury at being so thoroughly ignored shaped her thoughts into a narrow tunnel out of which she peered like a sailor seeking a safe harbor with a spyglass. She found one, just where it had always been.

Mother. She would go to Mother. She would tell her about the others, about their nasty plans and plots. Mother would be happy and proud. Mother would make her a princess—a princess just like Sapphire.

Everything would be wonderful. Citrine knew it, and if the traces of common sense that clamored to rise through her anger and resentment tried to tell her otherwise, Citrine simply didn't listen.

By the afternoon of the day when Firekeeper had returned and told how Edlin and Peace had been captured by Peace's angry sister, the household had returned to some semblance of normalcy. Firekeeper was sleeping off bone-deep exhaustion. Elise had gone to the Hawk Haven embassy, just in case Ambassador Redbriar's spies turned up something significant. Wendee was searching for rumors on the streets. Doc was seeing patients. Derian was pulled two directions at once—tending to all of his and Wendee's usual routine and assisting Doc when he needed another set of hands.

It was easy to slip away. Indeed, the ease of it added fuel to the raging fire of Citrine's resentment. Step one had been telling Derian she needed to lie down, that she was tired from sitting awake worrying all night. Derian hadn't questioned her, only given a tight smile.

"Go," he had said. "I only wish I could join you."

Citrine knew Derian was actually glad to have her gone away. She'd heard the grownups discussing their fears that her lack of New Kelvinese—brilliant though her ability was for one who had spoken none of the language a few moonspans before—would give her impersonation away to Hasamemorri or one of her maids.

Citrine had gone into the sleeping room she shared with Wendee and Elise—Firekeeper preferred to be outside—and lay down, keeping the door open a crack so she could hear what went on in the rest of the house. When she heard Doc call for Derian and guessed from the rising note in his voice that Derian would be busy for more than a few minutes, Citrine rose, straightened her New Kelvinese attire, picked up a small bundle of personal possessions wrapped in a square of silk, and went into the kitchen.

From there she had simply walked out the kitchen door, out the back gate, and down the alley behind. Even though she longed to run, Citrine had learned when she was very young that running attracted attention. She strained her ears to hear Derian calling or the shriek of Bee Biter, Firekeeper's kestrel.

There wasn't a sound. No one came after her. No one on the street looked twice at her. Panic flooded Citrine when she realized she was going to get away with it, almost washing away the anger.

Almost, but not quite. With a firm, steady step she went to the market from which she'd posted her letter to Mother. The letter should have arrived by now. Indeed, she might miss the messenger Mother was certain to send for her. She envisioned a coach and four, later changing her mental picture when she recalled that the New Kelvinese tended to use litters for smaller human cargo.

The litter her mother would send for her had been hung with red-gold curtains, just a touch lighter than her own citrine namestone. The men who carried it had been muscular, their bodies painted in fanciful swirls that shone beneath the oil they rubbed on themselves.

Indeed, the image was so vivid that Citrine nearly turned around to go and wait for what seemed so certain and so real. But the sight of the Earth Spires at the city's northern edge drew her on. Certainly Mother wouldn't mind if she came of her own accord. She might even be pleased. After all, it would take a great while to find a litter with curtains just the right shade.

So Citrine hurried on, pausing once to buy some candied ginger root—a New Kelvinese delicacy for which she'd developed a liking. Buying it would provide an excuse if she accidently met up with Elise or Wendee—though it was likely to earn her a scolding as well.

With the ginger root's spicy sweetness in her mouth, Citrine hurried through the crowded streets. For once not even the most elaborate costume could distract her. She had a more fascinating image in her mind—her mother kneeling down to welcome her, her arms spread wide, a smile of pure pleasure softening her lips.

As Citrine drew close enough to Thendulla Lypella that she could see the walls, she paused to consider which gate she should enter by. There was the trade entrance, of course. That was the one most discussed by her companions, for if they had any hope of sneaking inside—other than through the sewers—it was through that gate.

Citrine supposed she might slip through there, posing as part of some merchant's party, but discovery would be too certain. In any case, once inside she'd be in almost the same situation as before. Numerous questions—mostly directed to various of Doc's patients or to Oculios the apothecary, for she was careful not to let any person know too much about her interest—had enabled Citrine to piece together the names of some of the more visible spires, including the Cloud Touching Spire, in which the Healed One and his wife lived. However, up close she could hardly tell one towering mass of stone from another. Clearly she'd need directions, probably a guide.

There were many other gates: the Petitioner's, the Processional, the Visitor's, and many whose names she had not learned. Citrine considered using the Visitor's Gate, but everyone coming through there had an invitation to show and she had none. She knew enough about guards to know that they were singularly unimaginative regarding alterations in routine.

That made the Petitioner's Gate her best choice. She joined the line there. It was quite short and Citrine smiled with joy. Just a few people in front of her, just a few more minutes between her and Mother.

"Not many people today," she said in her best New Kelvinese to the man ahead of her in line.

The man blinked, showing stars on his eyelids.

"This line isn't for today, boy," he said, sharply but kindly. "It's for tomorrow."

Citrine's spirits plummeted. She didn't think she'd be able to avoid the others all afternoon and all night, too.

The man must have understood.

"You speak to the clerk inside," he explained, "tell who you need to see, then get a ticket that tells you when to come back. Much better than long lines come morning."

Citrine nodded, afraid to try her New Kelvinese around the lump in her throat. The man smiled and patted her on the head.

"You'll do all right, boy. They're used to folk from the country."

He might have been inclined to chat further, but the line was moving. In a moment, he entered one small kiosk and hardly a breath later Citrine was waved into its mate.

A rather round fellow with whiskers like a catfish's and greenish stains near his eyes looked up as she came in. His robe was a deep blue-black the exact shade of spilled ink.

"Yes? And who do you wish to see, young man?"

"Consolor Melina, sir," Citrine said, her voice very small.

The clerk's eyebrows rose to where his hairline should be.

"Really, the Consolor doesn't see petitioners."

"Please, sir," Citrine said. "I have to see her."

To her horror, she felt tears welling in her eyes. She wanted to wipe them away, but didn't want to be rude and touch her face.

"Consolor Melina doesn't see petitioners," the man repeated, his tone firm but not unkind. "Perhaps if you tell me what the matter is, I can direct you to the right department."

"There is no department for this," Citrine said, hoping she was saying the words right. Despairing, she pushed back the strip of cloth tied over her forehead to hide her gemstone band. "I'm her daughter. I'm Citrine Shield."

IT WAS HOURS BEFORE SHE SAW MOTHER. First she was taken to a guardroom and made to wait. Her only advantage here was that they assumed—despite her New Kelvinese attire—that she had no real command of the language and so spoke freely in front of her. Knowing that they really were trying to find Mother made the waiting bearable.

Then she was taken to another, nicer room, bathed—though she wasn't really all *that* dirty—and given girl's clothes to wear. They were New Kelvinese girl's clothes, which meant they weren't that much different in cut from the robes she had been wearing, but the fabric was softer: a pretty apricot silk printed with flowers growing from graceful green stems. Best of all, the robe smelled of some marvelous perfume that made Citrine feel like the nicest parts of summer.

The maids who helped her were quick and obedient. They didn't ask many questions—only whether she wanted this clip for her hair or that one, or maybe about the style of slipper she preferred. Citrine might have been fooled into thinking they were completely uninterested, but she'd spent a little time with Hasamemorri's maids and knew that their manners when on duty were quite different from their sparrow-like gossiping when off.

Citrine was glad for her lessons in New Kelvinese deportment now, though they had seemed quite tedious when Peace was drilling her. Watching the elegant grace of the servants, Citrine was glad that she would not embarrass herself with some rude gesture and so anger her mother.

Now that Citrine was closer to her mother, she found herself remembering all the things she'd tried so hard to forget. How quick mother's temper could be. How mysterious she was. How little time Melina had for her youngest and—after three others—quite superfluous daughter.

Citrine was nearly regretting her temerity at coming uninvited when the broad double doors on the other side of the chamber opened and Consolor Melina swept into the room.

She looked so like a New Kelvinese lady that at first Citrine didn't recognize her. Her robes swept the floor, the outer skirts emerald green, the inner, just visible when she walked, a violet so dark that in some lights it seemed black. Her silvery blond hair was drawn up into a long, thick braid, coiled at the back of her head and fastened with gemstone pins.

But what made Melina a stranger were the designs painted on her face. They weren't overtly unnatural, only distorting. Carefully contoured lines made her pale eyes seem to slant. Her lips seemed fuller, her nose very thin. Delicate crisscross patterns had been worked across her forehead, around her temples, and gradually faded to near invisibility near her jaw. Doubtlessly they were terribly significant, but to Citrine they just seemed odd.

More important than even the heavy face paint was the absence of the necklace Melina had worn everywhere—even in her bed—for as long as Citrine had known her. The scoop neck of her robe left the upper portion of her bosom bare, and its only adornment was a small pendant of some carved stone.

Citrine felt lost, as if her mother's relinquishing the necklace was the final proof that she had no further need for her youngest daughter.

But Melina was rushing across the floor, gathering Citrine into her arms, pressing her against that astonishingly unadorned bosom. The stone pendant, Citrine could see now, was smooth and resembled a cloud.

"Leave us! Leave us!" Melina said to the maids in a voice that was high and—to that tiny cynical core in Citrine's being—a shade theatrical. "I would be with my poor, lost lamb."

And the maids did leave, and when the door was closed behind them, Melina rocked back on her heels, released Citrine from her embrace, and looked at her through those strangely slanted eyes.

"You've grown," she said in Pellish, her words sounding completely natural. "At least a finger span. They haven't starved you then, though I hear you've been ill."

"Yes, Mother," Citrine said, curling closed her left fist so her mother wouldn't see the lost fingers. "I was, but I'm better now."

"Good," Melina purred. "Come and sit on the divan with me and tell me all about everything that has happened to you."

"Everything?" Citrine said in some amazement. "That could take a long time."

"Well, why don't you start backwards," Melina suggested, "and we'll work our way to the present."

So Citrine started talking, telling about Hasamemorri's and about being ignored, about Edlin and Peace, about Firekeeper, and all the fuss.

"And you weren't happy with this?" Melina asked.

"No, Mother."

"So you decided to run away across all the city and find me yourself?"

There was a curious tightness in Melina's voice, but her expression remained kind.

"Yes, Mother. They were supposed to find you and they didn't, so I did."

She felt proud of herself, so proud that Melina's next words were like a blow.

"And you expect me to believe that, you little brat?"

"It's true, Mother!" Citrine heard her voice break and felt deeply embarrassed. "Every bit!"

"You didn't come here to find me and see if you could wheedle out of me some information about where your beloved companions are?"

Citrine stared uncomprehendingly for a moment. Then she realized that Mother must mean Peace and Edlin.

"No, Mother. Honest, no!"

Melina was looking distinctly mean.

"Information you would pass on to one of that damned feral child's spies? Slip to some little birdie, maybe?"

"No!"

"I've foiled you, dear child," Melina went on as if she hadn't heard. "This room has no exterior windows—not one. The windows you see are all false. I thought to trick you, to see what the messenger was, but why wait?"

"There is no messenger!" Citrine wailed. "I came to find you all on my own. I don't care about Edlin or Peace. I wanted you!"

Melina's expression softened, just a trace.

"Maybe you did," she said. "Maybe. For now, you'll remain here and we shall see."

She rose to depart and Citrine grabbed her flowing sleeve.

"Mother!"

For a moment she thought Melina would slap her. Then the severe expression softened. She continued to walk, but only as far as a braided bell-pull.

"Bring dinner here for me and my daughter," she said to the servant who came to her call. "And have messages brought to my maid Tipi and His Honored Grace the Healed One informing them where I can be found."

"Yes, Consolor," replied the servant, bowing his face into his hands before hurrying away.

"Now," Melina said, coming back and resuming her seat, "where were we? Ah, yes. You were telling me about your adventures. Tell me more. Tell me everything."

Citrine obeyed. Most of her was very happy, but deep inside her heart there was a rapidly beating pulse that felt very afraid.

❧

FIREKEEPER WOKE as late afternoon was merging imperceptibly into evening to hear Wendee shouting Citrine's name—or rather that of Rios. She sat up in the hayloft, picking straw from her hair. Wendee didn't sound annoyed. She sounded anxious.

Wendee came into the stable and called for Rios. When Firekeeper poked her head over the edge of the loft, Wendee glanced up, concern in every line of her face.

"Is Rios there?" she asked. "No games now!"

Firekeeper tilted her head to one side inquiringly.

"No games," she said. "No Rios either."

She swung herself lightly down from the loft. Blind Seer thumped down beside her.

Wendee, who had taken an inadvertent step back, looked as if she'd say something about nearly being pounced, but instead she bit her lower lip and frowned.

"Citrine told Derian she was going to take a nap, but when I came back from errands and went to check on her she wasn't there. Neither were several of her possessions—a comb, a drawing set Edlin gave her, a scarf. I'm worried."

Firekeeper considered.

"You think she is gone away?"

"Yes. She's been acting strange again, ever since we came to Dragon's Breath. I'm worried she's decided either to try and rescue Edlin on her own or . . . or to go to her mother."

Hating Melina as she did, Firekeeper found it hard to imagine that anyone would want to go to her. It seemed more likely that Citrine would have tried to rescue Edlin and Peace. She had seemed fond of Edlin, and Peace had acted as her father for these moonspans past. And the deed—should she succeed—would garner for Citrine the attention the girl clearly craved.

The missing drawing set seemed to confirm Firekeeper's theory. Citrine might have made a new map of the sewers for herself, copied from the one Edlin had done.

"I go look for Citrine," Firekeeper offered. She touched Blind Seer on one shoulder. "We both."

"And don't forget to come back and tell us what you've found," Wendee called after. "We don't need two of you to find."

When Wendee had gone, Firekeeper turned to Blind Seer.

"What can you find, clever nose?"

The wolf cast around for a bit, expanding his search through the yard in back of Hasamemorri's house. His task was complicated by the scent trails accumulated over the days they had been in residence.

Finally, he snorted.

"Something here," he said. *"Interesting. Open the back gate, Firekeeper."*

Firekeeper complied and the wolf went forth, casting his nose along the ground, sneezing once at something cast into the alley, but otherwise very attentive.

"Tell," she suggested.

Never lifting his nose from the ground, Blind Seer did.

"She came out this way, recently, for the spoor is fairly fresh. If you look, you may see sign."

Firekeeper did look. The alley, unlike the streets in front of the houses, was only intermittently paved. The soft shoes Citrine wore left no deep marks in the dirt, but here and there she saw a likely trace.

"Is this hers?" she asked the wolf.

"It is," he confirmed.

"She walked steadily," Firekeeper commented. *"Can you track her from here?"*

"I can only try."

They went forth, but once they were on the paved main streets Firekeeper had to rely on the wolf. Even a lesser street in Dragon's Breath saw a fair amount of traffic, plenty to wear away any small signs the girl's shoes would have left.

"She walked toward the market," Blind Seer said. *"The trace is there— for me."*

Firekeeper tugged his ear, but didn't gainsay him. Side by side they walked to the crowded market. The residents did not stare or express any astonishment at the great wolf and his odd human companion, but they did leave a broad passage down the crowded street for them to pass along.

In the market, Blind Seer lost all but the faintest traces, but they met Wendee, there before them. The woman looked more worried than before.

"I found a sweetmeats seller," she said without greeting, "who says our 'boy' bought a small bag of candied ginger from her. The seller did notice that the boy didn't go back in the direction from which he had come, but went into that street."

She gestured.

Firekeeper nodded.

"Is this at right time?" she asked. "Not an earlier buy? We know she—he—like candy."

"It is the right time," Wendee confirmed. "The seller noticed the bundle the boy carried. That's why she looked after him, to make certain he hadn't pilfered anything."

Firekeeper frowned, but she gestured with her head in the direction of the indicated street.

"We can only see if his nose," she thumped Blind Seer on the skull, "is as sharp as he boasts."

Briefly, she filled Wendee in on the little they had learned.

"Go back and tell the others," the wolf-woman suggested. "We will track from here. Is Elise come home again?"

"Not yet," Wendee said. "Maybe the boy has gone to her."

She brightened at the thought. Firekeeper, however, thought this optimistic. She was beginning to doubt her own initial conclusion that Citrine was off to the rescue. If Citrine had been planning to use the sewers then she should have gone to the same entry they had used the night before. That she had been seen in Aswatano was not a good sign.

Blind Seer had come to the same conclusions.

"I'll track Citrine as far as I can," he said, *"but I'll lose her on some busy street. Best then that we go directly to the walls of Thendulla Lypella. I'll give up blood-hot meat should we not find her trail there."*

"Shall we go directly?" Firekeeper asked.

"No, I wish to learn if anyone joins her, speaks to her, steers her. It could tell us if she chose this trail alone or was forced to it."

"Wisdom," Firekeeper said.

"Running feet do not prove choice," the wolf quoted, *"only speed."*

Though the proverb was usually quoted to remind young wolves that they could steer a stampeding herd, it made sense here. Firekeeper wondered how much wolf wisdom could be adapted to human ways—and what that might mean should the Beasts choose to war against humankind.

She put that thought from her as she had a dozen dozen times before. They padded along the cobbled streets, moving slowly until at a busy crossing Blind Seer lost the trail in a wash of ox piss.

"Not deliberate," he said, waving his head to clear his nose, *"and Citrine was alone to here. Very well. Let us go to Thendulla Lypella."*

They did this. By carefully checking the quiet spots across from the thick stone barrier, they found trace of Citrine once again. The girl had stood in several doorways out of the crush of traffic, where she could study the scene before her.

"*Recent, too,*" Blind Seer reported with satisfaction. "*There is the scent of fresh ginger mixed in with her own spoor. Does it taste better than it smells?*"

Firekeeper, who had little taste for sweets—though she appreciated the quiet rush of energy they granted—didn't deign to reply.

"*Can you tell which gate she went to or shall I ask at each?*"

Blind Seer cast along the ground, growling to himself in annoyance at all the muddling scents, apparently unaware of the grumbling of those who were forced to detour around him. Firekeeper, hanging back in order to avoid being asked to control "her dog," watched with amusement.

"*I am not certain,*" the wolf said at last, padding over to her, "*but that gate seems most likely. What did Bee Biter tell us it was called?*"

"*The Petitioner's Gate,*" Firekeeper replied promptly. "*For those who wish to grovel to the Ones. Yes, that makes sense. Wait here, sweet hunter, and guard my back. It occurs to me that in our worry for Citrine we have come to our enemy's hunting grounds while there is yet daylight. If Melina has watchers like Peace she will know of our interest.*"

"*What of it?*" the wolf said. "*Melina would wonder more if we didn't hunt.*"

Firekeeper crossed to the Petitioner's Gate. There were two lines and both were short. She had been to market frequently enough to know that she was supposed to wait her turn, but it made her feel like the tiniest of pups to do so. By the time she reached the head of the line she was irritable enough to wrestle three times her weight in bears.

A round-faced man in blue-black robes blinked at her, looking her up and down with that supercilious expression that the New Kelvinese managed with such ease.

"Yes?" he said in New Kelvinese.

Already short-tempered from her wait, Firekeeper couldn't manage the right phrases in New Kelvinese and decided to try Pellish.

"I am looking for a boy who come here earlier today. Maybe," she held a hand toward the sky, "when the sun was some fingers younger."

The man blinked, but her guess had been correct. Those who guarded this gate spoke other languages than their own. How else could they deal with those petitioners who might not be New Kelvinese? And how else could they keep looking so superior?

"A boy," the clerk said, his accent quite heavy. "This tall?"

He held his hand to Citrine's height.

Firekeeper nodded.

"Wearing a headband?" the man continued.

Firekeeper nodded.

The man paused, seemed to consider.

"No such boy was here."

The stress on the word "boy" was unmistakable.

Firekeeper nodded.

"A girl, yes?"

The man frowned, considered, made a gesture with one hand.

Firekeeper studied him, remembered some of Derian's stories about how he had gotten some good deal, thought the man might want to be paid for his information. She, of course, carried no money, disdaining it. Strong wolves took what they wanted.

"If this we speak of is the girl I think," she said, "her mother would be so very angry at what you just try."

The man jerked back his hand as if burnt.

"Then there was no boy and no girl either," he said haughtily and pulled back into his booth.

Firekeeper wanted to shake him, but decided it wasn't worth the effort. She'd learned what she wanted and without giving the clerk anything but another story to sell—and that was unavoidable. Her feet suddenly light, she crossed to where the blue-eyed wolf waited.

"Citrine was here," she said. *"And the man know she was girl not boy and who her mother is."*

"A good end to a bad trail," Blind Seer said, wagging his tail once in satisfaction.

"Good in that we know," Firekeeper said, beginning to walk more rapidly, *"bad, I think, in what we now know Citrine has done."*

However, nothing Firekeeper could do would change what had happened. Dutifully recalling her promise to Wendee, she slapped Blind Seer on the shoulder and darted through the crowd at a run, disregarding anything but the need to report to the others.

XXVII

"DARLING," said Melina, fixing Toriovico with her brilliant gaze, "how nice of you to come so quickly."

The Healed One stared at her blankly, wondering what she was talking about. He hadn't seen her since that morning over breakfast.

She had been late coming in the night before, but he had very carefully neglected to mention this fact in obedience to orders she had given him after she had slipped between the sheets, orders that took for granted that his will was still enslaved to hers.

Had he forgotten some other command? Panic touched Torio's soul. It was so very important that she not realize that he was free of her. Columi might know the truth, but could an old man be trusted to act independently, especially when his own life would be at risk?

But apparently he had not forgotten, for Melina was looking at him with puzzlement to match his own.

"Didn't you get my note? I sent messengers around to your studio and to your office as well."

Toriovico hid his relief in a brilliant smile. Then he crossed to her, caressing her silk-clad shoulder affectionately—an act that not only demonstrated his continuing devotion, but took him out from under the direct gaze of those enchanting eyes.

"No, my dear, I did not," he said. "I was at the cobbler's having slippers fit for the coming festival. The last pair pinched my toes dreadfully and didn't give nearly enough support to my instep and ankle. Don't you remember? I mentioned it at breakfast."

Melina had been very distracted at breakfast, breaking shell into her soft egg, and scolding Tipi for some minor infraction.

"I remember now," she said, all apologetic sweetness. "Now you are here like an answer to a wish."

He kissed her lightly on the top of her head.

"I came hoping to find you," he said.

Or rather hoping to find where you've been, he corrected mentally.

"Then we both have had our wishes granted," she replied, and her tones were so affectionate that Toriovico nearly forgot everything he had learned these past few days.

Then Melina drew him to a seat on a long couch and pulled his feet into her lap. Rubbing his tired arches with strong fingers that had rapidly picked up the trick of what felt best, she said rather hesitantly for her:

"Torio, I have something important to tell you."

He tried to remain casual, the perfect servant to whom his mistress's least wish is law.

"Yes, darling?"

"Torio, yesterday afternoon a visitor arrived for me."

"Oh?"

"Yes, darling. Someone from Hawk Haven."

Torio frowned.

"Can't they leave you alone?" he asked, doing his best to sound indignant on her behalf. "Haven't they troubled you enough? You belong to me and to New Kelvin now."

Melina sighed, a deep, wistful sound that would have torn his heart if he hadn't believed it as false as his own indignation. Lots of problems would be solved if Hawk Haven desired to reclaim their wandering noblewoman. But such a request would have come to him or to Apheros—or would it?

"I thought you might feel that way, Torio," Melina said plaintively. "I know you always have my best interests at heart."

"I do," he said fervently. "Always, darling."

Melina paused and for a moment Toriovico thought he might have overdone his adoration. Then she went on:

"This is a visitor I welcomed, once I adjusted to the shock. It was a member of my family."

Torio thought quickly. Melina had left several brothers behind, one of whom was a reigning duke, another who was a soldier. Or did she mean one of her children? He felt an unexpected flash of jealousy as he thought of the five children she had borne to another man.

Easy, Torio, he counseled himself. *She still has claws in you, even if they're not as deep.*

Still, he thought that jealousy was probably an appropriate reaction, for she had not as much as mentioned her Hawk Haven family for a long time now.

"Go on," he said stiffly, making as if to draw his feet back from her caress.

Melina held his feet and massaged with even more enthusiasm. Torio felt his mind slipping into patterns of relaxation and fought against them. With sudden insight Toriovico realized that she could use more than her eyes to work her charm. Anything that relaxed the subject so his will could be reached unguarded was a tool.

One of his hands was hidden from her view by the couch. Now Torio drove his nails into his palm, seeking to distract himself from her soothing touch. His mind cleared sufficiently for him to listen with true alertness as Melina went on.

"You know I left my little ones behind when I came here," she said.

"Yes," Torio agreed. "Three girls and a youth."

He didn't include the Crown Princess Sapphire in his count, for her mother denied the young woman's existence unless she was very angry.

"The youngest of these girls was quite small," Melina said, "only nine."

"Citrine," he said automatically, his tones rather flat.

He had a nagging feeling that there was something he should remember about Citrine, but the information belonged to the days when Melina had clouded his mind and he could not remember.

"Yes, little Citrine," Melina said. "She's been cruelly treated since I went away and finally she ran away. She made her way to Dragon's Breath and yesterday came trembling to the Petitioner's Gate."

From the slow, wonderfully relaxing circles that Melina was kneading into his instep, Toriovico felt pretty certain that he was to accept this explanation with asking any of the questions that had sprung so readily to mind. Run away? How had she managed that? And how had she managed to make her way this deep into New Kelvin without arousing suspicion? How had she even known of the Petitioner's Gate? Why had they had no forewarning?

He suspected that Melina knew the answer to all these questions. Even so, he didn't ask, just smiled lazily and thrust his foot a little deeper into her hand.

"You said you welcomed her," he said. "How nice for the poor child. You did say she had been cruelly treated, didn't you?"

"That's right," Melina acceded. "The child is troubled in mind as well as body. She needs me, and I need her."

"Oh?" Toriovico tried to sound affronted, but not too much so.

"Yes, darling," Melina lifted his foot and kissed it. "You are wonderful and all my new friends are marvelous, but there are times I long to hear my own tongue, to trade gossip with someone who knows the people of Hawk Haven as more than names."

"We could buy you a slave or something," he said with thoughtful seriousness. "One who speaks the tongue."

Then he grinned at her with boyish playfulness.

"But that's not what you want. Is it darling? You want your own little girl."

"Torio," she said passionately. "I do. No one else will do so well. You and she would get along so well."

"Then you must have her," Torio said firmly, thinking *And maybe Citrine's presence will slow you down in whatever scheme you're working*. "I admit that I have missed the sound of girlish laughter. You do remember that I have six sisters, don't you? Since they've all grown old enough to take up positions as ritual directors in various parts of the country, I have felt quite bereft."

Torio knew that the custom of splitting up the siblings of the Healed One was an old one, dating back to the First Healed One's need to do something with his superfluous daughters. It had been one of his many ways of assuring that continuity of rule remained with his direct heirs. True, distance did make it easier for factions to form undetected, but the need to conduct incredibly complex rituals—rituals that were believed to help maintain the kingdom's borders safe from invasion—kept the exiled siblings very busy.

He thought it a shame that his own very intelligent and creative sisters should be wasted this way, but it was the law.

Melina hugged his feet to her breast with what seemed genuine joy.

"Then you don't mind?"

"Mind?" Torio repeated. "I want whatever will make my darling wife happy. Citrine cannot be my heir—she is not male, nor is she of our blood. Therefore, no one should be threatened by her living with us as your companion."

"Thank you, Torio," Melina said. "I am very glad that you accept her."

Torio fought back an urge to say something flippant. He had a feeling that he had just succeeded in some rather difficult test. Maybe Melina had believed that his charm would break under the strain of accepting this invader to their cozy intimacy. He had a vague sense that she had drawn him in by lavishing affection on him—and making him feel that their bond was exclusive. Certainly even the strongest charm might weaken under the strain of admitting her need for another.

I must be very careful, he thought. *She will be watching me, checking for any sign that my resentment is weakening her control.*

Swinging his feet from Melina's lap, Torio sprang up.

"You said you had written for me to come to you," he said jovially. "Now that I have your news, where's the little girl? Isn't it time I met her?"

Melina beamed up at him and for a moment he once again had to struggle not to lose himself in the warm embrace of her gaze.

"Yes, darling," she said. "I will have Tipi bring Citrine to us. The two of you mean so much to me. I can't wait for you to meet."

For a moment, Torio caught something cool and calculating in the blue pools of her eyes, something so cold that it thrust him out and into himself again. Then Melina smiled and were it not for memory, he could believe her a happy mother, about to introduce her new husband to her youngest child.

ELISE INSISTED Derian ride with her when she returned to the Hawk Haven embassy, for she no longer felt confident about her safety out on the streets.

On her previous return from the embassy, sitting at ease in the litter, reviewing what she had discussed with Ambassador Redbriar, Elise hadn't immediately noticed anything out of the ordinary. Then one of the litter bearers had stumbled.

"Someone tried to trip me!" the man had called back in response to Elise's startled cry.

Thinking this a weak excuse, Elise had begun to watch the crowds, remembering Edlin's concern when they made their first call on the ambassador—had that only been two days before?—and seeing now that the situation had grown far worse.

She might not have Peace's gift for seeing deeply into other's actions, but even so she became aware of the angry glares that were turned on her, the clenched fists, mouths pursed as if to spit. Yet few acted as aggressively as had the unknown who had sought to overturn her litter. Most turned away, and Elise thought she saw fear mingled with the anger.

Attending more closely now, more than once Elise heard "Consolor" muttered, with the suffix that meant "kin" or "family" attached to it. So the anger was not directed toward Elise personally, but to her as one of Melina's people.

By the time Elise reached the door of Hasamemorri's house, she had realized that all the sullen and hate-filled faces seemed to belong to people of the lower, serving classes. The sodality members who passed, often carried in litters of their own, looked upon her with either curiosity or indifference, as did the obviously prosperous.

What was it the servants feared? What was it that made them so angry? How was it their masters seemed comparatively ignorant? Elise might dread Melina's strange powers, but she did not believe the woman could have worked her trance induction on all of the upper classes. Something more—maybe simple ignorance—must explain it.

Ambassador Redbriar's informants, the majority of whom were disaffected politicians from within the Dragon Speaker's court, had reported nothing that might account for this surge of almost uncontrollable anger, nor was Ambassador Redbriar particularly helpful regarding what might be done for Edlin.

"He is a lord," Violet Redbriar said, "and that is good, except that his title and position—and his father's well-known ambitious nature—will make it seem more likely, rather than less, that Lord Kestrel was spying."

"And to make matters worse," Violet continued, draining her goblet of white wine, "from what you say, Edlin Norwood *was* spying. This deeply restricts what we can do. However, I shall put some feelers out, and send you word when I know something. Don't come to call too often. Feeling against us has become very strong. We had a window broken by a well-thrown rock and one of our footmen was assaulted when he went to the market."

Indeed, Elise's hired litter bearers—who had been promised a substantial payment if they remained to take her home—were waiting very nervously when Elise came to take her leave. Ambassador Redbriar had offered guards, but Elise had not thought there would be any trouble—and had nearly been very wrong.

Yet this late afternoon, despite the ambassador's warning, Elise and Derian were returning. Citrine's disappearance and her probable destination were matters too sensitive to trust to a note that might be read by any number of people before—or after—it reached the ambassador.

Elise had insisted on waiting a full day's span before going to the embassy. Citrine might not have gone into Thendulla Lypella, no matter what Firekeeper reported. Or she might not have found the welcome she desired. It hardly made sense to raise a fuss if the girl was soon to reappear on their doorstep.

And it would be dreadfully embarrassing.

However, by the next morning, Elise was as eager as any of them to seek what assistance Ambassador Redbriar might offer. Bee Biter had reported that Citrine had been seen walking in one of the sheltered gardens that were lavishly spread between the Earth Spires. Her companions had been her mother and the Healed One and she had strolled hand in hand between them.

That the girl looked well and content was no comfort to Elise—or to any of Citrine's friends. Many of Melina's victims looked quite happy and placid—Ruby and Opal were fine examples of this—but this was the stillness of a frozen will, not true tranquility of spirit.

Ambassador Redbriar received them in her study, but it was clear that she was not pleased to see Elise again so soon. Had Derian not worn his counselor's ring rather prominently, he might have found himself relegated to the kitchens.

Violet was too much a diplomat to turn away people who might rise to positions of influence. She offered them refreshments, filled her own glass with white wine from a carafe set in a bed of crushed ice, and listened to Elise's account.

She frowned when Elise completed her tale.

"And what is it you want me to do? You seem to know where the girl is, and that she is happy and safe."

Violet's mouth drew into a little wrinkle of disapproval. It was quite clear that she did not precisely believe what she had been told about how Blind Seer and Firekeeper had tracked Citrine to the gates of Thendulla Lypella, nor about Bee Biter's report.

Or maybe, Elise thought with sudden insight, *she fears this as any sane person would—as hints of magic beyond the honest talents. It is good that she isn't intended to learn what Melina can do.*

Elise had been prepared for the ambassador's protest, though not for the rather breezy way in which it was presented. She wondered if Violet was frightened. Certainly the attacks on her residence and her servants gave reason, and it might explain her sudden fondness for quantities of wine.

"It is not a matter of Citrine's happiness," Elise said rather haughtily. "It is a matter of right. Consolor Melina was exiled from Hawk Haven, declared a traitor, and had all her property stripped from her. That includes her right to her children. Citrine does not belong to her. Citrine belongs to the family that is now headed by her older brother, Jet Shield.

"Moreover," Elise went on, continuing through the ambassador's attempted interruption, "Citrine was given into my custody, and, should something happen to me, to the custody of my companions in order of precedence. Therefore, my rights have been violated. The girl may have foolishly run away, but if she is kept after I request her return then it is no longer a case of a runaway child. It is kidnapping."

Elise finished with a flat finality that jolted Violet Redbriar out of whatever comfortable haze the wine had cast over her. She looked quite grim, reached for her glass, reconsidered, and poured herself some of the chilled tea that had been brought for Elise.

"The matter is quite serious," Violet admitted, "when presented in that fashion. What do you wish me to do?"

"I have drafted a letter requesting my charge's return to me," Elise replied promptly.

She put out a hand and Derian placed in it the final draft of the missive that they had labored over for several hours the night before. It had been essential that the request be firm, but not so firm that making Citrine disappear permanently would be the easiest way to eliminate any uncomfortable situation between the two kingdoms.

"I would like you to review this," Elise said. "Offer suggestions as to how it could be rephrased, have it recopied onto better paper, and then arrange for the signed document to be delivered to the appropriate person in Thendulla Lypella."

Violet fumbled in a side pocket of her chair, removed a spectacle case, and perched a round-lensed pair of glasses on her nose.

"The letter is admirable," she said when she had concluded her perusal. "I suggest a few minor changes to make certain that there is no room for misinterpretation—a matter of schematics, nothing more. I would also like your permission to include a copy in New Kelvinese. I can do the translation myself—I would insist on doing so, given the sensitivity of the matter. I simply do not wish to leave the choice of which word to use for certain technical terms to some clerk in Thendulla Lypella, especially one who might be prompted to shift the tone to make us seem more aggressive than we are—or less."

"That sounds wise," Elise agreed with a crisp nod. "Derian and I will wait so that I can sign both copies."

And in that way I can assure myself that you're not slipping anything into the text. I hate not being able to trust even one of my own king's sworn representatives!

Violet Redbriar gave a slight smile that hinted she knew precisely the drift of Elise's thoughts—and approved of them.

"Since security is to our interest," she said, "and I hate to think what might happen if the word that Consolor Melina's birth daughter has joined her reached the street, I will also do the scribe's copy myself. I write a good hand."

Elise nodded her acceptance, and was surprised when Derian spoke up. He'd kept his silence to this point, serving as witness now that the need to bodyguard her through the streets was—until they headed back to Hasamemorri's—ended.

"I wonder if that very information is what has stirred up the people," he said thoughtfully. "It would match. Firekeeper did not meet any but the usual hostility . . ."

"Not uncommon for someone who travels about with a huge wolf, I suspect," Violet said, rising from her chair.

"Not," Derian agreed, "though less here than in Hawk Haven. The New Kelvinese seem to take the peculiar in stride. However, what I was thinking is that Firekeeper and Wendee both searched for Citrine and didn't have any difficulties. Elise, coming home a few hours later, met some. That would be enough time for some loose-tongued clerk—say the one at the Petitioner's Gate Firekeeper mentioned—to spread a few delicious stories."

Violet nodded approvingly.

"That could well be the case, and such rumors would spread to his peers among the working classes—common clerks are not members of the sodalities—faster than among their betters. However, this does not answer all our problems. My embassy had been troubled before any word of Citrine's disappearance could have been known."

Derian looked disappointed.

"I guess I'm wrong then. Kind of you to listen to my wanderings."
Violet smiled.

As Elise had nothing to add, she studied the titles of various books Ambassador Redbriar was removing from her shelves, all of which proved to be guides to etiquette and language.

"I hadn't realized there were so many," Elise said, picking up one, "and so varied."

"There are more than these," Violet said, moving over to her desk and pulling out a clean sheet of paper. "These are simply my favorites. I am rather surprised that you didn't translate your letter yourself. Your command of the language is good."

"Better spoken than in composition," Elise admitted promptly. "Though I do well enough with the written material when I have dictionaries to hand."

They waited while Ambassador Redbriar made both her translation and her copy. Elise found herself a fairly simply written textbook that proved to contain stories that were almost familiar, for many of them had been adapted into Wendee's beloved plays. Derian amused himself with a book relating local history and legends, translated and annotated for the foreigner by none other than their host.

"All done but the direction," Ambassador Redbriar announced some time later. "To whom do you wish this sent? Consolor Melina herself?"

Elise frowned.

"It would be too easy for her to ignore it," she said. "This must become a public matter. Who do you recommend? The Dragon Speaker, perhaps?"

"Once perhaps," Violet said slowly, "but these days . . . Apheros has not seemed himself, and as we have discussed, his policies seem so closely linked to those of Consolor Melina. If you wish the information to become public, then I would suggest Xarxius."

"The Dragon's Claw?" Elise asked.

"That's right," Ambassador Redbriar said. "Such would be quite within proper etiquette. Xarxius is in charge of foreign trade and this could be seen—especially in a slaveholding state—as a matter of goods misappropriated."

Elise choked slightly at the concept, but she couldn't disagree. Derian, too, was nodding, clearly pleased to have Xarxius brought into the matter.

"Xarxius, then," Elise said.

She bent over the letters the ambassador had finished dusting with sand, scanned them, and found them accurate to a fault.

"Beautiful," she said, speaking louder than she meant in her admiration.

Derian was looking over Elise's shoulder—though, of course, the New Kelvinese script meant nothing to him.

"I'm not surprised," he said. "I've been reading your book, ma'am, and it's wonderful. Where could I get a copy? I like to take one home to my family."

The ambassador surprised them all by flushing with pleasure.

"I have a few spares," Violet said, "and would be pleased to make a gift of one to the king's newest counselor."

Elise and Derian left the embassy after witnessing the packet containing the letter and its copy being handed to a messenger. Hours had passed and the streets were much quieter than when they had arrived. Even so, Elise thought she could feel hundreds of pairs of angry eyes watching them from the shadows. Despite herself, she shivered.

NORTHWEST WAS NOT THE ONLY Beast agitating for going after the humans during the several days the settlers continued their rooting in the earth to retrieve bones and dead bodies. In some cases, the settlers consigned these bodies to fires, then inexplicably shifted wood from ash and carefully packed up the ash.

"They've been bitten by rabid squirrels!" Northwest exclaimed during one particularly odd interlude involving the hauling of boxes of bones to one of the wagons and lots of wailing on the part of the humans. "We would be doing their own kind a favor by slaughtering them, for surely the madness is contagious. Look how even some of those new come here are dripping water from their eyes and howling like the rest."

A bear rose on his hind legs to get a clearer look and dropped heavily down again, waggling his heavy head in consternation.

"They do seem out of their wits," he agreed. "I can understand digging up dead meat. The maggots and worms are sweet and flavorful, but they're burning the ripest carcasses. Madness indeed!"

"And it would be so simple," hissed a young puma, sleek in her young strength and half-mad herself from the proximity of easy hunting in the form of the well-fed horses. "Drop from above and a quick bite—even a whack from a paw would be enough. These two-legs are so frail."

Elation beat her wings in frantic disapproval.

"I tell you, they are not mad—not as two-legs go—and you might find their hides tougher and their teeth sharper than you imagine. Those new-comers are rated great killers among their own kind."

Her protest alone wouldn't have been enough, but Shining Coat and Rip, supported by an old raven and a more temperate puma, reminded the others that the greater will of the Beasts was not to move against the humans—at least not at this time and in this place.

The bear alone had the seniority to disagree—at least on the part of his own people—but was by nature a calm creature unless angered. Moreover, he was not at all certain that dining on meat from clearly mad creatures would be healthy, and argued against the attack on the grounds that the Beasts might become infected.

"We have enough to contend with," he grumbled, "fattening for winter, without having our eyes run with water and our throats fill with meaningless howls."

So the humans were permitted to depart unharmed, never realizing how close they had come to not departing at all. When their long line of wagons and burdened beasts had crossed the gap and made the descent far enough that all the Beasts were sure they were well and truly gone there was much celebrating.

Watch would be kept on the keep being constructed to guard the gap, but as a good deal of time must pass before the wooden structure now being erected could be fully replaced by a more impregnable one of stone, the Beasts felt content that their territory was their own again, unthreatened by two-legged presence.

Elation was among those delegated to watch the remaining humans, a task she was flattered to accept but for one thing.

"We should send word to Firekeeper," she said, decisive in her awareness of her new importance as an expert on humanity. "She will be worrying lest the promise made to her by King Tedric not be kept."

Shining Coat looked up from the punishing tongue-lashing she was giving to an overadventurous pup, and considered.

"Falcon, your wisdom shames me," she replied. "Little Two-legs was my pup for many seasons, and I have seen the changes in her since she went among the humans. You are right. She will worry."

Rip added, "Let the wolves handle the matter—at least to a point. We can howl the news north in relays. Our people venture farther east in the lands to which Firekeeper has gone because there are mountains to hide our traces. It should be easy enough to contact one of the wingéd folk who nest in that area."

"I can give you a sign from the Mothers that will assure cooperation from all in that region," Elation said, delighted with this plan. Wings were good when distance must be traveled in person, but wolf howls were even faster than flight. "I learned them when Bee Biter was being counseled before he accompanied Firekeeper north."

"Good then." Shining Coat let the puppy go, ignoring the indignant growls that asserted its summer maturity. "We can start the calls tonight. They will ripple through the rocky reaches. Firekeeper will know before many more sunsets that faith has been kept—on both sides of the mountain."

THE SUN HAD JUST FILLED THE MORNING SKY when Bee Biter came to where Blind Seer and Firekeeper were wrestling in the hayloft of the stable.

"News!" the little kestrel shrieked.

"Of Citrine?" Firekeeper asked, rolling over and brushing straw from her hair.

"No," squawked Bee Biter, somewhat annoyed, "from home!"

"Even better," Firekeeper said. "Tell!"

"Three days ago, the humans in New Bardenville left. West of the Iron Mountains is ours again, but for a small flock left to act as watchers against their own kind in the gap—and those watchers are watched carefully lest they become too bold and forget their place."

Firekeeper and Blind Seer howled their pleasure—completely outraging the much put-upon horses and bringing Derian from the kitchen at a run.

"What are you up to?" Derian shouted angrily, soothing Roanne as best he could. Being who he was, his best was enough.

"News from home," Firekeeper said, somewhat contritely. "New Bardenville is no more. King Tedric has kept his promise."

"Did you ever doubt him?" Derian asked, moving among the rest of the horses and assuring them that mad wolves were not about to eat them.

"Until the prey is dead, the hunt may fail," Firekeeper said stiffly, not wanting to confess just how much she had worried, and how heavy her heart had been.

Blind Seer asked Bee Biter, *"Was anyone killed in this hunting?"*

Firekeeper froze, her joy trembling like an icicle in the wind.

"No," Bee Biter replied. *"The report does not go into details, but does say that two-legs and Beasts never met in open conflict. Rather, more two-legs came and took the other flock away."*

Firekeeper felt herself melt and knew from Derian's expression that he was aware of her distraction, if not the cause.

"And no one was hurt or killed in the breaking of New Bardenville," she explained. "Not human, not Beast."

"That's good news," Derian said sincerely, "good enough that I can forgive you for upsetting the horses—and the neighbors. How'd the news get to you so quickly?"

"Wolf howls and falcon wings," Firekeeper answered, her expression smug. "When the Beasts choose they are terribly strong."

Only afterward did she regret her boast, for Derian went away very thoughtful and looking less happy than he had just a moment before.

BY THE TENTH DAY of Hummingbird Moon, Lord Polr was certain that he would be able to get all the New Bardenville members safely away. They were over the mountains and already dissolving from a community into smaller groups looking toward their own advantage.

He wrote King Tedric:

Although the delay needed to deal with the settlement's dead was regrettable, I think it was for the best. The settlers departed with some dignity. They hope Your Majesty will accept the remains of the dead of the first Bardenville for respectable burial. The decision is, as I most humbly assert, your own and no other's, but I think acceptance of their request would go far toward bringing them back into the fold.

We also brought away their own dead, most of them victims of the illness and accidents such a venture must be prone to, but some killed in rather sinister circumstances. This last I would prefer to report to you in person, when I have had more of an opportunity to collect information from as many of the settlers as possible and so to construct a complete picture.

Cremation was necessary in the case of these more recent dead since we could not move partially decayed bodies without inviting the sicknesses that hover around them as a ward against disrespectful treatment of the deceased. The settlers accepted this necessity with grace, but the rude facilities we could construct for the purpose meant that they were greatly shaken by the event. I regret the necessity, but saw no way to avoid it.

The remaining garrison is constructing a keep from which they can view the surrounding area and prevent unwelcome passage west. Materials scavenged from New Bardenville, thanks to Your Majesty's foresight and preparation, will hasten the construction and the keep should be solidly in place well before winter. As you instructed, immediate work on stone sheathing for the base will begin when the first phase of construction is complete.

A few of the settlers offered to remain and assist. I refused lest we end up with the rebels all using this excuse to remain. I am returning to Eagle's Nest as soon as the rebels are dispersed. Some have requested relocation, for they gave up everything they had to make this venture. I have written to my brother, Duke Gyrfalcon, to request that he take in some of these. I do not doubt that he will do so, for even the settlers' children are seasoned beyond their years by this experience. Perhaps other heads of houses can be convinced to do the same. I do not think that these people were so much rebels against your authority as they were ambitious beyond prudence.

Upon my return, I hope to beg audience with Your Majesty. There are things I have learned that may be of interest to you and guide your future decisions regarding the western reaches of your kingdom.

Polr considered writing more or saying less, but the fast rider was saddled and waiting. If he hurried, this missive could be relayed to the capital in a handful of days. He settled for signing and sealing the letter, but his heart was not easy as he posted it.

Eyes once opened to what might live in the darkness do not close easily again in sleep.

XXVIII

IN THE DAYS that had passed since Citrine's arrival in Thendulla Lypella the girl discovered that life with her mother was not going to be anything like what she had dreamed.

At first it was promising indeed. She was moved from her first room into a suite in Cloud Touching Spire. It was a lovely place, like a private palace, decorated all in pale shades of green and gold. The bed was huge and had a canopy with gauzy side curtains that could be drawn shut or left open. The sitting room—or playroom, depending on Citrine's mood—was quite elegant. One of the tall cabinets held about a hundred dolls. A big chest held puzzles and games that just one child could play alone.

Citrine wasn't left alone very often, though. A maid of her very own was assigned to her. This was a complete novelty. At home only Mother had had her own maid, and the women Sapphire had sent to care for Citrine had been more nurses.

Rillon was a young woman with long black hair and eyes almost as dark. She was very serious about her new duties, and used the dolls to show Citrine the refinements of New Kelvinese attire. Sometimes she'd play tea parties, but not with much imagination or enthusiasm, and so playmates were found for Citrine among the children of the court. Many of these were the Healed One's nieces and nephews.

It turned out that he had six sisters. They were all away performing official duties, but each one had left at least one child at court. Having been such herself, Citrine knew hostages when she saw them, but that didn't make the New Kelvinese children any less fun to play with—even if they did talk too fast, sometimes.

The Healed One had a name, it turned out, not just a title, and that name was Toriovico. Toriovico was quite a long name for a Pellish-trained tongue. Had she not practiced her New Kelvinese with Grateful Peace, Citrine would have found it quite difficult to say. The Healed One told her she could use the short form of his name, which was Torio, but Citrine preferred the longer version. It made her feel quite exotic and entirely New Kelvinese.

Toriovico seemed like a nice man, even if he did have green hair and things tattooed onto his face. He was a dancer when he wasn't being a king, and invited Citrine to come and watch him practice. She did and then he asked her if she wanted to dance with him. Afterward, he said thoughtfully:

"You are light on your feet, little Citrine. Would you like to learn to dance as I do? With your coloring—especially your lovely hair—you would make a fine autumn leaf."

Citrine was quite excited by this. New Kelvinese dancing was very different from the measured court dances that she had been learning in Hawk Haven. It told stories. To be a leaf she had to learn to be light on her feet—to skitter in tiny motions like a leaf before the wind. She had to learn to sway and to drift softly to the ground.

It wasn't easy and the practices were harder work than anything else she had ever done before. However, she threw herself into them. They let her forget the thing she couldn't bear.

Her mother still had no time for her.

Every day Citrine would see Melina at least once, sometimes at breakfast, sometimes at lunch, sometimes looking in at her when the assistant Choreographer gave his little charges a rest. One of her proudest times came when she heard the Choreographer telling her mother:

"She is light on her feet, this little gem, and very strong for her age."

Citrine knew that learning she possessed strength would surprise Consolor Melina. Before the journey from Hawk Haven Citrine hadn't been very strong at all, but posing as Jalarios's son had meant that she must lead horses and carry bundles and haul water—any number of undignified things that a young lady of an almost noble household wouldn't ever do.

Melina hadn't shown any surprise at all, just haughty satisfaction. She'd smiled at Citrine, though, and it was all the girl could do not to run over and hug her tight.

But this was one of the many things she had been told she must never do.

"Public displays of affection between us must be eliminated," Melina had explained that first night, "unless my husband is with us. I will not have anyone thinking that I am less than loyal to my new alliances. It would not do."

So Citrine didn't, and felt all the lonelier for having her mother so near but still unapproachable. The hostage children were fun and Toriovico was very nice to her, but she had run away from Elise and Derian and Firekeeper because she wanted to be with her mother. Now it seemed that even here she could not be.

Citrine took to stealing out of her room at night and going to where her mother's suite was. Many nights, Mother wasn't there. At first Citrine thought that she was sleeping with Toriovico, but then, overcome with loneliness and something like jealousy she crept from shadow to shadow until she came to the conjugal suite.

No one was awake because the Cloud Touching Spire was guarded from downstairs and outside. Anyhow, everyone inside was trusted. Citrine slipped from room to room, until she came to the royal bedchamber.

Knowing what she was doing was forbidden, Citrine pushed open the door. A small lantern, its wick turned down very low, burned on one of the bedside tables. It didn't give much light, but it was enough for her to see that Toriovico slept alone.

Where then did Mother go at night when her own bed was empty?

Wanting to know, but desperately afraid of what she would learn if she did know, Citrine forgot caution and fled to her own bed, terrified that she would find Melina standing by it, terrible anger burning in her eyes.

Her bedroom was empty, but Citrine, plagued by fears she couldn't even focus, much less put a name to, slept no more that night.

DERIAN WAS AWARE of Doc's relief when the knock on the door sounded. For several days now, business had been tapering off. First there had been fewer new patients. Now even those who should have returned for follow-up visits were not doing so.

It didn't help that Ambassador Redbriar had sent word that Xarxius was away from Dragon's Breath, although the Dragon's Claw was expected to return shortly. She had offered to send a copy of their letter requesting Citrine's return to someone else in Apheros's organization, but they had decided against this. One letter might already be one too many.

Ambassador Redbriar had also sent word that she had learned nothing at all about the whereabouts of either Edlin or their "New Kelvinese servant, Jalarios." This last, combined with the fact that although Bee Biter and his wingéd-folk allies had spotted Citrine a few times, nothing had been seen of either of the men, added to everyone's anxiety for them.

And for Doc worse than for the rest of us, Derian thought, *since Edlin's close kin. Now more than ever Doc could use the distraction of patients.*

Rather than waiting for Wendee to answer the door as would have been the case a few days earlier, Doc dropped his cards on the table and shoved his chair back.

"I'll get it," he said, rather unnecessarily, for he was already out of the kitchen and heading toward the front door.

Derian followed, more out of idleness than for any other reason. Their small company didn't require what Doc earned through his practice, but the activity had been a constant backdrop to their New Kelvinese residence—its absence had accented the tension they all felt.

"May I speak with Sir Jared?" asked an unfamiliar male voice.

"I am he," Doc replied.

Derian could hear the smile in his voice. The New Kelvinese were rarely prepared for Doc's informality. No wonder this caller didn't believe that the great healer himself had answered the door.

Derian expected to hear a further exchange along this line. Instead, the caller said:

"My mother is very ill. Could you come out to see her? Our home is not far."

Derian frowned, biting his lower lip. Something wasn't quite right here. He struggled to place the incongruity even as Doc replied:

"Certainly. Let me get my bag."

As Doc, the abstracted air he always acquired when contemplating a new challenge not quite banishing his expression of pleasure, crossed from the front door to get his bag from the consulting room, Derian placed what was out of order.

The caller had spoken Pellish. Moreover, he had said he didn't live far away. Hasamemorri's house was in a very working-class neighborhood, not at all the type where diplomats who might have learned Pellish would reside.

"Doc," Derian said, keeping his voice low and rushing after the physician. "Something's not right here."

Rapidly, he explained his conjectures. Doc nodded as he listened, but more of his attention seemed fixed on which herbal preparations he should place in his bag.

"He didn't say what was wrong with his mother," Doc said, his tone half agreement. "Go ask him for me. Heart? Stomach? A recent injury? I wish Elise was here. She could ask him in his own language. The fellow may not have the Pellish."

Elise, however, had gone out with Firekeeper, partly in an effort to pick up rumors, partly to distract the still guilt-ridden and consequently less than even-tempered wolf-woman.

Derian hid his frustration and headed for the door. At least this way he'd get a look at their caller.

He reopened the door to find a hulking fellow on the doorstep. His first thought was that the man looked as if his mother had been a bear rather than someone delicate enough to need a healer. His second thought was that the man looked vaguely familiar.

In the time they had been in New Kelvin, Derian had begun to learn to look beyond the omnipresent facial decorations to the features behind them. Indeed, he was coming to suspect that he saw more of the original face than might a New Kelvinese. Their caller's features were weathered; moreover, even the thick orange and yellows lines he'd drawn around eyes and mouth couldn't hide that recently he'd been exposed to great heat.

One of Derian's more regular girlfriends had been a baker's daughter. He'd seen similar coloring on the baker's face near festival times when the demand for some special delicacy meant he spent more time than usual peering into the ovens.

"Doc wants to know," Derian said, deliberately making his Pellish more colloquial than he usually would, "what's wrong with your mother. So he can pack the right things, you see."

Their caller didn't hesitate.

"It is her heart," he said. "She is not young and the summer has been difficult for her."

Derian nodded. "We'll be just a moment."

He returned to Doc.

"The man says heart," he reported. "And he understands Pellish like a native, and I think I've seen him somewhere before. I'm going with you."

"He could have worked on the river near Gateway or Zodara," Doc protested mildly, taking some items out of his bag and replacing them with others. "But come along if you'd like."

Derian darted back into the kitchen to tell Wendee that he was escorting Doc on a call. On his way out the door, he snatched up his weighted walking stick from the stand, then hurried after Doc. Their caller was hurrying Sir Jared toward Aswatano. Again Derian frowned. That wasn't a residential section at all—and even if Doc had done so, Derian hadn't forgotten Ambassador Redbriar's warnings about unrest or the attacks on the embassy.

Yet even though Derian was certain something was distinctly wrong, he didn't vocalize his thoughts. As long as there was a patient who might need his help, Doc would only find some excuse to continue. Now more than ever, Derian didn't want their unnamed caller to be aware of his concerns.

As the two Hawk Havenese entered the marketplace, Derian was acutely aware of the angry looks and ugly gestures directed their way. Even Doc noticed them and gripped his bag more firmly. Indeed, the only person who didn't appear to notice was their guide.

Instead, the guide slowed and turned toward the market, gesturing at the stalls. As he spoke, he began talking rather loudly—and this time he spoke New Kelvinese.

"Slaves?" he said, as if responding to a question Doc had asked. "This is not the market for slaves."

Doc, of course, understood only a fraction of what had been said, and the key term "slave" had not been among the basic vocabulary Peace had thought necessary for his charges to learn.

Doc's response didn't make matters any better.

"What about your mother?" he said, in Pellish, only knowing that his guide had slowed and was waving his arm.

Derian doubted that anyone understood what Jared had said—and even if they had, his words were certain to be misunderstood. What the market-goers would have seen was the foreigner urgently questioning the man who had just told him this wasn't a slave market.

Recalling the rumors that had reached New Kelvin about Melina's practices—say the one about feeding spiders on human blood—Derian wondered for the first time what stories might be being told about the Consolor among her new subjects. The New Kelvinese might be magic crazy, but he'd never heard of them being particularly cruel. The same stories should be equally repulsive to them.

"I tell you," their "guide" said in New Kelvinese, "I know nothing about where you can get these people."

Doc turned away in disgust, obviously seeking Derian and finding instead an angry man holding a cleaver. He might even have been the same butcher with whom Derian and Wendee had tangled on an earlier visit to the market.

"So you want slaves, Hawkus," the butcher said in New Kelvinese. "It is true then that your people are hypocrites who long to break your own rules."

He might have said more, but Doc, understanding only the bastardized "Hawkus," interrupted eagerly:

"Yes, I'm from Hawk Haven. This man told me his mother was ill and asked me to treat her. I'm a doctor."

At this juncture an anonymous voice called out in New Kelvinese, "Don't believe him. He wants slaves to drain for his barbaric rituals. He's the man who claims he can heal with a touch."

Some of the increasingly restive crowd looked at Doc with surprised respect, but the majority looked even more infuriated. Derian had learned enough of New Kelvinese theories of magic during their last venture to realize that Doc's talent would seem impossibly easy to these people. Their magic was vested in elaborate rituals—not in a simple internal gift.

"Doc!" Derian called out. "It's a setup of some sort. Get back to the house."

At almost the same moment their guide, perhaps trusting that Doc would not have understood what he had said in New Kelvinese, cried out in Pellish:

"Sir Jared, this way! That butcher means you harm."

"Doc, no!" Derian began, but quickly realized he had problems of his own. Perhaps his height and distinctively bright hair color had caused him to blend into the motley throng more easily than the obviously foreign Jared. Perhaps his silence had protected him, but now many of those nearest to him were raising threatening fists or fumbling for makeshift weapons.

Various shouts of "Murderers!" or "Baby stealers" inflamed the crowd further. Rational thought had clearly gone by the wayside.

Derian started backing, hoping to get a wall or something else solid behind him. He was glad that he had seized up his walking stick on the way out the door, very sorry that Firekeeper and Blind Seer were not with them. In the press he could no longer see Doc and he had to hope that the other man's soldier's training was coming to his aid.

The world had become a muddle of brightly colored faces. The air reeked of sweat and grease and overwhelmingly of spices.

Derian glanced quickly behind him. He had backed against a stall selling a variety of dried herbs, certainly the same one where he and Wendee had shopped. He wasn't carrying the powder Wendee had bought for them both that other day, but he thought he recognized it among the neat open bags set on display.

Wildly, he grabbed a handful of the powder, feeling it burn against his skin on contact with his sweat. He flung the spice into the faces of those nearest to him, his own eyes burning as some blew back at him.

The spice vendor was shrieking insults at those who threatened to overturn her livelihood, so violent in her imprecations that they stepped back as if her curses had real force.

Derian took advantage of the distraction to duck around the edge of the spice vendor's booth and into some more open space. As he ran he glanced around for Doc, but the other man was nowhere to be seen.

Knowing it was futile, Derian shouted, "Firekeeper! Elise! Doc! Wendee!"

No welcome howl—or even human shout—answered his cry, only voices raised in New Kelvinese shouting things like: "There he goes!" "He was seeking a baby to butcher!" "He's a foreigner, just like the bride!"

Melina sure has made herself popular, Derian thought wildly.

A fist caught him in the ribs, missing his kidneys by a finger's width. Derian swung without aiming and felt his stick hit solidly. His flash of satisfaction ebbed as quickly as it had risen, for the man's yelp of pain seemed to signal the others to close in. The only good thing was that they were getting in each other's way and so Derian was able to jam himself into the angle between two walls. These kept him from getting trampled, but also imprisoned him. Derian was big enough to make a pretty good target and blow after blow found its mark.

The beating might not be systematic enough to do a lot of damage, but it hurt. Derian found himself concentrating on nothing more than hitting back and shielding himself from the worst of the blows. Escape no longer seemed an option. He only wondered if they'd be content to knock him unconscious or if they'd only be satisfied with killing him. A vague certainty that the latter was likely kept him from feigning unconsciousness.

Unconsciousness was precariously close when Derian became aware of a brassy trumpet call followed by someone shouting commands from what seemed like a vast distance. Moments later, he realized that there were fewer people hitting him—and fewer close enough for him to hit. He sagged against the wall, stick held defensively, grateful that his parents had insisted he have arms training.

There was blood on the cobbled ground and Derian felt pretty certain it wasn't all his own. His head throbbed when he turned to look for the source of the now dominant commands.

A contingent of the city guard was quelling the riot, for once the brawl had begun several of the stall holders had entered the fray, seeking to protect their property. Derian recognized the spice vendor speaking in rapid fury to someone who—if the number of feathers in his helmet was any indication—was probably in charge.

I hope I don't go to prison for shoplifting, Derian thought, and in the sudden exhaustion that flooded him the idea seemed very funny.

Laughter tortured his battered ribs so that he collapsed to his knees, still gasping and wheezing. A pair of strong hands raised him up.

"Are you in need of a doctor?" a woman's voice asked.

Derian looked into a painted face beneath an unplumed helmet and for the first time in what seemed like a lifetime thought of Doc.

"Doc!" he gasped. "Sir Jared. My companion. We were lured here. A man said he needed a doctor for his mother."

Seeing the woman's expression flow from genuine concern to complete confusion, Derian stopped, realizing he'd been speaking an incomprehensible mixture of New Kelvinese and Pellish. He started again:

"My companion, Sir Jared, is he all right? We came this way together, following a man who said his mother needed a doctor."

The guard shouted to her nearest companion.

"This one's alive. He says he had a companion—a foreigner like himself. See if you can find him."

As he hauled himself back onto his feet, Derian realized for the first time the extent of the damage. Numerous people lay unconscious or nursing a variety of wounds. No wonder the guard was uncertain about Jared.

Derian allowed her to escort him to a stone bench near the very fountain Wendee had thought so disquieting. Beneath the battling wizards and their amorphous foe, Derian repeated his story, then repeated it again when the many-plumed commander came over. Their experience at the Mushroom

Stanza Inn with Captain Brotius had not prepared Derian to expect to be given the benefit of the doubt by New Kelvinese law, but this was a different situation.

"Several of the vendors confirm much of your account," the commander said. "They did not understand your foreign babble, but they confirm that you and your companion did nothing to incite the riot."

Derian asked hesitantly, "And my companion?"

"Sir Jared has an odd tale to tell," the commander said. "I have had him speaking to one of my company who speaks some of your language. Perhaps you could serve as translator in case we have missed something?"

In his deep relief, Derian didn't waste energy resenting that he hadn't been told sooner that Doc was well enough to talk, nor did he miss that the commander had taken care to get both of their accounts before letting them speak to each other.

"I would be pleased to assist, sir," Derian replied, trying to remember the appropriate formal gestures. "Could I beg the favor of a message being taken to our residence? News of this riot may have reached there and our friends may worry."

"This has already been done," the watch commander said with a slight smile, "at the request of Sir Jared, as soon as he was certain you were alive."

Doc looked far better than Derian did, and would have immediately begun on the redhead's injuries if the commander hadn't made quite clear that anything short of life-threatening damage would wait until he had his report. Doc's tale matched Derian's right up to where the riot began. Then it took an odd turn.

"I didn't know which way to go," he said, addressing the commander, though speaking through Derian, "and as I couldn't reach Derian, I went toward the man who had brought us here. I didn't really trust him, but I thought he could explain what was going on.

"As soon as I was within arm's reach, he drew me into a alley between two of the buildings bordering the market—bakeries. I remember the scent of fresh bread distinctly. I thought something strange was going on and pushed away. It seemed like he wanted me to go into one of the shops."

"Perhaps he meant to keep you safe," the commander suggested.

"Perhaps," Doc agreed, "and I would have believed that myself if at that moment I hadn't realized I recognized him. Derian had tried to warn me there was something odd about him—odder even than his being our only patient today—but I hadn't listened. I guess I'd been too glad to have work. Now that we were close and I had no patient to worry about, I gave him a good look and that's when I realized that I did know him.

"Well," Doc paused to qualify, "not really know him, but that I'd seen him before. I'm absolutely certain that he was one of the men who attacked Fire-keeper and Blind Seer at the Mushroom Stanza Inn."

Derian interrupted Doc long enough to explain. The watch commander frowned thoughtfully.

"I believe I read a report on that incident," he said. "Continue."

"There isn't much more to say," Doc shrugged. "Once I realized that this was likely some sort of plot—maybe revenge for our being part of him and his buddies being sent to Urnacia—I decided that the riot might be safer after all. When I reemerged into the market, you and your guards were already breaking things up. I started helping the nearest injured and looking for Derian."

"Very interesting," the commander said. "If I permit you to return to your residence, will I find you there if I have further questions?"

Derian answered for them both.

"Yes, sir, and if Hasamemorri throws us out, we'll make certain you know where to find us."

"I will take your word on that," the commander said. "Can you, Counselor Derian," he asked, surprising Derian by his awareness of his title, "walk or do you need a litter? In either case, I will delegate a few of my people to escort you safely to your door."

Derian wasn't at all sure he could walk the distance, but he'd rather collapse trying than admit it.

"I'll be fine, Commander," he said, "and thank you."

"Thank rather," the watch commander said with one of his quicksilver grins, "the keeper of the spice booth. Not only does she not wish to press charges for your theft of her goods, she has spoken most loudly about how you were attacked."

"I'll bring her my thanks," Derian said.

"But not now," the commander said, looking around at the still roiling throng. "But not now."

Derian, his head throbbing with the sudden release of tension, thoroughly agreed.

⚛

TORIO HAD HOPED that having Citrine learn to dance would break Melina's obviously sorcerous control over her daughter, but although the girl threw herself into the patterns of the Harvest Joy dance with a natural talent that would have had the Sodality of Dancers looking to recruit her had she been New Kelvinese, Citrine remained enslaved.

Studying her covertly when they were together, the Healed One wondered what the girl's childhood had been like. She spoke of it infrequently and when she did the subjects were inconsequential: a younger cousin who was apparently a favorite playmate, the pony she had left behind, dancing lessons with her sisters.

She never spoke of the things Torio really wanted to know about. What trauma had maimed her hand? Was it only her father's recent death and her mother's exile that caused the unease that lurked behind her eyes like fire behind a hearth screen? How did she feel about her family's dissolution?

Toriovico could not ask Melina these things. The one time he'd asked about Citrine's missing fingers, Melina had pushed his queries away with a light laugh and a suggestion that he think about something more intimate.

He obeyed, of course, though increasingly he was having trouble performing sexually with his wife. His pride had been stung when he realized that Melina didn't particularly care if he was able to bed her or not. All that mattered was her ability to order him to try.

One night, lying in the darkness with her lightly mocking laughter still ringing in his ears, Torio resolved that he would learn what it was that had cost Citrine her fingers. Perhaps it was somehow linked to how Melina controlled her victims.

Horrible images of ground bone dust and ointments made from blood and fat swarmed against the back of the Healed One's closed eyelids. It was too easy to imagine that omnipresent gemstone on Citrine's brow soaked in such potions before being bound onto the child's head.

If he was to learn what had happened to Citrine, he might find a way to ward himself against Melina's power. He was growing tired of fearing that some casual statement on his part might make her realize that her hold had slipped—and as he saw more and more the contempt in which she held him his deepest self was wounded. Toriovico might not have been reared with the expectation that he would be the Healed One someday, but all his father's children had known they were of a select line. That inherent pride did not care at all for Melina's treatment of him.

True freedom might not be beyond him. He fell asleep with that hope keeping the more visceral horrors from becoming anything worse than nightmares.

A few days later, Toriovico decided to take advantage of another meeting with Xarxius, Dimiria, and Apheros on the question of Waterland trade to secure a private interview with the Dragon's Claw. As before, Xarxius was the obvious dissenter on a variety of matters. It was quite simple for Toriovico to request that Xarxius remain after the others had left.

If the other two had thought anything about the Healed One's request, it would have been to gloat that their rival was getting a dressing-down from on high.

What frightened Torio was that he didn't think they thought about it at all.

"How was your recent trip?" he asked Xarxius when they were alone. "You were in the south, weren't you?"

"That's right. Down near Zodara," Xarxius replied. "A matter of smuggling that needed to resolved."

"Ah."

Toriovico thought about asking more, decided that he was stalling, and went directly to the matter that really interested him. After all, he didn't know how long they would have before they were interrupted. He'd shifted the meeting to this room precisely because it was—as far as he knew—impossible for an outside observer to spy on what was said, but that meant that if anyone was curious, they would find an excuse to come in.

I'm getting paranoid, Toriovico thought with sorrowful pride. *I don't think I ever was before. My father's death may have made me the Healed One, but it seems that it took Melina to make me a ruler like any other.*

"I suppose you have heard about the arrival of Citrine Shield."

Xarxius nodded and there was a peculiar emphasis in his voice when he answered. "I had indeed. There is a matter related to Citrine's arrival that I had wished to speak to someone about, but I had not decided whether you or Consolor Melina would be best."

Toriovico was completely taken aback.

"Is the matter urgent or may I ask a few questions of you first?"

"It is urgent," Xarxius replied, "but not so urgent that a few questions will matter."

Toriovico almost told Xarxius to go ahead with his report, but he feared that he might become distracted. It was essential that he learn everything he could about Citrine in case her situation might shed some light on his own.

"Citrine seems a nice enough child, but neither she nor her mother will speak of certain matters," Torio began a touch awkwardly. "I thought it possible that with your knowledge of foreigners you might be able to brief me."

"I can only try, Healed One."

"How did the child lose her fingers? From how she holds her hand I sense that it is not an old injury but is one about which she is still sensitive."

Xarxius's hound-dog features sunk into even more mournful lines.

"The Healed One is correct," he said. "The injury is not old. It occurred last winter when Citrine was held captive by pirates in the eastern swamps of Hawk Haven."

"The pirates injured her?"

"After a fashion," Xarxius said carefully. "My sources say that the man who actually did the deed was the former Baron Waln Endbrook of the Isles."

"I believe I met him once," Toriovico said, wrinkling his brow in concentration. "He came bringing his queen's greetings. He hardly seemed like a man to mutilate a child."

"Men often are not what they seem," Xarxius said. "Women either, to be fair. Baron Endbrook was very deceptive. As you may recall, his diplomatic career in relation to our own land ended with him a hunted fugitive."

Toriovico thought he should remember, but his memories of that time were mingled with the cloudy imprecision that he was coming to associate with Melina's influence.

"Something to do with his treatment of my wife, wasn't it?" he asked.

"Yes, Honored One. Melina reported that one night when he had too much to drink Baron Endbrook attempted to seduce her. When she refused him he became violent."

Not too long ago, Torio would have failed to hear the emphasis on the word "reported." Now he did and found himself wondering if, like Columi, Xarxius was among those who had not fallen prey to the lady's charms.

"Melina put Baron Endbrook off," Xarxius continued, "and he apparently came sufficiently to his senses to realize the implications of what he had done. He fled. Grateful Peace, who had arrived to escort Melina and the baron to Dragon's Breath, sent his escort after Baron Endbrook but they failed to find him. Apparently, Endbrook took refuge with the pirates. The

Isles have long been a haven for their sort, and this has not changed since Queen Valora ascended to the throne."

"And Citrine Shield was with these pirates?"

"That is what I have heard."

"How did a noble-born child come to be with the pirates?"

Xarxius looked uncomfortable.

"I cannot say, Honored One."

"Cannot or will not?"

Xarxius took a deep breath and let it out in a shuddering sigh. Toriovico felt that Xarxius's indecision was genuine, but also that the Dragon's Claw was playing a part as he might in one of his negotiations.

"What I know is the result of rumors," Xarxius said after thoughtful pause. "Some little more than tavern tales."

"If I give you my word that I will consider your sources," Toriovico replied, "will you tell me what you have heard?"

Xarxius nodded slowly.

"Speak then."

"What I heard is that Citrine Shield was left with the pirates—or their agents—by Baron Endbrook."

"And how did he come to have custody of her?"

Xarxius looked pleading, and again Torio felt that the emotion was genuine—and the portrayal theatrical.

"I heard that her mother gave the child to him as a hostage to assure her own cooperation in the matter of the artifacts for whose interpretation Baron Endbrook had recruited her."

There was no need to ask which artifacts. Torio frowned, remembering.

"Yes, I recall that when Baron Endbrook first came to New Kelvin it was for the purpose of soliciting our skilled assistance in awakening the power of those artifacts. He was sent away, though. I cannot remember if I ever knew why. Apheros handled the matter, not me."

"Baron Endbrook was sent away because," Xarxius said heavily, "he was an ignorant Islander. Someone had the thought that we needed a fresh point of view—a new expertise—in order to have the best chance of awakening the artifacts' power."

Toriovico frowned, sensing all manner of intrigue. It hardly mattered now. The artifacts were stolen—some said destroyed—and only Melina remained. She was his current problem.

"You are telling me," the Healed One said very carefully so that Xarxius would not think him either distracted or angry, "that Melina gave her own youngest daughter as a hostage for her behavior, that Baron Endbrook cut off that daughter's fingers as a threat, and that Melina did not act?"

"That is what the rumors say, Honored One," Xarxius said stiffly. "Of course, Melina may have acted in a manner of which we know nothing."

Toriovico thought, *Yes. She remained here, seduced me, beguiled me into wedding her, and now is working on reigning through me and my ministers. I know. I wonder if Xarxius does.*

Somehow, the Healed One thought he might.

"But the child is no longer with the pirates," Torio said, returning to safer topics. "Did her mother redeem her?"

"No, Honored One. Citrine was rescued from captivity by her sister, Crown Princess Sapphire of Hawk Haven, acting—so it is said—on information brought to her by those perfidious criminals who were responsible for the theft of the artifacts."

"I see. And how came Citrine here, then?"

Xarxius drew in a deep breath.

"She was brought here."

"At her mother's request?"

Torio suddenly felt a rush of suspicion against the girl. What plans had her mother for her? Was she to inherit New Kelvin as Sapphire would Hawk Haven? Did Melina mean to set all her children on thrones? He'd heard that Princess Sapphire bore no love for her mother, but that could be false.

Xarxius, however, was shaking his head.

"Not that I have heard. I have only just begun looking into the matter, but it seems that Citrine was brought here by a trade commission headed by a Lady Archer and Lord Kestrel, both heirs apparent to important houses in Hawk Haven. It is uncertain why the child came with them, but what is clear is that Citrine fled her guardians and came seeking her mother of her own accord."

"How do you know this?"

"Her guardians have written me"—Xarxius removed several sheets of paper from the sleeve of his robe—"explaining the situation and requesting the child's return. As I understand the matter, since her exile Melina is regarded as holding no legal rights to Citrine. Therefore, Melina's continued custody of the child—who is a minor and therefore considered property of her House—could be viewed as theft. If a stricter interpretation was made, the situation could be viewed as kidnapping."

"Even if the child ran away of her own accord?"

"Even so," Xarxius said, toying with the letters. "Our own legal code would view the matter in a similar light. Indeed, given that we have upheld Waterland laws regarding slaves and have asked that Hawk Haven do the same in the matter of our slaves who flee across the White Water, those who drafted this request are not only within rights granted by their own laws, they are also within reasonable interpretation of our own."

Toriovico was fascinated, and had to fight against being diverted into a discussion of legal matters.

"So what you wanted to speak to me about was whether or not Melina should be permitted to retain custody of Citrine."

"Yes, Honored One."

"If Melina wishes to keep Citrine, what can these guardians do?"

"They hint at taking legal action," Xarxius said, "and that could have very unpleasant ramifications for trade. You must recall that Citrine is the biological sibling of Princess Sapphire. There would be no delays in this case being heard. The only delays would be in the speed the messages could be carried. However, Citrine's guardians may choose another course."

"Oh?"

"They may try to take her by force."

"From Thendulla Lypella?"

"It is completely possible, Honored One. You see, I have done some checking and these are the very people suspected of stealing the artifacts last winter, the people who suborned the loyal Grateful Peace. They might try to take Citrine—and never mind who might be hurt in the process."

Torio wasn't completely certain he cared whether or not Citrine remained, but he was positive that, having taken the girl in, Melina would not let her go for any reasons but her own.

"These guardians then are criminals?" he asked.

"I perhaps used the word too freely," Xarxius said.

By my own left hand, I am certain you did not, Torio thought. *What game are you playing at, old schemer?*

"Lady Archer, Lord Kestrel, and their companions are suspected of complicity in the matter, but no formal charge has ever been entered in the books. It is a matter of circumstance."

"Oh?"

"Well, the artifacts were stolen by a small group which included several people dressed—unconvincingly, it seems—as New Kelvinese. Among these people was a woman accompanied by a large wolf. Although she wore cosmetics, robes, and had her hair styled in the New Kelvinese fashion, there is little doubt that this was Lady Blysse Norwood."

"The feral child?" Torio asked, vaguely recalling some minstrel tales from the mists in his memory.

"The very one, though no child, rather a young woman and apparently as vicious as the monster that accompanies her everywhere. On the same night as this strange group in the company of the traitorous Grateful Peace infiltrated Thendulla Lypella, the other members of their company vacated their hired lodgings in the city. None of them were ever caught, though a group matching the description of those who came into the Earth Spires attacked an isolated guard post at the end of the sewer line. It is assumed they escaped from there."

"And were never captured?"

"Grateful Peace was with them," Xarxius said apologetically. "He may have known secret ways. It was also winter and the weather was so horrid that normal communications were slowed or stopped entirely."

"But no formal action was taken?"

"No, Honored One."

Xarxius looked at the tip of one curled slipper, though whether in shame or in embarrassment that the Healed One recalled so little of these monumental events, Toriovico could not tell.

"Further investigation showed that Baron Endbrook and his queen may have been precipitous in offering us the artifacts. They were taken—many said illegally—from the treasury of Bright Bay. The question, then, was open as to whether these people were guilty of theft or merely of repossessing property belonging to their allies.

"Moreover, both Hawk Haven and Bright Bay have proven of late that they will go to war to enforce their prerogatives. The Primes decided that it was best to overlook the matter and not risk similar confrontation. There was also the fact that several members of the group were well placed in Hawk Haven society."

For a moment Torio forgot everything but that he was the ruler of a kingdom whose rights had been violated.

"They had the gall to return here?" he asked indignantly.

"They were under no official ban," Xarxius reminded him, "and there was good reason. Lord Kestrel will someday inherit a major holding just across the White Water. His father is known to be very ambitious. Lady Blysse is his adopted sister and therefore will have the family interests at heart. Lady Archer's prospective holding is of lesser stature, and she may be eager to enhance it. She is also said to be a linguist and an admirer of our culture. The letter I mentioned was written by her."

"Let me see it."

Xarxius obeyed, and Toriovico studied the version in New Kelvinese.

"They do seem concerned for Citrine," he said, handing the documents back. "Even as I am. Let us look into this matter, you and I, but I think Consolor Melina need not know anything just yet."

Xarxius nodded and slid the letters into his sleeve pocket once more.

"I understand, Honored One."

I think you do, Toriovico thought as he recited ritual farewells, then watched the other man walk out the door. *I think you understand a great deal more than you are saying, Xarxius, but I am not quite ready to take you into my confidence . . . not just yet.*

XXIX

FIREKEEPER WOULD WAIT NO LONGER. The moon's face had grown full since the terrible night that she had been forced to abandon Edlin and Peace in the cavern beneath Thendulla Lypella. As she saw it, nothing good had been achieved in that long time. Matters, had, if anything, grown worse.

Citrine was still in Melina's hands—and they seemed to have no more hope of retrieving the girl than they did of finding Edlin and Peace, no matter what letters Elise had written. The citizens of Dragon's Breath had progressed from acting arrogant but being secretly curious, to being nervous and hostile, to indulging in active assault.

If it wasn't that Hasamemorri was a defiant sort, devoted to Doc for the relief from pain his treatments brought her overburdened joints, they might have found themselves thrown out into the streets. As it was, they lived with the shutters along the front of the house closed against thrown rocks and one of the ground-floor tenants awake and on watch at all times.

"I must do something," Firekeeper argued with Blind Seer.

They were out in the shady stable yard, her favorite refuge now that the streets had become unsafe and the house so closed and crowded.

The wolf stretched and licked one forepaw as if bored, but she wasn't fooled. Little hairs stood raised along Blind Seer's neck, the beginnings of hackles raised as he contemplated her madness.

"And what will you do?" he asked as idly as if they had not discussed this same matter dozens of times in the days that had passed.

"I will go into the sewer again," she said, "with you if you have the courage. I will take with me a copy of the map—Derian has made several and stealing one will be easy as breathing. Then I will make my way to where we last saw Edlin and Peace. I shall track them from there, find them, and if I can, bring them away. If not, I shall at least know more and be able to make better plans."

"And the traps that we met with before?"

"Peace showed us how to disarm them," Firekeeper said with more confidence than she felt. "Most we can move around. If you do not trigger them, they are no danger. I have more to fear from your nose betraying you than from any wire or arrow."

The wolf ignored this, saying instead:

"And the locks?"

"They can be broken. If I must, I will tear apart the gate itself."

"In complete silence," the wolf said sardonically.

"Would you have me abandon them then?"

"We do not even know if they are there any longer. There are many buildings in the Earth Spires. Melina could have cached them far away from the tunnels."

Privately, Firekeeper feared that the wolf might be right, but her desire to do something was stronger than her reason.

"Then the tunnels will not be guarded or trapped," she said, "for they will have no need of either."

"Except, perhaps, as a snare for eager puppies," Blind Seer replied. "Had you thought of that?"

"They know we are too wise to make the same mistake twice," Firekeeper said, inspired by this new vision, "and the moon has turned over a third of her cycle since last we went that way. They will think we have given up, that we wait for Elise and Ambassador Redbriar to solve our problems."

Blind Seer seemed inclined to be convinced, and so Firekeeper pressed on.

"Do you go with me or not?"

"Will you tell the others of this full-moon madness," the wolf asked, "or will you go without telling them and give them yet another worry?"

Firekeeper, pack creature that she was, had been almost as troubled over this as she had over the finer details of her planned expedition.

"If I tell them," she said, "then someone will insist on going with me."

"Is that an entirely bad thing?" Blind Seer asked. "You are not the wisest when keys and doors and written speech are concerned."

Firekeeper glowered at him.

"I can follow a map," she said, though with more confidence than she actually felt, "and I have told you that locks can be broken. If you and I had been alone the last time no one would have been captured."

"Oh?"

"Didn't we get away?" she challenged.

"Only because of Edlin's cleverness."

"Edlin's cleverness let us take away the map," Firekeeper said, "but my own skills carried me away."

"If you insist."

Firekeeper refused to argue further a point about which she wasn't completely confident, and returned to the first question.

"If I don't tell them," she said, "you are right and they will miss me and worry. Therefore, I have a solution."

"Do tell," said the wolf, but he seemed more scornful than interested.

"There are many writing things left in Edlin's kit," she said. "I shall take a piece of paper and make on it a mark like my hand and another like your paw. Then I shall make lines like the sewer map—maybe I shall even leave this note on the place where Derian has been making maps. This will tell them where I go and that you go with me."

"Can you make these marks?" Blind Seer asked, genuinely curious.

Firekeeper demonstrated in the dust.

"It is not too like my paw print," Blind Seer said, inspecting her work and sneezing when he breathed in some chaff, "but it may be good enough. Our lives would be easier if you would learn to read and write."

"I try," Firekeeper said, "but the words do not like me."

"Or you them," the wolf replied, and she knew he was the more correct.

Wendee claimed to have some difficulty clearly reading words that otherwise had been faultlessly written. She said that the letters swam and changed places on the page. Firekeeper had appropriated this excuse for her own. Who, after all, could see through her eyes? Not even Blind Seer could be sure.

"I will learn in time," Firekeeper temporized. "Now, I have answered many questions for you. Will you come with me or not?"

"I could," the wolf said slowly, "make your plans known. Derian would understand a little, perhaps. Or I could just sit on you. Then, however, you would abandon me also and go away some other night."

"So you will come?"

"I will, but only because you are foolish enough to drown while snapping at your own reflection in a pond."

Firekeeper didn't like this, but she also couldn't bear even one more night of waiting. Tonight, then, they would go.

LEAVING WAS EASY. They left after nightfall when the others were relaxing until those who had drawn the watch for later in the night needed to get their first sleep.

Even Derian, who had watched Firekeeper closely the first several days following Edlin and Peace's capture, had grown more relaxed about her occasional disappearances. Of course, it had helped that he always found her quickly enough, usually sleeping, for she had never lost the wolf's sense that ample sleep and food were the two greatest luxuries.

And perhaps, Firekeeper thought, trotting quickly down the alley toward the sewer, *Derian will not look too soon, for in his heart of hearts we are doing what he would do if he had the skill.*

Beneath the moon's caress the wolf-woman felt quick and bright and strong. No one was anywhere near the sewer opening and in less than the time it took her to take three deep breaths—a thing she did in anticipation of the stench below—the cover was up and she and Blind Seer had made their descent.

The sewer smelled even worse than she had remembered, a thing Firekeeper had not thought possible. Yet she made not the least complaint. It was her choice to hunt in these subterranean grounds in defiance of advice and, perhaps, even common sense.

Firekeeper had carried a lantern with her so she could consult the map, and now she opened one side shield the smallest amount so that they would have some illumination. She had told Elise that she had learned how to see in the dark, but that did not apply to this completely sealed cavern. When she and Blind Seer had fled from Idalia, the wolf had been able to backtrack along their own scent trail. They had made their way underground until they found an access ladder that led into the city above.

The small amount of light from the lantern made all the difference for eyes accustomed to navigating by starlight, and soon the pair were moving through the tunnels at a fair pace, slowing themselves deliberately so that they could check for trip wires and other indications of traps.

The only thing they found was absence. There were no traps or tricks, and when they reached the point where Peace had unlocked the first gate they nearly missed it. The gate was gone, only the scarring in the stone left to prove that it had ever been there.

Though they both tried to take comfort from this—humans were the great masters of inexplicable actions—neither Firekeeper nor Blind Seer was particularly happy.

"Is it taken away so that we will be lured on?" Blind Seer asked, sniffing around the scoring in the stone in hope that he might find some explanation.

"Or is it merely that the sewer workers complained of the inconvenience?" Firekeeper offered. "Look how often we must chase around Hasamemorri's looking for a key now that we are keeping the doors locked. Perhaps the workers grew aggravated at the inconvenience?"

Blind Seer shook his entire body as if uncertainty was a physical pressure.

"I recall, now," he said, "that Edlin chaffed Peace for not putting in such gates himself when he was the guardian of the city and Peace defended his action by saying that these tunnels were meant to let the sewage pass and that such gates might provide blockades when the water ran high. Perhaps the gates were removed for that reason."

Firekeeper nodded. Whichever reason—or another entirely—might be correct, they had found a kind of sense behind the removal of the gate. Turning back from a nothing that might be a reason for fear rather than from something physical and solid seemed to make little sense. So thinking, Firekeeper urged Blind Seer on.

The wolf came more willingly now, his head dipping intermittently to sniff the stone while Firekeeper cast about for sign of a trip wire or other trap. They found none for there was none to find. When trouble came it was far less subtle.

They had stepped from their tunnel into the area where several such tunnels met to form a larger river when, without warning beyond the hissing of ropes running rapidly through well-greased pulleys, a large, weighted net plummeted from the shadows overhead. The net was quite wide, meant to catch them both and entangle them in its mesh, but at the first sound out of the ordinary, Firekeeper leapt back.

Her lantern guttered out and darkness blanketed them, a darkness so complete that she could not tell whether her eyes were open or shut.

"*Hold your place,*" Firekeeper called softly to Blind Seer, who, larger though no less alert, had not escaped the trap, "*and I will see if I can free you.*"

"*You must, for I cannot free myself,*" Blind Seer replied with a whine of frustration. *"I am so wrapped and tangled I fear that if I move I will only draw the strands more tightly."*

Firekeeper patted him.

"This was dropped by human hand," she said, *"not by any loose rock or wire we failed to see. The one who loosed it will come to check his catch. Listen for someone coming while I see what I can do here."*

The wolf growled his agreement. For her part, Firekeeper tried to make sense of the tangle of ropes. She didn't waste time trying to find her lantern and light it. Her nose had adjusted somewhat to the stench of the sewers by now, enough that she could smell spilled lantern oil. Moreover, even if she could manage a light, it would give her away. Better that she see the trappers before they could clearly see her and Blind Seer.

Rapidly, Firekeeper's fingers examined the net, finding the mesh very heavy, of a type used to catch and hold large prey rather than to snare birds or rabbits. The strands had been coated with something sticky that caused them to cling to her fingers, making it difficult to locate an edge or manipulate the heavy mass of rope.

This alone would have made her reluctant to dull her Fang against its edge; then, too, there was the fear that she might slip and cut Blind Seer. Better to work more slowly until she was certain.

As she struggled with the net, Firekeeper recalled the roadhouse tales of giant spiders that fed on human blood. Hadn't it been said that Melina kept many of these creatures, that she was gathering slaves with which to feed her pets? The wolf-woman shivered, almost paralyzed with fear. What if one of these spiders and no human was coming upon them? A spider might not need a light. A spider might make no sound but the faintest tapping of chitinous legs on the stone.

The wolf-woman strained to hear, her fingers moving independent of any conscious will on her part. Imagining a hairy leg reaching out to grasp her, Firekeeper fought down a scream of terror as irrational as that which came to her sometimes after the nightmares she could never remember.

Then her fingers touched a knot, and near that knot a heavy lead weight. These proofs of human agency banished the spiders back into imagination. Still breathing hard, Firekeeper felt her way from weight to another knot. Surely this would be near the edge.

"I'll have you free soon, dear heart," she said to Blind Seer.

The wolf growled. Perhaps he, too, had been imagining what might be coming for them. Perhaps he only hated having his freedom restricted.

"*Don't worry for my fur,*" he ordered. "*When you have an edge lift it and I will creep out.*"

Firekeeper grunted her agreement, working as rapidly as she could.

"*Do you hear anything?*" she asked.

"*I think so,*" the wolf said. "*Work faster!*"

Firekeeper didn't bother to tell Blind Seer that she was working as fast as she could. The mesh was not only strong, but it had been made so that it would bind to itself as well as to its target, and she was frequently forced to stop and relocate her edge.

"*Light!*" the wolf cried a moment later, his excitement making an echoing bay of the announcement. "*It reflects off the tunnel walls, coming, I think from the same that Peace led us to before. Am I free?*"

"*Not yet,*" Firekeeper admitted. "*This is hard to do in the darkness.*"

She could feel the wolf straining against the mesh.

"*Take care,*" she warned. "*If you rise while tangled, you may pitch yourself into the waters and drown.*"

The wolf subsided, but she could feel his nervous panting, and the wash of heat coming off him as his tension grew.

There was a thud and clang, then the faintest glow of light broke the absolute darkness. Without looking up from her work, Firekeeper knew that those who had trapped them were coming closer. She could not tell how many sets of feet trod the stone, only that there were more than one.

She pulled and was rewarded by feeling a large section of the net come loose, freeing the wolf's hindquarters, though she suspected at the cost of a great deal of fur.

She had time to do no more. There was a thump as the bridge joining their walkway to the next was lowered. The light grew brighter and shone from a higher point so she knew that someone had lit one of the many lanterns hung for the convenience of those who worked here. In but a breath or two she would have lost whatever advantage she might have.

Standing, Firekeeper tossed the edge of the net forward, hoping to throw it entirely off the wolf. Without waiting to see if she had succeeded, she leapt over Blind Seer's recumbent bulk and drew her Fang. In the improved light, she could see at least four coming over the narrow bridge. Men, she thought, enormous, bulky figures.

Even in the lantern light, they were hardly more than shapes. She, however, was only a shadow, a darker form against the dark.

The man in the lead barely suspected her coming. Then she was against him, pitching him into the stinking waters before he could raise an alarm.

The man behind him was not so easily taken. He waved the short sword he carried and moved forward, clearing the way for his fellows to exit the bridge, shouting back at them in some incomprehensible garble.

Firekeeper was kept busy dodging the man's blade. He was skilled with it, but not so skilled that he thought to vary the pattern of his attack and defense. When she had learned his movements, she brought her Fang up and cut his throat as neatly as if he had been a rabbit.

He sprayed blood enough to soak her and the stone on which they both stood before sliding into the river.

Spitting his gore from her mouth, Firekeeper readied herself for the next attack. She could hear Blind Seer's claws scraping against the stone, accompanied by his furious and frustrated whines, and guessed that the wolf was still pawing himself free from the net. That he had not called for her assistance assured Firekeeper that he thought he could manage.

All she had to do was win them both enough time.

The remaining two men were more cautious than their fellows had been, for the first had thought to find netted captives and the second, frightened by the suddenness with which his leader had vanished, had not thought at all.

These moved forward with care, neither side by side nor one after the other. Rather one came forth hugging close to the wall while his companion moved a pace behind, but over slightly so that he gave his fellow room. The man on the outer edge moved his hand in a slow looping motion that Firekeeper found vaguely familiar. Only after the man made his cast did she recognize it.

She jumped into the air, but could not completely avoid the weighted rope that lashed out to snare her. The man had been trying to pin her arms to her sides and had succeeded only in snaring her about the waist and hips. Even so it was enough to throw her off balance.

He yelled his triumph and shouted something in a language Firekeeper did not understand as he hauled back on the rope, drawing it more tightly around her and dragging her closer. His fellow gave an answering cheer and moved in, intent on either killing or disarming Firekeeper.

Regaining her balance was nearly impossible with blood-wet stone beneath her feet and the rope jerking around her waist, so Firekeeper did not dare lower her guard long enough to try to slash her Fang through the restraint—and she feared that it would take more than one attempt to cut the supple coil that wrapped her round.

The second man was closing, cautious in his awareness of both the chancy footing and the knife that had so easily opened his companion's throat. Firekeeper spat at him, darting her Fang in little motions that made clear what would happen if he came much closer. The swordsman was no fool, but he was also aware of how much of her mobility had been sacrificed.

All he had to do was take care while his comrade reeled her in. Firekeeper knew this and wondered if somehow she might turn the rope to her own advantage. She pulled back against the rope, seeking now not only to maintain her distance, but to force the other man to pull even harder. Her strength was tremendous, but she was far smaller than her opponent and weight was against her. Moreover, her feet slid on the blood of the man whose throat she had cut while the man on the rope's other end had comparatively solid footing.

Still, Firekeeper did not hope to drag him forward, rather to force him to pull as hard as he might. When she judged this moment had been reached, Firekeeper leapt forward, dodging wide around the man with the sword so that the rope caught him across his lower body. He fell, dropping his sword, his weight dragging at the rope and making Firekeeper lurch and drop her Fang.

The man holding the other end of the rope staggered back, unbalanced by pulling against a force that was suddenly no longer there. He reeled back several paces, then fell over into the sewer.

Now Firekeeper became aware of a flaw in her hastily devised plan. In the faint light she had not seen that the man had the other end of the rope fastened onto his body. When he fell, she was jerked forward into the disarmed swordsman. He, unaware of this complication or uncaring now that he was the lone survivor of what had been four strong men, beat at her with his fists, screaming what must have been curses or insults.

Firekeeper warded off the blows as best she could, but she was more concerned about getting free from the dragging rope. Without her Fang, she could not cut it. The rope man had been caught by the strong current formed by the flooding together of these several streams, and whether living or dead was providing an anchor pulling her inexorably after him.

She howled her fear and frustration, hammering at her adversary. The world narrowed to the weight that dragged her toward the edge of the walkway and the man who struck at her. In frustration rather than with forethought, Firekeeper shoved her attacker, pushing him away from her.

He tripped on the taut rope, stumbled, and, grabbing at the rope as if to stay his fall, went toppling over the edge. Firekeeper, unbalanced by the momentum of her own attack, felt herself going down after him. She dove over the edge, her head and shoulders sliding into the stinking waters, and knew that she would die choking on human filth.

At that moment, a searing heat on her left calf divided Firekeeper's world into twin pains: the quiet one of suffocation paired with a loud screaming from muscles and bone clamped onto by strong jaws, jaws that pulled back and upward, dragging her out of the water.

The rope about her waist still hauled her down. Though Firekeeper could hardly think through the sharp pain to her calf, she knew that if Blind Seer was to succeed in drawing her up she must release herself from this competing grasp. Laboriously, she plucked at the rope, untwined the weighted end from where it held the coils close to her, and at last felt it slide free.

With a final jolt of pain, Firekeeper felt herself dragged level across stone that reeked now of her own blood mingled with that of the man she had slain. Never before had she longed for anything as she did now for unconsciousness and the release from pain it would bring, but she knew that if she slept now she would never waken.

"Get me," she managed, speaking as much with a toss of her head as with words, "closer to that one. His clothes may make bindings for my wounds."

In reply the great grey wolf instead went and dragged the dead man over to her.

"No need," he said, snuffling at her injured calf and licking the blood away, "to move you when he is so far beyond protest."

Firekeeper didn't waste energy agreeing. The lanterns hanging high on the walls gave enough light that she could examine the dead man. He did not carry a first-aid kit, but his shirt was good cloth, easily torn into bandages with scraps left over for her to use as towels to mop away the worst of the filth that still dripped over neck and shoulders.

Doc had given Firekeeper some training in medicine and she knew that this stuff was as great or greater a danger to her healing as were the wounds themselves. Therefore she did not protest when Blind Seer, having licked her wounds clean, took it upon himself to begin to wash her.

"Foul stuff," he commented, panting, his breath like heated sludge, "but better gone from you."

Binding her wounds hurt so much that Firekeeper had to keep pausing to let bright flashes of pain fade from behind her eyes. By the time she had finished her labors she knew that though Blind Seer had been as careful as he might—a thing she knew for her leg bone was not crushed to splinters—still his fangs had sorely lacerated her flesh. She wrapped her makeshift bandages around and around, partly to stay the bleeding, partly to soak up what would inevitably flow.

"My Fang," she asked him. "Did it go into the muck?"

The wolf nosed around and came back, bearing the bare blade very carefully in his mouth. She took it from him, and slipped it into its sheath, for she knew it would take all that she had merely to move. There would be no more fighting for her.

"No convenient walking staff," she asked, trying to make light of her need.

"None," the wolf said, "and no time to hunt. These will be missed and we do not want to await the searchers."

Firekeeper agreed.

"I shall make do with your shoulder then," she said.

Bracing herself against Blind Seer, she hauled herself up so that she stood balanced on her good leg, her heavily wounded one throbbing so that she didn't dare put any weight on it.

They made their escape, leaving behind betraying light, entering darkness that now seemed sheltering rather than obstructive.

Their travel was very slow. Whenever they came to a turning, Blind Seer would pace ahead, leaving Firekeeper leaning against a wall in absence of his support. More than once he offered to let her rest and go seek the others so that she might be carried, but always she refused.

"I would sleep," she said, "for I can barely keep awake now. Then if I was found I could offer no defense. This is better."

Whether the wolf agreed or not, he remained with her. Firekeeper hardly knew who she was or where. Her entire world had been reduced to the throb in her calf, to the dozen lesser aches, and a pleasant lassitude that continually beckoned her. She didn't know when she ceased to move of her own accord and Blind Seer was forced to drag her by one shoulder, the leather vest providing some slight armor against his teeth, but the bruising going to the bone.

At last they came to the entry into the sewer nearest to Hasamemorri's house. Blind Seer could not haul Firekeeper up, but he managed the rung ladder, and shouldered the cover aside.

He emerged into the greyish light of false dawn, a blood-streaked horror so like something out of the worst legends that the few early risers who saw him fled, not even pausing to scream.

ELISE PACED ABOUT THE KITCHEN, brewing tea and refining the lecture she was going to give Firekeeper when the wolf-woman returned from this latest impulsive foray.

Derian had noticed Firekeeper's note and the missing map when he went to ready himself for bed. He had returned to the kitchen, his shirt open, revealing what Elise recalled with a slight blush as a rather attractive chest. Normally, Derian was modest to a fault around her—a lingering remnant of his respect for her as both a woman and a noble. It had been his abandoning this that had given Elise the first sense that something was wrong.

"Does everyone else read this the way I do?" he asked, dropping a grubby sheet of paper on the table where they could all see it.

Sir Jared had answered first.

"Firekeeper's gone back into the sewers," he said, slamming his fist into his palm, too polite to curse in the presence of the ladies.

"That's what I thought, too," Derian agreed. "She's taken one of the map copies I made—a finished one, thank the Horse."

They'd debated about someone going after woman and wolf, deciding at last that Firekeeper and Blind Seer would be too far ahead of any pursuit, that their already attenuated group could not risk any further losses.

"Likely," Wendee said, drying the same plate for the third time, the only sign of distress she permitted herself, "Firekeeper will be back sometime in the middle of the night, smelling to the skies and as pleased as if she's done something clever. I'll set a stew kettle filled with water over the coals to warm before I go to bed. That way whoever is awake can make her bathe."

Wendee's practicality, forced as it was, had a good influence on them all.

Derian returned to readying himself for bed. Doc left to check the lock on the front door before taking the early watch. The women soon followed Derian's example and went to bed.

When Derian woke Elise for her turn on watch, her first words had been: "Are they home?"

He'd shaken his head.

"No sign. I'd better get some rest. Who knows what tomorrow will bring?"

Once she was alone, Elise found herself growing angrier and angrier. Maybe if she'd had siblings or children she would have been better prepared to deal with Firekeeper's behavior, but she had not. The Archer family had taken "Responsibility" as a motto rather than the more poetic "Arisen from the Soil" suggested by Grandmother Rosene to her suitor. Now Elise was facing just what that responsibility meant, and realizing what a trial some of her own escapades must have been to her parents.

"I wonder if Mother and Father have gone ahead and adopted Deste," she thought, and realized that she hoped they had. *"Or perhaps if they have not we can take custody of Citrine when we get back. Jet certainly has done no good for her."*

Homesickness and the routine kitchen chores that fell to the dawn watch kept Elise busy. When she heard the thump on the kitchen door, her first thought was that Derian must have slipped out while she'd been in the pantry and had his arms full with a load of wood for the fire.

Elise opened the door to find Blind Seer on the stoop, his fur spiked with mire and blood, his entire being reeking of filth. Though her mind knew perfectly well that he was no danger, her heart thought differently.

Her scream brought the others—including one of Hasamemorri's maids—running in. Derian ran directly to the wolf.

"Firekeeper!" he said. "Where is she?"

Blind Seer replied by tugging at Derian's shirt then turning his piercing, blue-eyed gaze directly on Doc and whining.

"I'll get my bag," the knight said.

"Elise," Derian ordered when she made as if to come with them. "If the two of us can't get Firekeeper, one more set of hands won't help. Get water on the boil and the surgery ready. All that blood isn't from the 'other guy' or Firekeeper would be here bragging about how tough she was."

Immediately realizing the wisdom in this, Elise hurried to obey, brushing past Doc in the hall. Wendee was urging Hasamemorri's maid out of the way, promising to bring the landlady's tray up herself.

Before the small kettle of water Elise had put on had time to boil, Doc and Derian were back, Firekeeper between them on a horse blanket that acted as a makeshift stretcher.

"Blind Seer grabbed it as we went out the back," Derian said, words flowing to cover his evident concern. "He obviously knew Firekeeper was in no shape to walk."

Doc, who was walking at Firekeeper's head, added, "If the water's boiled, bring it. If not, Derian can put on more. Bring what you have."

Blind Seer hovered in the doorway, obviously wanting to come in but not wanting to get in the way. Elise patted him on the head as she grabbed the kettle.

"Let Derian or Wendee wash you off," she suggested, "before you come in. You're a disease waiting to happen."

The wolf whined in resignation and Elise repeated her suggestion to Wendee as she hurried past.

"Right after getting breakfast ready for Landlady Curiosity," Wendee snapped, exasperated.

Elise offered a wan smile by way of apology, but didn't pause.

Once in the surgery, Elise got her first look at Firekeeper and had to stifle another scream. Doc and Derian had stripped off the wolf-woman's vest, revealing a left shoulder that was black and blue where it wasn't bleeding. Every inch of exposed skin on Firekeeper's upper body was scraped and scratched. It looked as if someone had wrapped a whip about her waist, leaving angry weals. Her left calf was wrapped in blood-sodden strips of cloth and caked with dirt.

"She's alive but lost so much blood that we must get liquid into her," Doc snapped, his hands moving as he checked and probed. "Derian, make sure there's more water heating. Prepare it in several small pots so they'll heat faster. Then bring in some tepid water and see if you can get Firekeeper to swallow some."

"Right!" The redhead was gone almost before Doc finished issuing his orders.

"Elise, is that water boiled?"

"Not quite, though it's hot."

"I want to wait until we have boiled water to unwrap the leg. Start sponging off the shoulder and upper body cuts. Use alcohol when the worst is off. The wounds must be clean before we put ointment on or we'll just trap the infection."

Elise nodded, then ventured, "What do you think happened to her? Did she meet some monster down there?"

Doc's lips twisted in a humorless smile.

"I'd say that this shoulder at least was done by Blind Seer. He must have dragged her I don't know how far. Poor creature must have wanted hands in the worst way."

Elise was horrified. She'd never really taken a close look at what the wolf could do, though she'd seen him kill and knew he was deadly. To think that this was what he was capable of when he was being gentle was enough to reawaken fears that she had thought forever gone.

"Is the shoulder broken?"

Abstractly she thought, *The shoulder. The leg. As if they don't belong to a woman we know, as if they're just body parts.*

"I don't think so," Doc replied, "though she may wish it so. It's going to hurt, even with the best I can do for her. We should be glad that she insists on wearing leather. It'll be easier to clean the fibers out and leather does offer protection that cloth would not."

Eventually Derian came in bearing two small pots holding a gallon or so of boiled water between them.

"More's on and Wendee says to tell you that the bigger kettle she put on last night is coming around now that the fire's built up."

"Good," Doc said. "Set your pots there. Elise, let's look at that leg. We'll want cold water to stanch the bleeding if it starts afresh when we unwrap the bandages."

Derian ran to haul fresh cold water from the well while Elise reached for the stoneware jugs in which they kept water boiled once and let cool. When Derian returned he set the bucket on the floor near where Doc could reach it, then took a bottle of clean water from his pocket and started nursing drops between Firekeeper's pale lips.

"Is she conscious?" Derian asked after he'd been at work for a time. "I thought I heard her whine when you moved her leg."

"Conscious or not," Doc said brutally, "she's not getting anything for the pain. I don't dare put her under so far that I might not be able to draw her back."

Elise knew that meant Firekeeper likely was conscious and feeling everything they did to her. She tried to be gentle, but that was nearly impossible. Some of the blood on the wrappings had dried, cementing the fabric so that it had to be cut away. Other strips had left long strands from the frayed ends of the cloth buried in the lacerated flesh and each of these must be pulled clear.

The injuries to Firekeeper's calf, once they were fully revealed, made the ones on her shoulder look like nothing.

"Blind Seer again," Doc commented, "or they met another carnivore of his shape and size. This time there was no vest to protect her skin. The teeth went right into the muscle. It's a wonder that he didn't break her leg."

"What happened, Jared?" Elise asked, hearing a plaintive note in her voice as if she would cry the tears Firekeeper did not. "Did something drive one of them mad down there so that he had to attack her? I'd more easily believe in the existence of another wolf than that either would harm the other."

Jared shook his head, sponging and cleaning the wounds as best he could.

"Only Firekeeper can tell us," he said. "Let's do what we can to save her. I'd hate to be left with a mystery."

When Firekeeper was as clean as they could make her, Doc and Elise stitched closed the longest cuts. Scrapes and bruises were liberally anointed with ointments and poultices made from calendula and comfrey. Then Doc placed his hands on Firekeeper's thigh and shoulder, and sent his healing talent into the injured parts with such force that he swayed and would have crumpled to the floor had Derian not caught him.

Derian lifted Doc onto the surgery cot with relative ease, as if Doc's use of his talent had made the man physically lighter.

"Now we have two patients," Derian said with a wry smile. "I'll go see if that broth Wendee was making is ready and pour a mug of honeyed tea for Doc."

Elise nodded and sank into a chair where she could watch over Firekeeper and Jared both. Outside the windows she could hear the bustle of the market day beginning. In pointed contrast there rose the howl of a freshly washed wolf who wasn't being let inside until his coat had dried.

XXX

FAILURE WAS THE END RESULT of Columi's attempts to locate pre-cisely where the Dragon of Despair was bound.

"I did read," the old man said, "that the spell that binds the dragon is so carefully formulated that releasing the monster would be nearly impossible. Perhaps we do not need worry so much about what Melina intends."

"I wish I was certain," the Healed One replied. "'Nearly impossible' is not enough when dealing with ambition on this scale. This is a woman who apparently has been willing to sacrifice her own children's well-being in order to gain what she desires. I cannot underestimate her.

"However, we must accept," Toriovico continued heavily, "that the task of tracking Melina is beyond me. I cannot follow her myself without risking her learning that I am free of her domination and I have yet to find a spy I can trust."

Columi looked both relieved and apprehensive.

"Then we must wait to react to what she does?" he asked, and he sounded almost hopeful. Some of his fervent desire to undermine the Con-solor had weakened now that he perceived what a difficult and potentially dangerous course of action this was.

Toriovico did not chide the emeritus Prime for his temerity. Raging against something that seemed wrong was easy when raging was all that could be done. Not everyone was suited for dangerous action. Unfortu-nately, the Healed One could not let Columi fade back into his retirement. He needed at least one agent he could trust.

"No," Torio replied. "I will not wait to react. That might be too little too late. I have done some preliminary investigation and I believe I know where agents can be found who will be glad to work against Consolor Melina."

"Members of the Defeatists?" hazarded Columi.

"No," Toriovico said, "for we don't know which of those might be trusted to keep silence. The Defeatists might view their first duty as to their political associates rather than to the abstract ideal of our kingdom."

"Then who?" asked Columi.

"Tell me," Toriovico asked rather than replying directly. "What do you think Xarxius's position on Consolor Melina might be?"

"Xarxius?" Columi seemed troubled and confused by this change in topic. "The Dragon's Claw?"

"The same."

Columi massaged the bald spot atop his head with one hand as he considered.

"I do not believe Xarxius has any great fondness for her," he offered at last.

"Then you do not believe Xarxius is among those you would include in her party?"

"No . . . I don't think so. He has never courted her, nor she him. Recently I have heard it bruited about that they had differences in opinion in the matter of Waterland trade."

"That is true," Toriovico agreed. "I was present at several such meetings. Very well. I believe that Xarxius is one with you and me regarding Melina's influence on New Kelvin. However, belief is not enough. I must be sure. I cannot ask him. Even if I told Xarxius that he was safe to speak with me on the matter, I would be the last one he would trust. Therefore, I want you to ascertain beyond a doubt his feelings regarding Melina and her influence."

"Me?"

"Don't look so startled, Columi," Toriovico reprimanded a trace sharply. "You may have retired to curate a museum, but in my father's day you were among the canniest politicians in this kingdom. I cannot believe that those reflexes are lost. Take them out and polish them—then go and speak with Xarxius."

Columi straightened and nodded crisply, not as if his previous reaction had been an act, more as if he could not but acknowledge the truth of what his ruler said.

"I shall use the excuse of wishing to acquire certain mineral samples for the collection as my reason for calling on Xarxius," Columi said after a moment's thought. "He is always looking for little things he can gain to make certain we have the advantage in a trade. Indeed, with all the rumors flying about that rare artifacts are to be brought from Waterland it would seem stranger if I didn't petition for my own sodality."

"Very well, then," Toriovico said, pleased. "Go to it. Once you are certain of Xarxius, I shall put a proposal to him myself."

"Might I know what that proposal will be?" Columi asked, his instinct for political predation aroused now in full.

"Let us say only that," Toriovico replied, "I think Xarxius knows of a spy I can use—and that I believe I already have the price that will pay for that spy's complete loyalty."

Columi looked neither offended nor angered that Toriovico refused to tell him more. Indeed, it took a moment for the younger man to realize what the emotion was that lit the elder man's round face.

It was pride.

FLEEING THE PAIN THAT THROBS IN HER LEG, Firekeeper leans over herself. With elaborate precision, she detaches herself from the feverish body unconscious on the bed. First she strips away the leg that hurts so much, then the other. Reaching behind her head, she pulls loose connections looped behind each ear and skins her face down. Arms need to be worked free, too. That's a little tricky since she needs an arm to undo an arm, but she manages.

Standing on blue-black darkness that puddles warm around her ankles, Firekeeper stretches. Her fingers brush the stars, spilling sparkling pollen from summer heavy blossoms. The stars are scented with mingled honeysuckle and wild rose. The strong odor drifts into her head and intertwines with her thoughts. The sensation is very pleasant.

Firekeeper doesn't know how long she stands there inhaling the breath of stars before she is aware of a voice. Calling. Her?

Pivoting as lightly as milkweed on the wind, Firekeeper searches for the source of the voice. She sees the comet swimming through the rich blue-black, sinuous as a snake or a vein of lighter rock within the dark or blood in a vein.

A vast thundering torrent of sparkling white light, the comet pours through the night sky, vigorous and purposeful. Mysteriously, though Firekeeper senses great speed from the comet, she is also aware that it is not moving at all.

Unlike a frozen waterfall, the comet is not the image of motion though motionless. It is truly immobile, yet truly moving at speeds beyond what even the most swiftly diving falcon might attain.

Firekeeper, embodied bodilessness rejects the contradiction as unworthy of consideration.

"Wise," the comet hisses, "for are you not both wolf and woman?"

"Wolf," she agrees, "and woman."

"As I am prisoner and yet a terrible master."

"You mean you are a prisoner of some fate," she offers, "as a king is prisoner of his throne while most believe him master of all."

"No," the comet hisses. "Truly, I am a great force, so powerful that hurricanes and tornadoes are nothing to me. I could swallow the living world in flames and never feel filled. I am captive, yet if I am freed, I will be more a captive than I am."

"Why do you tell me this?"

"Few have ears that can hear me, even in sleep. I am a thundering torrent. Incomprehensible."

Pollen shakes from the stars as Firekeeper struggles with the comet's words.

"I hear you," she says, "but I do not understand you. Captive yet free? More captive if freed? What is it you desire?"

"My freedom," the comet replies. "But not my captivity."

"I thought that the one brings the other," she protests.

"Free me, and I will be your master."

"I don't want a master!"

"You would desire the alternative less. . . ."

DERIAN WATCHED at Firekeeper's bedside as she slept from dawn through dusk. Sometimes she tossed with pain or nightmare, but mostly she was so still that he found himself watching for the rise and fall of her breathing.

Before retiring to his own bed for most of the day, Doc had said that sleep would be Firekeeper's best healer now that he had done what he could for her. However, he had insisted that the wolf-woman be roused every few hours and given something to drink.

At first Firekeeper hardly seemed to notice, sucking at the bottle Derian held for her like a nursing foal given an artificial teat. By midday, however, she was drinking thirstily of whatever was offered, and by evening she was protesting that broth, juice, and water were not enough for a wolf who needed to regain her strength.

"Doc told us to take care," Derian insisted, pushing her back onto the bed when she tried to rise, "that you did not overstrain your system. Liquids are what you need to replenish the blood you left all over New Kelvin."

"Meat," Firekeeper replied with certainly, lying back as ordered, "is better. I will take drink with it."

Doc arrived in the doorway of the infirmary at that moment, his black hair still sleep-tousled and the expression of affectionate amusement in his grey eyes tinged with annoyance. It was at moments like these that Sir Jared most reminded Derian of his cousin the earl.

"Still wiser than every other head?" Doc asked, coming over and reaching for Firekeeper's wrist so that he might test the strength of her pulse. "I thought last night might have taught you otherwise."

Firekeeper looked so ashamed that Derian was reminded of a puppy cringing.

"Am I wrong?" she said softly. "I am very hungry."

"I shall be the judge of what is best to feed your hunger," Doc continued severely. "Now, how do you feel?"

Firekeeper replied with an accuracy that reminded Derian of a young solider reporting.

"I hurt everywhere, like time when I fall out of tree when hunting squirrel nests. I was growing then," she added inconsequentially, "and didn't climb well for my limbs were strange to me."

"Where do you hurt worst?" Doc asked.

"In my leg and shoulder," she said, indicating the places with a movement of her chin, "though not as bad as I remember I should. You have fixed me again."

She sounded very pleased at this and Doc frowned severely.

"I thought about not doing so," he said, his tone leaving no doubt that he was completely serious. "Had it not been that we might need you and Blind

Seer to help save Edlin and Peace—Eagle's Eye watch over them if they live—and to free Citrine from Melina if the need arises, I would not have done so."

Firekeeper looked at him wide-eyed.

"Truly?"

"Truly," Doc said firmly. "I think your foolishness comes in part from a good heart, but in part from the belief that you will not suffer the consequences of your actions. What good would I do you if I made you lose the caution that kept you alive in the wilds?"

His voice rose, and again Firekeeper cringed. Derian thought that the bandits who had run from her should see her now, cowed by nothing more than words.

Or maybe, he thought, *she knows that Doc's right and what has her beaten is the awareness that she's been an idiot.*

Firekeeper looked up through her lashes at Doc, not in the least flirtatious, rather like a child who is checking to see if the scolding is over.

"May I please have something to eat?" she pleaded. "And is Blind Seer well?"

"You may have something to eat," Doc replied evenly. "Stewed chicken and vegetables, I think."

"Blind Seer is well," Derian added, ignoring her grimace at this invalid's fare. "He has been sitting with you most of the day. I believe he just went out into the yard to run off some excess energy."

Firekeeper smiled.

"Blind Seer saved me," she said. "When I would have fallen. I remember that now."

"Save the tale until we all can hear it," Derian suggested. "I'll tell Elise and Wendee that you both are awake and coherent. We'll put a tray together and after she eats Firekeeper can give us a full recital of what happened last night."

THE RECITAL TOOK QUITE A WHILE, for there were many questions, and as Firekeeper did not have all the answers there was much conjecture and discussion.

"My guess," Derian offered, tracing his fingers over one of the copies of the map, "is that whoever it was who went after Firekeeper has had watchers down there all along. They heard our pair coming or saw the light and dropped the net. Firekeeper says they came from two bridges away—the same tunnel Peace led them up last time. That's suggestive."

"But of what?" Elise said impatiently. "We don't know enough to act. Edlin and Peace could be dead. Xarxius has sent a bread and butter note saying that he will take up the matter of Citrine with his ruler. Do we stay and try to confirm that Edlin and Peace are out of our reach? Do we risk ourselves again in those tunnels?"

Elise paled as she made this last suggestion, but Derian felt only admiration for her. It took a lot more courage to suggest doing something that scared you than to do as Firekeeper had done and charge in confident of your own strength and invulnerability.

Firekeeper, too, seemed to recognize this, for she said:

"Going again be stupid. It stupid to go first time. It lose us Edlin and Peace. The second time was purer stupid. I nearly lose us me."

She didn't look as if she expected either praise for admitting her own fault or reassurance. Nor was she wallowing in self-pity. This was just a blunt admission of fact.

"No. We not go there again. Still, I not leave without knowing what happen to Edlin and Peace. If they live, they live expecting us."

Wendee spoke quickly. "I agree with Firekeeper. I just can't believe in my heart of hearts that Edlin is dead. Selfishly," she gave a self-deprecating smile, "I can't bear the idea of going back to the North Woods and telling Duchess Kestrel that I don't know whether her grandson and lineage heir is living or dead."

"I agree with Wendee," Doc said. "House Kestrel has been good to me. I owe them at least confirmation of Edlin's status. The question is what do we do?"

Derian had been thinking about this and was about to outline a proposed plan of action when Elise spoke as authoritatively as if she were Grand Duchess Rosene.

"We concentrate on the problem that we can deal with," she said. "Citrine. Xarxius may or may not successfully plead our cause to the Healed One. I am comforted that we know our advocate is a man with a sense of justice, but that does not mean his master is one as well."

"Or," Wendee added tremulously, "that if he is that Consolor Melina's influence will permit him to be so."

"Right," Elise said, nodding crisply. "Doc, how long will Firekeeper be bedridden?"

"Several days, if I have my way," the knight said in a tone that left no doubt that he would. "Blind Seer broke none of her bones when he dragged her, but those muscles he tore will mend better if she isn't pulling at them."

"Fine," Elise said. "Do you have a problem with Firekeeper being outside as long as she isn't walking?"

"No . . ."

Doc looked rather uncertain, and Elise hastened to explain.

"I want Firekeeper to coordinate some of her bird friends to pin down where Citrine spends her days. It will be easier to do so if Firekeeper isn't inside."

"That's fine with me," Doc said, "if Firekeeper promises to give her parole."

Firekeeper clearly had no idea what the word meant, but she was still smarting from his earlier scolding and promptly replied:

"If I am not to walk I not walk, run, or even crawl."

"That's good enough for me," Doc said with a slight smile.

"Firekeeper," Elise said, "can you get the birds to work with you?"

"Bee Biter will," Firekeeper said with that hesitancy she always showed when asked to turn her Royal allies to human cause. "I cannot promise other."

"It's a start," Elise said. "I know you don't like doing this, but the rest of us cannot poke around asking questions. It would have been hard at the best of times, but the last several days have not been the best. The embassy was attacked again—nothing more serious than a few broken windows, but Ambassador Redbriar is adamant that we take precautions."

Wendee nodded.

"I'm already paying one of Hasamemorri's maids to do most of our shopping," she said, "and Oculios has said it is no longer safe for him to bring his goods here but insists that we send someone to fetch them."

Firekeeper looked worried. Derian suspected that she was thinking of how some of the Beasts were already looking for any excuse to reopen their abandoned war with humanity. Such a use of the wingéd folk could be considered cause.

"I will do my best" was all she said.

Elise smiled briefly, then returned to explaining her plan.

"Meanwhile, I want Derian and Wendee to put together packs and things so that we can get out of Dragon's Breath quickly."

Derian grinned at her.

"My thought exactly," he said, quite pleased. "We're suspicious characters now. We can't expect an easy escape."

"Or any escape at all," Doc added. "That's what worries me. I wish we could relocate to outside the wall of the city. This last escapade of Firekeeper's makes us even less secure than before."

"I'm working on that," Elise said, her grin nearly as bright as Derian's had been. "I think we may 'quarrel' with our landlady. I want to make certain that we have somewhere relatively safe to go when we do. I'm going to put Ambassador Redbriar to work on the matter. This is one case where the unrest in the local population may work to our favor. It makes sense that we move."

"It sounds good," Doc said, speaking for them all. "A well thought-through plan. You reminded me of your father as you spoke."

Elise acknowledged Doc's praise without the faintest blush and Derian wondered a trace sadly if she had ceased to care for Doc. He hadn't thought the end of that ill-omened romance would make him grieve, but the thought of it did.

"I had to do something," Elise replied practically, "while you and Firekeeper slept out the day."

"Night again now," Firekeeper said, dropping a hand to scratch Blind Seer behind one ear. What she added next made Derian wonder if she had been injured more severely than even Doc could diagnose. "I wonder where the comet is and what it sees."

"XARXIUS IS TRUSTWORTHY," said Columi the day after Toriovico had sent him on his mission, "at least as far as I can tell, that is. I've sounded him out and he loves Consolor Melina even less than I do.

"Of course," the Lapidary went on, suddenly dubious, "Xarxius could be playing a very deep game. He could want to lead me on to my own destruction. Still, from what he said, he doesn't think Consolor Melina's ambitions are focused on what will bring the best for New Kelvin—rather for herself with New Kelvin as the horse she'll ride to some other goal. New Kelvin's good is her good—but only for as long as she needs it. Then she'll let us founder."

Toriovico nodded. He'd allowed Columi to run on, though he longed to get to the point. He could see that the emeritus Prime was still overcharged with the latent tension of his mission.

"I doubt," Toriovico said a trace dryly, "that we can count on Xarxius making a more open declaration. Indeed, I'd trust him less if he did so, for such might be a trap. I will meet with him. Happily, he has already given me a good reason. Citrine Shield's guardian has requested her return. Xarxius brought the matter to me rather than to Melina."

"And have you mentioned this request to Consolor Melina?" Columi asked, his eyes round in apprehension.

"No," Toriovico replied. "I have not. Therefore, I may act on the matter as I see fit without risking that the lady will think her hold on me weakening."

Columi looked uncertain as to what Citrine's fate might have to do with their larger problem. Toriovico chuckled.

"Come with me," he suggested. "All your questions will be answered and it is time we took a risk or two.

"Besides," he added darkly, "if something happens to me, it is better that there be those ready to carry out my plans."

THAT XARXIUS FOUND BOTH TIME and privacy to meet with them might simply have been an indication of his respect for the Healed One. Toriovico chose to be encouraged to think it rather more. After all, Xarxius was skilled in the intricate games of trade and politics. He was not likely to have missed Columi's probing.

"The reason for this council," Toriovico began after the necessary formalities and rituals that hobbled even the least meeting were concluded, "should any inquire, is bound within veils of secrecy. If pressed, you may hint that I sought your mutual advice on an appropriate Harvest Festival gift for my wife.

"Recently," Toriovico went on, spinning the cover story as if it were a tale, "I have been consulting with Columi as to an appropriate gift for Consolor Melina. Knowing her fondness for gemstones, taking one of our greatest and most senior Lapidaries into my confidence was only reasonable. We examined several possibilities before Columi had a brilliant idea."

"I did, Honored One?" Columi said amused.

"You did," Toriovico said with solemnity. "You recalled the rumors that Waterland was offering potentially magical artifacts for trade. We then decided to consult Xarxius, who—other than Dimiria of the Stargazers—would have the best idea of what precisely is offered for sale and whether among those items is one which would delight my wife."

Xarxius nodded slowly.

"And so here we are," he said, "but from how you began this speech, I think you have more than gift shopping in mind."

Toriovico nodded, running his hand through his hair, thinking with the incongruity that so often interrupted serious matters that soon it would be time for the hairdressers to highlight the rich green with yellow and orange.

"I do," he said. "Several days ago, you brought to me a request from Lady Archer of Hawk Haven requesting assistance in assuring the return of her ward, Citrine Shield. I have reflected on that matter and have decided that Citrine should indeed be returned to those who have legal right to her."

"You have, Honored One?" Xarxius said. "And have you spoken to Consolor Melina about the matter?"

"I have not," Toriovico said, "nor will I. You see, Xarxius, there will be a price for the child's return, and I do not think her mother will approve."

Both Xarxius and Columi were listening with active interest, neither holding enough pieces of the puzzle to guess where Toriovico was headed. Still, neither was looking as if he had suddenly gone insane.

Torio was relieved. The Healed One took more interest in government than many who viewed his position from outside the system realized—indeed, more than many inside realized. They chose to see his attendance at meetings as largely ceremonial rather than functional.

This was how it should be, for such little deceptions permitted the Healed One to fulfill his inherited mission of keeping certain lines of research in check. Yet it had the drawback that when the Healed One must act as a ruler rather than a figure of awe and majesty, some found the transformation as shocking as if a trained dog had risen onto its back legs and started giving commands.

But neither Xarxius nor Columi seemed inclined to shock or confusion, and Toriovico permitted himself to marginally relax.

"I have reason to believe," Toriovico said, "that Consolor Melina is involved in some complicated plot whose end result would not serve to the long-term benefit of New Kelvin."

He went on then to brief Xarxius as to Melina's disappearances, the inspection of her soiled robes, the research he had done in the Restorer's writings and which Columi had supplemented. When Xarxius listened thoughtfully, asking no more questions than were absolutely necessary to clarify some point, Toriovico went on to explain why he had kept his suspicions secret.

"First," he said, "I would know what my wife does, the better to prevent some future action along similar lines. Second, I cannot speak too publicly of my fears for I do not know who she has in her hold. Third, having been in her hold myself, I have no wish to be made her slave again. Too public speech would risk that. Sadly, Healed Ones have been known to go insane. Consolor Melina has read enough of our history to learn that. She would have ample allies to support her claim that I had merely suffered a lapse of my mental faculties—and I fear that as soon as she worked her charm on me I would be among those most heatedly supporting her claim."

Xarxius nodded slowly.

"You have planned well and carefully, Honored One, and I am deeply grateful that you have taken me into your trust. May I ask what—other than Columi's word—made you do so?"

Torio smiled, a grim and wistful expression.

"I recalled your daring to speak out against Melina's wishes when others enthusiastically supported her. I recalled, too, how often you kept from her presence. Your role as Dragon's Claw explained some of this, but when my mind cleared I was able to consider how much your travel away from the capital had increased of late. Most pointedly, I recalled—then confirmed from observation—how you avoided meeting the lady's gaze, though normally you are fond of using your own forlorn visage to great advantage."

Xarxius bowed his head in acknowledgment.

"I can only pray that the lady herself was not so observant. Past evidence shows that she can overextend her power over others and that her arrogance is such that she does not notice."

Toriovico felt rather hurt, as if Xarxius was dismissing the usefulness of his own carefully maintained charade. Xarxius did not miss the change in the Healed One's expression and hastened to explain.

"I did not refer to you, Honored One, but rather to another upon whom Melina laid her will and then let him slip."

"Who is this other?" Toriovico asked sharply. "Perhaps we can add him to those who share our secrets."

"I fear he is not among us," Xarxius said. "The man I refer to is Grateful Peace, the former Dragon's Eye. Unlike you Grateful Peace did not break Melina's hold through his own art. Rather she let her attention to him lapse.

It seems she mistook the self-effacement he practiced as an indication that he was unimportant, a mere messenger for greater rulers."

"And later Grateful Peace attempted to defeat her aims," Toriovico said, understanding. "Well, wherever he is he may someday feel satisfaction for I plan to take a page from his book."

"Peace was an Illuminator before he took to other arts," Xarxius said, friend speaking of friend now. "I think he would like your choice of metaphor—almost as much as knowing that in the end you understood and approved his actions."

"Perhaps when all of this is over and the truth out," Toriovico said, "we can bring Grateful Peace home again, but such hopes must wait until we have succeeded in ousting this foreigner who has made herself my wife and has tried to take my rulership from me."

He was fierce then, remembering the wrongs done to himself as well as to others, and in that fierceness he spelled out the details of his plan.

"I have told you," he said, nodding to Xarxius, "how Columi and I have tried to discover where it is that Melina goes on these nocturnal ventures and how despite our best efforts we have failed. For very good reasons, I cannot recruit anyone from the watchers already among us. With their Eye gone, it is impossible to know who might have been subverted and my own watchers would have been among the first Melina took care to place her own advocates among.

"Indeed, after careful thought I would prefer not to recruit any from Thendulla Lypella. Consolor Melina's powers seem limited to those she has met and fascinated. Therefore, those whose enmity of her is without doubt remain our best allies."

Xarxius was nodding now, but Columi looked uncertain—though Toriovico's comment about taking a page from Grateful Peace's book might have offered the Dragon's Claw a hint. Toriovico hastened to clarify, not wishing this faithful adherent to feel slighted.

"When Xarxius told me about Lady Archer's request to regain Citrine Shield, he also told me who had accompanied Lady Archer to Dragon's Breath."

Columi raised a hand.

"Slowly, Honored One. I think it would be best if you clarified even more. Who is this Lady Archer? How did she come to Dragon's Breath at all?"

Between them, Xarxius and Toriovico explained the intricacies, then Toriovico resumed:

"It seems peculiar to me that this group, who left New Kelvin in such haste and under such unhappy circumstances, should return to Dragon's Breath with, of all things, Melina's birth daughter in their keeping. The child is said to be deeply troubled emotionally—I have seen evidence of her pain myself. Perhaps they hoped for something from Melina and the girl's running away was something they had not anticipated."

Toriovico made a sweeping gesture that wiped the past away in one decisive blow.

"What is most important are three factors. First, they are here and have no love for Melina, so little that it is doubtful that they are her allies. Second, they have in their number one whose assets are said to include skill at tracking and the companionship of a large wolf. This creature might track by scent what its mistress misses by sight. Third, we have something they want—the child Citrine. My plan is to offer them Citrine in return for their help in finding where Melina goes and what she is doing."

There was silence then, but not shocked silence, rather the careful pondering of the two older men weighing Toriovico's plan, testing it, and, judging from the approval that crept into both of their features, finding it sound.

"Interesting," Xarxius said at last, "and possibly quite valid. Where do we begin?"

Toriovico spread his hands on the table, feeling tension flow from him as water from a burst dam. He knew it would return as they worked through the details, but for now all he felt was considerable relief.

"Xarxius, you have been contacted by Lady Archer. I suggest that you meet with her—perhaps in the Hawk Haven embassy. It would be beneath your dignity to go to this boardinghouse where they are staying, yet I would not have Consolor Melina hear of her enemies coming into the Earth Spires."

Xarxius nodded.

"I have a good relationship with Ambassador Redbriar. I even think I can assure use of a parlor where eavesdropping would be quite difficult."

Torio turned to Columi.

"Your task, old friend, will be even more difficult."

Columi paled, then straightened in his seat.

"Whatever the Honored One wishes."

"You must keep silence," Torio said, "all the while acting the garrulous old man overwhelmed by honors, busy selecting stones and metals for a truly elaborate piece of jewelry."

❦

PEACE AND EDLIN were drafting a map section when Consolor Melina burst into their cave unannounced and obviously in a foul temper.

"I want to know," she hissed, motioning the guards back out of hearing range, "about this map."

She dropped a map segment onto the work table between them. The map showed a section of the artificial tunnels beneath Thendulla Lypella, focusing on a route that permitted subterranean travel from the Cloud Touching Spire to the Dragon Speaker's residence.

"I followed your directions," Melina continued, "and came up in the kitchen of the next building over. Happily, the hour was late and no one was present."

Peace studied the map.

"I assure you," he said. "This map is drawn as I requested and according to the best of my memory."

"The best of your memory," Melina taunted. "I had heard you were infallible. This is failure!"

Peace forgot himself, forgot the threat he had been living under during these long days of captivity. Immersed as he had been in knowledge acquired as the Dragon's Eye, he had become that important personage once more.

He glowered at Melina, forgetting she was now the Consolor and his captor. She was only the rather annoying foreigner who had thought him a minor servant of a greater master.

"I am pleased," he said with stiff arrogance, "that my reputation is such, but I assure you, I have never claimed infallibility. Indeed, if you would bother to recall, you would remember that I cautioned you that my memory of those passages was less than perfect. My Speaker never needed to skulk unseen to report to the Healed One, nor would the Healed One so lower himself."

Melina went starkly white beneath her facial ornamentation, but only when Peace heard Edlin whisper, "I say, easy, my good man," did he realize what he had done.

Frozen, one element in a tableau in which even the uncomprehending guards did not stir, Grateful Peace waited to hear his doom pronounced. Gradually, color flowed back into Melina's face and she pursed her lips in thought.

"You did warn me," she said. "I remember now."

Something in her inflection told Peace that she had not only remembered his caution, she had remembered how she had pushed him to outline that particular section when he would have preferred to stay with areas he better knew. But Peace also knew that Melina would not forget how he had insulted her. Clearly, she had decided she still needed him, otherwise Idalia would have been given her reward.

His fear intensified as he faced off against an opponent who could calculate so carefully even when in the grip of fury.

"Have you," Melina said stiffly, "any suggestions as to how such errors might be avoided in the future?"

"If I cannot be permitted to stay with those areas I know well," Peace replied promptly, knowing nothing was to be gained from groveling or apologies, "then I would need to tour the appropriate regions. With that stimulus, I am certain I would remember more accurately."

"And perhaps slip away?"

"I am certain that you could prevent that. You have taken great care thus far."

He gestured around the cave as he spoke.

True to her promise to Edlin, Melina had made the cave more comfortable for its inhabitants, but they were permitted nothing that they could turn into a weapon. The table at which they now sat was a perfect example.

Rather than resting on four sturdy legs, this table was supported by thin pieces of flexible wood cross-jointed to each other in an elongated X. The individual legs might have remained unbroken for a blow or two, but as their guards always wore at least light armor and were never without helmets, those blows would have been useless. The tabletop itself was made from a slice of wood hardly thicker than a piece of paper. It served to steady Edlin's drawing paper or the vessels that held their meals, but could be used for nothing else.

Their chairs were made along a model similar to the table, but with seats of stretched canvas rather than wood. Their beds were pallets stuffed with wool and rags, and were taken away each morning. The prisoners ate from translucent porcelain as fragile as eggshells. Even their simple clay cup had been replaced with a vessel so delicate that they almost feared to use it.

The chamber pot could not be made of such fragile stuff, so it was bolted to the stone wall, its lid attached by a short hank of chain. When Edlin wished to sharpen one of his drawing implements, he must ask a guard for assistance.

Moreover, Peace and Edlin had been assured that if every item in the cave was not intact for each of the frequent but erratic inspections Idalia conducted they would find themselves deprived of the item in question. Thus the lanterns, which with their reservoir of burning oil offered a logical temptation, were left untouched lest they find themselves sitting in the dark.

Melina glanced around at the precautions and smiled a slow smile of satisfaction.

"You are right," she said. "I do believe your escape could be prevented. Let me put some thought to the matter. In the meantime, I desire that you review this flawed map and consider where your memory might have led you astray."

Peace bowed his head in polite humility.

"As you wish," his lips said, but his heart was singing at the prospect of getting even a few steps away from this cave. Surely once on his own ground again he could manage to win them their freedom.

XXXI

THE MESSENGER from Ambassador Redbriar was clearly nervous, but he delivered his mistress's words with perfect polish.

"Ambassador Redbriar is in possession of news that she does not wish to commit to writing," he said. "If you would call on her in an hour's time, she would be willing to receive you. An important guest will also be present."

Elise nodded, feeling her breath come fast as she realized who that guest must be.

"Tell the ambassador that I will be there. May I bring one or more of my companions?"

"She advises that you do so. As your own company's experiences have shown, the streets are not safe for foreigners traveling alone."

Elise did not ask why Violet Redbriar had not sent an escort. The embassy had been the focus of much of the local unrest. Foreigners escorted by more foreigners might upset the precarious calm the local guard had managed to maintain.

Derian had answered the door when the messenger had arrived. Now he stood by just in case there was trouble when the messenger departed.

"He's off safely," he reported, closing the peephole they'd installed in the front door. "Had a couple of men waiting for him."

Elise nodded, considering various options.

"Will you come with me, Derian?"

"Of course."

"And see if Doc will come, too."

Sir Jared appeared at that moment.

"If you can excuse me," he said apologetically, "I should remain here. Firekeeper is restive and I don't trust her to stay put without me to remind her of her duty. Besides, Wendee should not be left alone."

Elise sighed her agreement, though privately she did not think that anyone left with Firekeeper and Blind Seer nearby—even if the wolf-woman *was* wounded—could be considered alone.

"Derian," Elise said, turning toward the redhead so that Doc would not see her disappointment, "do you think we can get a litter?"

"No," Derian replied promptly. "Even Oculios isn't speaking to us anymore. Hasamemorri has exhausted her credit with the neighbors just keeping her house safe and her maids unmolested when they do the shopping."

"We must attend this meeting, even if we must walk," Elise said. "The guest of whom the messenger spoke must be Xarxius or someone speaking for him."

"It could be Prime Nstasius," Doc reminded. "Ambassador Redbriar has relayed his messages to us."

"True," Elise admitted, "but Nstasius has been much less interested in playing at politics since we of Hawk Haven became so publicly unpopular."

Doc nodded. Elise felt a surge of warmth when she realized that Sir Jared had been trying to cushion her against disappointment.

"I can carry my walking stick," Derian said. "It served me well enough when Doc and I were assaulted. It's better than a sword in that it doesn't look like a weapon. Do you think you could handle a similar weapon?"

"Perhaps," Elise replied dubiously, "but a bow is the only weapon I've practiced with and that would be more obvious than a sword."

They had drifted into the kitchen as they talked in order to include Wendee and Firekeeper in the discussion. Now Firekeeper spoke from where she rested propped up on a cot just outside the kitchen door.

"I have weapon for you," she said, thumping Blind Seer on one flank. "He can wear collar and be a dog."

The wolf snapped at Firekeeper's hand, but when he turned his blue-eyed gaze upon Elise he wagged his tail in a lazy agreement with his friend's plan.

"And I see if I can get Bee Biter to watch from above," the wolf-woman continued. "He should be coming soon."

"Bee Biter's too small to be much help," Derian said dubiously. "Not like Elation would have been."

Firekeeper shrugged, but persisted.

"Bee Biter can watch and no one notice. If someone is hurt, he know and come for help. If someone is taken, Bee Biter can follow. We have too many missing pack members to lose another."

From Firekeeper this was a veritable oration. Derian and Elise accepted the wolf-woman's suggestion, not so much because they were certain the kestrel could help, but because it was clear Firekeeper would wait with an easier mind if she knew they were being watched over.

Besides, Elise thought as she hurried into her room to comb her hair and put on a fresh dress, *how could we stop her from sending him?*

Perhaps because of these precautions, perhaps because Dragon's Breath's city guard was out in force, Elise and Derian arrived at the Hawk Haven embassy physically unscathed, though their ears were burning from the crude insults that had been shouted at them from people who remained within their houses to be safe from Blind Seer.

Elise thought it was a relief that Derian had understood only a portion of what had been said—his command of colloquial New Kelvinese being a bit less than his formal—but what he had understood had brought the color mantling high in his cheeks.

If Derian had understood some of the things being implied about them both she doubted he would have settled for blushing. His battle with the mob had not taught him fear, but instead had raised his martial ardor and his confidence in his abilities.

Elise herself had kept her blushes at bay by imagining the retorts Grandmother Rosene would likely hurl back. It had been a frail defense, but sufficient to keep her walking forward in the force of the storm of hatred and her own rising fear.

The embassy's front door was opened by an armed retainer. The man nearly slammed the door in their faces when he caught a glimpse of Blind Seer, even though the wolf was sitting politely at Elise's side on the steps, doing his best—though not very convincing—imitation of a docile dog.

Derian thrust his walking stick into the aperture and announced briskly, "Lady Elise Archer and Counselor Derian to see the ambassador. I believe we are expected."

The retainer admitted them, sidling to keep from turning his back on Blind Seer. Elise had learned enough about the wolf's body language to realize that Blind Seer's slightly gaping jaw and rhythmic panting was the lupine equivalent of loud laughter, but the man could not. She resisted an impulse to boot the wolf in the ribs as she had seen Firekeeper do on similar occasions. That might be taking too great a liberty.

Instead Elise glanced past the doorkeeper and saw the ambassador emerging from her study. Violet Redbriar, too, was taken aback by the presence of the wolf, but unlike her retainer she controlled her reaction with admirable poise.

"Lady Archer, Counselor Derian," she said, offering each of them a polite inclination of her head by way of greeting. "This must be Blind Seer. I have heard much about him."

The wolf stood and stretched in a slight bow of his own before sitting again. The acknowledgment of her introduction was so obvious that Elise could see Violet catch herself before she bowed in return.

"Prime Xarxius arrived shortly before you," Ambassador Redbriar said, "and is waiting in one of the front parlors. Will Blind Seer accompany you, or shall I see him made comfortable in the yard?"

"He's coming with us, thank you," Elise said. "Don't worry. He's completely house-trained."

Elise could have sworn that the stare the blue-eyed wolf turned on her was distinctly annoyed, but other than offering an apology for the affront by dropping her hand onto his head for a quick moment, she let it go by.

The parlor into which they were taken was furnished in a mixture of New Kelvinese and Hawk Haven styles that proved surprisingly pleasing to the eye. Elise did not doubt that many of the choices had been Ambassador Redbriar's own. They bore a similar style to the prose in the book with which Violet had gifted Derian, though in arrangement of physical space rather than words.

Xarxius rose from a chair with a spare, carved wooden back after the New Kelvinese style, and offered them all—including Blind Seer—versions of the complicated New Kelvinese bow calculated to a nicety for their social status relative to his own. Since Elise's teachers had taught her that the Dragon Speaker's Three were about the equivalent of dukes in Hawk Haven this meant that their own response should be even more prolonged and elaborate.

I suppose the idea is, Elise thought, working through the motions Peace had tutored them all in and pleased to see that Derian was handling his own quite well, *that the lower-ranking people will spend so much energy on remembering the exact form of their reply that they won't have time to think about what they're going to say.*

It was a pleasing notion and she filed it away for later reflection.

Once greetings were over and refreshments proffered, Ambassador Redbriar surprised Elise by making excuses that she was needed elsewhere. She left briskly, shutting the door behind her with a finality that suggested no one would be listening in on the conversation.

"I told the ambassador," Xarxius began almost apologetically, "that what I must speak of to you was strictly private. Violet Redbriar has greatly benefitted from her association with my kingdom and complied without argument."

"I see," Elise said, though honestly she did not. "Ambassador Redbriar's letter said that you have information for us regarding Citrine. Is my ward well?"

"Citrine is physically healthy," Xarxius said, "but troubled in her mind. Yet I believe that this latter affliction dated to before her coming to us— before even you had custody of her."

Elise nodded, more as an acknowledgment that she understood that Xarxius was offering no insult to her and her companions than in agreement.

"Then Consolor Melina is being kind to her?"

"I am not intimate with the domestic life of the Healed One's family," Xarxius replied with a faint note of reproof, "but I have not heard otherwise. Citrine has a slave of her own and new robes. As the girl is frequently seen about Thendulla Lypella and is even taking dancing lessons with some of the other children, I must believe she is not abused."

Elise thought, *Poor Citrine, running away to cling to her mother's skirts and being farmed out to dance instructors and maids just like always!*

Even as she framed the thought, Elise wondered if Xarxius had intended her to reach that conclusion. The man had a reputation for cunning. He might want her to know that Citrine's situation was less than everything for which the girl might have hoped. Very well, Elise would remember that.

"As requested," Xarxius went on, "the matter of Citrine's custody has been reviewed. The Healed One himself took an interest and has ruled that your claim is valid. The child will be returned to you . . . ."

An "if" was so obviously forthcoming that Elise withheld any comment, though Derian, perhaps because he was less schooled in the nuances of New Kelvinese, let a short, delighted laugh slip through his lips before catching Elise's expression and sobering.

"If," Xarxius said a flicker of a smile incongruous on his hound-dog lips, "you and your companions would agree to do a service for us."

"And this is?" Elise said, promising nothing.

"We wish you to find where Consolor Melina has been taking herself when she vanishes from her rooms at night," Xarxius said, clearly aware that his words were going to open a floodgate of questions, "and then we will progress from there."

FIREKEEPER ALREADY KNEW the gist of what Elise would report, for Blind Seer had filled her in when he returned. The wolf did not understand New Kelvinese very well, but Elise and Derian had discussed the matter in low voices all the walk back to Hasamemorri's house.

Melina was up to something that even her new pack did not like. They could not find her, but trusted in Firekeeper's skills and Blind Seer's nose to search her out. Although Firekeeper didn't feel very strong yet, no cuts and bruises won through her own foolishness were going to keep her from carrying out this commission.

Yet the others must chatter and chatter. Humans, Firekeeper thought in fond exasperation, surely must be kin to squirrels.

At last the debate took a turn that interested Firekeeper and she propped herself up on her pillows to listen more attentively.

"On impulse," Elise said, her tones still filled with indecision, "I confided in Xarxius that Edlin and Peace were missing."

"Peace?" Wendee asked sharply. "Not Jalarios?"

Elise looked even more unhappy.

"Peace," she agreed. "I felt Xarxius could not help us without knowing who it was we sought. I'm worried I've overstepped."

"Why?" Firekeeper asked. "We want Peace and Edlin back. Xarxius can help us find them."

Elise nodded. "I know. That's why I told him, but I'm afraid that now that Xarxius knows how much we want to get into those tunnels and make a search for ourselves he might become less eager to return Citrine to us."

"Why would he?" Wendee asked. "Didn't he say that the Healed One acknowledged your claim?"

"He did," Elise said, "but I could not help but recall that Citrine is Sapphire's birth sister. If Xarxius thought he could get our help without turning Citrine over to us, then what a hostage he would have."

"I think," Doc protested mildly, "you may underestimate the Crown Princess's ability to withstand such persuasion."

"No, Doc," Elise said sternly. "I think Sapphire would show remarkable tenacity, far more than the New Kelvinese might realize. Who would suffer for this in the end? Citrine. It is best that we get her away from where she will be a pawn to others' ambitions."

There was an uncomfortable silence that Firekeeper broke.

"I think you do right. Edlin and Peace might not be in tunnels. Xarxius can find."

"And Peace did say," Derian added, his tones less than certain, "that he and Xarxius were friends as well as fellows in this Dragon's Three. He may help us for that reason alone."

"I hope so," Elise said, "but it does mean we must take additional care."

"Speaking of which," Derian said, "I have a question for Doc. I know what Firekeeper insists, but do you think she's ready for an outing like this? I had the distinct impression that, though he of course said nothing directly, Xarxius thought we might run into more than rock and empty corridor down there."

Firekeeper started to insist on her readiness, but restrained herself. There would be time enough to argue after Doc said she was unwell—if he did.

"I think she might manage," Doc replied, giving Firekeeper a critical look, "especially if I use more of my talent on her this evening. You say this venture is not going to begin tonight?"

"No," Derian replied. "Xarxius made the interesting point that Melina usually can be found during the day—though she has taken to indulging in long naps, as if she isn't getting quite enough sleep at night. To prowl in these new haunts of hers when she is about is not necessary—not with Blind Seer's ability to track by scent."

"Then we are set," Elise said, "as soon as one more question is answered: Do we trust Xarxius or is this an elaborate attempt to make several more of our number conveniently disappear?"

"It would hardly be convenient," Derian protested. "Our families know where we went. Most of us have been writing home. We were negotiating with local merchants before the city's mood got so ugly. Anyhow, Xarxius came to our aid when Firekeeper got tangled up with those men and their dogs. I'm inclined to trust him."

Firekeeper watched anxiously, not certain what she would do if the decision went against the plan, and was relieved to see each head dip in a nod of agreement.

"Then we are committed," Elise said, rising from her chair. "Xarxius told me to put a lantern turned up bright close behind the shutter where its glimmer could be seen from the street."

She rose and did so.

"The next move is theirs."

SNEAKING AFTER MOTHER took a great deal of courage, but Citrine's curiosity had become so all consuming that she could not sleep. Nor was the girl watched as closely at night. Rillon slept in the servants' quarters. For her own reasons, Melina discouraged the servants from wandering.

Citrine had been told to ring for Mother's servant, Tipi, rather than Rillon if she needed anything at night—an instruction that had been accompanied by a clear hint that such summons would be unwelcome unless the need was serious.

So after she had been washed for bed, Citrine had the night to herself. There were earth-toned robes among the garments in her new wardrobe. Her dancing slippers were soft yet strong and made no sound against the floor. She cast a dark scarf over the red-gold light of her hair, smudged paint over the fairness of her skin, and played at being a shadow.

Dancing was honing the remaining baby fat from her, revealing, if Citrine had known what to look for, the first similarities between her mother's features and her own. Dancing had made the girl lighter on her feet as well. She amazed herself the first time she skirted a night guard and he didn't see her. Within a few nights of such games, Citrine grew more confident.

Perhaps knowing Firekeeper and regularly witnessing the seemingly miraculous way the wolf-woman slipped in and out of shadows gave Citrine confidence. Perhaps it was merely that the girl had grown accustomed to no one paying her any heed and so no one did. For whatever reason, Citrine soon developed sufficient confidence in her abilities that she did not hesitate to follow Consolor Melina on her nocturnal prowls.

The first time Citrine stopped short of following Mother through the trapdoor in the cellar floor. The next she tested the door and discovered that not only could she lift it, the door had been recently oiled and moved without a sound.

Citrine had heard the tale of how Grateful Peace had led the others into Thendulla Lypella via such tunnels the winter before. It did not surprise her that her mother, always the mistress of so many secrets, should use similar routes. What Citrine desired was not the knowledge that her mother had secrets, but to know what those secrets were.

Citrine could not see in the dark, but then neither could Mother. Several lanterns, all filled with oil, waited at the base of the ladder. There were a few candle lanterns as well.

Citrine took one of these along with one of the tinder boxes so conveniently provided, but she did not light the candle. Instead she trusted to her mother's light and her own shadows. After all, her reason for descending beneath the Earth Spires was to learn what Mother was doing. Why should she stray?

Melina never looked behind her, but moved as purposefully as if she were walking through more conventional streets. Citrine followed, skirting heaps of stone that concealed nearly invisible tunnels, ducking through doors that opened into corridors that gradually changed in character from the normal cellars and corridors of the city above to caverns and tunnels sculpted by primeval heat.

Eventually a dull glow shone from ahead. Noises—first unrecognizable, later revealed as scraps of conversation carried by the unpredictable acoustics of the underground—broke the relative silence through which they had traveled. Citrine dropped back, unwilling to lose her mother, but even less willing to be discovered.

Peeking around a corner, Citrine glimpsed what could only be called an underground town inhabiting a vast cavern dimly lit by hundreds of lanterns.

No one seemed surprised to see the Consolor of the Healed One in such a hidden place. Indeed, Melina was greeted with—if possible—even more deference and respect than she was in the upper world. A stiffly elegant lady emerged from a roofless hut set slightly apart from the other structures, many of which were little more than spaces marked off from those surrounding them by lines of rocks or some other largely symbolic barrier.

Citrine was reminded of the way she and her friends had played house just like this, and how their imaginations had made the pretend walls so real that they felt a shiver when someone stepped over and through a wall, rather than using the gap that stood for a door. The stiff lady must be very important if she had real walls instead of pretend.

Mother and this woman walked into one of several tunnels that branched off from the larger cavern. Citrine longed to follow, but didn't dare. The "town" was not thickly populated, but there were enough people moving about that Citrine felt certain she would be seen. There seemed to be few children here, and most of these were infants tied to their mother's backs or resting in makeshift cradles, rather like the dolls with which Citrine and her playmates had populated their pretend houses.

She waited, torn between a desire to follow Mother and fear of discovery for what seemed like an eternity. She had just decided that discovery was preferable when Mother and the stiff lady re-emerged. Mother carried several rolled pieces of paper in her hand. They paused under a cluster of lanterns to consult over these, then Melina handed the lady one of the rolls.

Each woman collected a pair of the townspeople, each of whom carried a lantern. Then, after exchanging formal New Kelvinese farewells, they went their separate ways. The stiff lady went off to yet another tunnel while Melina, to Citrine's infinite relief and satisfaction, returned the way she had come.

The next several hours had been spent creeping along behind while Mother followed what was written on the rolls of paper. She hadn't said much, so Citrine had only the vaguest idea of what they were doing. It reminded her of a scavenger hunt, though, and she wished she knew what they were after so she could help.

This first venture laid the pattern for the next several nights. Citrine even took to sneaking ahead to the room in the Cloud Touching Spire with the trapdoor so she wouldn't miss Melina's departure. Melina never noticed her shadow, but being in her company somewhat satisfied the gaping hole in Citrine's heart. The voices in the girl's head stopped arguing so much.

The only person who wasn't happy was Citrine's dance instructor. He was so frustrated by her exhaustion and inability to follow his instructions that he risked Toriovico's anger and demoted the girl from a graceful skittering leaf to a dumpy apple who did little more than stand near the edges of the stage and rise and fall with the music.

Citrine didn't even care. She pretended that Melina knew her daughter was accompanying her and made up elaborate conversations between them. The hard part was when Melina did or said something that didn't fit in with

Citrine's imaginings. That was what happened on the night Citrine remembered about Edlin and Peace.

The two men had become like dreams to her since her arrival in Thendulla Lypella. All her companions had, all part of some uncomfortable version of reality she didn't care to recall. It raised too many questions.

But during this particular night, Citrine was forced to remember. She knew that something had not been right the night before. Mother had climbed up a series of rungs set into a cellar wall with the same brisk confidence with which she had essayed a dozen similar sets. This time, however, she raised the trapdoor over her head and let it down so quickly that, had the hinges been better oiled, it would have slammed.

Mother had then motioned the lantern bearers to a retreat so rapid that Citrine, half drowsing in her dream conversation, had nearly been discovered.

Other nights Mother had parted from the lantern bearers and gone back to the Cloud Touching Spire unescorted. This time she went back to the subterranean town and popped down one of the side tunnels. When she had returned, she had looked less angry.

The next night, Citrine was padding along behind in a fashion that was rapidly becoming routine when her daydream was interrupted by the sound of voices. They were speaking so quietly and guardedly that she immediately knew they were not inside her head. Those voices were never less than outspoken.

She expected to see Mother hide or run or motion for a retreat, all things she had done when they had unexpectedly encountered some servant or laborer in the more trafficked sections of the tunnels. This time Mother merely paused, listened, then nodded in a sharp, self-satisfied fashion and motioned for her lantern bearers to step lively.

Within a few twists of the tunnel they had encountered a group twice the size of their own headed by the stiff woman. Citrine had learned that her name was Idalia. Her name seemed vaguely familiar, but it was a familiarity associated with discomfort so Citrine didn't think too hard about where she'd heard it.

Idalia was accompanied by several people who, at first, Citrine believed were lantern bearers like Mother's. She noticed differences right away.

These were all men—big men—whereas Mother's lantern bearers were often women, and often seemed chosen for their lightness of foot and willingness to take orders without question. Idalia's escort all wore leather armor and carried in addition to their lanterns short spears.

These were being used to prod along the last segment of the group, two figures in kilted robes who moved with a strange, halting gait. When they drew closer, Citrine realized that they walked funny because they were hobbled about their ankles. With mild curiosity, she looked more closely, wondering what they had done to merit such treatment. That was when she realized that she was looking at Edlin Norwood and Grateful Peace.

Both men looked thinner than when she had last seen them and more pale. Edlin carried a writing tablet and a short pencil. Peace was empty-handed, his one arm bent behind his back and bound. He moved as if he hurt and there were reddish lines near his mouth.

In a moment, Citrine understood why. As Idalia's party paused to greet Consolor Melina, the guard closest to Peace took a hank of twisted cloth that hung around the former Dragon's Eye's throat and used it to gag him.

"I didn't want him to try anything clever," Idalia explained in a stuffy, puffed-up fashion that made Citrine really dislike her. "There are all sorts of levers and pressure plates down here as we've discovered—often to our loss. I didn't want him hitting one or calling out through some hidden speaking tube."

Even Citrine could see how stupid Peace would need to be to do any of these things, hobbled as he was and with Idalia's spear-holding guards behind him, but Melina only nodded approvingly, as if what Idalia had said was the smartest thing in the world.

"We cannot be too cautious," Mother agreed, "especially with a proven traitor. Have you located anything?"

"We have mapped several more tunnels and Grey Pee has shown us a shortcut to one of the interior parks," Idalia replied, "but that is all."

A new voice cut in, kept soft so it would not carry but nonetheless vibrant and assured.

"I say," said Edlin Norwood, "it would be easier to find what you're looking for if we knew what it was, don't you know?"

Idalia struck him across the face with the same casualness Citrine had seen applied to puppies or other overly enthusiastic young creatures. Mother frowned.

"How do you know I am looking for something? I may only wish to understand the extent of my kingdom."

"True," Edlin replied, licking at a trickle of blood from one corner of his mouth. "Just seems that you're putting a lot of energy into it all of a sudden, given you have a life tenancy and all, what?"

Mother's eyes narrowed and Citrine held her breath thinking Mother, too, was going to hit Edlin, but she only glowered at the young man.

"What do you think I might be seeking, Lord Kestrel?" she asked in silky tones as dangerous as another woman's shout.

"Treasure," he said bluntly. "The Founders couldn't have taken it all with them. Must cost a lot to run a place like you have down here. Not just the slaves—lantern oil, food, clothing. Adds up, what?"

"It does indeed," Mother agreed. "And I am looking for treasure—of a type."

Interested as Citrine was in what Edlin and Mother were saying, Citrine could hardly hear them for the sudden ruckus raised by the voices inside her head. She gripped her ears and squeezed them as if she could drown the angry voices out.

"Edlin was bleeding! She hit him like you'd hit a dog."

"Like a dog! Edlin would never hit a dog. Remember how he cried when he saw that Firekeeper and Blind Seer had killed those bandit dogs? He didn't think anyone saw him, but you did. Edlin's really very sweet."

"Grateful Peace looks horrible. I bet it really hurts him to have his arm twisted that way. And I bet he falls a lot."

"What do you mean?"

"Look at the way his robe is all dirty on the front. He's fallen. He told you that his balance has been off ever since he lost his right arm. Now they took his left."

So it went, the voices forcing Citrine to consider things she would rather not have noticed. When the others—Derian and Elise and all the rest—had talked about Melina being responsible for Edlin and Peace not coming back with Firekeeper, Citrine had ignored them. Hadn't Firekeeper herself said it was someone else? Someone named . . .

Memory hit her with the truth before Citrine could flee from it. Someone named Idalia, Idalia who Firekeeper had said was Peace's own sister who hated him. The same Idalia who Citrine herself had seen was Mother's ally, the mayor of Melina's underground town.

And now here was proof that Citrine could not evade. Melina stood talking to Edlin, not reprimanding the woman who had struck the young lord, not even offering him a cloth to blot his cut. There stood Peace, bound and gagged, treated like less than dirt.

With a chill certainty, Citrine recognized the man's resignation as that of someone who already believes himself dead, who only looks to delay the inevitable execution. And Peace had been kind to her, kinder in many ways than Citrine's real father, for Rolfston Redbriar had been a man too beaten by events to have much kindness left in him for a late-born, extra, extraneous daughter.

And Mother knew about this and Mother approved of this. Peace's humiliation and dread was the coin in which she paid Idalia for her faithful support.

Citrine realized that the voices had drowned out a large portion of the discussion. She was brought back into the present by the sight of the guard wrenching the gag from Grateful Peace's mouth.

"So," Consolor Melina said to the Illuminator, "do you have any idea where treasure rests?"

"I have . . ." Peace coughed, a hollow sound from a throat dry as bone, but no one, not even Edlin, offered him water, "no certainty but a few ideas."

Melina smiled.

"Very good," she said. "Tonight is nearly gone, but tomorrow we shall see how your ideas manifest into reality."

XXXII

EXHAUSTED FROM HER EXPLORATIONS during the night before, Melina was not at all pleased when Tipi shook her awake near mid-morning.

"Mistress," Tipi pressed, "I think this is important. Your caller is Kiero, and despite his many reasons to stand in awe of your power and authority, he persists in insisting he must speak with you."

Melina did not allow her sudden interest to show, but her head no longer felt so cloudy.

"Very well," she said, covering a yawn. "Have Kiero attend upon me in my private sitting room. You may bring me hot tea and honey."

Tipi abased herself out of the room, leaving Melina to perform her own ablutions, a time she used to arrange her thoughts as well as her appearance.

When she swept into her office some time later, Melina's appearance in no way revealed her exhaustion. The omnipresent cosmetics worn by the New Kelvinese had more uses than she had realized when she had studied them from her unsophisticated Hawk Haven perspective. They could be as practical as any other form of attire when it came to concealment—and therefore certainly no more shameful than the wig King Tedric regularly wore.

Kiero had not the effrontery to sit without her invitation so awaited her standing. When she entered the room, he abased himself appropriately, not abbreviating one gesture or bow though his excitement radiated from him like heat from the sun.

"Speak," Melina said, settling herself into a chair behind her reading desk and motioning for Tipi to pour tea and then leave them in privacy.

Kiero stood straight, his hands clasped behind his back, his gaze directed respectfully toward her. Melina's servants rapidly learned that she did not appreciate their studying the opposite wall or the carpet while they addressed her—a discipline she wished she could enforce on everyone with whom she must regularly interact.

It would make life so much easier.

"Consolor Melina," Kiero began, "as I well know, I have been less than perfect in my service of you."

He was not hoping for reassurance as a similar servant in Hawk Haven might have done. He really meant what he said. Such awareness that promotion was based upon personal achievement rather than inheritance was one of the things Melina greatly approved of in the New Kelvinese.

She sipped her tea, graced him with the faintest inclination of her head, and Kiero continued:

"After my attempt to bring Sir Jared Surcliffe into your personal service met with disappointment, I set myself with renewed enthusiasm to watching the foreigners in hopes that I might be offered some other opportunity to do you service.

"Yesterday, I believe that my fidelity met with some reward. I was observing the boardinghouse wherein the foreigners have residence when I noticed the arrival of messengers from the Hawk Haven embassy. One man went in, stayed only briefly, and then retreated.

"I sent one of my associates to follow him and kept my vigil on the foreigners. A short time later, Lady Archer and Counselor Derian departed. Although they were on foot, they had with them the large wolf which is their pet. Therefore, I made no move to agitate the population against them. In any case, I thought it would be interesting to learn what I could about their business."

Melina awarded him a smile.

"Very good. We have already seen an alarming tendency in the legal system to tolerate misbehavior on the part of that beast. Information is of infinitely greater value."

The tips of Kiero's ears colored a deep red—the only part of his blush clearly visible beneath the burning Urnacia had inflicted on his skin.

"I am grateful that you approve," he said. "When I arrived at the embassy, the associate I had sent in advance informed me that the messengers had returned directly from their errand. My associate had waited to see if anyone was sent out again. While he did this a visitor arrived at the embassy.

"The visitor was carried in a hired litter and wore a loose robe over his head and shoulders so that his features were not recognizable. At this point, I sent my associate to locate the hired litter and to question the bearers as to the identity of their fare. I took up the vigil at the embassy myself.

"After a long time, the foreigners emerged. Their bearing and what I could hear of their parting comments to the doorkeeper seemed to indicate that they intended to return to their dwelling. My associate had not returned from his errand, therefore I let them depart unescorted. I waited instead to follow the unidentified visitor.

"Shortly following the foreigners' departure, the doorkeeper sent a runner for a litter. Despite the local unhappiness regarding the foreign presence in Dragon's Breath, a litter was found borne by menials willing to trade their self-respect for the inflated prices foreigners are willing to offer.

"I positioned myself so I could follow the litter without myself being noticed. At Ronorialla Market Square, the passenger ordered—speaking very good New Kelvinese—the litter to halt. At Ronorialla he was able to acquire another litter without difficulty, and did so. He was borne directly to Thendulla Lypella.

"Using the pass given to me by Your Gracious Ladyship, I entered after him. Following him within the Earth Spires without being detected was more difficult, but I succeeded and saw him admitted without question to White Rock Spire, the tower occupied by the Dragon's Claw. After the man had passed within, I came up, moving as if I carried a message. When I queried the door guard if his master was within, the man replied easily that I was in luck, that Xarxius had just returned. I then created some fairly routine message to be passed onto the Dragon's Claw and departed.

"I intended to report to you immediately, but a message from the associate I had sent to trail the litter was waiting for me at my quarters whence I had gone in order to make myself fitting for your august presence. It requested that I meet with him immediately at the watch house we had established across from the foreigners' residence. I hastened there and learned two things.

"One, the litter bearers reported that they had acquired their fare at another of the large market areas. Two, the foreigners had returned from the embassy and had apparently gone into private conference—this being judged by the closing of windows in one of the more secure rooms, a thing that would not be usual on such a warm evening.

"Even as my associate related this, we saw a lantern blossom behind one of the shutters, a clear signal to someone without. Although we saw no one react to this signal, it was not difficult to assume that Xarxius had—as your esteemed self has had the foresight to do—posted watchers on these uncertain elements. Clearly, some message was being sent.

"By the time I had acquired this information, the hour was past that which I had been told I could bring to you anything but the most dire information. I therefore waited until this morning. I hope I have judged correctly."

Melina nodded almost absently.

"You have behaved fittingly," she said. "Who knows of this?"

"Only I know the entire story," Kiero replied promptly, "though my associate knows much."

Melina sipped her tea, no longer in the least sleepy.

"This is interesting, Kiero, but I will need to consider how to act. Speak of this to no one."

"I will not."

"Have someone you can trust to be subtle keep an eye on Xarxius. I want a record of where he goes. I want warning if he makes any plans to leave the city."

"Yes, Consolor Melina."

"Very good, Kiero. For now you are dismissed, but leave word of where you may be found. I may have an essential task for you."

"Should I wait here within Thendulla Lypella?"

"No. You may go about your duties, just make certain that you can be found if I want you."

Kiero heard the dismissal in her tone and began the departure ritual. Melina hardly paid him any mind—a thing perfectly fitting given the difference between their ranks. A few moments later, she rang for Tipi.

"Prepare my breakfast," she commanded, "and learn for me where the Healed One may be found."

"Yes, Mistress."

BY THE TIME SHE'D FINISHED a grilled lamb cutlet and several cups of tea, Melina knew what must be done next.

"Tipi, did you learn where my husband is?"

"In his studio, Mistress. Dancing."

Melina frowned slightly. Toriovico was always most difficult to deal with when he had been dancing.

"Bring a message asking him to call upon me when he finishes his rehearsal. Then inquire when the Dragon Speaker can see me. Don't make an appointment, just learn Apheros's schedule for the day."

"Yes, Mistress."

"And, Tipi?"

"Yes, Mistress?"

"Where is Citrine?"

"I believe she is at a dance rehearsal."

Melina nodded, satisfied.

"Leave a message for Citrine's maid telling her that Citrine is not to bother me today. I will do my best to stop by before the child is put to bed."

"Yes, Mistress."

Melina next retrieved her research from the double-locked box in which she kept it. Last night's prowling had tickled some memory of what she had read and she could do nothing on the Xarxius problem until she had spoken to Toriovico—or rather she could, but she preferred to keep her involvement shielded under proper forms. This was not a land that would be comfortable with a woman ruler.

Melina wondered how Hawk Haven would take to Sapphire when she was queen. After all, both of Zorana's successors had been male: her son Chalmer, her grandson Tedric. Still, Sapphire should do well. After all, wasn't she her mother's daughter? And it wouldn't be long before she had her mother's help in that difficult task.

Melina turned over her notes. Something Edlin Norwood had said made her want to look at these again, something about treasure. . . .

For a long while Melina turned over page after page, reading her own thin, spidery handwriting, trying to remember her own abbreviations. She'd taken her notes in Pellish, but knowing this would not be precaution enough against determined snoops she'd created her own cipher. Nothing more than abbreviations and word substitutions, but enough to slow someone down.

Even herself.

Melina's broad grin would have surprised all those who perceived her as cold and humorless. Perhaps that grin was what slowed Toriovico as he stepped over the threshold.

"Melina, darling?" he said. "Tipi said you wanted me."

Melina looked up, biting her lower lip to keep from reprimanding him for entering unannounced. The Healed One was the single person with whom she must observe the forms—at least before witnesses, and who knew what escort had trailed him here?

"Yes, Torio," she said, filling her voice with warmth and enthusiasm. "I see you came straight from practice."

"My lady called," he replied warmly, lifting her hand and nibbling along the back of her wrist beneath the form of a polite kiss. "How may I serve you?"

"My lord," Melina began seriously, "I have learned of that which hints at a plot to undermine you, perhaps through me. Most certainly Apheros's government is in danger."

Toriovico dropped her hand and lowered himself into a chair.

"What?"

"My lord, a man who had been spying upon those same Hawk Havenese who brought Citrine to us came to me hoping to sell information. I agreed to listen and he told me that one of Apheros's Three was seen meeting with these foreigners."

"Which one?" Toriovico asked.

"Xarxius."

"My sweet," the Healed One replied, his tone a trace condescending, "Xarxius is responsible for our trade with other nations. It is part of his usual duties to deal with foreigners."

"Then why did Xarxius go to his meeting disguised? My lord, I fear something more than trade was under discussion. I would like you to support me in having Xarxius brought for questioning."

The Healed One looked very grave, and for a moment Melina actually thought Toriovico would refuse her. She chided herself for spending so much time away from him—this was the one bond she should never risk weakening. Then, to her relief, the Healed One nodded.

"Very well, if Apheros agrees. Remember, his advisors are not mine to choose."

"But they are yours to dismiss," Melina said, "if they act in a fashion of which you do not approve. True?"

"True," Toriovico replied. "Will you go to Apheros next?"

"In your company, my lord. I would never overstep my place."

"Then I must shower and otherwise prepare myself," Toriovico said. "It is barely permissible that I call upon my dearest wife in this state."

Toriovico rose and Melina crossed to him, rising up on her toes to kiss him on one cheek.

"I will request a meeting with Apheros," she said.

"Very good," Toriovico replied.

He sketched a bow and left with flattering speed.

Melina smiled and glanced over at her notes. A pause to clip the Dragon's Claws, then back to her true work. She smiled, hearing the rush of flames light her imagination.

DISBELIEF MINGLED WITH HORRIFIED SHOCK flooded Toriovico's heart as he listened to Melina's words. Xarxius discovered? Melina's spy web so thorough? More than ever, he resolved that this Consolor who insisted at playing queen would not rule his land in his stead.

However, his hands were tied. If he took action against Melina now she could claim he was insane. Those who followed her would support her most outrageous claims—especially with such evidence as his apparent paranoia regarding his own wife to support them. He didn't doubt that Tipi, among others, would supply ample evidence. Toriovico needed more information, proof that would sing out no matter how many of the higher-ranking members of the Primes Melina held in thrall. She could not hold them all, of that he was certain.

With new insight, Toriovico praised the enormously cumbersome government the First Healed One had designed. It might have been originally intended to slow the New Kelvinese's ability to become a power that could challenge the Founders, but had their land possessed a simple monarchy as did Hawk Haven or even an oligarchy like that which reigned in Waterland, New Kelvin would already have been doomed by this unanticipated threat.

Or perhaps the threat of a single powerful, charismatic leader had not been unanticipated by the First Healed One. Wasn't that what had led to the fragmentation of the Gildcrest colony across the White Water? Who knew what history the Old Country possessed that would have given the First Healed One warning?

UNSURPRISINGLY, THE DRAGON SPEAKER "just happened" to have a few meetings he could reschedule to make time for the Healed One and his

Consolor. In the five years of his reign, Torio had never requested such an interruption to the Dragon Speaker's schedule, so it was not unreasonable that the Dragon Speaker would hurry to honor his request now. However, with his fresh awareness of the extent of Melina's influence, Toriovico found Apheros's haste to cooperate rather sinister.

When Torio and Melina arrived in the Dragon Speaker's private office, Xarxius was there before them. He and Apheros were calmly discussing the projected wool harvest, but halted politely as soon as the Healed One and his Consolor came through the door.

As formal greetings were exchanged, Toriovico couldn't help but notice how Apheros's gaze, animated and direct when they had entered the room, was now grown still and calm. The Dragon Speaker did not stare at Melina, but his gaze strayed to her periodically, as a dancer uncertain of his steps might look toward the choreographer for guidance.

"How may I be of service to my rulers?" the Dragon Speaker inquired when the greeting ritual had ended.

Melina, in the company of two she believed puppets and one she suspected was an enemy, spoke with more bluntness than tact.

"Apheros, I want Xarxius to explain why he was seen at the Hawk Haven embassy."

Xarxius replied directly to her, although in proper form he should have spoken to Apheros. As a member of the Three, one of Xarxius's rights was to answer to the Dragon Speaker and to no one else—though the Dragon Speaker was required to answer for his Three if the Healed One so demanded.

Toriovico silently cursed Xarxius's lack of caution. Xarxius should observe the forms lest he give away too much of what he knew about Melina's influence in the court.

The Dragon's Claw's words showed a caution his manner of address did not, so perhaps he realized his error.

"I went there to negotiate trade," Xarxius replied. "Such is my responsibility."

His tone was just a trace condescending as if to say "But a foreigner like you couldn't be expected to know that."

Toriovico saw that Melina heard Xarxius's scorn and that it stung, but she did not react.

"Trade?" she said. "Apheros, I want Xarxius to explain why he went to discuss trade with Lady Elise Archer and Derian Carter. They are no great merchants such as would deserve his attention."

Xarxius again replied directly to Melina, bypassing Apheros.

"They have the ear of King Tedric," he said, his scorn even more evident, "and of the king's heirs. In the not too distant future, they will be important. A wise government should cultivate such potential allies now rather than later."

The Dragon's Claw's tone added, "As you would know if you knew anything," and Melina shifted restively.

Her next question was addressed directly to Xarxius.

"Tell me, then, why you disguised yourself to go to this meeting if the circumstances were so direct and without reproach. Why did you change litters so that the bearers who carried you to the embassy would not know your identity?"

Xarxius replied, "Since your marriage to our great and glorious Healed One, O Consolor, there has been much anger among some segments of our population—many of whom believe that a foreigner should not be permitted such privileges. Since you have remained almost completely sequestered here in the Earth Spires that anger has been taken out on representatives of your natal country. I did not wish to be seen going to the Hawk Haven embassy for that reason."

"Because you feared for your safety?" Melina sneered.

"Let us say that was so," Xarxius agreed.

Toriovico observed Apheros stirring and looking less than happy during this last exchange. After a moment, he realized why.

Xarxius is doing it on purpose! he thought with barely hidden glee. *He is trying to make Apheros angry that his privileges are being infringed upon—that Melina is ignoring his importance. Politics are Apheros's dance, the force at the core of his heart, and Xarxius hopes to use those instincts to break Melina's hold upon him.*

Barely daring to breathe lest he somehow interfere with Xarxius's design, Toriovico listened as Melina snapped out her next question.

"So, fearful for your safety lest the populace see you performing your duties, you went to the Hawk Haven embassy in disguise and using various litters. What business did these two striplings wish to discuss with you?"

Apheros frowned.

"Lady Archer and Counselor Derian," he reproved with a dry cough.

Melina stiffened, then nodded. She turned to Apheros and Toriovico felt his heart sink.

"Of course, Dragon Speaker," Melina replied with silky respect. "I forgot. I have known Elise Archer since she was an infant. She was even engaged to my son, Jet. It is difficult to remember that such infants grow into young baronesses."

Apheros's smile had once again become fatuous and agreeable.

"As long as you understand, Consolor," he said in the fond tones of a teacher reproving a favored pupil, "that we must always be respectful of our neighbors, no matter how we think of them in private."

"Yes, Dragon Speaker."

Very carefully, Melina directed her next question to Apheros.

"Dragon Speaker, I wonder what business these foreign emissaries, favorites of their monarch and his heirs, had with your Dragon's Claw."

Apheros glowered at Xarxius, and Toriovico saw the unspoken sorrow in Xarxius's hound-dog eyes. He, too, knew his attempt had failed.

"In addition to matters of trade," Xarxius said, "they wished me to inquire as to the return of Lady Archer's ward, Citrine Shield."

"And what did you tell them?"

"I said I would make inquiries."

"Ah."

The single syllable was potent with emotion but gave away no information. Clearly, Melina had realized how her own anger had endangered her. Whether or not she also realized how Xarxius had deliberately triggered that anger, Toriovico could not tell.

"Apheros," she said after a long pause, "is it right that Xarxius should be trading in human flesh?"

"No," the Dragon Speaker replied sternly, "not if that human is a citizen of Hawk Haven. It has long been our law to trade only in what our trade partners agree is legal."

"So in agreeing to make inquiries, Xarxius has overstepped his prerogatives?"

"It is as you say, Consolor."

Xarxius didn't protest. Toriovico knew that Xarxius had made his effort. They both knew that what came next would have nothing to do with law or rights. It would have everything to do with what Melina desired. She only had to find the correct veneer of legality for her wishes so that Apheros would not question his agreement with her.

Melina was about to speak again when Xarxius said in a rather dreamy tone of voice.

"They also inquired after two members of their party who have been missing for many days now. One is Lord Kestrel, son and heir of the duchess who rules the western reaches across the White Water River. The other posed as a New Kelvinese guide called Jalarios, but in reality this man was the former Dragon's Eye, Grateful Peace. I made inquires after these men, but they are nowhere to be found."

Toriovico swore in astonished surprise, though his reasons were doubtless quite different from what an observer might deduce. Xarxius had clearly taken this opportunity to pass on information Toriovico must have. Grateful Peace here in New Kelvin, but Xarxius had been unable to locate him? What might that mean? Where might the former Dragon's Eye be?

Melina hardly glanced at Xarxius and Toriovico knew this must be because she too had something to conceal. Surely it would be reasonable for her to express some indignation at the return of a confirmed traitor. Instead, with glacial calm she turned her attention once more to Apheros.

"More trading in human lives," she said indignantly. "Does the Dragon Speaker keep one who violates the law in his service? I should think not!"

"I think not," Apheros echoed sternly.

Torio couldn't help but notice how, now that Melina had found another excuse to attack Xarxius, the question of treasonous plotting against the Dragon Speaker had suddenly vanished. She was far too clever to use anything that might show to her own detriment if other opportunities presented themselves.

Apheros tugged at a bell-pull and two guards entered.

"Take Xarxius away. I have found him in violation of the law and of his duties. This is a matter to take before the Primes."

Melina interjected quickly, "Surely you must do some further investigation before troubling the Primes."

"Indeed," Apheros snapped, his voice decisive. "Xarxius is to be restricted to his personal quarters with no visitors and no servants. His food is to be . . ."

Toriovico listened as routine security precautions were outlined to the startled guards. His gaze rested on Xarxius with what he hoped was an expression of mild interest, and he saw the other man's slight smile.

Torio inclined his head, a marginal bow of acknowledgment.

I understand, the Healed One thought, wishing he could say more.

Grateful Peace and Edlin Norwood are Melina's prisoners or you would have located them already. As her enemies, they may be my friends. In any case, they are too valuable to be left in her hands. Peace alone is a mine of information, information Melina must not have.

When the guards departed with Xarxius, Melina began issuing orders—always phrased as suggestions, but orders nonetheless—as to how the case against Xarxius should be constructed. Taking his lead from Apheros, Toriovico spoke when spoken to and listened for cues in Melina's own words as to how and in what manner he should reply.

Evidently, she was satisfied, for she dismissed them—there was no other word for her action—and announced that she would be returning to her study as there was a matter she must continue working on.

After separating from Melina, Toriovico wrote a short note to Columi. Newly warned of Melina's spreading web, he phrased it with careful innocuousness.

> *Do continue your work on our project. It begins to seem as if the other purchaser will be unable to deliver his goods for the Harvest Festival. I myself may be so involved over the next few days as to be unable to further my own interests in this matter. If so, I rely upon you to carry on alone.*

Toriovico could only hope that this note—combined with news of Xarxius's disgrace—would be warning enough to Columi, as well as notification that this setback would not stop the Healed One in his course. If it was intercepted, Torio could quite honestly admit to a plot—one to acquire a secret gift for Melina. He hoped it would be enough.

Hope was beginning to seem the only thing he did have, and that was a frail net with which to catch a falling kingdom. Toriovico also had the unsettling feeling that although he might have broken Melina's spell, her control over his actions was as tight as ever.

DERIAN WATCHED in enthralled silence as the latch to the back gate began to rise. The yard was dark, its only occupants himself, Blind Seer, and Firekeeper. It was the latter who had hushed him and pointed toward the gate. It was her hand on his arm that kept him still and quiet, though his fingers tightened around the weighted walking stick without which he no longer went anywhere.

They'd been out enjoying the coolness that now came with evening, watching the stars and looking for the comet with which Firekeeper was once again obsessed. They had no lantern with them, but the light that shone from the kitchen window gave enough illumination that they could read each other's expressions—and watch the slow, stealthy raising of the latch.

The latch reached its apex with a faint snap and the gate eased inward with an audible groan. The movement of the gate halted, then resumed.

By now, Derian was fascinated rather than afraid. Someone coming to do them mischief wouldn't be so stealthy—at least, the rioters they'd dealt with to this point hadn't been. However, more than his own reasoning, what steadied his nerve was the glimpse he had had of Firekeeper's face. The wolf-woman was smiling, her hand coiled in Blind Seer's scruff as if she expected some entertainment.

Xarxius? Derian thought. *Firekeeper would find going after Melina beneath Thendulla Lypella amusing, even if any sane person would be scared stiff.*

But it wasn't Xarxius who came around the corner of the gate and eased it closed behind him. It was Nstasius.

The least Prime was clad much as when they had first seen him, robe and facial ornamentation alike meant for moving unseen through the darkness. Derian guessed that Firekeeper—or Blind Seer—had known who their visitor was by scent and he tried to word his response in keeping with their odd sense of humor.

"Hello," Derian said in New Kelvinese, his tones soft and conversational. "Out for a late-night stroll?"

Firekeeper's slight chuckle assured Derian that he'd been on target, but the least Prime jumped.

"Counselor Derian! I didn't know you were there."

"Stargazing," Derian explained laconically. "To what do we owe the honor of your visit?"

"I'll explain," Nstasius said, "inside, if you don't mind." He glanced at Firekeeper and added, "I wasn't spying."

Derian translated this for Firekeeper.

"I not think so," the wolf-woman said, getting to her feet with an apparent ease that Derian knew actually cost her a considerable amount of effort. "He come straight."

Derian didn't ask how she knew. Explanations would ruin Firekeeper's mystique and they were learning how valuable at least a semblance of magical ability could be when dealing with the New Kelvinese. Instead he motioned toward the door.

"Come in. I'll gather the rest of the household. We can meet in Doc's consulting room."

No one had yet retired for the night, though Elise was brushing her hair in preparation. She joined them with the fair mass still loose, looking, Derian thought, incredibly pretty and a whole lot softer than she had these last several days when worry and her assumption of responsibility for everything that had gone wrong had rested on her like some physical burden.

Wendee and Doc had been playing a two-handed version of a complex New Kelvinese board game Wendee had learned from Hasamemorri. Wendee, Derian saw at a glance, was winning. From Doc's momentarily unguarded expression when he caught his first glimpse of Elise, he wouldn't be feeling his losses for long.

"I have news from Thendulla Lypella," Nstasius began as soon as greetings were concluded. "News that may have a great effect on you and your safety. Xarxius has been taken into custody pending question of possible treason. Rumor says that the reason for his arrest has something to do with his meeting with some of your household."

Elise replied with such promptness that Derian knew she was trying to forestall anyone saying anything foolish.

"How can our meeting with him be treasonous? Isn't he your minister for trade?"

Nstasius looked very unhappy.

"Apparently—and what I know originates with the guards who arrested Xarxius at the Dragon Speaker's command—Consolor Melina and the Healed One were present at the arrest. There was some talk of slave trading—and something to do with the former Dragon's Eye Grateful Peace having been part of your company."

Xarxius has betrayed us! was Derian's first thought, then he wondered, *But why would they arrest him for giving news about Grateful Peace? There's more here than Nstasius knows.*

Elise apparently reached a similar conclusion, for she asked, "And why would you warn us? Is this some sort of trap?"

Nstasius glanced to where Firekeeper—who had been following via Wendee's whispered translation—had begun to growl.

"No!" he cried as if vehemence alone could shield him. "Not at all. I told you how the party to which I belong favors our kingdom's advancement. We can't do that if we're at war with our neighbors. Hawk Haven has proven itself a military power not to be ignored. I have no desire for my government to create a situation that would cause your king to declare war on us."

"And treason," Elise said, "is not something that can be done by oneself. If Xarxius is convicted of treason then we will be convicted—by association if nothing else—as spies. Is that how you see it?"

"Rather," Nstasius agreed. "What will you do?"

Elise glanced at the others.

"Stay right here," she said. "We have done nothing and my ward is in the Earth Spires. I have no desire to leave without her."

Derian nodded his agreement, though he wondered if the wisest thing would be to cut their losses and get out. So far, it seemed, Melina had all the victories on her side.

Nstasius surprised him.

"Good," he said. "My political associates and I think this may be our opportunity to undermine Apheros's government. Xarxius has not been brought up for formal examination yet, but when he is, we plan to use this situation to call for a vote of confidence. If we win, Apheros will be Dragon Speaker no longer."

"And you will be," Derian said dryly.

"Oh, no," Nstasius laughed. "I am far too junior, but I may be one of the new Three. We shall have to see. The point is, we can demonstrate how the actions of Apheros's government have made our international political situation precarious in the extreme, how the questioning of Xarxius's actions in regard to you could be seen as an insult to your kingdom. If you planned to leave, we would have had to structure our criticism to say we would mend the breach. Now we can say we will prevent the breach. It's much nicer that way."

Elise looked as exasperated and confused as Derian felt.

"I'm sure it is," she said, "and in the meantime, what will you do for Xarxius?"

"Xarxius?" Nstasius looked genuinely puzzled. "I suppose he'll return to some post in the Stargazers."

"So you'll set him free?"

"Certainly," Nstasius said. "Our entire point will be that he was only doing his job, and that if Apheros cannot trust his own Three, how can he be trusted to run New Kelvin?"

"There is a certain amount of sense there," Derian agreed, "but your way of thinking makes my head spin."

"Prime Nstasius, aren't you worried," Elise said, "that we might have been involved in treasonous talks with Xarxius?"

Nstasius looked momentarily unhappy, then shook his head.

"The slave-trading charge is all nonsense. It has to do with that ward you mentioned a moment ago, Citrine Shield. The guard said that when Xarxius mentioned that you wanted the girl back, Consolor Melina immediately said something about trading in human flesh with people from Hawk Haven being against our law and Apheros supported her. That's when Xarxius said what he did about Grateful Peace."

He paused and smiled apologetically.

"Secondhand information and not the best. Apheros doesn't want his guards to be the type who remember too much, but this fellow has a cousin who is of my party—Apheros doesn't know that, of course—and who routinely passes information our way. Most of it isn't worth much, but this!"

For a moment, Nstasius looked as pleased as a cat who'd gotten into the cream. Then he suddenly became apprehensive.

"I need to leave. Who knows what the charges would be if I'm seen here?"

"Treason at least," Derian offered. "Though isn't it legal for your government to overthrow itself from within?"

"We don't think of it as overthrowing," Nstasius said, "just changing the old guard for one that is fresh."

Wendee looked up from her whispered translation.

"How did you get here? Do you know you weren't seen?"

"I don't think I was," Nstasius replied. "I rode with a friend in a hired litter, then slipped out and into the alley. I stayed near the wall and I don't think there's anyone in that alley."

"I not think there is," Firekeeper replied after a moment. "Blind Seer and me make it not so nice."

Derian decided not to ask just how they had done this. On reflection, just knowing the two of them were prowling out there periodically could dissuade even the bravest. Hasamemorri's yard was screened by trees still fully in leaf, so it was doubtful that anyone was spying on the back of the building from adjoining buildings.

"I'll leave by the alley again," Nstasius said, "until I link up with some more populous streets. Then I'll rejoin the crowd."

"And we," Firekeeper said, "will go with you."

WHEN THE WOLF-WOMAN RETURNED some time later she was visibly exhausted.

It may be a good thing that Xarxius didn't come for us tonight, Derian thought. *Firekeeper still isn't strong.*

He didn't say anything, of course, only brought Firekeeper a thick slab of bread and cheese.

"I not think," Firekeeper reported between bites, "that anyone see Nstasius. I have Bee Biter go and fly high to see if anyone in trees or too interested at windows. He say he not see anyone. Blind Seer and me, we not see anyone either."

"That's something," Elise said, "but it doesn't solve our current problem. Simply put: I don't think Xarxius is going to be slipping anyone into the Earth Spires to find out where Melina goes at night, and now it's more important than ever that we know what she is doing."

Doc nodded.

"I agree. I don't think any of us missed that Melina was there when Xarxius was arrested—or that she seemed to have a lot to do with it."

Firekeeper seemed hardly herself as the voice of caution.

"But we no can go in there looking for Peace and Edlin. They are bait in a snare for us. We know that."

"You're right," Elise agreed, and Derian caught a strange light in her sea green eyes. "We can't charge in there looking for Peace and Edlin—but I can go to the Earth Spires and demand that Citrine be returned to me."

They all stared at Elise in amazement.

"We've made our requests through the usual channels," Elise explained with a patient deliberation that was at odds with the glow in her eyes. "Within a day or so it will be perfectly reasonable for us to have heard about Xarxius's disgrace. Right?"

Nods all around, and Derian heard himself saying:

"If you want confirmation as to how well the rumor has spread, you could ask Ambassador Redbriar."

"Good." Elise twisted a coil of her loose hair around her finger. "When we met with Xarxius, he said that he'd spoken with the Healed One, that the Healed One had taken a personal interest in Citrine's case."

"He did," Derian confirmed in response to questioning glances from those who had not been present. "He said we could have Citrine back *if* we found out where Melina has been going nights."

"Right," Elise said, not in the least daunted. "As I see it, we've got this Healed One in an interesting situation."

Wendee interrupted, "The Healed One could deny that Xarxius ever spoke with him about Citrine. That's what I'd do if Xarxius is really in disgrace. Maybe Xarxius did lie about the Healed One. Maybe the Healed One knows nothing about your request."

Elise refused to be shaken from her purpose.

"I don't see why Xarxius should lie about something that big. After all, he's basically a duke himself. He doesn't need to make himself more important by saying he's talked to the king, not to us, not when we're supplicants."

"Except," Derian broke in, catching Elise's excitement, "if Xarxius was a sort of supplicant! He did want us to do something for him. His mentioning the Healed One gets really interesting then. Either he was just trying to make us feel like dirt—sort of I take your lady and counselor and raise you by a king—or he was mentioning the Healed One deliberately, saying basically that the Healed One himself was interested in knowing what Melina was up to."

Doc nodded agreement with a thin smile.

"Well, I certainly would want to know if my wife was prowling around nights, especially if that prowling wasn't for any of the usual mischief."

Derian grinned at him.

"So you wouldn't mind if your wife was prowling for the 'usual mischief'?"

Doc colored slightly and punched Derian in the shoulder.

"If we could be serious for a moment," Elise said, and Derian thought her own color was a bit high, "my plan is to get an audience with the Healed One and then insist in my best high and mighty manner that I must have Citrine back."

"Could you really do that?" Wendee asked, and Derian recalled his own awe regarding monarchs. "March in to a king?"

Elise giggled.

"Have you ever met my Grandmother Rosene? I plan to model myself on her."

"Eagle's Wings over us all," Doc murmured.

Elise stuck her tongue out at him.

"As I see it," she continued, "if the Healed One wants us to do something for him he will arrange a private interview—after all, he can't come to us. If Xarxius did lie about the Healed One's involvement or the Healed One is afraid of what he once would have dared, we won't be granted our audience."

"And Melina?" Wendee asked a bit breathlessly. "All this time we've been working to avoid a direct confrontation with her. There's no way she won't learn about this."

Elise nodded.

"As I see it, by using Xarxius's interview with us to arrest him she has made it impossible for us to continue acting as if we're unaware of her influence. Really, from the moment she kept Citrine rather than sending her back to us she has opened a door."

Firekeeper, clearly remembering the traps she had encountered during her second venture into the sewers, frowned.

"I hope that this door is not into a pit or room of armed soldiers."

"Me, too," Elise agreed. "But in case it is I think we should all go to call on the Healed One together—more of us to deal with whatever we encounter."

"All of us?" Wendee squeaked.

"All of us," Elise repeated firmly. "Two titled ladies, a knight, a counselor to the king, and a confidant of a duchess. It will be hard for Melina to justify making all of us disappear."

Derian nodded slowly.

"And if she plans to do so," he added, "we're only making it easier for her by waiting here, trapped indoors by the unrest of her subjects."

He rubbed his hands across his face, suddenly weary.

"Yes," Elise agreed. "It's too late to contact Violet Redbriar and learn if news of Xarxius's arrest has become public and we can't reasonably act until then. We'll call on the ambassador first thing in the morning."

"All of us?" Wendee asked hesitantly.

"Not quite yet," Elise assured her. "For this call the only danger is being attacked in the streets."

"Only," Derian said, thinking of the riot he and Doc had been in and rubbing his still healing bruises. "Only."

XXXIII

"I MUST REST!" gasped Grateful Peace, leaning hard against the rough rock wall, then sliding to the ground so heavily that his robes tore.

He knew what was coming next. With booted feet, one of the guards kicked his side until Peace's only choice was to stagger upright or have his ribs broken.

The Illuminator heard the flutter of paper as Edlin dropped his sketch pad, the clank of chains as the young man lurched to his assistance.

"I say!" Edlin demanded angrily, interposing himself between Peace and the guard. "Wouldn't it be easier to let him rest a moment? Give him some water? We've been at this for hours."

Edlin received a backhand across the face—a punishment that had become so frequent that there was a thick swelling at one corner of his mouth. This hadn't stopped Edlin from speaking out, though, taking full advantage of his value as a hostage to make the protests that might get Peace killed.

"Those hours," Consolor Melina replied from where she was studying some sigils etched into a rock at the juxtaposition of two tunnels, "are precisely why we cannot stop. I shall need to retrace my steps far too soon. It would not do for my loving husband to find me gone from my bed as well as from his. I would like to find where this tunnel goes before then."

Peace indicated to Edlin that he could stand on his own.

"I believe it leads to one of the hot springs, Consolor," he said as respectfully as he could. "That horizontal wavy line with similar vertical ones above it usually indicates such. I have not been this way myself."

"Well, you shall lead the way now," Melina said, silkily kind. "Just in case you remember more than you are saying. I have no wish to lose my guards to some conveniently forgotten pit."

Melina did, however, pause long enough to order one of the guards to stir some honey into a tin cup of water and let Peace drink the mixture. The sweet stuff was little enough treatment for his injuries and exhaustion, but Peace accepted thankfully. He knew full well that had Idalia been present his ribs would have been cracked, not bruised, and he would have been offered no refreshment.

Melina had a use for him, which was why she stopped her guards from injuring him too severely, but she had a use for Idalia as well and Peace's pain was payment for his sister's services. Melina weighed the two needs against each other very carefully, but Peace was the one who paid the price. Tonight, Idalia was exploring another network of tunnels, so Peace was safe from her abuse—and so had dared this small rebellion.

Within the last few days, Melina had become very interested in those tunnels which led to hot springs or other areas where the subterranean temperature was highest. She had not precisely confided in Peace what she hoped to find in these tunnels, but neither Peace nor Edlin believed any longer—as Melina's guards still did—that what she sought was as mundane as a treasure hoard.

Melina's new intensity meant that Idalia could not be spared to accompany Melina in her search, but that Idalia must conduct some portion of the search on her own. Peace wondered why there was this sudden rush. Surely it was not because Melina thought he might be rescued. More likely she thought Peace might need to be executed soon, either to placate Idalia or because pressure had been brought to bear for his or Edlin's return.

Grateful Peace wondered if those well-meaning young people he had guided into New Kelvin realized that his discovery would mean his death. Even if Idalia would not demand it, he was thought of as a traitor by his peers—and traitors were not permitted to live.

WHEN MELINA DEPARTED for her chambers in the Cloud Touching Spire, Peace and Edlin were permitted to retire to their cave. Peace collapsed onto his pallet. When Edlin knelt beside him to inspect his wounds the Illuminator whispered urgently:

"Are we watched?"

Edlin, after long days of shared captivity, had learned that Grateful Peace rarely asked an idle question. The two men had also detected the probable spy holes and often had some sense whether these were being used.

Now, with a casual deceptiveness that Peace quite admired, Edlin rose to his feet, sopped up water from the cave's tiny spring, and returned to his place beside the injured man.

"Only the usual spot by the door," Edlin replied softly, adding in a more audible voice, "Can you raise that bit of robe for me so I can clean the skin along your side before the cloth sticks?"

Peace did as instructed, a movement that conveniently hid his mouth from sight if the guard was watching. He had told Edlin early on in their captivity that they must always assume they were being watched. By now such misdirection had become nearly second nature. They hadn't had much to hide, but teaching Edlin the skills he needed to keep their secrets had given them both a small feeling of control.

Speaking rapidly, Peace said, "Consolor Melina has a shadow. Citrine has been following her these last several nights. I believe I am the only one who has noticed the child."

Edlin replied in a completely normal tone of voice, "Amazing. Can you roll to one side or shall I shift you?"

Peace accepted the young man's assistance—in truth he needed it—though the actual reason was to permit him to continue his soft-voiced explanation unobserved.

"I hoped to make the child pity us, so she would bring assistance."

Edlin's reply was again spoken in a normal voice.

"I can't believe you let them beat you like that!"

"Let us say I," Peace replied, also in a normal voice, "took the opportunity to rest and hoped the guards would not be too vicious."

In a softer voice Peace added, "I dare not make my actions too obvious or Citrine will suspect. She is canny beyond her years, as wounded creatures often are."

"If Firekeeper were here . . . ," Edlin said, rising and filling the cup with water.

"Firekeeper is not," Peace replied firmly. "We must work with what is here. In my case that is a battered, one-armed body. You must take care not to defend me too strenuously. Although Consolor Melina wants you as a hostage, and it would be better if you were returned unharmed, a certain amount of 'carelessness' on the part of her guards could be excused."

Edlin shook his head. His thick, curly black hair had grown mop-like and was still too short to tie back, so he was constantly brushing it out of his eyes. He did so as he held the cup of water to Peace's lips.

"You're the one who needs to be careful."

Peace nodded, thinking of Idalia.

"I know."

FIREKEEPER KNEW her wounds weren't mending as quickly as Doc expected them to. She suspected she knew the reason, too, but she couldn't bring herself to explain. To do so would be to try and explain things that were so abstract that they didn't seem worthy of a wolf.

Simply put, she wasn't sleeping well at night, not because of pain— though the bruised and lacerated muscles in her leg throbbed constantly— but because the comet kept haunting her dreams.

Firekeeper had never much remembered her dreams, though sometimes she awoke so weary in body and soul that she suspected that she must have dreamt heavily. However, those sleep-time explorations always faded to wisps of cloud, burnt from memory by the light and heat of awakening.

Now, however, whenever she fell asleep she dreamed and always, no matter how innocently those dreams began, the comet entered in. Firekeeper might be hunting with her family and run to Shining Coat's side only to find that the silvery-grey wolf had become the brilliant comet compressed into a wolf's shape. She might be talking to Dawn Brooks in her cabin in New Bardenville and the fire in the hearth would spread out, creeping up the walls and across the floors, speaking in the comet's voice.

And worst of all her dreams remained with her in some form or another when she woke. For Firekeeper, who had suspected that the dreams her human friends often related over breakfast were simply an excuse for weaving wild and improbable stories, this was a torment. Sleeping and waking were no longer distinct. One no longer brought rest. The other no longer brought clarity.

Blind Seer was the only one aware of her difficulty and he couldn't really understand why she wouldn't talk about it to the others.

"I can't," she said, leaning her head against his flank as they sat under one of the trees in Hasamemorri's yard. She was aware that she was dangerously close to drowsing off and struggled against it. "They wouldn't understand."

Blind Seer turned and nipped her arm.

"The proverb says, 'Hunt when hungry, sleep when not, for hunger always returns.' Isn't that a way of saying that sleep is as important as food? You never hesitate to grab whatever you want from the table, to whine when you are empty. Why hesitate to ask for help with filling this hunger?"

Firekeeper's head was so heavy that the wolf's words almost made sense.

"But how can I explain that I hunger for sleep but fear it as well? They will mock me as a fool."

"I don't think they will," Blind Seer said, "but even if they did, wouldn't mockery be a small price to pay to regain your strength? Aren't you being unfair to them? They believe that when the hunt is called you will lead. Any wolf pack would tear you to shreds at the scent of such deception, but these two-legs are too gentle. They will be the ones torn to shreds in exchange for their trust."

Firekeeper didn't like that thought at all—and she knew that no matter how Elise or Derian directed things, when a fight was expected they did count on her. Guilt for abandoning Edlin and Peace still weighed heavily upon her, no matter how many times she was assured she had done the right thing in leaving.

"I will speak to Doc," Firekeeper said at last, "in a bit. The sun feels so good and your fur is so soft."

And Blind Seer, wise enough to sense her drifting off, said nothing, only moved himself as her weight grew heavy against his shoulder, lowering so she slept collapsed against him, his body curled strong and protective around her.

ROCK, BROKEN ALONG JAGGED ANGLES, not by hammer or fist, but by the shattering absence of heat. Heat still rising, though only from pockets now. A rock face hot enough to raise blisters, springs that steam and reek of dissolving minerals.

The comet's voice speaks from a glittering vein coiled through the matte-black stone.

"Motion is not freedom, though it is often mistaken for such. Do you understand?"

Firekeeper, uncertain where she is or even if she is embodied in this place, tries to shape an answer: "You can choose stillness?"

"That is one way of seeing it, I suppose. I was thinking of those who go about their days bounded by invisible walls."

"Like slaves?" Firekeeper is still trying to understand this concept. She thinks the comet might help.

"The walls that bind slaves are often very physical indeed," the comet hisses. "I was thinking of those walls by which you bind yourself, wolfling."

"I am not bound!" Firekeeper replies indignantly.

"Are you not? Duty, obligation, custom. All of these bind you as strongly as any chain or prison wall. They master you, yet you call yourself free."

Firekeeper refuses to reply.

A rippling flow that might have been laughter—but might not—courses along the glittering vein in the rock.

"I am bound," the comet voice says, "but I would not harm the one who bound me, rather the one who freed me. It is all a matter of perception. There are things that bind one that make one free; there are things that free only to further bind."

Firekeeper considers her own refusal to tell Doc about her dreams, about how her apparent freedom to keep her secret has bound her more firmly to these unsettling dreams.

"Why do you keep bothering me?" Firekeeper asks, her anger lighting the dark rock walls though she still cannot tell where she stands.

"I have told you before," the comet hisses. "You can hear me. What good would shouting to deaf ears do?"

"I only hear you when I am asleep," Firekeeper replies, confident of at least this freedom.

"Are you so certain?" the comet asks.

HAD MELINA REALIZED the argument and uproar that Xarxius's arrest would generate, she would either have let him continue with whatever he was about and made certain that Kiero caught him doing something truly damning or she would have arranged for the Dragon's Claw to be called away on urgent business—and meet with a bit of bandit trouble along the way.

Now Melina was faced with sitting through a long hearing in front of the Primes, a hearing meant to answer the question of what degree of treasonous act—if any—Xarxius was guilty of committing and, when that was ascertained, assigning the appropriate punishment.

The hearing had superseded all normal business. Moreover, as one of the accusers—Toriovico was the other—Melina was required to sit off to one side and make herself available for questioning at any time.

The honest truth was, Melina admitted to herself, she had not adjusted to the fact that the Healed One was not a true king—not as she had grown to adulthood understanding the term—nor was his Consolor a real queen.

King Tedric's nobles might present their differences of opinion to him, they might question his judgment, they might even make their unhappiness with his policies known to him by being grudging with some tithe or duty they owed the throne. However, when the king pronounced a decision, that decision became law.

Queen Elexa did not hold the same power, but when she acted as regent for her husband her decisions were also binding as law, law that could be appealed upon King Tedric's return to court, but law nonetheless.

Fleetingly, Melina wondered how such matters would be dealt with in Hawk Haven when King Tedric died, and Sapphire and Shad took the throne. Theoretically, the new king and queen were to hold equivalent power and authority. That would work nicely when the couple agreed on a point, but what if they disagreed? As Melina herself was learning through wearisome experience, having more than one person holding equivalent authority was a recipe for chaos.

In her naive misunderstanding of New Kelvinese government, Melina had thought that if Apheros used apparent treason as justification for renouncing his Claw this would be sufficient to get rid of Xarxius, ruin the man's reputation, and maybe even get him executed.

Indeed, by law and custom, the Dragon Speaker was permitted to replace any of his Three without offering any reason other than that this was his desire. In reality, some excuse should be offered lest the friends and supporters of the demoted Prime take exception—exception that could, in extreme cases, bring the Speaker's government to face a vote of no confidence.

Melina had thought that having the Healed One and his Consolor bring the accusation would make the matter final, for surely no one would question either their word or their authority.

In reality, her and Toriovico's involvement and the entire question of treason had complicated a matter that should have been simple. Treason was a serious matter under the New Kelvin legal code, carrying with it a sentence of death, a death that was administered in various increasingly ugly ways depending on the severity of the treasonous acts.

Mere conspiracy, such as that with which Xarxius was charged, carried with it a fairly painless death—beheading or suffocation accompanied by the administration of soporific drugs. Violent actions against the kingdom or leading an invading force, both of which Grateful Peace stood accused of committing, carried with them the penalty of death by slow torture.

At least, Melina thought, a trace of whimsy touching her lips, *I got that part right.*

Melina quickly schooled her expression to seriousness when she saw several of the Primes frown at her. When she thought of the ramifications of what she had unwittingly done, it was easy for her to be serious.

One of the rumors flying through Thendulla Lypella was that the Progressives were planning to use Xarxius's disgrace—following as closely as it did on the heels of that of Grateful Peace—to challenge Apheros's government. Even if the Progressives could not win the Speaker's chair, rumor said that certain of Apheros's supporters were likely to ask him to step down in favor of another Dragon Speaker, his image and reputation having been irreparably tarnished.

Listening to the arguments and counterarguments on the floor, Melina thought how little any of them had to do with Xarxius's apparent treason. The real issue concerning the Primes was whether Apheros's long hold on the Speaker's chair had been broken at last—and who would sit in it after him. Xarxius's guilt and innocence would be decided on that basis and no other.

Melina looked at where Xarxius sat, his face scrubbed clean of all but his tattoos as a sign of his disgrace, and thought that he knew this as well, but he, like she and Toriovico, was not permitted to speak except in response to a direct question.

The worst of this was that Melina could no longer participate in her own important and essential explorations. True, the hearings did not extend beyond normal business hours, but afterward both she and Toriovico were constantly being requested to attend meetings and strategy sessions.

Apheros was now as eager to save his Claw as he had been to dismiss him, for he saw this as the only way to redeem his own honor. However, the charges made against Xarxius could not merely be dropped, for dropping the charges would not save Apheros's reputation. The Dragon Speaker must find a way to twist the accusations that he himself had brought in order to make them seem innocuous.

This was a task for which Apheros needed every ounce of his conniving mind and Melina had to struggle to keep him under her control without damping his abilities. It was a challenge like none she had ever faced and she was not yet certain she could handle it successfully.

Fortunately, Melina's control over Toriovico was based on assuaging his loneliness and isolation, not on making him feel that his political standing was unchallengeable. A few foot rubs and a bit of passionate sexual attention were all she needed to keep her husband neatly curled within her control.

Idalia was another ally Melina didn't need to worry about. The more responsibility with which she entrusted the other woman, the more excuse she gave Idalia for tormenting Grateful Peace—anything but gross injury or death had been agreed upon as acceptable—so Idalia labored to serve Melina's wishes.

And Melina needed Idalia's labors more than ever now that her own movements were so restricted. With Apheros's government unraveling with every word spoken at Xarxius's hearing, Melina needed the power represented by the entrapped dragon more than ever. If she had read the old texts aright, time was ripening toward when the dragon could be freed, but, as Melina was all too aware, time was also running out.

By the time Melina was offered an opportunity to work her will upon the beast, even a dragon's power might not be enough to save her.

AMBASSADOR REDBRIAR SENT A NOTE midmorning of the third day following Nstasius's nighttime visit. Elise hardly waited to retire to the privacy of the now unused consulting room before tearing the missive open.

"I thought you might be interested in knowing," wrote the ambassador, her wording, as they had agreed, making no mention of the fact that they had been given prior warning of these developments, *"that the Dragon's Claw, Xarxius, with whom you met here at the embassy in order to discuss various trade proposals, has been taken in arrest on charges of treason subsequent to his meeting with you. Apparently, the Healed One and his Consolor took*

exception to some of the matters discussed, viewing them as contrary to New Kelvinese law and custom.

"My understanding is that although Xarxius was arrested several days ago, his hearing was postponed in order that evidence might be organized and an emergency council of the Primes convened. As of this writing, it does not seem as if you or any of your company will be summoned to testify, the crime being viewed as wholly that of the Dragon's Claw.

"Xarxius's hearing is already under way, but I do not believe that the matter will be resolved easily. I shall inform you of the outcome as soon as I myself am informed, and then you may act in order to advance your trade plans."

"And that," Derian commented as Elise folded the letter once more, "gets our careful ambassador off the hook if we do anything impulsive. I'd bet Roanne that she kept a copy of this and, if questioned, will assert that she told us to wait on the trial to do anything."

"So should we wait?" Wendee asked.

Elise didn't hesitate, though inwardly she longed for someone else to make the decisions.

"No. Acting immediately is our best course. Indignation and concern for Citrine would look rather feigned if we wait until the trial is over."

Doc shook his head.

"We could wait," he said, "and still take that course. We would simply say we had been waiting until we knew whether our contact in the Earth Spires had been convicted or not."

Elise nodded.

"I see your point," she said, wondering if the vague annoyance she felt would have been the same if Derian or Wendee had made the suggestion.

She'd grown so accustomed to Sir Jared's support that she hadn't looked for him to question her decision. Then again, maybe her annoyance was due to someone having given her a way to escape the need to act immediately. No matter how brave a face Elise put on for Wendee's sake, she wasn't looking forward to marching up to the Petitioner's Gate and demanding an interview with a king.

Firekeeper spoke from where she sat on the floor with Blind Seer.

"I think we go now. Citrine is only part of reason. Other is Edlin and Peace. If Healed One really was with Xarxius against Melina, then he may know something."

Derian nodded.

"I agree. I like Doc's reasoning and we can use it later if we can't get past the gates this time, but with Melina feeling pressed—as she must be to accuse Xarxius of treason—then we can't waste time."

Wendee bit into her lip, but nodded.

"Whatever you decide, I'm with you."

Elise swallowed around a lump in her throat, suddenly more nervous than she could ever remember being before—except, maybe, the night she had sneaked into Melina's tent. Remembering that venture and how it had turned out steadied her.

"We may not be able to get an audience for today," she said, "but I want to make certain the Healed One himself hears of our request."

Derian quirked half his mouth in a humorless grin.

"Bribes should do it. Anyone have any idea how much a gatekeeper gets?"

"Shopping has given me a fair idea of the value of New Kelvinese credits," Wendee offered. "We can work something out."

"Last question," Elise said. "Do we all go to schedule this appointment or just a few of us?"

"All," Firekeeper growled. "Somehow I think if all of us come, they let us in."

Beside her Blind Seer opened his jaws in a huge, wolfish laugh and Elise was reminded that fear might open gates as easily as money.

"I see your point," she said, rising and smoothing her skirts. "Everyone get dressed in your finest, but don't linger. It's a long walk to Thendulla Lypella and I, for one, don't want to be on the streets after dark."

ELISE WAS NEVER CERTAIN whether it was Blind Seer's smile or Derian's tactfully offered bribe that opened the gates for them. Perhaps neither was necessary, for the line they had expected outside the gate was not there.

"Business is suspended," the inky-robed clerk said in a tone of feigned boredom, "for the hearing. No appointments are being made."

But he could not completely hide his interest at their foreign attire, or that he probably guessed exactly who they were—a thing that Blind Seer's presence alone would have given away, even if there had not been increasingly few foreigners of any nationality in Dragon's Breath since the unrest had mutated into violence.

Elise looked down her nose at him, easy enough to do since as a mark of his indifference the clerk had not bothered to rise.

"I think that the hearing alone would be reason for the Healed One to grant us an audience. Do you want to take the risk that he would wish to see us?"

Apparently, the clerk did not, and the appearance of a flood of people coming from one of the larger towers gave him excuse to comply.

"I see a recess has been called," the clerk said. "If you will step into my office, I will send a message."

Soon after the flood of people had drawn back into the large tower, word came that the Healed One would graciously make time to see them. They were escorted to the audience by a tall, lean man wearing very serviceable armor instead of the usual robes—although over this he wore a long, dark green tabard embroidered with a fallen tree, a fresh sapling rising from the ruin. This, Elise knew, was the emblem of the Healed One. The same emblem was tattooed on one side of the man's face. He wore no other facial adornment.

Their guide did not balk even at the inclusion of Blind Seer in their party. Indeed, there was a steadiness about him that reminded Elise of Sir Dirkin Eastbranch, King Tedric's most trusted guard. She took comfort in this until she remembered to what extremes Sir Dirkin would go if he believed his king in danger.

Without any explanation of the wonders and fancies that met them at every turn, their guide led them along curving paths between a maze of buildings until, at last, they stopped before one ornate twisting spire that stood isolated in a private garden.

"The Cloud Touching Spire," their guide explained. "The Healed One will grant you audience here."

His tone made quite clear the honor he thought the Healed One was doing them—and that he quite disapproved. Elise wondered what this dour, loyal man thought of the Healed One's foreign-born wife, and suspected that she knew.

Take rock from the wall and watch it tumble, she thought with wry amusement. *Obviously the rats are swarming in the grain.*

Once they had entered the spire, the guard knocked at a solid door a short way down the corridor. It was opened from within by another guard wearing a similar costume to their guide's. Guide and guard flanked the door and motioned the five foreigners to pass between them into the room beyond. Then, to Elise's complete astonishment, they shut the door, leaving themselves on the outside.

For a moment, Elise thought that she and her companions had walked into a trap. Some of this must have shown on her face, for the first words spoken by the man who rose from a high-backed chair of polished wood were:

"Do not be afraid. No harm will come to you by me or those loyal to me. I am Toriovico, the Healed One."

Elise, remembering her manners, carefully worked her way through the elaborate New Kelvinese greeting that Grateful Peace had taught them all on the unlikely chance that they might meet with their enemy's new husband. It was very difficult and she was certain that she got parts of it wrong, but when she—and her companions a few gestures behind her—completed the motions the Healed One seemed pleased.

"You have studied," he said in very stilted Pellish. "I too have, but not so well. Can you speak with me in my language?"

Elise nodded, then remembered that now that the greeting ritual was completed she was permitted to speak.

"Yes," she said. "Two of us, however"—she gestured at Firekeeper and Sir Jared—"do not speak your graceful language well or understand it perfectly. I beg permission to translate periodically."

"Certainly," the Healed One replied. "I will permit this. Please seat yourselves and tell me what brings you before me."

Repeatedly tutored in the formalities of New Kelvinese society, Elise had not expected such concessions from its ruler. All her mental rehearsals for this meeting had put her at the foot of some great throne, speaking her piece to some elevated figure who glowered down at her through a violently intimidating mask. She took advantage of seating herself to adjust to this new reality.

The Healed One—Toriovico—was younger than Elise had imagined Melina's husband would be. Elise didn't think he was more than ten years older than herself. Since she had grown accustomed enough to face paints and dyes that the guards' minimal ornamentation had been a touch startling, the Healed One's numerous facial tattoos didn't distract her from seeing that he had quite a nice face.

What did startle her was that the Healed One's hair was a vibrant green and that cosmetics around his eyes were clearly meant to enhance the green in his hazel eyes. His robe was rich silk dyed in graduated hues of brown mingled with hints of green. After a moment, Elise realized that the entire effect was meant to evoke a tree in leaf.

She wondered what kind of king dressed as a tree and whether this had something to do with the sprouting sapling in the Healed One's family arms, but these weren't the questions she had come to ask and she schooled herself to discipline.

"What has brought us before you," Elise said, doing her best to echo the pattern of the Healed One's speech, "is a little girl named Citrine Shield who was last seen coming into Thendulla Lypella. The Dragon's Claw, Xarxius, told us that she was here and that you had listened to our request to have her returned and that you acknowledged our right to her."

To one side Elise heard Wendee translating a quick summary of what had just passed and blessed the day that Saedee Norwood had decided this multi-talented woman would be a fit chaperon for Firekeeper.

The Healed One waited until Wendee had finished, then asked, "Do you know that Xarxius is in disgrace, under arrest for treason?"

"We do. That is why we came to you, Honored One, because we long to have Citrine back again and did not know if Xarxius could help us."

"Xarxius," the Healed One said with what Elise was certain was a trace of sorrow, "cannot even help himself any longer. Why did you come to me and not Citrine's mother, my wife?"

Elise's heart was pounding so hard she was certain the vibrations must be visible through the front of her dress, but she kept her voice steady as she replied.

"By our laws, Melina is no longer Citrine's mother, though her body bore her. Citrine's guardian is her older brother, Jet Shield. Therefore, I did not go to Melina because by our custom she has no greater claim over Citrine than would a stranger."

"Citrine," the Healed One said, "may feel differently."

"I know," Elise said. "That's true. Even so, this is a time when the wisdom of adults must rule over the emotions of children."

Elise thought she sounded dreadfully stiff and pompous, hoped she didn't see a twinkle in the Healed One's eye when she referred to herself as an adult—after all, her majority was comparatively newly achieved.

Toriovico's reply, however, held no trace of mockery.

"It is true what Xarxius told you, that I agreed to have Citrine returned to you."

"*If,*" Elise thought frantically. *He's going to remind us of that "if."*

"I would do so," the Healed One continued, "if I could do so without considerable danger to myself. The difficulty is that my wife would oppose the returning of Citrine, and I dare not oppose her, even at this time—or, perhaps I should say, especially at this time."

Derian said with a simplicity that Elise could not have managed, "Honored One, I don't understand."

"No more you should," the Healed One replied, and this time Elise was certain of the bitterness in his voice. "After all, I am the king."

He used the Pellish word, clearly meaning it to mean "ruler" or "absolute authority." He paused to let Wendee's translation catch up, then continued.

"Lady Archer, Melina said she had known you from your infancy, that you were at one time engaged to be married to her son, Jet. Is this so?"

"Yes, Honored One."

"Tell me with the same directness what they say of Melina in Hawk Haven—not about her character, but about her talents."

"She is said to be a sorceress, to have control over the minds of others."

"What would you say," the Healed One leaned slightly forward in his high-backed chair, "if I told you this was true, really true, not the fancy of a 'magic-crazed' people?"

Elise drew in a deep breath.

"I would say that I know, that I have not only seen evidence of her powers but have been a victim of them myself."

The Healed One flung himself back in his chair, the motion so eloquent of relief that Elise realized for the first time how hard asking such a question of members of the magic-phobic peoples of Hawk Haven must have been.

Derian added, "I've seen the evidence, too, Honored One. So has Firekeeper—that is, Lady Blysse. Sir Jared, too."

The Healed One held his hands palm up, level with his chin, and exclaimed, "First Healed One be thanked! I had hoped this would be your answer—though I am sorry that you, Lady Archer, have suffered under her domination. What dance freed you from Melina's spell?"

Elise was a bit puzzled by his phrasing but replied, "She bound me through an ornament. I put off the ornament and with it her power."

Derian grumbled, "It wasn't quite that easy."

The Healed One nodded. "So I believe. I have seen evidence of how Melina uses artifacts to make her hold stronger."

Firekeeper spoke as soon as Wendee finished translating.

"Citrine."

"Yes," the Healed One replied.

He spared a glance for the wolf-woman who—despite her gown—sat on the floor next to the great grey wolf. Then he went on.

"Did you know Melina can work this control without an artifact?"

Elise nodded.

"We have seen this, though her hold does not seem to be as strong."

The Healed One shook his head.

"Oh, it is very strong, especially if she is able to reinforce her control daily—as she could with me."

"But not anymore," Elise said confidently. "You would not be able to talk to us like this if you were still bound."

"No, I could not," the Healed One agreed, adding rather mysteriously, "It was my dancing that freed me. However, I have led Melina to believe I am still hers to command. I fear that she holds rulership over enough key members of my government that I could become as Xarxius—not tried for treason, for I cannot betray myself, but facing accusations that would make me ineffective. Ineffective, that is, until she had command over me again."

Elise frowned.

"What accusations could she make against you?"

"Insanity," the Healed One replied with pained simplicity. "It is not unknown in my family. Once I was under Melina's control again, she would claim me cured."

"That's horrible!" Derian exclaimed. "Can't you just divorce her?"

"Nothing is so simple," the Healed One said, "not even, I suspect, in your own land, where the king is truly king. Here, where I share my rulership with the Primes and the Dragon Speaker, it is more complicated."

"No wonder," Elise said, "you wanted us to find out where Melina was going at night."

She hadn't meant to say the words aloud and clapped her fingers over her mouth, but she had spoken—and the Healed One had understood her. The angry reprimand she feared did not follow; instead he nodded.

"Precisely. If I can prove that she is the true conspirator then I will have no difficulty putting her from me. Indeed, the shock of her workings may be enough to break her hold on several of my ministers. They move to the call of power as I do to music."

"Music?" Firekeeper said, this being one of the New Kelvinese words she had learned. "What?"

The Healed One looked puzzled, then nodded.

"I forgot for a moment that custom keeps those outside the walls in distant awe of those within. Before I became the Healed One, I trained as a dancer. Dancing is still near to my heart, an art I practice daily. Dance, it seems, has an even stronger hold on my mind than those things Melina used to bind me."

He might have expected Firekeeper to ask more questions, but the wolf-woman thought dancing and music were among the few things that made humans interesting and worthy of emulating. Elise knew that the Healed One's explanation would only have raised him in Firekeeper's estimation.

Elise didn't bother to explain this, though. Such personal details weren't important in comparison with the question that loomed unanswered in the forefront of her thoughts.

"Do you still wish us to find where Melina goes?"

"Yes," the Healed One replied, "but there are other things you must know, things I did not have Xarxius confide in you because I thought them unnecessary. Now, Melina's willingness to move so openly makes me believe she may feel she needs none of us much longer—that she is near her goal."

"Goal?"

"Last winter Melina came to New Kelvin bearing three artifacts of proven provenance," the Healed One said. "I believe she is seeking something here in New Kelvin that will make those artifacts as nothing, an old power bound in the days of the Founders. Our legends call it the Dragon of Despair."

XXXIV

FIREKEEPER WAS FAR LESS BOTHERED by her inability to follow the conversation than the others might have imagined. Although she understood a great deal more Pellish than she had a year before, much of what was said in more complicated discussions was still lost to her.

She had learned to compensate by watching expressions, coming to the decision that though humans lacked proper ears and tails, they really did give a great deal away—even when they did not intend to do so. This watchfulness, combined with Wendee's whispered translation, gave Firekeeper more than enough information to keep her interested.

After a few minutes, she decided that she liked the Healed One. His robes might hide his body, but nothing could hide the muscular power of his movements from eyes trained to look for signs of a healthy—and therefore dangerous—beast. She wondered how someone who stayed locked within this walled city could so remind her of a stag in his prime. When she learned the Healed One was a dancer, Firekeeper was content.

The tale of the Dragon of Despair—which Toriovico began by telling how the dragon came to be—reminded the wolf-woman of the stories Queen Elexa had told her when her winter cold had kept her in bed. Firekeeper wondered how much of this tale was true and how much fancy, but the sincerity of the Healed One's tone as he related the tale—even to a tight, strained note barely detectable beneath his words—gave credence. Clearly, the Healed One believed the tale and equally clearly he did not expect them to do so.

Firekeeper decided to keep an open mind as to its truth. After all, not much over a year before she wouldn't have believed in human cities. She'd hardly believed in humans, come to that, and humans had not believed in Beasts.

The wolf-woman felt a momentary twinge of fear that humans might now believe, and what that belief could mean to her people, but she put the fear from her, though she did tighten her hand in Blind Seer's fur.

When the story of the Dragon of Despair, its binding, and the Healed One's belief that Melina was seeking it to turn its terrible power to her own uses had ended, Firekeeper listened a trace impatiently as the others asked the Healed One various clarifying questions—none of the answers to which seemed to make them very happy.

After some time had passed, Derian glanced around the room uneasily and said, "Isn't this dangerous, our meeting with you like this and for so long?"

The Healed One's lips twisted in that odd expression that seemed like a smile but held no warmth.

"Usually, it would be dangerous," he agreed. "Indeed, I fully expect word of this meeting to get to Melina, but that was something I had to risk. I sincerely hope to convince her that we were simply discussing the customs of your country."

"But," Derian pressed, "it sounds like Melina has a lot of influence here in Thendulla Lypella. Won't she just come walking in when she gets wind of this?"

The Healed One shook his head so vigorously that his long green braid whipped over his shoulder.

"Not this time. Melina is in a trap of her own making. Since she brought the accusation against Xarxius to Apheros she is required to be a witness at the hearing. As Healed One I could insist I had duties that require me to be elsewhere. My Consolor does not have that excuse.

"Moreover, I do not believe Melina will be willing to leave Apheros. She knows—for Xarxius nearly freed Apheros from her power by appealing to his pride of office—that this hearing is the greatest danger to her hold over the Dragon Speaker there could be. Therefore, even if someone brings her word that I am meeting with you—and I do not think her agents could get a message into the sealed judicial chamber—she will be reluctant to leave."

"Why," asked Doc through Wendee, "is your civil ruler called the Dragon Speaker? I'd expect him to be called something like Number One Prime. It better fits your nomenclature."

The Healed One looked momentarily annoyed, then suddenly he turned serious.

"Actually, the title is tied in with that same legend I was relating a moment ago. Although the Founders' government was different from our modern one—for one thing, the Founders didn't have a Healed One—they did govern via a council. After the binding of the Dragon of Despair, the Star Wizard was given the position of head of the council in recognition of his heroic deeds. Since the Star Wizard had spoken to the dragon—some said he continued to hear its laments for the rest of his life—he was given the title Dragon Speaker. When my ancestor the First Healed One created the Primes he retained the title for its ancient honor and tradition."

Firekeeper felt unaccountably uncomfortable at this snippet of information. To distract herself, she asked a question of her own.

"What about Peace and Edlin?"

Now it was the Healed One's turn to look uncomfortable.

"Xarxius said something about the two of them being missing," he replied. "He mentioned it after he was arrested. I had the impression he was trying to let me know that Melina had them. However, I must admit I have no idea where they are—or how she acquired them in the first place."

As Elise explained how Peace and Edlin had been captured, being far kinder to Firekeeper in the telling than the wolf-woman would have been to herself, Firekeeper considered the task the Healed One had set for them with a sense of dread that intertwined with her own weariness and the continued pain of her injuries.

Not only did they need to find where Melina went at night, they needed to learn what they could about her investigations into this dragon. The Healed One had admitted that he believed the story, but that he had no idea whether the dragon might be a symbol for something else.

Firekeeper understood about symbols, but in her gut she thought that Melina would not be looking so hard and taking so many risks if she wasn't fairly certain that there was a real dragon to be had at the end of the chase—or at least an artifact so powerful that it had raised a mountain and caused vast destruction.

So Firekeeper had to find the truth of this dragon story. From what the Healed One was now telling Elise, it looked as if Firekeeper would need to find Edlin and Peace as well. Rather than simplifying matters, she thought that their visit to the Healed One had complicated their tasks greatly.

Firekeeper said as much to Blind Seer and the wolf replied, *"The spider's web is tightest at the center, dear heart. Trails cross most when you near the deer yard."*

"Proverbs," she said, punching him.

"Truth."

MOTHER DIDN'T come. Citrine waited, crouched for hours on the cold stone floor of the storeroom, waited until she worried she would fall asleep, sleep there until morning, and give away Mother's secret.

Citrine wanted to go to look for Mother, to make certain she hadn't left without her, but she was afraid that Mother would come and leave without her.

Then Citrine remembered a trick Grateful Peace had shown her, a trick for telling if someone had opened a letter or drawer. She reasoned that the trick would work as well for a trapdoor. Peace's trick called for something small to be laid across the fold or opening, something so small and unremarkable that it would be moved or broken when the letter was unfolded or the drawer opened—but the person who had left it there would know the marker had been moved.

So Citrine moved a bit of cobweb from where the spider had left it behind a barrel and carefully stuck it over the edges of the trapdoor. The storeroom wasn't swept very often and certainly wouldn't be this night. She could trust the cobweb to tell her if Mother had come through in her absence. Thus reassured, Citrine went looking for her mother.

The first thing Citrine was aware of was that the Cloud Touching Spire was a great deal busier than it usually was at this hour of the night. The second was Tipi sweeping down on her.

"There you are you bad girl!" Tipi exclaimed, all fury and relief. "Where have you been?"

Citrine stayed close to the truth.

"I was looking for my mother."

"Your mother isn't here," Tipi scolded. "Consolor Melina sent me a message saying that she would be in meetings through much of the night. She told me to bring you her good-night wishes."

Citrine doubted this last. Melina never had indulged in such sentimental overtures. Tipi must have had some other reason for prowling around Citrine's chambers. Thinking of the handsome guard she had snuck past on her way out, Citrine thought she knew why Tipi had wanted an excuse to be in that part of the tower.

She giggled to herself when she thought of how surprised Tipi must have been to find the bed empty but for a bundle of cloth.

"And why are you dressed like that?" Tipi demanded, indignant that the girl was not afraid and noticing Citrine's tunnel-prowling robes for the first time.

"It's my costume for one of the dances," Citrine lied. "I'm an evening shadow."

Tipi snorted to show what she thought of such ridiculous nonsense. Despite having lived in New Kelvin for many years, the slave paid little attention to the local religion and Citrine had counted on her not knowing that there were no shadows in the Harvest Joy dance. Tipi's private cult was one of profit and survival with Melina as her personal goddess.

Citrine decided to invoke that goddess now.

"I wonder if Mother will be angry with you when she learns you were out tonight?" she asked with mild curiosity.

The fashion in which Tipi stiffened made Citrine think that Melina would indeed be angry. The restriction on wandering the Cloud Touching Spire at night didn't apply as strictly to Tipi as it did to the lesser servants, but apparently it did apply.

"Nonsense," Tipi retorted, her words more confident than her bearing. "Consolor Melina sent me to check on you and check I shall. You'll need another bath or you'll rub off paint on your sheets."

Citrine surrendered, even to the extent of another bath, though she knew from experience that she could remove the paint quite well with just a small amount of the cream on her dressing table and a damp cloth.

The next morning Citrine heard, along with everyone else in Thendulla Lypella, about Xarxius's disgrace and the treason hearing. That morning at breakfast, even beneath her skillfully applied face paint, Melina looked tired and worried.

"Can I help you, Mother?" Citrine asked.

Melina's reply had been uncharacteristically gentle.

"Only if you could find a way for me to be three or four places at once, chick. I have to attend Xarxius's hearing all day and I don't know how I can possibly do that and still attend to everything else that demands my attention."

"Maybe I could stand in for you," Citrine offered hesitantly.

Melina's expression balanced between a scowl and a smile, but the smile won.

"That's very sweet of you, dear, but you can't take my place. Now don't trouble me any further. Off to dance practice with you."

Citrine had been about to offer to take a message to Idalia, but Melina's command effectively sealed her lips.

DESPITE CITRINE'S FEAR that Tipi would check on her, the girl slipped out of her room at the usual hour the next night.

Although Xarxius's hearing was sequestered, enough rumors were circulating that Citrine's rational mind knew that Mother wouldn't be venturing into the tunnels tonight. But her rational mind was nearly smothered beneath clamoring howls of fear, for over supper, Tipi had told Citrine that the Healed One had excused himself from Xarxius's hearing to entertain emissaries from Hawk Haven.

"Five people and a great, huge wolf," Tipi had said with malicious relish. "I can guess who they are. I bet you can, too. I wonder what their business could be?"

Citrine had no doubt. They were going to take her away, away from Mother. Elise and the others. They would mean well, but they didn't understand how Citrine needed to see Mother, needed to be reassured that Mother still loved her and took some pleasure in having her littlest girl near.

The fear that filled her mind with noise came not from the fact that the others wanted her back, but from a growing certainty that Mother wouldn't fight to keep her. Mother was having a lot of trouble now. Citrine didn't understand all the government talk, but she understood enough to know that Apheros, one of Mother's greatest friends in Thendulla Lypella, was in trouble, that he might lose his place as Dragon Speaker.

Citrine had also gathered—mostly from sly looks and chopped-off sentences whenever she came in hearing—that Xarxius had gotten himself and Apheros into trouble over her. Citrine didn't need to be as clever as Mother or Grateful Peace about government workings to guess that the easiest way to solve all of this trouble was to give Citrine back.

No Citrine. No trouble.

But Citrine didn't want to be given back, so she crouched on the cold stone floor, hoping Mother would come and that they could be together just like always. Citrine would explain to Mother how much she wanted to stay, how helpful she could be. She'd show her how well she knew the tunnels. That she knew about Idalia and the underground town. Then Mother could make Citrine her go-between.

Citrine hugged herself, almost giggling at the thought of their sharing that cozy secret. She determinedly didn't think about how Mother might be angry at her for sneaking around, nosing into her business. Instead she thought about how proud Mother would be that Citrine had some backbone, not like Ruby or Opal or even Jet, though Mother seemed to think so highly of him.

Cold seeped up through the soles of Citrine's slippers. It was this more than conscious planning that caused Citrine to creep from her hiding place and raise the trapdoor. The tunnels weren't any warmer than the storeroom, but she could move around there and keep herself warm.

Once Citrine was down below, it seemed quite natural to light a lantern. Almost as if struck to life by the same flint and steel, a brilliant idea lit the girl's mind.

Hadn't Mother said just that morning how she was worried about all the things she couldn't keep up with because she needed to be at Xarxius's hearing? Well, Citrine could mind this bit of business for her. Citrine had a pretty good idea of where Idalia might be checking for whatever it was that Mother wanted. Idalia and Mother had discussed their search pattern the last time Citrine and Mother had been down here.

Citrine would go and check on Idalia's progress. If there was nothing substantial—as there had been thus far—she would keep silent. But if Idalia had found something wonderful!

Soft-shod feet ghosted silently down the tunnels as Citrine dwelt on this wonderful vision. Idalia sent Mother messages through special couriers, but these messages didn't come very promptly—and Citrine knew that if one came while Mother was attending the hearing Mother wouldn't be given it until there was a break in the proceeding.

That would mean that Mother wouldn't learn of the wonderful discovery until late—maybe even a day late. But Citrine could learn everything and this very night go to Mother's room and tell her everything about . . .

The fantasy wavered somewhat as Citrine came up against the obstacle that she had no idea what Mother wanted to find down here. Treasure of some sort, that was certain.

Well then . . .

Citrine would tell Mother about the treasure and Mother would be proud and happy and announce to all the Primes: "This is my daughter and she is worth all her sisters and even her brother and all of you, too. She's staying with me and so there!"

Versions of this happy vision swept the fears from Citrine's mind and kept her fancy occupied while her feet concentrated on being as quiet as possible and her eyes checked the walls for the markers that showed the way and her ears stayed alert for sound that would tell her where Idalia was attending to her mistress's business that night.

Citrine located the searchers in the second section of tunnels she checked. They had paused in a small cavern where steam rose from a vent in the wall and the air smelled foul. Peace was there and Edlin, sketchbook in hand. Idalia was there, too, along with a young man Citrine had gathered from earlier encounters was her son, Varcasiol.

As if the shackles they wore were not enough to hold the prisoners, four guards flanked the group. The guards doubled as lantern bearers so the immediate vicinity was brilliantly lit, bordered in a dancing aura of stark black shadow in which Citrine hid as among the trees of a dense forest.

Reassured by the sour expression on Idalia's face that she had not missed witnessing the finding of the treasure hoard, Citrine turned her lantern down as low as the flame could go and made sure the shutters were tightly closed. Then she settled behind a heap of rocks to watch.

The first thing Citrine noticed was that Grateful Peace looked as if he'd had a terrible fall. There were cuts and bruises on his face and he moved as if every bone in his body ached. Whenever he could, Peace braced his one remaining arm against the wall, as if he couldn't stand on his own. When he must move without that support, he wrapped his arm across his front to hold his side.

Edlin also showed signs of battering. His lower lip was swollen so that his normally cheerful features were set in a permanent grotesque pout. He had a black eye and a welt across one side of his face. Edlin hovered as near to Grateful Peace as he could and that protectiveness told Citrine more than she wanted to know.

Confused as her thoughts could sometimes be, Citrine was not a fool. She had seen various guards strike Peace, even when Idalia was not present. She had seen the hatred Idalia bore her brother. She was also no stranger to the rivalries and resentments that can grow between those who—by an accident of birth—are supposed to be natural allies.

Citrine did not need to make a great leap of imagination or memory to know why in less than two full days Grateful Peace had gone from being a bruised cripple to a physical wreck who could hardly move without assistance. Nor did it take any tremendous reasoning power to realize how Edlin had received his own disfiguring injuries.

As this unhappy information flooded Citrine's brain the voices began their clamoring.

"Idalia's killing him!"

"What of it? When Mother was here she didn't stop the guards from beating him."

"She stopped them from hurting him too badly."

"Did she really? She started talking to him, sure, but she didn't really tell them to stop."

"But Mother has a use for him. That's obvious to the dimmest eye. If Idalia keeps this up, Peace won't last much longer."

A new voice, gentler, more wistful, entered the debate.

"And Peace was very kind to me when he was Jalarios and I was Rios. Doesn't it make you even a little sad to see what's happening?"

"No! What's important is that Mother needs him."

"But that doesn't mean Idalia can kill him, right? I mean, if Peace dies, Mother won't be happy."

"No wonder Mother feels she needs to be everywhere at once. Idalia doesn't realize what's really important. She hates Peace too much. She'll kill him and then Mother will be very angry."

"Idalia's crazy!"

"And what about what Idalia's doing to Edlin? I tell you, she's going too far there. She has no reason to hurt him. What did he ever do but protect a one-armed old man?"

The arguing continued in this fashion until Citrine pressed her hands to the sides of her head, certain that her head would split.

A thin, shrill keen of pain and frustration burst from her lips and echoed off the tunnel walls.

The guards jumped, stiffening to alertness. Idalia looked around wildly, then turned accusingly to Grateful Peace.

"What was that?" she demanded.

"I have no idea," Peace replied in a voice so full of pain that Citrine hardly recognized it.

"Echo?" Edlin offered. "Someone's sword scraping against the rock?"

Idalia looked as if she wanted to be convinced, but Varcasiol—a youth of about seventeen—was unconvinced.

"Is it true that the Founders still walk these tunnels?" he asked. "That's what the storytellers say."

"Nonsense," Idalia said, but she sounded less than convinced.

One of the guards raised his lantern high so that the upper reaches were illuminated.

"Maybe bats?" he proposed. "Or rats?"

"That's it," Idalia replied with certainty. "Bats disturbed by our lights. Are you ready to move on, Grey Pee?"

Grateful Peace was studying some characters etched into the rock with such close attention that Idalia had to repeat herself before he looked up.

"Oh, yes. If you wish."

"I do wish," Idalia said, then paused. "What do you mean, 'If I wish'?"

Grateful Peace looked as if he'd been about to shrug but winced instead.

"These writings," he said, "are a warning against going any further down this tunnel. Quite reasonable."

Peace stopped talking, caught in a fit of dry coughing. Edlin handed him a canteen, his defiant gaze daring anyone to prevent him.

"Can you talk now, old man?" Edlin asked kindly. "I think our fair hostess is interested in what you have to say."

Peace looked back at the etched rock face. The finger he traced them with, Citrine noticed with a horrified acuteness of perception, looked as if it had been stepped on repeatedly.

"Really," Peace said, with what was clearly meant to be a reassuringly urbane smile but which looked ghastly when the leaping lantern light reflected off a broken front tooth, "it's nothing to be alarmed about. Just about what one would expect if treasure were hidden near here."

He coughed and Edlin offered him more water.

"Beware of the dog, what?" Edlin said brightly. "Property guarded?"

"Rather like that," Peace agreed.

Idalia looked so alarmed that Citrine couldn't help giggling. The shrill sound caught against a rock and broke into myriad echoes. The guards jumped and several unsheathed their swords. Varcasiol looked about wildly.

"Give a complete translation," Idalia insisted, frowning at her son.

Peace gave one of his wince-shrugs, and Edlin put his hand out for one of the lanterns so that he could hold it nearer to the inscription.

The nearest guard, eager to get a more solid grip on his sword, handed the lantern over without question.

Citrine waited eagerly for what Peace would say, certain she was the only person here who wasn't afraid. After all, she knew where the noises were coming from. She smothered a giggle behind her hand and leaned a little closer.

" 'Pass not beyond this point,' " Peace read, " 'lest you wish your blood to boil even as does the water in the rocks.' "

He paused as if reluctant to continue. Idalia raised one hand as if to strike him and Peace quickly bent his head again to the task.

" 'Your eyes shall melt in their sockets, the very marrow in your bones turn to fire. Trespass at your peril.' "

Peace looked up, letting his hand drop to his side from where it had been tracing beneath the characters.

"Rather theatrical," he said, almost apologetically.

Varcasiol had come forward to peer more closely at the inscription.

"I recognize the characters for boiling," he said, his voice tight and anxious, "and there's one that looks like eyes and another like a thighbone. Why couldn't the First Healed One have had the old script taught more widely!"

Peace looked down his nose at the nervous young man.

"It is, Nephew, in the Illuminator's college, and several others, but the old symbols are rather cumbersome for daily business."

Citrine sensed a well-worn family argument in the glare Idalia turned on her brother, but before Idalia could put her indignation into words Edlin set the lantern down near his feet and straightened.

"I say," he said, running his free hand inside his collar, "is anyone else feeling rather hot?"

The guards shifted nervously, obviously unwilling to admit anything. Varcasiol immediately nodded.

"I do," he said, brushing his hand along his forehead.

It came away covered with white paint. Citrine giggled at this social error. Everyone jumped.

"It's just the hot spring," Idalia snapped. "You weren't hot until Grey Pee read this warning. The sounds are bats or perhaps steam escaping."

"I say," Edlin cut in, "actually I was rather hot. Had the water bottle out several times, don't you know."

Citrine noticed that the guards were now all edging away from the invisible line marked by the inscription. She eased herself away from their light. Pebbles rolled from beneath her feet, their bouncing rattling directionless echoes from all around.

You could help Edlin and Peace, you know, the gentle voice said. *Peace was kind to you and Edlin let you ride Moonkissed. Mother wouldn't mind. She'd be pleased that you saved Peace from Idalia.*

Citrine stiffened, bracing herself for the onslaught of voices.

"Go away!" she wailed frantically, and though she would have sworn that the words burst from her without warning, perhaps this was not so, for she spoke not Pellish—as would have been natural—but New Kelvinese.

Upon hearing this desperate, misery-laden cry, one of the guards broke and ran, carrying his lantern with him. Idalia's son grabbed for the lantern that Edlin had set down, but the young lord had grabbed it before him.

"I say," Edlin protested, "get your own light!"

"Give it to me!" Varcasiol insisted, clawing for the lantern.

Edlin swung at Varcasiol, the panicked blow landing so solidly that Varcasiol's feet slipped out from under him and he fell on his backside. His scream was more shocked than pained, but the sound of it echoing off the rocks was too much for the nerves of the other guards.

Two fled outright. The one who had given Edlin his lantern paused a moment, but seeing Edlin's fist rise in challenge and his fellows vanishing he took to his heels.

"Cowards!" Idalia shouted after their retreating backs. "There is nothing here."

"Oh, yes there is," Peace said, rising stiffly from where he had remained crouched by the rock. "We are and now we two are as many as you."

Idalia sneered and Citrine admired the woman for her brave defiance.

"You," Idalia retorted, "a one-armed wreck and this youth? Both of you chained?"

Peace looked steadily at her.

"If you think it will be so easy, then take the light from Edlin and drive us before you."

When Idalia didn't move, it was Peace's turn to sneer.

"Not so quick to act without your slaves to order about, are you? I'd be careful of those slaves now. They're afraid of something bigger than you. If I've caught rumors that some political debacle is keeping Melina away, you can guess the slaves know three times as much. How long before they lose confidence in her promises of freedom and luxury? How long before you have a full-blown rebellion on your hands? Do you dare stand here arguing with me when your pocket kingdom might even now be fragmenting?"

Citrine could see that Peace's words had struck home, but Idalia wasn't about to give up her prisoners.

"Do you really think you can defeat us?" she asked.

"I do not," Peace said, "but I do know one thing we can do that you cannot prevent."

"What?"

"We can break the lantern and leave you in the dark."

Varcasiol gave a thin cry of terror, but Idalia was unmoved.

"And what good would that do?"

"I am very skilled at moving in darkness," Peace replied. "Remember, I was once the Dragon's Eye. My strong young friend here is a hunter in his own land. His sister the wolf has taught him many secrets about moving without light."

Citrine knew this last was a lie, but she admired Peace no less for it. Idalia wavered.

"You have a deal in mind," she stated.

"Yes. Trade us for the lantern in return for unlocking these chains. Leave us in darkness. Go. Reestablish your hold on your slaves. Edlin and I will have our opportunity to escape. Likely we will not get far and you will recapture us."

"And if I do not take your offer?" Idalia asked in the tones of one who already suspected the worst.

"Then Edlin will smash the lantern. As I said, I am very good at moving in darkness and so is he. Will you be so confident that we are evenly matched when there is no light?"

"Mother," Varcasiol said, "Uncle has a point."

"Cowardly clerk!" Idalia spat.

"Time," Peace reminded her, "is precious. Every moment that passes is a moment during which your hold over Melina's slaves could be slipping. Then, too, the supply of lamp oil is not infinite. I believe the guards took the refills with them."

Idalia decided.

"Very well," she said, her mouth twisting as if she was tasting something very sour. "Edlin, come here."

"No," Peace countered instantly. "Me first. Edlin will hold the lantern while you unlock my chains. He is stronger than I am, but you two might hope to overthrow him if there was no one free to guard his interests."

Idalia shrugged, her very gesture admitting the trick she had hoped to play. Peace shuffled forward and the cuffs were unlocked from around his ankles. He picked the metal weight up and stepped back to Edlin's side. He traded the lantern for the chains, which Edlin looped around his fist.

"Something of a weapon, what?" the young man said cheerfully, scooping up his own chains once they were unlocked.

Peace handed over the lantern.

"I'd go quickly," he advised with false kindness. "There isn't too much oil remaining."

"The map," Idalia demanded, pointing toward where Edlin's sketch pad lay on the rock.

"I say. It wasn't part of our agreement," Edlin said, "but we wouldn't want you getting lost, what?"

Idalia snatched the papers from his hand and with Varcasiol behind her hurried in the same direction as the vanished guards. The light dropped away sharply as Idalia and her son retreated. It wasn't long before the two men were in darkness.

"Not bad," Edlin said cheerfully. "Of course, I hope you're as good in the dark as you said. I'm nothing at all like Firekeeper."

"You may not need to be," Peace responded, and Citrine was struck by how the pain and exhaustion had returned to his voice. He must have been putting everything he had into arguing with Idalia.

"What?" Edlin said.

In response Peace called softly, "Citrine? Are you there?"

XXXV

TORIOVICO EXCUSED HIMSELF from a portion of Xarxius's hearing the morning following his interview with the Hawk Havenese. He was glad not to have to sit all day next to Melina in the council chamber.

Melina had accepted his reason for meeting with her erstwhile enemies with so little argument or questioning that Torio realized how genuinely worried she was about the situation with Apheros. It was enough for her to see her husband smile and tell her how curious he was about a land that could let a wonderful and talented woman like her go.

Even so, Toriovico was very relieved not to need to keep up the deception at such close quarters for most of a day. What if he forgot himself and gazed into those pale blue eyes? He might find himself drowning before he knew he had slipped in over his head.

Happily, though Melina might grumble that she had better things to do than sit and listen to the Primes debate, Toriovico really did have responsibilities that demanded he be elsewhere.

The moon had entered her fourth quarter and the Healed One must preside at the ceremonies that assured nothing untoward would happen during the waning of her light. The Harvest Festival would not begin until the new moon was into her second quarter, but the Choreographer had been heard complaining that he could not continue much further in his preparations without the Healed One present to dance the Harvest Lord's part.

And Toriovico's hairdresser wanted a chance to strip the green from his master's hair in preparation for tinting it in varied shades of red and orange for autumn.

This last, at least, could wait. The Choreographer, however, did have a reasonable argument—and Torio's semireligious role as Healed One took precedence over his civic duties.

Toriovico trotted lightly up the stairs to his private studio, eager for a return to the joys of the dance. Formal practice would not begin for at least an hour. He would stretch and go through his part a few times without music, without any companions other than his reflections in the polished copper mirrors on the walls of his studio.

Torio's surprise when one of those mirrors slid to the side, admitting two dirty and battered men into the shining tranquility of his studio, could not have been greater if his own reflection had started to converse with him.

"Honored One," said the leaner and more battered of the two intruders, "pray do not call out."

Toriovico had been about to do so, but, knowing that there was a guard just down the hall—and that these were strange times—he restrained himself.

"Who are you?" he asked.

The speaker's bruised lips twisted in a wry grimace.

"I am Grateful Peace. My companion is Edlin Norwood, Lord Kestrel of Hawk Haven."

The second man gave a Hawk Havenese bow. The curly mop of dark black hair he shook back from his eyes as he rose testified more than any words to his identity. Elise Archer had included Edlin's idiosyncratic hairstyle in her description of the missing man.

"Not quite attired to meet a king, what?" Edlin said by way of greeting, his Pellish accent quite strong but the words understandable.

"What am I to do with you?" was the question that fought up through the horde that competed for Toriovico's attention.

"Hide us," Grateful Peace replied simply, "and then help us escape the Earth Spires."

His statement was so lucid that Toriovico was instantly in control of himself once more.

"Can you continue to hide wherever you came from?" he asked. "If I arrange for you to have food and water and such?"

Peace nodded.

"For a time. I believe no one but myself knows of this particular passage."

"Is there one into my bedroom?" Torio asked curiously, crossing the room to fetch the carafe of cool well-water that a servant had brought to the studio.

"No," Peace replied with a forced grin that revealed a badly broken tooth.

"This room was once an office. A painting hung where the mirror is now. This is one of the few secret passages within the Cloud Touching Spire. I believe that is why your ancestor selected this building for his residence."

Toriovico nodded, understanding far better than Grateful Peace could ever know why his ancestors would covet privacy.

"I know what happened to you," he said, "to the moment Lady Blysse was forced to abandon you. I can only offer you water now and I must dance or there will be questions. Stand where you cannot be seen if someone comes down the corridor and tell me what has happened since."

Edlin Norwood smiled brightly, despite a swollen and disfigured mouth.

"Then you have spoken to the others," he said. "Citrine said that was the rumor and that was why Peace dared bring us to you. We've had quite a time of it since Sister left us in the tunnels."

Torio listened to their account without question, interrupting only once to indicate a small cabinet stocked with a variety of salves and bandages meant for his own strained muscles. When they finished their account, his mind was again reeling from the implications of what they had reported.

"So Citrine assisted you in your escape? Where is she now?"

"Asleep," Edlin replied. "We convinced her to have a cup of wine before retiring," he added rather ashamedly, "so she should sleep heavily for some time now."

"I will make certain she is not disturbed," Toriovico said. "Now, I must attend a rehearsal. Your mention of wine makes me think you have not been without refreshment."

"Raided the larder," Edlin admitted. "Honored One, will you help us?"

"I already have," Torio reminded him; then he took mercy on the youth's obvious concern. "I need time to think and if I do not show up at rehearsal there may be awkward questions. Return to your refuge and rest. I will return as soon as I can."

The fugitives could do nothing but accept the Healed One's decision, Peace with resignation, Edlin with evident distrust.

Torio didn't blame him. They had been through far too much for Edlin to easily trust a man he'd never before met. Grateful Peace knew better. Perhaps he could calm his companion's unease.

Arranging for Citrine not to be disturbed was quite simple. Toriovico stopped in to see her, ostensibly to see if she wanted to accompany him to practice. Citrine had trouble rousing enough to talk to him, but he managed to get her to drink some water in which he had dissolved a small dose of a powder his apothecary had given him when a torn muscle had made sleep impossible.

He felt bad about drugging the child, but she could not be permitted to wake and possibly say things that would endanger Grateful Peace and Edlin. Then Torio told Citrine's maid that the child was not to be troubled.

Racing down the corridors in a fashion he had not since he was a boy, Toriovico reached the large dance studio located in one of the towers near the center of Thendulla Lypella. The Choreographer—a highly ranked member of his sodality—was too assured of himself to be honored at Toriovico's attendance, but he did offer a small sniff of approval at his lead dancer's return.

For a time Toriovico had attention for nothing beyond the intricate movements of the dance. However, once the company had gone through the same passage several times—a handful of the younger fruit and vegetables were having difficulties—his mind was free to wander. A solution came to him about halfway through the practice. He tried it out, mapping it as he would the steps of a dance, and found no flaw in it.

It would mean hiding the two fugitives until the next day, finding a way to get them clean and more appropriately costumed, but it should work. Columi's services should be needed, but happily the emeritus Prime was not attending Xarxius's hearing.

Toriovico's greatest worry was how to keep Melina in ignorance of her prisoners' escape. Grateful Peace and Edlin had questioned Citrine extensively regarding how Melina communicated with Idalia and the slaves she supervised. From what Citrine said, communication was roundabout at best, involving notes dropped at public pedestals and then routed from there to Thendulla Lypella. Melina had preferred to go to Idalia herself, and Idalia was forbidden to come to Melina or to send any human messenger.

This, combined with the fact that Idalia would doubtless prefer to hide her failure from her mistress as long as possible, gave Toriovico hope that waiting until tomorrow would not be too great a risk to take.

At the conclusion of practice, Toriovico spoke with the Choreographer. The man was all enthusiasm for the Healed One's suggestion.

"Just what we need," he said, "during this time of doubt and crisis, a public display of all that is good about our land. Pageantry, color, respect for the wonders of the past. I am honored to serve you in this way."

"Very good," Toriovico said. "I will leave you to your preparations. I have one or two things to do myself."

DERIAN FOUND THE NOTE late in the afternoon, resting on the carpet in the front hallway. From scuff marks on the paper, it had clearly been slid under the door.

The folded paper bore no address, but somehow Derian did not think that a missive for Hasamemorri would have been so delivered. Despite her continuing support of her tenants—or maybe because of it—Hasamemorri had lost no respect with her friends and neighbors. The people who threw rocks at the shuttered windows or left offal on the doorstep were—at least according to Bee Biter's eye and Blind Seer's nose—strangers.

The tall redhead carried the paper into the room that had been Doc's consulting room and now, in the absence of patients and the occurrence of their own semi-imprisonment, had become their sitting room.

Doc sat reviewing a text of medical drawings sent to him by Oculios the Alchemist while Wendee and Elise worked at the mending. Firekeeper disdained either reading or hand work but lay drowsing by the cold hearth, her head on Blind Seer's flank. She was still mending from her injuries, and though he kept quiet about it, Derian was worried about her.

"I found this in the hall," Derian said, holding up the folded sheet of paper. "There's no address."

Elise dropped her stitchery in her lap with rather too much eagerness. "Let me see!"

Derian held it out of her reach, teasingly, as he might have with Damita. "I found it," he chided. "I get to read it."

He broke the blob of wax that sealed the fold and frowned. He read some New Kelvinese, but except for a few words this was beyond him.

"I guess you get it after all," he said, handing the paper to Elise.

She accepted the missive with an slightly arrogant arching of her brow—then stuck her tongue out at him.

"It's very strange," she said after puzzling over the writing for a long moment.

"Read it," Doc prompted.

Elise did so without further hesitation.

"Be at the Processional Gate within the crowd at the noon hour. Seize the gem that is your own and additional riches will fall into your hands."

Derian felt his blood thrill.

"Is it signed?" he asked.

"Not even with an initial or a sign," Elise replied, turning the paper over in her hands and inspecting it carefully. "The paper's very fine quality, though, even by New Kelvinese standards."

Wendee extended her hand and Elise dropped the paper into it.

"'The gem that is your own,'" Wendee read. "That has to be a reference to Citrine! I think someone is telling us that she's going to be at the Processional Gate at noon tomorrow."

Derian didn't disagree, but he wasn't as confident as Wendee that they'd understood the entire message.

"What's that bit about 'additional riches,' then?"

Wendee gave an airy wave of her hand.

"Diversion. Something to make anyone who reads this think the note was about an assignation or maybe even thieves planning a crime. There are lots of messages just like it in the plays."

Derian wasn't going to give in so easily.

"Maybe," he said. "Still, I don't suppose we dare not show up at the appointed time and place."

"Not in the least," Elise said in her Grandmother Rosene manner. "What if this letter is from the Healed One? He would have taken great risks communicating with us—in addition to whatever he's done to arrange that Citrine be within our reach."

"What are we going to do about the crowds?" Wendee asked. "We hardly dare walk to Aswatano for vegetables. Now we're going to go all the way across the city to the gates of Thendulla Lypella—and hide ourselves in a crowd?"

Doc grinned mischievously and leaned forward.

"Wendee, it is time you returned to your roots on the stage. The one thing certain to be overlooked in New Kelvin is a group of people dressed in some colorful or peculiar manner. We have until noon tomorrow. What can you manage by then?"

THAT WAS HOW Derian found himself standing at the front edge of a festival crowd close to the Processional Gate. He was dressed like a giant carrot, Wendee having decided that each of their costumes must cover their heads at least to the hairline so that they wouldn't need to resort to shaving their hair.

To escape that humiliation, Derian would have dressed as almost anything, but he thought that a carrot was going a bit far. Wendee had, however, quizzed Hasamemorri's ever useful maids and learned that criers from Thendulla Lypella had announced a special preview of a portion of the Harvest Joy dance—with the Healed One himself dancing the part of the Harvest Lord.

"It is meant," the maid explained, "to hearten our people. Many have been greatly disturbed by recent events within the Dragon Speaker's court."

"Lots of people will be dressing up following a harvest theme," Wendee had explained to them later, "and Hasamemorri's maids say that those who are costumed will be given privileged places at the front—it's the usual custom apparently."

Orange fabric had been what Wendee could acquire at both short notice and in sufficient quantities to cover Derian's lanky form, so a carrot was what he must be. They didn't have time to make entire costumes for each one of them, so a common brown robe made the foundation for a respectable potato costume for Doc.

Doc kept complaining, however, that the hooded upper-body garment, which had been cobbled from a burlap sack, itched and was full of dust. However, since shaving the front portion of his scalp was the only other option, like Derian, Doc surrendered.

Elise was rather more fortunate than either of the men. Among her belongings was a pale green New Kelvinese robe. This, when accompanied by a loose white silk coif and appropriate face paint, transformed her into quite a convincing young onion.

Wendee was either the least or most fortunate of the lot, depending on how one was inclined to think. Nothing in her wardrobe lent itself to the general theme of fruits and vegetables, and creation of Derian's carrot robe had occupied all available hands. After some consultation, Hasamemorri herself suggested that Wendee attire herself as a wheat mother.

"The Mothers are lesser figures," she said, "not the wives of the Harvest Lord, so you won't be out of line. You've a woman's figure," Hasamemorri added approvingly, "not a mere slip of a girl's like Lady Elise."

Hasamemorri helped Wendee dye a plain robe golden brown. Braids of golden straw attached to a sturdy cotton coif, and a basket containing ears of wheat completed Wendee's accessories. Her face was painted in a rather unsettling mosaic in which her eyes and mouth became elements within the harvest bounty.

"I think it is a shame and a disgrace," Hasamemorri said, leaning back in her chair and inspecting her work, "that you Hawk Havenese have been treated so poorly this last moon or so. I take great pleasure in thinking how now you'll go out and enjoy some of Dragon Breath's brightness."

But Hasamemorri's shame on behalf of her fellow citizens did not extend to accompanying her tenants. She cried off on the grounds that her knees would not stand the strain, but Derian thought that Hasamemorri was far too acute not to have noticed that strange events seemed to be plaguing her tenants and far too canny to get intimately involved with them.

One other member of their party cried off as well.

Firekeeper said she hurt too much to put them at risk by accompanying them. No one doubted the truth of her words. Though the lacerations to her leg had closed and daily looked less angry, Firekeeper herself was becoming more and more withdrawn.

"Firekeeper seems worse since we went to Thendulla Lypella," Derian confided in Doc as they helped each other put on their costumes. "Could she have caught something? Or could someone have cursed her?"

He offered the last suggestion hesitantly, but surely the New Kelvinese were capable of such.

Doc shook his head.

"Firekeeper's not sleeping enough. Worried, I think, about the others. Maybe if we get Citrine back and see our way toward getting Edlin and Peace she'll relax."

Doc frowned slightly, then went on, hesitantly, as if confiding something in rather bad taste.

"In fact, I took the liberty of giving her something this morning that will help her sleep while we're gone. I don't want her changing her mind and doing herself—or someone else—an injury."

Unspoken was the fact that Doc had done this without consulting Firekeeper, who barely tolerated medicines that reduced pain and hated anything that dulled her wits.

But Derian couldn't waste energy worrying about Firekeeper or her possible reaction now. Indeed, as much of an asset as the wolf-woman could be in a crisis, as the hour drew closer to noon and the crowd surrounding the Processional Gate grew Derian was glad that she was not being subjected to this cacophony. Who knew what she would do?

Or perhaps "almost glad" was a more honest reaction. Part of Derian dreaded discovery as a foreigner as he had never feared anything before and knowing that Firekeeper would be there to get him and the others out would have been reassuring.

Promptly at noon, a series of resounding cymbal clashes and shouts from the guards at the gate announced that the event was beginning. The crowd hushed so rapidly that Derian was reminded of those days when King Tedric himself would come to address his subjects from the speaker's balcony at Eagle's Nest Castle. Even the vendors who moments before had been hawking everything from sweets to plaster figures shaped like various vegetables settled to watch.

Though the sense of expectancy was similar to what Derian had experienced, there was something more as well. Joyful anticipation mingled with intense reverence could be seen on face after brightly painted face. Derian was tall enough to see through the gates and realize that the crowd was two-sided. The inhabitants of the Earth Spires had left their daily round and were watching with expressions no less reverent than those of their less privileged fellows outside.

In those expressions, Derian was reminded yet again that to the New Kelvinese the Harvest Dance was no mere civic celebration like the fourteen society festivals in his homeland, it was a magical ritual meant to somehow influence the coming year. Today's performance might only be a rehearsal, but that made it only slightly less important than the real thing. As Hasamemorri had explained, the magic would still be there.

The soles of Derian's feet tingled and his heart beat more wildly than it had even when he had contemplated a potential riot. It took all his self-control not to rush away lest this magic—like that which had brought into being the Dragon of Despair—rage out of control. He calmed himself with a physical effort, straightening the point of his hat and looking toward the Processional Gate, which even now was swinging slowly and smoothly outward.

A series of deep drumbeats set the tempo, and then an unseen orchestra burst into a soaring piece that replaced the conventional melodies with which Derian was familiar with complex themes that evoked, even to his city-bred imagination, the entirety of the harvest.

Emerging first through the gates came six women, their long legs bare, their robes kilted up almost to their hips. The motions of their dance were those of stoop labor, the bend and toss, bend and toss so eloquently expressed that Derian found himself looking to see what they were picking.

These were followed by burly men, their coordinated arm gestures evoking the scything and binding of sheaves. They were followed by apple pickers, grape stompers, diggers working root vegetables loose from the soil. Somewhere in the course of their circling, whirling dance, Derian realized that he was seeing the same dancers over and over again, but they merged their motions into each other's so smoothly that the entire process of the gathering in of summer's bounty was evoked and celebrated.

Around the fringes of these workers and their complex dance skittered little children dressed in robes the colors of autumn leaves. Their costumes were so carefully constructed that Derian could tell oak from maple, elm from ash, beech from birch without even looking to see the leaf patterns block-printed on the fabric. The leaves were chased by winds in robes of silvery white touched with icy grey. Every so often a rumble just like thunder would drown out the music. Then the harvesters would increase their tempo, glancing upward, their posture so eloquent of worry that Derian found himself inadvertently checking the clear noon sky.

Gradually, the gathering of the harvest segued into a celebration of its bounty. Men hauled out a wagon laden with piles of fruit and vegetables. Over this bright treasure stood the Harvest Lord himself—dressed in girded robe, his hair the brilliant color of autumn leaves. He posed for a moment of sudden hush on a small platform suspended over the wagon's bed; then, on this small stage, he began to dance. His motions incorporated the gathering in of the harvest, but also recalled its planting and somehow reminded the watcher of all the labor involved.

Watching, Derian forgot he had ever been afraid, caught up in the joy and wonder of what a human body could achieve—and disbelieving, even as he watched and knew it was real, what he was seeing.

Derian had seen the Healed One in person just the day before. He could recognize something of that man in the figure who towered over his subjects now, but he had to struggle to do so. This seemed no man but a vibrant force of nature.

But wonders did not end with the Harvest Lord's dance. At a wave of Toriovico's hand, the gathered crops in the wagon bed rose and joined him in his celebration, spilling over the sides with such effortless grace that Derian's mind had to fight to see costumed men and women and not grain, fruits, and vegetables suddenly brought to exuberant and joyful life.

And in the midst of this, Derian spotted Citrine. She was dressed in bright red robes, the hat on her head shaped exactly like an apple. Her skills were not markedly less than those of the other child dancers in the fruit and

vegetable group—though the autumn leaves that still skittered and pirouet-
ted around the fringes clearly represented the most skilled.

Wendee's hand closed around his arm and Derian nodded. Then he realized what they were going to have to do. To the little fruit and vegetables,
possibly because their dancing was not up to that performed by their fellows, had been given the task of distributing gifts to the crowd. Like the
rest, Citrine had danced back to the wagon and been given a basket containing—as Derian saw when a shy little boy dressed as a cucumber thrust a
piece into his hand—miniature vegetables and fruits, molded from sugar
paste.

"Spread out," he whispered to the other three, "and try to get near Citrine. Make it look like part of the fun."

That wasn't as hard as it might have seemed. The reverently watching
audience had evolved into a good-natured scramble for some of the candy.
The fruit and vegetable children circulated through the throng, handing out
their gifts and often giving little impromptu performances.

Citrine was hardly the center of all eyes, though Derian could have sworn
that the Harvest Lord—though he continued his own stylized motions—was
rather more aware of her than he might have been expected to be.

Knowing that the voluminous skirts of his carrot costume offered a perfect place to conceal Citrine should she resist, Derian made an extra effort to
reach her. He was rewarded, coming up on her just as she was handing out
her last bits of candy—and incidentally becoming even less of interest to the
foraging crowd.

Derian knelt in front of her.

"Remember me?" he asked with a grin.

"You're a carrot!" she laughed, and he swept her up into his arms.

Citrine's outraged shriek was dismissed by those nearby as part of the
fun. Derian tried to look as if he was dancing with her, whirling her in the air
as he hustled her toward the edge of the crowd. His deception might not
have worked, but at the very moment Derian took hold of the girl the orchestra suddenly surged into what was—even to his unsophisticated ears—a
recessional.

Attention shifted back toward the Processional Gate.

I bet the Healed One was watching, Derian thought, *and provided the best
diversion he could. And I'll bet anything that most of the crowd just figured
that Citrine was my little girl and had gotten out of hand. Her costume isn't
all that much different than a dozen I've seen today.*

"No!" Citrine squealed indignantly. "I've got to go back!"

She spoke Pellish, so no one understood her words, but her tone did awaken some interest. Worried that Citrine would remember to use New Kelvinese next time, Derian tried to silence her without being too obvious. Citrine took advantage of this to bite him hard on one hand.

Derian's yelp of pain was covered by the music, but there was no way he could recover the temporary loosening of his grip. In that instant, Citrine wriggled free and in no time at all she had joined the last trailing dancers as they swept back behind the walls of Thendulla Lypella.

Derian decided that it was time he, too, retreated lest when the rehearsal performance was over some of his neighbors in the crowd decided to ask a few uncomfortable questions. He wished he were dressed a little less obviously as he found Wendee and the two of them headed back toward Hasamemorri's house, trying hard not to hurry.

They'd become separated from Doc and Elise in the crush, but Derian was only mildly worried about them. He trusted that the pair would have made their way safely back to the house—especially as his straining ears did not catch the roar of a rioting crowd. Therefore he was relieved but not surprised when Elise—her hair freed from its coif though otherwise she was still clad in her spring onion costume—opened the front door for them.

What made Derian's jaw drop was who waited for them inside the consulting room.

"Edlin! Peace!" Derian nearly sank to his knees in the rush of sudden relief. "You're all right!"

Derian almost regretted the words even as he spoke them. Edlin Norwood and Grateful Peace might be present, but they certainly were not all right. Both showed ample evidence of hard use. Bruises and lacerations were visible beneath the cosmetics they had been wiping from their faces. Both Edlin's eyes had been blackened. Peace had at least one broken tooth.

As Derian entered, Edlin set aside the rag he'd been using to clean off his own face paint. When he rose to offer Derian a heartfelt embrace—honoring the tall redhead as he might a kinsman—Derian could feel how much weight he'd lost.

But what Edlin had suffered was nothing compared with the injury inflicted on Grateful Peace. The Illuminator sat slightly slumped in a chair near the side window, passively permitting Doc to wipe away his face paint and inspect his injuries all at once.

As with Derian, Wendee's initial joy at the return of their companions was muted when she saw what had been done to them.

"I'll make tea," she said, sweeping out.

Elise nodded.

Turning to Derian, she asked, "Citrine?"

He shook his head.

"I had her," he replied ruefully. "Then she bit me."

Holding up the swollen digit as proof, he went on, "I couldn't very well knock Citrine out and that was the only way I could have gotten her away without her screaming herself silly."

"I'm sure you did your best," Elise said, but Derian couldn't help but feel he had to explain.

"If I'd thought I could make people think she was my kid acting up," he said, "I'd have hit her and taken their disapproval, but too many might have seen her out there dancing. What if she'd said the wrong thing? I guess I was afraid there'd be another riot."

Elise put her hand on his arm.

"Derian, we understand, really. You at least got close to her. Doc and I didn't even manage that."

Derian felt marginally better.

"It looks," he said, looking at Edlin and Grateful Peace, "that at least part of the Healed One's plan worked. Or is this just good luck?"

"Some luck," Edlin agreed, "but the Healed One, too. He arranged it all."

He was clearly ready to launch into an explanation, but Derian forestalled him with a raised hand.

"Wait for Wendee to get back with the tea. Where's Firekeeper? She'll want to hear this. I'm surprised she's not in here rejoicing in your return. You've never seen anything like her mood since she left you behind in the tunnels. She nearly got herself killed trying to rescue you single-handedly."

"It sounds," Grateful Peace said, "as if we all have a considerable amount to tell each other. As for us, we owe our escape largely to Citrine."

"It does sound," Derian said slowly, "as if we do have a lot to tell each other."

Along with the tea, Wendee brought Firekeeper and Blind Seer from where they had been drowsing in the yard. Despite the wolf-woman's enforced sleep, she had shadows under her eyes so deep that they looked nearly as bruised as Edlin's. Seeing unguarded shock touch both Edlin and Peace's expressions, Derian realized how ill Firekeeper must appear.

By common consent, the story began when Firekeeper left Edlin and Peace. Edlin did much of the talking for the pair, Peace being subjected to Doc's ministrations. In addition to filling in gaps in their knowledge, as Edlin spoke two things rapidly became apparent. One was that Edlin's respect and admiration for Grateful Peace verged on awe—and that Peace's affection for the younger man was just as sincere. Two, it became clear that Edlin had done a considerable amount of maturing during the time he had spent as Melina's captive.

Odd, Derian thought, *if Earl Kestrel owes this improvement in his son to an enemy.*

Initially, Derian's group had little to contribute to the tale. Citrine's defection was dealt with lightly, though no effort was made to hide their worry about her or the various attempts they had made to get her back. Later, they had more to tell: the attempt to kidnap Doc, their visits to Ambassador Redbriar, the meeting with Xarxius. When they reached the point where Xarxius had been arrested for treason, Peace looked very grave.

"We were told something of this by one of the Healed One's close confidants. I am deeply saddened," Grateful Peace continued, "that Xarxius's attempt to help us may cost him his life. He is a good and loyal servant to New Kelvin—no more a traitor to his kingdom, Speaker, and Healed One than am I."

"Maybe," Elise offered, "we can help him. Certainly, the Healed One doesn't believe these accusations."

"I certainly hope we can help him," Peace replied, but his tone was without conviction.

"But," Edlin added, "whatever else, Xarxius's arrest was why we got away from Idalia. We never would have managed if Melina had still been around."

With a glance at Peace, Edlin told how they'd made their escape owing to Citrine's fortuitous intervention. She had provided the light by which they made their way into familiar reaches, but had not wished to come away with them.

"Treated us like enemies one moment," Edlin said, "friends the next."

"She is," Peace agreed, "a troubled child. Part of her is in rebellion against her mother. I firmly believe that, but that part is nearly smothered beneath waves of guilty indebtedness and a desire to have her mother's approval."

After making their way to the Cloud Touching Spire by means of various tunnels, Edlin and Peace had petitioned the Healed One for assistance. He had not only agreed but had contrived a way that the gates would be opened for them.

"I think," Edlin added, "that the Healed One wants to make it up to Peace for thinking him a traitor. He knows now what Melina is really like—and how terrible it would have been if she had gotten her hands on working magical artifacts."

An agent of the Healed One had taken them to a place where they could get clean and conceal the worst of their injuries with face paint. He had also provided them with robes identical to those worn by many workers within Thendulla Lypella. Edlin's had included a hood that covered his hair. As with Derian's own group, New Kelvinese eclecticism had worked in favor of their disguises. The large population of the Earth Spires had assured that no one would notice a couple of strangers.

"I wish we could have managed something similar last year," Wendee said, touching her still short front hair.

"But then," Peace reminded her, "you needed to be able to pass for workers on a specific project. This time we could be from any of a number of walks of life."

As the crowd within Thendulla Lypella began to gather to watch the rehearsal of the Harvest Dance, Peace and Edlin's unnamed guide had positioned them near the gate. During the distribution of candy, the two men had simply walked out. There had been a tense moment when a man had knocked Grateful Peace to the ground in his eagerness to get a candy onion. Edlin had been ready to knock him down in turn, but the man had been so ashamed by his own behavior that he had helped them out of the more crowded areas and had even given them his own carefully assembled hoard of sweets.

"I say," Edlin grinned, looking more like himself than he had, "he nearly made it impossible for us to get away. He'd seen us come out of Thendulla Lypella and wanted to escort us safely back to our offices within. Peace made up some nonsense about our having to visit someone at the Sericulturalists' sodality and the man escorted us to their gate instead."

Peace's smile showed his broken front tooth all too plainly.

"We would have been inviting further difficulties if the porter had answered the gate promptly, but I had been correct in my assumption that he would have climbed to the wall to watch the dance from there."

"So the entire public rehearsal," Elise said, wonder erasing the weariness and tension from her features, "was to provide an excuse to open the front gates of Thendulla Lypella and a crowd to cover your sneaking out."

"That's about it," Edlin agreed. "I only wish the Healed One's plan had succeeded in bringing Citrine out, too."

"So do all of us," Wendee agreed.

"And what," Derian said to cover the uncomfortable silence that followed, "do we do next?"

"Prepare dinner," Wendee said, her practicality a welcome interruption. "I could use help in the kitchen and I'm sure that Edlin and Peace could both use some quiet rest."

Elise agreed. "We can't hope to achieve anything more today. I'll come out to the kitchen with you, Wendee. Doc can help Peace and Edlin if they're too sore to get out of those robes without help."

She smiled at Jared when she added, "And maybe Doc can use a nap, too. He's given a lot of himself today."

Derian thought that Doc's answering smile showed no sign of weariness, and knew that one of them, at least, felt well rewarded for the day's efforts.

XXXVI

"THEY DID what?"

Melina looked up from the papers she had just spread out on her desk, papers she had thought she would have a few hours to study before needing to surrender to sleep.

Bright Eagle! She could sleep during the trial tomorrow. It wasn't as if she was needed there. Maybe she'd send Tipi with a message she was ill. Woman's complaints. Something vague. Maybe even intimate it was morning sickness. That would make the ground under them roll.

But here was Citrine standing in front of her desk, still in her dance costume, her ridiculous apple hat pushed to one side, interrupting her mother's work once more. The child had burst in almost before Melina had her books open, babbling so rapidly Melina hadn't grasped a quarter of what she was saying, but now she had fallen inexplicably silent.

"They did what?" Melina repeated sternly. Her gaze dropped to the page in front of her: "*Bounded by streams of liquid fire, deep beneath the Earth Spires, we trapped it, forcing it within the living rock and sealing that rock with cold until it became dead.*"

The pronoun use was difficult, but Melina was certain that the second "it" referred to the rock, not the dragon. What use the rest of the account if the dragon had been killed?

"They tried to kidnap me, Mother. Derian was in the carrot costume, I'm sure. He talked to me."

Melina wrested her gaze from the text.

"You are saying that Derian Carter tried to kidnap you? When?"

"Just this afternoon, Mother. At the end of the rehearsal—the rehearsal for the Harvest Joy dance."

Melina remembered Toriovico telling her something about this public rehearsal over breakfast, an event to hearten the people of the city, people whose morale had been badly shaken by recent events and rumors.

Rumors, Melina knew well, that arose from her—or if not from her specifically, from residual unhappiness related to the Healed One's marriage to her. Melina didn't mind Toriovico showing himself to his people in an accustomed role, but they had better get used to her. She wasn't going anywhere.

"I would have come to you earlier, Mother," Citrine said, clearly dreading a reproof, "but Tipi said that you couldn't be interrupted while you were in court."

"And she was right," Melina reassured the girl. "Now, tell me everything that happened. Speak slowly and clearly, as benefits a matter of such grave importance."

And Citrine did so. One of the great advantages, Melina thought complacently, of her influence over her daughter was this ability to override anxieties.

When Citrine concluded, describing her biting of Derian Carter's hand with such relish that Melina wondered if the child had spent too much time with that feral woman of the Norwoods, Melina gave an appropriately grave nod.

"You did well, Citrine," she said, and the child all but wriggled like a puppy beneath her mother's praise. "I am pleased by this proof of your love and devotion."

"Thank you, Mother," Citrine replied, her eyes shining.

"Now, go and get out of your costume and get cleaned for dinner. You haven't had your dinner yet, have you?"

"No, Mother."

"Go then and get ready."

Melina looked longingly at her pages; then a chance thought stirred, a seed splitting but not yet fully sprouted. It had to do with Citrine and with bypassing a difficulty. . . . Never mind, it would come to her. In the meantime, the child needed rewarding for her loyalty.

"And when you are ready, Tipi is to come and get me. I," Melina pronounced in the tones of one bestowing a great honor, "will eat the evening meal with you."

Citrine shaped the appropriate ritual of temporary leavetaking and skipped out the door. Melina was turning back to her book when she noticed several folded sheets of paper, heavily sealed, sitting at the top of the rest of her ignored mail. The seals were among those Melina had given Idalia.

Checking that Citrine was truly gone and the door securely closed, Melina reached for the missive. Snapping open the heavy wax, she recognized the seemingly incomprehensible words as one of the codes Idalia used. Almost automatically, Melina deciphered it and read:

> *Consolor Melina,*
>
> *With heavy heart I write you to report that the two uninvited guests to whom you so kindly extended your hospitality have taken leave of my care. We were touring as you directed should be done when strange noises— which I firmly believe originated with bats—frightened the guards. They fled and our guests took advantage of their absence to also flee.*
>
> *I have searched for the guests and can find no trace. Therefore, I have no reason to think they remain in the vicinity. Moreover, the frightened guards carried their fear back to their fellows. My family and I spent much energy over the following day securing their continued fealty.*
>
> *I write this one full day and night after our guests' departure. If you wish further report of any of these events you have only to ask.*
>
> *I remain your . . .*

Melina hardly saw the flowery closing phrases, though once their unctuous flattery would have soothed her anger—at least somewhat. Her gaze kept returning to certain phrases, understanding their meaning perfectly despite Idalia's carefully evasive phrasing.

". . . have taken leave of my care." Escaped.

". . . the frightened guards carried their fear back . . ." That sounded as if there had been a near revolt among the slaves.

". . . one full day and night . . ." Given how long messages from Idalia usually took to reach Melina, that meant that the escape had been not last night, but two nights ago. With any other prisoners, Melina would have thought them gone beyond finding, but with these two . . .

She yanked the bell and when a clerk came to the door said, "Send for Kiero."

The clerk ducked his head and vanished. Melina had hardly begun rereading the letter for the third time and contemplating how she might slip away unnoticed to meet with Idalia later that night when there came a sharp rap on her door.

"Come!"

Kiero entered, the expression on his heat- and weather-worn features part quizzical, part pleased. He shaped various greeting gestures, then said:

"I understand from the clerk outside that you require me, Consolor Melina?"

"I do," Melina replied. Then, because it never did to skip the little courtesies with those you needed but didn't completely control, "I compliment you on the promptness of your arrival."

"Pure coincidence," Kiero said humbly, "though surely a power such as yourself may warp the very fabric of time to her needs. I was coming here," he added more bluntly, "because I had news for which I thought you would not wish to wait."

"Speak," Melina said calmly, though her thoughts added, *And dispense with the flattery.*

"I have just checked in with the man I have watching the house of Hasamemorri from the rooms across the street. He had interesting information for me—so interesting that I am docking his pay for not finding a way to get it to me more quickly."

Talk more quickly . . . , Melina thought, and perhaps her gaze held some of the malice she felt, for Kiero did so.

"Late this morning, the remaining four foreign tenants of that house departed in costume to see the rehearsal of the Harvest Joy dance. Costumed as they were, they would not be easily recognizable as foreigners, therefore, my agent did not try to instigate any anger against them in the streets.

"Sometime later, presumably following the performance, Lady Archer and Sir Jared returned without their companions. These two were hardly inside when two New Kelvinese my agent had never before seen came to the house. They were admitted by Lady Archer.

"Shortly after that, Derian Carter and Wendee Jay returned. Neither of these strangers have reemerged, although the hour has grown late for visiting. My agent reported this to me a short time ago when I went to collect his report before he was relieved."

Kiero paused.

"That is your complete report?"

"Yes, Consolor Melina."

He stood so very stiff and proper, yet vaguely pleased with himself for all his formality. Melina wondered if he'd heard of the kidnapping attempt and thought he was providing information about the probable kidnappers. How little did he know!

"What you say is interesting," Melina replied. "You did well to report to me. Is anyone now watching the house?"

"Yes, Consolor Melina. I ordered the first agent to remain alert. As I was leaving to report to you his relief arrived."

"Well done."

Melina had strong suspicions as to who those two "New Kelvinese" strangers might be. It was too much of a coincidence that two would arrive there when two were missing elsewhere. Kiero didn't need to know that, of course. As of yet Melina had not told him about the underground area where Idalia kept order. Melina would prefer as few people as possible to know about that.

"Where exactly is this house of Hasamemorri?" Melina asked. "I know it is across the city from the Earth Spires, but in what district?"

"The Aswatano district, Consolor Melina, called so for the closest market square, named in turn for a famous fountain from the time of the Founders."

"I wonder if I have been to this Aswatano?" she mused aloud, trying to picture it.

"The fountain," Kiero said, self-effacingly, as speaks one who supplies information he has not been directly asked for, "depicts the Star Wizard and his allies taming the Dragon of Despair. It is famous both for its artistry and because it runs with both hot and cold water."

Melina stared at Kiero in disbelief. Could it be that the entire time she had been delving beneath Thendulla Lypella, the place she sought was out in the city proper—and so clearly marked?

Kiero was looking at her, concerned that his words would have met with such an unexpected result.

"The fountain is in a public area, Consolor Melina," he said. "I could take you to see it if you wish."

"I may indeed wish," she said slowly, then turned her mind to more immediate matters, "but I cannot go tonight."

"Of course not, Consolor Melina," Kiero said, rather shocked that the Healed One's wife should think to play tourist at such an hour. "In any case, the sculpture is best appreciated by daylight. The moon is waning and her light would not be enough for you to appreciate the subtleties of the carving."

Melina tapped her fingers along her jawline, so agitated that for a moment she forgot the enormity of this social gaffe. Then she looked at Kiero.

"I want an even more complete watch kept on those foreigners. Put several watchers there, even if you need to pull them from other points. If anyone leaves the house, I want him or her followed."

Kiero nodded.

"Make certain back exits are covered as well," Melina continued. "I recall you were concerned about difficulties with the neighbors noticing and complaining. Tell any who complain that a ring of burglars has been operating in the area and you are trying to stop them."

Kiero grinned, approving of her deception—and the greater freedom it offered him to operate.

"Make certain I can always get a message to you," Melina concluded, "in the shortest time possible. Now go!"

Kiero did. When she was alone Melina turned almost lovingly to the biography of the Star Wizard. There were a few things mentioned within those pages she thought would be useful. And when she had the dragon under her control, then she could end this wearisome juggling of the claims and desires of various people who thought they were important.

At last they would realize that she was the only one whose wishes truly mattered.

HASAMEMORRI WAS, of course, curious about the two visitors who transformed into her long-absent tenants, but she had learned that knowing less rather than more about her foreign guests was the best course of action if she wished to keep a happy and peaceful home.

Therefore, after exchanging a few pleasantries with Edlin—Peace in his role as Jalarios had never come under her inspection—she retired to her apartment. Her parting words were unsettling, nonetheless.

"I am sorry that the little boy, Rios, did not return with his father. A child is such a bright thing to have about the house."

For Elise, Hasamemorri's comment recalled Citrine as she had briefly been on their trip to Dragon's Breath, closer to the bright-eyed girl Elise had known most of her life, laughing and playing, eager to help, that weird, fey streak nearly vanished. They had lost more than the child's physical presence when Citrine had run away; they'd lost the progress they had made toward her healing.

And Elise couldn't help wondering what—if anything—Citrine had now told Melina about the afternoon's events and what repercussions that report might have for their household here. However, although they kept their usual guard shifts with more than usual alertness throughout the night, nothing untoward happened.

After breakfast the next morning their reunited household again gathered in the consulting room. Derian and Elise had hoped to start making plans for their next course of action the night before, but Doc had refused to have his patients disturbed.

"Edlin and Peace are getting the first decent sleep they've had in who knows how long. My talent can speed healing, but even it cannot work without sleep to help it along."

Doc said this with a rather pointed glance at Firekeeper, but the wolf-woman did not respond. She seemed drawn inward on her own thoughts, and as soon as she learned there would be no further planning session that night she had retired to the stable yard—presumably to sleep.

The following morning, although both Edlin and Peace looked markedly improved, Firekeeper did not—dashing both Derian and Elise's hopes that her sleeplessness would end with the return of the two men.

"Last night," Elise said, "we rather glossed over why the Healed One agreed to help us."

"Didn't do it out of a sense of justice, what?" Edlin asked impudently.

"I didn't say that," Elise shot back. "But I must say that I trusted the Healed One's goodwill toward us and our interests all the more because he wanted something from us in return."

"Fair," Edlin agreed. "And what was that?"

"Lady Archer would tell you," Peace interrupted, "if you would only still your tongue."

The words were a rebuke, but the tone so affectionate that Elise suppressed a smile. Yet despite the warmth of Peace's tone, Edlin came to heel like one of his own chastened pups.

Elise resumed, "When we first dealt with Xarxius regarding the possibility of Citrine's return, the Dragon's Claw intimated that the Healed One would see his way to supporting our right of custody if we would do something for him. That thing was finding where Melina went at night."

Elise thought again how odd a situation this was, and how even odder was the matter-of-fact way they all accepted it.

"I say," Edlin exclaimed, "we know where Melina goes well enough now—and what she does there. Peace and I told the Healed One about Melina's underground slave complex. Maybe the debt is paid and we'll find Citrine gift-wrapped on the stoop later this afternoon."

"Did the Healed One tell you about the Dragon of Despair?" Elise asked.

Edlin looked puzzled, but over Grateful Peace's battered features there spread the beginnings of understanding.

"He did not," Peace said, silencing Edlin with a gesture. "And I, of course, know the tale and have since my childhood. What part does such an old story play here?"

Elise tugged a lock of her hair straight as if by doing so she could straighten this entire mess.

"The Healed One thinks—for various reasons that made sense when he spelled them out for us—that Melina is seeking the place where this dragon was bound. He thinks that she plans to release it, hoping that it will give her even more power than she currently holds, power that won't be tied to any alliances or to the fortunes of those she holds under her will."

Peace nodded with grudging approval.

"Melina's choice is wise. Of all the legends I studied in my early apprenticeship as an Illuminator, the tale of the Dragon of Despair seemed among those that held the most substance. It was a tale that belonged to the New World, you see, not, like so many of the others, to the Old World."

Doc leaned forward, his posture holding the same tense alertness Elise had seen when he was working his way over a badly damaged limb seeking where to best apply his talent.

"So you think there really is a dragon?"

Peace gave a shrug that, despite its stiffness, held some of his former cosmopolitan insouciance.

"Who knows? But whether what Melina seeks is a dragon or merely an artifact with power enough to raise mountains and level cities, does that matter? We cannot have Melina find this thing and gain control of it."

Wendee cleared her throat.

"I remember the story, both from your telling it to us on the road and from allusions to it in various plays. Wasn't there a tremendous cost for using the dragon? Didn't it kill Kelvin and haunt the Star Wizard?"

Peace nodded.

"That is what our tales tell, but either Melina does not believe that this cost exists or she believes what she would gain would be worth paying the price."

"Or," Derian added with all the cynicism of a merchant's son late come to politics, "she thinks she's found a way to defer paying."

"There is that, too," Peace agreed. "Now, based on Melina's treatment of Edlin and myself, I think Melina believes she has some indication of where the dragon is hidden."

"The hot springs!" Edlin interjected. "That's where we were directed to do much of our mapping these last few nights."

"Correct," Peace said. "However, now that Lady Elise has told us what Melina is seeking, I believe that Melina is misdirected."

Elise hardly dared hope.

"You mean she's on the wrong track?"

"I think so," Peace said. "You see, any legends—especially in the older texts Melina must have been perusing—would say that the dragon is trapped beneath the Earth Spires. What Melina may have overlooked—indeed her actions seem to prove that she has overlooked—is that the Earth Spires is the old name for the entire city. It was only after the Restorer's time that the lower city came to be called Dragon's Breath . . ."

"For this very legend!" Wendee inserted triumphantly.

"True," Peace said, "for this very legend. If Melina has been misled, then she is searching beneath the wrong part of the city. She thinks much of personal privilege. It would be antithetical to her nature for her to believe that such a valuable thing might have been imprisoned where any commoner might get to it."

Elise's hope was turning into creeping horror.

"You mean out here?"

"Yes," Peace replied, "very near to here. I think that Aswatano, the Fountain Court where we go to market, is adorned with that remarkable statue for a reason. I think it may have been placed to commemorate where the Dragon of Despair was brought to earth, and where, so some say, the Star Wizard and his allies bound it."

Elise suspected that her own expression was mirrored on the faces of her companions. Glancing from one to another, she saw fear, shock, and something like disgust. Why, they'd even drunk water from that fountain!

"I guess," Wendee said, obviously trying to lighten the mood, "there was good reason for me to dislike that statue."

Grateful Peace shrugged.

"Or not. After all, if the dragon is imprisoned there, the statue marks a prison that has been secure for several hundred years."

Elise's mind was already racing to the next step.

"Very well, if the dragon is there, what can we do? We can't go poking around in broad daylight and the streets have become less than safe for us in any case."

"We may need to risk the ire of the populace," Peace said. "Melina is a persistent woman. How long will she leave you abroad now that you have made your intentions toward Citrine so plain? Surely as soon as Xarxius's trial is ended she will find an excuse to demand your banishment."

"I say," Edlin added, "I seem to recall that Melina was pushing a bit, said something about time being important. Maybe that's just because her hold on Apheros is threatened, but what if there's some other reason, something to do with when the dragon can be freed."

Grateful Peace nodded thoughtfully.

"I had forgotten that, Lord Kestrel. Melina's need did seem rather urgent. However, whether that urgency had its heart in an ancient spell or in modern politics is immaterial. She is moving as swiftly as she may. Therefore, so must we."

Firekeeper, silent to this point, cleared her throat. It was such an unaccustomed gesture—normally she spoke out bluntly without asking leave—that all fell silent.

"I think I know some things," Firekeeper said stiffly, "and, yes, we must go for the dragon, and soon."

Elise looked over to where the wolf-woman sat bolt upright and tense, eschewing even her usual arm about Blind Seer.

"Have you been holding out on us, Firekeeper?"

Firekeeper shook her head.

"No. Nightmares were all I thought. I have them forever, though I not remember them. These I thought were more of that, but now, after what Peace says, after what Doc did, I think I know something."

"Whoa!" Derian got down on the floor next to Firekeeper and put a comforting arm around her. "Steady, Firekeeper. What did Doc do?"

"He made me sleep," she replied accusingly, "and Blind Seer let him."

The wolf did not look in the least abashed, though Elise was certain he understood Firekeeper's accusation, but then neither did Doc. Both of them apparently felt that they had known better than Firekeeper did herself what was good for her.

"Go slowly," Derian said to Firekeeper, his tone level and reassuring, full of a patience Elise suspected he did not feel. "Tell us exactly what happened."

Firekeeper sat still and silent for a moment, then nodded.

"I have dreams since a long time," she began, "but after I go into tunnels and get so hurt, then I start having other dreams—different dreams. In these dreams, I am talked to by the comet."

The comet? Elise longed to ask, but she saw the slight warning shake of Derian's head and held her tongue.

"Comet tell me things I am troubled by," Firekeeper went on, "things about freedom and stillness and captivity. I am very confused, for I think that comet want me to free it, but it promises terrible things to who frees it.

"Dreams grow worse," Firekeeper continued, looking directly at Doc, "and are why I not sleep. When I sleep comet talks to me and I wake more tired. If I stay awake I am tired but I not have to listen to comet."

Doc nodded, "I see."

"But you want to make me sleep," Firekeeper said, "and because I am tired my nose does not tell me what you give me and Blind Seer—who like you thinks I must sleep—he does not tell me either. So I sleep and am pushed down into sleeping and cannot wake.

"And because I cannot wake comet flies into my dreams and talk and talk and I cannot wake. Maybe because I cannot run this time I surrender to listening and looking. Before I am always trying to get away, but now I am as trapped as comet."

Fleetingly, she looked sad.

"Maybe because of what the Healed One tell us, but this time I see comet is something other. This time I see that comet is a . . . dragon."

Perhaps they looked disbelieving or perhaps the wolf-woman didn't quite believe herself, but she hurried to justify this statement.

"I have seen what dragons look like, what people think they look like. Queen Elexa showed me pictures and there was inn along the road."

Firekeeper's posture remained defiant and Elise hastened to reassure her.

"I believe you, Firekeeper. Why shouldn't you dream of a dragon after everything you've seen and heard? It makes sense, really."

But Firekeeper was having nothing of easy reassurances.

"I did not dream of a dragon because of these things," she said. "It came to me. It wants to be free, but it does not want to be freed."

There was a confused silence which Grateful Peace broke.

"I think I understand you, Firekeeper, maybe better than you do yourself. The dragon is held and wants to be free, but it does not want to be freed—that is, it does not want Melina to break the spell that holds it. Am I correct?"

The tension that had been infusing every line of Firekeeper's body fled so suddenly that Elise only became aware how extreme it had been in its departure.

"I think so," the wolf-woman answered. "Comet tells me things like this, but I do not understand. I think maybe it is my own mind and heart talking to me."

She looked deeply ashamed.

"I have feeled so trapped since spring came and Derian and I go to my pack's hunting grounds only to find humans already there. I have feeled—felt—that the Beasts need me for this thing, humans need me for that thing. All I want to do is run free and have no one need me!"

Her voice rose to a shrill wail that reminded Elise for the first time in a long time that Firekeeper was probably several years younger than herself—that in human ways and the complexities of human needs she was barely a year and a half old.

Elise knew how her own new awareness of her position as heir to a barony and the responsibilities that role brought had weighed her down and shaped her, but that was nothing to Firekeeper's weird position as the only person who could understand—and perhaps even love—two worlds so different that neither quite believed in the existence of the other.

But Firekeeper had never been much for pity—much less self-pity—and she shook herself as if to shed the emotion like so much water.

"But when Doc make me to sleep and sleep," she said, and this time her glance toward Sir Jared held no resentment, "I realize that these dreams are not from my unhappy heart. Somehow, someways, this dragon is real and is talking to me. When I accept this, it can tell me things."

Firekeeper sat up very straight and ticked these things off on her fingers.

"One, as I say, somehow it knows that Melina wishes to free it. It wants to be free, but not as her slave.

"Two, it knows that freeing of it is difficult thing. I don't understand all that dragon tells me, but somehow this Star Wizard made it one with living rock. Stories are not true that land here is hot and full of steam because dragon is bound in it, but it is because the land is hot and full of steam that dragon could be bound in it."

She answered Edlin's half-voiced query before he could form more than an "I . . ."

"No, Edlin, I not know how or why of this. I am not a wizard, nor is dragon. I am not even certain dragon is really a dragon, but is word we can use."

Edlin looked as if he wanted to say more, but Peace laid a hand on him.

"Let your sister finish her speech. Talking doesn't come as easily to her as to you."

Edlin nodded and pressed his still swollen lips tightly together.

"Three, though dragon not know exactly what thing is that will free it—for it does not use magic—it is very aware of the price the spell-sayer will pay."

The wolf-woman seemed reluctant to speak further, and Elise coaxed her.

"Go on, Firekeeper. If we can find what this price is, maybe we can take the means to pay from Melina and so prevent her."

Firekeeper shook her head.

"You could take, but not without catching her—and if we do that then she not be problem. Price is this: One who holds dragon will age one year faster for each year dragon is held. Each year, then, is two."

Derian, confident in youthful strength, looked concerned.

"That's not too bad, is it? I mean, a young sorcerer could have control of the dragon for twenty years or more, then release it to someone else and still have a bit of time."

Grateful Peace, thirty years or more older, was not so certain.

"I doubt a young sorcerer could work the charm, but even if one such could, consider the price. He starts at twenty, twenty years later he is sixty. For an older man, the side effects of aging would begin to be felt much sooner—loss of vision and hearing, stiffness of joints, reduced vitality."

Grateful Peace pushed the unbroken spectacles he had taken from his luggage up the bridge of his nose and stared at Derian as if challenging him to say the cost was light.

Firekeeper broke in, her voice crisp with distaste.

"That is cost for *holding* dragon," she said. "To command cost is three times that—three years for every one. And there is no breaking bond and handing it on. Link is for life. Even if dragon gets second master, first continue to pay."

"Who would use it at such a cost?" Wendee asked, appalled.

"Perhaps," Peace said with terrible gentleness, "only those who thought their lives were nearly ended in any case. The Star Wizard would have wanted the price to be allocated in such a way, otherwise the dragon might be released lightly."

Sir Jared frowned.

"Firekeeper, do you think Melina is aware what she is inviting?"

Firekeeper shrugged.

"I not know. Dragon did not say, but I think it not like this bond being forced on it. Right now it is prisoner. Then it would be slave."

She looked sad.

"For a long time, I not really understand slave, but now I think I do. That was last thing dragon could tell me, the difference between being bound by ties of the heart—as I am to my wolves and to some humans—and being slave who must do for those she hates."

"What I still don't understand," Derian said when Firekeeper leaned back against Blind Seer to indicate that she was finished, "is why the Star Wizard and his people didn't destroy this dragon rather than binding it."

Peace replied, "I can think of two reasons. One, they might have had the strength to bind it but not destroy it. Two, they were faced with a great dilemma. Here was power that could be harnessed again if the need arose. Remember that Kelvin's original raising of the dragon was tied in with an effort to forestall an invasion from Waterland. We have not been invaded from that direction—or any other—since."

Derian persisted, "But if your stories are true, the dragon is terribly dangerous!"

"And swords and bows and ballista are not?" Peace countered. "All weapons are dangerous. However, I understand what you mean. This bound dragon is a weapon meant to be used as a last resort. I expect that is why the cost to free it is so high. The Star Wizard desired that no one would release it without knowing what the price would be—and that it was a price that would be paid repeatedly, not just once."

Elise asked, "Firekeeper, do you know if the price for commanding the dragon is exacted with every command—'fly here' or 'burn that'?"

Firekeeper shook her head.

"I am not sure, but I think is more for a space of time, not for a command. One year of commanding cost three extra years of life. One year of holding but not using cost one extra year of life."

"Maybe that's what Melina plans to do," Elise mused, thinking aloud.

"One year of threat and devastation could do a great deal to solidify her as the real power in New Kelvin. After that, she's speeded her aging along, but after all she is only in her mid-forties. Her family is long-lived. Maybe she thinks that exchanging thirty or so years of normal life for fifteen or so of power is worthwhile."

Grateful Peace looked unsettled and pale, as if his thoughts had gone down even darker roads.

"And maybe Melina thinks she can get around even that cost," he said. "Melina has shown a great deal of interest in New Kelvin acquiring a harbor. Leaving aside the more usual benefits of possessing a harbor, what do all our legends—those of my land as well as yours—associate with the sea . . . with across the sea?"

"The Old World?" Wendee answered. "You think she wants to go there?"

"Why not?" the Illuminator said, suddenly weary. "Melina has shown herself hungry for magic—not merely for power. Where else will she find magic now that she has learned that New Kelvin holds far less than she imagined?"

Wendee, steeped as she was in the folklore of two countries, was quicker than the others to follow Peace's train of thought.

"And what more wonderful find could there be than something that would slow or eliminate aging? The old stories are full of such things—or at least of the search for them!"

"I doubt," Peace said, "that the means to rejuvenate lost youth are as common in reality as in the tales. Otherwise, the Star Wizard would not have thought aging such a stern price to pay to control the dragon. Still, we all have evidence that Melina is not one to be turned away when she wants something. Perhaps she has convinced herself that the means toward rejuvenation will be easy for her to find."

Elise forced herself to be the voice of practicality though she suddenly felt very young and unsure.

"You may be right, Peace, but if we can find a way to stop Melina before she finds the dragon then we will never need to deal with what she planned to do with it."

"True," Peace said, and Elise was uncomfortably aware of the faintest of twinkles in his eyes. Did she seem like a child playing at general?

She glanced at Doc, hoping for a touch of reassurance, but Jared was looking at Firekeeper.

"Tell me," he said to the wolf-woman, "you said that this dragon wants to be free. Can we release it and then tell it we'll let it go free if it promises to return to wherever it was before Kelvin freed it and do no harm to any? I mean then it would be out of Melina's reach for good."

"We could," Firekeeper replied, "but not without someone paying the price."

"Just as the Star Wizard did," added Grateful Peace somberly.

XXXVII

PLEASED AS HE WAS by the success of his plan to get Grateful Peace and Edlin Norwood out of Thendulla Lypella, Toriovico couldn't help but kick himself for forgetting that the littlest dancers were instructed to defend themselves against just the sort of assault Derian Carter had attempted—a practice that dated back, so one of Toriovico's teachers had said, to the Old Country when the little dancers stood for the fruits of the harvest far more literally than they did today and possession of one of them was thought to guarantee prosperity for the new year.

Still, Toriovico had gotten two of the three out and had survived Melina's indignant rant on the matter of the indignities to which her daughter had been subjected. He had been forced to promise to consider the matter of these irritating foreign visitors, but had dared to point out gently that Citrine was hardly the most reliable witness and that no one else had identified the kidnapper with this Derian Carter.

When Toriovico mentioned this, Melina looked as if she might add something more, but she had paused in midbreath and had only made him repeat his promise that as soon as Xarxius's trial left time for such matters Torio would see about the best way to tactfully eject these irritations to her peace and tranquility from the kingdom.

Toriovico had agreed with humble enthusiasm, and had hoped that he would not see much of Melina for a few days, but the next morning Melina came to him, her expression drawn.

"Torio," she said, laying her hand on his arm, her manner at its most ingratiating, "someone has told me that today the Primes mean to conclude Xarxius's trial. You will be there—perhaps do something for him?"

Toriovico bent to kiss the top of his wife's head—an affectionate gesture that incidentally kept his gaze from her own—and indulged in a cynical smile. He found it telling that Melina should now attempt to ameliorate a process she herself had begun. If she was a wiser person this mistake might make her reflect on the wisdom of her larger goals, but that was too much to hope for.

"I will be present for the conclusion of the trial," he promised her, "but whether I can do anything . . ."

Toriovico let his words trail off. Actually, giddy with his earlier success, he had lain awake last night trying to find a way to save Xarxius. He had the barest threads of a plan in place, but refused to speak his thoughts aloud. Melina might not be the only one with spies within the Cloud Touching Spire. Coming as she did from a monarchy where nothing short of mass murder would unseat the king and his heirs, Melina might have been surprised by the alliances being formed to bring down Apheros's government, but Toriovico was not.

In a more normal situation Toriovico would have let events run their course. After all, a shifting domestic government would make it more difficult for Melina to play her games. But he couldn't passively stand by when Xarxius's life and reputation were about to be swept away in the torrent. At least, he couldn't without a struggle.

AS RUMOR HAD promised, Xarxius was found guilty of treason that afternoon.

Lips moving as stiffly as if he condemned himself, Apheros issued the death sentence. This was tantamount to letting the axe drop, for the New Kelvinese legal code did not hold with delayed executions. Toriovico knew, as many of his contemporaries did not, the reason for this provision.

Some of the Founders had practiced human sacrifice in the course of their magical arts and immediate execution was meant to forestall any stockpiling of potential victims. The tradition of immediate execution had carried forward from the Old Country to the present, though the rationale had been lost to all but scholars of obscure legal codes—and the Healed One, who was admonished by his forebears to uphold the practice.

This time, however, Toriovico felt he must interfere or sacrifice not only Xarxius but all of Apheros's government to Melina's meddling.

The guards were stepping forward to lead Xarxius to the Death Spire when Toriovico rose. Taking a deep breath so that his voice would project to all corners of the chamber, he said:

"The lore that is the heritage entrusted to me by the First Healed One warns against executions at this time."

Every face in the room turned toward him and though Toriovico saw unguarded hope on a few, most were either neutral or actively hostile. He shaped his next words accordingly.

"We are moving toward not only the death of the year, but dark of the moon. An official execution at this time, in this place, would overbalance the tides, enhance those very forces that our Moon Rituals and Harvest Festival keep in check."

The sculptured dragon gripping Apheros's skull nearly touched the tips of his shoes, so low did the Speaker bow.

"Are you saying, Healed One, that Xarxius's life is not to be taken?"

Toriovico wished he could indeed say this, but he knew he must not overstep. He made his lip curl in disdain.

"Not at all, Apheros," he replied, deliberately eliminating the man's title in order to give hope to his opponents. "The execution is to be delayed until the first day of the new moon, when life energies will be on the flood rather than the ebb."

Prime Dimiria of the Stargazers, doubtless happy that such a valuable associate was being given even a few more days of life, spoke up quickly.

"That's in five days," she said. "Five days counting today. I request that Xarxius be locked securely in the upper rooms of the Death Spire until that day. I further advise that the execution take place as the edge of the sun peeks over the Sword of Kelvin Mountains so that the sun's rising energy can counter any weakness in the new moon."

Least Prime Nstasius of the Sericulturalists, clearly disappointed at what he feared would be interpreted as a sign of the Healed One's favor toward Apheros's retainer—and too inexperienced to hide this disappointment—spoke out before his allies could stop him.

"Could such an arrangement be made for tomorrow morning? Wouldn't the power of the sun counter the ebbing of the moon?"

Toriovico cocked an eyebrow at him.

"Not at all, Prime Nstasius." This time he placed the faintest emphasis on the man's title, as if questioning that one so ill-educated had risen to such prominence within his sodality. "If the sun's force alone could counter the moon we would not have a Moon Ritual at the ebbing of each phase."

Rebuked and belatedly aware that he had embarrassed both his Defeatist allies and his sodality, Nstasius offered no further protest. His embarrassment had the added benefit of stilling any other debate on the issue. Toriovico could almost hear the thoughts filling every mind in the room.

After all, it's not as if the Honored One pardoned Xarxius or questioned his sentence. He's only delayed it for a brief time.

Apheros is still vulnerable to a vote of no confidence. We don't even need to wait until after the execution—though maybe that would be wisest.

Toriovico knew that Melina would be wondering whether she should use this reprieve to find a way to clear Xarxius or whether she would do better to identify who was likely to succeed Apheros and set about digging her claws into the prospective new Speaker.

Then Toriovico wondered if he was wrong about her thoughts. Melina's expression when he glanced her way was withdrawn, as if now that the immediate issue of Xarxius's innocence and guilt was settled—if not completely to her satisfaction—she was concentrating on something that interested her more.

That worried Toriovico. He had bought Xarxius five more days of life. He had the strangest feeling that those five days were a countdown to something far more significant than the life or death of a innocent man and the rise or fall of a Speaker's prominence.

THOUGH MELINA PRAISED TORIOVICO lavishly for his clever delaying of Xarxius's execution, she decided that she would do nothing further to interfere with the course of those events. In her anger she had misjudged the power of the Speaker and the Healed One to protect her interests, but she had been right about Xarxius's treason. If Apheros could not maintain his position after everything she had done to try and help him, then he was not the strong ally she desired.

It was time to seek that ally—and to eliminate the need for all other allies. From the hints Melina had gathered from various histories, she had deduced that the best time to work the spells freeing the Dragon of Despair would be during the dark of the moon. As Toriovico had said, elemental forces were at an ebb then and as this dragon had been raised from the elements it should also be weakened—and easier to control.

She felt certain that Kelvin's error had been working his spell at a time when elemental forces were on the ascendance. She had no proof of this, but felt certain nonetheless. It fit.

Melina didn't blame that long-ago sorcerer for his error. After all, he had been working to defend his land against an invading force—an invading force that had already shown itself powerful enough to push the sorcerers of New Kelvin away from the coast and into the western mountains.

She was aware that Kelvin himself would probably consider her an invader, but she preferred to think of herself as a savior. New Kelvin had certainly drifted far from its initial glory. She doubted whether its current thaumaturges could raise a rain shower, much less a dragon. With her in charge, though, the kingdom would achieve the glory its founders certainly intended for it.

And then, and then . . .

Kiero requested audience with the Consolor of the Healed One almost as soon as Melina's foot crossed the threshold. Melina shook herself back into practical considerations.

"You have information for me?"

Kiero's hand crossed his chest right to left in an emphatic Yes!

"My watchers report that several of the foreigners left their house this morning, attired as New Kelvinese, and went directly to Aswatano. While one of their number, the woman called Wendee Jay, did some shopping, the others showed undue interested in the fountain."

Melina felt her blood chill.

"Did they do anything other than show interest?"

Kiero shook his head.

"They did not. Indeed, they seemed rather nervous about being in public."

"Did your agent do anything to help intensify this nervousness?"

"No. You seemed to wish to know what their plans were and another uprising would have been counterproductive."

Melina nodded muted approval, her mind racing. Truly there was no time for delay. The full dark of the moon wouldn't be for another four days, but she did not think she could afford to wait for that most propitious time.

Kiero was standing, his posture that of perfect servile waiting but his eyes alive with interest. Melina made up her mind quickly.

"Keep the watch as before. If any of them attempt to do more than show interest in the fountain, find a way to stop them. Stop short of violence if you can, but do not hesitate if that is the only way you can stop them. Do you have someone under you who is skilled in research, especially research into the work done in the time of the Restorer?"

Kiero looked surprised, but nodded.

"I have one who is well acquainted with the city archives. I am certain she could find what you seek."

"Very well, have her find any and all plans for the area surrounding Aswatano, including the Fountain Court itself. I want maps of the street layouts and of any sewers or tunnels beneath the area. Inspect these maps yourself before bringing information to me. If there is any other way that the Fountain Court could be reached, set impediments at those points."

"Impediments? Could your gracious self clarify?"

Melina nodded a trifle impatiently.

"I don't want the foreigners to have access to Aswatano from either above or below ground. Be subtle. If locks and alarms will do the job, then use them. If they won't, use guards, but have them remain out of sight. Set a roving patrol to check each point on a regular basis."

Now Kiero looked alarmed.

"I am not certain that I have enough agents to do all of this."

Melina frowned, then made up her mind.

"I will send you reinforcements. Whoever brings them to you will have a password so that you will know they are from me."

Kiero looked as much interested as relieved at this information and Melina knew he was wondering just how much she had at her command that he had not managed to learn about.

You would be surprised, she thought. *But take comfort. You would be less surprised than most.*

Kiero departed, promising that he would regularly leave messages regarding his location with the clerks at the Petitioner's Gate.

"Report on your progress," Melina said, "only in person and only to me. If you cannot locate me, act according to your best judgment. Under no conditions should you create a fuss if Tipi cannot locate me for you. I may have business about with which I do not entrust her."

Or you, she thought, seeing Kiero trying to mask his curiosity.

"Have no concern," Melina said to him by way of reassurance. "You will know more than any other as soon as I have confirmed that certain arrangements are in place."

This soothed the spy, reaffirming the sense of self-importance that had been growing since he had ingratiated himself into her service.

After Kiero left, Melina dealt with a long line of petitioners. Most of these were concerned with the outcome of Xarxius's trial and its possible implications for Apheros's government. She dealt with these as swiftly as possible, reminding them that the house of the Healed One did not meddle in matters of the Primes.

This satisfied those who were looking for reassurance that Xarxius's preservation was not meant to sustain Apheros's government and puzzled those who had noticed her interest in the Primes. Melina did not care as long as they left her alone.

Some hours into this process, a packet arrived from Kiero. It included the maps she had requested and a note that for all its businesslike tone couldn't quite hide the writer's pleasure in his own cleverness and efficiency:

> *Consolor Melina,*
>
> *My researcher was as excellent as I expected her to be. At my behest, she produced the maps you requested. She also used her connections at the Sodality of Illuminators to inspect their archive of city maps.*
>
> *Aswatano proves to be approachable from numerous points above ground, a thing unsurprising as it is the major market square for that district. However, the Fountain Court is only reachable underground from three channels, two of which are really sections of the same thing. The enclosed maps will assist you, but as they were rather quickly drawn, let me offer some clarification.*
>
> *Beneath the Fountain Court the maps show a series of interconnected chambers, doubtless associated with maintenance of the fountain itself.*

Melina looked at the map, which showed an extensive network of subterranean chambers. She recalled her earlier discussion with Kiero and smiled dryly.

Doubtless, she thought.

> *These are accessible from an opening located within the body of the sculpture that is central to the fountain. The other entry points appear to*

be portions of natural conduits for carrying away excess water. The roughly northern segment originates beneath the Earth Spires. The southern segment is a continuation of this, picking up where the waters leave the Aswatano chambers and carrying them to join up with the conduits that eventually end in the river.

The segment that originates beneath the Earth Spires does not connect above ground at any point until Aswatano. The southern segment, however, could be entered at numerous points. I will be using the bulk of the additional agents you will be entrusting to me to guard these entrances.

I have not entered the chambers beneath Aswatano and will not without your express command.

And how you want that command, Melina thought with cynical amusement, *but I do not think I will give it—at least not yet.*

Kiero's note intensified Melina's feeling of urgency. When early evening brought an end to her stream of callers, she fled to her private suite. Tipi was there, trying to look busy.

"I must go out," Melina told the slave, "alone. Tell those who seek me that I am meditating. Give them to believe that I am within my chambers. If any press, tell them I went for a walk among the spires and you have no idea where."

Tipi looked interested, but Melina's tone told her this was not the time to pry.

"Shall I tell the same to the Healed One and little Citrine?"

"Tell the same to the Healed One," Melina replied. "If Citrine comes looking for me reassure her that I will be back, though perhaps not until late. Tell her to eat her supper and get her rest. I will come to her."

Melina spoke with such force that she knew her assurance would be communicated to Citrine. It was very important that the girl wait. Very.

She paused only long enough to change from the ornamented robes she had worn to the conclusion of the trial and to gather certain essential items in a sturdy bag. Then, using back stairs and little-used corridors, she made her way to the storage room and from there to the tunnels beneath Thendulla Lypella.

The bag was heavy, and Melina wasn't accustomed to using the tunnels when the business of daily life was still under way. Several times she was forced to damp her lantern, drop into a shadowed corner, and wait while some servant went by, but as her course took her farther from the more populated areas the only footsteps she heard were in her imagination.

First Melina sought out Idalia. Idalia's mood was an odd mixture of defiance and groveling, from which Melina deduced that the other woman's husband and children had been trying to influence her—and were having an effect. That changed Melina's plans slightly. She had been about to order Idalia to choose a dozen or so of the most trustworthy slaves and put them— with herself in command—at Kiero's disposal.

Now she saw a way not to risk her valuable property and to make Idalia's no-good family pay for their attempted treachery. Of course she didn't present it this way to Idalia.

"I have seen portents that your brother, Grateful Peace, means to act against me," Melina began. "We must take precautions. I want you and Varcasiol to stay here and supervise the slaves. Your husband and other children can each take three trustworthy slaves and put themselves at the disposal of my surface agent, Kiero."

For a moment, Idalia's conflicting loyalties were visible on her pinched features, but her allegiance to Melina and hatred of Grateful Peace won out.

Melina turned to Pichero, Idalia's husband.

"The slaves are quite valuable to me," she said, acidly sweet, "and so I must request receipts for them. Do include their names and a brief description. If you return them all safely, I shall show my gratitude by gifting one of each group to you."

This bit of largesse on her part would be expensive, but it would assure loyalty. Idalia's family was not wealthy or Idalia would never have had to turn to her brother's patronage for Kistlio's advancement. Melina's promised gift would also assure that the best slaves were chosen for the task at hand—and that they were all returned. New Kelvinese law extracted rather stiff penalties for slave stealing.

Idalia's older daughter, the one who had been least happy about relocating to these subterranean reaches, was quickest to realize both the benefits and problems of this arrangement.

"Will the gracious lady tell us to what purpose this Kiero will be turning the slaves? So we might choose the most appropriate ones," she added hastily in reply to Melina's haughty glower.

"As watchers and possibly guards," Melina replied. "Choose for physical well-being, intelligence, and initiative—but not too much initiative."

The young woman nodded, drumming two fingers against her collarbone as she reviewed possibilities.

Melina had Idalia dismiss her family members to their new duties, then drew the other woman aside.

"You must remain alert," Melina said, looking deeply into Idalia's eyes and fixing her with her own will. "Grateful Peace now knows of this refuge and may invade it with the power of his allies behind him. I must go forth to battle his treachery, but I trust you to hold this place and my slaves for me."

Idalia's eyes shone with fanatical determination when Melina broke the contact, and Melina felt sure that she would defend Melina's interests no matter what her husband or children might say.

Leaving Idalia and the subterranean colony, Melina made her way to a cavern she had found during her searches for the Dragon of Despair. Although the final rituals must be done in the presence of the dragon, her researches suggested that the initial segments could be performed at a distance.

The cavern Melina had chosen for these preparatory rituals was an elegant place, egg-shaped and honeycombed with millions of tiny bubbles frozen within the black rock. It was in just such a place she had thought to find the dragon and therefore very appropriate for shaping her mind for its binding.

Steam rose from the crevice through which the cavern was entered, a momentary scorching immersion that made Melina feel cleansed each time she made the passage. The closeness of the cavern—it was hardly wider than Melina herself was when she was lying down—intensified the sensation of entering an earth womb. However, air entered along with the steam and the lot recirculated through a narrow slit at the apex of the egg, so the closeness never became smothering.

Even better than the natural sculpture of the cavern were signs and sigils still partially readable where they had been painted on the rock long ago. Not enough remained for Melina to understand their former meaning, but knowing that she had located a place once selected by the Founders themselves made her tremble with proud ecstasy. She even hung her lantern from a hook one of the Founders had set within the apex of the cavern's ceiling, feeling a kinship with those long-ago sorcerers each time she did so.

From her first interest in magic, when she had been hardly more than a child, Melina had always worked little rituals to intensify her personal powers. Dances in isolated moonlit groves or the deliberate shaping in beeswax of the forms of those she wished to control were two of her favorites. These personal rites helped Melina focus her abilities, to drown any uncertainty she might feel.

She had continued these practices after her arrival in New Kelvin, gradually incorporating motions and incantations she learned from her readings and from the various ritual celebrations doting Toriovico had arranged for his new bride to observe. Tonight, however, was the first time Melina was going to attempt a wholly New Kelvinese ritual.

For a brief moment, as she bent to remove certain items from the bag she had carried with her, Melina felt afraid, all the fear of magical power and its abuses that had been ingrained into her from her infancy rising and clamoring their protests. *This,* her infant heart seemed to cry, *is* real *magic, not the playing around you have attempted so far. This is the forbidden.*

Melina shook those protests from herself with a single angry gesture. Was the magic of New Kelvin more real than that which she had evolved for herself? She could not—would not—believe that. From what she had observed, she was three times the sorceress of any of these New Kelvinese who claimed such grand traditions.

Then why bother with their rituals at all? the doubt within her teased. *Perhaps their sorcery is as much sham as are their sorcerers.*

"Because," Melina defiantly answered that inner debate, "it is I who will use their lore. I have the power that they do not."

Moving swiftly but with every motion careful and calculated, Melina dropped her robe to bare her upper body to the waist, then removed the day's paints. Using a small hand mirror whose surface must be frequently wiped when steam clouded it, she adorned the empty canvas of her face and upper body with a series of potent symbols.

Next Melina exchanged her day robe for one of tightly woven fiery red silk, embroidered in gold thread with signs for earth and fire. Matching slippers went onto her feet.

Melina combed out the silver blond of her hair and rebraided it with a chain of gold strung with rubies. She then draped around each wrist bracelets from which hung dozens of charms, each promising its own protection or power. A thin girdle from which depended a pair of stylized but perfectly functional knives—one with a ruby in the hilt, the other with a dragon's-eye opal—looped loosely about her waist.

A heavy, enameled breast pectoral shaped like a dragon with its wings outspread was her last adornment. This had belonged—so they said—to the Star Wizard and usually resided in the Dragon Speaker's treasury. Melina had permitted Apheros to offer her a long-term loan.

Melina wished she could see herself in all her finery but settled for remembering how the ensemble had looked when she had tried it on before the long mirror in her rooms. She knew she looked impressive, draped in wealth to attract the dragon's greed and wrapped in powerful charms to contain its ability to harm her.

She didn't allow herself to wonder if the carefully constructed costume would work as planned, but set about placing on points carefully coordinated with the directions nine items she had collected in accordance with her research. Each was meant to distract and bribe the dragon, to focus its greed so that it would not resist the binding she would lay upon it. They were beautiful things, constructed in secrecy to her precise order.

To the eye the Nine were vases and weapons, boxes shaped like strange creatures, and elegant jewelry. The hand, however, would find their weight wrong, their balance strange, for in reality they were facsimiles of the things they represented. Each was carved of scented wood impregnated with rare oils. The metal was a delicate tissue overlay, the "gems" cunning replicas made from resins and pastes.

Nodding with almost housewifely approval as she reviewed the collection, Melina began her first recitation, the invocation to awaken the dragon. The invocation was long, but nothing in Melina's research had said that she could not read this piece, rather than recite it from memory as with so many of the others, so Melina read, paying particular attention to stress and cadence, giving the words their antique pronunciation wherever she could.

Melina was about to move to the second part of the ritual, an incantation that reminded her of some of the things she said to those she wished to impose her will upon, when she heard the sound of rocks rattling against each other from the other side of the steamy barrier that cloaked the entrance to the egg-shaped cavern.

Melina froze, for a moment as frightened as if she'd been caught doing something forbidden by the late duchess her mother. Then she remembered where and who she was. She stiffened and snapped out:

"Who is there? Come forth and show yourself!"

Such perfect silence followed that Melina could almost believe she had been mistaken, but she knew she had not. Reaching up, she removed the lantern from its hook and stepped through the steaming veil.

Immediately, her light fell upon the spy and for a long moment they froze—one in fear, the other in purest astonishment.

XXXVIII

"AWAKEN, WOLFLING! This is no time for sleep. Melina comes for me, even now."

Firekeeper knew she was asleep but, resigned to the dragon's invasion of her dreams, replied as if she were not:

"How do you know?"

"I hear her will untwining the bars that hold me. Do you think I would not know?"

Firekeeper really had no way to judge what the dragon would or would not know. However, in all the host of annoying dreams the dragon had thrust upon her, it had never told her anything like this.

"Where are you?"

"Where your friends have guessed, beneath Aswatano."

Firekeeper had gone with Peace and Derian when they ventured out to investigate the statue that adorned the Fountain Court. Her task had been to keep watch for any indication that the merchants and their customers had seen through the disguises Peace had constructed for them. She had remained alert, but felt her alertness wasted, for not only did no one give the three of them even a passing glance, the dragon had given her no hint that they were near its prison.

"Why didn't you tell me where you were before this? It would have been useful to know."

"I only learned the name of the place today when you explored with the others and I sensed your closeness."

"I have been to the Fountain Court before. Why did you never sense me then?"

"Perhaps I did. Perhaps I did not. Perhaps your focusing so on me forged a connection that had not existed before."

"Why didn't you say something to me this afternoon?" Firekeeper persisted, piqued.

"I sought to avoid unwise action on your part. You can be impulsive."

At this moment, Firekeeper felt anything but impulsive. Memories of her last failed venture were as sharp as the remaining pains in her leg. Only slightly less sharp were her recollections of her last meeting with Melina—and how Melina had bested her.

"What do you want me to do now?" she asked, suspecting she knew perfectly well what the dragon wanted.

"Consider," the dragon replied, "whether you want Melina to bind me—for she will succeed if she comes here unimpeded. Consider, too, who will be her first targets once I am hers to command."

The voice in Firekeeper's head fell silent and after a moment Firekeeper realized that she was no longer asleep. The night air was distinctly autumnal, with a bite in it that tasted of the north. Somehow she had missed the change. That made Firekeeper realize how wrapped up in herself and her own concerns she had been. Once she would have known without question. Now the seasons could change with her unaware.

But there was something else she realized. The dragon had good cause for leaving her to reason out what she must do on her own. Certainly it dreaded she would be frightened away beyond its ability to convince her otherwise.

How best to stop Melina? How best to prevent her from binding the dragon?

Simple. Finish the hunt before her. Claim Melina's prize before she could. The only other answer was to kill her, and though Firekeeper would much prefer that option, it had its dangers. Melina alive was Melina who could claim the dragon. Claim the dragon first and Melina could still be killed after.

Firekeeper swung herself upright on the grass lest the mere thinking of what she must do freeze her into inaction. Blind Seer was awake almost before she had steadied herself on her feet.

"Where are you going?" the wolf asked, blue eyes narrowing in suspicion even as he stretched.

"The dragon woke me," Firekeeper answered bluntly. "Melina is coming for it. I go to stop her."

The wolf growled softly, low in his throat.

"How will you do that? Surely you don't think Melina would be foolish enough to come alone?"

"She might," Firekeeper replied evasively. "What she does will not be even as these New Kelvinese wish. We know that from both Peace and the Healed One."

Blind Seer growled again.

"You don't believe she will come alone, no matter how bravely you speak."

"No," Firekeeper admitted. "I don't, but still I must try to stop her."

"Alone? Haven't you learned to keep a pack strong around you if you are to be strong?"

"I have," Firekeeper admitted, "but I think that for what I must do more hands and feet are not needed."

"What do you think to do?" Blind Seer asked sharply, but something in his bearing told Firekeeper that he had guessed.

"If I bind the dragon to me, then Melina cannot bind it to her."

"But it will eat your life!"

Oddly, Firekeeper found herself remembering her curiosity some moons past regarding how long the Royal Wolves lived compared with humans. Was she trying to hasten her living to match what she dreaded was their shorter span? She knew Blind Seer would be the last one to approve of such behavior, so sealed her lips and mind against the thought.

"One way or another," Firekeeper said aloud, "act or not, I think the dragon will have our lives. Now, do you come with me or do I go alone?"

"Rabid as a summer skunk!" the wolf protested. "Do you even know how to reach this dragon?"

"I do," Firekeeper said. "I watched today when Derian and Peace poked at the rocks and listened carefully to what they said. There is a door in the center of the fountain. We go through that."

She had been readying herself as they argued, checking the sharpness of her Fang, straightening the fit of her clothing where it had twisted while she slept. When she caught herself combing her hair with her finger ends she realized she was delaying and that made her angry with herself.

"Do you come with me?" she asked again.

Blind Seer snapped, gripping the heavy leather of her vest in his teeth.

"Not alone," he growled, and his insistence made the horses in the nearby stable restless. Bee Biter awoke, swooping down with the awkwardness of a day bird managing at night, but not liking it at all.

Firekeeper struggled against Blind Seer's hold, thinking to slip out of the vest, but he knew her too well and simply knocked her down and pressed her to the ground.

The kestrel perched on a section of fence and looked down at them.

"I take it this is not one of your usual games," he said. "I scent real fury here. What is it?"

"Grip this idiot by his tail," Firekeeper said by way of answer, "and when I am free I will tell you."

The kestrel stayed on his perch.

"I think Blind Seer would not knock you down without reason."

"She means to go after Melina herself," the wolf managed, his communication less hindered than a human's would be for he spoke with ears and tail as well as sound. "Or if she cannot stop Melina, to bind the dragon to herself."

To Firekeeper's relief and Blind Seer's evident astonishment, the kestrel didn't immediately think that Firekeeper was being foolhardy.

"There is some wisdom in this, but why go alone?"

"Because I don't need the others to do this!" Firekeeper said, her words thin from Blind Seer's weight on her chest. "That's what the dragon couldn't—or wouldn't—quite tell me. I don't need a ritual to talk to it as Melina does. Nor do I need to bind it to my will. It would gladly accept me as an alternative to her."

"But the cost!" Blind Seer insisted.

"The dragon is death, free or bound," Firekeeper replied. "Would you stop me if I was hunting?"

"If your prey was something too big for you," he said.

Firekeeper changed tactics.

"Time is flowing even as we argue," she reminded him. "Melina will not wait. I can hear the dragon's awareness of her pounding at my mind even though I am awake."

This was no evasion. Indeed, Firekeeper realized that some of her own eagerness to be moving was not her own but the dragon's. That made her pause, unwilling to be so suggestible.

"Will you let me go," she asked Blind Seer, "if I agree to tell the others where I go and why?"

The wolf trembled, torn between his desire to keep her safe and his awareness that none of them would be safe if Melina achieved her end.

"I would," he choked out.

"Then I will tell them," Firekeeper said, "but I will not stay to argue as humans will."

The wolf raised his weight from her.

"Done."

Bee Biter ruffled out his feathers, making himself twice his usual size, then shrunk down again.

"And I will scout around Aswatano. The area should be deserted at this time of night, but somehow I fear that this is not a usual night."

Firekeeper trotted over to the back door of the house. To her relief, Derian had drawn this particular watch. His mildly sleepy smile of greeting turned into one of concern when he saw the mauled edge of her vest.

"What happened to . . ."

Firekeeper cut him off.

"The dragon woke me. Melina is active this night. She comes to bind it. If we are stopping her, it is now."

Derian's drowsiness vanished.

"Where? How does it know?"

Firekeeper was already turning away.

"I don't know how, but I can feel the dragon in my head. It feels like a coal licking tinder. It does not want Melina, but it want less to be bound. When she comes, it will not fight her."

"Aswatano?" Derian asked.

"As you thought," Firekeeper said. "I go ahead and clear the way."

Derian nodded, but his expression was unhappy. Perhaps he had guessed why her vest was torn and perhaps he knew he had even less hope of holding her back than had the wolf.

Firekeeper did not let herself think about Derian or his unhappiness. The dragon's thoughts were washing against her own, making it very hard for her to think about anything other than what she must do at this very moment.

Bee Biter swept out of the darkness when Firekeeper and Blind Seer had covered half the distance to Aswatano. He landed on Firekeeper's shoulder, his claws biting even through the leather.

"The Fountain Court is even emptier than it usually is by night," the kestrel reported, "but the few who are there are not the type I have learned to expect. There are men there, armed and trying to stay hidden while keeping near the fountain."

"City watch?" Firekeeper asked, slowing to a trot so she would not charge in unwarned.

"I don't think so," Bee Biter replied. "These don't share their bearing, nor do they carry their lights openly."

"Do they carry bows?" Firekeeper asked.

"I will check."

The kestrel was away and back again almost before Firekeeper knew he was gone.

"No."

"Good. We will not bother with them then unless they bother with us."

"If they leave us alone," Blind Seer said, "I will never again eat bone marrow."

"Is that a promise?" Firekeeper teased him, suddenly very glad that the blue-eyed wolf was beside her.

"One easily made," he replied, "for I don't believe they will leave us alone."

"Still, this time we must allow them first strike. We must take care not to harm those who could be allies sent by the Healed One. Even if these prove to be enemies, try not to kill them. I think that these New Kelvinese would make trouble over that."

Blind Seer's snort of laughter indicated both his agreement and his exasperation.

The near moonless night was dark but slightly overcast so not even starlight lit their path. The streetlamps set widely spaced along the main streets were more hindrance than help, for Firekeeper would not risk diminishing her night vision by staying too close to them.

More such lamps were spaced around the fringe of Aswatano, and Firekeeper and Blind Seer tried to keep to the dark spaces. Bee Biter had told them where the guards lurked, and they chose their route to put the statue between them.

Aswatano by night was a place very different from Aswatano by day. As Bee Biter had noted, it was almost deserted of human life. The busy stalls where the merchants sold their wares were empty, stripped even of the brightly striped fabrics that provided shade from the sun. The timber frames were revealed as mere skeleton structures, providing not even enough shelter to invite a stray cat to linger.

The fountain, with its larger-than-life-sized tableau of the sorcerers battling something that might be a dragon, was at the center of the court, a wide apron of space left around it.

Earlier that day Peace and Derian had located the doorway hidden in the statue, concealed within the lines of the Star Wizard's outspread cloak.

Peace had guessed that the door would be locked, but that they need not worry that the mechanisms would have frozen from disuse.

"The fountain itself," he had said, "will need regular cleaning within as well as without, since the minerals in the water will adhere to the pipes."

Now, huddled in the shadows next to what was by day a butcher's stand, Firekeeper and Blind Seer inspected their goal.

"What do you intend to do about the lock?" the wolf asked.

"Ignore it," Firekeeper replied. *"I thought we could break the door. If we are lucky, we will be in and gone before those not dreadfully alert watchers even see us."*

Blind Seer made a wuffling grunt that might have been agreement, might have been resignation, but didn't argue—though Firekeeper had the distinct impression he wanted to.

"Ready?" she asked.

Blind Seer crouched. With Firekeeper's first footfall they left the shadows for the marginally better lit area surrounding the statue. Unfortunately for the success of the wolf-woman's plan the guards must also have known where the door was—and were watching it. Firekeeper had hardly touched foot to the wet stone of the statue's base when a cry went up. Blind Seer turned to cover her back, standing chest-deep in the fountain basin to do so.

When an experimental thump of her shoulder against the door didn't budge it, Firekeeper wheeled, drew her Fang, and leapt down on the pavement around the fountain. Blind Seer, soaking wet but no less impressive for that, leapt to join her.

The four men rushing at them seemed at least as interested as Firekeeper was in keeping the city watch out of the action, for other than the initial shout of alarm, their attack had been in relative silence.

Firekeeper feinted at one man with her Fang and when he drew back rushed at him. He jerked away, slipped on the wet stone, and fell. Pausing only to grab his sword and throw it clattering across the pavement, Firekeeper leapt onto the back of a man who was threatening Blind Seer.

The pressure of her knife on his throat made him suddenly tractable.

"Drop sword," she suggested in a husky whisper, "and go on your face."

The man did, and Firekeeper turned to find that Blind Seer had knocked the other two down.

"They ran," he explained, shaking a great shower of warm water over them all. *"I just had to chase."*

Firekeeper laughed and quickly took the guards' weapons. Then she bound their hands behind their backs, bound their ankles together, and for good measure gagged them. Blind Seer's glowering presence was enough to ensure that they didn't make a sound.

"I like," Firekeeper said to Blind Seer, *"that these New Kelvinese wear so much cloth."*

"And aren't very brave," the wolf agreed.

Firekeeper had just finished dragging her captives to the side of one of the market stalls, where she propped them as Citrine might a line of dolls, when Derian and Edlin arrived.

"What happened?" Derian asked, looking from side to side, his weighted stick held ready to challenge any comers.

"These were trying to stop us," Firekeeper explained. "We stopped them. Where is Peace? I want him to open the door."

"He should be here in a moment. Edlin and I came first in case you needed help."

"First? Who else comes?"

Derian sighed slightly and Firekeeper could imagine the argument there must have been as each member of the household demanded the right to be part of tonight's venture.

"Everyone but Wendee. She's going to carry a message to Ambassador Redbriar telling her what we're doing. Then she's going to tell the Healed One."

"Alone?"

Derian looked pleased.

"No. Hasamemorri came down from above, announced that she didn't have any idea what we were up to but that she had divined that whatever we were up to must be dangerous, and offered her help. She will escort Wendee, who will be disguised as one of her maids."

Firekeeper shook her head, amazed by this new evidence of human insanity.

"Only I really need go," she said, returning to her real concern, but Derian was having no more of this than Blind Seer had.

"Tough."

Grateful Peace, Doc, and Elise hurried up at that moment.

"I try," Firekeeper said to Peace, hoping to stop any discussion, "to break the door, but it didn't want to break. Can you open it?"

Grateful Peace pulled out a small ring of keys.

"Idalia has my other set," he said, "but I did manage to acquire new ones. Someone come and hold a lantern for me."

Edlin hurried to obey and the rest waited near Firekeeper's captives.

"It looks," Elise said, looking at the four bound figures, "as if Melina does indeed have an idea where the dragon is."

Firekeeper stiffened and Elise reached out a soothing hand.

"I didn't think you were lying," she said, "but the dragon might have been."

Firekeeper blinked in astonishment.

"I never think of that," she admitted, but touching the dragon's waiting intensity in her mind she added, "I not think if you hear what I do you would think so either."

"Probably not," Elise agreed. "Look! Edlin's motioning us over."

Firekeeper could leap from the edge of the fountain basin to the island holding the statues, but the others needed to wade, pausing first to remove their footwear. Impatient, Firekeeper went ahead, Blind Seer sloshing behind her.

"Don't you dare shake all over me," she warned him.

The wolf ignored her, taking advantage of a wide space between two sculpted sorcerers to get rid of the excess water clinging to his coat.

Glowering, Firekeeper picked her way between the figures to where Edlin was motioning for her to hurry.

"Pretty good, what?" he whispered.

Firekeeper, noting that the door swung outward, and that therefore no amount of pounding would have opened it, agreed.

Having noted the same thing, Blind Seer was panting wolfish laughter behind her.

"Peace?" she asked Edlin, glaring at the wolf.

"Inside."

Firekeeper ducked through the low doorway and found herself in a small room. Those walls that were not a confusing array of pipes were lined with cabinets of tools. At the room's farther end a trapdoor had been opened, revealing a steep flight of curving stairs lit from below—doubtless by Peace's lantern.

"Can you make it down these?" she asked Blind Seer.

"The fit will be tight," he admitted, *"but I believe I can manage."*

Firekeeper took the lead and went down, gripping the railing tightly. Something about the twisting stair—or maybe the throbbing increase of the dragon's presence within her head—made her own feet seem alien to her. She was glad when she was on level floor again, and sought to hide her disorientation by drawing her Fang and polishing it dry on a bit of her vest.

Grateful Peace stood barefoot near the base of the stair, holding his lantern up to better examine the larger room in which they found themselves. More pipes and various incomprehensible bits of machinery crowded along the walls.

"Mostly," Peace stated without preamble, "these are for working the fountain. The hot water emerges from a natural spring and is piped up. The cold is piped from somewhere below—another spring I would guess. However, I wouldn't be at all surprised if at least some of this intricate mess is a blind to cover another door."

Firekeeper nodded, though she had only understood part of what he said.

"What can I do?" she said, focusing on something concrete to keep the dragon's unspoken but intense anxiety from clouding her thoughts further.

"There should be other lanterns here," Peace replied. "Find them and light several."

Firekeeper did as Peace requested, locating the proper locker immediately with the assistance of Blind Seer's nose. While she checked the wicks and oil, she heard noise from above and then bare feet on the stair.

Elise was the first one down and promptly sat on a narrow bench to dry her feet and put on her shoes.

"Derian and Edlin," she informed them, grinning mischievously, "decided to relocate the four guards from outside to that upper room. If the stones of Aswatano have a chance to dry, their friends may think they got bored and went off for a glass of wine."

"Good idea," Firekeeper said, touching flame from Peace's lanterns to those she had prepared. "Can we lock door again?"

"Edlin is going to try," Elise replied. "If not, he and Derian will at least move a cabinet or two into the doorway to make it harder to get through."

"Good thought," Firekeeper agreed, "or if cabinet not move, put men tied up against door."

Elise relayed this suggestion upward via Doc, who was making his own descent.

Six humans and one Royal Wolf, all more or less damp, made the lower chamber rather close, so Peace sent Derian and Edlin back upstairs while he continued looking for the exit he knew must be there.

"At least I believe it is," he confided worriedly. "Firekeeper, can the dragon tell you anything about how we reach it?"

"No," the wolf-woman answered promptly. "This place is all since it was bound. It knows there is live water near it, for the water is involved with its binding. Live water and living stone. That is all it knows."

"Do you feel the dragon's thoughts more intensely in any direction?"

"Down," Firekeeper said. "When we come down it grew louder."

"But not east or west?"

Firekeeper shook her head. Her own emotions were in an uproar. If this was a dead-end and Peace could not find the way to the dragon then Firekeeper couldn't be blamed for not stopping Melina. She would not have to bind the dragon herself. She would not have to pay the price. But then Melina would win.

Hope warred with fear until Firekeeper didn't know what she hoped or what she feared, but the dragon's awareness that Melina was coming for it was as real to her as the odor of Blind Seer's wet fur.

Firekeeper could tell from Peace's expression that he was about to admit defeat when Doc said:

"Grateful Peace? I think I may have something here."

Peace turned, his gaze alight with surprise.

"Yes, Sir Jared?"

"I've been looking at the pipes," Doc said, "tracing them like I would the vessels in the body that carry blood."

"Yes?"

"And this lot over here," Doc indicated a mass of piping on the northeast segment of the wall, "doesn't seem to do anything."

Peace hurried over to the section Doc was inspecting.

"See?" Doc said, pointing to a curving pipe that looked no different from any of the others to Firekeeper's eye. "It starts there and ends there, but as far as I can tell it links into neither the hot nor cold water systems."

Peace held his hand up to the pipe in question, then gripped it in his hand.

"Neither hot nor cold, simply chill." He rapped it with his knuckles. "Nor does it carry water. Sir Jared, this may be our answer!"

It did not take long then for Peace to find how this one section of pipes swung clear from the wall. Once the pipes were moved away, Peace's expert eye found the thin outlines of a door cut into the dressed stone and a keyhole concealed in what appeared to be a natural flaw in the stone.

Firekeeper stood close, holding a lantern so that Peace would have light enough to pick the lock.

Blind Seer spoke to her. *"So, Little Two-legs, we could have done this without a pack, you and I, could we?"*

Firekeeper wanted to kick him, but felt the truth of his accusation.

"If we were not about to go on a hunt," she said, *"and this room were not so small, I would lay myself at your feet and show you my throat and belly."*

Blind Seer sneezed his satisfaction.

"Just don't forget. Like knows like best."

A sharp click announced that Grateful Peace had convinced yet another lock to yield to his skill.

"This door also pulls outward," he said. "There do not appear to be any traps, but we should take care when we go through. Tell Edlin and Derian they can join us now."

"I go first," Firekeeper said, "with Blind Seer."

"So the lantern light doesn't spoil your vision," Peace agreed, but something in his tone made her think he might be teasing her. "Then I will go second since I may see things you two do not."

Firekeeper did not disagree—though her real reason was that she wanted no one to stop her if she decided to do something they might find impulsive. When all were ready and lanterns turned to the merest glows and shielded so that their light would not give undue warning of their coming, Firekeeper put her fingers into small depressions in the stone and pulled against the heavy stone door. It glided easily on unseen tracks, swinging back and revealing a steep stone ramp curving gently downward.

"Now," Firekeeper said, almost to herself, "very careful, very quiet. We go."

XXXIX

FOR A LONG, SILENT MOMENT Citrine stared at her mother, awed and intimidated by the wonderfully terrible vision in crimson, gems, and gold that had emerged from the steaming portal.

Then, realizing she was cringing, Citrine straightened her shoulders, ready for whatever punishment Melina might deem fit. As the moments passed in slow, shuddering breaths, Citrine realized that there was no anger upon Melina's intricately painted features, only wonder and a strange, gleeful calculation.

"How long have you been following me, Citrine?" Melina asked, the jewel-hung chains on wrists and waist ringing as she knelt to meet Citrine's gaze.

"Since you left your rooms," Citrine replied softly. "You were carrying a heavy bag. I thought I could guess where you were going. So I followed."

"You could guess," Melina prompted. "How could you guess? This place is a secret."

"Our secret," Citrine replied in a nearly inaudible whisper. "I have known about it for days and days now. I . . ."

She decided to give up the entire truth and be done with it.

"I've followed you before, Mother. I had to know where you were going."

She waited for the slap across her cheek, the angry admonishment that would make her ears ring and her face blaze brighter than the rising welt. Neither came. Melina only looked thoughtful and maybe the tiniest bit sad.

"Why did you need to know where I went, Citrine? To tell your friends what I am doing?"

Citrine choked around a sob she didn't know was hidden in her throat.

"I don't have any friends. Nobody cares about me. The others only care about the things the king wants. I was just a tag-along, crazy baby."

Melina reached out and, careful not to mar her attire, drew Citrine close. The elaborately detailed dragon that spread its wings across Melina's breast made a hard pillow, but close to her mother's scented warmth Citrine didn't care. And when Melina finally spoke she said what Citrine had always wanted to hear.

"I think, Citrine, that you have turned out the best of my children, the very best of all. Sapphire was always so headstrong, so sure of herself. Jet was just a sniveling flatterer underneath. Ruby and Opal . . ."

Melina dismissed her middle two daughters with an indignant puff of breath.

"But you, little Citrine, so devoted, so passionately devoted. You're the very, very best of all."

Citrine wanted to weep she was so happy, but she knew she daren't. Close up she could see that Mother's paint went all the way down her neck and even lower. Tears might smear the tiny little characters written upon Mother's pale skin. That might make Mother mad and Citrine wanted nothing at all to spoil this perfect happiness.

Eventually, Melina released Citrine and rose with regal majesty to her feet. Her beautiful silk robe was soiled with dust from the floor and Citrine hastened to brush it clean. Her happiness when the dust didn't cling and ruin Mother's beauty made the child's smile radiant.

Melina took Citrine by the hand.

"Come, darling, let me show you the secret place I've found. It's hidden behind this steaming curtain. Close your eyes and follow me."

Citrine obeyed the gentle tugging of Mother's hand. She'd never dared cross the steam herself. Though she had followed Melina to this point, she had never been this near. When Mother had not returned for so long Citrine had crept closer, wondering if the steam concealed a tunnel rather than a cave, as she'd always assumed. In her haste to make sure she wasn't left behind, Citrine'd forgotten to be stealthy and the clatter of rolling pebbles had brought Mother forth.

Now the steaming heat filled Citrine's lungs with wet fire and made her head light, but that lasted only for a moment.

"Open your eyes," Melina said, and Citrine gratefully breathed in mouthfuls of marginally cooler air.

Citrine found herself in a cozy room shaped something like an egg.

Mother's bag rested on the smoothed stone of the floor along with the clothing she'd been wearing when Citrine had followed her. Lovely ornaments were placed here and there on the floor, but Mother didn't give Citrine time to closely examine them.

"Tell me, Citrine, did you hear what I told Tipi to tell you?"

"Yes, Mother. You said you'd come to see me, even if it was late. That I needed to eat a good dinner."

Melina smiled, evidently pleased, even though Citrine hadn't obeyed her commands. This puzzled Citrine a little, but then she realized that Mother was happy that Citrine loved her so much that she would disobey to be close.

"Do you believe I would have come to see you?"

"Oh, yes, Mother!"

Melina pinched Citrine gently on one round cheek.

"It's nice to be believed, but let me show you proof of my intentions, darling. Look what's in my bag."

Melina handed Citrine a folded bundle of fabric. Its weight warned Citrine that it contained more than cloth and so she unwrapped it very carefully. She soon found herself gaping in astonishment at a crimson silk robe not too different from Mother's own, a pair of embroidered slippers, and a tangle of jewelry. To Citrine's delight, there was even a dragon breast pectoral — it was made from dry paper mash, like the costumers had used to make her apple costume, but it was beautifully painted so unless you looked closely you couldn't tell the difference.

"Mother! Everything, it's just like what you're wearing!"

"That's right, my darling," Melina purred. "Tonight I planned to reward you for being such a wonderful, faithful daughter. I am going to let you help me with a very important project."

Citrine stood straighter, trying very, very hard to be worthy of her mother's trust.

"I'd like to help, Mother."

"I am going to work a great magic tonight, Citrine. Does that scare you?"

"No, Mother," Citrine insisted, though in reality her insides were twisting at the thought. She remembered how she and her cousin Kenre Trueheart used to scare themselves silly with the rumors that Mother worked magic.

Melina didn't seem to see her fear, but went on calmly, "This magic will make me the mistress of something so powerful that you and I will no longer need to worry about what those fools in the Primes think. They will listen to what I want and be glad for an end to their endless bickering and debate."

Citrine nodded, almost understanding. Certainly she got tired of the way the voices in her head could argue at her. It seemed reasonable that the Primes would be glad to stop arguing, too.

"The spell we will work tonight will awaken a dragon, Citrine." Melina's pale eyes were shining now, lit from within by the intensity of her vision. "A real flying, fire-breathing dragon! I was going to bind the dragon to myself, but a few days ago I had a thought . . ."

Melina paused dramatically. Citrine folded her hands around the folds of the brilliant scarlet robe and waited, her heart pounding.

"Citrine," Melina said, once again sinking down so she could meet Citrine's gaze, "do you ever get tired of being just a baby? Do you ever wish you could grow up quickly?"

Citrine had never realized that this was what she wanted, but she realized so now. How much easier life would be if she were grown-up! Adults never had to worry about what anybody thought. Adults were in charge of things.

"Oh, yes!" Citrine answered almost surprised at the fervor in her own voice. "I've always wished I could grow up quickly!"

"Well," Melina said, lowering her voice so that Citrine had to listen very carefully, "there's a secret to the dragon, a secret most people don't know, but I'll share it with you."

Citrine leaned closer.

"If you are in control of the dragon," Melina said, "then you grow up faster."

"Because you have to be grown-up to manage the dragon?" Citrine asked, trying to show that she understood.

"Something like that," Melina replied with a gentle smile. "Now, I could control the dragon, but then you'd stay a little girl, but if you controlled the dragon for me, then you'd grow up faster. Why, by the end of a year, you'd be twelve."

"Really?" Citrine gaped in wonder. "That's almost as old as Ruby!"

"That's right. You'd be almost a young lady, and you'd continue to grow up faster than usual. Do you know about Idalia?"

Citrine nodded, no longer at all hesitant about letting her mother know how much she had learned.

"She's the lady who is mayor of your underground city, Mother."

"That's right," Melina said, looking pleased. "Well, Citrine, when you were grown-up and controlling the dragon, I wouldn't need Idalia anymore. You'd be my assistant in her place."

One of Citrine's voices, very faintly, tried to cry out that there was a problem hidden in the folds of this strange offer, but Citrine didn't listen. Her mind was too full of wonderful images: of herself an elegant young lady in beautiful robes, of flying on the back of a dragon with Mother sitting close behind her, of being a princess at last, just like Sapphire.

"Mother, would you really let me do this?"

"I would," Melina said. Her tone grew stern. "First you must promise me from your heart of hearts, cross the river and never come back, that you'll never ever let the dragon do something unless I give you instructions first."

"I promise, Mama!"

"Promise that you'll go blind before you'll disobey me?"

"I promise, Mother. May I go blind and deaf and dumb if I disobey you."

"Good girl."

The severity left Melina's face and she lifted the red silk robe from Citrine's hands.

"Take off your dirty clothes, and we'll wash that dark stuff off your face and make you pretty again. While we get you ready, I'll tell you just what you'll need to do."

Heart fluttering wildly, Citrine reached to undo the toggles fastening the neck of her robe. She noticed that Melina's expression had turned dreamy.

"What are you thinking, Mama?" she asked shyly.

"I'm thinking that tonight, at long last, the Dragon of Despair will be mine!"

DERIAN PLACED HIMSELF LAST IN LINE, Elise directly in front of him, Doc before her, and Edlin shadowing Grateful Peace as if he had made himself the older man's protector for so long that it was unthinkable for him to do otherwise now. Firekeeper and Blind Seer, leading the way, were lost to Derian's sight.

The stone ramp was slightly rough, providing steady enough footing, but Derian found he kept reaching out with his free hand to touch the wall. The weight of the stick thrust in his belt was little comfort, for the corridor down which they moved was narrow enough that he could not have swung it.

He found himself hoping that they were on the right course. The New Kelvinese were so weird and their Founders seemed to have liked underground nearly as much as they liked sky-pointing spires. It seemed all too likely that these chambers beneath Aswatano might have nothing to do with the dragon—no matter what Firekeeper said. She hadn't been at all herself lately.

It was during one of those times he reached out to steady himself against the wall that Derian realized that the ramp had broadened. At almost the same instant, he knew from the sudden ache of calf muscles that no longer needed to tighten against the slope of the ramp that their course had leveled off.

Peace had reminded them against whispering, for the hissing sounds would carry farther than normal speech, so Derian asked in the softest voice he could manage:

"Are we in a room now?"

The sound of his own voice gave answer, echoing slightly against walls unpadded and unadorned but certainly wider set than the tunnel or the room above.

Peace's voice spoke in reply.

"I'm going to turn up my lantern just a little."

The pale beam Peace freed and turned back illuminated a small chamber, barren except for curling bits of what Derian knew was the older New Kelvinese script painted on the walls. An opening in one wall showed that their journey was not over, and Derian saw Firekeeper and Blind Seer cross to inspect it.

The painted inscription was well preserved and once Peace had confirmed they were alone and no traps awaited them, he motioned for them to wait while he brought his light over and directed it at the text.

"Any idea what it says?" Derian asked Elise, his lips nearly touching her ear.

"No," she answered. "A few words here and there, but the old writing isn't much like what they use these days."

Edlin had followed Peace and to Derian's surprise actually seemed to understand some of the characters. Then he remembered how Melina had forced her prisoners to systematically map the tunnels beneath Thendulla Lypella and thought he understood.

"Hot water again, what?" he could just hear Edlin say. "And the dragon. We're on the right road."

Derian felt strange relief that he was not the only one who had wondered, but Peace's reply awoke a new uneasiness in him.

"We are," the New Kelvinese replied, "and so was Melina. We must hurry."

The Illuminator walked briskly toward the other opening. Derian, turning to take up his place in line once more, saw that Firekeeper and Blind Seer had already passed through.

Before Grateful Peace turned his lantern low, Derian glimpsed his expression. To the redhead's consternation, the older man looked less annoyed—as Derian might have expected—than deeply worried, and a little bit frightened.

Peace's expression stayed with Derian, illuminating his inner landscape as the minute glow shed by his lantern illuminated the area around his feet—and with similar consequences. Every time that small glow showed Derian a place where without light he might have twisted an ankle or worse on the increasingly rough surface of the descending ramp, Derian found himself watching his feet more carefully. All the while his internal eye strained after Firekeeper, trying to guess what had disturbed Grateful Peace's usual urbane composure.

True light, when it came, seemed so unreal that Derian realized he had been seeing it for some time before he believed in its existence. It shone from ahead, a pale diffuse glow that silhouetted Elise's slender grace moving in front of him and revealed Doc as a solid shadow holding up his hand to signal them to slow.

Even as Derian did so, he strained to see what was creating this elusive and welcome light, taking advantage of his greater height to look over the others' heads, questing for the source. When he found it, the revelation was hardly welcome.

Their ramp had ended in a wide cavern that seemed natural in that no beams supported its walls, no tools marked its shaping, but was markedly unnatural in its very shape and in the evidence that something had rubbed the surface of the stone to such a high polish that the black rock gave back the light.

In form the cavern was like a moon almost half full, but not yet so far in her course that the horns at each end were lost. The ramp down which Derian's group was still carefully picking its way was near the rightmost horn.

A steaming river flowed from the center of the crescent, its waters gathering against the curve of the farther wall, creating a pool nearly as long as the wall itself. Derian guessed that the waters must drain away, else the chamber would have completely flooded long ago.

The basalt walls of the chamber were highly polished along the moon's curve, the polish diminishing and becoming irregular nearer to the horns. Viewing this odd and terrible cavern, Derian had a sudden vision of an enormous dragon sweeping down along where the central river course now ran, breathing fire in its fury, fire so hot that it melted the very rock that barred the dragon's way, forcing solid stone to curve and polishing basalt's roughness into glass wherever the fire licked.

It was such a stark and terrible vision that Derian did not doubt that reality had been forced into his mind. For the first time he pitied Firekeeper her nightmares.

Then pity, nightmares, and anything past was banished at the moment Derian caught his first glimpse of the present.

In front of the far wall, set close along the edge of the pool, were a series of braziers—the source of the light that had so confused Derian. All this while Firekeeper had been leading the group forward, keeping them to the densest shadows, which Derian realized would be nearly as good as a solid barrier in hiding them from the light-blinded eyes of those nearer to the braziers. Now, his view unrestricted by the ramp, Derian saw that the river was bridged a short distance from where it flowed out to create the pool. On this bridge stood twin figures, alike except for their height.

The taller, gaudy in crimson and gold, sparkling with gems that held every color the cold earth has ever pressed into stone, was Melina. The small one, Derian realized, must be—despite her ornate costume and stiff, unnatural posture—Citrine.

Derian saw Elise start as she realized the same thing, saw Doc rest his hand on her arm to warn her to silence. Ahead Edlin was raising an arm to point, the gesture as eloquent as one of his more usual vocal outbursts. Slightly ahead of Edlin, Grateful Peace remained watchful and calculating, but Firekeeper was drawing her Fang, angling the blade so it would not catch the light. Beside her, Blind Seer crouched, every line of his form eloquent of the desire to spring.

But Peace said something that held the wolves, and the slight gesture of his hand drew Derian's attention away from the bridge and to the shore.

Only then did he realize that Melina was not alone. Standing near the braziers on either side of the bridge were less ornately clad figures. Each held something that glittered richly in the light. With the first sound other than the flowing of the subterranean river and the hiss and crackle of the braziers Melina's voice sang out a few pure notes.

The scene shifted for Derian and he realized that they had arrived not at the inception of Melina's ritual but in the middle—and if the rising of the chanting was any indication, that middle was moving toward an end.

SOUND REACHED GRATEFUL PEACE'S EAR even as his eyes were realizing that not all the light was coming from the lantern in his hand. A few steps in front of him, Firekeeper paused, also listening.

"Melina," the wolf-woman informed him softly, "but I not know what she say."

Peace set his lantern to one side, seeking to free his one hand. Motioning for Edlin to remain back a few paces, he moved with silent skill to Firekeeper's side. She then led the way forward, reaching out from time to time to guide him around some obstacle with such thoughtless thoughtfulness that Peace experienced a momentary insight into the workings of a wolf pack where nothing was lost in accepting the aid of others.

As they crept closer to the source of the sound, Peace could distinguish individual words set in the measured rise and fall of a chant. His hearing wrapped itself around an initial strangeness, becoming comfortable when he realized that what he was hearing was the old form of the language—a language old even in the Founders' day and the traditional form used for magic.

He was impressed that Melina had managed to learn not one but two foreign languages. Moreover, judging from what he could catch of Melina's inflections, she understood what she was saying. This chant was not being sounded out from an ancient text but being spoken, and, he realized as he listened further, improvised upon.

The reluctant admiration Peace always felt for his opponent rose within him, then fluttered and died as he realized just what it was Melina was saying . . . and who she had with her.

Whether guided by some long-ago writings or by her own flawless sense of drama, Melina had positioned herself at the apex of a delicate arching bridge that spanned the hot waters of the underground river. She was attired in rich and brilliant robes after the fashion of the Founders, as was the small figure standing beside her. Indeed, the small one was Melina's silent copy, imitating her every gesture a moment after it was made.

Citrine, Peace thought, surprised only by his own pain at seeing the girl so deeply in thrall to her mother's will, trapped within a prison far worse than the one in which he and Edlin had been kept.

Well, Citrine had—if inadvertently—helped free himself and Edlin. Now Peace must do his best to free her.

Following Firekeeper's steady guidance, Grateful Peace moved closer until even his weak vision could distinguish who else accompanied Melina. On this side of the bridge, Idalia and several members of her family stood positioned near various braziers, each one holding a glittering ornament.

On the other side of the bridge stood four others, two other members of Idalia's family, a man Peace vaguely recalled as a spy in the Healed One's service, and Toriovico. The Healed One's hands cupped a golden vase, his face held the same expression of detached entrancement that Peace saw on the faces of his sister and her family.

Did Toriovico become careless? Peace thought. *Or did Melina somehow learn of his involvement in our escape? Columi's nerves were so on edge that even a less astute judge of human character might think to question him. . . .*

Grateful Peace had no attention to spare for such thoughts. At last he was close enough to follow Melina's speech in full.

He listened carefully, trying to judge just how much time they had—reaching out to place a restraining hand on Firekeeper's arm. The wolf-woman had drawn her omnipresent knife and was apparently preparing to attack—never mind that four people stood between her and Melina.

"Wait," Peace cautioned. "We may yet have time."

"Not much," came Firekeeper's reply, her voice even huskier than usual. "Dragon say."

Peace nodded, but kept his hand on her arm, though he knew such light restraint would serve no purpose if Firekeeper was determined to act. He concentrated on Melina's words.

"Dragon!" she was saying in what Peace recognized as a verse within a series of invocations he had been hearing for some time now. "See you the gifts we have brought for your honor. Symbolic, they are, of the respect we feel for your power. Flames send them to you, substantial, insubstantial, to give you form and strength."

As Melina spoke the phrase "form and strength" she dropped a golden dagger into the brazier in front of her. At the same moment, her lackeys dropped the items they held into the braziers before them. The actions were so perfectly coordinated that Peace knew Melina must have used her power to make certain that no one would spoil the moment.

As the items were engulfed by flame, the braziers flared high, devouring what smelled like scented woods and curling the soft metals into wisps of colored flame. The smoke was intense, even at the distance where Peace crouched listening, and he had to shove his sleeve against his mouth to keep from coughing aloud. Firekeeper—lacking a sleeve—had to settle for her forearm and Peace could see that her dark brown eyes were running with tears.

Weirdly, neither Melina nor her servants appeared to be at all affected by the smoke, a thing that made Peace shudder inside even as a cynical corner of his nature was wondering what precautions had been taken in advance.

The smoky onslaught lasted only a short while and was forgotten even before it had faded. The white smoke was being sucked in by the farther wall, etching upon the wall's curved and polished surface the lean skeletal form of an enormous reptilian figure. Within moments the lines of a dragon were present, complete to every bone and joint, its sinuous curves fleshed out in living flame.

Grateful Peace could not smother a gasp of wonder, but his imprudence did not give him away, for each of Melina's retainers had shouted aloud—an echoing cry that mingled exaltation and fear. Only Melina and Citrine stood stiff and silent.

Then, when even the echoes had faded, Melina stepped back and knelt behind Citrine, her hands on her daughter's shoulders, her lips close to the girl's ear.

"Dragon!" cried Citrine's childish treble, her inflection not as perfect as her mother's, but no less intense. "I am here to free you. My life will be bound with yours as you are now bound within rock and water. My honored parent has opened the way. Accept myself as the final offering to . . ."

Loud and terrible, belling from the polished walls and echoing from every stony surface, twin wolf howls overwhelmed the slender notes of Citrine's voice.

One with the sound, Firekeeper and Blind Seer leapt forward, pent up energy exploding from coiled muscles so that they were halfway to Melina before anyone thought to interfere.

How did Firekeeper know? Peace asked himself, even as he was rushing forward. *The dragon must have told her, somehow. What advantage would there be for it in that? Certainly it wants its freedom.*

And then Peace thought he knew and his heart wept acid as he realized what the dragon must expect. It was not relinquishing its freedom out of some sense of righteousness. It was bartering with another master—one who it must think would not exact nearly as much from it.

And who would be the master and who the slave? Peace wondered before there was no room for wondering.

Idalia had seen Peace coming and her hatred for him was greater even than her desire to protect Melina. Keening in a shrill parody of the wolves' howl she was rushing toward him, a long-bladed dagger raised high.

Peace never doubted Idalia could use the weapon. Despite their association with the Illuminators' sodality their parents had not been well off, their earnings hardly enough to keep their growing family. Especially when Idalia was a girl, the family had lived in the less prosperous parts of Dragon's Breath and knowing how to defend oneself had been a necessity.

However, whatever Idalia's skill with the dagger, it was diminished to some extent by her nearly mindless fury. Melina had twisted a mother's sorrow and rage, fed it with childhood jealousy, and transformed it—and the heart that held it—into a monstrous parody.

For Idalia at this moment there was no one else in the universe but Grateful Peace. Indeed, as Peace clumsily blocked the first downthrust blow, seeking to disarm his sister but disadvantaged by his single arm and latent injuries, he thought that Idalia probably didn't even know where she was or what had been about to happen. All she knew was he was there and the restraints that had kept her from killing him when he was her prisoner were no longer in place.

But Peace was not alone. Edlin had been next behind him as their group crept forward and now he leapt to Peace's defense. He closed the gap with long-legged speed and Idalia's expression of purest shock as the young man wrested the dagger from her confirmed Peace's suspicions.

"She is ensorcelled," Peace warned Edlin in Pellish. "This is not wholly her own doing. Be gentle."

He was not certain whether Edlin would heed him. The young lord had suffered intensely when Idalia had taken advantage of Peace's helplessness to torment her brother, and clearly Edlin longed for nothing so much as to pay her back in kind—at least to the extent of a solid blow or two. But Edlin's innate respect for Peace held his hand and he settled for twisting Idalia's wrist so that the dagger clattered to the stone floor of the cavern.

"Good thing Derian and I brought more rope, what?" Edlin said, producing several short lengths and starting to efficiently truss the struggling woman.

It was horrid to see how Idalia continued to spit and scream, struggling even as she was restrained, to get at the brother she hated so intensely.

Peace longed for the luxury of mourning this ruin, but he dared not pause.

When Idalia had slowed Peace, Firekeeper had continued her forward rush. Two of Idalia's grown children had sought to stop her, but Firekeeper and Blind Seer had dodged them as easily as they might a pair of unmoving boulders. The remaining defender on this side of the river, Idalia's husband, Pichero, had moved to the base of the bridge and stood blocking their progress, a long sword in one hand, a shield hung on his arm.

Like most able New Kelvinese, Pichero had received some military training—a necessity in a land that kept no standing army but expected to raise a competent force at need. Moreover, seeing his stance, Peace suspected that Pichero had taken advantage of managing Melina's small slave army to polish his fighting skills.

But if Peace feared for Firekeeper's safety, the wolf-woman herself did not hesitate. Howling, her dagger in hand, she raced at Pichero and when Pichero moved to answer her feint, Blind Seer struck. Smashing his entire weight into Pichero's shield, the wolf bowled the man back, off balance, and into the river. Pichero screamed as the near boiling waters closed around him, dropping both sword and shield in a frantic attempt to swim for the bank opposite his former opponents.

From behind Peace came running footsteps against stone as Derian and Sir Jared moved into action. Their goals, however, were different. Swinging his weighted stick wildly, Derian took on Peace's nephew, Varcasiol, as the young man was about to throw something at Firekeeper's back. Sir Jared, however, paused to make certain that Peace and Idalia had not been injured.

"Here, cousin," Edlin said, thrusting the rope with which he had been binding Idalia at Sir Jared. "Take over, what?"

Then Lord Kestrel was bounding away, swinging the sword he carried with such enthusiasm that it was no wonder that Linatha, Peace's niece, balked at confronting him, instead backing away, whatever control Melina had placed on her clearly weakened by her mother's insanity and her father's cries of pain.

Yet though the four on the nearer side of the bridge were no longer an obstacle, Peace saw that Melina had not maintained her position on the bridge. Instead she had hustled Citrine to the farther side. Once there, leaving her four remaining servitors to hold the bridge, Melina had once again turned the child to face the dragon-embellished wall and knelt behind her, whispering in her ear.

Melina's not going to stop! Peace thought, glancing at the wall and seeing that the outline of the dragon had not diminished. Indeed, it was taking on substance, now no longer a smoky skeleton barely fleshed in fire, but instead a sculpture in low relief, a sculpture that horribly was beginning to ripple like the muscles of a snake moving beneath scaled skin.

About to take on the first of those holding the bridge, the spy, Kiero, Firekeeper suddenly froze, aware on some level none of the rest of them shared of the reinception of the spell.

The wolf-woman stepped back a pace, then darted away from Kiero, moving instead to face the wall. With a howl in which Peace heard a note of purest despair, Blind Seer rushed Kiero's sword, leaving Firekeeper free to sacrifice herself to the dragon.

XL

WITHOUT THE COMFORT of Mother's hands on her shoulders, Citrine would have been terrified. Even with those two warm spots radiating heat through the thin silk of her robe, Citrine was trembling, though from excitement rather than fear—or so she tried hard to make herself believe.

When Firekeeper's attack had interrupted the orderly progress of the ritual, Citrine had been so deep within the convolution of the spell that she had hardly felt Melina carry her a safe distance away, set her down again, and urge her to resume the repetition of ordered phrases that was taking Citrine into a shadow realm where the dragon within the wall seemed more real than the screaming and fighting across the river.

Deep inside the curving passages of Citrine's mind, the voices that had been stilled since Mother had discovered Citrine lurking outside the egg cavern had taken advantage of the temporary disruption to shout for her attention. Unwilling to listen, Citrine focused even harder on perfectly repeating the strangely shaped syllables Mother was once again reciting into her ear.

Her ploy worked, for the voices were drowned out as the dragon's heated presence sliced through her internal fog. The dragon's intensity burned away the shadows that clouded her vision until Citrine saw herself standing before the dragon, its long tongue snapping like a whip a hand's breadth from her nose.

Though Citrine had understood perhaps one word in ten of the ornate incantation she had been reciting line by line, she understood every word the dragon said.

"So you are the one who offers to command me," it said, its voice hissing like the steaming river. "Do you really think you can manage me?"

There was mockery in that hissing intonation, but Citrine—youngest child of an unloving brood, younger cousin of an unkind mob—had lots of practice standing firm in the face of derision.

"I can," she replied stoutly, realizing that she had departed from Mother's prepared text. "Are you scared I can't?"

"It is you who should be afraid, little girl," the dragon hissed. "You have no idea what you are doing. I would not even warn you if it were not ordained by those who put me here that I must so warn whomever would set me free. Hear this warning and know it is true: I will be your death."

Melina's voice, incantorial and faint, came then, as if she shouted down a long tunnel. Distantly, Citrine's outer ears registered that Mother was shouting.

"Life will be the death of all living things," Melina responded as from a long way away. "What you say holds no fear for my daughter."

The hissing of the dragon's laughter rose as it glided forth to entwine Citrine in its coils, a single one of which rose almost higher than Citrine's head. She held her breath as if she was about to jump into a river from whose waters she would never emerge, feeling, too, a thrill of anticipation at what drowning in those waters would bring.

Then a new voice, strong and solid, challenged the dragon. Craning her neck to look over the dragon's coils, Citrine saw that Firekeeper had entered the shadow place.

"You don't want Citrine," the wolf-woman said, speaking without the hesitation and searching for words Citrine had come to expect. "You've been sniffing around the backside of my mind this moon's waxing and before. You know what Citrine hides from herself. You dread it as she would if she were wiser. Leave this little one. Let us make a pack between us."

The dragon's coils loosened and Citrine could see Firekeeper clearly. The wolf-woman stood easy and insouciant, staring up at the dragon without fear.

Citrine knew the dragon was greatly interested in what Firekeeper offered and she felt more than heard the shrill, panicked cry that broke from her lips at the idea of failing Mother.

And at her cry Mother, blessed Mother, came to Citrine's rescue. Her voice still came as from a great distance—an odd thing, for Citrine could feel herself flinch as Mother shouted only a finger's breadth from her ear.

"Dragon of Despair," Melina intoned, "we abjure and command you using the spells of the Star Wizard, he who won over even your might. Petrified by the light from his mirror was your bone, boiled into rank water were your flesh and organs. Desire you to feel this again or desire you freedom?"

It was a powerful threat and Citrine repeated it, marveling how she understood the archaic New Kelvinese that had been a mystery moments before.

"That is because," the dragon hissed, "you are hearing the words through my mind."

Impatient, Firekeeper spoke.

"Come to me, dragon. I will not need to threaten you, for I will not use you as Melina will."

"Truly?" the dragon hissed, leaving Citrine and gliding toward Firekeeper. "Can you honestly promise that, wolfling? Promise not to use my power though all you hold dearest is threatened? I must warn you that if you break that promise, the flow of life between us will be intensified so that in the end I will suck you into a shriveled husk—and may not obey you even then."

Citrine saw Firekeeper hesitate, heard one of her own voices murmur: *"She's worried about those Beasts. What if she gives her word and then can't help them? She's not as brave as you. You'll live your life faster to help your mother. What a coward Firekeeper is!"*

Turning, Citrine saw the speaker beside her, a version of herself but with a cynical twist to her features Citrine didn't at all like. Startled, she looked around and realized that she stood at the heart of a small cluster of Citrines—brave ones and frightened ones, one who looked as innocent as a baby, and one who looked sad and all too knowledgeable, one upon whom the dragon pectoral had been transformed into Melina's face radiating confidence and wisdom, one upon whom the same pectoral became Melina herself, arms outstretched, reaching upward, her hands curved to strangle Citrine's exposed throat.

Citrine shrieked and the crowd of selves vanished, but she couldn't forget their existence.

"The decision," the dragon said conversationally, turning to face Citrine, "doesn't require all of you to agree. I'll eat you as well without agreement, but it does raise some troubles for the troubled."

"Eat me?" Citrine asked, puzzled.

Firekeeper snorted, her expression blending pity and derision.

"What do you think a dragon does?" she asked.

"Mother said it will let me grow up faster," Citrine said defiantly. "So I can help her better."

"And so I shall," the dragon said, "for a while. Then someday you will be older than your mother, and someday you will die before her, wrinkled and bent, age eating your bones as you feed me."

From the distance, Melina's voice could be heard strong and certain, carrying on the incantation. Citrine was aware of Mother urging her to repeat the words, to go forward as Mother was going forward, though all the world was against her.

"Why do you think Melina is not here with us?" Firekeeper asked almost kindly. "You take the risks for her—you face the monster."

"What else do I have to give to deserve her love?" Citrine cried. Sucking in a ragged intake of breath, Citrine raised her voice, repeating the words Melina had been drumming into her ears. "Dragon of Despair, come into my heart, make a bond between us, make a strong road in which power is granted for power given."

She closed her eyes and pressed the tips of her fingers to them, but somehow she could still see. Firekeeper was hesitating, but Citrine could see into the hot red coal of her heart and knew that hesitation would not last, that Firekeeper would beat Citrine to the goal, that Citrine would fail, fail, and Mother would die and hate her and Citrine would be tortured forever and ever by her failure to do this one little thing right.

Shrieking, Citrine departed the formula, racing forward to impale herself on the spikes that rose like a thorn forest from the dragon's crest. She was running, her feet slipping on a floor made slick by what she knew with a sick sense of self-betrayal was her own doubt bleeding out before her in a oily red pool that she must leap.

And a calm voice spoke from behind her, a level voice well known and on some level loved.

"Melina has it wrong, dragon, doesn't she?" said Grateful Peace. "One small but important point of her research is flawed. Is that why you drive these children to immolate themselves in your fire? Not because you do not wish to serve Melina, but because you know that she lacks one of the keys to set you free."

Citrine found herself unable to move. Mother wrong? Impossible! But the dragon's eyes were narrow slitted now, amber-gold lines focusing on Grateful Peace so completely that Citrine knew herself and Firekeeper both forgotten. Mother's shouts faded to an echoing stillness and Citrine could do nothing but listen to what Peace said, for true knowledge of the spell had never been hers.

"I thought I had it right," Peace said with conversational pedantry. "I was reminded of the facts as presented in the old stories by what was written in the room above this one. The Star Wizard was a deeply conflicted man—especially for a sorcerer of his time. He had seen what Kelvin's impulsiveness had wrought and feared it, but he knew, too, how pitiful this little kingdom was. How long would Waterland or other enemies hold back if they thought the dragon gone? A generation, maybe two. Make clear that the dragon was only bound, though, and it remained a threat that would last for generations."

The dragon neither protested nor confirmed this version of history. Over to one side, Firekeeper struggled to make herself heard, but the dragon's indifference was so complete that she might as well have been howling at the moon.

He's locked us out of his mind, Citrine thought, *but Peace has not. He wants us to understand.*

She felt a sudden affection for the man, realizing how different he was from Melina. Peace had always wanted her to understand, to follow because she realized how important things were. Mother wanted her to obey—to prove her worthiness by perfect trust.

Feeling she owed Peace at least this, Citrine tried hard to listen, to understand every word.

"The Star Wizard had other difficulties. How to bind something so powerful without tempting every power-hungry soul to use it as a weapon? The penalty he created was horrid enough to stop all but someone insane—or perhaps very young. He did his best, so that even those who would free you would need to overcome many obstacles. He crafted these, playing fair by the rules of sorcery in his day, even to hiding your own name in plain sight. That's the element Melina has wrong—why she has not succeeded. She has been calling you by the wrong name, and as long as she does this none of her chants can free you."

The dragon coughed, slit eyes dilating in ironic laughter. Peace did not laugh in return.

"But what Melina did not know—and you knew all too well—is that there is a way to free you that has nothing to do with elaborate rituals, burning incense, and all of that trivia. The Star Wizard may have foreseen a day when the forms of ritual magic would be lost. Or perhaps he was just eager to hedge his bets. In addition to the calculating provisions everyone knew about, he also allowed that if someone freed you not for his own good but for the good of others—sacrificing his own life so that others might live—then you can be freed.

"You have tormented Firekeeper longer than I think she has admitted. You have sought to make Citrine sacrifice herself for what she thinks is her mother's good. Yet each time the Star Wizard has balked you, forcing you to warn against the very thing you desire most. I have heard the spells Melina recites. Indeed, she has shouted them over and over again until I think they will haunt the dreams of all who have heard them.

"None of those other hearers possess my memory. I can recite the appropriate words. I can give you your name. I can bind you and I can set you free."

The dragon hissed, "Such knowledge does not free you from paying the price, Illuminator."

"I know. The price frightens me as it would any but a child who has not yet learned the joy of living. Answer a question for me."

Citrine sensed that the dragon's mood had shifted, become eager, anticipating, and yet subtly frightened. What did something so enormous, so reeking with power have to fear?

Then she realized what the dragon must fear. It had been bound here for more years than Hawk Haven had existed as a kingdom. The dragon wanted its freedom—and it feared that Peace would not make the bargain that would set it free.

"What is your question?" the dragon replied guardedly.

"What happens to you when the one who has released you dies?"

The dragon answered with the same self-defeating honesty that Citrine was coming to recognize as the Star Wizard's mark.

"Unless he or she dies of injury or illness, the one who binds me will know to a year when I will drink the last of what they have to give. My master may then arrange for a substitute or attempt to bind me again as I am bound here. If neither of these things is done, then I return to where I was when Kelvin's magic pulled me forth."

Grateful Peace looked raptly fascinated.

"And where is that?"

The dragon's eyes narrowed again.

"That is not yours to know."

Peace sighed and rubbed his one hand across his face.

"Perhaps you will be more confidential at another time."

"Do you leave me then?"

"To be set loose once someone else with more time and knowledge comes along? The Star Wizard thought the threat of you would be enough to protect us forever. He was wrong. You are a temptation to those who have forgotten just what damage you can wreak. I will . . ."

Firekeeper finally broke through the dragon's indifference—or perhaps she suddenly realized that the one she needed to speak with was not the dragon, but Grateful Peace.

"No, Peace!" the wolf-woman cried. "You cannot do this. You are afraid of it. I am not afraid."

Peace faced her and narrowed his eyes so that he rather reminded Citrine of the dragon.

"Or is it that you are afraid of such power in any hands but your own?"

Firekeeper glared at him.

"Who sane would not be so afraid?" she shot back. "But still I do not think I fear aging and death as much as you do. The wolves do not hoard life. Why should I?"

"For those very ones you would spend it," Peace answered. "They'll need more from you than power in the years to come. Think, child, if they had wanted mere strength and ability to cause terror would they have raised a human?"

Firekeeper looked considering.

"But fear of the dragon would protect my people."

"Only for a time," Peace reminded her, "and only while you live. The dragon does not make the one who binds it immortal—rather the opposite. You would need to live your life in hiding, for any good tactician would see that you were the weak spot."

"The dragon could protect me," Firekeeper returned stubbornly.

"And if it protected you, it could not be defending the Beasts. Let it rest, Firekeeper. The dragon is not the answer to the looming conflict between humans and Beasts."

Firekeeper stepped back, as if physically relinquishing her claim; then she froze.

"And will you turn the dragon against my people?"

Grateful Peace's laugh was as harsh as a raven's croaking call.

"Oh, no, Firekeeper. I treasure the life I have left far too much to squander it. If I have my way I will guard my remaining years by invoking the dragon's power as little as necessary."

Citrine, recalling how Mother had said that she would grow up faster as she used the dragon in Mother's cause, thought she understood—and approved. Suddenly, it seemed dreadfully important to her that Peace not age and die too quickly. She had so much she could learn from him now that she saw how willing he was to teach.

"But you have not done the rituals," the dragon reminded Peace. "I am not yet yours to command."

It was a hint, not a taunt.

Looking down at his remaining hand as if seeing in it everything he had already lost, Peace nodded.

"I know, but if there are no further protests . . ." Here he looked at Firekeeper, who shook with shame. "Then I will."

Grateful Peace felt himself smile. Somehow, now that all the decisions were made, his fear was gone.

He sought the opening of Melina's incantation and substituted the dragon's true name for the bastardization born of fear that had come down through time:

"Despairing Dragon, I invoke and command you . . ."

ELISE COULD HARDLY BELIEVE HER EYES when Firekeeper suddenly broke away from the attack she herself had instigated and darted to the pool alongside the wall on which the outline of a dragon had appeared. Elise's shock that Firekeeper would abandon her allies in the midst of a battle was nothing to what she felt when the wolf-woman sank down onto her haunches and stared blankly at the wall.

Firekeeper must have been ensorcelled! Elise thought, looking side to side for help.

Apparently unaware of Firekeeper's plight, a growling and snapping Blind Seer was holding the near side of the bridge. Derian and Edlin were fully occupied by battles of their own. Doc was binding a slavering madwoman who Elise thought must be Grateful Peace's sister, Idalia. Peace stood near, his expression twisted with concern.

I guess I'm the only one left, Elise thought, and darted toward Firekeeper, meaning to shake the wolf-woman out of her stupor.

"Stop!" Grateful Peace shouted, rushing to intercept Elise.

For a moment Elise thought the Illuminator had changed sides, but Peace hastened to explain.

"Look across the bridge. Melina continues her spell. Firekeeper certainly must be trying to stop her. Our task must be to keep Firekeeper safe—and to stop Melina if we can."

Glancing in the direction Peace pointed, Elise realized he was right. She realized something else, too. The man now fighting Blind Seer was none other than Toriovico, the Healed One.

The bloodied wreck of the man who had been Blind Seer's prior opponent was eloquent enough proof of what the Royal Wolf could do. It seemed to Elise, though, that the wolf had recognized his opponent and was trying his best not to harm him, though his self-imposed restraint was becoming increasingly difficult to maintain.

Toriovico possessed the strength and flexibility of a dancer. He also had more than a little familiarity with the long-handled axe he spun and jabbed at the wolf. Thus far the wolf had defended himself by darting back and forth, giving ground when necessary, but it was clear that if Blind Seer was to continue to hold the bridge—and defend Firekeeper—he could not use such tactics much longer.

Visions of what would happen to them all if Blind Seer killed the Healed One nearly paralyzed Elise. The repercussions would not be reserved for this side of the White Water River, but would certainly carry over into Hawk Haven and Bright Bay. The entire group of them might even find themselves exiled. Yet in defending Firekeeper—who seemed to be the only one of their number who had any chance of reaching Melina, no matter that her manner of doing so was outlandish—Blind Seer was doing the right thing.

Elise ran toward the bridge, not certain what she would do when she got there, but knowing that she must do something. She had drawn close enough that the sulphurous taint of the water mingled with the raw scents of spilled blood and torn bowel, when revelation came.

"Toriovico!" Elise shouted as loudly as she could. "Toriovico! Dance!"

Elise felt like a complete idiot, but she continued shouting, "The Harvest Joy dance, Toriovico! Remember it? Dance!"

Toriovico's attack grew less forceful, his limbs jerking as if two sets of commands were warring for control of his muscles. Confronted with this much less effective assault, Blind Seer was no longer threatened. Elise was horrified to see the gigantic wolf drop back a few paces, then crouch and spring toward his opponent.

Her scream tore into audible shreds the words she had been trying to form, distorting them into an inarticulate cry that mingled warning and despair. Toriovico faltered in his internal battle, then brought his long-handled axe around in a too sloppy and too slow defense.

At that moment Blind Seer's leap carried him over the Healed One's axe, bringing the wolf to balance for a precarious moment on the curving rails of the bridge before he leapt down again, landing squarely on the chest of a man who, unseen from Elise's lower perspective, had been about to press his own attack.

The man fell, his head cracking solidly against the stone floor of the bridge, but another defender held the base of the bridge against the wolf's advance. In the cramped space Blind Seer could not gather the momentum to leap as he had before.

His new opponent held a long sword and shield. Behind him, a woman slowly rose from the side of the man Blind Seer had pushed into the river, readying her own long-handled spear.

Elise became aware of other developments as well.

Although Melina's attention had seemed entirely centered on Citrine and the continuation of whatever convoluted ritual they were working between them, the sorceress proved she had some awareness for what went on around her. As the battle grew violent enough that it might disturb even Citrine's fixed concentration, Melina raised her own voice, shouting her incantations loudly enough that distinct passages could be heard even where Elise stood.

Against the power of Melina's voice, Toriovico's attention was shifting. Once again, the Healed One raised his axe, his motions regaining some of their former grace and power as he turned toward Blind Seer's defenseless back.

Not seeing anything else to do, Elise raced forward. Grasping the haft of Toriovico's axe, she shouted in New Kelvinese:

"Dance, Toriovico! Dance! It's what you love. It's what you are. Dance!"

Only after she had spoken and felt his hazel green eyes focus on her did Elise feel strange about calling a foreign ruler by his first name. Yet she knew she'd done the right thing. She must reach his essential self and somehow she knew that deep inside Toriovico no more thought of himself as "the Healed One" than she thought of herself as "Lady Archer."

Even as she steeled herself to meet Toriovico's gaze and will him to win his internal battle, Elise felt a warm, strong presence next to her. She glanced to one side and there was Derian, pulling the axe from the Healed One's now unresisting hands.

"His Majesty doesn't seem quite sure," Derian said, trying the heft of the weapon and shoving past to help Blind Seer, "whose side he's on. Get him off this bridge."

Elise nodded, guiding the unresisting but strangely numb Toriovico off the span's curve and to the farther shore.

Edlin darted to intercept her.

"I say, Elise. What's wrong with Peace?"

The Illuminator had crossed to stand next to Firekeeper, his face so pale and strained with concentration that the tattoos stood out as if they'd been etched with green ink on bleached paper.

"I think he's trying magic," Elise answered. "Help Derian. Silence Melina. That's the best thing you can do to help him."

With a final worried glance at his mentor, Edlin did as Elise had ordered. Elise continued to guide the still unresisting Toriovico, stopping where Doc was neatly binding a very battered young woman, inspecting her wounds as he did so.

"Don't waste your gift on these," Elise told him bluntly. "We may need it to save others who have more right to it."

Doc looked unhappy, but nodded.

"This one's only bruised," he admitted, "but neither Derian or Edlin were gentle with her. The man I'm worried about is the one Blind Seer pushed into the river."

Elise shook her head, marveling at a nature so committed to healing that the fact that the man in question would have gutted Firekeeper and her wolf meant nothing now that the threat was ended. Oddly, Doc's skewed perspective did not annoy her as it might have in another, only warmed a part of her soul she hadn't known until then was cold.

"Help me with this man instead of worrying about one across the river," she suggested. "The Healed One seems trapped within Melina's control. I thought he was breaking free, but now I'm not certain."

"What was he doing when you thought he was breaking free?" Doc asked, for all the world as if he were diagnosing a more usual illness.

"I tried to get him to dance," Elise said. "I remembered he told us that was what broke the spell before."

Doc nodded, rising to his feet.

"That therapy seems more likely to succeed than anything I can offer. I'll see if I can help the others."

Unlike Elise or Edlin, Doc seemed able to sense that neither Firekeeper or Grateful Peace were in immediate danger. His attention was riveted by those battling on the bridge.

The fighting there was constricted by both the narrowness of the bridge and Blind Seer's bulk, but blood was flowing nonetheless. Making matters more difficult was that neither Edlin nor Derian wanted to do overmuch harm to their opponents—not knowing who they were or how they fit into the local hierarchy—while for their part those opponents were determined to do as much harm as possible.

This stalemate was broken all at once and in a manner that no one but Melina might have hoped—and certainly not in the manner she would have expected.

With a sound like ice breaking on a river, the far wall of the cavern cracked and shattered, showering the room with countless fragments of obsidian. Though her eyes squeezed shut on reflex, Elise felt blood well up from minuscule cuts on every piece of her exposed skin.

The clatter of weapon against weapon ceased as both sides dropped to the ground, seeking in vain protection against the hail of glass. The shrill shrieks and cries of panic that rose within every throat were swallowed lest an open mouth give entry to the obsidian shards.

Then, with a tinkling patter, the cutting rain ceased. Elise dared raise her head and open her eyes. The first thing she beheld before slick blood dimmed her vision was the vast bulk of the dragon, freed from its prison, poised sinuous against the farther wall. Its scales were black washed with red, taking color chameleon-like from its surroundings. Its eyes were amber, slitted like a cat's but as cold and hard as polished stones.

Carefully shaking her sleeve free of myriad shards of glass, Elise wiped the blood from her face. Near to her, she saw Toriovico doing the same and knew that shock had finished what dance had begun. The Healed

One's gaze was alert and full of questions for which Elise did not have the answers.

Indeed, now that Elise's vision had cleared, she saw that the subterranean chamber had been severely altered.

The hot river had sunk to a trickle. The curved wall against which the dragon had first been outlined was completely shattered, creating a dark cave back into which the dragon's bulk uncoiled. The bridge on which battle had raged only moments before had snapped inward, spilling those who had stood upon its arch into the now empty riverbed. A weak howl echoed by a human cry gave Elise a slim hope that Derian and the others had survived.

Firekeeper and Peace stood near the now empty pool. No color had returned to the Illuminator's face, but somehow he looked more relaxed. Firekeeper was not. The wolf-woman was collapsed on one knee, her head hung low, her bloody features washed with tears.

Looking from Firekeeper to Peace, Elise's skin crawled as she realized something else. Peace was unmarked by the explosion that had ravaged the young woman who stood not an arm's length from him. What had he done to protect himself? Suspicion filled Elise and she glanced around for confirmation.

On the farther bank, Citrine and Melina held much the same poses they had before, but like Elise their features were obscured by a sheen of still flowing blood. For a shocked moment Elise thought they might have been killed where they stood, so still did they stand. When Melina stirred, Elise half expected her body to topple forward in death.

Then, without even bothering to wipe the blood from her face, Melina took a few staggering steps toward the dragon—the dragon, Elise now realized, that had been bound by Grateful Peace.

THIS WASN'T HAPPENING. It couldn't be. Not after everything she'd done, after all the plans she'd made. Work hard and you'll get your way in the end. That's what her mother had said. That's what Melina's own experience had confirmed.

Somehow the only contingency Melina had never contemplated in all her plans, counterplans, and adaptation of plans was that in the end she wasn't going to get her way.

But now it seemed as if she wasn't. She had heard Grateful Peace reciting the words that bound the dragon to him. The Dragon of Despair had been bound, but it served her enemy. It shouldn't be possible, but it was.

All around the cavern the evidence was there. The survivors among her servitors were either surrendered or captured. Even Toriovico had somehow escaped her control. The dry riverbed that separated them was nothing to the gulf of horrified realization that she saw on his face.

Her enemies all seemed to have survived, though they were in rather bad shape, sanded and bloodied by flying glass or fallen among the ruins of the bridge. She felt a vague dissatisfaction when she realized that one man still stood uninjured.

Grateful Peace.

Melina puzzled over the wreck of her expectations, gazing up at the magnificence that was the Dragon of Despair. With a clarity like truth, Melina realized that there was something still left for her to do. It was so simple that she laughed aloud.

She could win. After all, now she knew the dragon's true name. To think that for a moment she had thought she could be defeated by a point of grammar!

Melina banished her earlier disappointment. First, eliminate Grateful Peace. Next, grab hold of the dragon. It was so easy. So simple.

She knew the dragon's name now. Despairing Dragon! What did it have to despair about? She'd give it reason for despair once she had ahold of it. She'd whip it into shape. Then the dragon would know that those long years of obsidian-locked sleep had held nothing to despair about. She'd show it . . .

A tug on Melina's sleeve slowed her forward progress just as she was stepping down the slope of what had once been a pool and was now only a mineral-encrusted sloping basin.

Melina glanced down, shaking blood from her face with an impatient gesture. The droplets splattered on the round-featured face looking up at her.

For a moment, Melina didn't recognize who this was, so like a distorted reflection of herself did it seem—a vision of herself cast onto nonexistent waters. Then she knew it.

Citrine.

"Mother?"

"Not now, dear. I'm busy."

She picked her way forward, across the level bottom of the pool. Bits of broken obsidian cut through the bottoms of her delicate embroidered slippers.

"Mother!"

Melina shook her sleeve from that annoyingly persistent grip. The fingers fell away but the voice persisted.

"You were feeding me to the dragon."

Melina had no time for niceties. There was the upward slope to consider, slick with obsidian flakes, some as fine as glass, others keen-edged as razors.

"I suppose you could see it that way, if you wished."

Melina pushed the child away, her gaze focusing on the one face in the room not hazed with blood. A dagger, very sharp, was one of the elements in the once beautiful costume Melina wore. She drew it now, seeing the steps to her success as clearly as if they were written on a page.

Grateful Peace. Can't kill him at once. Must hold him. Threaten him. Make him name you heir to the dragon upon his death. Then kill him.

It was so easy. So perfectly easy. She saw her way so clearly that she didn't even glance at the looming figure of the dragon.

It didn't move to prevent her, and Melina knew that Grateful Peace was afraid to use it, afraid of the cost.

She laughed to herself, shock fading, her own clear calculation returning.

It was going to be so easy.

THE PAIN FIREKEEPER FELT was like nothing she had ever experienced before, like nothing she had even imagined. Chunks of obsidian the size of fists had slammed into her torso, one narrowly missing her head. The tiny razor cuts covering bare arms, lower legs, neck, and face didn't hurt at first, making the burn and sting when blood flowed from them worse for being unexpected.

Yet her own pain was nothing to her shock when she saw that the bridge had collapsed carrying Blind Seer, Edlin, and Derian down into the bed of the river.

She howled in desperation and Blind Seer answered, his voice weak, but alive.

"Get us out of here!"

"I will," Firekeeper called, leaping to act and crumpling instantly as her bare foot was sliced by the myriad obsidian shards.

The razors buried themselves in her naked flesh and she fell onto one leather-protected knee. Tears flooded from her eyes as she realized she was afraid to move any further.

The frozen tableau that had held the others was broken as Melina stepped delicately down the slope. The woman's eyes were focused tightly on two things—the dragon and Grateful Peace. Indeed, Firekeeper doubted she saw anything else. Certainly she did not seem to see Citrine, who followed her for a few steps, tugging at her, begging for attention.

Then the child fell back and Melina came on alone.

"Peace," Firekeeper said urgently. "Peace!"

The Illuminator did not stir.

A familiar voice within her head said, *"He is yet with me, wolfling, unaware of what has happened without."*

"Tell him!" Firekeeper demanded aloud.

"And extend my own captivity?" The dragon's laughter was cruel. *"I think not. He has not ordered me to defend him. It was the Star Wizard's rule that saved him from the breaking of my prison, not my wish. Dream on, wolfling. I scent my freedom coming to me, carried to me by one I once feared."*

In that instant, Firekeeper knew that none of them would survive if Melina killed Grateful Peace. Elise and Doc didn't seem to realize what danger still remained. They were hurrying to assist those trapped by the fallen bridge.

"And what could they do?" Firekeeper asked herself. *"They are farther than I. Doc would resist doing harm because he does not understand the danger. Elise lacks the skill."*

Her bloodied foot screamed at her to be reasonable, but Firekeeper was beyond reason. Even so, Melina was within stabbing reach of Grateful Peace before Firekeeper moved to intervene, not because the wolf-woman was being cunning, but because she dreaded the pain when at last she must move.

It was seeing that Melina's slippered feet left red stains whenever she stepped that gave Firekeeper courage.

Am I less brave than she?

And as she leapt forward, Firekeeper answered herself.

No. Only more sane.

Stumbling slightly, Firekeeper thrust herself between the oblivious Grateful Peace and the all-too-focused Melina. It was only then that Melina seemed to register the wolf-woman's presence—and the hunting knife she held poised.

Striking like a snake, Melina feinted with her own blade, but Firekeeper knocked it easily from her hand. Then at last did Melina seem to realize her danger.

"No!" she cried, cringing. "I am unarmed!"

Firekeeper stared at the woman, remembering another time, another place. Then she raised her arm and her Fang bit deep, and tore into the elaborate pectoral on Melina's breast, biting through the metal and enamel as if it were tissue. Melina stared down at her chest and the dark heart's blood that welled from the ragged hole.

She sunk to her knees and looked up at Firekeeper.

"I would have so liked to see the Old World," Melina confided, and then she died.

Not even Citrine, dropping her gem-studded headband as a grave offering on her mother's corpse, had tears to spare for Melina, once Consolor, once Lady, now nothing but cooling flesh.

XLI

TORIOVICO INSISTED THE HAWK HAVENESE REMAIN within Thendulla Lypella, in the Cloud Touching Spire itself.

"I can't risk you in the city proper," he explained, "not until this is cleared up and the rumors die down. I'll have all your property and livestock brought to you. In any case, all of you need waiting on—far more labor than Goody Wendee deserves thrust upon her."

"We not prisoners?" Firekeeper asked from where she knelt near Blind Seer.

Neither wolf nor woman looked very strong. Blind Seer's fur was matted with blood from injuries sustained when the bridge collapsed. Firekeeper had ruined the soles of her feet. Even so, Toriovico didn't doubt that they would resist imprisonment.

"Not prisoners," Torio hastened to assure her. "You have done myself and my realm a great service. Let us serve you in return."

This seemed to make sense to Firekeeper, and she subsided.

"A question, Honored One," Derian Carter asked from where he was testing his own limbs and seeming surprised to find them sound.

"Yes?" Toriovico replied, vaguely amused by the young man's tone of conversational respect.

"How did you end up here?" Derian asked bluntly. "Last we spoke with you, you were free of Melina's influence."

"I don't know precisely," Torio admitted. "All I recall clearly is Melina coming in to see me. I remember thinking her attire was rather fantastic, even for her. Then everything sinks into a comfortable fog."

"Melina may have needed," Grateful Peace offered, "a certain number of people to help perform her ritual. Without you, she would have been one short. Perhaps in your eagerness not to let Melina know you had broken her hold, you accidently did something that enabled her to recapture you."

"That," Toriovico said, "is as good an explanation as any I can offer—better indeed. I wouldn't doubt Melina told me to forget what she was doing and, sadly, I have done so."

During this time, Sir Jared Surcliffe had completed his preliminary inspection of the wounded. Derian Carter was judged the least injured among those who could be spared, and so was sent to make the long climb to the surface of Aswatano and summon aid.

Among the survivors, Lord Kestrel had broken his left wrist. Idalia's youngest daughter had suffered several blows to the head. The rest of the group had suffered varied degrees of cuts and bruises from when the dragon had broken free from its centuries-long imprisonment.

The rest of the group, that is, except for Grateful Peace. The former Dragon's Eye was physically unharmed, but as they waited and Sir Jared did his best to treat the worst of the injuries, Grateful Peace told the Healed One his tale.

The one-armed Illuminator did so without either false modesty or overt self-praise, but as he spoke, Toriovico realized that Grateful Peace had truly been the hero in a night filled with heroic acts.

"And what will happen with the dragon now?" Toriovico asked, glancing to where the huge figure still lurked in the shadowy recesses of the newly revealed cave.

"I could command it to remain here," Grateful Peace said, "and it must, but that would be a misery for it. It is not a kind creature. I am not completely certain that it is a creature as we understand such. What I am certain of is that if we treat it harshly we will make an enemy of it."

"It isn't already?" Toriovico asked, thinking over what he had been told.

"It is not our friend," Peace replied, weighing his words carefully, "but it is not yet our enemy."

Torio wasn't certain he understood, but he was willing to take Grateful Peace's word on the matter.

"And your counsel on the matter is?"

"The Star Wizard wished to keep it near as a weapon. Let me permit it to return to the wilds from which Kelvin inadvertently summoned it."

Toriovico remembered the old stories, how the dragon had attacked the city and its people.

"Won't it be a danger to us?"

"It is very willing to give its word that it will not trouble us. Indeed, it seems to hint that we will not even be aware of its presence—not unless I call it."

"And if you let it free," Toriovico asked, hoping that perhaps there was a way for Grateful Peace to escape the terrible price he had paid, but the Illuminator was shaking his head.

"No," he said sadly. "My letting it 'free' will not end what it will take from me. That is irrevocable. All this would assure is something of a mellowing of the animosity it feels toward humanity."

Toriovico thought how he would feel if he had been summoned from his life and been bound by another. He thought of Melina and how the only emotion he had felt on seeing Firekeeper kill her was relief.

"I do not blame the dragon for its feelings," he replied, "but it seems to me that you will have given a great deal for very little return."

Grateful Peace looked at him in astonishment.

"I have served my land, the Healed One, and been permitted home from exile. My reputation will be restored to me. I have given a great deal—and I will regret that life I will not have to live—but never think I have not had anything in return."

Toriovico nodded, glad that even before he had learned how central Grateful Peace had been to his rescue he had told the Illuminator that he would be publicly cleared of all charges.

"And Idalia, her surviving family members?" he asked. "What would you have done about them?"

Peace smiled sadly, his gaze wandering to where Idalia waited docilely for whatever would come. Her expression was confused, as if she still sorted through her memories, wondering how she had come to this point.

"Perhaps in time she will hate me less, for Melina did not create that hatred, only used it. I think it would be wise if she and her family were sent in truth to some isolated portion of the kingdom—even as was given out in the first place. Perhaps one of your sisters could be trusted to report on them and advise you when she thought they had served sufficient penance."

"Then you don't think them traitors?" Toriovico asked, obscurely relieved. He had little taste for punishing those Melina had used, having been so soundly used himself.

"Not really. After all, they were serving the Consolor of the Healed One—that is hardly the same as acting in the service of a foreign power."

"Good." Toriovico nodded crisply. "Not many will need know of their role in any case. Melina kept what they did for her secret enough."

The clatter of boots on stone announced the arrival of Derian Carter and a large contingent of the city watch.

Toriovico rose and gathered his dignity to him, prepared for everything but how to deal with the inevitable shock and horror when the dragon was sighted. He glanced across to its cave and found the dark space empty.

"Where?" he said to Grateful Peace.

The Illuminator smiled.

"I have already told it to return home."

"Is there another tunnel then?"

Peace's gaze grew distant and misty with wonder.

"I don't think so. As I told you—I am not at all certain the dragon is a creature quite as we would understand."

ONE BY ONE, Citrine's voices fell silent. She realized that this was not because she no longer had things that bothered her, but because at last she trusted other people enough to talk with them about her problems.

Nearly the worst of those problems had been watching her mother die under Firekeeper's knife. The worst was that Citrine hadn't wanted to stop Firekeeper, not one bit. Once Citrine might have tried to fool herself: telling herself she had been too far away or that Firekeeper was too strong or if she'd called out she might have distracted Mother.

Now Citrine didn't try to tell herself any of that. The revelation of exactly what the dragon did to those who commanded it had been too fresh in her mind when Firekeeper attacked Melina, as had Citrine's realization that Mother had meant Citrine to pay the cost. Nor did she doubt that Mother would have burned her life away without hesitation.

Right now Citrine was nine, in a year she would have been twelve, in two years fifteen, in three—when she should have only been twelve she would have been eighteen. And inside she would have still been just twelve.

Peace had explained this last to Citrine, explaining that age alone did not give wisdom or certainty—only living and making decisions did that and not perfectly even then. That was why Firekeeper sometimes seemed so old, though she couldn't be more than about sixteen. Her life had forced her to make choices.

All through the days immediately following Mother's death, when the shock was greatest, Citrine kept doing those figures over and over again in her head. She'd look at Derian, who she guessed was about twenty, at Doc, who was maybe twenty-five, and try to imagine what it would have been like to be that way outside and herself inside.

In the end, Citrine decided that she'd live with her voices, her grief, and her anger. At that moment, oddly enough, the voices had begun to quiet.

She tried talking more and discovered all sorts of things she'd never known—how Elise had been afraid of Mother when she herself was a little girl, how Firekeeper needed to explain that she had killed Mother because sometimes that was the only way to end a problem.

"If I not then, maybe knock Peace to one side and hope I can hold Melina, then someday Melina will hurt someone else. I am only sorry you had to see."

Citrine had patted Firekeeper's scarred and callused hand, realizing that this was what Grateful Peace had meant about dealing with things making you wiser.

"I didn't like seeing it," Citrine answered honestly, "but I think I had to. Otherwise Mother would be a voice in my head forever."

She lowered her voice to a whisper and added, "And Firekeeper, I think I would have tried the same, but not because Peace had to be rescued, because I was so hurt and angry. You saved me from that."

Firekeeper had grinned wryly.

"I was angry, too. Not think other. I have been angry at Melina for a long time. Now, though, she is no more. Dry bones don't ease hunger, only splinter in the belly."

Citrine thought this last must be some bit of wolf wisdom since she didn't understand it at all. The words stayed with her, though, and she kept worrying over them as a real wolf might have a bone.

At last she thought she understood and went to Grateful Peace to share her insight.

"I think," she said, taking a seat on a footstool and looking up at the Illuminator, who had set his book aside as Mother never would have done. "I think that what Firekeeper means is that worrying over things that are over and done with only makes you think you're full—like a belly full of dry bone. Really though the worries are poking at you, maybe even making you sick.

"I asked Edlin," Citrine added a touch inconsequentially, "about bones and he says that the dry ones aren't really good for dogs. He doesn't know about wolves."

Grateful Peace smiled at her.

"I think you are right about what Firekeeper meant," he said, and Citrine glowed with pleasure, "and her advice is good to a point. However, humans are not wolves. We cannot put the past from us without trying to learn from it. I think that someday Firekeeper will realize this."

"Firekeeper?"

"No one has nightmares like she does without something haunting them," Peace replied. "However, now may not be the time or place for Firekeeper to look into her past."

"I guess we're going back to Hawk Haven soon," Citrine said. "The moon is already showing a crescent. It was nearly waned when all that happened—when Mother tried to summon the dragon. I heard Doc say that Edlin's wrist is mending nicely."

"And that all of you were fortunate that obsidian is so sharp," Peace added, "that cuts from it don't usually scar—not if they're kept clean. Let me see your face."

He reached out with his one hand and Citrine marveled how his mutilation didn't bother her anymore. Indeed, it seemed a proud thing—a sign of something survived. She considered her own mutilated hand and for the first time felt a little proud—not of the missing fingers, but that she'd come through everything that had led to her losing them.

With new understanding Citrine looked closely at Grateful Peace's tattooed features, taking advantage of their proximity as he tilted her chin, turning her face side to side to inspect the healing cuts.

"That one," Citrine said, indicating the mark across the bridge of his nose. "That means you'll never get married again, right?"

Grateful Peace nodded.

"I was young when Chutia died, but on that matter I knew my mind well. I have never regretted not remarrying, only sometimes I have regretted not having children."

"You don't have any children?"

"Only nieces and nephews," Peace said with a levelness that did not hide his sadness, and Citrine remembered that the nephew he had loved best had died. "And none I am close to any longer."

Citrine took his hand when he let it drop.

"I don't have any parents, not anymore. I wish I could be your daughter for real, not just pretend like Jalarios and Rios."

Peace studied her with the smallest of smiles.

"So do I, Citrine. So do I."

ELISE WAS RATHER NERVOUS when she received a summons from the Healed One a few days before their planned departure for Hawk Haven. She wondered if Toriovico was going to prevent them from leaving. So far they had been well treated by the New Kelvinese, who, in response to carefully prepared speeches, were even seeing them as heroes of a sort, come to rescue the Healed One from an evil force out of their own land.

Knowing how calculated and unheroic their mission had really been, Elise felt a bit uncomfortable about this, and worried that someone would turn it back against them. She'd seen how quick the New Kelvinese were to condemn their own. What might they do to foreigners?

Toriovico looked tired when Elise came into his office, but that was no surprise. Not only had the Healed One needed to deal with the immediate results of Melina's death, there also had been larger repercussions as well. Although Xarxius had been saved and his honor restored, Apheros's government had indeed fallen. The new coalition functioned far less smoothly than the old and Grateful Peace had confided that he was not at all certain that Apheros would not be in power again before the winter ended.

Then there was the Harvest Joy dance, rehearsals for which were moving along at a considerable pace. Finally, Elise did not need to have been the Castle Flower of Eagle's Nest to notice the large number of unmarried female callers at the Cloud Touching Spire—callers who glared rather pointedly at either Elise or Wendee if their paths happened to cross.

That had made both women giggle privately.

"Not that Toriovico isn't a fine-looking man," Wendee said, "but I'd no more want to be his second foreign bride than I'd want to cut my head off and use my skull as a handbag."

The allusion to the Old Country tale made Elise smile, but beneath the smile she was wondering about Jared. He'd been busy since their arrival within Thendulla Lypella, so much so that Elise had hardly seen him. Part of this could be accounted for in his assumption of responsibility for all those injured during the struggle against Melina, part to the New Kelvinese's fascination with his talent.

Eager volunteers had made Elise's assistance unnecessary, and Derian reported that Doc was sleeping nearly half the day, recovering from his continual expenditures. Even so, Elise couldn't help but think he was avoiding her.

Toriovico rose when Elise entered, and this, combined with his asking her to meet in the relative informality of his office rather than the awe-inspiring precincts of his reception hall, made Elise certain that what he needed to discuss with her was quite serious. This was confirmed when he sent all but his personal guards away.

"I have asked you here," the Healed One began, after they were seated, "to discuss something important, with potentially complicated ramifications for future relations between our kingdoms."

Elise nodded, trying to stay calm, but beneath her folded hands she was gripping her fingernails into her palms in the hope the pain would give her composure.

He's going to tell us we can't leave, she thought. *Firekeeper will go over the wall. She's already impatient to be away. The others will want to escape, too. What will I do!*

"You are scheduled to depart at the conclusion of the Harvest Festival," Toriovico continued, "but I have had a rather singular request. Citrine Shield wants to remain. She came and asked me herself. It seems that she feels she has little to go home to—and that she has formed a deep attachment to Grateful Peace."

Elise said nothing, though she managed a considering nod, and the Healed One went on.

"Grateful Peace has agreed to act as Citrine's guardian. Indeed, if the arrangement works, he would offer to legally adopt her and make her his heir. He has a substantial fortune, and as he is being courted by those who feel they wronged him, stands to see that fortune grow."

Elise wondered what her expression must have shown, because Toriovico clearly thought she disapproved. He said quickly:

"This isn't an attempt to acquire the girl as a hostage. Indeed, Grateful Peace has said he would relocate to the Hawk Haven side of the White Water River if necessary. He admits he would prefer to remain in New Kelvin, in Dragon's Breath or its environs, but realizes that this may not be possible."

The Healed One stopped speaking, leaning back in his chair, and with one of those eloquent New Kelvinese gestures indicated that she was invited to speak.

Elise composed her thoughts before beginning.

"Citrine asked to stay?"

"Yes. You can ask her yourself. She," and here Toriovico couldn't restrain a smile, "told me that she knew I couldn't take care of her because her mother had made so many enemies, but that she would do everything she could to show my people that the Hawk Havenese were not all like Melina."

Elise found herself smiling as well, thinking that speech sounded very much like the suddenly articulate Citrine who had emerged with the waxing of Deer Moon.

She wondered what kind of life Citrine would have back in Hawk Haven. Sapphire might try to be kind to her youngest sister, but when Melina's final plot was explained to her—and Toriovico had insisted that on this matter there should be no secrets between his court and the throne of Hawk Haven—Sapphire would never be able to look at Citrine without remembering how close Melina had come to ruining all their lives.

Then, too, Sapphire and Shad would have their new child and the children who would follow. Already there were those who felt the inheritance picture was complicated enough with the two heirs to two thrones—and the potential competing claims of all their siblings should the worst occur. Removing Citrine from the picture would actually help.

"There is precedent," Elise said aloud, "in the marriage of Princess Caryl of Hawk Haven to Prince Tavis of Bright Bay, back in the reign of King Chalmer. That marriage was arranged in the hopes of soothing old wounds. We could argue that this adoption was meant to ease new ones, to show New Kelvin's forgiveness of Melina. You have no children of your own, so a marriage couldn't be arranged, and you could not adopt Citrine without complicating the inheritance picture. This could actually be presented as astute politics—especially if Citrine visited Hawk Haven often enough that she does not become a stranger."

"I am surprised," the Healed One said, "that you go so far back in history to find precedent. Wasn't the marriage of Princess Sapphire and Prince Shad arranged for similar reasons?"

"Yes," Elise agreed. "I suppose that I didn't think of it because so much else rests upon its success."

"Then you would be in favor of Citrine remaining?" Toriovico asked.

"I will need to speak with her and with Grateful Peace," Elise said. "It would also need to be understood that the decision is not mine to make. I am Citrine's guardian for this journey. Her elder brother, Jet, is her legal guardian. He would be the one who must first be asked."

Elise knew her expression had grown cynical, but she didn't care.

"I will tell Grateful Peace that two things will be certain to sway Jet as to the wisdom of this plan. First, Princess Sapphire's approval. If she disapproves, I don't think he will dare approve."

"And second?"

"Jet took over management of a nice estate on his father's death. With Melina's death he will inherit in full. However, the property needs work and Jet is required to provide a marriage portion for each of his three sisters. If Citrine was adopted, he would not need to provide for her, but if Grateful Peace was willing to supply funds . . ."

"Perhaps specifically earmarked for the marriage portions of Citrine's sisters, Opal and Ruby?" the Healed One interjected delicately into the pause.

"That would be nice," Elise said. "I don't trust Jet not to spend anything he can lay his hands on for his own purposes."

"Then a present to him as well," Toriovico said, "would be wise."

"Don't make it look like Citrine is being bought," Elise hastened to add. "Our people aren't as easy about slavery as are yours."

"We will consult Ambassador Redbriar," Toriovico assured her. "She is well versed in our ways as well as yours."

Elise nodded.

"Then all we need is a legitimate excuse for me to leave Citrine behind, since in doing so I would be in violation of my guardianship."

"Citrine told me," the Healed One said, obviously a bit uncomfortable with what he was about to say, "that one of the reasons she accompanied you on this journey was to enable her to regain health she lost when she was captive of some pirates . . ."

Elise appreciated his not mentioning precisely what type of health Citrine had lost.

"Yes, that is true."

"Then perhaps you could suggest that Citrine is remaining where she can be in her physician's care," Toriovico suggested, "and continue the healing this journey has begun."

"Her physician?" Elise echoed blankly. "Do you mean Grateful Peace? His kindness has certainly done a great deal to heal what ailed Citrine."

The Healed One frowned slightly.

"I meant Sir Jared Surcliffe," he said. "Hasn't he told you and your companions that he intends to remain in New Kelvin after the Harvest Festival?"

"I WON'T STAY FOREVER," Doc said when Elise found him—by good fortune alone—in the main room of the suite he shared with Edlin and Derian. "Though it sounds like it's convenient that I decided to stay."

Elise stared at him, disbelieving.

"But you *are* staying?"

"I am."

For all their mutual attraction, Doc had rarely touched Elise and then such contact had usually been in the informal context of work or the formal one of dancing.

Now he reached out and took her hand with such contained intensity that for the first time Elise realized that she'd stormed in here without a chaperon.

How I have changed! she thought. *Maybe Grandmother Rosene was right all along and I shouldn't have been let out alone. Certainly, it never occurred to me to find Wendee.*

"Elise," Doc said, "we both know that I love you. That hasn't changed. I also know what you told me last Wolf Moon outside the Smuggler's Light, that I had your affection but not your promise."

Elise nodded, thinking how cold those words sounded. She knew, too, that she had been cool to him since they had re-met at Duchess Kestrel's dower house. What she hadn't realized until this moment was how cool she had been to everyone. Even Citrine, who could have deserved better of her, had suffered under her disapproval.

I can't seem to do anything halfway, Elise thought ruefully. *Either I'm an idiot flinging myself at Jet or I'm some parody of my father, commanding and rebuking. What's wrong with me that I can't find a balance?*

"You're young," some kinder part of herself answered, but Elise shook her internal colloquy away and gave Doc the attention he deserved.

"Go on," she prompted, offering his hand a gentle squeeze.

Doc relaxed.

"You also told me something else, something your mother said."

Elise tilted her head, trying, then remembering Aurella Wellward's words, and blushing at the cool cruelty that she could have repeated them—and thought them a kindness.

Doc clearly thought she didn't remember, and went on:

"Lady Aurella said that I would never be so impolite, so unaware of the differences in our stations, to propose marriage to you. She said that burden would be on you."

Elise nodded, unable to speak.

"I accepted that then," Doc went on. "Sometime during this trip I realized that I was indeed what I had named myself half in jest then. A coward."

"No!"

He waved her protest aside.

"I put the burden on you, the burden of proving to your parents, to those people who will rely on you when you are Baroness Archer, that you had chosen your husband wisely. I did nothing to prove myself."

"You're a knight!" Elise burst out. "A healer."

"Past deeds promising perhaps present patronage," Doc replied levelly. "I want to offer you more than that, but I know my strengths and weaknesses. I am not a warrior. My glory in battle was accidental."

Elise didn't agree, but held her tongue. It was only fair to give Doc a chance to say what he'd obviously been thinking about for a long while.

"I am not a merchant. I am, however, more than the healer you named me. I am a doctor. I have studied the workings of medicine and the body. The talent my ancestors were kind enough to pass on to me enables me to save those I might otherwise lose, but it is not all I have."

"I didn't mean," Elise said hesitantly, "to imply that."

"I know," Doc assured her. "You meant to offer me a compliment. The fact is that in this past year of blood and battle, I started to forget I had more than the talent. What has been needed from me was that quick ability to keep the breath in the body. My more painstakingly acquired skills came into play later, if at all. Do you want to know what started me thinking I might have overlooked something?"

"I do."

"On my way to meet you at Duchess Kestrel's, I stopped to help one of her tenants, Widow Chandler. My talent helped, but it was the ointments I could leave behind me that I knew would assure her recovery."

Elise, remembering her flash of jealousy at Doc's tending this woman, had the grace to blush.

Doc, intent on his own memories, didn't question her.

"I thought about that. I thought about Sapphire's pregnancy and how we all wish there were some ointment that would assure a healthy child. I thought about how Queen Elexa sacrificed her health to bear the kingdom three living children."

His voice dropped and now he flushed dark red.

"I thought how your mother is Elexa's niece and how she, too, carries that weakness. How the only thing your father could do to help Aurella was insist that she have no more than the one child. I thought how you, too, might carry that weakness. I realized that as a doctor I would not want to stand by and watch you transformed into a frail wraith by the natural act of bearing a child."

He took a deep breath.

"I'd feel that way even if I wasn't your husband. I'd feel it even more if I was."

Elise nodded.

"And so . . ."

"I'm staying here to study everything I can lay my hands on regarding what the New Kelvinese know about pregnancy, childbirth, and its after-effects. I have been promised the cooperation of several sodalities, all of which want a chance to study my talent.

"I have promised the Healed One a copy of my results, but what I plan to do with what I learn is to come home—hopefully before Sapphire's child is born, but if I cannot to send what I can to the Royal Physicians in both Hawk Haven and Bright Bay."

"And?"

"And to your parents as well, for if I find a way to overcome whatever it is that plagues the Wellward women, I will have something to offer House Archer in return for the privilege of marrying its heir. And then . . ."

He paused for so long that Elise thought he was going to leave the thought unfinished.

"And then I am going to ask you to marry me—and I hope you will consider me worthy."

Elise knew she couldn't promise, couldn't even promise to wait, for she knew enough about medicine to know that the research Doc was hoping to complete in a few moonspans might take years. Still, she hoped that her smile would give Doc the encouragement he needed to carry on.

THE NEW KELVINESE HARVEST FESTIVAL was something that Derian knew he would be telling tales about not just this winter but for winters to come. Their position as the Healed One's guests—and the heroes who had saved the land from Melina—meant that they were welcome wherever they went. He took advantage of this freedom to escape the formality of Thendulla Lypella and join the townspeople, who proved, despite their robes and masks, not too different from their counterparts in Eagle's Nest when it came to enjoying a public festival.

Indeed, as Derian joined the crowd in Aswatano, he found it hard to believe that not too long ago he and Doc had hardly escaped that very crowd with their lives. The butcher who had been so cruel thrust a sausage on a stick at him by way of apology and Derian accepted with a grin. His waistcoat pockets bulged with the lucky sweets shaped like fruits and vegetables, until he started handing them out again—an act that made him very popular with the children.

When the dancing started, Hasamemorri and her maids undertook to teach him the steps until Derian felt confident joining in. After a few rounds, he felt a tap on his elbow and there stood the little spice vendor, smiling up at him.

Later that evening, Derian discovered just how successfully he could communicate even with his limited New Kelvinese, for the spice vendor had only a few words of Pellish, but a considerable amount she wanted him to learn.

Derian couldn't say he was sorry to leave Dragon's Breath when the time came. Indeed, he was eager to tell his family more than he could ever remember to put into letters. Still, it was hard to leave Citrine and Peace behind—even though he was assured that he would see them both again. The spice vendor hinted that she might visit Eagle's Nest someday, and made him promise to call on her if he came back to Dragon's Breath.

With an escort provided by the Healed One and captained by Brotius—though Derian wasn't certain whether this was a reward or a punishment for the man whose sense of duty had given them so much trouble—their small party made good time. Grateful Peace had taken charge of their budding business, saying that it really wouldn't be a bad idea for House Kestrel and House Archer to set up trade—and that now he was no longer in government, he needed a new venture.

They reached the Gateway to Enchantment and, leaving Brotius and his guard company behind, crossed into Stilled. There the innkeeper at the Long Tail Winding had heard rumors and wanted facts. They provided them willingly, having decided that secrecy would serve no one, themselves least of all.

On a stretch of road between Stilled and the Kestrel estate, Firekeeper suddenly spoke, raising her voice so that everyone could hear her clearly.

"Here we leave you," she said, taking a small pack down from one of the mules.

"Leave?" Derian said.

"I say, leave?" Edlin echoed.

"I'm going home," Firekeeper said. "Too much has happened. I want to see my pack—my parents. I want to learn if they think I have been right in what I did."

Her posture left no room for argument, but Elise tried.

"You know you did, Firekeeper. Come back with us, share the celebration." Firekeeper shook her head.

"You eat my share. I . . . we . . . want to go home. The weather will be kind for a time. The deer fat. There is a litter of pups that will hardly know us."

She paused and Derian thought of the other things she would want to see: the gatehouse going up at the gap through the Iron Mountains, proof that New Bardenville was indeed gone. It was one thing to be told, another to see. And she would want to tell her parents, those impossible wolves he still hardly believed in, about everything she had been through.

"And I think," Firekeeper added, almost as if she had been reading his thoughts, "that I want to ask the Ones about dragons."

His voice sounding rusty even to his own ears, Derian said, "Tell Elation hello for me."

Firekeeper smiled.

"I will, and I think that if life stays with me I will come see you all again."

She held up one foot, showing Derian that she still wore boots—a necessity, for the skin had not yet toughened after the obsidian cuts had healed.

"I have learned many good things."

With the same rambunctious spirit that she had heretofore reserved for her romps with Blind Seer, Firekeeper gave everyone hugs and planted enthusiastic kisses on both Derian's and Edlin's cheeks.

Blind Seer wagged his entire body with such energy that Derian knew without translation that the wolf, too, was saying good-bye and wishing them all the best.

Then wolf and woman ran ahead down the road a short distance, before darting into the forest. Even the sound of their feet vanished after a few paces, but a high clear howl, two voices raised as one, called back a final farewell.

Agneta Norwood: (Lady, H.H.) daughter of Norvin Norwood and Luella Stanbrook; sister of Edlin, Tait, and Lillis Norwood; adopted sister of Blysse Norwood (Firekeeper).

Aksel Trueheart: (Lord, H.H.) scholar of Hawk Haven; spouse of Zorana Archer; father of Purcel, Nydia, Deste, and Kenre Trueheart.[2]

Alben Eagle: (H.H.) son of Princess Marras and Lorimer Stanbrook. In keeping with principles of Zorana I, he was given no title, as he died in infancy.

Alin Brave: (H.H.) husband of Grace Trueheart; father of Baxter Trueheart.

Allister I: (King, B.B.) called King Allister of the Pledge, sometimes the Pledge Child; formerly Allister Seagleam. Son of Tavis Seagleam (B.B.) and Caryl Eagle (H.H.); spouse of Pearl Oyster; father of Shad, Tavis, Anemone, and Minnow.

Alt Rosen: (Opulence, Waterland) ambassador to Bright Bay.

Amery Pelican: (King, B.B.) spouse of Gustin II; father of Basil, Seastar, and Tavis Seagleam. Deceased.

Anemone: (Princess, B.B.) formerly Anemone Oyster. Daughter of Allister I and Pearl Oyster; sister of Shad and Tavis; twin of Minnow.

Apheros: (Dragon Speaker, N.K.) long-time elected official of New Kelvin, effectively head of government.

Aurella Wellward: (Lady, H.H.) confidant of Queen Elexa; spouse of Ivon Archer; mother of Elise Archer.

Barden Eagle: (Prince, H.H.) third son of Tedric I and Elexa Wellward. Disowned. Spouse of Eirene Norwood; father of Blysse Eagle. Presumed deceased.

Basil Seagleam: see Gustin III.

Baxter Trueheart: (Earl, H.H.) infant son of Grace Trueheart and Alin Brave. Technically not a title holder until he has safely survived his first two years.

Bee Biter: Royal Kestrel; guide and messenger.

Bevan Seal: see Calico.

Blind Seer: Royal Wolf; companion to Firekeeper.

Blysse Eagle: (Lady, H.H.) daughter of Prince Barden and Eirene Kestrel.

Blysse Norwood: see Firekeeper.

Bold: Royal Crow; eastern agent; sometime companion to Firekeeper.

Brina Dolphin: (Lady or Queen, B.B.) first spouse of Gustin III, divorced as barren.

Brock Carter: (H.H.) son of Colby and Vernita Carter; brother of Derian and Damita Carter.

Brotius: (Captain, N.K.) soldier in New Kelvin.

Calico: (B.B.) proper name, Bevan Seal. Confidential secretary to Allister I. Member of a cadet branch of House Seal.

Caryl Eagle: (Princess, H.H.) daughter of King Chalmer I; married to Prince Tavis Seagleam; mother of Allister Seagleam. Deceased.

Ceece Dolphin: (Lady, B.B.) sister to current Duke Dolphin.

Chalmer I: (King, H.H.) born Chalmer Elkwood; son of Queen Zorana the Great; spouse of Rose Rosewood; father of Marras, Tedric, Caryl, Gadman, and Rosene Eagle. Deceased.

[1.] Characters are detailed under first name or best-known name. The initials B.B. (Bright Bay), H.H. (Hawk Haven), or N.K. (New Kelvin) in parenthesis following a character's name indicate nationality. Titles are indicated in parenthesis.

[2.] Hawk Haven and Bright Bay noble houses both follow a naming system where the children take the surname of the higher ranking parent, with the exception that only the immediate royal family bear the name of that house. If the parents are of the same rank, then rank is designated from the birth house, great over lesser, lesser by seniority. The Great Houses are ranked in the following order: Eagle, Shield, Wellward, Trueheart, Redbriar, Stanbrook, Norwood.

Chalmer Eagle: (Crown Prince, H.H.) son of Tedric Eagle and Elexa Wellward. Deceased.

Chutia: (N.K.) Illuminator. Wife of Grateful Peace. Deceased.

Citrine Shield: (H.H.) daughter of Melina Shield and Rolfston Redbriar; sister of Sapphire, Jet, Opal, and Ruby Shield; aka Rios.

Colby Carter: (H.H.) livery stable owner and carter; spouse of Vernita Carter; father of Derian, Damita, and Brock Carter.

Columi: (N.K.) retired Prime of the Sodality of Lapidaries.

Culver Pelican: (Lord, B.B.): son of Seastar Seagleam; brother of Dillon Pelican. Merchant ship captain.

Daisy: (H.H.) steward of West Keep, in employ of Earl Kestrel.

Damita Carter: (H.H.) daughter of Colby and Vernita Carter; sister of Derian and Brock Carter.

Dawn Brooks: (H.H.) wife of Ewen Brooks, mother of several small children.

Dayle: (H.H.) steward for the Archer manse in Eagle's Nest.

Derian Carter: (H.H.) also called Derian Counselor; assistant to Norvin Norwood; son of Colby and Vernita Carter; brother of Damita and Brock Carter.

Deste Trueheart: (H.H.) daughter of Aksel Trueheart and Zorana Archer; sister of Purcel, Nydia, and Kenre Trueheart.

Dia Trueheart: see Nydia Trueheart.

Dillon Pelican: (Lord, B.B.) son of Seastar Seagleam; brother of Culver Pelican.

Dimiria: (N.K.) Prime, Sodality of Stargazers.

Dirkin Eastbranch: (knight, H.H.) King Tedric's personal bodyguard.

Donal Hunter: (H.H.) member of Barden Eagle's expedition; spouse of Sarena; father of Tamara. Deceased.

Edlin Norwood: (Lord, H.H.) son of Norvin Norwood and Luella Kite; brother of Tait, Lillis, and Agneta Norwood; adopted brother of Blysse Norwood (Firekeeper).

Eirene Norwood: (Lady, H.H.) spouse of Barden Eagle; mother of Blysse Eagle; sister of Norvin Norwood. Presumed deceased.

Elation: Royal Falcon, companion to Firekeeper.

Elexa Wellward: (Queen, H.H.) spouse of Tedric I; mother of Chalmer, Lovella, and Barden Eagle.

Elise Archer: (Lady, H.H.) daughter of Ivon Archer and Aurella Wellward; heir to Archer Grant.

Evaglayn: (N.K.) senior apprentice in the Beast Lore sodality.

Evie Cook: (H.H.) servant in the Carter household.

Ewen Brooks: (N.K.) spouse of Dawn Brooks, father of several children.

Faelene Lobster: (Duchess, B.B.) head of House Lobster; sister of Marek, Duke of Half-Moon Island; aunt of King Harwill.

Farand Briarcott: (Lady, H.H.) assistant to Tedric I, former military commander.

Fess Bones: a pirate with some medical skills.

Firekeeper: (Lady, H.H.) feral child raised by wolves, adopted by Norvin Norwood and given the name Blysse Norwood.

Fleet Herald: a pirate messenger.

Fox Driver: (H.H.) given name, Orin. Skilled driver in the employ of Waln Endbrook. Deceased.

Gadman Eagle: (Grand Duke, H.H.) fourth child of King Chalmer and Queen Rose; brother to Marras, Caryl, Tedric, and Rosene; spouse of Riki Redbriar; father of Rolfston and Nydia Redbriar.

Garrik Carpenter: (H.H.) a skilled woodworker.

Gayl Minter: See Gayl Seagleam.

Gayl Seagleam: (Queen, B.B.) spouse of Gustin I; first queen of Bright Bay; mother of Gustin, Merry (later Gustin II), and Lyra. Note: Gayl was the only queen to assume the name "Seagleam." Later tradition paralleled that of Hawk Haven, where the name of the birth house was retained even after marriage to the monarch. Deceased.

Glynn: (H.H.) a soldier.

Grace Trueheart: (Duchess Merlin, H.H.) military commander; spouse of Alin Brave; mother of Baxter Trueheart.

Grateful Peace: (Dragon's Eye, N.K.) also, Trausholo. Illuminator; Prime of New Kelvin; member of the Dragon's Three. A very influential person. Husband to Chutia; brother of Idalia; uncle of Varcasiol, Kistlio, Linatha, and others; aka Jalarios.

Gustin I: (King, B.B.) born Gustin Sailor, assumed the name Seagleam upon his coronation; first monarch of Bright Bay; spouse of Gayl Minter, later Gayl Seagleam; father of Gustin, Merry, and Lyra Seagleam. Deceased.

Gustin II: (Queen, B.B.) born Merry Seagleam, assumed the name Gustin upon her coronation; second monarch of Bright Bay; spouse of Amcry Pelican; mother of Basil, Seastar, and Tavis Seagleam. Deceased.

Gustin III: (King, B.B.) born Basil Seagleam, assumed the name Gustin upon his coronation; third monarch of Bright Bay; spouse of Brina Dolphin, later of Viona Seal; father of Valora Seagleam. Deceased.

Gustin IV: (Queen, B.B.) see Valora I.

Gustin Sailor: see Gustin I.

Hart: (H.H.) a young hunter.

Harwill Lobster: (King, the Isles) spouse of Valora I; during her reign as Gustin IV, also king of Bright Bay. Son of Marek.

Hasamemorri: (N.K.) a landlady.

Hazel Healer: (H.H.) apothecary, herbalist, perfumer, resident in the town of Hope.

Heather Baker: (H.H.) baker in Eagle's Nest; former sweetheart of Derian Carter.

Holly Gardener: (H.H.) former Master Gardener for Eagle's Nest Castle, possessor of the Green Thumb, a talent for the growing of plants. Mother of Timin and Sarena.

Honey Endbrook: (Isles) mother of Waln Endbrook.

Hya Grimsel: (General, Stonehold) commander of Stonehold troops.

Idalia: (N.K.) assistant to Melina. Sister of Grateful Peace; spouse of Pichero; mother of Kistlio, Varcasiol, Linatha, and others.

Indatius: (N.K.) young member of the Sodality of Artificers.

Ivon Archer: (Baron, H.H.) master of the Archer Grant; son of Purcel Archer and Rosene Eagle; brother of Zorana Archer; spouse of Aurella Wellward; father of Elise Archer.

Ivory Pelican: (Lord, B.B.) Keeper of the Keys, an honored post in Bright Bay.

Jalarios: see Grateful Peace.

Jared Surcliffe: (knight, H.H.) knight of the Order of the White Eagle; possessor of the healing talent; distant cousin of Norvin Norwood, who serves as his patron. Widower, no children.

Jem: (B.B.) deserter from Bright Bay's army.

Jet Shield: (H.H.) son of Melina Shield and Rolfston Redbriar; brother of Sapphire, Opal, Ruby, and Citrine Shield. Heir apparent to his parents' properties upon the adoption of his sister Sapphire by Tedric I.

Joy Spinner: (H.H.) scout in the service of Earle Kite. Deceased.

Kalvinia: (Prime, N.K.) thaumaturge, Sodality of Sericulturalists.

Keen: (H.H.) servant to Newell Shield.

Kenre Trueheart: (H.H.) son of Zorana Archer and Aksel Trueheart; brother of Purcel, Nydia, and Deste Trueheart.

Kiero: (N.K.) spy in the service of the Healed One.

Kistlio: (N.K.) clerk in Thendulla Lypella; nephew of Grateful Peace; son of Idalia and

Pichero; brother of Varcasiol, Linatha, and others. Deceased.

Lillis Norwood: (Lady, H.H.) daughter of Norvin Norwood and Luella Stanbrook; sister of Edlin, Tait, and Agneta Norwood; adopted sister of Blysse Norwood (Firekeeper).

Linatha: (N.K.) niece of Grateful Peace; daughter of Idalia and Pichero; sister of Kistlio, Varcasiol, and others.

Longsight Scrounger: pirate, leader of those at Smuggler's Light.

Lorimer Stanbrook: (Lord, H.H.) spouse of Marras Eagle; father of Marigolde and Alben Eagle. Deceased.

Lovella Eagle: (Crown Princess, H.H.) military commander; daughter of Tedric Eagle and Elexa Wellward; spouse of Newell Shield. Deceased.

Lucho: (N.K.) a thug.

Lucky Shortleg: a pirate.

Luella Stanbrook: (Lady, H.H.) spouse of Norvin Norwood; mother of Edlin, Tait, Lillis, and Agneta Norwood.

Marek: (Duke, Half-Moon Island) formerly Duke Lobster of Bright Bay but chose to follow the fate of his son, Harwill. Brother of Faelene, the current Duchess Lobster.

Marigolde Eagle: (H.H.) daughter of Marras Eagle and Lorimer Stanbrook. In keeping with principles of Zorana I, given no title as died in infancy.

Marras Eagle: (Crown Princess, H.H.) daughter of Chalmer Eagle and Rose Rosewood; sister of Tedric, Caryl, Gadman, and Rosene; spouse of Lorimer Stanbrook; mother of Marigolde and Alben Eagle. Deceased.

Melina: (H.H.; N.K.) formerly entitled "lady," with affiliation to House Gyrfalcon; reputed sorceress; spouse of Rolfston Redbriar; mother of Sapphire, Jet, Opal, Ruby, and Citrine Shield. Later spouse of Toriovico of New Kelvin, given title of Consolor of the Healed One.

Merri Jay: (H.H.) daughter of Wendee Jay.

Merry Seagleam: see Gustin II.

Minnow: (Princess, B.B.) formerly Minnow Oyster. Daughter of Allister I and Pearl Oyster; sister of Shad and Tavis, twin of Anemone.

Nanny: (H.H.) attendant to Melina Shield.

Nelm: (N.K.) member of the Sodality of Herbalists.

Newell Shield: (Prince, H.H.) commander of marines; spouse of Lovella Eagle; brother of Tab, Rein, Polr, and Melina Shield. Deceased.

Ninette Farmer: (H.H.) relative of Ivon Archer; attendant of Elise Archer.

Northwest: Royal Wolf, not of Firekeeper's pack. Called Sharp Fang by his own pack.

Norvin Norwood: (Earl Kestrel, H.H.) heir to Kestrel Grant; son of Saedee Norwood; brother of Eirene Norwood; spouse of Luella Stanbrook; father of Edlin, Tait, Lillis, and Agneta; adopted father of Blysse (Firekeeper).

Nstasius: (N.K.) Prime, member of the Sodality of Sericulturalists, sympathetic to the Progressive Party.

Nydia Trueheart: (H.H.) often called Dia; daughter of Aksel Trueheart and Zorana Archer; sister of Purcel, Deste, and Kenre Trueheart.

Oculios: (N.K.) apothecary; member of the Sodality of Alchemists.

One Female: also Shining Coat; ruling female wolf of Firekeeper and Blind Seer's pack.

One Male: also Rip; ruling male wolf of Firekeeper and Blind Seer's pack.

Opal Shield: (H.H.) daughter of Melina Shield and Rolfston Redbriar; sister of Sapphire, Jet, Ruby, and Citrine.

Oralia: (Isles) wife of Waln Endbrook; mother of three children.

Ox: (H.H.) born Malvin Hogge; bodyguard to Norvin Norwood; renowned for his strength and good temper.

Pearl Oyster: (Queen, B.B.) spouse of Allister I; mother of Shad, Tavis, Anemone, and Minnow.

Perce Potterford: (B.B.) guard to Allister I.

Perr: (H.H.) body servant to Ivon Archer.

Pichero: (N.K.) spouse of Idalia; father of Kistlio, Varcasiol, Linatha, and others.

Polr: (Lord, H.H.) military commander; brother of Tab, Rein, Newell, and Melina.

Posa: (N.K.) Prime, member of the Sodality of Illuminators.

Purcel Archer: (Baron Archer, H.H.) first Baron Archer, born Purcel Farmer, elevated to the title for his prowess in battle; spouse of Rosene Eagle; father of Ivon and Zorana Archer. Deceased.

Purcel Trueheart: (H.H.) lieutenant Hawk Haven army; son of Aksel Trueheart and Zorana Archer; brother of Nydia, Deste, and Kenre Trueheart. Deceased.

Race Forester: (H.H.) scout under the patronage of Norvin Norwood; regarded by many as one of the best in his calling.

Rafalias: (N.K.) member of the Sodality of Lapidaries.

Red Stripe: also called Cime; a pirate.

Reed Oyster: (Duke, B.B.) father of Queen Pearl. Among the strongest supporters of Allister I.

Rein Shield: (Lord, H.H.) brother of Tab, Newell, Polr, and Melina.

Riki Redbriar: (Lady, H.H.) spouse of Gadman Eagle; mother of Rolfston and Nydia Redbriar. Deceased.

Rillon: (N.K.) a maid in the Cloud Touching Spire; a slave.

Rios: see Citrine Shield.

Rip: see the One Male.

Rolfston Redbriar: (Lord, H.H.) son of Gadman Eagle and Riki Redbriar; spouse of Melina Shield; father of Sapphire, Jet, Opal, Ruby, and Citrine Shield. Deceased.

Rook: (H.H.) servant to Newell Shield.

Rory Seal: (Lord, B.B.) holds the title Royal Physician.

Rose Rosewood: (Queen, H.H.) common-born wife of Chalmer I; also called Rose Dawn; his marriage to her was the reason Hawk Haven

Great Houses received what Queen Zorana the Great would doubtless have seen as unnecessary and frivolous titles. Deceased.

Rosene: (Grand Duchess, H.H.) fifth child of King Chalmer and Queen Rose; spouse of Purcel Archer; mother of Ivon and Zorana Archer.

Ruby Shield: (H.H.) daughter of Melina Shield and Rolfston Redbriar; sister of Sapphire, Jet, Opal, and Citrine Shield.

Saedee Norwood: (Duchess Kestrel, H.H.) mother of Norvin and Eirene Norwood.

Sapphire: (Crown Princess, H.H.) adopted daughter of Tedric I; birth daughter of Melina Shield and Rolfston Redbriar; sister of Jet, Opal, Ruby, and Citrine Shield; spouse of Shad.

Sarena Gardener: (H.H.) member of Prince Barden's expedition; spouse of Donal Hunter; mother of Tamara. Deceased.

Seastar Seagleam: (Grand Duchess, B.B.) sister of Gustin III; mother of Culver and Dillon Pelican.

Shad: (Crown Prince, B.B.) son of Allister I and Pearl Oyster; brother of Tavis, Anemone, and Minnow; spouse of Sapphire.

Sharp Fang: a common name among the Royal Wolves; see Northwest and Whiner.

Siyago: (Dragon's Fire, N.K.) a prominent member of the Sodality of Artificers.

Steady Runner: a Royal Elk.

Steward Silver: (H.H.) long-time steward of Eagles' Nest Castle. Her birth-name and origin have been forgotten as no one, not even Silver herself, thinks of herself as anything but the steward.

Tab Shield: (Duke Gyrfalcon, H.H.) brother of Rein, Newell, Polr, and Melina.

Tait Norwood: (Lord, H.H.) son of Norvin Norwood and Luella Stanbrook; brother of Edlin, Lillis, and Agneta Norwood.

Tallus: (N.K.) Prime, member of the Sodality of Alchemists.

Tavis: (Prince, B.B.) son of Allister I and Pearl Oyster; brother of Shad, Anemone, and Minnow.

Tavis Seagleam: (Prince, B.B.) third child of Gustin II and Amery Pelican; spouse of Caryl Eagle; father of Allister Seagleam.

Tedric I: (King, H.H.) third king of Hawk Haven; son of King Chalmer and Queen Rose; spouse of Elexa Wellward; father of Chalmer, Lovella, and Barden; adopted father of Sapphire.

Tench: (Lord, B.B.) born Tench Clark; right-hand to Queen Gustin IV; knighted for his services; later made Lord of the Pen. Deceased.

Thyme: (H.H.) a scout in the service of Hawk Haven.

Timin Gardener: (H.H.) Master Gardener for Eagle's Nest Castle, possessor of the Green Thumb, a talent involving the growing of plants; son of Holly Gardener; brother of Sarena; father of Dan and Robyn.

Tipi: (N.K.) slave, born in Stonehold.

Toad: (H.H.) pensioner of the Carter family.

Tollius: (N.K.) member of the Sodality of Smiths.

Toriovico: (Healed One, N.K.) hereditary ruler of New Kelvin; spouse of Melina; brother to Vanviko (deceased) and several sisters.

Tris Stone: a pirate.

Tymia: (N.K.) a guard.

Ulia: (N.K.) a judge.

Valet: (H.H.) eponymous servant of Norvin Norwood; known for his fidelity and surprising wealth of useful skills.

Valora I: (Queen, the Isles) born Valora Seagleam, assumed the name Gustin upon her coronation as fourth monarch of Bright Bay. Resigned her position to Allister I and became queen of the Isles. Spouse of Harwill Lobster.

Valora Seagleam: see Valora I.

Vanviko: (heir to the Healed One, N.K.) elder brother of Toriovico; killed in avalanche.

Varcasiol: (N.K.) nephew of Grateful Peace; son of Idalia and Pichero; brother of Kistlio, Linatha, and others.

Vernita Carter: (H.H.) born Vernita Painter. An acknowledged beauty of her day, Vernita became associated with the business she and her husband, Colby, transformed from a simple carting business to a group of associated livery stables and carting services; mother of Derian, Damita, and Brock Carter.

Violet Redbriar: (Ambassador, H.H.) ambassador from Hawk Haven to New Kelvin; translator and author, with great interest in New Kelvinese culture.

Viona Seal: (Queen, B.B.) second wife of King Gustin III; mother of Valora, later Gustin IV.

Wain Cutter: (H.H.) skilled lapidary and gem cutter working out of the town of Hope.

Waln Endbrook: (the Isles) formerly Baron Endbrook; also, Walnut Endbrook. A prosperous merchant, Waln found rapid promotion in the service of Valora I. Spouse of Oralia; father of two daughters and a son.

Wendee Jay: (H.H.) retainer in service of Duchess Kestrel. Lady's maid to Firekeeper. Divorced. Mother of two daughters.

Wheeler: (H.H.) scout captain.

Whiner: a wolf of Blind Seer and Firekeeper's pack, later named Sharp Fang.

Whyte Steel: (knight, B.B.) captain of the guard for Allister I.

Wind Whisper: Royal Wolf, formerly of Firekeeper's pack, now member of another pack.

Xarxius: (Dragon's Claw, N.K.) member of the Dragon's Three; former Stargazer.

Yaree Yuci: (General, Stonehold) commander of Stonehold troops.

Zahlia: (N.K.) member of the Sodality of Smiths. Specialist in silver.

Zorana I: (Queen, H.H.) also called Zorana the Great, born Zorana Shield. First monarch of Hawk Haven; responsible for a reduction of titles—so associated with this program that overemphasis of titles is considered "unzoranic." Spouse of Clive Elkwood; mother of Chalmer I.

Zorana Archer: (Lady, H.H.) daughter of Rosene Eagle and Purcel Archer; sister of Ivon Archer; spouse of Aksel Trueheart; mother of Purcel, Nydia, Deste, and Kenre Trueheart.